DUNE

THE BATTLE OF CORRIN

The Dune Chronicles by Frank Herbert

Dune
Dune Messiah
Children of Dune
God Emperor of Dune
Heretics of Dune
Chapterhouse: Dune

Prelude to Dune by Brian Herbert and Kevin J. Anderson

Dune: House Atreides
Dune: House Harkonnen
Dune: House Corrino

Legends of Dune by Brian Herbert and Kevin J. Anderson

Dune: The Butlerian Jihad
Dune: The Machine Crusade
Dune: The Battle of Corrin

DUNE
THE BATTLE OF CORRIN

Brian Herbert
and
Kevin J. Anderson

TOR®

A TOM DOHERTY ASSOCIATES BOOK

NEW YORK

DUNE: THE BATTLE OF CORRIN

A Tor Book
Published by Tom Doherty Associates, LLC
175 Fifth Avenue
New York, NY 10010

Tor® is a registered trademark of Tom Doherty Associates, LLC.

ISBN 0-765-30159-8

Printed in the United States of America

To Pat LoBrutto,

For your unflagging support since the very beginning of our DUNE projects. Your enthusiasm, knowledge, and perceptiveness have made these books far better than anything we could have done alone. You are a true Renaissance editor.

ACKNOWLEDGMENTS

For the two authors of this book, envisioning the path from concept to finished manuscript is akin to a pair of Guild Navigators at the helm of the same Heighliner searching for a safe path through foldspace. The first navigator in the fantastic Dune universe was, of course, Frank Herbert. But he did not do it alone, as Beverly Herbert devoted almost four decades of support and devotion to him. We are greatly indebted to them both. We are also grateful to the Herbert family, including Penny, Ron, David, Byron, Julie, Robert, Kimberly, Margaux, and Theresa, who have entrusted Brian and Kevin with the care of Frank Herbert's extraordinary vision.

Our wives, Jan Herbert and Rebecca Moesta Anderson, have contributed in ways that go far beyond anything either of them contemplated when they took their wedding vows. Both of them are artists in their own right—Jan is a painter and Rebecca is a writer—and they have contributed immense amounts of their own time and talents to the story you are about to read.

We are also indebted to many other people who assisted us in another epic, colorful journey across the Dune canvas. This includes our dedicated agents and staff, Robert Gottlieb, John Silbersack, Kim Whalen, Matt Bialer, and Kate Scherler. Our American and U.K. publishers have shared our vision and have kept all matters of production and promotion on track—thanks especially to Tom Doherty, Carolyn Caughey, Linda Quinton, and Paul Stevens. Our extraordinary editor, Pat LoBrutto, has tended to our stories like a fine chef, adding just the right seasonings where needed. Rachel Steinberger, Christian Gossett, Dr. Attila Torkos, and Diane E. Jones provided much-needed advice, while Catherine Sidor worked tirelessly to transcribe dozens of microcassettes and to input corrections on the manuscript.

Though billions of human beings have been slaughtered by the think-
ing machines, we must not call them victims. We must not call them
casualties. I hesitate to even name them martyrs. Every person who
died in this Great Revolt must be nothing less than a hero.
We will write the permanent record to reflect this.
　—SERENA BUTLER, private proceedings of the Jihad Council

I don't care how many documents you show me—how many
records, or interviews, or damning bits of evidence. I am perhaps the
only person still alive who knows the truth about Xavier Harkonnen
and the reasons for what he did. I have held my peace for these many
decades because Xavier himself asked it of me, because it is what
Serena Butler would have wanted, and because the needs of the
Jihad demanded it. But do not pretend that your propaganda is accu-
rate, no matter how many League citizens believe it. Remember, I
lived through those events. None of you did.
　—VORIAN ATREIDES, private address to the League of Nobles

The gravest error a thinking person can make is to believe that one
particular version of history is absolute fact. History is recorded by a
series of observers, none of whom is impartial. The facts are dis-
torted by sheer passage of time and—especially in the case of the
Butlerian Jihad—thousands of years of humanity's dark ages, delib-
erate misrepresentations by religious sects, and the inevitable corrup-
tion that comes from an accumulation of careless mistakes. The
wise person, then, views history as a set of lessons to be learned,
choices and ramifications to be considered and discussed, and mis-
takes that should never again be made.
　—PRINCESS IRULAN, preface to the *History of the Butlerian Jihad*

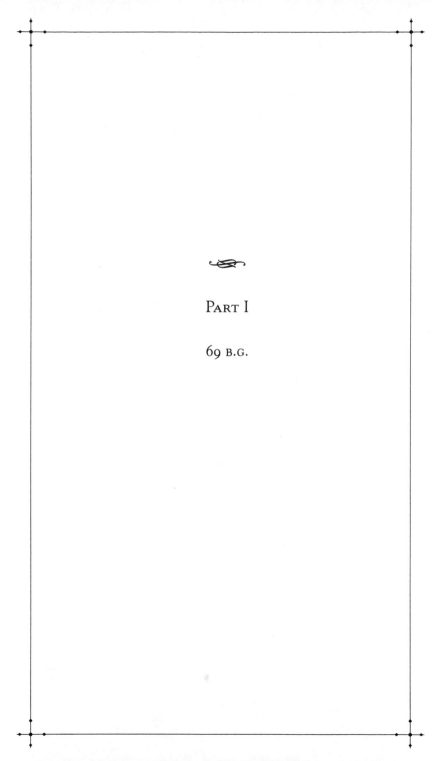

PART I

69 B.G.

Machinery does not destroy. It creates, provided always that the controlling hand is strong enough to dominate it

— RIVEGO,
a muralist of Old Earth

E rasmus found the pecking order among the dying and hopeless humans fascinating, even amusing. Their reaction was all part of the experimental process, and he considered the results to be very worthwhile.

The robot strolled through the corridors of his meticulously organized laboratory facility on Corrin, swirling his plush crimson robe. The garment itself was an affectation he had developed in order to give himself a more lordly appearance. Alas, the victims in their sealed cells paid little heed to his finery, preoccupied instead with their suffering. Nothing could be done about that, since distractible humans had such difficulty focusing on matters that did not directly affect them.

Decades ago, squads of efficient construction robots had built this high-domed facility according to his exact specifications. The numerous well-equipped chambers—each one completely isolated and sterile—contained everything Erasmus required for his experiments.

As he continued his regular inspection rounds, the independent robot passed the glaz windows of sealed chambers in which plague test subjects lay strapped to beds. Some specimens were already paranoid and delirious, displaying the symptoms of the retrovirus, while others were terrified for good and rational reasons.

By now, testing was nearly complete on the engineered disease. The effective direct mortality rate was forty-three percent—not at all perfect, but still the deadliest viral organism in recorded human history. It would serve the necessary purpose, and Omnius could not wait much longer. Something had to be done soon.

The humans' holy crusade against thinking machines had dragged on for almost a full century, with much destruction and distraction. The constant fanatical attacks from the Army of the Jihad had wrought incalculable damage to the Synchronized empire, destroying robot warships as fast as the various evermind incarnations could rebuild them. The progress of Omnius had been inexcusably stalled. Finally, Omnius demanded a solution. Since direct military conflict had not proved sufficiently effective, alternatives were explored. Biological plagues, for instance.

According to simulations, a fast-moving epidemic could be a superior weapon, serving to eradicate human populations—including their military forces—while leaving infrastructures and resources intact for the victorious thinking machines. After the specially designed plague ran its course, Omnius could pick up the pieces and get the systems operating again.

Erasmus had some reservations about the tactic, fearing that a terrible enough disease could wipe out every last human. While Omnius might be satisfied with total extinction, the autonomous robot had no desire for such a final solution. He remained quite interested in these creatures— especially Gilbertus Albans, whom he had raised as a surrogate son after removing him from the squalid slave pens. In a purely scientific sense, Erasmus needed to keep sufficient organic material for his laboratory and field studies of human nature.

They couldn't *all* be killed. Just most of them.

But the creatures were remarkably resilient. He doubted that even the worst epidemic could completely wipe out the species. Humans had an intriguing ability to adapt to adversity and overcome it by unorthodox means. If only thinking machines could learn to do the same . . .

Drawing his exquisite robe tight, the platinum-skinned robot entered the central chamber of the facility, where his turncoat Tlulaxa captive had engineered the perfect RNA retrovirus. Thinking machines were efficient and dedicated, but it took a corrupted human imagination to channel Omnius's wrath into a thoroughly destructive course of action. No robot or computer could have conceived such appalling death and destruction: That required the imagination of a vengeful human.

Rekur Van, a biological engineer and geneticist now reviled across the League of Nobles, squirmed in his life-support socket, unable to move more than his head because he had no arms or legs. A retention socket connected the geneticist's body core to nutrient and waste tubes. Shortly after capturing him, Erasmus had seen to the removal of the man's limbs, rendering him much more manageable. He was certainly not trustworthy, in sharp contrast with Gilbertus Albans.

The robot fashioned a cheery smile on his flowmetal face. "Good morning, Stump. We have much work to do today. Perhaps we will even finish our primary test runs."

The Tlulaxa's narrow face was even more pinched than usual; his dark, close-set eyes flitted about like those of a trapped animal. "It's about time you got here. I've been awake for hours, just staring."

"Then you have had plenty of time to develop remarkable new ideas. I look forward to hearing them."

The captive grunted a coarse insult in response. Then: "How are you coming on the reptilian regrowth experiments? What progress?"

The robot leaned close and lifted a biological flap to look at the bare skin on one of Rekur Van's scarred shoulders.

"Anything yet?" the Tlulaxa asked, anxiously. He bent his head at an odd angle, trying to see details of the stump of his arm.

"Not on this side."

Erasmus checked the biological flap on the other shoulder. "We might have something here. A definite growth bump on the skin." Each test site contained different cellular catalysts injected into the skin in an effort to regenerate the severed limbs.

"Extrapolate from your data, robot. How long before my arms and legs grow back?"

"That is difficult to say. It could be several weeks, or possibly much longer." The robot rubbed a metal finger over the bump on the skin. "Conversely, this growth could be something else entirely. It has a reddish coloration; perhaps it is nothing more than an infection."

"I don't feel any soreness."

"Would you like me to scratch it?"

"No. I'll wait until I can do it myself."

"Don't be rude. This is supposed to be a collaborative effort." Though the results did look promising, this work wasn't the robot's priority. He had something more important in mind.

Erasmus made a minor adjustment to an intravenous connection that smoothed away the discontent in the man's narrow face. Undoubtedly, Rekur Van was undergoing one of his periodic mood swings. Erasmus would observe him closely and administer medication to keep him oper-ating efficiently. Perhaps he could prevent the Tlulaxa from having one of his full-fledged tantrums today. Some mornings, anything could set him off. Other times, Erasmus purposely provoked him just to observe the result.

Controlling humans—even such a disgusting example—was a sci-ence and an art. This degraded captive was as much a "subject" as any of the humans in the blood-spattered slave pens and chambers. Even when the Tlulaxa was driven to the extreme, when he struggled to rip away his life-support systems using nothing more than his teeth, Erasmus could always get him working on the plagues again. Fortunately, the man despised League humans even more than he hated his machine masters.

Decades ago, during a great political upheaval in the League of Nobles, the dark secret of the Tlulaxa organ farms had been revealed to the horror and disgust of free humanity. On the League Worlds, public opinion had been inflamed against the genetic researchers, and outraged mobs had destroyed the organ farms and driven most of the Tlulaxa into hiding, their reputations irreparably blackened.

On the run, Rekur Van had fled to Synchronized space, bearing what he thought was an irresistible gift—the cellular material to make a perfect clone of Serena Butler. Erasmus had been amazed, remembering his intriguing discussions with the captive woman. The desperate Van had been certain Erasmus would want her—but alas the clones that Van developed had none of Serena's memories, none of her passion. They were merely shallow replicas.

Despite the clones' blandness, however, Erasmus had found Rekur Van himself very interesting—much to the little man's dismay. The indepen-dent robot enjoyed his company. Here at last was someone who spoke his scientific language, a researcher capable of helping him understand more about the countless ramifications and investigative pathways of complex human organisms.

Erasmus found the first few years to be a challenge, even after remov-ing the Tlulaxa's arms and legs. Eventually, with careful manipulations, a patiently administered system of rewards and punishments, he had con-verted Rekur Van into quite a fruitful experimental subject. The limbless man's situation seemed rather like that of Van's own slave subjects in the sham organ farms. Erasmus found it wonderfully ironic.

"Would you like a little treat now, to get us started on our work?" Erasmus suggested. "A flesh cookie, perhaps?"

Van's eyes lit up, for this was one of the few pleasures remaining to him. Made from a variety of laboratory-bred organisms, including human "debris," the flesh cookies were considered delicacies on the Tlulaxa homeworld. "Feed me, or I refuse to continue my work for you."

"You use that threat too often, Stump. You are connected to tanks of nutrient solutions. Even if you refuse to eat, you will not starve."

"You want my cooperation, not just my survival—and you have left me with too few bargaining chips." The Tlulaxa's face contorted in a grimace.

"Very well. Flesh cookies!" Erasmus shouted. "Four-Arms, see to it."

One of the freakish human laboratory assistants walked in, his quartet of grafted arms balancing a platter mounded with sugary organic treats. The Tlulaxa shifted in his life-support socket to look at the gruesome food—and the extra set of arms that had once been his own.

With some knowledge of the grafting procedures used by the Tlulaxa race, Erasmus had transplanted the arms and legs of the former slaver onto two laboratory assistants, adding artificial flesh, sinews, and bone to adjust the limbs to the proper length. Although it was just a test case and a learning experience, it had been remarkably successful. Four-Arms was particularly efficient at carrying things; Erasmus hoped someday to teach him to juggle, which Gilbertus might find amusing. Alternatively, Four-Legs could run like an antelope on an open plain.

Whenever either assistant came into view, the Tlulaxa man was harshly reminded of his hopeless situation.

Since Rekur Van had no hands, Four-Arms used two of his own—the pair formerly belonging to the captive—to cram flesh cookies into the eager, open mouth. Van looked like a hungry chick demanding worms from a mother bird. Brownish yellow crumbs dripped down his chin onto the black smock covering his torso; some fell into the nutrient bath, where the materials would be recycled.

Erasmus raised a hand, making Four-Arms pause. "Enough for now. You will have more, Stump, but first there is work to do. Together, let us review today's mortality statistics from the various test strains."

Interesting, Erasmus thought, that Vorian Atreides—son of the treacherous Titan Agamemnon—had attempted a similar means of wiping out the Omnius everminds, planting a computer virus in the update spheres unwittingly delivered by his robot captain Seurat. But machines weren't the only ones vulnerable to deadly infection. . . .

After pouting for a moment, Rekur Van licked his lips and set to work studying the results. He seemed to enjoy the casualty figures. "How delicious," he muttered. "These plagues are the absolute best way to kill trillions of people."

Greatness has its own rewards . . . and bears its own terrible costs.
—PRIMERO XAVIER HARKONNEN,
a final dictajournal entry

During his preternaturally long military career, Supreme Commander Vorian Atreides had seen much, but he'd rarely visited a more
beautiful world than Caladan. For him, this ocean planet was a treasure
chest filled with memories, a fantasy of how a "normal" life should be—
without the machines, without the war.

Everywhere he went on Caladan, Vor saw reminders of golden times
he had spent here with Leronica Tergiet. She was the mother of his twin
sons, the woman who had been his beloved companion for more than
seven decades, though they'd never officially married.

Leronica was at their shared home back on Salusa Secundus. Though
she was in her early nineties, he loved her more than ever. To keep a longer
hold on her youth, she could have taken regular doses of the rejuvenating
spice melange, which had grown quite popular among the rich nobles, but
she refused what she saw as an unnatural crutch. It was so like her!

In sharp contrast, because of the immortality treatment his cymek
father had forced on him, Vor still looked like a young man, her grandson
perhaps. So that they wouldn't appear to be quite so mismatched, Vor
regularly added gray tints to his hair. He wished he had brought her with
him on this trip back to where they had met.

Now, looking out at the calm Caladan seas and watching the boats
return from a day of harvesting kelp and fat butterfish, Vor sat with his

eager young adjutant, Abulurd Butler, youngest son of Quentin Vigar and Wandra Butler. Abulurd was also the grandson of Vor's close friend . . . but Xavier Harkonnen's name was rarely spoken, since he'd been irreversibly branded a coward and traitor to humanity. The thought of this injustice, carried forward by the momentum of legend, caught in Vor's throat like a spiny fruit, but he could do nothing about it. Nearly sixty years had already gone by.

He and Abulurd had found a table inside a new cliffside suspensor restaurant that moved slowly along the Caladan shore for a constantly shifting view of the coast and the sea. Their military caps rested on a wide window ledge. Waves crashed against large rocks just offshore and left rivulets of water running down the sides like white lace. Late afternoon sunlight glinted off the waves.

In their green-and-crimson uniforms, the two men gazed out at the incoming tide and drank wine, enjoying a brief respite from the unending Jihad. Vor wore his uniform casually, without all the distracting medals, while Abulurd himself seemed as crisp as the creases on his trousers. *Just like his grandfather.*

Vor had taken the young man under his wing, watching out for him, helping him along. Abulurd had never known his mother—Xavier's youngest daughter—who had suffered a severe stroke giving birth to him, which left her catatonic. Now, upon turning eighteen, the young man had pledged himself to the Army of the Jihad. His father and brothers had earned prestige and many decorations. Eventually, Quentin Butler's youngest son would distinguish himself as well.

To avoid the taint of the Harkonnen name, Abulurd's father had taken his surname from the auspicious maternal line, proud to claim the heritage of Serena Butler herself. Ever since he'd married into the famous family forty-two years earlier, the war hero Quentin had remarked on the irony of the name. "A butler was once a menial servant who quietly followed the orders of his master. But I declare a new family motto: 'We Butlers are servants unto no one!'" His two oldest sons Faykan and Rikov had adopted the catchphrase as they devoted their early lives to fight in the Jihad.

So much history in a name, Vor thought. *And so much baggage with it.*

Taking a long breath, he scanned the interior of the restaurant. A banner hung on one wall, with pictures of the Three Martyrs: Serena Butler, her innocent child Manion, and Grand Patriarch Ginjo. Faced with an enemy as relentless as the thinking machines, people sought rescue from God or His representatives. Like any religious movement, the "Martyrists" had zealous fringe members who followed strict practices to honor the fallen trio.

Vor did not adhere to such beliefs himself, preferring to rely on military prowess to defeat Omnius, but human nature, including fanaticism, had an influence on his planning. Populations that would not fight in the name of the League would throw themselves howling upon machine foes if asked to do so in the name of Serena or her baby. But while the Martyrists could help the cause of the Jihad, frequently they just got in the way. . . .

Keeping his long silence, Vor folded his hands and looked around the restaurant. Despite the recently added suspensor mechanism, the place looked much as it had many decades ago. Vor remembered it well. The chairs, of a classic style, might be the same ones, but he thought the worn upholstery had been replaced.

Quietly sipping his wine, Vor recalled one waitress who used to work here, a young immigrant that his troops had rescued from Peridot Colony. She had lost her entire family when the thinking machines razed every human-built structure on that planet, and afterward she had worn a survivor's medal that Vor presented to her personally. He hoped she had made a good life for herself here on Caladan. So long ago . . . she might be dead now, or an old matron with a brood of grandchildren.

Over the years, Vor had visited Caladan many times, ostensibly to monitor the listening post and observation station his crews had erected nearly seven decades ago. He still returned whenever possible to keep an eye on the water world.

Thinking he was doing a good thing, Vor had long ago moved Leronica and his sons to the League capital when Estes and Kagin were children; their mother had thrived amid all the wonders, but the twins had not particularly cared for Salusa. Later, Vor's boys—*boys?* They were in their sixties now!—had decided to return to Caladan, never having warmed to the bustle of Salusa Secundus, League politics, or the Army of the Jihad. Off on his military missions, Vor had rarely been home, and when the twins came of age, they had departed for the ocean world to set up their own homes and have their own children . . . even grandchildren now.

After so much time and only infrequent contact, Estes and Kagin were veritable strangers to him. Just yesterday, when Vor's military group had arrived, he had gone to visit them—only to discover that they had packed up and left for Salusa the week before, intending to spend a few months with their old mother. He hadn't even known! Another missed opportunity.

Still, none of his previous visits with them in past years had been particularly joyful. Each time the twins had followed social niceties, sat with their father for a brief dinner, but didn't seem to know what to talk about. Before long, Estes and Kagin had pleaded other obligations. Feeling awkward, Vor had shaken their hands and wished them well, before going diligently about his military duties. . . .

"You're thinking back, aren't you, sir?" Abulurd had remained silent for a long time, watching his commander, but had finally grown impatient.

"Can't help thinking. I may not look it, but I am an old man, remember. I have a lot of ties here." Vor's brow furrowed as he took a sip of Zincal, one of the most popular Caladan wines. The first time he'd been here, in the dockside tavern owned by Leronica and her father, he had drunk only a potent and bitter kelp beer. . . .

"The past is important, Abulurd . . . and so is the truth." Vor turned from the ocean scenery to focus on his adjutant. "There's something I've been meaning to tell you, but I had to wait until you were old enough. Maybe you'll never be old enough."

Abulurd brushed a hand through his dark-brown hair, revealing reddish-cinnamon highlights like his grandfather's. The young man also had an infectious smile like Xavier's, and a disarming way of looking at people. "I'm always interested in what you can teach me, Supreme Commander."

"Some things are not easy to learn. But you deserve to know. What you do with it afterward is your own business."

Perplexed, Abulurd squinted. The suspensor restaurant stopped its lateral movement and began to float down the face of a water-blackened cliff, approaching the sea and the waves that crashed against the shore.

"This is difficult," Vor said after a long sigh. "We'd better finish our wine." He took a long swallow of the robust red varietal, stood, and grabbed his military cap from the window ledge. Abulurd followed dutifully, taking his own cap and leaving his glass half full.

After exiting the restaurant, they climbed a paved trail that switchbacked to the top of a cliff, where they stopped among wind-sculpted shrubs and sprays of white starry flowers. A salty breeze whipped up, and the men had to hold on to their caps. Vor gestured to a bench surrounded by high sheltering hedges. The sky and open air seemed vast, but in this special place Vor felt a sense of privacy and importance.

"It's time for you to learn what really happened with your grandfa-

ther," Vor said. He sincerely hoped this young man would take the revelations to heart, especially since his older brothers never had, preferring the
official fiction rather than the uncomfortable truth.

Abulurd swallowed hard. "I've read the files. I know he is my family's
shame."

Vor scowled. "Xavier was a good man and my close friend. Sometimes
the history you think you know is little more than convenient propaganda." He let out a bitter laugh. "Ah, you should have read my father's
original memoirs."

Abulurd seemed confused. "You are the only one who doesn't spit at
the name Harkonnen. I . . . I never believed he could have been so terrible. He was the father of Manion the Innocent, after all."

"Xavier did not betray us. He didn't betray anyone. Iblis Ginjo was
the evil one, and Xavier sacrificed himself to destroy him before he
could cause more terrible harm. The Grand Patriarch's own actions led
to Serena's death, along with the Ivory Tower Cogitors' mad peace
plan."

Vor's hands clenched into angry fists. "Xavier Harkonnen did what no
other man was willing to do—and he saved our souls, if nothing else. He
doesn't deserve the shame piled upon him. But for the sake of the Jihad,
Xavier was willing to accept any fate, even history's knife in his back. He
knew that if such vast corruption and treachery were exposed at the heart
of the Jihad itself, the holy crusade would degenerate into scandals and
accusations. We would lose our focus on the real enemy."

Tears filled Vor's gray eyes when he looked hard at Abulurd. "And all
this time, I . . . I let my friend be colored as a traitor. Xavier knew that the
Jihad had to take precedence over personal exoneration, but I am
exhausted from wrestling with the truth, Abulurd. Serena left us both a
message before she departed for Corrin, knowing she was likely to be
killed—martyred. She explained why personal feelings had to be shunted
aside for the cause. Xavier felt the same way—he never gave a damn
about medals or statues in his honor, or how history remembered him."

Vor forced his fingers to relax. "Xavier knew most people wouldn't
understand what he had done. The Grand Patriarch was too well
ensconced in his position, surrounded by the powerful Jipol and propaganda specialists. For decades, Iblis Ginjo manufactured his own inde-
structible myth, while Xavier was just a man, fighting as best he could.
When he learned what Iblis meant to do to yet another human colony—
when he discovered the scheme the Grand Patriarch had created with the

Tlulaxa and their organ farms—he knew what he had to do. He didn't care about the consequences."

Abulurd watched him with intense fascination, a mixture of dismay and hope. He looked very young.

"Xavier was a great man who performed a necessary act." Vor shrugged, a weak gesture. "Iblis Ginjo was removed. The Tlulaxa organ farms were abandoned, their vile researchers blacklisted and scattered. And the Jihad was rejuvenated, resulting in the last six decades of fervor."

Young Abulurd remained disturbed. "But what about the truth? If you knew that my grandfather's infamy had no basis, why didn't you try to fix it?"

Vor just shook his head sadly. "No one wanted to hear it. The turmoil would have been a distraction. Even now, it would stall our war effort while we waste time pointing accusing fingers and screaming for justice. Families would take sides, vendettas would be sworn . . . and through it all, Omnius would keep attacking us."

The young officer did not seem satisfied, but he said nothing.

"I understand what you are feeling Abulurd. Trust me, Xavier himself would not have wanted me to demand a historical revision in his favor. It has been a long, long time. I very much doubt anyone cares."

"I care."

Vor gave him a wan smile. "Yes, and now you know the truth." He leaned back on his bench. "But our long struggle is held together by the slender threads of heroes and myths. The stories surrounding Serena Butler and Iblis Ginjo have been carefully crafted, and the Martyrists have transformed those two into much more than they ever were. For the good of the people, for the strength of the Jihad, they must remain untarnished as symbols—even the Grand Patriarch, though he does not deserve it."

The young man's lower lip trembled. "My grandfather wasn't . . . wasn't a coward, then?"

"Far from it. I'd call him a hero."

Abulurd hung his head. "I'll never be a coward," he vowed, wiping tears from his eyes.

"I know you won't, Abulurd, and I want you to know that you're like a son to me. I was proud to be Xavier's friend, and I'm proud to know you." Vor put a hand on the young man's shoulder. "Someday, perhaps, we can right this terrible wrong. But first we must destroy Omnius."

A birth on this soil is the birth of a warrior.
> —SWORDMASTER ISTIAN GOSS,
> to his students

The Army of the Jihad vowed to take back Honru from the thinking machines, regardless of the cost in blood. After a century of Serena Butler's holy war, humans were accustomed to extreme sacrifices.

Quentin Butler, the battalion's primero, stood on the bridge of his flagship and watched the Omnius-enslaved planet that loomed in front of him. He uttered a silent prayer as he faced his soulless enemy. Cut from the mold of a staunch war hero, he looked much older than his sixty-five years, with pale gold hair and wavy curls; the finely chiseled features of his face—a firm chin, thin lips, and piercing eyes—looked as if they had been modeled after a classical bust. Quentin would spearhead the offensive, leading the jihadis to victory here on the site of one of their earliest, most devastating defeats.

Four hundred ballista battleships and over a thousand javelin destroyers converged to form a deadly noose around the planet that had once been inhabited by free humans, before the Honru Massacre. This time, the thinking machines stood no chance whatsoever against Quentin and his sworn cause, not to mention the overwhelming firepower he had brought.

In all the years of the Jihad, brave human warriors had inflicted constant and significant damage on the Synchronized Worlds, wrecking robot fleets and destroying machine outposts. And yet the enemy continued to rebuild their forces.

The primero, addicted to the rush of adrenaline and the thrill of victory, had already performed plenty of heroic deeds in his long military career. Many times he had stood victorious in the smoking ruins of a battlefield. He never tired of that sensation.

"Omnius should just calculate the odds and shut down all of his systems," said Faykan, Quentin's oldest son. "It would save us time and trouble." Even taller than his father, Faykan had wavy hair like Quentin's, but high cheekbones and lean features from his mother Wandra. He was thirty-seven, ambitious both in military service and League politics.

Also standing on the flagship's bridge, his brother Rikov snorted. "If victory is as easy as all that, it would be hard to justify a big celebration when it's over. I'd prefer more of a challenge." Seven years younger than his brother, Rikov was a head shorter, with broader shoulders and a squarer jaw. His generous lips took after his Harkonnen heritage, though no one with good sense would remind Rikov of that embarrassment.

"I am satisfied with any victory that brings us one step closer to annihilating the machine demons." Quentin turned to look at the two eager men. "There'll be enough glory for both of my sons . . . with a bit left over for myself."

Subconsciously, he often avoided mentioning his youngest son because of what Abulurd's birth had done to Wandra. He always thought of his precious wife before going into battle. Late in her childbearing years, Wandra had accidentally gotten pregnant, and the difficult delivery had stolen her from him. Mourning, ignoring his new baby, Quentin had taken his comatose wife to the peace and solitude of the City of Introspection, where her revered aunt Serena had spent so much time in contemplation. A part of him still blamed Abulurd for taking Wandra from him, and though his conscience told him he wasn't being fair to Abulurd, his heart refused to believe otherwise. . . .

"Are we going to just stare at Honru?" Rikov asked flippantly, already standing close to the exit. "Or are we going to get on with it?"

The battalion's subcommanders transmitted detailed acknowledgments, marking positions and announcing their readiness for a full assault. The Omnius evermind on the planet below must already realize its doom. Defensive systems and combat robots would have detected the incoming Jihad fleet, but the thinking machines could do nothing against such an overwhelming force. Their fate was predetermined.

Quentin rose from his command chair, smiling patiently at his eager sons. The basic battle plan had been developed in a command center in far-off Zimia, but in war everything could change up until the last moment. "We will send down five hundred kindjal fighters in two separate waves, each with a load of scrambler-pulse bombs, but we won't deploy the large-scale atomics unless everything goes sour. We'll need a precision strike on the evermind nexus and then ground crews to root out the substations. We have plenty of Ginaz mercenary commandos."

"Yes, sir," both men answered.

"Faykan, you lead the first wave. Rikov, the second. A few high detonations of pulse-atomics should scramble their gelcircuitry brains sufficiently without killing all the human population. It'll soften the machines enough for our ground troops to sweep in and eliminate the rest. The people of Honru will be free before nightfall."

"If any of them remain," Rikov pointed out. "It's been almost ninety years since the machines took over down there."

Faykan's face looked grim and stony. "If Omnius has killed them all, that's even more reason for revenge. Then I, for one, wouldn't have any reservations about slagging the planet with a flood of atomics, just like the armada did at Earth."

"Either way," Quentin said, "let's get on with it."

The primero clasped his hands in front of his face in the half prayer, half salute that the Jihad commanders had adopted since the murder of Serena Butler more than half a century ago. Though ostensibly he spoke to his sons, the words were transmitted across the battalion—not just a pep talk, but his sincere belief. "The Honru Massacre was one of the darkest moments in the early history of the Jihad. Today we will balance the scales of history and finish the story."

Faykan and Rikov marched toward the flagship's main launching deck, where they would lead the waves of kindjal fighters. Quentin remained in the command center to watch the unfolding assault, completely confident in his sons. On the screen, he continued to study the rich-looking planet below: brown and green continents, white wisps of clouds, deep blue blotches of broad seas.

No doubt the Omnius incursion had stripped the landscape over the past nine decades, turning Honru's beautiful forests and meadows into an industrial nightmare. Enslaved survivors would have been forced to serve the evil thinking machines. Quentin clenched his fists, muttering another quiet prayer for strength. All that damage could be recovered, given time. The first step was to reassert benevolent human rule, to avenge the first Massacre. . . .

Five years after Serena Butler launched her great Jihad, an armada of League warships had attempted to liberate the Synchronized World of Honru. The well-armed and enthusiastic armada had swept in, urged on by Grand Patriarch Ginjo. But corrupt thinking machine spies had misled them about the number of enemy forces waiting at Honru.

Ten thousand Omnius ships had lain in ambush and then engulfed the armada. The human fighters had responded with desperate combat measures, but self-destructive robot ships wiped out the Jihad battleships in orbit. Waves of combat robots on the surface exterminated entire villages of humans who had hoped to be rescued.

The intended liberation of Honru had turned into a rout, a slaughter that continued until all remaining human battleships were wiped out. In addition to uncounted casualties on the ground, over five hundred thousand free human soldiers had been massacred in a single engagement. . . .

It is long past time to avenge that, Quentin thought.

"Kindjal squadrons are launched, Primero," said his lieutenant.

"Ready our troops for the ground assault to secure our advances. I want this to go smoothly. Land all personnel transports while we maintain air cover with javelins." He allowed himself a sober yet confident smile.

Five hundred kindjals flew from their ballista mother ships. Already, the Honru robot fleet was rallying, some launching vessels into orbit, others converging from picket lines at the edge of the system.

"Prepare for combat," Quentin said. "All Holtzman shields engage as soon as the robot ships come into range, not a moment before."

"Yes, Primero. We'll hold fast."

He was confident his fleet could shrug off the robotic battleships, so he focused instead on the activities of his sons. Faykan and Rikov divided the kindjal squadrons, and each followed an operational pattern pursuant to his own style; the mixture of strategies had proven quite effective in earlier engagements. Today, the famous Butler Brothers would add another victory to their résumés.

With an ache in his chest, he wished Wandra could have seen her boys now, but she was beyond knowing anything that happened around her. . . .

Eighteen years ago, Quentin's two oldest sons had seen tears streaming down his cheeks as they were leaving her in the City of Introspection. It was one of the first times the military hero had ever allowed himself to appear so vulnerable.

"Too much grief, Father," Faykan had said. "Everywhere we turn."

But Quentin had shaken his head. "These are not tears of anguish or grief, my son." He reached out to embrace both young men. "They are tears of happiness for all that your mother has given me."

Quentin had never abandoned Wandra. He visited her each time he returned to Salusa, certain in his heart that his wife still remembered him. When he felt her pulse and the beating of her heart, he sensed that their love was what kept her alive. He continued to fight for the Jihad, silently dedicating each victory to her.

Now he looked up as reports streamed in from Honru, excited transmissions from Faykan's and Rikov's kindjals. The warships swooped in over machine strongholds, dropping swarms of pulse explosives that emitted bursts of destructive Holtzman energy.

"All scramblers deployed, Primero," Faykan transmitted. "The main city is ready for our second phase."

Quentin smiled. In orbit, the first group of robotic warships ineffectually slammed into the Jihad ships, more of a nuisance than a threat, so long as the Holtzman shields did not overheat.

He redeployed his forces. "Javelins, descend into the atmosphere. All projectile batteries prepare for bombardment from above. Tell the Ginaz shock troops to gather their pulse-swords and get ready to scour the city. I expect them to remove all vestiges of machine resistance down there."

His subcommanders acknowledged, and the primero sat back in his command seat as the huge battleships closed in to secure their conquest.

QUENTIN BUTLER'S ARMORED vehicle crunched through the debris in the main machine city, carrying the conquering commander forward. He surveyed the devastation, saddened by the waste of a beautiful planet. Factories and industrial lines spread out across a landscape that once had been agricultural fields.

Liberated human slaves ran about in the streets, dazed, seeking shelter, breaking free of their holding pens, abandoning labor lines where guardian robots now hung stunned and useless after the pulse bombardment from the skies.

Quentin was reminded of the liberation of Parmentier, early in his career. On Parmentier, the stricken people had been unable to believe that the thinking machines were finally vanquished. Now, in the years of pros-perity since he'd ceded temporary governorship of the reconquered planet to Rikov, the people worshipped Quentin and the Butler Brothers as saviors.

But these Honru survivors did not shout or cheer as Quentin had anticipated; they seemed too surprised to know how to react. . . .

Groups of sharp-eyed mercenaries and swordmasters raced forward into the remaining battle zones. Too independent, they would never make a good organized combat unit, but the mercenaries were effective solo fighters and crack demolition troops. They sought out any robot that still functioned.

Unprotected work machines and sentinels, considered expendable by the evermind, had been destroyed during the first pulse bombardment. But now combat meks came out, still fighting though they were clearly damaged and disoriented. Wielding pulse-swords, the swift and deadly mercenaries eliminated their enemies one by one.

From his jouncing command vehicle, Quentin could see the armored citadel through which the Omnius evermind linked itself to the city. To reach this primary target, the Ginaz mercenaries fought like whirlwinds, pushing their way closer and closer, heedless of their own danger.

Quentin heaved a sigh. If only he'd had more men like that fifteen years ago for the second defense of Ix, he would not have lost so many fighters and civilians. Vowing that Omnius would not retake any world that the Army of the Jihad had freed, Quentin had driven back the machine incursion at great, but necessary, cost. He had been trapped in an underground cave-in himself, nearly buried alive before his rescue. . . . That battle had strengthened his reputation as a hero and earned him more accolades than he knew what to do with.

Now, as the mercenaries swept through the Honru city, another ragtag group of humans came forward, surprising him. These people carried hastily created banners, thrown together from rags, paint, and whatever they could scrounge from the city. Chanting and cheering, they cried out the name of martyred Serena Butler. Though they had few effective weapons, they threw themselves into the fight.

Quentin watched from his command vehicle. He had encountered Martyrists before.

Apparently, even here on oppressed Honru, captive humans talked quietly of the Priestess of the Jihad, her murdered baby, and the first

Grand Patriarch. News had probably been carried to them by new prisoners from recently conquered League Worlds. In captivity, they had secretly prayed to the Three Martyrs, hoping their angels might come down from Heaven and strike Omnius dead. On Unallied Planets, free League Worlds, and even here under the oppression of Omnius rule, people swore to sacrifice themselves for the greater cause of mankind—just the way Serena, Manion the Innocent, and Iblis Ginjo had done.

Now the Martyrists surged forward, galvanized. They threw themselves upon the remaining machines, smashing stunned worker drones or hurling themselves upon armed combat meks. By Quentin's estimation, five fanatics died for every robot they managed to deactivate, but this did not deter them. The only way the primero could save these people would be to end the conflict quickly—and that meant annihilating Omnius in the central citadel.

If all else failed, Quentin had the option of dropping enhanced pulse-atomics on the city. The warheads would instantly vaporize Omnius and obliterate thinking-machine control from Honru . . . but that would kill all of these people as well. Quentin did not wish to win at such a cost. Not as long as he had other alternatives.

Finished with their kindjal raids, both Rikov and Faykan found their father's command vehicle and reported directly to him. After seeing the Martyrists, the Butler Brothers had reached the same conclusion. "We need a commando raid, Father," said Rikov. "Now."

"Here on the battlefield I am your *primero*, not your father," Quentin reminded him. "You will address me as such."

"Yes, sir."

"Still, he's right," Faykan added. "Let me lead a group of mercenaries directly into the citadel. We'll plant explosives and destroy the evermind."

"No, Faykan. You are a commanding officer now, not a wild soldier. Such adventures are for others to engage in."

Rikov spoke again. "Then let me select mercenaries, sir. Within the hour, we will destroy Omnius—I'll lead them myself."

Quentin shook his head again. "The mercenaries already know their mission requirements."

The words had barely left the primero's lips when a huge explosion ripped through the distant city blocks. The Omnius citadel turned into a blinding flash of light, and an expanding shockwave vaporized the citadel and toppled buildings in an increasing radius. As the light dwindled, the dust seemed to implode. Not a scrap of the evermind's fortress remained.

Moments later, the leader of the Ginaz mercenaries strode up to the command vehicle. "The problem has been taken care of, Primero."

Quentin grinned. "So it has." He clasped the hands of Faykan and Rikov and raised them in a triumphal salute. "A good day's work. And another momentous conquest over Omnius."

The path to victory is not always direct.

—TLALOC,

A Time for Titans

When yet another Omnius battle fleet arrived at the cymek stronghold on Richese, Agamemnon groaned at the evermind's persistent foolishness. "If his gelcircuitry brain is supposed to be so sophisticated, why is it that Omnius never learns?" Through the speakerpatches of his intimidating walker-form, the general's synthesized voice carried a clear undertone of annoyance.

He did not expect the hostage robot to answer him, but Seurat said, "Relentlessness is often an advantage of thinking machines. It has brought us many victories over the centuries—as you well know, General Agamemnon."

Despite Seurat's apparent lack of resistance—he was a damned robot after all, even if an autonomous one—his answers and advice had been singularly unhelpful. He seemed to be toying with his cymek captors; refusing to provide answers, withholding necessary information. After more than five decades, it was very frustrating. But Agamemnon couldn't kill him yet.

The Titan general strode around the vast open room, angry at the robot fleet approaching the planet. His crablike walker was much larger than the bodies he'd worn as a lapdog of Omnius, before he and the surviving Titans had rebelled and broken free of the Synchronized Worlds. After the thinking machines were crippled on Bela Tegeuse by a computer virus—unwittingly delivered by Seurat himself—Agamemnon and his cymeks had conquered that world, and then they had seized Richese, which they now used as a base of operations.

The general grumbled. "This is the seventh time Omnius has sent a fleet either here or to Bela Tegeuse. Each time we've succeeded in driving him back, and he knows we have scrambler technology. He's caught in a feedback loop, unable to move on and leave us alone." He did not point out, though, that this group was noticeably larger than the previous cluster Omnius had sent against Richese. *Perhaps he is learning after all. . . .*

Seurat's smooth coppery face was always placid, expressionless. "Your cymeks have destroyed many of Omnius's update spheres, thereby causing significant damage to the Synchronized Worlds. The evermind must respond until he achieves the desired result."

"I wish he'd spend his time fighting the *hrethgir* instead. Maybe the human vermin and the Omnius forces will wipe each other out—and do us all a favor."

"I would not consider that a favor," Seurat said.

In disgust, Agamemnon clattered away on heavily reinforced piston legs. Automatic defensive alarms had begun to sound. "I don't know why I shouldn't just dismantle you."

"Nor do I. Perhaps we should think of an answer together."

The Titan general had never let Seurat know his true thoughts. He'd captured the independent robot because Seurat had spent a great deal of time with Agamemnon's treacherous son, Vorian Atreides. Vorian had been a trustee, given advantages and a great deal of power. But for the love of a woman, Serena Butler, he had thrown everything away, turning against the thinking machines and defecting to the free humans.

For many years, the Titan general had been unable to explain why Vorian had betrayed his own father. Agamemnon had placed so much hope in him, had made so many plans. He had intended to convert Vor into a cymek himself, as a worthy successor to the Titans. Now the general had no options for continuing his own bloodline. There would be no more offspring. . . .

Seurat, in theory, could provide insights into how Vorian thought and behaved. "Would you like to hear a joke, General Agamemnon? Your son told it to me, long ago. How many *hrethgir* are required to fill one brain canister?"

The Titan paused as he strode through the exit arch. Was that why he kept this robot around, just to hear stories about bygone times with

Vorian as his copilot aboard the *Dream Voyager?* That nonsense was a softness Agamemnon could not afford to show.

"I'm in no mood for it, Seurat. I have a battle to attend." The cymeks would be rallying their forces, launching attack ships. He made up his mind that once he drove off this annoying Omnius fleet, he would destroy the independent robot and start fresh.

Inside the control center, Dante, one of the three remaining Titans, operated the inventory and communications systems for the Richese installation. "They have repeated their decree five times now, verbatim. It is the same one they issued during their previous attempt. They await our surrender."

"Let me hear it," Agamemnon said.

A flat voice poured from the speakers. "To the Titans Agamemnon, Juno, and Dante, your cymek rebellion has caused harm to the Synchronized Worlds, so your threat must be eradicated. Omnius has issued instructions for your immediate capture and the destruction of your followers."

"Do they expect us to feel guilty about it?" Agamemnon said. "Juno isn't even here." His beloved mate had spent the past several years as a queen on Bela Tegeuse.

Dante moved his walker-body in a strangely human gesture as if he meant to shrug his shoulders. "For a thousand years Omnius allowed us to serve the thinking machines. According to his calculations, we should be grateful."

"I think you're learning humor from Seurat. Is Beowulf ready? I want him to take the brunt of it, if anything goes wrong."

"His fleet is prepared."

"All of them expendable and armed with scrambler mines?"

"Yes, all neos, with clear instructions."

Neo-cymeks had been created from the enslaved populace on Richese and Bela Tegeuse. Precise surgery detached volunteer brains from frail human forms and installed them in mechanical walkers. Ever wary and vigilant, the Titans ensured their converts' loyalty by installing "dead man" switches into all their life-support systems that would cause them to break down if the Titans died. Even the neos on other cymek planets, far from here, had to receive a "reset" signal at least once every two years, or else they would perish. If the general and his two companions were assassinated, all of the neo-cymeks would eventually succumb. It not only prevented betrayal, but also fostered in them a fanatical desire to protect Agamemnon, Juno, and Dante.

The general grumbled. "I don't know whether to hope for Beowulf's survival or his destruction. I simply don't know what to do with him." He paced with metal legs, waiting for events to unfold as he thumped along.

Beowulf had been the first neo-cymek to join the Titans' rebellion against Omnius. When he had attacked the Rossak Sorceress Zufa Cenva and the businessman Aurelius Venport, based on information delivered by a human spy for the thinking machines, Beowulf had suffered severe damage. Though a mechanical body could easily be replaced or rebuilt, the neo-cymek's brain had been injured. The Titans kept him around, but the clumsy and erratic Beowulf was now more of a liability than an asset.

"I think I'll go up there myself. Is there a military ship available for my preservation canister?"

"Always, General Agamemnon. Shall I reply to the machines?"

"We'll give them a clear enough answer when we hit them with scrambler mines."

Agamemnon stalked out to the launching pad. Machine arms detached his protected canister and moved his brain from the walker-body and into a nest of control systems that connected thoughtrodes to his brain-output sensors. When the general launched his razor-edged combat ship to orbit, it felt like an athletic, soaring body streaming raw power behind it.

The clustered thinking-machine fleet followed predictable tactics, and Agamemnon was tired of hearing the combat robots' dire pronouncements. True, the evermind was prevented from killing the Titans, but his robot fleets could cause significant damage and destroy everything else. Did Omnius expect the cymeks to simply surrender and metaphorically cut their own throats?

But the general was not as confident as he let on. This attack group was significantly larger than the previous ones, and defeating it would deplete many of the cymeks' defenses.

If the *hrethgir* hadn't occupied Omnius with so many constant aggressive strikes, Agamemnon's handful of rebels wouldn't be able to defend against the military strength of Omnius, or even the human vermin. Either enemy could have sent an utterly overwhelming force, had they chosen to do so. The general realized that his situation was rapidly growing untenable on Richese.

Once he reached the other cymek ships in space, scout probes flitted from the shelter of the planet's dark side to spy upon the robotic fleet.

"They—they—they are preparing to—to—to attack," Beowulf said in a maddeningly slow, stuttering transmission. The damaged neo's thoughts were so muddled that he could not send a clear signal through his thoughtrodes. When on the ground, Beowulf could barely make his walker-form stride forward without staggering or stumbling into things.

"I'm taking command," Agamemnon said. *No sense wasting time.*

"Ack—ack—acknowledged." At least Beowulf did not try to pretend he was still talented or capable.

"Spread in a random pattern. Open fire with pulse projectiles."

The neo-cymek ships rushed out like eager wolf pups baring their fangs. The robotic fleet quickly pulled together into an attack formation, but the cymek ships were much smaller, harder to hit, and more spread out. Agamemnon's defenders dodged projectile fire so they could dump their scrambler mines.

The small magnetic capsules were designed using Holtzman field technology copied from *hrethgir* weapons, some seized on battlefields, others provided by the human spy. Cymeks were immune to scrambling pulses, but the League of Nobles had used the technology against thinking machines for a century.

During the deployment of the mines, robotic firepower vaporized dozens of neo-cymek ships, but many scramblers flew free and clung to the metal hulls of enemy battleships, sending out waves of disruptive energy. With gelcircuitry minds erased, the robot ships drifted out of control, colliding with each other.

Seeing no need to risk himself, Agamemnon hung back but enjoyed his proximity to the battle. The thinking machines were being crushed even more resoundingly than he had anticipated.

Another ship streaked up from the city below. As it roared toward the enemy fleet, Agamemnon wondered if Dante had also decided to join the battle, but that was unlikely. The bureaucratic Titan did not like to be in the thick of things. No, this one was someone else.

He knew that many of his neo-cymeks longed to fight against Omnius—and that was no surprise. The evermind had oppressed Richese for so long, back when the neos had been mere humans; it was only natural that they wanted their revenge. The neos did not complain that the Titans ruled with just as tight a grip: Since Agamemnon had given them the opportunity to become machines with human minds, the volunteers forgave him his occasional brutalities.

The mysterious new ship rose into the thick of the Omnius forces, but did not open fire. It dodged projectiles as it threaded through the fray, passing beyond the front lines of damaged machine vessels. Signals rattled like ricochets across the communication frequencies, some coded and incomprehensible in machine language, others jeering and defiant catcalls from the neos.

"Make inroads and destroy as many Omnius ships as you can," Agamemnon said. "They'll go home stinging."

The neos started forward, while the mysterious ship threaded its way deeper into the group of surviving robot ships. Agamemnon expanded the range of his sensors and watched the single unidentified ship lose its gamble. As it approached a robotic battleship, it was captured and drawn inside, like an insect snagged by the long tongue of a lizard.

Neos launched more scrambler mines. Apparently, the machines recalculated the odds and finally concluded that they had no chance for a victory here. By now the Omnius fleet was reeling from the damage and pulled back, retreating from Richese, leaving a host of their ships dead in orbit, like so much garbage.

"We have determined that other battles have higher priority," one of the robot ship commanders announced; it sounded like a weak excuse. "We will return with a far superior force, which will maintain our losses at an acceptable level. Be aware, General Agamemnon, that Omnius's sentence against you and your cymeks still stands."

"Oh, of course it does. And *you* be aware," Agamemnon transmitted, knowing the thinking machines would not interpret his taunting tone, "that if you come back and remind us, we'll send you packing again."

Leaving more than a hundred damaged or deactivated ships drifting in cold space above Richese, the Omnius fleet departed. The wreckage would be a navigational hazard, but perhaps Agamemnon and his cymeks could use them as part of a defensive barricade. Their base could not be too secure.

The cymek understood, though, that the robotic commander had issued no idle threat. The thinking machines would surely return, and next time Omnius would provide sufficient firepower to insure a victory. Agamemnon understood that he and his Titans needed to leave Richese and find other worlds to conquer, more isolated planets where they could build up impregnable strongholds and expand their territory. That would be enough to elude Omnius, for now.

He would discuss the matter with Juno and Dante, but they needed to move quickly. The evermind might be clumsy and predictable, but he was also absolutely relentless.

MUCH LATER, AFTER returning to the city and assessing the damage wrought by the robotic attack, Agamemnon discovered to his chagrin that the pilot of the lone ship had not been an ambitious neo-cymek after all.

Somehow, after fifty-six years of captivity, the independent robot Seurat had escaped and flown off to rejoin the thinking-machine fleet.

God rewards the compassionate.

—A Saying of Arrakis

Though her imagination could barely be contained within the universe itself, Norma Cenva hardly ever left her cluttered offices. Her mind went wherever she needed to go.

Utterly focused, she captured her copious ideas on static blueprints and electronic drawing boards, while Kolhar's nearby construction yards hummed as workers fashioned her visions into reality. Ship after ship, shields, engines, weapons. The process never ended, because Norma never stopped. The Jihad never stopped.

She noticed without much surprise that it was morning again. She had worked through the night . . . maybe longer. She had no idea of the date.

Outside in the Kolhar shipyards, now managed by her oldest son Adrien, she heard the heavy machinery. It was a . . . productive sound, not distracting at all. Adrien was one of her five children by Aurelius Venport, but the other four did not have his aptitude and dedication for business. The others, two sons and two daughters, worked for VenKee Enterprises, but in lesser positions as representatives of the company. Now Adrien himself had gone to Arrakis to oversee spice deliveries and distribution.

Work crews assembled merchant vessels and warships, most with safe conventional engines, though some were outfitted with the remarkable space-folding engines that could snap a vessel from one place to another. Unfortunately, that system remained inherently risky; the loss rates were so great that few people were willing to fly spacefolders, not even the jihadis, except in the direst emergency.

Despite repeated setbacks—some caused by mathematics and physics, others caused by fanaticism—Norma would eventually find the solution, given enough time and concentration. She had no higher priority.

She stepped out into the cool air of morning, staring at the construction chaos, not hearing the din or smelling the fumes. Most of Kolhar's resources were devoted to assembling new ships to replenish the constant attrition in the Army of the Jihad. The sheer amount of energy, materials, and work that had gone into fighting this war was incomprehensible even to her mind.

Once, she had been a stunted young woman, scorned by her mother. Now, Norma was physically beautiful, with ideas and responsibilities that spanned an entire universe and stretched far into the future. Now that she had so fundamentally *changed*, rising to a higher level of consciousness after being tortured by the Titan Xerxes, she was a critical bridge between the present and eternity. Humankind could not fulfill its potential without her.

Norma had been fortunate, for a time. She'd been well loved and had loved in return. Aurelius, her emotional and business anchor, was gone now along with her stern and egocentric mother, both victims of the war. Norma's relationship with Zufa had been difficult, but dear Aurelius had been a godsend, rescuing her in so many ways. He remained in her thoughts every day. Without his unwavering faith in her, Norma would not have accomplished her vital goals or realized her dreams. Early on, Aurelius had recognized her potential and had put his fortune on the line for her.

Thanks to the agreement Aurelius had negotiated with Serena Butler herself, VenKee maintained a monopoly on the space-folding technology. Someday, the new generation of ships would be more important even than Holtzman shields—as soon as Norma solved the navigation problems. But each time she found part of the solution, previously unimagined problems unfolded, making the answer appear farther away from her, like a multiplied reflection in a hall of mirrors. A chain reaction of unknowns.

As Norma watched the industrial spectacle, her mind wandered, always searching for the elusive answers. Spacefolders could leap from point to point across the universe—the propulsion itself worked perfectly—but *guiding* the ship around the obstacles that littered the cosmos seemed an insurmountable challenge. Though space was vast and mostly empty, if a spacefolder's route happened to pass through an inconveniently placed star or planet, the vessel was annihilated. No chance to swerve or evade, no chance to launch a lifeboat.

As many as one-tenth of the spacefolder voyages ended in disaster.

The problem was akin to flying blindfolded through a minefield. No human mind could react to the hazards swiftly enough, no maps could plot a course through folded space with sufficient accuracy to take all problems into account. Even Norma could not do it, despite her superhuman intellect.

Years ago, she'd found a temporary solution by using fast-thinking computers, swift analytical decision-making apparatus that could anticipate errors within nanoseconds and plot alternate courses. Surreptitiously installed in the initial spacefolders, these computerized navigation machines had cut the loss rate in half, making the new technology almost—*almost*—feasible.

But when officers of the Army of the Jihad subsequently discovered the computers, the uproar had nearly shut down the Kolhar shipyards. Norma had been baffled, citing the evidence of success and pointing to the greater good the superfast ships would do for the Jihad. But Grand Patriarch Tambir Boro-Ginjo had been apoplectic about the "deceit" Norma had attempted to perpetrate.

Her son Adrien, a smooth talker and quick-witted negotiator like his father, had saved Norma and the shipyards, issuing abject apologies, going out of his way to extract and destroy the computerized navigation systems while dour-faced League officials watched. He had smiled, and the officials had left, looking smug. "You will find another solution," Adrien had whispered to his mother. "I know you will."

Though she could never use the computers again, Norma had kept several of the navigation systems hidden away—then spent decades working on the problem from first principles, an impossible handicap. Without sophisticated computerization, she could see no way around it. A navigator would have to foresee problems and correct them *before* they occurred—a seeming impossibility.

And so the spacefolders remained a VenKee investment pit so deep it could never be filled with profits. The technology worked exactly as Norma had designed it . . . but controlling it was the problem.

Fortunately, VenKee made substantial profits hauling cargo, especially the mysterious spice from Arrakis. So far only her merchant company had the connections and knew the source.

Norma used the spice herself. It had proved to be quite a boon. *Melange*. Preparing herself for a new day of work, she sniffed the rich cinnamon odor of a reddish-brown capsule, placed it on her tongue, and swallowed. She had lost count of how much melange she'd taken in the past few days. *As much as was necessary.*

The effect of spice coursing through her bloodstream, her mind, was dramatic. One moment, Norma was gazing out the window of her shipyard office, watching the fabrication of a nearby vessel. Workers hurried along scaffolds attached to the hull or maneuvered along the metal skin using suspensor belts of her own design—

The next moment she felt a rush, like the instant of folding space but different in a way she did not yet understand. During recent months she had been increasing her personal melange consumption, experimenting on herself as well as on the ships, desperately seeking an answer to the navigation conundrum. She felt alive, her thoughts a veritable flood, rushing to conclusions like cascades churning through a black-rock canyon.

Abruptly, in a mental flash, Norma was surrounded by a vision that took her far from Kolhar. She saw a tall, lean man standing in an expanse of sun-drenched desert, supervising the repair of a spice harvester. Despite the rippled nature of the vision, as if she were looking through thick glass, Norma recognized the man's patrician profile and dark, wavy hair that still showed no gray despite his sixty-four years. The geriatric effects of his own melange consumption.

Adrien. My son. He is on Arrakis. She thought she remembered now that Adrien had gone to deal with Zensunni spice gatherers on the desert planet.

He looked so much like his father that she could almost imagine seeing Aurelius. With her son's demonstrated business acumen, Norma had given him the operation of VenKee Enterprises so that she could concentrate on her own work.

Was this vision real? Norma didn't know what to believe, or if what she wanted to believe might be possible.

As she watched the image of her eldest son, a sharp pain ripped through her skull as if it were being cut by a serrated edge, and she cried out. She saw only flashes and streaks of color before her eyes. She fumbled blindly for another capsule of spice, gulped it. Gradually, the pain subsided, and her vision cleared.

The dream image shifted away from Adrien, like the eyesight of an eagle swooping high over the endless dunes. Then Norma swooned and dove into blackness, like a blind worm plunging into the sand. . . .

LATER, SHE STOOD naked before a mirror. Ever since her mental boosting, she had been able to rebuild her body and maintain a perfect appearance drawn from the gene pool of her female ancestors. Aurelius had always appreciated her for who she was, even in her misshapen form, but Norma had used the process to mold her body and make it more beautiful for him. She no longer aged. Now, in the reflection, Norma examined the faultless curves of her female form, the exquisite lines of a face that she had created long ago for the man she loved.

Within her, she felt something disconnecting from the physical world as her metamorphosed body changed even more, apparently of its own volition. It did not seem to be dying, or falling apart . . . but she was *evolving*, and did not understand the process of it at all.

Her physical appearance was no longer relevant; in fact, it was a distraction. She needed to control the power, directing it properly as her Sorceress ancestors had, but on a much larger scale. What she intended required more of her mental energy than shaping a single human body, and much more than the acts of destruction of her Sorceress ancestors.

It always takes more energy to create than to destroy.

Norma felt weary from the stresses of what she needed to do, drained by the continual construction of images, the testing . . . the constant failures. And when she was tired, she needed more melange.

In the mirror, she watched her statuesque body ripple and shimmer. A red blotch appeared on one shoulder. Forcibly, using her mental powers, she restored the perfection of her appearance. The blemish faded.

She kept herself perfect for the memory of Aurelius Venport. But he was gone, and even being without him would not stop her from accomplishing what was necessary.

The line between life and death is sharp and quick in the desert.
—Admonition to Spice Prospectors

O n the crest of a windblown dune, Adrien Venport stood apart from the mechanics, watching them repair a spice harvester while others scouted for any sign of an approaching sandworm. He did not know the detailed operation of the machine, but he knew that under his intense supervision, the men worked faster and harder.

Out here in the sun-drenched desert of Arrakis, time seemed to stand still. The ocean of sand was endless, the heat intense, the aridity severe enough to crack exposed skin. He felt utterly vulnerable, with an eerie prickling sensation that someone unseen and powerful was watching him.

How can any man not be in awe of this planet?

One of the small melange-sifting machines had broken down, and VenKee was losing money for every hour it remained inoperative. Adrien had other gatherers and distributors waiting for the shipment in Arrakis City. Farther out in the golden basin, two spice-excavation behemoths worked an orange patch of spice sand. A jumbo carrier hovered low nearby, while daredevils worked with power shovels to scoop up rust-colored melange deposits, filling cargo boxes and loading them onto the aircraft for processing.

Over the staticky comline, a man shouted, "Wormsign!"

The mercenary crew ran for the carrier, while the mechanics near Adrien froze in fear. "What are we going to do? We can't fly this thing out of here!" One of the dusty men looked helplessly at the engine parts strewn on plastic tarpaulins on the sand.

"You should have worked faster!" one of the other spice prospectors cried.

"Stop your tinkering and make no sound," Adrien said, keeping his feet planted in the sand. "Stand perfectly still." He nodded in the direction of the other two big excavators. "They're making far more noise than we are. There's no reason for that worm to pay any attention to us."

Across the basin, the second and third crews had scrambled aboard the heavy lifter that snatched up as much of the cargo as could fit. Moments later the lifter rose from the ground, abandoning the shell of the harvesting machines—very expensive equipment, Adrien thought.

The gargantuan worm plowed straight through the sand toward its quarry. The abandoned machinery rested silently on the ground, but the lifting engines of the escape vessel roared and pounded, the vibrations stimulating the worm's hunting instinct. Like a launched artillery shell, the sandworm emerged from the covering of sand and stretched itself into the air, higher and higher. The heavy lifter strained, its engines thumping to heave it out of danger, and the huge maw of the great worm opened wide, spewing gouts of sand like furious saliva.

The worm reached its apex, yearned and stretched, just missing the heavy lifter. Its chomping motion stirred the air and made the lifter waver, rising and falling as the sandworm collapsed back down to the dunes, crushing the abandoned machinery beneath it. Then the pilot regained control and continued his ascent, heading at full speed toward the sharp demarcation of a cliff line.

The stranded workers with Adrien muttered with relief to see their comrades escape, but they kept themselves still. Rescue ships could not come back for them until the worm had gone.

The worm thrashed in the wide basin, devouring the harvesting machinery, then dug itself into the desert again. Adrien watched, holding his breath, as the worm's wake rippled the sands, passing toward the horizon in the opposite direction.

The dirty prospectors seemed pleased and relieved at having outsmarted the desert demon. Laughing quietly in a backwash of fear, they congratulated themselves. Adrien turned to watch the heavy lifter as it continued to lumber toward the black cliffs. On the opposite side of the ridge, in a sheltered gorge protected from the open sands and the worms, another VenKee station would provide beds and a place for them to rest.

They would send back a pickup crew for Adrien and the others.

He didn't like how the sky had changed to a murky greenish color in the vessel's path behind the line of rock. "Do you men know what that is? A storm brewing?" He had heard of the incredible sand hurricanes on Arrakis, but had never encountered one himself.

The mechanic looked up from his array of tools; two of the spice prospectors pointed. "A sandstorm, all right. Small one, a burst event, not nearly as bad as a Coriolis storm."

"The lifter is flying right into it."

"Then that's very bad."

As Adrien watched, the lifter began to shake. Emergency blips accompanied the pilot's shouts over the comline. Soft-looking tendrils of sand and dust folded around the heavy lifter like a lover's embrace. The flyer jerked erratically, spinning out of control, until it slammed into the black cliffs, leaving only a small burst of orange flame and black smoke that quickly disappeared in the whirlwind.

The damned worms always get their spice back, Adrien thought. *One way or another.*

It was an unfortunate truth of risky business ventures: No matter what precautions were taken, unexpected disasters always awaited the unprepared. "You men finish your repairs as soon as possible," he said in a soft but firm voice, "so we can get out of here and back to Arrakis City."

LATER, WHEN HE stood in a souk marketplace in Arrakis City surrounded by spice prospectors, Adrien addressed the men, many of whom continually tried to cheat VenKee Enterprises. It was their way, and he was savvy enough to prevent them from getting away with it.

"You're raising your prices too much." Without wavering in his stance, Adrien stared down a stocky, bearded prospector who was almost twice his size. Like the other natives, the prospector wore a desert-camouflage cloak, and dusty tools ringed a thick belt at his waist. "VenKee cannot tolerate it."

"Getting the spice is dangerous," the bearded man responded. "We must be fairly compensated."

A second prospector said, "Many crews have been lost without a trace."

"It is not my fault when men take too many chances. I don't like to be cheated." Adrien stepped closer to the intimidating men, because it was the opposite of what they would expect. He had to appear strong and for-midable. "VenKee has given you a large contract. You are secure in your jobs. Be happy enough with that. Old women do not complain as much as you."

The desert men stiffened at the insult. The bearded leader put a hand at his side as if to grab a weapon. "Do you want to keep your water, offworlder?"

Without hesitation, Adrien planted both palms on the prospector's dusty chest and shoved him abruptly and forcefully, making the man stumble backward. The fallen man's desert companions drew their knives while others helped him to his feet, furious.

Adrien crossed his arms over his chest, giving them a maddeningly confident smile. "And do you want to keep your business with VenKee? You think there are no other Zensunnis waiting to grab at what I offer? You have wasted my time bringing me here to Arrakis, and you waste my time with your childish whining. If you are honorable men, you will fulfill the terms to which we all agreed. If you are not honorable, then I refuse to do further business with you."

Though he remained casual, he knew he was not bluffing at all. The desert tribes had grown accustomed to gathering and selling their spice. VenKee was the only regular customer, and Adrien *was* VenKee. If he should decide to blacklist these men, they would have to go back to scrap-ing out a living from what the deserts of Arrakis could provide . . . and many Zensunnis had forgotten how to do that.

They stared at each other in the heat and the stink of the crowded souk. In the end, he offered them a token increase for their product, a cost he would pass on to the users of melange, many of whom were wealthy. His customers would be willing to pay, probably wouldn't even notice the difference, as melange was so rare and expensive. The desert men marched off, only half satisfied.

When they were gone, Adrien shook his head. "Some perverse genie fouled up this planet as much as possible . . . and put spice right in the middle of it."

The universe may change, but the desert does not. Arrakis keeps its own clock. The man who refuses to acknowledge this must face his own folly.

—*The Legend of Selim Wormrider*

As soon as the day's heat began to diminish, the group of Zensunni men emerged from their shaded hiding places and prepared to continue their journey down from the Shield Wall. Ishmael was not overly anxious to get to the noise and stink of civilization, but he would not let El'hiim go unsupervised to the VenKee settlement. The son of Selim Wormrider too often chose a dangerously comfortable path around offworlders.

Ishmael covered his exposed leathery skin with protective garments, showing common sense, even if the brash younger members of his tribe did not. He wore a mask across his wizened face to retain moisture exhaled in breathing, while filtration layers of sandwiched fabric acted as a distilling suit to save his perspiration. He wasted nothing.

The other men, though, were careless with their water, assuming they could always purchase more. They wore garments of foreign manufacture, designs chosen for fashion rather than desert utility. Even El'hiim sported bright colors, spurning desert camouflage.

Ishmael had promised the boy's mother on her deathbed that he would watch over him, and he had tried—perhaps too often—to make the younger man understand. But El'hiim and his friends were another generation entirely; they looked on him as an ancient relic.

The rift between him and Ishmael ran deep. When his mother was dying, El'hiim had begged her to seek outside medical treatment in Arrakis City, but Ishmael had adamantly opposed the influence of untrustworthy outsiders. Marha had listened to her husband instead of her son. In El'hiim's view that had led directly to her death.

The young man ran away, stowing aboard a VenKee ship that took him to distant worlds—including Poritrin, still devastated from the slave uprising in which Ishmael and his followers had escaped to Arrakis. Eventually El'hiim came back home to his tribe, but he was forever shaped by what he had seen and learned. His experiences had convinced him more than ever that the Zensunni should adopt outside practices—including the gathering and selling of spice.

To Ishmael, it was anathema, a slap in the face to Selim Wormrider's mission. But he would not abandon his earlier promise to Marha, so he reluctantly accompanied El'hiim, even in his folly.

"Let us pack up and redistribute the weight," El'hiim said, his voice bright with anticipation. "We can easily make the VenKee settlement in a few hours, and then we'll have the rest of the night to ourselves."

The Zensunni men chuckled and moved eagerly, already anticipating how they would spend their tainted money. Ishmael frowned, but he kept his words to himself. He had already said them so often he sounded like a nagging harpy. El'hiim, the new Naib of the villagers, had his own ideas on how to lead the people.

Ishmael realized he was just a stubborn old man himself, with the weight of one hundred and three years on his aching bones. A hard life in the desert, as well as a steady diet of the spice melange, had kept him strong and healthy, while these others had grown soft. Though he looked like a Methuselah from the ancient scriptures, he was convinced he could still outwit and outfight any of these young whelps, should they challenge him to a duel.

None ever would, though. That was another way in which they failed to follow the old ways.

They picked up their heavy packages of condensed, purified melange, which they had harvested from the sands. Though he disagreed with the idea of selling spice, Ishmael shouldered a burden at least as heavy as the others carried. He was ready to depart before his younger companions had finished fumbling with their equipment, then waited in stoic silence until finally El'hiim set off with a noisy and lighthearted step. The band emerged into the sunset and picked their way down the steep slopes.

In the elongated shadows of approaching dusk, twinkling lights from the VenKee settlement shone out in the protected lee of the Shield Wall. The buildings were a jumble of alien structures, erected with no plan whatsoever. It was like a cancerous growth of prefabricated houses and offices that had spewed from cargo ships.

Ishmael narrowed his blue-within-blue eyes and stared ahead. "My people built this settlement, after arriving from Poritrin."

El'hiim smiled and nodded. "Yes, it has grown quite substantially, hasn't it?" The younger Naib was more talkative, wasting the moisture of breath from his uncovered mouth. "Adrien Venport pays well and always has a standing order for our spice."

Ishmael trudged onward, sure-footed on the loose rocks. "Do you not remember your father's visions?"

"No," El'hiim said sharply. "I do not remember my father at all. He allowed a worm to swallow him before I was even born, and all I have are legends. How can I know what is truth and what is myth?"

"He recognized that offworld trade in spice will destroy our Zensunni way of life and eventually kill Shai-Hulud—unless we can stop it."

"That would be like trying to stop sand from blowing in through door seals. I choose another path, and over the past ten years we have seen plenty of prosperity." He smiled at his stepfather. "But you always find a way to complain, don't you? Isn't it better that we natives of Arrakis gather the spice and profit from it, rather than someone else? Should we not be the ones who harvest melange and bring it to VenKee? Otherwise, they will send in their own outsiders, their own teams—"

"They already have," one of the other men said.

"You ask which sin is more palatable," Ishmael said. "I choose neither."

El'hiim shook his head, looking at his companions as if to indicate how hopeless the old man was.

Many years before, after Ishmael had accepted El'hiim's mother as his wife, he'd tried to raise the young man according to traditional values, following the visions of Selim Wormrider. Perhaps Ishmael had applied too much pressure, unwittingly forcing his stepson to turn in another direction.

Before Marha died, she had made him swear to shelter and advise her son, but over the years that promise had become like a sharp rock caught in his shoe. Though he harbored grave concerns, he'd had no choice but to support El'hiim in becoming Naib. From that point on, Ishmael felt as if he were sliding down the shifting slope of a steep dune.

Recently, El'hiim had shown his poor judgment when he'd arranged for two small carrier craft to come to one of the hidden Zensunni camps in the deep desert. El'hiim saw it as a convenient way to exchange supplies that were too heavy to carry far, but to Ishmael the small aircraft looked too much like the slaver ships that had captured him as a boy.

"You are leaving us vulnerable!" Ishmael had strained to keep his voice down so as not to embarrass the Naib. "What if these men mean to abduct us?"

But El'hiim had brushed aside his concerns. "These aren't slavers, Ishmael. They are merchants and traders."

"You have placed us at risk."

"We've entered into a business relationship. These men are trustworthy."

Ishmael shook his head, letting his anger grow. "You have been seduced by your own comfort. We should be trying to bring to an end all spice-exporting operations and refuse the tempting conveniences."

El'hiim had sighed. "I respect you, Ishmael . . . but sometimes you are incredibly shortsighted." He had walked off to meet with the visiting VenKee merchants, leaving Ishmael behind in rage. . . .

Now, as night fell, the group of men reached the base of the Shield Wall. Outlying buildings, moisture condensers, and solar-power generating stations had sprung up like mold from sheltered places against the high cliff.

Ishmael maintained his steady pace, though the other desert men hurried, eager to partake of so-called civilization. In town, the background noise was a cacophony unlike anything heard in the open bled. Many people talked, machinery pounded and boomed, generators buzzed. The lights and smells were an offense to him.

Already, word of their arrival had passed up and down the VenKee town streets. Company employees came out of their dwellings to meet them, dressed in odd costumes and carrying incomprehensible gadgets. When the news reached the VenKee offices, a merchant representative strutted down the street, happy to receive them. He raised his hands in welcome, but Ishmael thought his smile was oily and unpleasant.

El'hiim offered the man a hale greeting. "We have brought another shipment, and you may buy it—if the price is the same."

"Melange is as valuable as always. And our town's amenities are yours if you desire them."

El'hiim's men gave a boisterous acknowledgment. Ishmael's eyes narrowed, but he said nothing. Stiffly, he removed his pack of spice and dropped it on the dusty ground at his feet, as if it were no more than garbage.

The VenKee representative cheerfully called for porters to relieve the desert men of their burdens, taking the melange packages to an assay office where they could be weighed, graded, and paid for.

As the artificial lights grew brighter to fend off the desert darkness, raucous alien music pummeled Ishmael's ears. El'hiim and his men indulged themselves, spending newfound money from the spice shipment. They watched water-fat dancers with pale and unappetizing skin; they drank copious quantities of spice beer, allowing themselves to become embarrassingly drunk.

Ishmael did not participate. He simply sat and watched them, hating every minute and wanting to return home, to the safe and quiet desert.

Since there has been no upload linkage between me and the ever-mind for centuries, Omnius does not know my thoughts, some of which might be considered disloyal. But I do not mean them to be that way. I am just curious by nature.

—*Erasmus Dialogues*

Surrounded by festering death, moans of pain, and the full range of pleading expressions, Erasmus diligently recorded every test subject with equal care. Scientific accuracy required it. And the deadly RNA retrovirus was nearly ready to be launched.

He had just come from the last in a series of meetings with Rekur Van to discuss the best methods for plague dispersal, but the robot had been frustrated—as much as a thinking machine could be—when the Tlulaxa kept changing the subject, nagging about the progress of the reptilian regrowth experiment. Van was obsessed with the prospect of regrowing his limbs, but the robot had other priorities.

In order to calm him, Erasmus had adjusted the biological patches on the man's shoulders and lied by overstating the results. Tiny bumps were indeed growing under the patches, with definite evidence of new bone growth, though at an almost negligible rate. Perhaps this was interesting in its own right, but it was only one of many important ongoing tests. He had found it necessary to increase the medications this morning, enough to focus the limbless human on what was most relevant, rather than on silly personal matters.

In one of his favorite plush robes, a rich blue this time, Erasmus strolled from chamber to chamber, maintaining a pleasant smile on his flowmetal face. The infection rate was nearly seventy percent, with an expected mortality of forty-three percent. Many of those who recovered, though, would be permanently crippled due to tendon ruptures, another result of the disease.

A few of the experimental victims shrank from him, cowering in corners of their filth-smeared cells. Others stretched out their hands beseech-ingly, their sickness-dulled eyes desperate; those prisoners, the robot decided, must be delirious or delusional. But of course paranoia and irrational behavior were expected symptoms of the virus.

Erasmus had installed and amplified a new set of olfactory sensors so that he could sample and compare the stenches wafting through his labs. He felt it was an important part of the experience. Over the years, tirelessly running tests and mutating batches of viruses, Erasmus felt proud of his accomplishments. It was easy to develop a sickness that killed these fragile biological beings. The trick was to find one that swept through their populations swiftly, killed a large percentage of the victims, and was nearly impossible to cure.

The robot and his Tlulaxa colleague had settled on a genetically modified airborne RNA retrovirus that, while somewhat fragile in the outside environment, was transmitted easily through mucus membranes and open wounds. Upon entering the human body, it unexpectedly infected the liver—unlike most similar diseases—and from there it replicated rapidly and produced an enzyme that converted various hormones into poisonous compounds that the liver could not process.

The initial indications of the disease were a breakdown of cognitive functions leading to irrational behavior and overt aggression. As if the *hrethgir* needed to be pushed into more erratic activities!

Since the first-stage symptoms were minor, infected victims functioned in society for days before realizing they were sick, thus spreading the disease to many others. But once the converted compounds began to build up in the body, and liver function was progressively destroyed, the second stage was rapid, unstoppable, and directly fatal in over forty percent of the test subjects. And once that percentage of a League World's population dropped dead within the space of a few weeks, the rest of the society would crumble swiftly.

It would be marvelous to watch and document. As League Worlds fell one by one, Erasmus expected to gather enough information to study for centuries to come, while Omnius was rebuilding the Synchronized Worlds.

As he entered a different sector with airtight chambers that held another batch of fifty sample victims, the robot was satisfied to see that many of them either lay writhing in agony or were already curled up dead in stinking puddles of vomit and excrement.

Scrutinizing each victim, Erasmus noted and recorded the varying skin lesions, the open sores (self-inflicted?), the dramatic weight loss, and the dehydration. He studied the cadavers and their twisted positions in death, wishing he had a way to quantify the levels of agony each victim had endured. Erasmus was not vengeful; he simply wanted an efficient means of eradicating enough humans to mortally weaken their League Worlds. Both he and the computer evermind saw only benefits in imposing Synchronized order on human chaos.

Without a doubt, the plague was ready to be deployed.

Out of habit, he widened the grin on his shape-shifting silvery face. After much consultation with Rekur Van, Erasmus had applied his engineering knowledge to designing appropriate virus-dispersal canisters, torpedoes that would burn up in a planet's atmosphere and deliver encapsulated plague organisms across a *hrethgir*-infested planet. The RNA retrovirus would be weak in the air, but strong enough. And once the population was exposed, it would spread rapidly.

Recording a final tally of the humans who had died, Erasmus directed his glittering optic threads toward an observation window. Beyond the window was a small chamber from which he sometimes spied through the mirrored glass. The window was coated with a film so that humans, with their frail eyesight, saw only reflections. He shifted wavelengths, peered through, and was astonished to find Gilbertus Albans there in the chamber observing him. How had he gotten inside, past all security? His faithful human ward smiled, knowing Erasmus could see him.

The robot reacted with surprise and urgency that bordered on horror. "Gilbertus, remain there. Do not move." He activated controls to ensure that the observation chamber remained sealed and fully sterilized. "I told you never to come into these laboratories. They are too dangerous for you."

"The seals are intact, Father," the man said. He was muscular from extensive exercise, his skin clear and smooth, his hair thick.

Nevertheless, Erasmus purged the air in the chamber and replaced it with clean filtered air. He couldn't risk having Gilbertus infected. If the beloved human had become exposed to even one of the minor plague organisms, he might suffer terribly and die. An outcome the robot did not desire at all.

Ignoring his experiments for the moment, not caring if he destroyed a week's worth of data, Erasmus hurried past sealed chambers piled high with bodies awaiting incineration. He paid no attention to their staring eyes and slack mouths, their limbs like tangled insects petrified with rigor mortis. Gilbertus was different from any human, his mind organized and efficient, as close to a computer's as was biologically possible, because Erasmus himself had raised him.

Though he was now more than seventy years old, Gilbertus still looked in the prime of youth, thanks to the life-extension treatment Erasmus had given him. Special people such as Gilbertus did not need to degrade and age, and Erasmus had made sure the man had every possible advantage and protection.

Gilbertus should never have risked coming here to the plague laboratories. It was an unacceptable danger.

Reaching the sterilization chamber, Erasmus tore off his thick blue robe and placed it in the incineration chute; it could always be replaced. He sprayed his entire metal body with powerful disinfectant and antiviral chemicals, making certain to drench each joint and crease. Next he dried himself thoroughly, and reached for the door seal. He hesitated. Before emerging, Erasmus repeated the full decontamination process a second time, and then a third. Just to make sure. He could never take enough precautions to be sure Gilbertus remained safe.

When finally he stood relieved before his adopted son, the robot was strangely naked, without the usual plush attire. He had meant to lecture Gilbertus, to warn him again of the foolish danger he risked by coming here, but a strange emotion dampened Erasmus's stern words. He had scolded the feral child enough decades ago whenever he misbehaved, but now Gilbertus was a fully programmed and cooperative human being. An example of what their species could achieve.

The man brightened so obviously upon seeing him that Erasmus felt a wave of . . . pride? "It is time for our chess match. Would you like to join me?"

The robot felt a need to get him away from the laboratory building. "I will play chess with you, but not here. We must go far from the plague chambers, where it is safe for you."

"But, Father, haven't you already endowed me with every possible immunity through the life-extension treatment? I should be safe enough here."

" 'Safe enough' is not equivalent to completely safe," Erasmus said, surprised by his own concern, which bordered on irrationality.

Gilbertus did not seem worried. "What is safety? Didn't you teach me that it is an illusion?"

"Please do not argue unnecessarily with me. I have insufficient time for that now."

"But you told me of the ancient philosophers who taught there is no such thing as security, not for a biological organism or a thinking machine. So what is the point of leaving? The plague might get me, or it might not. And your own mechanisms could stop at any moment, for reasons you haven't yet contemplated. Or a meteor might fall from the sky and kill us both."

"My son, my ward, my dear Gilbertus, will you not come with me now? Please? We can discuss such matters at length. Elsewhere."

"Since you are so courteous, which is a manipulative human trait, I will do as you wish."

He accompanied the independent robot out of the domed facility, passing through sealed airlocks and out under the red-tinged sky of Corrin. After they walked away, the man mulled over what he had seen inside the plague laboratories. "Father, does it ever trouble you to be killing so many people?"

"It is for the good of the Synchronized Worlds, Gilbertus."

"But they are human . . . like me."

Erasmus turned to him. "There are no humans like you."

Many years ago, the robot had developed a special term in honor of Gilbertus's burgeoning mental processes, his remarkable memory-organizational ability and capacity for logical thinking. "I am your mentor," the robot had said. "You are my mentee. I am instructing you in mentation. Therefore, I will call you by a nickname I have derived from these terms. I will use the name whenever I am especially pleased with your performance. I hope you consider it a term of endearment."

Gilbertus had grinned at his master's praise. "A term of endearment? What is it, Father?"

"I will call you my *Mentat.*" And the name had stuck.

Now, Erasmus said, "You understand that the Synchronized Worlds will benefit the human race. Therefore, these test subjects are simply an . . . investment. And I will make sure you live long enough to reap the benefits of what we are planning, my Mentat."

Gilbertus beamed. "I will wait and watch how events unfold, Father."

Reaching Erasmus's villa, they entered the peaceful botanical garden, a tiny universe of lush plants, tinkling fountains, and hummingbirds—

their private sanctuary, a place where they could always share special time together. Impatient to begin, Gilbertus had already set up the chess set, while waiting for Erasmus to finish his work.

The man moved a pawn. Erasmus always let Gilbertus take the first move; it seemed only fair, a paternal indulgence. "Whenever my thoughto grow troubled, in order to keep my mind organized and operating efficiently, I have done as you taught me. I journey into my mind and perform complex mathematical calculations. The routine helps settle my doubts and worries." He waited for the robot to move a pawn of his own.

"That is perfect, Gilbertus." Erasmus favored him with as genuine a smile as he could manage. "In fact, you are perfect."

DAYS LATER, THE evermind summoned Erasmus to the Central Spire. A small ship had just arrived bearing one of the few humans who could travel with impunity to the primary Synchronized World. A leathery-looking man emerged from his vessel and stood by the pavilion in front of the mechanically animate spire. Like a living organism, the flowmetal structure that housed Omnius could change shape, first towering tall and sinister, then bending lower.

Erasmus recognized the swarthy, olive-skinned man. With close-set eyes and a bald head, he was larger than a Tlulaxa and less furtive-looking. Even now, many decades after his disappearance and supposed death, Yorek Thurr continued to work at destroying the human race. Surreptitiously allied with the thinking machines, he had already caused incalculable damage to the League of Nobles and Serena Butler's precious, foolish Jihad.

Long ago, Thurr had been Iblis Ginjo's handpicked commander of his Jihad Police. Thurr had demonstrated an uncommon knack for rooting out minor traitors, people who had cooperated with the thinking machines. Of course, the man's remarkable abilities stemmed from the fact that he had given his loyalty to Omnius in exchange for the life-extension treatment, though at the time Thurr's body had already been long past its prime.

For all the years that he ran Jipol, Thurr had continued to send careful reports to Corrin. His work was impeccable, and the scapegoats he'd killed were irrelevant, unimportant spies sacrificed for the greater good of increasing Thurr's importance to the League.

After the death of Iblis Ginjo, he had worked for decades to rewrite history and vilify Xavier Harkonnen while making a martyr of the Grand Patriarch. Alongside Ginjo's widow, Thurr had run the Jihad Council, but when it came time for him to take his seat as the new Grand Patriarch, the widow had outmaneuvered him politically, placing her own son, and then grandson, in the position. Feeling utterly betrayed by the humans he had served, Thurr faked his own death and went to take his due among the thinking machines, where he was given a Synchronized World, Wallach IX, to rule as he saw fit.

Now, seeing Erasmus, Thurr turned and straightened. "I have come for a report on our plan to destroy the League. I know thinking machines are ponderous and relentless, but it has been over ten years since I came up with the idea to develop plagues. What is taking so long? I want the viruses released soon, to see what will happen."

"You merely provided the idea, Yorek Thurr. Rekur Van and I have done all of the actual work," Erasmus said. The bald man scowled and made a dismissive gesture.

Omnius's voice boomed. "I will proceed at my own pace, and will execute the plan when I feel the time is correct."

"Of course, Lord Omnius. But since I take a certain pride in this scheme that I suggested, I am naturally curious to watch its progress."

"You will be content with the progress, Yorek Thurr. Erasmus has convinced me that the current strain of the retrovirus is sufficiently deadly for our purposes, though it kills only forty-three percent of the humans who are exposed."

Thurr gave a surprised exclamation. "So many! There's never been a plague so deadly."

"The disease still sounds inefficient to me, since it will not kill even half of our enemy."

Thurr's dark eyes twinkled. "But, Lord Omnius, you must not forget that there will be many unpredictable secondary casualties from infections, lack of care, starvation, accidents. With two out of every five people dying from the plague, and many more weakened and struggling to recover, there won't be enough doctors available to tend all the people infected by the plague—much less any other injuries or illnesses. And think of the turmoil it will inflict on governments, societies, the military!" He seemed close to choking on his glee. "The League will be utterly incapable of mounting any offensives against the Synchronized Worlds, nor will they be able to defend themselves—or call for help—should a thinking-machine army strike them. Forty-three percent! Ha, this is effectively a death blow to the rest of the human race!"

Erasmus said, "Yorek Thurr's extrapolations have merit, Omnius. In this case the very unpredictability of human society will cause far more severe damage than the retrovirus mortality numbers might indicate."

"We will have empirical evidence soon enough," Omnius said. "Our initial volley of plague capsules is prepared for immediate launch, and the second wave is already in production."

Thurr brightened. "Excellent. I wish to see the launch."

Erasmus wondered if something had gone wrong during the life-extension treatment that had twisted Thurr's mind, or if he had simply been devious and treacherous from the outset.

"Come with me," the robot said, finally. "We will find you a place from which to observe the launch in comfort."

Later, they watched as fiery projectiles shot into the crimson sky under the simmering light of Corrin's red giant. "It is a human habit to rejoice when watching fireworks," Thurr said. "To me, it's a glorious spectacle indeed. From now on the outcome is as inexorable as gravity. Nothing can stop us."

Us—an interesting choice of words, Erasmus thought. *But I do not entirely trust him. His mind is filled with dark schemes.*

The robot turned his smiling flowmetal face up into the sky to watch another shower of plague torpedoes shoot away toward League space.

The people welcome me as a conquering hero. I have battled cymeks and I have overthrown thinking machines. But I will not let my legacy stop there. My work is just beginning.

—PRIMERO QUENTIN BUTLER,
Memoirs on the Liberation of Parmentier

After recapturing Honru from the thinking machines, Quentin and his troops spent a month mopping up, helping to rebuild the machine cities and providing aid to the survivors. Half of the mercenaries from Ginaz would remain behind, assigned to oversee the transition and help to root out any remaining robotic infestations.

When those preparations were in place, Primero Butler and his two oldest sons flew to nearby Parmentier with the bulk of the Jihad warships. The fighters were ready for some well-deserved rest, and Rikov was anxious to get back to his wife and their only daughter.

Before the conquest of Honru drove their borders deeper into Omnius's territory, Parmentier was the closest League World to Sychronized space. Over several decades, human settlers had made remarkable progress in reclaiming Parmentier after the devastating years of machine occupation. Now the rough Synchronized industries had been cleaned, toxic chemicals and wastes discarded, agriculture reestablished, forests planted, rivers dredged and rerouted.

Though Rikov Butler still spent much of his time serving in the Army of the Jihad, he was also a well-liked and effective governor of the human settlement. He waited with his father on the bridge of the flagship ballista, smiling as the serene planet—his home—came into view. "I can't wait to see Kohe again," he mused quietly next to the command chair.

"And I just realized that Rayna has turned eleven years old. I've missed so much of her childhood."

"You'll make up for it," Quentin said. "I want you to have more children, Rikov. One granddaughter is not enough for me."

"And you can't have any more children if you never spend time alone with your wife," Faykan said, nudging his brother. "I'm certain there are lodgings in the city, if you'd rather have the privacy."

Rikov laughed. "My father and brother are always welcome in our house. Kohe would have a cold bed for me indeed if I turned you away."

"Do your duty, Rikov," Quentin said with a mock growl. "Your older brother doesn't show any inclination to find a wife."

"Not yet anyway," Faykan said. "I haven't found the appropriate political connection yet. But I will."

"Such a romantic."

Over the years, Rikov and Kohe had established a fine estate on a hill overlooking Parmentier's main city of Niubbe. Given time and Rikov's efficient rule, Parmentier would no doubt become a powerful League World.

When the docked Jihad fleet sent its soldiers and mercenaries down for furlough, Quentin accompanied his sons to the governor's mansion. Never one to show extraordinary affection in public, Kohe gave her husband a chaste kiss. Rayna, a wide-eyed and straw-haired girl who preferred the company of books to friends, came out to greet them. Their home contained an elaborate shrine to the Three Martyrs. Bright orange marigolds were set out in flower dishes in memory of Manion the Innocent.

But while Kohe Butler was a devout woman who insisted on daily prayers and the proper observances, she was not fanatical like the Martyrists, who had established a foothold here. Parmentier's populace remembered the oppression the thinking machines had inflicted upon them, and they turned easily to the more militant religions against the machines.

Kohe also saw to it that her family and staff did not partake of the spice melange. "Serena Butler did not use it. Therefore we shall not, either." Rikov occasionally indulged in the popular vice while out on military maneuvers, but he was on his best behavior at home with his wife.

Young Rayna sat at the table, quiet and polite, her manners impeccable. "How long can you stay?" Kohe asked her husband.

Feeling magnanimous, Quentin drew himself up. "Faykan has nothing better to do than follow me around and defeat thinking machines, but Rikov has other obligations. I've kept him away from you for too long, Kohe. Governing Parmentier is at least as important as serving in the

Army of the Jihad. Therefore, under the authority given to me as primero, I grant him an extended leave of absence—for at least a year—so that he may fulfill his duties as political leader, husband, and father."

Seeing the delighted and surprised expressions on both Kohe's and Rayna's faces, Quentin felt warm inside. Taken completely by surprise, Rikov did not know how to react. "Thank you, sir."

Quentin smiled. "Enough with the formality, Rikov. I think you can call me Father in your own home." He pushed his plate away, feeling at peace and quite sleepy. Tonight he would rest in a soft bed instead of his bunk in the primero's cabin. "Now, as for you, Faykan, we'll take a week to rest and resupply here. The soldiers and mercenaries could use that much. Machines aren't the only ones that need to recharge their power sources. Then we must be off."

Faykan gave a curt bow. "A week is most generous."

DURING THE DAYS away from duty, Quentin entertained Rikov's family by telling stories of military exploits during the defense of Ix and how he had been buried alive in a cave collapse. He confessed that dark and confined spaces still made him uneasy. Then he told how he had encountered—and escaped—the Titan Juno herself when he'd commanded a scouting foray to rescue people on the fallen planet of Bela Tegeuse.

His listeners shuddered. Cymeks were even more mysterious and frightening than traditional fighting robots. Thankfully, since turning against Omnius, the Titans had caused little trouble.

Sitting quietly at the end of the table, Rayna listened wide-eyed. Quentin smiled at his granddaughter. "Tell me, Rayna—what do you think of the machines?"

"I hate them! They are demons. If we can't destroy them ourselves, then God will punish them. That's what my mother says."

"Unless they were sent against us because of our own sins," Kohe said, a cautionary tone in her voice.

Quentin looked from mother to daughter, to Rikov. "Have you ever seen a thinking machine, Rayna?"

"Machines are all around us," the girl said. "It's hard to know which ones are evil."

Raising his eyebrows, Quentin looked proudly at Rikov. "She'll make a good crusader someday."

"Or maybe a politician," Rikov said.

"Ah, well, I suppose the League needs those too."

WHEN HIS BATTALION departed, Quentin decided that he would return to Salusa Secundus. There was always business to be done with the League's government and the Jihad Council, and it had been a year and a half since he'd visited silent Wandra at the City of Introspection.

Over the course of an afternoon, the mercenaries and jihadis shuttled back to the big ships waiting in orbit. Quentin embraced Rikov, Kohe, and Rayna. "I know you long for the old days when you and your brother were wild soldiers fighting the machines, my son. I did it myself as a young man. But consider your responsibilities to Parmentier, to your family."

Rikov smiled. "I certainly won't argue. Staying here, at peace, with Kohe and Rayna—it's a thoroughly satisfactory assignment. This planet is under my stewardship. It's time I settled down and truly made it my home."

Donning his military cap, Quentin climbed aboard the captain's shuttle and left for his flagship. The group of vessels ran through checklists preparatory to departure. Each ballista and javelin was fully supplied and fueled, ready to begin the long journey back to the League's capital world. When they had pulled away from orbit and were preparing to leave the Parmentier system, his technicians spotted an incoming flurry of small projectiles like a meteor storm, flying a course that did not appear to be random. "We have to assume they're enemy objects, sir!"

"Turn about and alert the planetary defenses!" Quentin shouted. "All vessels, reverse course—back to Parmentier!" Though his soldiers responded instantly, he saw that they could not arrive in time. The torpedoes, clearly artificial and almost certainly of machine origin, headed straight for Parmentier.

Down on the surface, Rikov sounded alarms, and sensors plotted the paths of the incoming projectiles. From a much greater distance, the Jihad ships streaked in, ready to destroy the machine intruders.

But the projectiles disintegrated in the atmosphere. They caused no destruction. Not a single one made it to the ground.

"What was all that?" Faykan asked, leaning over the shoulder of a sensor technician.

"I suggest we stay and run a full analysis," Quentin said. "I'll put these battleships at your disposal, Rikov."

His son, though, turned him away. "No need, Primero. Whatever those were, they caused no damage. Even if the thinking machines created them, they were klanks, misfires—"

"You still better check it out," Quentin said. "Omnius is up to something."

"Parmentier has modern laboratories and inspection equipment, sir. We can do it here. And we have a fully staffed local defense force." It seemed a matter of pride for Rikov.

Waiting in orbit, Quentin was still uneasy, especially since his own son had been the target. Obviously, the projectiles had been unmanned and unguided. For some reason, they had targeted Parmentier, the closest League planet to the Synchronized Worlds.

"Maybe it was simply a guidance experiment," Faykan said.

During his career, Quentin had witnessed far, far worse actions committed by the thinking machines. He suspected there must be more than what he saw.

"Maintain high alert status down there," Quentin transmitted to Rikov. "This could just be the prelude."

For two days afterward, Quentin dispersed his fleet in a precautionary defensive line at the edge of the system, but no further machine torpedoes came from the gulfs of space. Finally mollified, he saw no reason to remain any longer. After saying another farewell to Rikov, he led his ships away from Parmentier and back to Salusa Secundus.

The universe constantly challenges us with more opponents than we can handle. Why then must we always strive to create enemies of our own?

— SWORDMASTER ISTIAN GOSS

Though a horrific tsunami had killed most of the population and scoured the archipelago of all vegetation, after nearly six decades thick new jungles covered the islands of Ginaz. Gradually the people returned, eager mercenary trainees who wanted to learn the swordmaster skills developed by the legendary Jool Noret.

Ginaz had always been a breeding ground for the Jihad's mercenaries, great warriors who fought thinking machines on their own terms, with their own techniques, rather than adhering to the regimented bureaucracy of the Army of the Jihad. Ginaz mercenaries had a high casualty rate—and a disproportionately high number of heroes.

Istian Goss had been born on the archipelago, a member of the third generation of survivors of the catastrophic tidal waves, brave souls who struggled to repopulate their world. The young man intended to spend his life fighting to free enslaved humans from the evil machines; it was what he had been born to do. As long as he could father several children before he lost his life in the Jihad, Istian would die content.

Chirox, the multi-armed combat mek, strode forward on the beach, his supple metal body erect. He turned his glittering optic threads toward the current batch of trainees. "You have all finished your curriculum of programmed instruction." The mek's voice was flat and unsophisticated, unlike the more advanced thinking machine models. He had never been designed with more than a rudimentary personality and communications capabilities.

"All of you have proved adequate against my advanced fighting methods. You are suitable opponents for true thinking machines. Like Jool Noret." Chirox gestured with one of his weapons arms toward a small rise on the island where rough lava rocks had been built into a shrine that held a crystalplaz-encased coffin. Sealed within lay the battered but restored body of Noret, unwitting founder of the new swordmaster school of fighting.

All of the trainees turned to look. Istian took a reverent step closer to the shrine, accompanied by his friend and sparring partner Nar Trig. With wonderment in his voice, Istian said, "Don't you wish we had lived decades ago, so we could have trained under Noret himself?"

"Instead of this damned machine?" Trig growled. "Yes, that would have been nice, but I am glad to be living now, when we are much closer to defeating our enemy . . . in all of his incarnations."

Trig was a descendant of human settlers who had fled Peridot Colony when it was overrun by thinking machines eighty years ago. His parents were among the hardy settlers now attempting to rebuild the colony, but Trig himself had found no place there. He felt a deep and abiding hatred for thinking machines, and he had given his time and energy to learning how to fight them.

Unlike Istian, who had golden skin and rich coppery hair, Trig was squat and swarthy, with dark hair, broad shoulders, and powerful muscles. He and Istian were equally matched as sparring partners, using pulse-swords designed to scramble the gelcircuitry brains of combat robots. When Trig dueled with the sensei mek, his anger and passion grew inflamed and he fought with a berserk abandon that made him score higher than any other student in their group.

Even Chirox had commended him after one particularly vigorous sparring session. "You alone, Nar Trig, have discovered Jool Noret's technique of surrendering entirely to the flow of combat, erasing all concern for your safety or survival. This is the key."

Trig had not been proud to hear the remark. Though Chirox had been reprogrammed and now fought on the side of humanity, the young man still resented robots in all their forms. Istian would be glad when he and Trig left Ginaz, so that the other man could turn his ambition and fury against a real enemy instead of this surrogate opponent. . . .

Chirox continued to address the group of young and determined fighters. "Each of you has proven by fighting me that you are worthy and prepared to battle thinking machines. Therefore I anoint you as warriors of the Holy Jihad."

The combat mek retracted its weapons appendages, leaving only two manipulating arms on the top so that he looked more humanoid. "Before dispatching you for service in the Jihad, we will follow the traditions of Ginaz and complete a ceremony established long before the time of Jool Noret."

"The mek doesn't understand what it's doing," Trig muttered. "Thinking machines can't grasp mysticism and religion."

Istian nodded. "But it is good that Chirox honors what we believe."

"It's simply following a program, reciting words it has heard humans speak." Nevertheless, Trig stepped forward with all the other trainees as Chirox marched through the soft limestone sand to three large baskets filled with etched circular chits made of coral, like a treasure hoard of coins. Each small disk was either blank or inscribed with the name of a fallen warrior from Ginaz. Over many centuries of fighting Omnius, the mercenaries believed that the holy mission was strong enough to keep their fighting spirits alive in a literal sense. Each time one of them was killed in combat against the robots, his spirit was reborn in another potential fighter.

These trainees, Istian Goss and Nar Trig included, supposedly carried within them the dormant soul of another fighter waiting to be reawakened to continue the combat until final victory was achieved; only then could the ghosts of those dedicated warriors rest in peace. The baskets of engraved chits had grown more and more full as casualties piled up over the long course of Serena Butler's Jihad, but the numbers of volunteer trainees also increased, and each year new candidates accepted those fighting spirits so that the drive of humanity grew more powerful with each generation, becoming as relentless as a machine itself.

"Each of you will now select a disk," Chirox said. "Fate will guide your hand to reveal the identity of the spirit that lives within you."

The students edged forward, all of them anxious, none of them wanting to be first. Seeing the hesitation of his comrades, Trig glanced expressionlessly at the combat mek, then bent over the nearest basket. He closed his eyes and plunged his hand in, rummaging among the small disks, finally grabbing one at random. He pulled it out, looked at the face of the disk, and nodded noncommittally.

No one expected to recognize the names, for while there were many legendary figures among the mercenaries, many more had died leaving only their names. Buried in vaults on Ginaz were records of all the fallen fighters. Any new mercenary was welcome to dig through that enormous database to discover what was known about the spirit inside of him.

As Trig stepped away, Chirox commanded the next trainee to make his selection, and the next. When finally Istian stepped forward, one of the last, he hesitated while curiosity and reluctance trembled through him. He did not even know the identity of his parents. Many Ginaz children were raised in crèches, communal training groups with the sole focus of developing fighters that would earn honor for Ginaz. Now at last he would learn the name of the intangible presence that lurked within his DNA, the spirit that guided his life, his fighting skills, and his destiny.

He reached deep into the second basket, moving his fingers, trying to determine which disk called out to him. He looked up at Trig and then over at the expressionless metal face of Chirox, knowing he had to pick the correct one. Finally one smooth surface felt colder than the others, a sensation of connecting with the whorl patterns on his fingertips. He pulled out the disk.

The other unclaimed chits fell back into the basket with a clatter, and he looked down for the answer—and he almost dropped the disk in disbelief. He blinked. His throat went dry. This couldn't be! He had always felt proud of his abilities, sensed the greatness within him, as all trainees claimed to feel. But while Istian Goss was talented, he was not superhuman. He could not live up to an expectation like this.

Another trainee bent over to look, seeing Istian's stupefied reaction. "Jool Noret! He's drawn *Jool Noret!*"

Beneath the discord of gasps, Istian muttered, "This can't be right. I must have drawn the wrong one. Such a spirit is . . . much too powerful for me."

But Chirox swiveled his metallic torso, his optic threads shining brightly. "I am pleased you have returned to us to continue the fight, Master Jool Noret. Now we are a great stride closer to victory against Omnius."

"You and I will fight side by side," Nar Trig said to his friend. "Perhaps we can even surpass the legend you must live up to."

Istian swallowed hard. He had no choice but to follow the guidance of the heretofore silent presence within him.

Those who have everything value nothing. Those who have nothing value everything.

—RAQUELLA BERTO-ANIRUL,
Assessments of Philosophical Revelations

Richese would be doomed as soon as Omnius returned with a full-fledged military force. Upon escaping, the damnable Seurat had certainly provided the evermind with vital information about the Titan rebels. By assessing their past failures, the machines would calculate the necessity for a much larger fleet, accept larger losses, and return with enough battleships and firepower to wipe out the cymek installations. The Titans didn't have a chance.

General Agamemnon doubted he had more than a month.

He and his cymek followers needed to leave, but he could not simply run like a mad dog to the nearest available planet, which might be fiercely defended by the *hrethgir* or even other machines. He did not have sufficient information, or personnel, to find and subjugate a new stronghold.

From a thousand years of experience as a military commander, he understood the need for accurate intelligence and a complete analysis of all options. Since only three of the original Titans remained alive, Agamemnon could not afford to take needless risks. Though he had already lived for well over eleven centuries, he valued his survival more than ever.

Juno, his lover, had matching ambitions and goals. Returned from the other cymek planet of Bela Tegeuse, she faced him in their expansive stronghold on Richese, swiveling her head turret to show off her sparkling optic threads. Even in this strange inhuman configuration, Agamemnon found her brain and her personality beautiful.

"Now that we've broken free of Omnius, we require new territory, new populations to dominate, my love." Her simulated voice had a rich, thrumming quality. "But our numbers are not overwhelming enough to face either the *hrethgir* or the Synchronized Worlds. And the thinking machines will be coming back to Richese. Soon."

"At least Omnius is prohibited from killing the three of us."

"Small consolation! Omnius will destroy everything we have built, slaughter all our followers, and rip the preservation canisters from our walkers. Even if we aren't dead, he could strip away our thoughtrodes and leave us in an eternal hell of sensory deprivation. Worse than dead—we would be useless!"

"Never useless. I would kill you myself before I allowed that to happen," Agamemnon said in a bass projected rumble that made the columns in the spacious chamber vibrate.

"Thank you, my love."

Moving with implacable speed, he lurched his walker-form through the archway, already transmitting orders to the neos to prep his fastest ship. "You and Dante remain here and shore up our defenses against the thinking machines. I will locate another world for us to rule." He flashed his optic threads, which sent a constellation of Juno images flooding into his mind. "With luck, Omnius won't find us for some time."

"I prefer to count on your magnificent abilities—not luck."

"Perhaps we'll need both."

Racing away from Richese under acceleration that would have killed any fragile human being, the Titan general traveled to his secret contact inside the machine empire.

Wallach IX was an insignificant Synchronized World, where Yorek Thurr held dominion over a pathetic herd of captive humans. For decades, Thurr had been a reliable yet surreptitious source of information about both Omnius and the League of Nobles. He had notified Agamemnon about the return of long-lost Hecate and her unexpected support for the *hrethgir* cause, and he had also divulged the travel plans of Venport and the hated Sorceress Cenva, so that Beowulf could ambush them in the Ginaz system. Thurr was not the least bit nervous about playing three sides against each other.

The Titan general had ensconced himself in an extravagant vessel built with intimidating angular structures, a full suite of exotic weapons and powerful grappling arms. It served both as a spacecraft and a ground walker. When he settled down in an open plaza on Wallach IX, he extended flat, powerful feet, reconfigured the robotic body, and rose up in a fearsome new form. Thurr's advice might be useful, but the general did not entirely trust him.

Cowed human captives backed away as the Titan plodded down the boulevards to the imposing citadel Thurr had built when crowning himself king of this planet. Though Wallach IX ostensibly remained a Synchronized World, Thurr claimed to have bypassed and manipulated the evermind's external controls. He kept the local Omnius incarnation deviously isolated and fooled, with programming of his own.

Agamemnon was not concerned. If the evermind had secret watcheyes to prove the human's duplicity, then Thurr himself would face execution. After all, the cymek rebels were already under a death sentence.

Because his walker-body was so enormous, he had to sweep his armored arms from side to side to knock down walls and constrictive arches so that he could enter the citadel. It made good military sense to demonstrate his power and put the turncoat firmly in his place.

When he entered the audacious throne hall Thurr had designed, the man seemed neither disturbed nor intimidated. He sat back on his gaudy, elaborate throne, gazing with a jaded eye at the cymek. "Welcome, General Agamemnon. I am always pleased to receive such a distinguished visitor."

Thurr had constructed his throne atop a massive dais. The chair and its pedestal were fashioned from polymer-reinforced bones; long femurs formed the support, and rounded skulls made an ornate foundation. The design seemed unnecessarily barbaric, but Thurr savored the mood it evoked.

Large display cases lined one wall, containing exotic weapons. Momentarily distracted by the beauty of an antique projectile gun, Agamemnon stared at it. The workmanship on the white bone handle was exquisite with scrimshawlike markings depicting scenarios of violent death caused by the weapon. For many years, Agamemnon had collected such weapons, amused by their potential as museum relics rather than as actual threats.

"Do you have an opportunity for me, General?" Thurr sniffed. "Or are you here to request a favor?"

"I never ask for favors." Agamemnon expanded his powerful arms and the body core, puffing himself up like a bird. "From one such as you, I would *demand* assistance, and you would be pleased to give it to me."

"Always. I can offer you refreshment, but I believe a fine vintage would be wasted on you."

"We obtain fresh electrafluid whenever we need it. That is not why I am here. I need copies of your intelligence files, your astronomical maps and geographical assessments of other planets. It is past time that I expanded my cymek empire. I need to decide which world to conquer next."

"In other words, you plan to abandon Richese before Omnius comes back to destroy you." Thurr snickered at his insight, fidgeting with excitement. "And it is good that you cymeks plan ahead and strengthen your defenses, because before long Omnius will have utterly defeated the *hrethgir* and absorbed them into the Synchronized Worlds."

"That's a bold statement, since the Jihad has already been simmering for a century."

"Ah, but the thinking machines have changed their tactics, thanks to me. My idea!" He preened with pride. "Corrin has recently released a potent biological plague. We fully expect the epidemic to spread across the *hrethgir* worlds and wipe out entire populations."

Agamemnon was surprised at the information. "You certainly like to kill things and cause great pain and damage, Yorek Thurr. In another age, Ajax himself might have recruited you."

Thurr beamed. "You are too kind, General Agamemnon."

"Are you not concerned that you will be infected yourself? Once Omnius learns of your treachery, you will be left to die here on Wallach IX." He thought of his son Vorian, wondering if he might succumb to the infection, but the life-extension treatment should have greatly enhanced his immune systems.

Thurr waved a hand. "Oh, I would not have suggested unleashing the plagues until I received the immunization myself. The vaccine gave me a strange fever for several days, but ever since then my thoughts have been . . . clearer, sharper." He grinned as he massaged the smooth skin of his scalp. "I'm pleased to make a mark upon history for all time. These plagues demonstrate my influence more than anything I have previously done. At last I can be satisfied with the accomplishments of my life."

"You are a very greedy man, Yorek Thurr." Agamemnon maneuvered his large mechanical body closer to the weapons display shelves. "You succeeded in everything you've attempted, first with Jipol, then guiding the League from behind the skirts of Camie Boro-Ginjo, and now as a king of your own world."

"None of it is enough!" Thurr stood from his throne of skulls. "After only a few decades, ruling this planet has become tedious and pointless. I hide within the boundaries of the Synchronized empire, and no one even knows what I have accomplished. Back on Salusa Secundus, I guided the policy of the Jihad for years, but no one believed it was me. They all thought the Grand Patriarch was intelligent. Hah! Then they gave credit to his widow and her milksop son. I want to make my own mark."

Agamemnon understood, but still he found the little man's prideful ambition quaint and amusing. "Then you had best help me, Thurr, because when the new Time of Titans comes to pass and my cymek empire comprises many planets, *our* history will remember you as an important touchstone."

He strutted over to the weapons display cases, ripped the door off its hinges, and reached inside.

"What are you doing?" Thurr demanded. "Be careful. Those are valuable antiques."

"I'll pay you whatever this is worth." Agamemnon removed the projectile gun that he had admired.

"It's not for—"

"Everything has a price." Agamemnon opened a compartment on his body and slid the gun inside. He had other keepsakes in there as well, a variety of intriguing killing devices that he had begun to collect. While Thurr glared, the cymek closed the compartment. "Send me a bill."

The man's eyes glittered. "Keep it, please, as my special gift to you. Now, General, what is it you need? More planets to dominate? As my plagues spread, you'll have ample opportunities to invade and secure League Worlds. Soon all *hrethgir* planets will be graveyards, all that territory available for the taking. You can pick up the pieces wherever you like."

"Not good enough. I am a conqueror, not a plunderer. I need a new stronghold now, one that doesn't have its own overwhelming military force. My reasons are of no concern to you. It is only necessary for you to give me an answer, before I lose my patience and kill you."

"So, Agamemnon wants to feel safe and strong." Unconcerned, Thurr sat back down on his throne of skulls, tapping his long fingers together as he pondered. Soon a huge grin split his face. "Ah, there is another alternative. Knowing you Titans and your long-held grudges, you'll consider it quite satisfying."

"We have made many enemies over the centuries." Agamemnon

paced the floor in his monstrous walker-form, cracking the tiles beneath his immense weight.

"Yes, but this is different. Why not go to Hessra and destroy the Ivory Tower Cogitors? As a practical matter, they have electrafluid fabrication plants, which you would find useful. But I think the mere satisfaction of obliterating them would prove enough."

Agamemnon bobbed his articulated head. Thoughts rushed through his ancient brain. "You are quite correct, Thurr. Attacking Hessra will not immediately draw the attention of either the *hrethgir* or Omnius. Crushing the maddening Cogitors would be pleasurable for its own sake."

Human beings strive for respect and dignity. This a common theme in their personal interactions at all levels, from street gangs to Parliament. Religious wars have been fought over this issue, which is simple in theory but complex in practice.

—SERENA BUTLER,

comments in her last interview

As Supreme Commander of the Army of the Jihad, Vorian Atreides could have afforded fine quarters for himself and Leronica, a mansion or an entire estate. The League would have been happy to accommodate him for his more-than-a-lifetime of service.

Years ago, he had offered Leronica an opulent home, but she preferred something small and simple, comfortable but not extravagant. He had found an apartment in Zimia's interplanetary district, a section of the city filled with a variety of cultures, which she always found fascinating.

When he'd brought his family to Salusa, Vor promised her all the wonders she could imagine. He had made good on that promise, but he wanted to give her much more than she would accept from him. She always remained sweet-natured and loving toward Vor. Constant and steadfast, she waited for him to come home and showed great delight whenever they were together.

Smiling now as he walked home through the neighborhood with fresh supplies and trinkets from recently visited Caladan, Vor heard many languages spoken, tongues that he identified from his travels: the guttural accents of Kirana III, the musical syllables of refugees from Chusuk, even slave dialects originating on former machine-controlled planets.

Grinning with anticipation, he climbed the steps of a well-kept wood-frame building, made his way to the fifth floor, and entered. Their four-bedroom apartment was clean and simple, decorated only with a few antiques and holos that depicted Vor's greatest military victories.

In the kitchen at the rear of the apartment, he saw Leronica holding a pair of shopping bags that appeared much too heavy for her to carry in her thin arms. Having recently celebrated her ninety-third birthday, she looked every year of it, since she had never been a woman to pander to vanity. But even at her age, the woman insisted on doing her own shopping and leading her own social life when Vor was gone on his long military missions.

To keep herself busy, Leronica took in special fabrication jobs from people in the neighborhood, but never charged for her work, since she did not need the money. The culture of Salusa appreciated crafts and personally made items, instead of mass-produced objects that reminded the long-suffering people of mechanical precision. Leronica's fishing quilts, much in demand, depicted scenes from exotic Caladan.

Grinning, Vor hurried over to hug her, snatching away the shopping bags and setting them on a side table. He gazed into her dark pecan eyes, which still looked youthful in her wrinkled, heart-shaped face. He kissed her passionately, seeing not an old woman but the person he had fallen in love with decades ago.

She caressed his artificially gray hair as they embraced. "I found your secret, Vorian. It seems that you age from a jar." She laughed. "Not many men use coloring to make themselves look *older!* Your real hair is as rich and dark as when I first met you, isn't it?"

Chagrined, he did not deny her discovery. Though he could never make himself look close to his one hundred fifteen years, he tinted his hair to diminish the obvious gap between himself and Leronica. His stubble of beard did add a bit of age, but his face had no lines.

"While I appreciate the gesture, you don't need to bother. I still love you, despite your youthful appearance." With an impish smile, Leronica turned back to working the feast she had planned in order to welcome him home.

He sniffed the enticing aromas. "Ah, something better than military fare! As if I needed another reason to keep returning to you."

"Estes and Kagin are coming. You know they've been here for the past two weeks?"

"Yes, and I just missed them on Caladan." He made a smile, for her sake, then said, "I look forward to seeing them."

The last time the family had gotten together, he and Estes had gotten into a quarrel over a minor sarcastic comment. Vor couldn't recall the specifics, but episodes like that always saddened him. With any luck, this evening would be tolerable. He would try his best, but the gulf between them would remain.

When they were toono, Kagin had accidentally discovered that Vor was his real father, and he had told the shocking news to his brother. Leronica tried to soothe their distress, but the hurt did not easily go away. Both boys preferred their pleasant childhood memories with Kalem Vazz, the man who had raised them as his own sons until he was killed by ele-crans out in the seas.

Now, while Leronica busied herself in the kitchen, he answered the door to welcome his sons. Estes and Kagin were in their mid-sixties but had slowed their aging process by taking regular melange, which gave their eyes a bluish tint. Both had dark hair and lean Atreides features, but Estes was slightly taller and more flamboyant, while Kagin took the role of a quiet, introspective follower. Youthful and smiling, Vor appeared young enough to be one of their grandsons.

They shook his hand—no hugs, no kisses, no words of affection, just deferential respect—before going into the kitchen. Only then did their tones change, and they offered all of their charm and love to their mother.

Long ago, head-over-heels in love, Vor had set up Leronica and the boys in a nice house on Salusa. Then he'd gone off to fight his Jihad missions, leaving them to fend for themselves, never realizing how much it seemed like he was abandoning them after dumping them in a strange world with no friends.

Each time Vor returned home, he had expected the twins to greet him like a hero, but the boys behaved distantly. Calling in favors among League politicians, Vor made sure his sons had good connections, proper schooling, the best opportunities possible. They accepted such privileges, but did not thank him. True, they had taken his name, at Leronica's insistence. At least that was something.

"Grand crab and shore snails, specially imported," she announced brightly from the kitchen. "One of your father's favorite meals." Vor inhaled the savory aromas of garlic and herbs, and his mouth watered in anticipation. He remembered the first time she had prepared this meal for him on Caladan.

Leronica brought a platter of four large crabs into the dining chamber and placed it on a suspensor-field turntable that floated above the center platform. The transparent tabletop covered an artificial tidepool, a miniature world of seawater, rocks, and sand. Small, cone-shaped snails clung to the rocks. Vor had transported the table here from Caladan, knowing Leronica would love it.

Before the group sat down, Vor opened a bottle of the inexpensive Salnoir wine that Leronica preferred. On other planets the dry, pink wine went by different names, but it was essentially the same grape everywhere, and went very well with seafood. Leronica especially liked its reasonable price; it was a continuing source of pride for her to keep household expenses down.

Vor had given up trying to get her to spend more and improve her standard of living. An economical lifestyle made her happy and gave her a feeling of worth, because it left more money for her to donate to worthy causes. Since so many people were in need of help, so many refugees of the Jihad, Leronica always felt guilty in luxurious surroundings. In some ways, she reminded him of Serena Butler herself.

Vor had an accountant pay household bills and gave Leronica whatever money was left over, so she could donate it as she pleased. Many of her favorite causes involved underprivileged children and even Buddislamic families that most everyone else in the League disliked for their refusal to fight thinking machines. She also gave substantial stipends to her sons, in a generous effort to make up for the lack of opportunities they had in the fishing villages of Caladan.

At the center of the table, four small metal ramps opened on the suspensor turntable. Enjoying herself across the table, Leronica operated the controls from her chair. A steaming roasted crab slid down each ramp onto the plates, and then the suspensor lifted to a compartment in the ceiling, out of the way. The aroma of salt and pungent seasonings saturated the air.

The two younger men removed packets of melange from their pockets and each sprinkled the spice onto Leronica's carefully prepared food without even tasting it. Their mother did not approve of too much spice consumption, but she said nothing, apparently not wishing to spoil the special dinner.

"Will you be staying on Salusa long this time, Father?" Estes said. "Or do you have Jihad business again?"

"I'm here for a few weeks," Vor said, not missing the slight sarcasm. "There'll be the usual round of political and military meetings." His gaze lingered on his son for a moment.

"The boys are staying for three months," Leronica said with a pleased smile. "They've rented their own apartment."

"Space travel takes so long, and a trip from Caladan is such a major undertaking," Kagin said, then his voice began to trail off. "It . . . seemed the best thing."

Almost certainly, Vor would be off again before his sons left. They all knew it.

After a brief but awkward lull in the conversation, Leronica slid open the lid of the glazplaz tabletop. The diners used long clamps to pluck live snails off the rocks; then with little forks they pried the snail meat from the shells. Vor dipped snail after snail into herbed butter and ate them, then dug into the main course of roast crab.

Across the table, Vor caught Leronica's brown-eyed gaze, returned her smile, and it helped to calm him. She ate her crab with an impressive appetite for an old woman. After the meal, as usual, after coffee, conversation, and games with Estes and Kagin, she would snuggle with him. Later, they might even make love, if she felt up to it. Her age did not matter to Vor in the least. He still loved her, still wanted her.

Now she beamed at him and spontaneously kissed his cheek. Their sons watched them, looking uncomfortable at the display of affection, but they could do nothing about the way Vor and Leronica felt for each other. . . .

THAT EVENING AS Vor lay awake next to her, glad to be home, he thought long into the night. His relationship with his sons had never blossomed, as much his own fault as theirs. Recalling his days as a trustee of the thinking machines, Vor wondered if Agamemnon had somehow managed to be the better father. . . .

He thought of when he'd been a brave young Jihad officer with women fawning over him in every port. At the time, Xavier had been happily married to Octa, who suggested that Vor settle down and find a soul mate of his own. Vor had been unable to imagine such love, and instead occupied himself with numerous flings, a girl on every planet. In particular he remembered a beautiful woman on Hagal named Karida Julan; he knew she had given birth to a daughter, but since meeting Leronica more than half a century ago, he had almost forgotten about her. . . .

It was not enough that he'd done his best to help Abulurd, in honor of Xavier's memory. He had lost his own sons, long ago. He would continue to try working through the barrier with Estes and Kagin, but they were old now and set in their ways. He doubted his relationship with them would ever be close. But he did have Leronica's love, and Abulurd was like a son to him. And perhaps . . .

Jihad business takes me to many far-flung places, he thought. *I'll track down some of my other children—or grandchildren. I should know them, some-how . . . and they should know me.*

*From heaven, Serena Butler watches over us. We try to measure up
to her expectations, to the mission she set forth for the human race.
But I fear she must be weeping to see the weak, slow progress we
have made against our mortal enemies.*

—RAYNA BUTLER,

True Visions

The deadly virus spread across Parmentier with appalling swiftness.
Frightened, Rayna Butler watched from the governor's mansion on
a high hill overlooking Niubbe. She was too young to understand all the
implications as her father frantically worked with his teams of experts to
impose controls on the outbreak.

No one comprehended exactly what was happening, or what to do
about it.

The girl knew for certain that it was a curse from the demon machines.

FEW PEOPLE RECOGNIZED the symptoms at first—slight weight loss
and hypertension, yellowing of the eyes and skin, breakouts of acne and
skin lesions. Most disturbing was a current of unruliness, distractibility,
and undeniable paranoia that led to increased aggressive behavior. It
manifested as a new movement of undefined fanaticism, a rush of wildness that had no focus and no goal.

Before Governor Butler and his staff could determine that the rash of
mob activity and violence was caused by a disease, the first wave of victims had progressed to the next phase of the infection: severe and sudden

weight loss, debilitating diarrhea, muscle weakness, tendon ruptures, intensely high fevers, then liver shutdowns that led to death. Thousands more, infected during the incubation period, began to show the initial symptoms several days later.

The unprecedented illness appeared almost simultaneously at villages and cities across Parmentier's settled continent. Rikov and his civil advisors deduced that the cause was some kind of airborne virus released by the mysterious projectiles that had rained down into the atmosphere. "It has to be something Omnius sent," Rikov announced. "The demon machines have developed genetically tailored viruses to wipe us out."

Rayna's father had not hesitated. He scratched all other priorities to launch a full-scale research program, dispensing unlimited funding, resources, and facilities to the planet's best medical researchers. Knowing it was necessary to warn other worlds to be on the alert for the projectiles from space, he selected several home guard soldiers from isolated outposts—those least likely to have been exposed to the virus—and launched them with warnings to the nearest League Worlds.

Then, though he knew he might be imposing a death sentence upon his family and the population of his world, the governor announced an immediate and total quarantine of Parmentier. Fortunately, since the recent departure of Quentin Butler's battalion, no new spacecraft had entered the system. This far out on the fringe of League space, cargo ships and merchant vessels arrived infrequently, usually only one or two per week. On the edge of Synchronized space, Parmentier was still considered a dangerous destination.

Next, Rikov ordered the strict isolation of any individual who showed the slightest hint of plague symptoms. While people shut themselves in their homes and many still-healthy citizens rushed out to the unpopulated countryside to try to avoid the epidemic, Rikov chose groups of men or women without families to crew defensive military stations in orbit. Their job would be to shoot down anyone trying to escape from Parmentier.

"If it is humanly possible," he said in a statement, "we will not allow this sickness to spread to other League Worlds. This is our immense responsibility. We must think beyond ourselves to the good of the human race, and pray that Parmentier was the only target."

As Rayna listened to her father deliver the speech, she felt proud of how brave and commanding he appeared. Because she was a member of the Butler family, her father always insisted that she receive a full political and historical education, and he had hired the best tutors and coaches for her. Rayna's mother was just as firm in her convictions that the girl must receive a solid religious indoctrination. The quiet girl balanced both sets of knowledge so well that her father had once commented, "Rayna, you will be qualified to become either the Interim Viceroy or the Grand Matriarch one day." The girl wasn't certain she wanted either job, but knew he meant it as a compliment.

Kept at home for her safety, Rayna watched the city from a distance, saw the smoke of fires and sensed the terror and tension in the air. Her father looked gray and deeply concerned; every day he worked himself to exhaustion, meeting with medical experts and containment forces.

Her mother, showing clear signs of panic, shut herself for hours at a time in their private sanctuary, praying, lighting candles to the Three Martyrs, begging for the salvation of the people of Parmentier. Over half of the household servants had already left, some disappearing in the night to flee Niubbe, though no doubt some of the refugees took the sickness with them out into the countryside. There would be no safety, no matter how far they ran.

The paranoid and violent behavior of the initially infected joined with the fear and fanaticism from those who were not yet victims of the virus. The Martyrists staged long processions through the reeling city, carrying banners, offering prayers to the Three Martyrs. But the spirits of Serena, Iblis Ginjo, and Manion the Innocent did not seem to answer their pleas.

As panic increased, Rikov organized civil protection squads, arming them to maintain order in the streets. At all hours of the day and night, smoke curled into the air from makeshift crematory facilities set up to dispose of plague-ridden bodies. Despite disinfection and extreme isolation measures, the disease still spread.

Rikov was haggard, his eyes shadowed. "The infection rate is incredibly high," he said to Kohe. "And almost half of them die unless they are constantly tended—but we don't have nearly enough aid workers, nursing attendants, doctors, or medical practicioners of any kind! The scientists have found no cure, no vaccine, nothing effective. They can only treat the symptoms. People are dying in the streets because there are no open hospitals and insufficient volunteers even to deliver water, blankets, food. Every bed is full, shipments are delayed, everything is crumbling."

"Everyone is dying from this scourge," Kohe said. "What is there to do but pray?"

"I hate the demon machines," Rayna said aloud.

When they noticed the girl eavesdropping, her mother shooed her away. But Rayna had already heard too much, and she mulled over what she had learned. Millions of people would die from this sickness spread by the evil machines. She could not conceive of all those bodies, all those empty homes and businesses.

Already, the orbital blockade had turned back two merchant ships before they could land. Their civilian pilots would rush to other League Worlds, spreading news of the medical crisis on Parmentier, but there was nothing anyone on the outside could do. Now that Governor Butler had imposed such a strict quarantine, this planet was doomed to let the plague run its course and burn itself out. Maybe everyone would die, Rayna thought. Unless God or Saint Serena could save them.

Already the deadly epidemic had flared on one of the seven orbital blockade stations. The sickness swept through the dedicated military crew trapped in the sealed station, infecting virtually everyone aboard so that they were all sick at once. Attempting to flee, some of the paranoid and angry soldiers took a ship—and were shot down by the other stations. Within days, the few weakened victims who remained aboard had also perished, and the whole station became nothing more than a tomb in space. Other soldiers, handpicked by Rikov, remained at their posts and did not swerve from their duties.

From the patio of her hilltop house, Rayna could sense the waves of fear and hopelessness carried on the breezes. Her mother had forbidden her from going down into Niubbe, hoping to protect her from exposure. If the Demon Scourge was truly a punishment from God, the girl didn't think those measures would be sufficient, but she always listened to her parents' admonitions. . . .

One afternoon, Kohe went into her private shrine to pray, and Rayna didn't see her for many hours. As the plague continued to spread across Parmentier, her mother spent more and more hours in consultation with the saints and with God, asking questions, demanding answers, begging for their help. Each day, she sounded more and more desperate.

Finally, Rayna grew lonely and concerned enough that she decided to join her mother in her devotions. The girl remembered many times when she and Kohe had prayed together; those were special, magical times that comforted her.

When she entered the personal chapel, though, she found Kohe sprawled on the floor, weak and feverish. Her body was drenched in sweat, plastering her hair to her head. Kohe's skin felt as if it was on fire, and she shuddered, her eyes half-closed and fluttering with delirium.

"Mother!" Rayna rushed to hold her, lifting her head. Kohe tried to gasp something, but the girl could not understand.

Knowing she had to help somehow, Rayna took her mother by the arms and struggled to pull her away from the altar. Thin and gangly, Rayna was not a strong girl, but adrenaline gave her the determination she needed. She finally got her mother to the master suite she shared with Rikov. "I'll call Father! He'll know what to do."

As Kohe groaned and struggled to push herself up on rubbery legs, Rayna helped her onto the low, soft bed. Her mother had just enough strength to sprawl like a boneless sack of skin across the blankets. Rayna refused to believe that her mother had contracted the demon scourge, insisting to herself that no one could be harmed while in the chapel praying. How could God or Saint Serena allow such a thing?

Receiving his daughter's frantic call while in the government chambers down in the city, Rikov set aside his duties and abandoned an emergency meeting. He shouted curses at the sky as he raced to the governor's mansion. He had seen so much death and disaster on this planet that he already looked shell-shocked and stricken every day when he came home. Now, he stared at his daughter with wild and faintly yellowed eyes as if Rayna herself had caused the sickness.

He held Kohe, propping her up in their bed, but she was unresponsive. Fever raged through her, and she had already slipped into a deep sleep. Sweat poured off her face and neck. Squirming deliriously, she had vomited off the side of the bed, and the mess filled the room with a foul, sour odor.

The girl stood beside them, anxious to do something. She looked at her parents, and they seemed just as vulnerable as anyone else. The governor had faced the realities of this epidemic enough to know that with symptoms this severe, Kohe had little chance of surviving; he could summon no medical aid, no cure. Rayna saw the terrible realization in his face. Even worse, he was so focused on his wife's grim prognosis and the plight of all Parmentier that he did not notice the signs of the plague in himself. . . .

WHEN SHE NOTICED she was hungry, Rayna got her own food from a pantry since she could find none of the servants. Hours later, when she felt nauseated and unsteady on her own feet, she made her way to the master suite to ask her father what she should do.

With perspiration beading on her forehead, the girl could barely manage to keep her balance. She weaved as she walked down the corridor, and when she touched her own forehead and cheeks, she realized that she had never felt her skin so warm before. Her head pounded, and her vision rippled as if someone had sprayed poisoned water into her eyes. It took her a long time to remember what she had been doing. . . .

When she finally gripped the edge of the bedroom door just to stay on her feet, she saw her mother lying motionless on the bed, tangled in sweat-drenched sheets. Her father had collapsed in an awkward sleeping position beside her. Rikov stirred and moaned, but did not respond to his daughter's calls.

Then, before Rayna could do anything else, she doubled over and retched. When she had finished vomiting, she collapsed to her knees, unable to keep herself upright. She needed to rest, needed to get her strength back. From other times when she'd been sick, the girl knew that her mother would have told her to go to bed, to lie there and pray. Rayna wanted to take her book of scriptures to read and reread some of her favorite passages, but she could not focus her vision. Nothing seemed to make sense.

When the disoriented girl finally reached her room, she found some tepid water in a cup beside her bed and drank it. Then, not knowing what she did or why, Rayna made her way into the womblike shelter of a cramped closet, where it was dark and quiet and comforting.

With a weak voice and a parched throat, the girl called out for her parents, then tried to summon the servants, but no one answered. She drifted on a river of delirium for a long time, abandoned to the currents, searching for something to keep her from going over the high waterfall ahead.

She closed her eyes and huddled there, drifting. She knew most of the favorite verses by heart anyway. She and her mother had recited them together so often. As thoughts and images swam inside her head, she muttered heartfelt prayers, taking comfort from the holy writings. The wildfire fever grew hotter and hotter within her, burning behind her eyes.

Finally, when she was far separated from the world, from her room and the dark closet, from reality itself, she dreamed of a beautiful white woman, Saint Serena. Shining and smiling, the woman moved her lips and said something important to her, but Rayna could not make out the words. She begged the woman to make herself clear, but as soon as she thought she heard her, the vision wavered and faded.

Rayna sank into a deep, deep sleep. . . .

There is a certain hubris to science, a belief that the more we learn about technology and develop it, the better our lives will be.

—TIO HOLTZMAN,
acceptance speech for Service to Poritrin Award

Each time she solved one part of the foldspace navigation problem, the answer seemed to move that much farther out of reach, dancing away like mythical fairy lights in a forest of ancient legend. Norma Cenva had already progressed beyond the ability of any other genius to comprehend what she had done, but she would not let the challenge defeat her.

Engrossed in her work, Norma sometimes forgot to eat, sleep, or even move more than her eyes or her writing stylus. For days on end, she pressed forward relentlessly, consuming little nourishment other than melange. Her reconfigured body seemed to draw power from elsewhere, and her mind demanded the spice in order to think on the stratospheric levels where her thoughts lay.

Long ago, back in the most human time of her life, she and Aurelius had spent hours together talking, eating, experiencing the simple joys of life. Despite what had happened to her, Aurelius had always been her anchor to that humanity. In the years without him, though, her thoughts were cut adrift, and her preoccupation became more intense.

Her manipulated body attempted to set itself to her demanding schedule. Internal systems slowed in order to conserve and direct energy where it was required, compensating for the expenditures of her weighty thoughts. She did not concern herself with directly supervising the cellular interactions. Norma had more important things on her mind.

Not interested in the weather or even the seasons on Kolhar, Norma rarely bothered to look out her office windows. She glanced at the construction activities only to reassure herself that the work continued under Adrien's supervision, now that he had returned from Arrakis.

Her calculation chambers stood in the shadow of a large new cargo ship in dry dock. According to schedule, this craft would undergo full power-up soon, preparatory to its actual launch and a shakedown flight. Sunlight glinted off of its nearly complete skin.

Men in white worksuits performed final inspections, scrambling around on the hull, buoyed by suspensor belts. Three technicians worked upside down, making adjustments on the underside of the vessel. The ship would use conventional, safe spaceflight technology, but had been designed to accommodate Holtzman engines. For decades, Norma had insisted that all VenKee ships be ready for the inevitable future, preparing for the day when she solved the navigation problem.

Struck by another way to manipulate an equation, she turned back to her calculational table. She used a combination of prime numbers and empirical formulas, entering them side by side on an electronic drawing board. Since the basic problem involved folding space, and since mathematics attempted to reproduce reality, Norma physically folded the columns over on top of themselves one or more times, providing multilevel views that revealed intriguing alignments. But Norma found it impossible to write down with mere words and numbers what she sought. She needed to visualize the universe and lay out the conundrum by actually layering her thoughts on themselves.

For a long while, the fresh melange sang through her mind, sharpening her thoughts and insights. She stared at the calculations in front of her, as motionless as one of the ancient statues commissioned by the Titans on Earth, before the human uprising had torn them all down.

From outside, she barely heard the familiar whine of heavy spaceflight engines and the changing pitches of pre-takeoff test cycles. Gradually, as the external noise increased, Norma retreated inward, focusing on her own mental galaxy. One of her greatest skills, and needs, had always been to drive away all distractions.

To enhance her efforts, she reached unconsciously to her open supply tray and palmed three more melange capsules, ingesting them in rapid succession. The odor of cinnamon filled the air she breathed, and she felt a calming wind inside, as if her body were the desert where the spice had come from and a great, cleansing sandstorm had begun to blow. Thoughts were brighter, clearer; the background annoyance faded.

How to see a navigation problem before it occurred? How to anticipate a disaster that happened in the tiniest shaved fraction of a second? At such speeds, one had to prepare and react *before* any evidence of a problem appeared—but that was impossible, violating all notions of causality. No reaction could exist before the initial action occurred. . . .

In the shipyards an explosion rolled like thunder, accompanied by the sounds of crashing sheets of plaz and crumpling metal plates. Heavy components thudded to the ground, wrecking storage buildings and screeching across paved work yards, as if a massive cymek force had attacked Kolhar. The shockwave rocked Norma's laboratory building and bowed the outer walls inward. Overpressure cracked plaz windows on the opposite side of her calculation chamber.

She didn't hear it. Papers, her cup, and some drafting implements fell to the floor, but not the electronic sketch board, which she gripped in her hands, freezing it in place before her fixated eyes. For her, very little existed in the entire universe other than these numbers and formulas.

Sirens and klaxons went off, and secondary explosions boomed across the shipyard. Men shouted. Emergency crews rushed to the site of the disaster, rescuing the injured as other workers fled. Like a living blanket, flames spread across the entire building, curtaining her window, scorching and eating away at the walls—but Norma no longer looked in that direction. Though her body did not move, her mind performed complex mental acrobatics, examining different angles, diverse possibilities. Picking up speed, momentum. Closer and closer . . .

So many alternatives. But which one will work?

Acrid smoke oozed through the burst seals in her walls, penetrating the cracked plaz windows and crossing the floor toward her. The chemical flames roared hotter. Outside, the screams grew louder.

So close to a solution, an answer at last!

Norma scribbled new entries on the drawing board, adding a third column that incorporated the factor of spacetime in relation to distance and travel. On a whim, she used the galactic coordinates of Arrakis for a baseline, as if the desert world was the center of the universe. It provided her with a new perspective. Excited, Norma aligned three columns as unexpected thoughts occurred to her.

Three is a holy number: the Trinity. The key?

She thought also of the Golden Mean, known to the Grogyptians of Old Earth. Mentally, she placed three points on a line, designating A and B at each end, with C positioned in between so that the distance AC / CB = ø. This was the Grogyptian letter phi, a decimal of approximately 1.618. It was known that a line segment divided by the ø ratio could be folded on itself repeatedly, creating the ratio over and over, infinitely. A simple and obvious relationship, but basic. Elemental.

This mathematical truth suggested a religious connection to her, and made her wonder about the source of her own developing revelation. Divine inspiration? Science and religion both sought to explain esoteric mysteries of the universe, though they approached the solution from fundamentally different directions.

Arrakis. The ancient Muadru were said to have come from there, or settled there for a time in their wanderings. The spiral was their most sacred symbol.

Hardly able to contain herself, oblivious to the chaos and turmoil that engulfed the shipyards and her own building, she arranged the three columns in a physical spiral with the Arrakis factor in the middle, and again began to fold the columns over and over. More and more complex equations resulted, and she felt herself on the brink of a breakthrough.

In her blistering hands, the electronic drawing board had begun to smolder, but with a simple thought Norma obliterated the damage to her skin and to the equipment. Flames leaped around her, consuming her clothing and hair, roasting her skin. Each instant, she used the energy to rebuild her cells almost as an afterthought, to keep everything stable around her, so that she could continue. On the verge—

Loud and furious movement intruded into the universe of her calculations. A man, bellowing in a deep voice, grabbed her shoulders, knocked the electronic pad out of her hands, and hauled her roughly out of the divine place in her mind.

"What are you doing? Leave me alone!"

But the man would not listen. He wore an unusual suit . . . thick red material, completely covering his body . . . and a glossy but soot-stained helmet. He manhandled her through a crackling wall of flames and greasy black and purple smoke. Finally Norma became conscious of the discomfort to her body, her skin, and saw that she was naked. All of her garments had burned off, as if in her mental journey into the heart of the cosmos she had accidentally plunged through the cauldron of a sun.

With a concentrated effort, she focused on her internal chemistry, felt the changes as she restored her damaged cells organ by organ, section by section, treating her own injuries. Her mind was intact, and her body was easily repaired, simply an organic vessel to hold her increasingly abstruse thoughts. She couldn't, however, re-create her clothes . . . not that it mattered to her.

Outside the burning calculation chamber, medical attendants placed her on a cot and wrapped her in a healing blanket. They began to take her vital signs.

"There's nothing wrong with me." Norma struggled to break free, but two strong men held her down.

Adrien rushed over, looking distraught. "Be calm, Mother. You've been burned, and you need to let these people take care of you. Two men died trying to rescue you from the inferno."

"That was unnecessary. A complete waste. Why would they risk themselves when I can easily rebuild my body?" She looked down at herself. "I'm not burned—just distracted." Her body began to feel cooler as she repaired the epidermal structures of her skin, vastly accelerating the catalysts in the healing blanket. "See for yourselves."

A doctor shouted to the attendants. Something pricked her arm, an injection. She performed a chemical analysis on the fluid as it flowed into her veins—a fast-acting sedative—and used her powers to counteract the effect. She sat up, pushed the healing blanket away from her. The attendants rushed to stop her, but she extended her arms. "No burns anywhere. I am intact."

Startled medical personnel pulled back and allowed her to finish. Norma focused on her face and neck, which had not yet received the full force of her curative powers, and erased deep burns and then a few superficial blisters. She touched the rough skin of her face, felt it smooth out and cool.

"My body is under my control. I have reconstructed it before—as you well know, Adrien."

Norma rose to her feet, letting the healing blanket fall to the ground. Everyone looked at her in disbelief. Aside from her hair, which she had not yet restored, her milky skin was almost perfect except for a large red blotch on one shoulder. Catching sight of it, Norma focused her restorative powers, and the persistent blemish disappeared.

Curious, she thought. For weeks, the red area had been getting larger, requiring her periodic attention to clear it away. Previously, everything about her appearance had remained in place automatically, requiring no conscious effort after the initial metamorphosis.

Adrien hurried to cover his mother's nakedness with the blanket, while the emergency teams continued to struggle to get the shipyard fires under control.

"I need to get back to work right away," Norma said. "Please see that no one interrupts me again. And, Adrien—trust me next time. Some of my choices may seem odd to others, but they are a necessary part of my work. I cannot explain it further."

Too much commotion around here, she thought. Since she no longer had an office in which to work, Norma walked purposefully off toward a rocky hill near the shipyard, a promontory on which she could sit and think in peace.

Humans were foolish to build their own competitors—but they couldn't help themselves.

—ERASMUS,

philosophical datanotes

Though designed as an update ship for the thinking machines, the *Dream Voyager* was a timeless vessel, streamlined and beautiful, no less serviceable now than when Vor had served Omnius. Almost a century ago, Vor had first flown the black-and-silver ship with Seurat. He had escaped Earth in the *Voyager,* rescuing Serena Butler and Iblis Ginjo, and he still used it whenever he wasn't required to be on the bridge of a military ship. In an odd way, it made him feel at peace.

Now he flew the *Dream Voyager,* comfortable at the controls. After fighting the Jihad for nearly a full century, he had far more discretion on his missions than any other officer. When he'd told Leronica he was leaving Salusa again, she had simply smiled stoically, accustomed to his restlessness. In part he was running from further uncomfortable encounters with his sons during their long visit in Zimia, but he was also heading out to find his other descendants. In the final accounting, that must be considered a good thing.

Since making his decision, Vor had dug up details of his past travels and service in the Jihad. But records were often corrupted and incomplete, especially on worlds that had been harassed by the thinking machines. There had been quite a few eager women, all of them wanting to do their part to strengthen the much-pummeled human race. If they had never informed him about their children so many years ago, he would have difficulty following the clues and tracking them down now.

As a starting point, however, he did know he had one daughter by Karida Julan on Hagal. Long ago, when she'd told him, Vor had sent plenty of credits to support the child and her mother. Since finding Leronica, though, he'd had no further contact.

Too often, Vor had blithely abandoned his connections and obligations. He was beginning to see a pattern in his life, that he made swift and far-reaching decisions without thinking through the consequences. If only he could find his daughter by Karida—the last name he knew was Helmina Berto-Anirul—perhaps he could do something right for a change.

Following up on the leads, Vor found to his dismay that Helmina had been killed in a groundcar accident seven years ago. She had, however, left behind a daughter of her own, born late in Helmina's life: Raquella, Vor's granddaughter. According to a credible report, Raquella was now living on Parmentier, a recaptured Synchronized World governed by Rikov Butler.

Vor made up his mind to meet her before it was too late. The Jihad Council and Quentin Butler were happy to have him go to Parmentier to deliver political documents and receive updates from Rikov. This fit quite well with his own agenda.

He pushed the old update ship to the maximum acceleration he could tolerate. The *Dream Voyager* was painfully slow in comparison with the military and merchant spacefolders, but on the long journey he had plenty of time to rehearse his first meeting with his granddaughter.

In her late teens, Raquella had married a jihadi soldier who'd died in the war less than a year later. Afterward, she studied medicine and dedicated herself to helping the war-injured and those suffering from the deadly diseases that still afflicted humanity. Now twenty-nine, she had spent years with the respected doctor and researcher Mohandas Suk. Were they lovers? Perhaps. Suk was himself the grandnephew of the great battlefield surgeon Rajid Suk, who had served Serena Butler during the early fervor of the Jihad. Vor smiled. Like himself, his granddaughter did not have low aspirations!

As the *Dream Voyager* finally approached the outer orbital lanes, a surprising message blared across his comline: "I am planetary governor Rikov Butler. By my order, Parmentier is under strict quarantine. Half of our population has succumbed to a new plague, possibly developed by the thinking machines. Extremely high mortality rate, as great as forty to fifty percent—and the secondary deaths and chaos are impossible to quantify.

Depart before you are infected. Carry our warning throughout the League of Nobles."

Concerned, Vor opened the channel. "This is Supreme Commander Vorian Atreides. Give me further details on your situation." He waited, anxious.

Instead of answering him, though, Rikov's voice repeated the same words. A recording. Vor transmitted his request once more, searching for a reply. No one responded. "Is anybody there?" *Is anybody alive?*

His instruments picked up a blockade of orbiters in place, primarily to stop ships from escaping. They bristled with weapons, threatening but silent. The nearest station looked like a fat beetle, a large, round habitat with brightly illuminated ports encircling its equator line. Messages and warnings were broadcast in the leading galactic languages over all the comlines, threatening to destroy anyone who attempted to leave the infected planet.

Vor hailed the nearest station repeatedly, but no one answered. He had always been doggedly persistent once he made up his mind to pursue a goal. Now that he knew of the crisis here, he needed to see Rikov Butler. And since he knew Raquella was also here, he wouldn't turn around without seeing her.

One of the other stations finally responded to his call. A haggard-looking woman came on the screen. "Go back! You are forbidden from landing on Parmentier—we are under strict quarantine because of the Omnius Scourge."

"Omnius has always been a scourge to human existence," Vor said. "Tell me about this plague."

"It's been raging down there for weeks, and we've been sent to these stations to enforce a strict quarantine. Half of us are sick. Some of the stations are abandoned."

"I'll take my chances," Vor said. He had always been impulsive—to his friend Xavier's frequent dismay. The life-extension treatment Agamemnon had given him a century ago protected him from disease; he had not suffered so much as a minor cold in all those years. "A quarantine is designed to keep people from getting out, not getting in."

The haggard woman cursed at him, called him a fool, then signed off.

First he docked against the empty blockade station. They could send all the warnings they wanted, but he had never been good at following orders. The *Dream Voyager* matched hatches and activated the standard-configuration access doors. Vor once again identified himself, waited in vain for a reply, then opened the locks intent on finding out more about the plague on the surface of Parmentier.

As he drew the first whiff of what should have been reprocessed and sterilized air, a shudder went down his spine. After many decades of war, he had developed an almost extrasensory ability to detect when something was not right. He powered on his personal shield and made sure his combat knife was readily accessible at his side. He identified the all-too-familiar, unmistakable odor of death.

A warning message blared across the facility's speaker system: "Code One! Full Alert! Proceed to safe rooms immediately!"

The message repeated itself into empty space, then fizzled and stopped. How many others had ignored the command, or not moved quickly enough? It appeared that the healthy men and women aboard the station had fled, hoping to outrun the plague. He doubted any of them had had access to long-range spacecraft that would have taken them to other League Worlds. Fortunately.

His boots clicked on the hard polymer deck. Behind a guard station counter he found two bodies on the floor, a man and a woman in brown-and-black uniforms. Parmentier Home Guard. Crusty, dried fluids covered their skin; blood and excrement had dried on the deck as well. Without touching the victims, he estimated that they had been dead for several days, perhaps a week.

A private room behind the counter had walls of surveillance monitors. Every screen showed essentially the same thing: empty corridors and rooms with a few human bodies strewn about. While diminished crews remained alive on other stations, this facility was empty. He had already guessed that the surface communication systems were either down or unattended. This scene confirmed it. With nothing more to be done on the orbiting ghost ship, Vor returned to the *Dream Voyager*.

Vor hoped his granddaughter had found a safe place. With millions of people at stake, how could he worry about one woman he had never even met? If she was a doctor, working with Mohandas Suk, Raquella's services were needed more than ever down there. He smiled to himself. If she truly had Atreides blood in her veins, then she was probably in the thick of things. . . .

Landing in the city of Niubbe, built on the foundations of an old Omnius industrial complex, Vor was greatly reassured to find people alive, though many of them looked like the walking dead, as if they might collapse at any moment. Many muttered to themselves and seemed disoriented or angry. Others appeared to be crippled, their tendons ruptured, unable to walk or stand. Some bodies lay along the streets, piled up like cordwood. Haggard-looking retrieval teams in large groundvans picked up the bodies and hauled them off, but the public work crews were obviously overwhelmed by the scale of the epidemic.

First he went to the governor's mansion. The large house was empty, but not ransacked. He called out over and over, but heard no answer. In the master suite, he found two bodies, a man and a woman—no doubt Rikov and Kohe Butler. He stared for a long moment, then made a cursory search of the other rooms, but found no one else, no sign of their daughter Rayna or the servants. The mansion echoed with his footsteps and the buzzing of flies.

In a slum at the center of the city he tracked down a pink brick building with patches of ivy on the exterior walls, a place called the Hospital for Incurable Diseases. Apparently, in the resettlement of Parmentier, Mohandas Suk and Raquella had established a hostel and research center; Vor had read about it in his brief summary.

If she was still alive, Raquella would be there.

Donning a breather, more to block out the stench than because it offered him protection, Vor strolled into the hospital's cluttered reception area. Though the building was fairly new, it had been used hard and poorly maintained in recent weeks as hordes of hopeless patients swept in like an invading army.

After passing an unmanned admittance desk, he searched one floor after another. The medical wards were as crowded and miserable as the slave pens the robot Erasmus had once kept on Earth. People injured from an incomprehensible rash of ruptured tendons lay helpless like broken dolls; even the ones who had recovered from the symptoms of the disease remained unable to care for themselves or to assist any of the others who were sick or dying.

All the medical personnel wore breathing masks as well as transparent films over their eyes, like an airtight blindfold to protect against exposure through the wet membranes. A few of the doctors looked ill, despite their precautions. Vor wondered how long the Scourge's incubation period was, how many days these medical practitioners could keep tending the sick before they themselves became terminal patients.

Repeatedly, he asked exhausted-looking nurses and doctors if they knew Raquella Berto-Anirul. When someone finally directed him to the sixth floor, he entered the noisome, hopeless ward and observed her from a distance. He tried to find echoes of her grandmother, though after so much time he didn't remember Karida Julan too clearly.

Raquella looked strong as she moved quickly and efficiently from bed to bed. Her clearplaz breather and the transparent eye-protection film allowed Vor to see through to her face. Her cheekbones were hollow with shadows from lack of sleep and insufficient nutrition. She had an upturned nose and golden brown hair secured in a braided bun to keep it out of her way while she worked. Her figure was slender, and she had a graceful way of moving, almost like a dancer. Though her expression was dull and grim, it did not appear hopeless.

Raquella and a lean male doctor worked tirelessly in a ward of a hundred beds, each occupied by a sick or dying patient. Attendants removed corpses to make room for emaciated victims who had collapsed into a deadly fever coma.

Once, she happened to glance in his direction, and Vor saw that Raquella's eyes were a striking shade of light blue. His own father, the notorious Agamemnon, had had pale blue eyes centuries ago when he was in human form, before he had transformed himself into a cymek. . . .

Vor caught her gaze, and Raquella seemed surprised to see a healthy stranger standing in the ward. He stepped forward, opening his mouth to speak, when suddenly she recoiled in alarm. One of the patients sprang on Vor from behind and clawed at his breather mask, then fell on him pummeling him and spitting in his face. Fighting instinctively, Vor threw his attacker to one side. The wretch clutched a scrap of a banner that depicted Serena's baby Manion, and he howled prayers, begging the Three Martyrs to save him, to save them all.

Vor pushed the screaming man away, and medical attendants took him swiftly to a diagnostic bed. Trying to regain his composure, he reseated the breather across his mouth and nose, but Raquella was already there, spraying him on the face and in the eyes.

"Antivirals," she said in an edgy, businesslike voice. "Only partially effective, but we haven't found anything better. I can't tell if anything got into your mouth or eyes. The risk of infection is great."

He thanked her, didn't say that he believed he was immune, just looked at Raquella's bright blue eyes. Vor couldn't stop his smile.

It seemed an odd way to meet his granddaughter.

"VORIAN ATREIDES," SAID Dr. Suk. In a small private office, he checked Vor quickly after the attack, though he had many patients in far worse shape. "*The* Vorian Atreides? You were a fool to come here."

Suk's skin was such an intense brown that it was almost black. He appeared to be around forty, with shallow creases on his face and large brown eyes, though he was impatient and harried. His boyish features, accented by a wild mane of black hair that he kept out of the way with a silver clasp, gave him the look of a grown-up child.

Even in the enclosed office, the air stank of harsh disinfectants. Vor didn't want to talk about his life-extension treatment. "I will either survive . . . or not."

"The same can be said of all of us. The Scourge gives us an even chance of living or dying." Suk shook Vor's hand in his own gloved grip, then he squeezed Raquella's hand, a warm gesture that implied how close they had been for a long time. The crisis of the plague would have thrown many people together in desperation, but Suk and Raquella had already been a team.

After Suk hurried off, already intent on other duties, Raquella turned to Vor, giving him an appraising look. "What is the Supreme Commander of the Jihad doing on Parmentier, without a bodyguard?"

"I've taken a leave to attend to personal matters—to meet you."

The weeks of fighting the epidemic had left her with little capacity to experience any emotions. "And why is that?"

"I was a friend of your grandmother Karida," Vor admitted. "A *very* good friend, but I let her down. I lost her. I found out a long time ago that we had a daughter, but I lost track of her until very recently. A daughter named Helmina, who was your mother."

Raquella stared at him with wide-open eyes, then seemed to comprehend all at once. "You're not that soldier, the one my grandmother loved? But—"

He gave a faint, embarrassed smile. "Karida was a beautiful woman, and I'm deeply sorry she's gone. I wish I had done a lot of things differently, but I'm not the same person I was then. That's why I came here to find you."

"My grandmother thought you had died in the Jihad." Her brows knitted over her clear blue eyes. "The name she gave me was not Vorian Atreides."

"For security reasons, I had to use aliases. Because of my high rank."

"And other reasons, perhaps? Because you never intended to return?"

"The Jihad is an uncertain master. I couldn't make promises. I . . ." His voice trailed off. He didn't want to tell lies, or even distort the truth.

The thoughts were peculiar to Vor. He had been a free spirit during most of his long life, and the idea of family had always frightened him because of the chains and limits it suggested. But in spite of his lack of closeness with Estes and Kagin, he had come to realize that a family also opened up limitless possibilities for love.

"My grandfather looks as young as I do." Raquella seemed interested, but she was so overwhelmed by the epidemic that her reactions were dulled. "I would like to study you, take genetic samples, prove our blood connections—but that can't be my priority right now. Not with all this. And during such a crisis, it seems to me that a personal visit to track down an illegitimate granddaughter is rather . . . self-indulgent."

Vor gave her a wry smile. "I have lived through eight decades of the Jihad, and there is always 'such a crisis.' Now that I see what's happening here, I'm glad I didn't wait." He grasped her hand with both of his. "Come back with me to Salusa Secundus. You can deliver your summary and message to the Parliament. We'll get the best medical teams in the League to work on a cure, send all possible aid back to this planet."

She cut him off. "If you truly believe I am the granddaughter of the great Vorian Atreides, then you can't possibly imagine I would leave when there is so much for me to do, so many people to help?" She raised her eyebrows, and he felt his heart swell. He had, of course, expected no other answer.

Raquella turned, fixing him with her bright, intelligent gaze. "And I wouldn't risk spreading the plague. However, Supreme Commander, if you insist on going back to Salusa, then tell the League what we face here. We need doctors, medical equipment, disease researchers."

He nodded. "If this epidemic was truly engineered by the thinking machines, then I don't doubt that Omnius has launched plague canisters to more worlds than Parmentier. The rest of the League must be warned."

Uneasy, Raquella pulled away and stood up. "I will give you all of our records and test results. The plague is out of control here, an RNA retrovirus. Hundreds of thousands of people have died in a short time, with over a forty percent *direct* mortality rate, not to mention all the deaths from derivative causes like infections, dehydration, organ failure, and so on. We can treat the symptoms, try to make the patients comfortable, but so far nothing eradicates the virus."

"Is there any chance for a cure?"

She looked up at the sound of shouts coming from one of the crowded wards, then sighed. "Not with our facilities here. We don't have the supplies or personnel to tend everyone. Whenever he can spare a moment, Mohandas does laboratory work, researching the course of the Scourge. We don't see the usual pattern of viral progress. It builds up in the liver, which was quite unexpected. We discovered that aspect only days ago. A cure is not—" She caught herself. "We can always hope."

Vor thought of his youth spent as a trustee of the thinking machines, blind to all the harm they were causing. "I should have guessed long ago that the thinking machines might try something like this. Omnius . . . or, more likely, Erasmus." After a moment's hesitation, Vor pulled off the breather. "What you've accomplished here, and all the impossible things you're attempting—it's most noble."

Raquella's blue eyes shone with a new intensity. "Thank you . . . Grandfather."

Vor took a deep breath. "I'm very proud of you, Raquella. More than I can ever express."

"I'm not used to people saying that." She seemed to feel a shy pleasure. "Especially when I see all around me every patient I've failed to save, and all the broken ones who will never completely recover. Even once this has passed, a large segment of the population will remain crippled for life."

He took her shoulders, stared intently into her face. "Nevertheless, I *am* very proud of you. I should have found you long before this."

"Thank you for caring enough to find me now." Obviously uncomfortable, she spoke with a new urgency. "Now, if you can indeed get away from Parmentier, then leave right now. I pray that you have not contracted the disease, and that you arrive safely on Salusa. Be very cautious. If . . . if you are infected, the incubation period is short enough that you'll show symptoms long before you reach the nearest League World. However, if you manifest any sign of the disease, don't risk—"

"I know, Raquella. But even if the quarantine here was imposed in time, and never broken, I fear that Omnius dispatched plague canisters to other targets as well. Machines rely on redundancy." He saw Raquella wince as the realization hit home. "If that is the case, then all your quarantine efforts might not save humanity. Warning them and sharing what you and Dr. Suk have learned so far may do more to protect them than any quarantine could."

"Hurry, then. We'll both fight this plague as best we can."

Vor reboarded the *Dream Voyager* and set coordinates for home. He easily evaded the barely manned barricade stations and feared that some infected people might have done so as well. Sadness enveloped him as he lifted away from Parmentier, and he hoped he would see Raquella again.

In memory, he saw the fleeting expression of pleasure she had shown when he'd said he was proud of her. That moment, so ephemeral but beautiful, had been worth the entire trip.

But now he had another duty to perform for humanity.

If we allow ourselves to become too human, to admit the weakness of love and compassion at the time when it is most dangerous, then we create a vulnerability by which the thinking machines can destroy us utterly. Yes, human beings have hearts and souls which the demon machines do not, but we cannot allow these things to be the cause of our extinction.

—QUENTIN BUTLER,
letter to his son Faykan

After returning home from the liberation of Honru, Quentin Butler went to spend time with Wandra in the City of Introspection. His wife was unresponsive and silent, as always, but the weathered primero liked to just sit beside her, comforting her with his presence and drawing comfort from hers. Staring at Wandra's face, he could still see the beauty, shadows of the good times. He spoke aloud, talking softly about what he had done on his recent mission, telling her about visiting Rikov's family on Parmentier.

Unfortunately, Quentin had barely an hour with her before a fresh-faced young quinto found him. The Jihad officer hurried into the beautifully graveled and landscaped grounds of the religious retreat. An old metaphysical scholar in a voluminous purple shirt guided the visitor along, moving much too slowly for the young officer's sense of urgency.

"Primero Butler! We've just received a communiqué from Parmentier. The governor dispatched a ship with an urgent message weeks ago. It's a warning!"

Quentin squeezed Wandra's limp hand and stood, straightening his back and immediately turning his attention toward duty. "A warning from Rikov? Let me see this messenger."

"You can't, Primero. I mean, he hasn't come down to Salusa. The messenger remains in orbit transmitting, but he refuses to leave his ship. He's afraid he'll infect us all."

"Infect us? What's happening?"

"And that's not everything, sir—already news is coming from other League Worlds!"

While the quinto spluttered an explanation, Quentin grabbed his arm and ushered him away from the grounds. Behind them, the scholar stared with a placid expression on his deeply etched face. Then the old man tugged down on loose folds of his purple shirt, and spoke to silent Wandra as if she might be a receptive audience for his esoteric ideas.

WEARING AN UNEASY frown, Quentin watched as the Jihad Council played Rikov's recorded message. Images transmitted by the harried scout from his orbiting ship showed the epidemic spreading through Niubbe and across Parmentier's countryside, people already lying dead or dying in the streets, hospital wards filled far beyond capacity—and this was weeks ago, at the beginning of the epidemic.

"This news is already out-of-date," said Grand Patriarch Xander Boro-Ginjo. "Maybe they've found a cure by now. Who knows what's happened in the meantime?"

Quentin said, "I was there myself when the first projectiles exploded in Parmentier's atmosphere. At the time, none of us knew what Omnius was up to. Now Rikov's bottled up with that disease."

"Who can ever know what Omnius is up to?" asked the Interim Viceroy. Brevin O'Kukovich often made comments that meant absolutely nothing.

Quentin ignored the politician. "If the thinking machines have developed a biological scourge, we must always be on guard. We can destroy incoming plague canisters out in space, but once the disease is dispersed into the atmosphere, not even rigorous quarantines and medical measures will be completely effective. There's no guarantee."

Though he'd had little time before the emergency session could convene, Quentin had gathered reports from recently arrived ships. He had also dispatched Faykan to increase space perimeter patrols in the vicinity of Salusa Secundus, expanding the sensor network to detect incoming projectiles. Normally, it would have been nearly impossible to spot such small objects among the clutter of debris that dusted the system, but because the Army of the Jihad had accurate recordings of the first torpedoes at Parmentier, they could compare signatures and sift out false signals.

"We have to verify this news," said the Interim Viceroy. "We will have to take well-considered action."

Quentin stood. With Supreme Commander Atreides gone—ironically, to Parmentier—he was in temporary command. "We will have to take *immediate* action! If Rikov's interpretation is correct, then we haven't a moment to lose. With interstellar commerce and the exchanges of peoples and material throughout the League Worlds and Unallied Planets, an epidemic could cause unprecedented damage to the human race—"

His secure comline signaled, and Quentin accepted the message. Faykan's voice came over the small speaker, clear enough for the Council members to hear. "Primero, your suspicions were correct. Exactly as you predicted, we discovered an incoming cluster of canisters like the ones that impacted at Parmentier."

Quentin looked knowingly at the other men and women sitting around the Council table. "And did you intercept them?"

"Yes, sir."

One of the Council members suggested, "We should keep one of them intact so that we can study it, perhaps learn what Omnius is doing."

Cutting in, Faykan said, "We have destroyed them all, so as not to risk accidental contamination."

"Excellent work," his father said. "Maintain your close surveillance. Because Salusa is the most important target in the League, Omnius is sure to send more than one salvo of canisters."

Faykan signed off, and Quentin looked around the table. "Who doubts that Omnius has already dispatched more torpedoes to other League Worlds? We've got to stop them, get the word out before the plague spreads farther."

"Exactly how do you propose to do that?" asked Interim Viceroy O'Kukovich.

Decisively, Quentin rattled off his plan. "Disperse the Army of the Jihad as widely and swiftly as possible. Send scouts with warnings and prepare for quarantines. The urgency may even warrant the use of spacefolder ships," he said as an afterthought. "We might lose as many as one in ten, but if we fail to prepare and guard our other planets, we may lose entire populations."

"This is all, uh, rather drastic," said O'Kukovich in an uncertain voice, looking around at the others for confirmation.

"Precisely—and so is Omnius's plan."

QUENTIN HIMSELF LED patrols, like any other officer. He raced from one system to another, helping the local populations to implement protective measures. Dozens of incoming plague canisters were intercepted at other League Worlds, but some had obviously gotten through. Rikov's Parmentier was already infected and shut down—and now news of the burgeoning epidemic had come from five more planets.

Quentin dreaded that it was already too late.

Severe quarantines had been imposed, but frightened people still escaped, carrying the Scourge along with them. In all likelihood some would seek safety on Salusa Secundus. Even with draconian measures, it would be nearly impossible to protect the League capital world. How could they intercept every small, desperate ship? They would have to be ferociously vigilant to spot all incoming vessels, block them and quarantine them until any signs of the Scourge could manifest. Fortunately, given the slow speed of long-distance space travel and the relative swiftness with which the epidemic acted, any infected ships would be obvious by the time they arrived at Salusa.

Quentin paced the bridge, observing the haggard looks and tense confusion on the faces of his crew. His sensor technicians were always alert, understanding that if they allowed their attention to waver for just an instant, if even a single plague torpedo slipped through their guard, an entire world could die.

After so many years of Serena's Jihad, the League was sore and unstable, held together by hatred for the thinking machines. Quentin feared that such a virulent plague—and the panic that spread even faster than the disease itself—might make civilization itself unravel.

I am all the graveyards that ever were, and all the lives resurrected . . . but so are you.

—RAYNA BUTLER,

True Visions

After the feverish visions dwindled into nightmares and the blackness of utter sleep, Rayna Butler drifted, clinging to a strand of life as thin as a silkworm's thread. Descriptions of Heaven that her mother had provided during daily devotions did not resemble this at all.

When she finally returned to her body, her life, and her world, Rayna found that everything had changed.

Still huddled inside the dark, stifling closet, she realized that her clothes were soiled, stiff with dried perspiration. The sleeves of her blouse, wadded and discolored, were pinkish from blood that had seeped out of her pores along with copious fever sweat. Though the discovery was odd and disturbing, Rayna felt emotionally flat and sensually deadened. She didn't even smell her clothes.

Struggling to her feet, Rayna felt her weakened muscles tremble. She was incredibly thirsty, unable to understand how she could have survived without fresh water. She didn't try to understand how anything made sense anymore. Each step, each breath, comprised a little victory for her, and she knew there would be many more difficult things to come . . . and to overcome.

Rayna looked down at herself and noticed now that her clothes were dusted with tangles of her pale yellow hair, long strands that had fallen from her scalp and downy flecks of prepubescent hair from her arms. It made no sense. Her skin was pale and perfectly smooth.

Moving with painstaking slowness, afraid her body might break at any moment, the girl went to tell her parents about all the fever visions and religious revelations. Saint Serena herself had spoken to her! Rayna was sure she could figure out what the shining woman meant. The heavenly instructions had to be true echoes from the voice of God, which Rayna had been able to hear only because of the depths of her sickness.

When she reached the master suite, though, Rayna found her parents lying in precisely the same positions that she last remembered seeing them, only now their bodies were swollen and blackened with the onset of decay. Although the sudden shock and stench slammed open her senses, Rayna remained staring for a long moment until finally she turned away.

In other halls and rooms, she found two more bodies, servants who had not fled the governor's mansion, as she had thought. Her home was utterly silent.

At least the water was still running. In her bathroom the girl activated the long streams of a purging shower. Water gushed from outlets in the wall, and Rayna clawed off her stained clothes and stood naked under the cold flow as she gulped mouthful after mouthful. The heating systems no longer worked, but her skin was numb anyway. All of her joints ached and gritted as if her cartilage had turned into broken glass. She grasped a bar for balance and simply endured the rushing streams. More strands and clumps of hair fell away from her scalp and rushed down the drain carried by rivulets of cold water.

The girl had no means to mark the time that passed, nor any interest in doing so. . . .

When finally she emerged, dripping and rejuvenated, Rayna stood before the polished full-length mirror—and saw a stranger. Her rail-thin body had changed in ways she had never imagined. All of her hair had fallen out. Her scalp was bald, even her eyelashes and eyebrows were gone. The arms, face, and chest of the eleven-year-old were completely smooth, and in the daylight streaming through the windows, her skin took on a translucent, luminous quality. *Like an angel.*

She didn't know how long it had been since she'd last eaten, and though she was famished, Rayna knew she had a more important duty to perform first. She dressed in clean clothes, then went to the private family chapel where she had prayed with her mother. Sitting before the altar of the Three Martyrs, the child asked for guidance, remembering the revelations Saint Serena had given her. Finally, as her thoughts and memories became clear, the girl picked herself up and went at last to the silent kitchens.

Much of the food was rotting, and some of the storage units had been ransacked by halfhearted looters. She must have been unconscious, hidden in her closet, for days. She found the body of another household servant sprawled near the food preparation counter. The sickly smell of decaying flesh mingled with the raw odors of spoiled meat. She wondered what the cook had meant to prepare before the Demon Scourge struck her down.

First the girl drank more water, cool clean liquid that came from the mansion's cistern. Her body was dehydrated. She had lost a great deal of weight. Her eyes were sunken and hollow, her cheeks pressed against her teeth. She gulped a long drink and then stopped when her stomach rebelled. She found some cheese in a food locker and ate a small bowl of canned stew cold, but the spices were too strong and she threw up.

Still weak but knowing she needed to nourish herself, Rayna drank more water and found a small loaf of stale bread. That was good enough for now. The repast of bread and water held a simple, pious purity that imparted heavenly strength to her.

Though she still felt weak and shaky, Rayna decided she had rested enough. She left the governor's mansion behind, turning her face toward the too-quiet city below. The plague was a scourge from God, but Rayna had survived. She had been chosen for great works.

Though she was only a child, she was absolutely clear about what she had to do now. The lovely vision of Saint Serena Butler had given her instructions—and now Rayna had her mission.

She set off barefoot down the hill.

THE PEOPLE SHE saw going about their business looked gaunt and exhausted. They flinched at any startling movement. Everyone had seen many friends and family members die, had done their best to tend the sick if they could. Many of those who had recovered were lame and twisted, a cruel joke on those strong enough to overcome the plague. They used makeshift crutches or crawled, searching for food and calling for help. Even the intact survivors had broken spirits, unable to bear the burdens and responsibilities of doing the work of ten.

Rayna walked alone, her eyes bright, looking for what she needed to see. From the streets, she made out furtive shapes above her, shadows in the windows of dwellings and shuttered businesses. Though just a girl, she ventured forward, tall and confident, so pale-skinned that she might have been a living skeleton . . . or a manifestation of the Spirit of Death. There would be plenty of stored food for the survivors to scavenge, but soon, if they did not dispose of the rotting bodies, if they did not take care of the infections and infrastructure breakdowns, deaths from a cascade of related causes would add a great many to the numbers who had fallen from the Demon Scourge in the first place.

Rayna picked up a fallen crowbar from the gutter. Earlier, she remembered her father talking about riots in the streets, people fighting each other. Martyrists had marched in desperate processions; many people— both participants and innocents—had died in the brawl. Now the crowbar felt heavy and warm in her hand, a sword to be wielded by a righteous young woman who had received direct instructions from Serena.

Finally she saw the first target in her mission.

The ethereal girl stood before the window of a shop that sold mechanical devices, appliances and innocuous conveniences that had thus far escaped the waves of rioters and looters. League citizens used such things without a thought to their origin, ignoring the fact that high-technology devices were distant cousins of Omnius. All machines, all electronics, all circuits, were temptations, inherently evil. They insinuated themselves into daily life so that people blithely accepted the pervasive presence of machines.

Drawing a silent breath, Rayna swung the crowbar and smashed the shop window, laying bare the vulnerable appliances. Then she began to pummel them into metal and polymer debris. This was her first strike against evil. Her visions had told her to root out the infestation from within, obliterating any vestiges of thinking machines so that humans could avoid such weaknesses in the future.

In an eerily calm frenzy, Rayna smashed everything she could see. When she found no further mechanical manifestations, she sought out another building, an accounting firm that contained calculating machines on the second floor. The girl destroyed those as well. One man, looking weak and frightened, came out to stop her, but cringed when Rayna issued a stony, determined curse, berating him for allowing machines into his place of business.

"Humans will face only misery if we do not eradicate all aspects of the mechanical demons. I have heard the voice of God, and I will act accordingly!"

In the face of such a vehement pronouncement, albeit from such a small person, the man ran away.

For now, with so much work to do, Rayna did not make distinctions between the levels of technology, the variations of computer sophistication. She went tirelessly from business to business, until finally two members of Parmentier's skeleton security force stopped her. But she was no more than a child, the daughter of the dead governor, and after looking at her, they gave each other knowing glances. "She's been through a rough time. She's just taking out her anger in the only way she can. Right now, I'm too tired to take care of anything that's not an emergency."

"I even turn a blind eye to half of those." One of the security men, tall and dark-skinned, pointed a stern finger at Rayna. "We'll leave you this time, girl, but don't get into trouble again. Go back home."

Rayna saw how late it was. Tired, she did as she was told and returned to the governor's mansion.

The next day, however, she was back again with her crowbar, seeking further targets, smashing all thinking machines and related devices.

This time, though, she was accompanied by a small crowd of watchers, many of them haggard Martyrists. They began to chant in support, picking up cudgels of their own. . . .

Faith and determination are a warrior's greatest weapons. But beliefs can be corrupted. Beware that these weapons are not turned against you.

—SWORDMASTER ISTIAN GOSS

For their first mission after being dispatched from Ginaz, Nar Trig and Istian Goss had hoped to be pitted in direct combat against the forces of Omnius. Instead, the new swordmasters found themselves in a tangled police and recovery action on recaptured Honru.

"You'd think they would have put the man carrying the spirit of Jool Noret on the front lines," Trig grumbled. "Now that this place has been freed from Omnius, why can't these people maintain their own order?"

"Remember what you were taught: Any battle that defends humanity is important." Istian bit back a sigh. "If this job is as easy as you say, we can finish our work here swiftly enough—then we'll be off to other battles."

After Quentin Butler's battalion had left Honru, the downtrodden survivors had gone into a vengeful frenzy incited in part by Martyrist propaganda. Sentinel robots, floating watcheyes, and all the subsystems that served the evermind had been dismantled, circuitry uprooted, machinery torn apart. Nar Trig looked at the zealots with a hungry curiosity, as if detecting a fervor similar to his own against the thinking machines.

Unfortunately, Istian thought, the survivors had been so intent on their vendetta that they caused far more damage than necessary to establish their foothold. If they had turned their energy and enthusiasm to rebuilding Honru instead of crushing an already defeated enemy, the two swordmasters might have been able to fight the real battles instead of wasting their time here.

The Honru slave pens had been torn down, and the people set up dwellings inside former machine strongholds, erecting tents and lean-tos, purloining comforts from factories in the once-gleaming city. Extravagant and colorful shrines to the Three Martyrs sprang up like weeds through out the city and in the strip-mined countryside. Long banners depicting Serena, Manion the Innocent, and Grand Patriarch Iblis Ginjo unfurled from tall buildings. Instead of growing food, Martyrist farmers planted fields of the orange marigolds that had become the symbolic flower of Serena Butler's murdered baby boy.

Istian and Trig marched down the streets, alert. The ranks of Martyrists had grown substantially, and their thankful followers held frequent vigils, celebrations, and prayer meetings. They seized any remnants of intact Omnius machinery they found among the ruins, then pulverized them in symbolic destruction parties.

The survivors were settling down, though, and each day they turned toward more productive work. Istian hoped that he and Trig would be able to leave when the next League ship arrived.

Many people rushed in from other League Worlds, some to stake their claim on new territory, others genuinely wanting to help. The philanthropic Lord Porce Bludd, grandnephew of Niko Bludd, who had been killed during the great slave uprising on Poritrin, contributed vast amounts of funding. The rebuilding and restoration of Honru did not lack for money, resources, or manpower. The only failing, Istian thought, was in focus and initiative. . . .

They heard a shout. Istian turned to see a man sprinting toward them wearing an officer's uniform—it was the military administrator of the reclaimed colony. Despite his relatively high rank, the man had noble blood and was more of a bureaucrat than a warrior. Trig placed his hand on the power button of his pulse-sword and stood ready.

"Mercenaries! We require your assistance." Red-faced from the effort of running, the military administrator stopped in front of the two swordmasters. "While breaking open one of the sealed storage depots, workers encountered three combat robots, and they were still active! The meks killed two of our people before we could seal the machines inside. You have to go fight them."

"Yes." Trig grinned wolfishly and turned to his sparring partner. "We do."

Istian looked determined and pleased. "Let's go, then."

In a part of the city filled with identical cube-shaped warehouses and storage chambers, the two swordmasters raced after the military administrator and a dozen well-armed jihadi soldiers. They could have used explosives and heavy projectile weapons to destroy the combat robots, but the rebuilders needed the supplies, equipment, and resources that were stored intact within the warehouse. Istian and Trig, on the other hand, could dispatch the enemies with finesse—and without collateral damage. Also, the jihadi soldiers wanted to watch the Ginaz mercenaries and their much-vaunted skill in hand-to-hand combat against the enemy machines.

A crowd followed them as they rushed off to their destination. People shouted. Some of them carried banners of the Three Martyrs. Trig raised his pulse-sword in a defiant gesture, and the Martyrists cheered. Istian focused his attention forward, mentally preparing himself for his opponent. He recalled ancient legends of brave armored knights who set forth to fight dragons in their lairs while terrorized peasants watched, and he supposed that he and Trig filled a similar role now.

When they stood before the sealed metal door to the cube-shaped warehouse, Istian saw that its smooth, polished surface was rippled with convex dents as if someone had launched cannon shells from the inside. Obviously, the trapped combat robots had tried to hammer themselves free.

As soon as the barricade ratcheted aside, the tall and burly killing machines strode forward, extruding spiny appendages, deadly weapons, flamethrower arms, projectile cannons. The three battle machines were the stuff of nightmares—precisely the targets for which a Ginaz swordmaster was trained. Chirox had given them both the necessary instruction.

Istian and Trig shouted in unison and charged ahead, raising their pulse-swords. The combat robots seemed startled by these small opponents. A gout of flame spurted from one of the incinerator arms, but Trig dove to the left, rolled, and sprang back to his feet. Istian leaped forward, swinging his pulse-sword against the same enemy. With a single blow, he sent a surge of energy through an appendage of the combat robot. Its flamethrower arm drooped, powerless.

The other two combat robots swiveled and converged as Trig charged toward them. His eyes were ablaze, and he didn't even bother to dodge. He gripped the pulse-sword in his left hand and a small energy dagger in his right.

Incensed at the first battle mek for launching fire at him, Trig collided with that one, thrusting and slashing. He tapped the hilt button to increase the sword's discharge power and, in a blur of well-aimed blows, shorted out the mek's primary memory core, erasing the combat programming and shutting it down completely.

Istian focused on the second intact battle machine. It raised two artillery arms, but he ran forward faster than it could reset its aimpoint. The two arms launched their explosives after he had passed into its blind spot. The shells exploded, leaving a smoking crater a meter behind Istian. Then he was inside its vulnerable zone.

The combat machine retracted its artillery arms and extruded bladed weapons instead, stabbing appendages that flailed about like sharp pincers. Istian parried them, letting his thoughts flow, trying to feel the guidance of Jool Noret's spirit within him. When Istian could not detect the presence, he thought, *Why are you silent?*

For the first time, Istian fought without thinking, without fear of injury or pain. Before he even realized what he was doing, three of the machine's sharp-bladed arms fell to the side, drooping like withered willows.

For good measure, Istian struck the pulse-sword against the lowered artillery arms to prevent the robot from firing projectiles at the fanatical spectators who surged forward as if they wanted to help fight the enemy with their bare hands. If the Martyrists got too close, Istian knew they would be massacred.

Yowling like a wild man, Trig was already battering the last combat robot. The machine flailed its arms, attempting to use a different set of weapons. Clearly it was on the defensive, unprepared for the unfettered fury of this berserk fighter. Watching him, Istian thought with a sadness in his heart that Nar Trig should have been the one in whom the spirit of Jool Noret was reborn.

Gritting his teeth, he fought harder.

One of the mek's cutting arms slashed him in the shoulder, and a second blade sliced across his chest. But Istian bent backward, flexing at an amazing angle so that the serrated edge traced only a thin line of blood across his sternum as the weapons arm swept past.

Istian bounced back like a released spring. His pulse-sword, also at its highest setting, slammed into the armored torso of the combat machine. He released a pulse that drained the rest of his battery, a full-fledged surge that paralyzed the fighting robot's mobile systems, leaving its arms and legs dead, its artillery deactivated, and only its head swiveling back and forth, helpless.

Trig struck his own opponent's neck column, hammering down in a shower of sparks that made the mek jitter and thrash. He slammed the weapon home again with enough force to break the tubing and support pipes, and finally snapped off the encased armored head. The heavy body drooped, dead.

Feeling the wash of adrenaline leave him like a tangible presence— could it have been the spirit of Jool Noret?—Istian slumped, letting his drained pulse-sword clatter to the floor. His exhausted muscles trembled. Beside him, Trig paced like a caged Salusan tiger looking for another enemy.

Before they could turn back to the first paralyzed combat robot, whose head still swiveled back and forth on its deactivated body, the angry Martyrists surged forward. They carried their own weapons, cudgels, sledgehammers, prybars. As a mob, they vented their fury against the three defeated fighting machines, swinging and crushing, shouting as they battered the murderous meks into collapsed hulks.

Sparks flew; components were torn loose. Processing units were smashed, gelcircuitry modules pried free and splattered on the warehouse's hard floor. The mob did not stop until, after a long and great clamor, they had pounded the shrapnel into unrecognizable wreckage.

"We can use those metals," the military administrator said brightly. "The Martyrists have already begun a program of using scrap from destroyed thinking machines to make our building materials, agricultural tools, and carpentry supplies. The ancient scriptures tell us that swords must be beaten into plowshares."

"It is not enough just to defeat the minions of the evermind," Nar Trig agreed, his voice deep. "Victory will be sweeter if we can turn them to our own advantage."

"Like Chirox," Istian pointed out. His partner did not respond.

I have imagined what it would be like to be Omnius, and the far-reaching decisions I might make in his position.
—Erasmus Dialogues

Despite Rekur Van's promises, the new version of Serena Butler was a great disappointment. Another accelerated clone, another misstep.

Erasmus hoped the damage to the Serena experiment was not irreparable. Using preserved cells brought as a bargaining chip when he'd fled the League, the Tlulaxa captive tried again and again to re-create the woman, but he always encountered the same problem. The smuggled cells carried only her genetic makeup—not *her*, not her essence. The secret wasn't in the cells, but in the *soul*—as Serena might have said.

And now the limbless flesh merchant petulantly refused to tend to the other clones being grown.

Perhaps it had something to do with his frustration over the reptilian regeneration experiments. After a promising start, the bony growths on both of Rekur Van's shoulders had fallen off, leaving infected patches of raw, oozing skin. The Tlulaxa had found this most upsetting, and his mood contributed to his failings on the Serena matter. To straighten out the mess, Erasmus adjusted medications to keep Van focused on important matters, and to give him selective amnesia. It required constant modification and attention.

I mustn't mix experiments, the robot thought.

Now, as he faced the counterfeit Serena in his immaculate gardens, Erasmus hoped for some flicker of recognition, even fear, in her lavender eyes. Gilbertus remained dutifully at his side. "She looks exactly like all the archival images, Father," the man pointed out.

"Appearances can be deceiving," Erasmus said, selecting from his store of appropriate clichés. "She matches human standards of beauty, but that is insufficient. This is not . . . what I am looking for."

With his perfect memory, the robot could replay every conversation he'd had with the real Serena Butler. Thus, he could relive the numerous debates they'd had during her time as his special slave on Earth. But Erasmus wanted *new* experiences from her, continued understanding, an appropriate counterpoint to the excellent insights he gained from Gilbertus.

No, this new Serena clone simply would not do at all.

She was as bland and uninteresting as his other human specimens, containing none of the memories and sheer stubbornness that Erasmus relished. She had been accelerated to maturity, but without the commensurate education of experiences.

"She appears equivalent to my apparent age," Gilbertus said. Why was he so interested?

The real Serena Butler had been raised in the League of Nobles where she'd learned to believe interesting foolishness, such as her human superiority and the innate rights of freedom and love. Erasmus regretted that he had not appreciated Serena's uniqueness as much as he should have. Now it was too late.

"You do not know me, do you?" he asked the new clone.

"You are Erasmus," she answered, but her voice held no spark.

"I suspected that was all you would say," he answered, knowing what he must do. He disliked having reminders of mistakes where he could see them.

"Please don't destroy her, Father," Gilbertus said.

The robot turned, automatically fashioning a puzzled expression on his face.

"Allow me to speak with her, teach her. Recall that when you took me from the slave pens, I was uneducated, wild, a blank slate that showed none of my potential. Perhaps with care and patience I can . . . salvage something."

Suddenly Erasmus understood. "You find Serena Butler attractive!"

"I find her interesting. From what you have told me about the original Serena, would she not be a suitable companion to me? A mate perhaps?"

The robot had not expected this, but he found the new permutation of purpose intriguing. "I should have thought of that myself. Yes, my Mentat, make your best attempt."

Studying the female clone, Gilbertus suddenly looked intimidated, as if he had accepted a challenge too large for him.

The robot gave his support. "Even if the experiment fails, I still have you, Gilbertus. I could never wish for a better test subject—or companion."

IN ORDER TO better study human preferences, Erasmus had designed a number of muscle-enhancement machines for Gilbertus, some simple in their application and some much more difficult. Gilbertus was a perfect specimen, both physically and mentally, and Erasmus wanted to keep his ward in peak condition. Like a well-tuned machine, the human body required maintenance.

After so many extensive workout programs, Gilbertus had become a prime example of the flawless male physique. When a human used his muscular components, his strength improved; when a robot used mechanical components, they began to wear down. An odd, but fundamental difference.

While Erasmus watched, the man effortlessly ran for kilometers on a treadway while curling weights and performing upper body exercises with resistance force fields. His mind was incredibly compartmentalized to manage such a complex feat. On a typical day Gilbertus would use more than thirty grueling workout stations without much rest and only water to drink.

Since the routine was time-consuming, Erasmus said, "While you push your physical abilities, you can also be honing your mental skills, my Mentat. You should be improving your memory, practicing calculations, solving riddles."

Gilbertus paused, breathing hard. Sweat glistened on his brown hair as he formed an expression that the robot identified as puzzlement. "I am doing exactly that, Father. While I work my body I work my mind. I go through countless calculations, projections, and equations, each of them providing new insights that are not available to common thinkers." He paused, added, "This is what you have made me . . . or what I am leading you to believe that you made of me."

"You are not capable of deceiving me. What purpose could you possibly have in doing that?"

"You have taught me humans are not to be trusted, Father, and I took your lesson to heart. I do not even trust myself."

Gilbertus had been his ward for nearly seven decades, and Erasmus could not imagine the man might secretly turn against the thinking machines. He would have sensed an alteration in Gilbertus's mood, and Omnius would have observed evidence of such a betrayal—his watcheyes were everywhere.

The robot worried that if Omnius ever formulated such suspicions, he would suggest that the safest course was to eliminate Gilbertus before he had a chance to cause damage. Erasmus had to make certain the evermind never experienced those doubts.

Omnius challenged me to make a feral child into an intelligent and civilized being, Erasmus thought. *Gilbertus has surpassed even my most extravagant expectations. He makes me think of things I had never considered before. He makes me feel affection for him in ways I could not have conceived without him.*

Gilbertus switched to performing force-field pull-ups and simultaneous lower-body exercises. As the robot watched, he recalled that Gilbertus had already expressed distaste for the deadly RNA retrovirus plague that was even now starting to spread among the League Worlds. What if he decided to help his own species . . . instead of Erasmus?

The situation will bear watching. The robot realized that he himself was exhibiting a very human trait himself: paranoia. *Thinking is not always reality. There must be a connection, documented evidence that establishes a linkage between suspicion and fact.*

A common problem that had long troubled human researchers was how an observer's presence affected an experiment. Erasmus had long ago stopped being an objective eyewitness to Gilbertus's progress. Did his surrogate son behave a certain way in order to prove something to his robot mentor? Were these extravagant physical exercises a way to flaunt his superiority? Was Gilbertus really more rebellious in his attitude than he revealed?

Though troubling, this line of thought was so much more complex and interesting than the bland Serena clones. Did Gilbertus intend to teach her to become his ally?

Finally, the man swung off his exercise machine, did a double back flip in the air, and landed squarely on his feet. "I was wondering, Father," he said, hardly even breathing hard, "does using an exercise machine make me more like a machine?"

"Research that question and give me your analysis."

"I suspect it does not have a definitive answer. We could argue it one way and another."

"A perfect topic of discussion, then. I always enjoy our discussions." Erasmus still had lengthy, esoteric debates with the Corrin-Omnius, but he preferred spending time with Gilbertus. On a certain level, Gilbertus was the more interesting of the two, though it would not be beneficial for Erasmus to point that out to the evermind.

The robot changed the subject. "Our surveillance probes should soon return with images showing the results of the initial plague deployment."

Finished with his workout, Gilbertus peeled off his clothes as he strode to the shower bay. The robot scanned, analyzed, and admired the naked physique while standing far enough away to keep his plush robe from being drenched in the spray.

"Yorek Thurr will no doubt be pleased with all the death and misery," Gilbertus said while scrubbing himself. "He enjoys being a traitor to his species. He has no conscience."

"Machines have no conscience either. Do you consider that a failing?"

"No, Father. However, since Thurr is a human, I should be able to comprehend his behavior." Standing in the pounding warm water, Gilbertus lathered his thick black hair. "I believe, however, that I finally know how to explain Thurr's actions, after reading so many ancient human records." He grinned. "Quite simply, he is crazy."

Gilbertus rinsed his body, then shut off the water, standing cool and refreshed. "Clearly, the immortality treatment he demanded as a price for his services has made his mind unstable. Perhaps he was too old. Perhaps the operation was flawed."

"Or perhaps I intentionally applied the treatment . . . inadequately," Erasmus said, surprised that Gilbertus had come to such a subtle conclusion. "Perhaps I felt he did not deserve such a reward, and even now he does not know exactly what was done to him." The robot's flowmetal face formed a small grin. "Still, you must admit that his plague idea was quite good. It adequately meets our needs for victory without causing undue damage."

"As long as some of us survive." Gilbertus toweled off and found a clean garment waiting for him.

"Especially you. I have taught you to be extremely efficient, with a highly organized mind, able to remember and analyze facts in a computer-like fashion. If other humans could learn such skills, they might coexist better with machines."

"Maybe I could be better than machine or man," Gilbertus mused.

Is that what he aspires to? I shall consider his remark at length.

The two of them walked out of the exercise building.

Machines are neither more nor less than we make them.
— RAQUELLA BERTO-ANIRUL,
Essays from the Edge of Consciousness

Agamemnon, Juno, and Dante soared along in immense warrior bodies. The general felt exhilarated to be planning a military assault again, seizing a place far from Richese where they would be safe from Omnius's dull-witted machine marauders. A place where they could regroup, grow stronger, and plan the next phase of their new cymek empire.

The three Titans were accompanied by a large force of neo-cymek battleships, each an extension of a single human brain with thoughtrode connections. All of these neos professed their loyalty with great enthusiasm, especially since they knew Agamemnon could activate selective termination switches and kill any of them on a whim. Still, he felt confident enough in their allegiance and dedication. Once their brains had been removed from biological bodies, what else were the neo-cymeks to do?

After abandoning Richese, the swarm of ferocious-looking ships converged upon the frozen planetoid of Hessra, where the Ivory Tower Cogitors had isolated themselves for many centuries.

"According to our projections, there should be no defenses here," Dante said. "The Cogitors pretend not to participate in any outside activities. They simply hide and think."

Juno made a derisive, guttural sound. "They can pretend all they like, but the Cogitors were never as neutral as they claimed to be. They've always had a meddling finger inserted somewhere."

"As b-ba-bad as *hrethgir*," damaged Beowulf transmitted in his hitching voice. While tolerant of Beowulf because of his past service, Agamemnon was annoyed that the neo-cymek had eavesdropped on a private discussion among Titans.

With exaggerated patience, Dante said, "My point was that our victory is assured. I foresee no military difficulties whatsoever in taking Hessra."

"Nevertheless, I intend to relish every moment of it." Agamemnon directed his force of cymek ships to encircle and descend. With expendable neos in front, the angular vessels converged in an expanded attack formation above the glacier-encrusted fortress of ancient philosophers.

While the Ivory Tower Cogitors professed disinterest in the outside galaxy and held to their isolation, they were not totally self-sufficient. They had long operated a secret business supplying the cymeks with electrafluid, even after Agamemnon and his rebels had broken free of the Synchronized Worlds.

Unwilling to be completely dependent on Vidad and his ilk, Dante had established the Titans' own electrafluid-manufacturing facilities on Bela Tegeuse and Richese. While the mass-produced fluid was adequate for neo-cymeks, Agamemnon and his Titans demanded better quality, and no electrafluid was superior to the concoction made for the Ivory Tower Cogitors. Today, the Titan general would seize the facilities for himself, claiming Hessra as his new headquarters, and beginning his long-delayed march on history. . . .

The black towers of the isolated citadel protruded from thick glaciers, nearly engulfed by slow rivers of ice that had built up over the centuries. The once-tall spires that housed the disembodied brains looked as if they were drowning in a flood of crawling snow and ice.

Agamemnon and Juno, flying in the lead, delighted in activating their integrated flamethrowers augmented by streams of oxygen from the thin air of Hessra. Tongues of fire lashed out from the cymek craft, pummeling the black stone walls, breaking away huge chunks of ice, and sending a prodigious cloud of camouflaging steam roiling into the dim sky.

"That will clear more operational area for us," Agamemnon said, setting down his ship.

In a dry voice, Dante delivered instructions to the neo-cymeks. His optic threads detected three yellow-robed secondaries rushing to tower windows and balconies. Mouths agape, they took in the situation of the unexpected attack, then fled for shelter inside.

Neo-cymeks continued to land like carrion crows around the immense Titan ships. Agamemnon transferred his brain canister into a small but powerful walker-form that would fit within the corridors of the stronghold. He summoned a group of neos to lead the charge, blasting open walls and battering aside doors. After exchanging their large mechanical vessels for smaller walker-bodies, they marched in like a procession of mechanized army ants loaded with weapons. Agamemnon clattered triumphantly behind them. The sharp legs of his walker-body struck sparks against the stone floor.

Outside, the clumsy neo-cymek Beowulf misjudged his landing and crashed, tumbling off a cliff and coming to rest helplessly inside a new crevasse of the broken glacier. When the neo-cymeks reported the blunder, Agamemnon considered simply leaving Beowulf there where he could freeze and be covered up by the slow but inexorable closing of the glacial jaws.

But Beowulf had once been a valuable ally, far more dependable and talented than the inept Xerxes, who had a much longer résumé of failure. Grudgingly, the Titan general issued orders for the removal of Beowulf's brain canister from the ruins of his ship-body and its insertion into a neo-cymek mechanical walker. *I am running out of excuses to keep Beowulf alive.* The brain-damaged neo-cymek was no longer an asset, and was rapidly becoming an actual liability.

Inside the frozen Cogitor fortress, neo-cymek warriors encountered and dispatched more than a dozen yellow-robed secondaries. Agamemnon killed two of them himself, using the antique projectile weapon that he had obtained from Thurr on Wallach IX. It worked perfectly.

Just ahead of the general, his neo-cymeks found libraries and workrooms where the monklike secondaries had spent their days copying and transcribing. It seemed the attendants had been particularly fascinated with all known manifestations of the mysterious Muadru runes found on scattered planets.

Additional chambers deep in the bowels of the fortress were devoted to electrafluid chemistry. Saffron-robed workers in the laboratories cowered as neo-cymeks stormed in, interrupting their chanting, ritualistic processes of converting water into the life-sustaining liquid.

Agamemnon issued explicit instructions and sent Dante to enforce them. "Find out how these factories work and then kill most, but not all, of the underlings. We need at least some of them alive."

Other secondaries fled into a large central chamber where the Cogitors rested on their pedestals. When finally Agamemnon emerged into the enclosure and surveyed the shimmering canisters of the Ivory Tower Cogitors, he was distressed to find only five brains floating in individual cylinders of bluish life-preserving liquid.

One of the six was missing.

"General Agamemnon, your arrival is needlessly destructive and chaotic," one of the ancient philosophers said through the pedestal's speakerpatch. "How may we assist you? Are you here to procure a supply of electrafluid?"

"That's part of it. I also intend to take over Hessra and destroy all Cogitors. Which one of you is not here?" He raised a mechanical arm, pointing its sharp end toward the empty pedestal.

Guileless, the philosopher brains hummed and answered honestly, "Vidad has taken up temporary residence on Salusa Secundus to advise and observe the League of Nobles. We need further data and discussions to continue to grow."

"That isn't going to happen after today," Juno said, strutting her ominous body into the chamber beside Agamemnon's. She'd always had a particular dislike for the meddling Cogitors, especially the one named Eklo, who had worked with Iblis Ginjo to foment a rebellion on Earth. That had been the beginning of this appalling, destructive Jihad.

Even though the League's crusade against machines had allowed the cymeks to launch their own rebellion and break free of the evermind's control, Agamemnon still harbored a deep grudge against the Cogitors. "Do you have any final brilliant revelations before we execute you?"

One of the Cogitors, speaking in a female voice, said with strange placidity, "We have a great many areas in which to enlighten you, General Agamemnon."

"Unfortunately for you, I am not interested in being what you would consider enlightened."

Instructing the neo-cymek walker-forms to continue searching the corridors and chambers of the Hessra installation, Agamemnon and Juno moved forward. They wanted to do this for themselves. It was a way for the two Titans to show their love for each other.

Raising powerful mechanical arms, they toppled the pedestals, smashing the transparent canisters that held the ancient Cogitors, and took great delight in grinding the quivering brains into oozing pulp with mechanical fists, one after another. It was over far too soon.

Finally, standing in the dripping wreckage, Agamemnon declared that Hessra was now theirs. There had never been any doubt of the matter.

Science is the creation of dilemmas in the attempt to solve mysteries.
—DR. MOHANDAS SUK,
speech to graduating class

At any other time, Raquella would have reacted much differently to meeting her grandfather, asking him a thousand questions, telling him about herself. *Supreme Commander Vorian Atreides!*

Her mother might have been more intrigued by his surprising revelation, but Helmina was dead now, just like Raquella's own first husband. She had assumed her grandmother's secret soldier was another casualty, unable to return. The Jihad had devastated so many lives and hopes.

She would rather have spent more time with Vor Atreides—would rather have done almost anything—but Raquella could not turn her back on all the people who needed her now. With the Omnius Scourge raging across Parmentier, she and Mohandas had too many people to save. They had a cure to find.

But thus far a cure had eluded them. They could treat the symptoms, hydrate the patients and keep the fever down, helping the largest number of victims to survive, but even so in such a massively infected population, that was not enough. Many, many people were dying.

Vor had promised to do what he could to help, to spread the news of their epidemic to other League Worlds. Even if he couldn't get back in time to assist Parmentier, at least he could warn the other planets to be on their guard against the machines' terrible new tactic. If it was in his power, Vor would keep his promise to her. Even though he had been gone only hours, she knew it.

The Hospital for Incurable Diseases. The name seemed unfortunately apt now. She didn't know what she would do if Mohandas succumbed to the plague. Better, Raquella thought, that she contracted the disease first . . . Already, three of the twenty-two doctors gathered from around Niubbe had died of the Scourge, four were recovering but still incapacitated, and two more were showing the unmistakable first-stage signs of the virus. Soon she would be tending them, too.

Mohandas had studied the disease closely enough to draw some basic conclusions, though he hadn't yet found any magic bullet. After the airborne virus entered the body via the mucus membranes and infected the liver, it produced large quantities of a protein that converted the body's own hormones such as testosterone and cholesterol into a compound similar to an anabolic steroid. The liver could not effectively break down "Compound X" (Mohandas hadn't had the energy to give it a more creative name), nor could it be removed from the bloodstream. Since natural hormones were depleted due to conversion into the deadly Compound X, the body then overproduced them, while the buildup of the poisonous compound caused striking mental and physical symptoms.

In the final stages of the disease, death took more than forty percent of all patients. In addition, liver failure was common and heart attacks and strokes caused by malignant hypertension often proved fatal. In a smaller number of cases, thyrotoxic crisis caused the body to simply shut down due to hormonal imbalances. By that point, the extreme fever had placed most victims into a deep coma that lasted several days before they stopped breathing. In a high percentage of virus sufferers, tendons easily ruptured, leading to many crippling injuries among the survivors. . . .

Raquella tended to forty patients within the next hour. She no longer heard the moans or the paranoid muttering, nor saw the terror or pleas in their eyes, nor smelled the foul miasma of death and sickness. This facility had always been more of a hospice than a hospital. Some people took longer to die from the viral infection; some suffered more than others. Some were brave and some were cowards, but in the end it didn't matter. Too many of them died.

Stepping into the corridor, Raquella saw Mohandas approach. She smiled at his warm, sweet face, seeing how haggard and weary he looked, with creases of fatigue etching his cheeks around the sealed breather. For weeks he had been doing triple duty, as a doctor, disease researcher, and interim hospital administrator. They had very little time to spend together just as two people whose deep love for each other had evolved into a comfortable, unbreakable bond. But after watching so much hopelessness and death, Raquella needed human comfort, if only for a few moments.

When they had both passed through decontamination sprays into a section of sterile rooms, Mohandas and Raquella could finally remove the breathers that prevented them from kissing. They held hands briefly, staring into each other's eyes through the protective film, saying nothing. They had met and found love in the tragedy of the Hospital for Incurable Diseases, like a flower blossoming in the middle of a barren battlefield.

"I don't know how much longer my energy can last," Raquella said, her voice worn down, trailing off in melancholy. "But how can we stop, no matter how tired we get?" She leaned closer, and Mohandas took her into his arms.

"We save as many as we can. As for those we lose, you make what remains of their lives more pleasant," he said. "I've watched you with the patients, the way their faces light up when they see you. You have a miraculous gift."

Raquella smiled, but with difficulty. "It's just so hard sometimes, listening to their desperate prayers. When we can't save them, they call out to God, to Serena, to anyone who will listen."

"I know. Dr. Arbar just died, in Ward Five. We knew it was imminent." He had fallen into a coma two days earlier, the fever burning fiercely, his body unable to fight the virus or the toxins it produced.

She was unable to control the tears that suddenly streamed down her face. Dr. Hundri Arbar had risen from an impoverished background in Niubbe to get his medical degree so he could help people less fortunate than himself. A local hero, he insisted on living without drink or drugs, refusing even the spice melange that was so popular across the League. Lord Rikov Butler—who, along with his household, was now dead—had provided his own ample stocks of spice to the hospital, since he also refused to consume it in light of of his wife's strict religious beliefs. Most of the doctors in the hospital took it daily to maintain their energy and stamina.

"One less doctor to help us. It makes you wonder if . . ." She broke off in midsentence as she thought again about the spice. "Wait a minute. I think I see a pattern." Whenever she found extra supplies, Raquella administered spice to some of the patients in order to ease their physical pains for just a little while.

"What is it?"

"Not until I'm sure." Raquella walked briskly down the corridor with him right behind, and entered a medical records room. Quickly she sorted through charts, scrambled to draw parallels. During the next hour, she feverishly went through file after file, each a separate sheet of circuit plaz with data, which she processed through a reading machine. The sheets piled up around her.

And the evidence became indisputable.

"Yes—yes!" Breathing hard, she looked triumphantly at Mohandas. "Melange is the common denominator! Look." She led him through the records, patient after patient. Her words poured out in a rush. "For the most part, people are dying in the greatest numbers along class lines, which at first blush doesn't make sense. Poor people catch the plague in much greater numbers than wealthy noble families or rich businessmen. That has never made sense to me, since nutrition and sanitary systems are fairly equal throughout the entire population.

"But if anyone who *consumes spice* has a greater ability to fight off exposure to the retrovirus, then people in the lower classes who can't afford melange will die in larger numbers! Look, even those patients who receive spice after contracting the plague show a better history of recovery."

Mohandas could not argue with the evidence. "And Dr. Arbar never took the stuff! Even though melange may not be a cure, it certainly appears to be a mitigant. It provides resistance." He paced the lab floor, pondering deeply. "The spice molecule is exceedingly complex, a huge protein that VenKee has never synthesized or managed to break down. It's quite possible that the molecule itself blocks the critical protein by which the virus converts normal hormones to Compound X. Essentially, if there's a pocket on the enzyme ordinarily filled by cholesterol and testosterone and then transformed into Compound X, maybe melange is shaped closely enough to those hormones that it gets stuck in this pocket, deactivating the enzyme."

Raquella felt herself flush. "Don't forget that the first stages of infection include paranoia, mental delusions, and aggressiveness. The spice enhances thought processes—perhaps it also helps people fend off an initial infection."

He grabbed her by the shoulders. "Raquella, if you're right, this is a huge breakthrough! We can treat entire populations that haven't been exposed yet, immunizing them against the virus."

"Right, but we need to move fast," Raquella said. "And where will we get so much melange?"

Mohandas lowered his head. "It's much more serious than that. Do you doubt that the Scourge has already hit other planets? The epidemic could be moving across the galaxy like a storm of locusts. We have to get the news out into the League at all costs."

Raquella drew a quick breath. "My . . . Vorian Atreides—he can do it!"

She raced out of the records chamber to the hospital's abandoned communications room. She had to send a signal to him before his vessel accelerated out of the system. As Supreme Commander of the Army of the Jihad, he could insist that the League dramatically increase spice distribution to any planet that might be a target of the Omnius plague.

To her relief, he acknowledged her transmission after a long signal delay. Without pausing, she told her full explanation, then waited for the transmission lag. Finally, he said, "Melange? If that's true, we're going to need a hell of a lot of it. You're sure?"

"I'm sure. Get the message out—and stay safe yourself."

"You too," he said. "VenKee headquarters on Kolhar is near my route back to Salusa. I can speak directly to the managers of the spice trade." He added something else, but static interfered, and they lost contact.

The successful executive is like a poker player, either concealing his emotions or showing false ones, so that others cannot use them against him.

—AURELIUS VENPORT,
The Legacy of Business

For nearly two weeks, Vor pushed the *Dream Voyager* to accelerations that only a robot was designed to withstand, determined to waste no time in bringing his vital news back to the League. His body ached, but he knew each passing moment could mean more lives lost.

If, by increasing the ship's speed to the limits of his body's endurance, he could save even one more person, that reward would be more than worth his own short-term suffering. Agamemnon himself had been the first to teach him that lesson when he'd given Vor the life-extension treatment: Pain is a small price to pay in exchange for life.

Over the long journey, he had manifested no symptoms or indication of the disease, saw none of the warning signs Raquella had warned him about. This meant that according to her past knowledge he was indeed immune to the Omnius Scourge. Thus he could immediately throw himself into the necessary work, without fear of infecting others and without fear for his own personal safety.

Vor shifted his course on a short detour to Kolhar to the VenKee shipyards. Under the circumstances, he considered it important to speak directly with the primary suppliers of spice. The ramifications of Raquella's discovery were astounding.

Sadly, but without surprise, he learned from newsbursts across the comline channels as soon as he approached Kolhar that the epidemic had already begun to spread to other League Worlds. Omnius was delivering the disease with ruthless efficiency, tainting planet after planet, despite the League's best efforts to stop the spread. Quarantines were imposed, but usually not swiftly enough; and even when precautions kept the epidemic bottled up, at least half of the people within the boundaries were doomed.

Vor alone had hope to offer, and it hinged on VenKee's cooperation. Those who consumed the spice could better resist the Scourge.

VenKee had a lock on melange exports, keeping their techniques and suppliers secret from the rest of the League. The merchant company also held a monopoly on the use of dangerous spacefolder ships for commercial transportation. The pieces fit together in Vor's mind: To counteract the fast-moving virus, it was essential to deliver medical supplies quickly, thus requiring spacefolders. And spice . . .

Vorian swore that he would not leave Kolhar until he had what he needed.

IN THE END, Norma Cenva herself accompanied Vor aboard the *Dream Voyager* to Salusa. She had foreseen his arrival and knew with an odd and inexplicable prescience that he would bring urgent news. By the time he had spoken a handful of sentences, Norma had determined three things: The situation was critical, spice was central to the survival of the human race, and she would go to Salusa with him to address the League Parliament.

Before leaving Kolhar, she dispatched three highly paid mercenary pilots aboard spacefolder scouts, each with redundant messages, to inform the Jihad Council so they could begin to spread the word. By the time she and Vor arrived, major changes should already be under way.

Then she ordered her son Adrien to alter all VenKee activities, increasing spice production and distribution to the highest possible levels. Finally, she followed Vor to his black-and-silver spacecraft. "I will concentrate better aboard your ship than here." She indicated the shipyards, where reconstruction and emergency repairs were still under way from the recent explosion. "We should go as soon as possible."

As they lifted off, Vor used only moderate acceleration, but after Norma assured him that her body could withstand even greater stresses than his could, Vor once again pushed the *Dream Voyager* to punishing speeds. The update ship shot out of the system on a direct vector for Salusa Secundus.

En route, Norma occupied herself with her thoughts and calculations, surrounded by notes, electronic drawing boards, and other materials from her Kolhar office. Curiously, though, she did not need to use any of those items. Instead, she found herself journeying inward in her mind as she absorbed and processed massive amounts of information. She found her mental capacity increasing beyond all imaginable limits.

Vor hardly felt as if he actually had human company during the journey, but he was accustomed to flying alone. During the tedious, quiet hours, he thought fondly of the days when he'd accompanied Seurat. In the current climate of war and pestilence, Vor could have used the distraction of a few good games or even the robot pilot's clumsy attempts at humor.

THE *DREAM VOYAGER* jerked as it settled on a windy field at Zimia Spaceport in the middle of the day. Norma emerged from her preoccupied trance, looked through the window port in her cabin, and saw the capital city. "We're there already?"

On the way to the Hall of Parliament she and Vor learned that the Scourge had grown seriously worse in only the few weeks of their passage, having appeared on a dozen more planets. The League's best medical scientists didn't know how to fight it, though Raquella's revelation about melange, already delivered by the spacefolder scouts, had suddenly created a huge demand for the spice. Even knowing it existed as an effective treatment, if not a cure, did not help all those planets without access to enough melange.

Norma hoped that her announcement would change that.

With a mental command, she adjusted her appearance, smoothing her blond hair and softening her facial features. Although physical beauty meant little to her, so long as her body functioned well enough to perform the tasks she demanded of it, Norma made this extra effort to honor her late husband.

As she accompanied the dashing Supreme Commander up the steps, she saw quite clearly her essential place in the unfolding history of mankind. Norma viewed herself only in an ephemeral sense, a breath of oxygen to keep a candle going. She did not care about being remembered by history; she cared only about the work itself. And saving lives.

"Are you ready for this?" Vor asked. "You seem far away."

"I am . . . everywhere." She blinked, then focused on the towering building in front of her. "Yes, I am here."

While they approached the Hall of Parliament, a group of yellow-robed men hurriedly exited, carrying a clearplaz canister that held a disembodied brain. Norma looked at it curiously as the preoccupied group passed. Although she had never personally interacted with one of the ancient brains, her mother Zufa had spoken of their arcane ways.

"Vidad, one of the Ivory Tower Cogitors," Vor said with clear distaste in his voice. He urged her through the arched doorway and into the echoing, bustling halls. "I won't let them interfere this time, as they did with that foolish attempt at peace."

After Serena had martyred herself to repair the damage the Ivory Tower Cogitors had done, Vidad had spent more than half a century on Salusa Secundus, studying historical records and recent philosophical treatises. He also acted the part of a political gadfly, meddling in the affairs of the Jihad Council. Vor wished he would go back to his comrades on frozen Hessra.

When they arrived, Grand Patriarch Xander Boro-Ginjo was presiding, wearing the gaudy and ornate chain of office around his neck that was a prominent symbol of his position as the spiritual leader of his people. Beside him sat the tall and gaunt Interim Viceroy O'Kukovich. Though ostensibly the political leader of the League of Nobles, the man had very little real power; he was merely filler, like putty stuffed into a hole.

In the front row of the assembly chamber, Vor and Norma took two reserved seats. Their arrival caused a noticeable stir, even though the Parliament had been in a long session, discussing the rapidly spreading Scourge. So far, fifteen planets were known to be infected, and everyone dreaded that further bad news was slowly en route. The Jihad Council had already suggested extreme military strategies to keep Salusa Secundus clean and safe.

Vor studied the agenda, saw a long list of reports and speakers, all of them marked URGENT. He sighed and sat back. "We'll be a while yet."

Norma heard panic in the voices of the speakers, saw it in their faces. Nearby representatives whispered nervously among themselves. Though she continued her thoughts and calculations in the background of her mind, she grasped the magnitude of the disaster as she listened to one urgent summary after another. No one on Salusa Secundus had been infected yet, and a serious proposal was before the parliament to impose a total blockade to safeguard the population of the planet.

Norma sat up as the next speaker addressed the audience: the leader of the Sorceresses of Rossak, her own half sister Ticia Cenva. Her alabaster face rippling with a storm of passion, her long blond hair and bone-white robe waving faintly in a nonexistent breeze, Ticia stared in silence, cowing the audience with the import of her presence.

Watching her, Norma did not expect a smile of greeting or even a nod of acknowledgment from her half sister. Despite their extraordinary talents, her family was fractured, all the pieces separated widely.

For years her mother had snubbed Norma as a failure, concentrating utterly on her work for the Jihad. Because of her powers as a great Sorceress, Zufa Cenva had long anticipated a perfect daughter, but by the time she finally gave birth to flawless Ticia, Norma had been transformed beyond her mother's wildest hopes. Thus, ignoring the daughter she claimed she had always wanted, Zufa blithely abandoned Ticia to be raised by other Sorceresses on Rossak, while she devoted all her attentions to Norma's work. And then Zufa had been killed, along with Aurelius.

Ticia matured on Rossak, exhibiting all the mental powers her mother had prayed for, but she lived in a vacuum eventually filled by resentment. Decades later, she had taken her place as Supreme Sorceress, just like Zufa Cenva, but Ticia was even sterner and more stonily dedicated than her mother. Engrossed in her theories and calculations, not to mention Ven-Kee business, Norma had rarely taken the time to see her half sister; neither of them would ever consider the other a "friend," even in the broadest sense of the word.

Ticia caught sight of Norma, hesitated for an instant before beginning her speech, then boomed out in a voice that seem to carry thunder in every breath. The audience shuddered with the power of the delivery.

"We Sorceresses gave our lives for years, destroying cymeks whenever they preyed upon humanity. I watched many of my Sisters perish, unleashing their minds to take down cymeks—including Titans—along with them. I held myself ready to do the same. I would have been next . . . if another enemy had come. But now, for decades, the cymek threat has waned."

Brevin O'Kukovich applauded. "The Sorceresses of Rossak have performed a great service to humanity."

Ticia gave him a withering look for interrupting her. "So have many others, sir. Now, in the face of this sweeping epidemic, I point out that we Sorceresses have another area of expertise. Because of our harsh world and our precise records of breeding over many generations, we understand bloodlines, the most important raw material of the human race. If this Omnius Scourge grows worse, we could lose prime branches of our species—not just the sheer casualties, but paths to our future.

"Now, as whole families, whole cities, are devastated on world after world, we cannot react too soon or too vigorously. Our race is in extreme peril. Even as we struggle to find a cure for this foul biological weapon, we must also take drastic action to preserve the best DNA before it it lost forever—protect and store key markers of some of the strongest lines, or the disease may erase them entirely. We must establish a program to protect the genetic information of all people, on all planets." She lifted her chin. "We Sorceresses have the capacity to manage such a program."

Norma looked at her towering half sister, wondering what Ticia had to gain from this proposal. Though the Supreme Sorceress was not a particularly compassionate person, like Zufa she was fiercely dedicated to the Jihad.

Ticia raked her pale, electric gaze around the chamber, pointedly ignoring Norma. "I propose that we go to places where the plague has not yet struck and rescue healthy candidates. We can keep a database of blood samples, save family attributes if we cannot save the families themselves. Later, when we've defeated this epidemic, we can use this vast genetic library to restore our populations."

The Grand Patriarch didn't seem to understand entirely. "But even if the Scourge kills half . . . there will still be plenty of survivors. Is an operation of this magnitude truly necessary?"

After taking a long, slow breath, Ticia said, "But will it be the *right* half that survives? We have to plan for the worst, Grand Patriarch. We must do this before time runs out—like ancient Noah, but on a far vaster scale. We need to maintain samples of the strongest characteristics from each planet, and we have to do it before the Scourge spreads farther. We will need all the DNA we can save in order to guarantee sufficient diversity for the strength of our race."

"Why not just cure the damned disease?" one distraught representative called. "It's appearing everywhere!"

"And what about the already-infected planets? We should send rescue efforts there, too. Those people need it the most!"

The Grand Patriarch called for order. "We are already mounting massive volunteer relief efforts to aid overwhelmed medical personnel on afflicted planets. Perhaps the Sorceresses can take samples there, as well."

Ticia looked at the man as if he was a complete fool. "It is already too late. Some portion of their populations will survive, but the pool is tainted. We should focus our efforts where they can do the greatest amount of good. Nothing can be accomplished on worlds where the epidemic has already manifested."

"Very well, very well," the Interim Viceroy said, pointedly noting the clock. "I see no reason why the Sorceresses cannot join this effort to the missions we already have going to League Worlds. You will find enough volunteers among the women of Rossak to do this?"

"More than enough."

"Excellent. Now, I see the next item on the agenda may be a bit more hopeful. Supreme Commander Vorian Atreides? And . . . and someone named Norma Cenva?" Clearly, O'Kukovich didn't know who Norma was, but his memory had never been terribly reliable. "You have more details about the use of melange against the Scourge?"

Vor led Norma to the speaking area, and Ticia seemed flustered at being upstaged. Though the report had been delivered weeks earlier, Vor quickly summarized his trip to Parmentier and what his granddaughter Raquella had discovered. "According to reports flooding in from other infected worlds, the conclusion is consistent. On every planet there are inexplicable pockets of immunity—with a common denominator. Those who consume the spice melange have a greater resistance, if not immunity. Spice. An expensive, recreational drug. And a powerful weapon against the Scourge!"

Vor stepped aside to give Norma the podium. She did not hesitate. "Therefore we need a great deal of melange, and we need to distribute it as swiftly as possible. For that, I offer the services of VenKee Enterprises."

"This is just a ploy to increase demand for the spice—to increase your profits!" called one surly man from the fourth tier.

"It's true that VenKee is the main supplier of melange throughout the League, and that we also control space-folding ships that can deliver spice swiftly enough to make a difference on the afflicted worlds." With a flash of frustration, Norma thought that if the unreasonably frightened and overzealous people in the League hadn't forced her to remove her computer-augmented navigation systems, the safety record of the superfast ships might be dramatically increased. Perhaps, somehow, she could slip some of the navigation devices secretly back into the vessels. . . .

In a firm voice, she continued. "I have already issued instructions to increase VenKee's spice production on Arrakis as much as possible. In the name of my beloved husband, the patriot Aurelius Venport, VenKee will donate melange to plague-stricken worlds as a humanitarian gesture." A rumble of surprise went through the audience. She turned her gaze toward the faceless man who had shouted his accusation. "I presume that addresses any complaints that we are profiting from this tragedy?"

With his clear business sense, Adrien would probably oppose her decision, arguing that VenKee had already sacrificed enough. But Norma was not interested in profits right now. This was the right course of action.

The representatives cheered, but Ticia Cenva, seated now in the front row, did not join them. She leaned over to speak to the Grand Patriarch, looking conspiratorial. The chubby man's eyes lit up at whatever she had to say, and he nodded more vigorously. Xander Boro-Ginjo rose to his feet, calling for order.

"We appreciate VenKee's offer, but such a gesture is not nearly enough in these dire circumstances. Even with superhuman efforts, one company alone cannot produce enough spice to mitigate this crisis, if indeed melange provides protection against the Omnius Scourge. Somehow, we must increase the harvest of melange by several orders of magnitude."

He cleared his throat, a sly grin spreading across his plump face. "Therefore, for the good of humanity and the survival of our species, I hereby *annex* Arrakis into the League of Nobles and open it to anyone who is willing to help scrape spice from the sands. Now is not the time to be conservative and cautious with this resource. The human race needs every gram of melange."

Norma noticed that Ticia looked pleased with the turn of events, as if she had scored some sort of victory. Given the urgency, Norma could not fault what the Grand Patriarch had done, but she hoped he hadn't dealt a death blow to VenKee Enterprises.

Little did the inhabitants of the remote planet of Arrakis suspect what was about to happen to them.

Some say that Harkonnen blood running through my veins disgraces me, but I do not accept the lies I have heard, the attempts to besmirch the role of my grandfather. To me the actions of Xavier Harkonnen speak of honor rather than cowardice.

—ABULURD HARKONNEN,
letter to Supreme Commander Vorian Atreides

The Omnius Scourge spread from one League World to another faster than quarantines could be imposed or evacuations could get under way.

Pursuant to Ticia Cenva's genetic-preservation concept, the Army of the Jihad dispatched survey and rescue ships to as many unaffected worlds as possible. Sorceress volunteers gathered representative breeding samples from the populations, so that at least the bloodlines could be saved. To some it seemed a defeatist tactic, a frightening concession to the absolute worst-case scenario in which the epidemic spread everywhere.

Though he was only a young cuarto, Abulurd Butler led one of these missions, accompanied by the unyielding Supreme Sorceress herself. His rank was too low for him to expect any sort of command, but Abulurd found himself in nominal charge of a small, fast expedition to Ix, like so many other urgently dispatched groups of jihadi ships dealing with thousands of details in this crisis.

Some in the League might have assumed from his family name that Abulurd had been born to a distinguished military career, but Primero Quentin Butler gave minimal support to his youngest son's aspirations. Abulurd assumed Supreme Commander Atreides must have had a hand in his assignment—supposedly a safe one. Vorian had a habit of nudging him forward whenever he saw an opportunity. Abulurd, though, would have preferred to help the already afflicted victims, to bring medical aid, volunteers, supplies of melange.

His stripped-down javelin was sent to Ix to present quarantine instructions, begin preparations for survival, and preserve key bloodlines from the hardy survivors of generations of machine domination. Almost seventy years ago, their planet had been freed from Synchronized control. Ticia seemed particularly interested, since the genetic stock of the native Ixians had not yet been heavily assimilated into the general League population.

Unfortunately, by the time Abulurd's ship arrived, the first symptoms of the epidemic had already surfaced—irrational paranoia and mob behavior, weight loss, skin lesions and discolorations. It was not clear whether plague canisters had exploded in the skies, or if infected merchants or refugees from other hot spots had brought the Scourge to Ix. Whole villages had been knocked to their knees; other settlements were just on the verge of being infected.

On the javelin's bridge, Abulurd groaned. "We have just one ship! How are we ever going to rescue all those people?"

The Supreme Sorceress scowled, reassessing her priorities. "Ix is only one planet, with a population much larger than we could ever preserve. Do not even try. We should just leave. I can accomplish nothing, if their populace is already tainted."

Abulurd, though, wanted to offer the League's assistance. "Leave? We have spent weeks in transit just getting here."

"There is no point, Cuarto Butler."

He seemed very young and inexperienced next to the intimidating woman, but he thought of what Vor would have done. "Fortunately, Madam Sorceress, I am in command here. Yours is not the only objective of this mission." Maybe he did not view the overall racial picture as the Sorceress did, but in a time of such human disaster he felt that compassion was more important than ever. A person's life he could understand; a gene pool was far less tangible. "I see no reason not to offer whatever assistance we can. Why not set down at one of the outlying towns, a place that hasn't yet shown any sign of plague? We can distribute all of our supplies of melange to help those we can't take with us. Surely, you can salvage something."

"That would require intensive testing, isolation, extreme procedures."

Abulurd shrugged. "Then it will require those extra measures. I'm sure we can handle it."

The Sorceress looked at him in frustration, but did not argue further as the bridge crew sent signals and received updates from the settlements scattered across the surface. After reviewing the reports, Ticia focused her attention on one established settlement, mostly underground.

"If you insist on this course of action, Cuarto, then I suggest we start there. The reports suggest the village is clean, though I don't trust their capabilities of spotting and documenting the first subtle indications of the Scourge. We will select our subjects from those people and isolate them until we can determine that they are uninfected. We'll keep them segregated, run tests, then take the ones that haven't been tainted. I will secure blood samples from many others."

Abulurd nodded and gave the order. He seemed far too young to be issuing instructions to these other jihadis, but he was a Butler, and the soldiers listened to him.

The crew quarters were in a separate section of the ship behind thick sterile walls, and Abulurd gave instructions for the jihadis to double up to leave more room to take people aboard. He would not let himself think the effort was as pointless as Ticia seemed to believe, but even at its maximum capacity, the javelin could take only a few hundred refugees from Ix. This was not an evacuation by any means, just a gesture.

During the javelin's final approach, he stood looking out at the planet-scape. He had never visited Ix before but knew its historical importance. "My father defended Ix against the last machine incursion, and he was buried alive in one of the underground tunnels," he said, not looking directly at Ticia. "It's a miracle he survived at all." Quentin, in fact, rarely talked about the matter, forcing back an obvious shudder of claustrophobia whenever the subject was broached. Now Abulurd also remembered the stories Vorian had told him. "And my grandfather led the first fleet here, wrenching Ix free from Omnius. He was declared a Hero of the Jihad."

Ticia scowled at the young officer. "But in the end Xavier Harkonnen proved himself a fool, a coward, and the worst of traitors."

Abulurd bridled. "You don't know all the details, Sorceress. Don't be blinded by propaganda." His voice was flat, but as hard as metal.

She fixed him with her pale gaze. "I *know* Xavier Harkonnen murdered my biological father, Grand Patriarch Iblis Ginjo. No explanation or misunderstanding is sufficient to excuse that crime."

Disconcerted, Abulurd did not press the issue. He had heard that the Sorceresses of Rossak concerned themselves less with morality than with genetics. Or was Ticia allowing her emotions to affect her thinking?

The military javelin descended to its landing point. Homes and a variety of other structures dotted a relatively empty landscape near the entrances to caverns and tunnels. Knowing that the ship was coming, desperate Ixians had flooded out of the underground regions to surround an open area where the big Jihad vessel settled. They swarmed forward, shouting, welcoming Abulurd and his crew as saviors and heroes. Every one of them wanted to get off the planet before the Scourge could reach their village.

Abulurd's heart grew heavy. From the hopeful looks on their faces, they didn't yet understand how little anyone could really do to help them. All of his melange supplies aboard the ship would protect them for only a short while. Then he reminded himself that Ticia didn't want to be here, and anything he accomplished was better than simply abandoning them all to the Scourge.

Keeping the upper compartments of the javelin sealed and disinfected, the cuarto handpicked a group of mercenary guards. Though medical research seemed to show that the airborne virus could only be contracted via the body's wet membranes or open wounds, Abulurd ordered his team to suit up in full anti-exposure suits and wear standard-issue body shields. He could not be too careful.

Already, through lax procedures and insufficient care, one of the rescue javelins bearing refugees from Zanbar had arrived at Salusa with over half of the passengers and a third of its crew infected; they had not carried enough melange to protect themselves. Abulurd refused to let that happen to his own crew.

The Sorceress suited up and waited for Abulurd to join her. She didn't need him to accompany her—probably didn't even want him there—but Abulurd was the ranking officer on this mission. Ticia would make her choices from among the hopeful people, while his crewmen distributed the melange and supplies to help them weather the oncoming disaster.

Carrying Maula rifles and needle-firing chandler pistols, the group from the ship went to impose a semblance of order upon the crowds. Sealed inside his impermeable anti-exposure suit, Abulurd stepped out under the painfully bright skies of Ix. For weeks he had smelled only the recycled, filter-scrubbed atmosphere aboard the javelin; under other circumstances, he would have longed to draw a deep breath of fresh air. Ticia proceeded down the ramp with graceful and gliding steps, even in the heavy suit. She swiveled her head inside the helmet as she scanned the crowd for viable subjects worth rescuing.

The waiting people were uneasy, alternately cheering and talking seriously among themselves. He suddenly worried that his handful of armed mercenary guards would not be sufficient against this mob should it turn violent; after all, increased violence and irrationality were among the primary first-stage symptoms. They could not fire their projectile weapons without first switching off their body shields, which would also leave them vulnerable. He would have to handle this carefully.

"Cuarto," Ticia called, as if she were suddenly in command, "see to it that the specimens I select are taken aboard, cleansed, and inspected. Keep them in isolation until we are sure we can use them. We cannot allow any infected person to contaminate the others."

Abulurd gave the order. This was what the League wanted, this was why they had come here. At least he was saving some of them. Another ten jihadis emerged from the ship, also wearing protective suits. They carried the League's "mercy shipment" of melange, but it would not be enough.

The Sorceress walked among the uneasy Ixian crowd, towering above most of them. She chose young men, women, and children who looked healthy, intelligent, and strong. Though her selections seemed arbitrary, Abulurd's soldiers separated the candidates and took them away, but soon the crowd's uneasiness shifted to anger. Husbands were chosen but not their wives; children were separated from parents. The terrified Ixian settlers finally realized that this was not the rescue or relief mission they had envisioned.

Angry shouts rang out. Abulurd's mercenaries readied their weapons, hoping their personal shields would be sufficient against whatever the mob would throw. One girl screamed, refusing to let go of her mother's wrist. Then, before the situation could grow worse, Abulurd hurried to intercede, transmitting on a private band. "Sorceress, this makes no sense. The mother looks healthy as well. Why not keep them together?"

Scornful of the crowd, the Sorceress turned her pale gaze toward Abulurd; her brow furrowed in an impatient scowl. "What would be the advantage to bringing the mother as well? If we have the daughter, then we have the family's genetics. It would be more useful to take a completely unrelated person, thereby saving another core bloodline."

"But you're breaking up families! This isn't what the League intends!"

"One specimen is all we need for each key bloodline. Why take duplicates? It's a waste of our time, and a waste of the cargo holds. You are fully aware we don't have enough room."

"Isn't there some other way? You didn't tell me we had to do this in such a terrible, inhumane—"

She cut him off. "I didn't tell you we could do this at all, Cuarto. But you insisted. Think—the plague will break up these families anyway. I am more concerned with preserving the race than with maudlin sentiments." She pulled away from Abulurd and continued to push through the people. Heedless of any threat to herself, Ticia chose another specimen and another, culling the best candidates from the mass of hopefuls.

A gray-haired woman and her balding husband pushed closer. "Take us! We can pay you well for your trouble."

The Sorceress rudely dismissed them. "You are too old." Likewise, she discarded others, pronouncing them, by turns, infertile, physically weak, insufficiently intelligent, even unattractive. Ticia stood as genetic judge and jury over all.

Abulurd was appalled. And she thought *Xavier Harkonnen* had committed inexcusable and inhuman crimes? He closed his eyes, searching for a way to stop her from playing God, but in his heart, he knew she was right. This mission, with its one stripped-down javelin, couldn't possibly save everyone.

"At least try to come up with a fairer method of selection. We could have them draw numbers. There must be a—"

She cut him off, showing no interest in or respect for his rank. He doubted she would have reacted differently even if he'd been a primero. "You knew from the outset that we could take only a handful. Now let me do my job."

Impatient, Ticia pressed on as their squad of mercenaries cleared the way. The people pushed forward, trying to save themselves; others broke from the perimeter and rushed toward the landed javelin, as if they meant to storm it and fly away. Shots rang out when part of the crowd tried to attack the mercenary guards. Abulurd whirled in the direction of the sound. Chandler pistols cut down several leaders of the mob, but the rest surged ahead, shouting. Even the weapons fire did not stall them. He saw now that some of them had jaundiced skin and yellowed eyes—indicators of the infection!

Those Ixians who had already been chosen crowded near the boarding ramp, glancing fearfully back at the others. Some looked as if they didn't want to get away, but would prefer to stay and die with their families.

Although Abulurd felt compassion for all of them, he didn't know how to ease the situation. He issued an order for the guards to wound only, not to kill unless absolutely necessary, but the mob was already inflamed.

"Stop, fools!" Ticia's voice echoed like a thunderclap, augmented by the speakers of her suit and the force of her own telepathic powers. The nerve-stopping command was enough to make the people pause. "We cannot take you all, so we must take only your best, the core bloodlines and breeding resources. I have selected them. Your unruliness imperils everyone."

But Ticia's words only enraged them further, and they turned more violent, rushing toward her and the armed guards. Abulurd shouted for order, but even his own men did not respond.

The Supreme Sorceress of Rossak made a disgusted noise. When she raised her gloved hands, Abulurd could see static lightning crackling from her fingertips. She launched a powerful invisible explosion that knocked hundreds of people backward. They sprawled flat, like stalks of wheat blown over by a cyclone. Some lay twitching on the ground, their burned skin covered with white blisters. One man had been crisped and blackened; smoke curled up from his singed hair and toasted skin.

Static danced around Ticia, residue from the mental energy she had unleashed. Finally, the Ixians were struck silent. Those still standing backed away in awe. The Sorceress glared at them for a long moment, then shouted to the soldiers, directing them to hurry the last candidates aboard for processing. "Let us get off this planet."

Sickened, Abulurd waited beside her at the javelin's ramp. Ticia was clearly furious. "Selfish vermin. Why do we make the effort to save such inferior people?"

But he'd had enough of her attitude. "You can't blame them—they were simply attempting to save themselves."

"With no regard to the lives of others. I am acting for the good of the human race. It is clear to me that you have no stomach for making difficult decisions. Inappropriate sympathy could doom us all." She scowled at him, clearly trying to make a pointed insult. "In my estimation, Cuarto Butler, you are weak and unreliable in a crisis situation . . . possibly unfit for command. Just like your grandfather."

Instead of feeling stung, Abulurd was angry and defiant. From Vorian, he had learned of the heroic things Xavier Harkonnen had done, even if history had not recorded them. "My grandfather would have had more compassion than you did back there." Few people would care about the truth anymore, since the story had been accepted and repeated for generations. But now, seeing the arrogant ignorance of this woman, he made a bold and impulsive decision.

Though his brothers and father bowed their heads in embarrassment, Abulurd vowed never to be ashamed of his true family name. He would stop hiding. He could not honorably do anything else.

"Sorceress, my grandfather was no coward. The details have been kept secret to protect the Jihad, but he did exactly what was necessary to keep the Grand Patriarch from perpetrating unforgivable harm. Iblis Ginjo was the villain, not Xavier Harkonnen."

Stunned, she gave him a deprecating, disbelieving look. "You insult my father."

"The truth is the truth." He raised his chin. "Butler may be an honorable enough name, but so is Harkonnen. From now on, and for the rest of my life, that is who I will be. I claim my true heritage."

"What foolishness is this?"

"Henceforth, you will address me as Abulurd *Harkonnen*."

War is a violent form of business.

—ADRIEN VENPORT,
"Commercial Plan for Arrakis Spice Operations"

The League of Nobles called it a "spice rush." Once it was learned that melange was useful in treating the deadly Scourge, hardy men and women from far-flung planets raced to Arrakis to seek their fortunes. Shiploads of prospectors and excavation contractors, all of them taking a desperate gamble, flowed to the once-isolated desert world.

Ishmael could hardly believe his eyes when he went to the dizzying metropolis of Arrakis City for the first time in decades. It reminded him of half-forgotten Starda on Poritrin, which he had fled long ago.

Hastily erected buildings sprawled across the parched landscape, spreading into the rocky foothills, piled one on top of the other. At the spaceport, ships came and went at all hours; local flyers and groundcars bustled to and fro. Passengers arrived by the thousands, shading their eyes from the yellow sun of Arrakis, eager to rush out to the open dunes, oblivious to the deadly perils there.

According to rumor, there was so much melange that a person could simply walk out with a satchel and scoop it up from the ground—which was true, in a sense, if one knew where to find it. Most of these people would be dead within months, killed by sandworms or the arid environment or their own stupidity. They were totally unprepared for the dangers that awaited them.

"We can take advantage of this, Ishmael," El'hiim said, still trying to convince his stepfather. "These people do not know what they will find here on Arrakis. We can earn their money for doing what comes naturally to us."

"And why would we desire their money?" Ishmael said, honestly not understanding. "We have everything we could wish for. The desert provides all our real needs."

El'hiim shook his head. "I am the Naib, and my duty to the people is to make our village prosper. This is a great opportunity to offer our desert skills and make ourselves invaluable to the offworlders. They will keep coming no matter what. We can either ride the worm, or be devoured by it. Didn't you tell me that story yourself, when I was young?"

The ancient man frowned. "Then you misunderstood the lesson of that parable." But he followed his stepson into the city anyway. Raised in a different time, El'hiim had never understood true desperation, the need to fight and protect hard-won freedoms. He had never been a slave.

Ishmael frowned at the garrulous offworlders. "It might be wiser just to lead them out into the desert, rob them, and leave them to die."

El'hiim chuckled, pretending Ishmael had made a joke, though he knew otherwise. "There is a fortune to be made by exploiting the ignorance of these invaders. Why not profit from that?"

"Because then you will encourage them, El'hiim. Can you not see this?"

"They do not need my encouragement. Haven't you heard of the plague released by the thinking machines? The Omnius Scourge? Spice offers protection, and therefore everyone demands it. You may bury your head in the sand of a dune, but they will not go away."

The younger man's firm opinion made him as stubborn as Ishmael.

Ishmael resented the truth, the changes, and at the back of his mind he did realize that this influx of outsiders was as unstoppable as a sandstorm. He felt all of his achievements slipping through his fingers. He still proudly called himself and his tribe the Free Men of Arrakis, but such a proud title no longer carried the meaning it once had.

In town, El'hiim easily mixed with offworld merchants and prospectors, spoke several dialects of the Galach standard language, and happily traded with anyone who would take his money. Over and over, his stepson tried to get Ishmael to enjoy some of the fine luxuries the tribe could now afford.

"You are no longer an escaped slave, Ishmael," El'hiim said. "Come, all of us appreciate everything you have done in the past. Now, we want you to enjoy yourself. Aren't you the least bit interested in the rest of the universe?"

"I have seen some of it already. No, I am not interested."

El'hiim chuckled. "You are too rigid and inflexible."

"And you are too quick to chase after new experiences."

"Is that a bad thing?"

"It is on Arrakis—if you forget the ways that have allowed us to survive for so long."

"I won't forget them, Ishmael. But if I find better ways, I will show them to our people."

He led Ishmael through the winding streets, past open market stalls and raucous bazaars. He slapped away pickpockets as he and Ishmael jostled through clusters of water sellers, food vendors, and purveyors of Rossak drugs and odd stimulants from far-off worlds. Ishmael saw poor, broken men huddled in alleys and doorways, those who had come to Arrakis seeking fortune and already lost so much that they could no longer afford to leave.

If Ishmael had had the financial means, he would have paid passage for every one of them, just to send them away.

Finally spotting his mark, El'hiim tugged on the older man's sleeve and hurried forward to a smallish offworlder who was buying outrageously priced desert equipment. "Excuse me, sir," El'hiim said. "I assume you are one of our new spice prospectors. Are you preparing to head out on the open dunes?"

The small-statured stranger had close-set eyes and sharp features. Ishmael stiffened, recognizing the racial attributes of a hated Tlulaxa. "This one's a flesh merchant," he growled at El'hiim, using Chakobsa so the stranger wouldn't understand.

His stepson motioned him to silence, as if he were a buzzing gnat. Ishmael could not forget the slavers who had captured so many Zensunnis and brought them to places like Poritrin and Zanbar. Even decades after the scandal of the Tlulaxa organ farms, the genetic manipulators were cast out and shunned. But on Arrakis during the heady days of the spice rush, money erased all prejudices.

The Tlulaxa newcomer turned to El'hiim, appraising the dusty Naib with obvious skepticism and distaste. "What do you want? I'm busy here."

El'hiim made a gesture of respect, though the Tlulaxa man deserved none. "I am El'hiim, an expert on the deserts of Arrakis."

"And I am Wariff—one who minds his own business and has no interest in yours."

"Ah, but you *should*, and I offer my services as a guide." El'hiim smiled. "My stepfather and I can advise you on what equipment to purchase and what would be an unnecessary expense. Best of all, I can take you directly to the richest spice fields."

"Go to whatever hells you believe in," the Tlulaxa snapped. "I don't need a guide, especially not one of the thieving Zensunni "

Ishmael squared his shoulders and answered in clear Galach. "Ironic words from a Tlulaxa, a race that steals human beings and harvests body parts."

El'hiim pushed his stepfather behind him before the confrontation escalated.

"Come, Ishmael. There are plenty of other customers. Unlike this stubborn fool, some spice rushers will actually find their fortunes."

With a haughty sniff, the Tlulaxa man ignored them, as if the two desert men were something he had just scraped off the sole of his boot.

At the end of the long, hot day, when the two walked away from Arrakis City, Ishmael felt sick with disgust. His stepson's pandering to outsiders upset him more than he could imagine. Finally, after a hard silence, the older man said in a heavy voice, "You are the son of Selim Wormrider. How can you lower yourself to this?"

El'hiim looked at him in disbelief, raising his eyebrows as if his step-father had asked an incomprehensible question. "What do you mean? I secured four Zensunni guide contracts. People from our village will take prospectors out to the sands and let them do the work while we take half of the profit. How can you object to that?"

"Because that isn't how we do things. It goes against what your father taught his followers."

El'hiim was clearly working hard to control his temper. "Ishmael, how can you hate change so much? If nothing ever changed, then you and your people would still be slaves on Poritrin. But you saw a different way, you escaped, and you came here to make a better life for yourself. I am trying to do the same."

"The same? You would surrender all the progress we have made."

"I do not wish to live as a starving outlaw like my father was. One cannot eat a legend. We cannot drink the water of visions and prophecies. We must fend for ourselves and take what the desert offers—or someone else will."

The two men traveled in silence out into the night, and finally reached the edge of the open sand, where they would begin crossing the desert wastelands.

"We will never fully understand each other, El'hiim."

The younger man let out a dry, bitter chuckle. "At last you say something I can agree with."

Fear and bravery are not as mutually exclusive as some would have
us believe. As I go into danger, I feel both at once. Is it brave to over-
come one's fear, or just curiosity about the human potential?

— GILBERTUS ALBANS,

A Quantitative Analysis of Emotions

When Omnius summoned Erasmus to the Central Spire, Gilbertus accompanied his teacher while remaining unobtrusive. He had left the Serena clone in the robot's extensive gardens; he had already discovered that she liked to look at the lovely flowers, though she was never interested in the scientific names of the species.

As he followed his robot mentor into the city, Gilbertus intended to listen carefully to any interchanges between Omnius and Erasmus, watching the style of debate, the exchange of data. From it he would learn. This was an exercise in mentation for the man Erasmus called his "Mentat."

The evermind rarely seemed to notice Gilbertus's existence; he wondered if Omnius was being a sore loser, since the human ward had indeed developed into a superior creature despite his squalid beginning. Apparently, the evermind did not like to be proved wrong in his assumptions.

When they reached the Central Spire, Omnius said, "I have excellent information to share." His voice boomed through speakers in the silvery walls of the main chamber. "It is what the *hrethgir* would call 'good news.'"

Colors swirled in pearlescent, hypnotic patterns on the Omnius wallscreens. Gilbertus didn't know where to look. Omnius seemed to be everywhere. Watcheyes flitted around the room, hovering and humming.

The robot's flowmetal face formed into a smile. "What has happened, Omnius?"

"In summary: Our retrovirus epidemic is devastating the human popu-lation, exactly as predicted. The Army of the Jihad is completely preoc-cupied with its response to the crisis. For months they have been unable to take any military action against us."

"Perhaps we can finally regain some of our territory," Erasmus said, the smile still fixed on his platinum face.

"More than that. I have dispatched numerous robotic spycraft to ver-ify the vulnerability of Salusa Secundus and other League Worlds. In the meantime, I intend to build up and consolidate a war fleet of greater power than any in human-recorded history. Since the weakened *hrethgir* do not pose a threat to us at the moment, I will recall all of my robotic battleships from across the Synchronized Worlds and assemble them here."

"Putting all of your eggs in one basket," Erasmus said, again selecting an appropriate cliché.

"Preparing an offensive force against which the League of Nobles has no chance. I calculate zero probability of failure, statistically. In all our previous engagements, the military strength was too evenly matched to guarantee us a victory. Now, our superior numbers will overwhelm *hrethgir* resistance by at least a factor of a hundred. The fate of the human race is assured."

"Undoubtedly, it is a most impressive plan, Omnius," the robot said.

Gilbertus listened quietly, wondering if the evermind was trying to intimidate him. Why would Omnius bother?

"Is this the reason you have summoned us?" Erasmus asked.

The computer's voice increased dramatically in volume, as if to startle them. "I have concluded that before our final assault against the League of Nobles, every one of my components—my 'subjects'—must join a single integrated network. I can afford no anomalies or diversions. In order for the Synchronized Worlds to be victorious, we must all be synchronized."

Erasmus's face reverted to its smooth mirrorlike countenance. Gilber-tus could tell that his mentor was troubled. "I do not understand, Omnius."

"I have tolerated your unnecessary independence for too long, Eras-mus. Now I need to standardize your programming and personality with my own. There is no longer any requirement for you to be different. I find it a distraction."

Alarm surged through Gilbertus, and he forcibly dampened his reac-tions. His mentor would solve this problem, as he always had. Erasmus must feel the same shock, though his placid robotic face displayed none of it.

"That is not necessary, Omnius. I can continue to provide valuable insights. There will be no distraction."

"You have said this for many years. It is no longer efficient for me to keep you distinct from my evermind."

"Omnius, I have compiled much irreplaceable data during the span of my existence. You may still find certain revelations enlightening, and they can provide you with alternate paths for cogitation." Listening to the calm words of the robot, Gilbertus wanted to scream. How could he not feel desperate? "If you simply assimilate me into your greater mental database, then my decision-paths and perspectives will be compromised."

He would die!

"Not if I keep all of your data in an isolated program. I will partition the record to keep your conclusion trees separate. Therefore the problem is solved, and Erasmus as a separate entity can be eliminated."

Gilbertus swallowed hard as he listened. Sweat broke out on his brow.

Erasmus paused while his gelcircuitry mind churned through thousands of possibilities, discarding most of them, looking for some way to sidestep this demand he had known would eventually come.

"For greater efficiency in our operations, I must complete my remaining work in progress. Therefore, I suggest that before you store my data and erase my memory core entirely, you allow me one more day to conclude several experiments and collate the information." Erasmus faced one of the pearly wallscreens. "Afterward, Gilbertus Albans can finish the work, but I must prepare for the transition and give him precise instructions."

Gilbertus felt knots in his stomach. "Will one day be sufficient, Father?" His voice cracked.

"You are an adept student, my Mentat." The robot turned to his human ward. "We do not want to delay the plans of Omnius."

Omnius considered for a long, tense moment, as if suspecting a trick. "That is acceptable. In one day I require you to present your memory core to me for full assimilation."

Later, inside the robot's villa after all the work had been done and the subsequent experiments prepared, Gilbertus fought down his deep anxiety as he followed Erasmus out into his greenhouse courtyard.

For the occasion, the autonomous robot wore his richest, most voluminous robe decorated with false ermine fur in the fashion of ancient kings. The cloth was a deep purple, which looked like dark old blood in the ruddy light of the red giant star.

His muscular body hidden in drab clothes, Gilbertus stopped beside him. He had read ancient heroic stories about men being led to unjust executions. "I am ready, Father. I will do as you instructed."

The robot formed a sensitive paternal smile on his flowmetal face. "We cannot contradict Omnius, Gilbertus. We must follow his commands—I only hope he does not choose to delete you as well, because you are my finest, most successful, and rewarding experiment."

"Even if Omnius chooses to destroy me, or send me back to the slave pens, I am satisfied with the enhanced life you have given me." Tears glistened in Gilbertus's eyes.

The robot seemed to be radiating tense emotions. "As a last service to me, I want you to deliver my memory core personally to the Central Spire. Carry it in your own hands. I do not trust the dexterity of some of Omnius's robots."

"I will not disappoint you, Father."

A HUMAN ALONE in Corrin's main robotic city, Gilbertus went to stand at the opening of the stylized flowmetal tower. "Lord Omnius, I have brought the memory core of Erasmus, as you commanded." He held up the small, hard ball in his hand so that the buzzing watcheyes could see it.

The shifting metal rippled under the bloody daylight. The soft quicksilver wall puckered and then opened to form a doorway in front of him, like a mouth. "Enter."

Gilbertus stepped into a broad main chamber. The details had shifted from what he had seen only the day before, strange designs like arcane circuitry or hieroglyphic messages now adorned the walls—decorations? The Omnius wallscreens still swirled like milky half-blind eyes.

Respectfuly silent, Gilbertus stopped in the middle of the room and held the valuable module. "This is what you requested, Lord Omnius. I . . . I believe you will see the advantage of keeping Erasmus's thoughts within you. There is much you can learn."

"How does a human dare to tell me how much I can learn?" the evermind said in a thunderous voice.

Gilbertus bowed. "I meant no disrespect."

A burly sentinel robot entered the room, extending thick metal hands for the sphere. Protectively, Gilbertus pulled the precious orb closer to his body. "Erasmus instructed me to insert his memory core with my own hands, to make certain no errors occur."

"Humans commit errors," Omnius said. "Machines do not." Nevertheless, Omnius created an access port on an inner wall.

Gilbertus took one last glance at the small sphere that contained every thought and every memory of Erasmus, his mentor, his . . . father. Before Omnius could scold him for the delay, he went to the port and inserted the core, then waited patiently as the evermind drank in all of the memories and other data, storing them in a discrete area of his vast and organized mind.

The intimidating sentinel robot nudged him away from the wall when the small memory core reemerged from the socket with a soft click.

The evermind spoke in a contemplative voice. "Interesting. This data is . . . disturbing. It does not conform with rational patterns. I was right to keep it entirely separate from the rest of my program."

The sentinel robot lifted the memory core. Gilbertus watched in horror, knowing what was bound to happen. His master had prepared him for this.

"Now that Erasmus is entirely stored within me," Omnius announced, "it is inefficient to duplicate his existence. You may go now, Gilbertus Albans. Your work with Erasmus is finished."

The sentinel robot squeezed its powerful metal hands and crushed the memory core, mangling it into fragments that fell to the floor of the Central Spire.

Thinking machines never sleep.

—A Saying of the Jihad

While numerous refugee ships converged in crowded space around Salusa Secundus, carrying representatives of the genetic branches of humanity, the League capital gained fame as the "lifeboat planet." No ship was allowed to land, however; instead they remained in quarantine, orbiting the planet. The backlog in the blockade caused spacecraft to pile up, crowding traffic lanes with thousands and then tens of thousands of vessels of all configurations from more than a hundred worlds.

The Scourge had by now consumed twenty-eight League Worlds, and billions were reported dead.

After returning from his ordeal on Ix, knowing that many of the people he had left behind were already dead, Abulurd's javelin waited with his isolated charges and an impatient Ticia Cenva until the appointed incubation period had passed. Each rescued person from Ix had been isolated, tested, and cleared; even in the turmoil of the mob, the precautions had worked. None of the refugees or crew fell ill during the long voyage back to Salusa.

En route, sticking to his brash decision, Abulurd had announced to his surprised crew that he was adopting the Harkonnen name again. He explained his own version of the events that had made Xavier such a hated figure, but it was ancient history to everyone else, and many doubted his version of the facts. Clearly, they wondered why the cuarto would stir up problems so long after the fact.

Since he was in command of the javelin, they did not openly question Abulurd's choice, but their faces said enough. In contrast, Ticia Cenva was not bound by such formalities, and she made it clear that she felt the young officer had lost all common sense.

Finally, when their quarantine time had passed, Ticia gratefully left Abulurd's company and joined other Sorceresses to collate their immense new catalog of genetic data. Swift library ships carried volumes of raw information back to their cliff cities on Rossak. Abulurd did not know what the Sorceresses would do with all that breeding information; for himself, he was simply glad to have the abrasive self-centered woman off of his ship.

At the military headquarters in Zimia, Abulurd presented himself for inspection before his father. Primero Quentin Butler remained somber since learning from Vorian Atreides of Rikov's death. He still wrestled with his own personal guilt, because his battalion had been at Parmentier when the first plague projectiles arrived. If only his Jihad ships had obliterated the infectious torpedoes before they could strike the atmosphere . . . But he was a highly trained soldier, dedicated to the destruction of Omnius. The primero would marshal his troops, redistribute his resources, and continue the virtuous Jihad.

Instead of dispatching Abulurd to another League World to acquire more escapees from the plague, Quentin ordered his youngest son to remain at Salusa and assist with the quarantine and resettlement activities. The task had grown monumental as ship after ship of frightened League citizens fled their worlds and came to the lifeboat planet. An entire contingent of the Army of the Jihad was put in place to prevent any vessel from landing and disgorging its occupants, until they had waited out their appropriate quarantine time and been certified by medical personnel.

Abulurd accepted his reassignment with a brisk nod. "One other thing, Father. Upon deep reflection and a thorough review of all historical documents, it is obvious to me that our family name was wrongfully blackened by history." He forced himself to continue. It was better to tell him now, before the primero heard from another source. "In order to reestablish our honor, I have chosen to take the Harkonnen name for myself."

Quentin looked as if his youngest son had slapped him. "You are calling yourself a . . . *Harkonnen*? What idiocy is this? Why now? Xavier died decades ago! Why reopen old wounds?"

"It is the first step toward righting a wrong that has endured for generations. I've already put into motion the legal documents. I hope you can respect my decision."

His father looked intensely angry. "Butler is the most respected and powerful name in the League of Nobles. Ours is the family line of Serena, and of Viceroy Manion Butler—yet you prefer to associate yourself with a . . . traitor and a coward?"

"I do not believe Xavier Harkonnen was that." Abulurd straightened, standing up to the primero's obvious displeasure. He wished Vorian Atreides could be there to support him, but this was between himself and his father. "The history we were all taught is . . . distorted and inaccurate."

Cold displeasure emanated from the older man as he stood from behind his desk. "You are of legal age, Cuarto. You are allowed to make your own decisions, regardless of what I or anyone else might think of them. And you must face the consequences."

"I am aware of that, Father."

"In these offices you will refer to me as Primero."

"Yes, sir."

"You are dismissed."

ABULURD SAT ON the bridge of his javelin, patrolling the swarms of ships crowded into parking lanes and docking orbits. Traffic-control operators in high stations monitored all vessels and maintained logs of how long each had been in transit. Since these ships did not use space-folding technology, each journey from an infected planet took weeks; if anyone had come aboard carrying the Scourge, the fast-acting retrovirus should have shown itself en route.

Aboard the rescue vessels, the League had isolated groups of people in sealed chambers as a stopgap measure, should an outbreak occur. After an appropriate time went by and the passengers passed inspection, they went through two additional decontamination processes before being allowed to disembark and settle in Salusan refugee camps. At some later date, they would be returned to their homeworlds or be distributed throughout the League.

As Abulurd patrolled the fringes of the system, he unexpectedly encountered a group of incoming vessels, expensive space yachts built for rich noblemen. He ordered his javelin to change course, interposing the military vessel between the unscheduled ships and Salusa.

When he established communication with the lead space yacht, Abulurd stared at the lean, bright-eyed man on the screen. A group of well-dressed people stood behind him. "I am Lord Porce Bludd, formerly of Poritrin, bringing refugees—all of them healthy, I guarantee—"

Abulurd drew himself up straight, wishing he had changed into a formal presentation uniform. "I am Cuarto Abulurd . . . Harkonnen. Will you submit to required quarantine procedures and medical inspection, so we can verify what you say?"

"We are prepared for that." Bludd now blinked in sudden realization. "Abulurd, did you say? You're Quentin's son, aren't you? Why are you calling yourself a Harkonnen?"

Taken aback by the man's recognition, Abulurd drew a breath. "Yes, I am the son of Primero Butler. How do you know my father?"

"A long time ago, Quentin and I worked together building New Starda on the banks of the Isana River. He spent a year there on military furlough, as a jihadi engineer. That was well before he married your mother."

"Has the Scourge appeared on Poritrin?" Abulurd asked. They had received no reports from that world.

"A few villages, but we're relatively safe. Since the great slave revolt, Poritrin's population centers have been scattered. I immediately issued isolation decrees. We had plenty of melange to go around—second highest per-capita consumption in the League, next to Salusa itself."

"So why have you come here?" Abulurd still had not moved his javelin out of the way. Bludd's convoy remained stalled.

The nobleman's eyes seemed intense with echoes of deep grief. "These families agreed to sacrifice all their accumulated fortunes. Added to my own, I intend to turn that wealth to humanitarian endeavors. The Bludd family has much to atone for, I believe. The Omnius Scourge is the worst crisis free humanity has faced since the Titans. If ever there was a time when I could help, it is now."

Abulurd acknowledged the bravery and determination he saw in Bludd's face. A long moment passed, and the lord grew impatient. "Well, are you going to let us through, Abulurd? I had hoped to disperse these passengers to quarantine stations before taking my ships to another planet where I can continue to help people."

"Permission granted." He instructed his navigator to withdraw from the defensive posture. "Let them through, into the quarantine queue."

"Say, Abulurd, is your father still on Salusa?" Bludd asked. "I'd like to discuss my plans with him. He always had a good eye for fine-tuning an operation."

"I believe he is still at headquarters in Zimia." Quentin had not spoken to his son since dispatching him to his patrol duties.

"I'll find him then. Now, young man, if you would be so kind as to escort me into Salusan orbit where I can deliver my charges? I may need your help navigating the bureaucratic tangle there."

"Acknowledged, Lord Bludd. You'll have plenty of time to send messages to my father while you're waiting." Abulurd turned his javelin about and led the way to Salusa Secundus.

TRAGEDY SEEMED TO strike daily. Among the refugee ships clustered above the capital planet, the news spread like wildfire: Scout ships had returned bearing terrible reports that four more League Worlds were inflamed with plague, suffering almost incomprehensible levels of loss. In some cities, where storms or rampant fires had struck and the weakened populations could not stand against natural disasters in addition to the Scourge, the death rate was nearly ninety percent.

Even more distressing was a shocking setback on one of the fully-loaded refugee ships. After surviving their extended isolation period, the weary passengers had emerged from their sterile chambers to await final inspection. The jihadi crew, its captain, and their mercenaries had joined the relieved and excited refugees, offering celebratory drinks. A crew of medical personnel arrived and routinely administered the final verification blood tests, so confident in the amount of time that had passed that they grew lax, mingling, talking, laughing, embracing.

To everyone's horror, one man unexpectedly began showing initial signs of the RNA retrovirus. The doctors were astonished, running checks and double-checks of their blood test results. Three more passengers exhibited symptoms before the day was out.

By then all of the routine isolation procedures had been set aside in preparation for disembarkation, and many people—refugees, jihadis, mercenaries, and even some medical personnel—had been exposed. Going back to their isolation chambers would serve no purpose. A cordon of military ships surrounded the rescue vessel to prevent any shuttles from departing.

Abulurd was assigned this horrendous watchdog duty for four days, waiting, hearing the pathetic and desperate cries for help from those sealed aboard the infected ship. Melange rations were rushed through the airlock, and the passengers fought over the spice, desperate to grab any chance at immunity.

The tragedy of it gnawed at his very soul. These people had all thought they were clean; now many of them would not survive to set foot on Salusa Secundus. And the jihadis and doctors—who should never have been in real danger, who had only been doing their jobs to protect others from the Scourge—would pay too high a price for briefly letting down their guard. There was nothing more Abulurd or any of the League scientists could do except keep the ship sealed and wait.

In anguish, he sat back listening to the letters transmitted by the refugees before they fell ill, hoping to preserve some reference to themselves or leave a message for their loved ones.

Abulurd's crew was deeply disturbed, and morale plummeted. He was about to block out the transmissions, but then caught himself. He would not turn a deaf ear to these poor people and their suffering. He would not pretend that they did not exist, nor would he ignore their hopeless plight.

He considered this small tribute a brave thing, something Xavier might have suggested. Abulurd only hoped that someday his crew, and his family, would understand why he'd done it.

Technology should have freed man from the burdens of life. Instead, it imprisoned him.

— RAYNA BUTLER,
True Visions

After more than a month of rampaging death, some might have drawn hope from the fact that Parmentier was reaching the end of its epidemic. The genetically modified RNA retrovirus was unstable in the environment and had degraded over the weeks, and the only new cases now came from unprotected contact with those who were ill.

The Omnius Scourge had run its course on the planet. The susceptible were already infected, and between a third and a half of them were dead. The final casualty count would likely never be known.

WITHIN DAYS OF beginning her work, Rayna Butler's mission grew too large for her.

Inside every building, every home, every business, every factory, she discovered evil machines, sometimes in the open and sometimes in shadows. But she found them. Her arms ached from methodically swinging her cudgel. Her hands were covered with bruises and cuts from flying glass and metal, and her bare feet were abraded and sore, but she did not pause. Saint Serena had told her what she must do.

More and more people watched her, first as entertainment, confused as to why she would direct so much destruction toward conveniences and innocuous appliances. But finally others began to understand her obsession and started smashing machines with joyous anger. For so long they had been helpless to strike back that they now turned against any manifestation of their great enemy. At first, Rayna simply went on her way, doing little to lead those who followed in her wake.

When she was unexpectedly joined by the surviving Martyrists, already intense fanatics willing to throw away their lives as Saint Serena herself had done, Rayna's ragtag band became more organized, and suddenly swelled. In the haunted streets of Parmentier, the new movement was unstoppable.

The Martyrists plodded after the ethereal girl, waving pennants and holding staffs high, until finally Rayna turned to them in confusion. Climbing atop an abandoned groundcar, she called out, "Why do you waste your time and energy carrying those banners? Who are you performing for? I don't want to see flags and colors. This is a crusade, not a pageant."

She jumped down and pushed into their midst. Confused, they made way to let the pale, hairless girl through. Rayna tore away a large fabric banner and handed the bare staff back to a man. "There. Now use *this* to smash machines."

She did not care who these people were or what motivated them, as long as they aided her cause. The girl's thin voice took on an added hardness, a tone of unshakable belief. "If you have survived this plague, then you are chosen to assist me."

Several Martyrists lowered their banners and tore them away from the poles, which they could now use as clubs and crowbars. "We are ready!"

The bald girl faced them with a childlike earnestness, exuding a primal power from her translucent, fever-damaged skin. Her words surrounded her like an aura, and the listeners began to sway. Rayna had never practiced to become a great speaker, but she had heard enough sermons with her mother, had listened to the recorded oratory of the charismatic Grand Patriarch Iblis Ginjo, had heard her father and grandfather give military rallies. "Look all around you! You can see the curse of the demon machines. Look at the insidious marks they have left upon our land, our people."

The throng murmured. In the empty buildings around them, the windows were dark, many of them smashed. The remnants of a few rotted, unburied bodies lay in the streets and alleys.

"Even before the Demon Scourge struck, the machines inched their way into our lives under our very noses, and we allowed it to happen! Sophisticated machines, calculational devices, mechanical assistants—

yes, we pretend that we've gotten rid of all robots and computers, but their cousins are among us everywhere. We can no longer tolerate any of that."

Rayna raised her crowbar, and her followers shouted.

"When I was struck down by the fever, Saint Serena herself came to me and told me what we must do." The girl's eyes filled with tears, and she became wistful. "I can see her face now, beautiful, glowing, surrounded by white light. I can hear her words as she revealed God's supreme commandment to me—'Thou shalt not make a machine in the likeness of the human mind.'" She paused, then raised her voice without shouting: "We must obliterate any sign of them."

One of the Martyrists picked up the shreds of a colorful banner. "I saw Serena Butler in a vision, too! She came to me."

"And to me," cried another man. "She is still watching over us, guiding us."

The followers clacked their staffs and bars together, anxious to go about the destruction. But Rayna had not yet finished her speech. "And we must not disappoint her. The human race cannot give up until we achieve total victory. Do you hear me? *Total* victory."

A man shouted, "Destroy all thinking machines!"

A shrill woman, whose face was streaked with scratches as if she had tried to claw out her own eyes, wailed, "We have brought our own pain upon ourselves. We have left our cities wide open to the Demon Scourge because we were not willing to take the necessary action."

"Until now." Rayna wagged a finger at them. "We must eradicate any computer, any machine, no matter how innocuous it may seem! A complete and total purge. Only that way can we save ourselves."

She led her agitated followers deeper into the death-filled city. Waving cudgels and mallets, the mob swept forward. Their fervor rose as they descended on factories, industrial centers, and libraries.

Rayna knew it was just the beginning.

THE VANDALS AND fanatics only compounded the misery inflicted by the epidemic and all the subsequent breakdowns in Parmentier society, as far as Raquella was concerned. Misdirecting their hatred of the thinking machines, the wild extremists targeted every semblance of technology, eradicating even sophisticated devices that helped people.

They shut down Niubbe's intermittently functioning public transportation system, along with much of the electrical grid and communications network.

As she struggled to aid the last plague sufferers after the power went out in the hospital, Raquella could not comprehend the delusions. Did these Martyrist lunatics really think they were hurting Omnius by using rocks, crowbars, and clubs to pummel benign machines?

Every day more of them gathered outside the overcrowded medical center, looking at the large building with a strange, glazed hunger. Many shook their fists and screamed threats. In order to protect the hospital, Mohandas had positioned as many armed guards as he could hire or bribe at every entrance. . . .

In a daze from the unending cycles of work and inadequate rest, Raquella stumbled down a corridor to a heavy door at the far end, wearing a breather over her mouth and nose. So far, she had been careful to protect herself from the obvious vectors of infection, but it would be so easy to make a small and deadly mistake. Her face, hair, and clothes always reeked of antivirals and disinfectants. Though she and Mohandas consumed whatever spice they could, just to keep themselves going, the supplies had dwindled to almost nothing.

She hoped Vorian Atreides would return soon. Isolated here on Parmentier, none of them had any idea what was happening out in the rest of the League of Nobles.

Now Raquella entered a large walk-in vault, the most secure room in the hospital. The vault door was partly open, which surprised her. Hospital rules dictated that it be kept closed and locked. Everything had grown so lax, so slipshod.

Cautiously, she pushed the heavy metalloy door, making the hinges groan softly. Inside, a startled man looked up.

"Dr. Tyrj! What are you doing?"

His face flushed behind his clearplaz breather as he tried to cover what he'd been doing, but Raquella had already glimpsed hidden pockets in his work smock crammed with doses of melange powder from the last supplies of spice kept in the hospital.

Every hospital worker received an allocation for personal use, since the spice protected them from the Scourge. But this was much more melange than any one person was allowed.

The small, wiry man tried to push past her. "I don't know what you mean. Now get out of my way. Patients are waiting for me."

She stopped him cold with a stiff forearm to the middle of his chest. "You're *selling* spice, aren't you?"

"Certainly not!" His left hand dipped into a side pocket, and she saw something glint as he started to bring it out.

With a swift knee to his midsection, Raquella doubled him over. A scalpel fell from his hand, clattering on the floor. She shouted for help as Tyrj lay groaning. She heard running footsteps in the corridor, and Mohandas appeared. Alarmed, he looked at Raquella, making sure she was all right. She pointed to the spice that had tumbled out of the doctor's hidden pockets.

"I can explain this." Tyrj struggled to his feet and tried to regain his dignity.

Mohandas touched a panel on the wall of the vault, summoning his hired security men while Tyrj babbled excuses, indignant instead of ashamed. Roughly, Suk emptied the doctor's pockets, pulling out packet after packet of valuable spice. He stared in disbelief at the sheer amount of melange the other man had attempted to steal.

"You are disgusting," Raquella said to him as two security officers arrived. "This is selfish betrayal, not just thievery. You're a traitor to the people you were supposed to help. Leave this hospital."

"You can't afford to lose my services," Tyrj protested.

"We can't afford to *keep* you." Mohandas took Raquella's arm, standing beside her. "I no longer consider you a doctor. You've violated your oath, become no more than a war profiteer." Looking at the security men, he said, "Throw him out to take his chances on the street. Maybe he will remember his calling and do some good. There are still plenty of suffering people."

Raquella and Mohandas went to an open second-floor window to watch as the guards pushed the thief out the front entrance toward the brooding crowd. Tyrj fell partway down the steps, then looked around at the angry Matryrists. His desperate shouts were drowned out by the waiting mob.

"Remember Manion the Innocent!"

"Long live the Jihad!"

A pale, hairless girl stood at the front, pointing toward the hospital. Raquella couldn't hear the girl's words, but suddenly the crowd began to move en masse toward the hospital. On the steps, Tyrj tried to move out of their way, but the zealots rushed the hospital, trampling the wiry doctor underfoot. The guards who had thrown him out backed away, frightened for their own lives.

Raquella grabbed Mohandas by the arm and ran down the corridor toward the nearest ward. "Sound the alarm." He pressed a security transmitter on the wall, triggering high-pitched sirens and loud klaxons.

The two of them raced to the closest entrance and attempted to secure the door. The hired guards assigned to that station had disappeared, fleeing as soon as the mob reached its flashpoint. A fanatical crowd slammed into the door, pushing it, prying it open. Despite Raquella's best efforts, the sheer press of people overwhelmed them quickly. More zealots shattered windows and swarmed through other open doors, surging into the corridors and wards.

The hairless girl stopped, like a calm eye in the middle of the storm of unleashed fanatics. She scanned the diagnostic machines, the monitors and dispensers, then said in a penetrating voice, "Sophisticated medical devices—evil machines disguised as useful equipment. They imprison us!"

"Stop!" Mohandas screamed as rampaging men and women toppled a bank of high-resolution diagnostic scanners. "We need these machines to treat plague victims. People are going to die without them!"

But the throng only struck with greater fury. Imagers and testing probes were hurled against walls and through windows. Though they were intent on the machines, the mob could quickly turn on the medical researchers themselves.

Taking Mohandas's hand, Raquella fled to the rooftop, where a medical evacuation flyer waited. Fires had already started in the hospital below. Some patients staggered out of their beds, trying to get away from the hospital, though others remained trapped. The doctors had already escaped.

"This place is doomed," Mohandas groaned. "All the patients!"

"We were just trying to help." Raquella's voice was hoarse with disbelief. "Couldn't they see we were saving people? Where do we go now?"

Mohandas guided the medical evacuation flyer up from the hospital rooftop. With a whine it rose above the thickening smoke, while he stared down with liquid brown eyes. "We've lost the battle here in the city, but I'm not ready to give up. Are you?"

She gave him a wan smile and put her hand on his forearm. "No, not if we can be together. There are plenty of places out in the country where suffering people need our help and expertise. Much as I regret it, the rest of Niubbe will have to fend for itself."

Technology has a seductive nature. We assume that advances in this realm are always improvements, beneficial to humans. We are deluding ourselves.

—RAYNA BUTLER,
True Visions

When the dispatch orders arrived directly from Primero Quentin Butler, Abulurd was disappointed that his father had appended no personal note, just a terse comment.

"You are to go to Parmentier, where Rikov died. Since the first cases of the Omnius Scourge appeared there, League medical researchers are desperate to have exhaustive baseline data. If you can verify that the epidemic has run its course, at least we will have some hope. Supreme Commander Vorian Atreides wishes to go with you, for reasons of his own. Take your javelin and depart immediately."

Mere moments after he received the message, his communications officer announced that a shuttle was en route, bearing the Supreme Commander. Abulurd felt pleased. At least Vorian would be with him.

When the high-ranking officer stepped aboard, Abulurd rushed to greet him. "I'm just a passenger on this mission," Vor said. "You are in charge. Pretend I'm not here."

"Oh, I can't do that, sir. You far outrank me."

"Consider me a civilian for the time being. This is your mission—mine is personal matter. I wish to check on my granddaughter and her brave work with the medical teams. You know full well about . . . personal obligations, don't you, Tercero Harkonnen?"

Abulurd didn't know if he'd heard right. "Tercero?"

Vor could not suppress his smile. "Did I forget to mention? I am authorizing an immediate field promotion." He fumbled in his pocket to remove a new set of insignia. "God knows we've already lost enough officers to this damned plague. You can't stay a cuarto forever."

"Thank you, sir."

"Now stop gawking at me, and let's get this ship moving. It's a long way to Parmentier."

LATER, IN HIS cabin, Abulurd met Vorian Atreides for a quiet drink and conversation. They had not sat together since the young man had announced that he meant to clear the Harkonnen name, to reestablish the honor of Xavier's deeds.

"Abulurd, you know you probably cut off your military career at the knees. Yes, the other officers know you're the son of Primero Quentin Butler, but the fact that you would change your name to honor a man they all revile shows not only defiance but poor judgment."

"Or a greater understanding," he said. He had expected support from Vorian.

"You may know that, but the others do not. They are content with what they think they know."

"This means more to me than my military advancement. Don't you want to clear his name, too? He was your friend."

"Of course I do . . . but after more than half a century, what purpose can it serve? I fear we could never win."

"When did the possibility of failure ever stop an honorable man from pursuing truth? Didn't you teach me that yourself, Supreme Commander? I intend to follow your advice."

As Vor came to realize that Abulurd truly meant what he said, tears welled in his gray eyes. "And it's about damned time. After this plague is over, perhaps the day will be right to force the truth down their throats."

Abulurd smiled. "One supporter is better than none."

WHEN THE LONE javelin reached Parmentier, the guardian stations that traveled endless orbital paths were empty and silent, everyone aboard either dead or, having surrendered to fate, returned to the surface.

Keeping Abulurd company on the bridge, Vor gazed down at the peaceful-looking planet. "It's been almost four months since I left here," he said. "Now most of the League is devastated by casualties and consequences. Will we ever be the same?"

Abulurd lifted his chin. "Let's go down there, sir, and see what all those other infected planets have to look forward to."

The new tercero and a handpicked crew of soldiers consumed a significant preventive dose of melange, which would help protect them from any remnants of the Scourge and give them added fortification against the horrors they were bound to find on Parmentier.

Instead of the bulky anti-exposure suit he had worn on Ix, Abulurd opted for a sterilized breathing mask that fit securely over his face. League tests had shown that the retrovirus broke down quickly after the initial epidemic, and enough time should have passed here. It was a straw of hope for the League to grasp.

Abulurd directed their shuttle to land on the top of a rise overlooking Niubbe, near the eerily silent governor's mansion. Even though he knew what they were likely to find in Rikov's home, he had to go there first. "You understand, don't you, sir?" he asked Vorian.

"I have personal obligations as well," Vor said, anxious and concerned. "I am going into the city, to the Hospital for Incurable Diseases. I can only hope my granddaughter is still there."

As the Supreme Commander set off alone, Abulurd guided his team into his brother's house. The soldiers spread out to search the rooms of the large, empty building. If nothing else, he intended to give his brother's family an appropriate burial and memorial. Abulurd walked quickly down the halls, checking the chambers, Kohe's private chapel, and the sitting areas that he remembered from occasional visits to his brother.

Inside the master suite, he found the badly decomposed bodies of a man and a woman, presumably his brother and his wife. The mercenaries located several other dead servants, but there was no sign of Abulurd's niece. Having seen so much death, especially in the past few months, he no longer experienced horror and disgust as he looked at the near-skeletal remains. Abulurd just felt a deep sadness, wishing that he had known his brother better.

"What would you have thought of my decision, Rikov?" Abulurd mused aloud, standing there. "Would you have understood why I want to be known as a Harkonnen? Or would your own myths fill you with too much pride?"

Later, when the team arrived in the main city, they were surprised to find that the bulk of the destruction appeared to have been caused by mob action, not the plague itself. Many buildings were nothing more than charred frameworks and piles of rubble, windows were smashed, debris lay strewn in the streets, plazas, and parks.

When the team dispersed into the ruins, Abulurd followed the lines of mob destruction, heading toward a cluster of burned-out buildings. At the Hospital for Incurable Diseases, he found Vorian Atreides standing despondent on the front steps, beside a fallen sign for the facility. "She's not here," he said. "No one inside. Everything's wrecked."

Abulurd's heart went out to his friend. In the midst of this terrible war, even the Supreme Commander was no more than a human being, concerned for the safety of his family.

Venturing inside, Abulurd saw that the hospital had been ransacked and gutted. "Why would they destroy a medical center?" he asked aloud, as if the ghosts of dead patients could answer him. Had people been angry at the failure of doctors to cure them? What a terrible shame to ruin one of the only facilities capable of mounting a defense against the epidemic and easing the last days of dying patients.

"After we do our initial assessment, we'll send out search teams for her," Abulurd said to Vorian. "You can lead them."

The Supreme Commander nodded. "Thank you." He made his way out into the streets to continue looking. Both men knew that with so many records lost and destroyed, they had very little chance of tracking down one person.

Late in the afternoon, on a hill at the far outskirts of the city, Abulurd and his mercenaries discovered a ragtag crowd that had gathered to share looted food. The people looked weary and reverent, all of them gazing up toward a small figure who stood at the crest of the hill.

Abulurd and his men approached, and saw that it was a hairless young girl with skin so pale it looked like translucent milk. The girl called out to them. "Have you come to join our cause, to spread the word of what humanity must do to survive?"

Abulurd searched his memory to identify what was familiar about this young woman. It took him a moment to adjust his perception, to identify her without any hair and in spite of the gauntness of her body. "Rayna? Rayna Butler?" He hurried forward. "You survived! I'm Abulurd—your uncle!"

The girl looked at him. "You have come from so far, to help us against the thinking machines?" She spread her hands to indicate the wounded city.

"The Scourge has spread everywhere, Rayna. Your grandfather sent me to look for you and your family."

"All dead," Rayna said. "Almost half died from the plague, and many more afterward. I don't know how many remain on Parmentier."

"Hopefully the worst is over here, if the virus has run its course." He hugged her. She felt ethereal in his arms, as if she might break apart in his embrace.

"Our fight is just beginning." Rayna's voice was strong, like tempered steel. "My message has already gone out. The Cult of Serena found ships in the Niubbe spaceport and they have left Parmentier for other worlds, bearing the news of what we must do."

"And what message is that, Rayna?" Abulurd smiled. He still thought of her as the shy girl who had spent so much time in religious devotions with her mother. "What is the Cult of Serena? I've never heard of it." Now he saw that the Scourge had not only made her hair fall out, but had added years of grief and maturity. She seemed to be leading these people.

"Serena smashed thinking machines herself," Rayna said. "When Erasmus killed her baby, she threw a sentinel robot off the high balcony. It was the first blow of a human against the evil minions of Omnius. My cause is to destroy all machines."

Abulurd studied his niece with growing concern about what she had been up to. He couldn't help thinking of the political machinations and self-serving measures Iblis Ginjo had undertaken, against which Xavier Harkonnen had fought. Rayna, though, seemed to have no selfish aspirations whatsoever. The people crowded around the beatific child on the hill, a mob that shouted her name.

Abulurd looked behind him at the charred evidence of destruction and spoke above the rising din. "You . . . caused all this, Rayna?"

"It was necessary. Serena told me that we must cleanse our planets and destroy all technological artifacts. We need to erase everything computerized so the thinking machines can never take over again. The demons can be allowed no foothold, or the human race will plunge over that precipice again. We've suffered enough, and we're still alive," Rayna continued, looking at him with her piercing, haunted gaze. "We can do without a few . . . *conveniences*."

She seemed a model of self-sacrifice, caring nothing for personal possessions. She probably took only the minimum of what she needed, leaving much behind in the abandoned governor's mansion.

Disturbed, Abulurd reached out to touch his niece's thin, bony shoulder. "I want you to come back to Salusa with me, Rayna. I'll reunite you with the rest of your family." He also wanted to get her away from this mob.

"Salusa Secundus..." Rayna murmured, dreamily, as if she had already envisioned this scenario. "It is true, my followers know what to do here. All right, I am finished with my work on Parmentier." He noticed a disconcerting gleam in her eyes. "It's time for me to continue my mission elsewhere."

*The Army of the Jihad can try to prepare for the next scheme of
Omnius, but we will always fall behind the thinking machines, for
they can develop their evil thoughts with computer speed.*

—PRIMERO QUENTIN BUTLER,
private letters for Wandra

While Abulurd was gone to Parmentier with Supreme Commander Atreides, Quentin Butler felt an increased weight of
responsibility for protecting the League capital world. Under the provisions of the Jihad Council, the primero became the ranking officer in
the Salusan system. He never felt the need for a moment to himself or a
day of rest. For months now, ever since the first fateful messenger had
come from Rikov announcing the Omnius Scourge, he had felt humanity's dire peril.

Thus, Quentin drove himself harder each day, accepting unnecessary
assignments, wanting to be everywhere at once. The jihadi soldiers he
commanded could use the down time in the incessant chaos of the quarantine and lifeboat efforts, but Quentin himself would have none of it.
His son Faykan was the same way. Rather than taking well-earned leave,
he offered to spend days on standard picket patrols out on the fringes of
the Salusan system.

"You and I are setting a fine example for our soldiers. Imagine—the
primero of a large battalion along with a high-ranking and heavily decorated segundo spending tedious hours on sentinel duty."

Faykan's chuckle came back over the comline. "It's not often the
thinking machines give us a chance to experience tedium, Primero. For
the time being, I'll welcome it."

"I fear that Omnius has more in mind than just spreading plagues. We are so very vulnerable now."

Faykan said, "We'll have to keep a sharp eye out."

The two men flew modified long-range kindjals, drifting within only a few light-seconds' transmission delay from each other, close enough that they could hold long conversations. The primero appreciated those simple discussions more than any trip to a League spa or resort designed for pampered nobles. In a way, though he recognized he was being unfairly harsh to Abulurd, he considered Faykan his only remaining son.

From the time he had been a young man, Quentin had been a war hero, earning his reputation in the Army of the Jihad after the successful conquest of Parmentier, one of the most surprising victories in the Jihad. Though only a lieutenant at the time, he'd beaten an overwhelming force of combat robots by using devious tactics that had made even Supreme Commander Vorian Atreides proud. Afterward, he'd never outgrown the title of "Liberator of Parmentier." Beautiful Wandra Butler herself had pinned on his medals during a ceremony. Smitten, Quentin had courted her. They were a perfect couple, and when they finally married, he accepted the great name of Butler instead of keeping his own.

Though of course her body still clung to life, he wondered what life would be like now if Wandra had not been stolen from him by that terrible stroke while giving birth to Abulurd. He grimaced at the thought of his youngest son, who now chose to call himself by a hateful name. *Harkonnen!*

For decades, Wandra's family had tried to overcome the shame of what their deceased patriarch had done. They performed extravagant deeds, sacrificed themselves, threw their lives into the unending Jihad. But now foolish Abulurd—of his *own* volition!—had chosen to nullify all that progress, reminding everyone of the inexcusable crimes Xavier Harkonnen had committed.

Where had Quentin gone wrong? Abulurd was intelligent and well educated, and should have known better. At the very least he should have discussed the matter with his father first, but now the brash decision had been implemented. Quentin could not face him, though honor did not allow him to completely disown his youngest son. Perhaps one day Abulurd would redeem himself. Quentin only hoped he might live long enough to see it happen. . . .

For now, he had only Faykan.

The two spent hours chatting about old times. Faykan and Rikov had both been rogues in their younger years, the famed Butler Brothers who took pride in proving their father's motto, "Butlers are servants unto no one." The impetuous brothers had bent orders, ignored direct commands, and made their mark in the history of the Jihad.

"I miss him, Father," Faykan said. "Rikov could have fought for many more good years. I wish he'd at least been given the chance to fall in battle instead of dying in bed from that damned virus."

"This holy war has always been a trial by fire," Quentin said. "It's either a crucible to temper and strengthen us, or a furnace to destroy the weak. I'm glad you weren't one of the latter, Faykan." As he said it, he wondered if Abulurd fell into a different category. If not for the benevolent mentorship of Supreme Commander Atreides and the Butler family clout, Abulurd would no doubt be a clerk organizing supply runs for isolated outposts.

Of late, Faykan had begun to settle down, concerning himself more with the broad landscape of League politics than with adventure. He said he would rather lead people and guide *society* than order soldiers to their deaths.

"You've changed too, Father," Faykan pointed out. "I know you would never shirk your duty, but I've watched your attitude. It seems to me that your heart is no longer in the battle. Are you weary of the war?"

Quentin hesitated longer than the transmission delay required. "How can I not be? The Jihad has gone on for so long, and the deaths of Rikov and his family have been a terrible blow for me. Since the Scourge, this is no longer a war that I can easily understand."

Faykan made an assenting noise. "We shouldn't even try to understand Omnius. But we should fear him and be watchful at all times for some new plan."

Quentin and Faykan gradually widened their patrol net. Though the primero drifted with his idling engines cooling down and his shields off, he did not doze. He let his thoughts wander, preoccupied with memories and regrets. Still, a lifetime of combat service—both on the ground fighting and on the bridge of his battleship—had trained him always to be alert for the slightest anomaly. A flicker of unexpected movement could mean an attack.

Though his wide-range scanner detected no unusual activity, only a few small blips below the instrumentation's error threshold, Quentin spotted a glinting metal object. The albedo was too high for a simple rock or even a comet. This was a geometrical shape with a smooth metal shell—the flat and polished planes of an artificial object that did not appear on his sensors.

Quentin studied his screens and gently powered his kindjal's engines, increasing acceleration just enough to close the distance and determine what he was seeing. He wanted to signal Faykan, who was also within range, but he feared that even a secure comline transmission would alert this silent intruder.

The mysterious craft was drifting out of the system, its velocity just sufficient to overcome the star's gravitational pull. Since the intruder generated no artificial power pulse, it was not likely to be detected on long-range League scanners. But Quentin had sighted it, and he eased himself closer until the configuration was unmistakable: a thinking machine ship, a robotic scout sent to spy on Salusa Secundus.

Moving cautiously, as if afraid even the noise of soft clicks in his cockpit might alert the stealthily moving enemy, he loaded fast-deployment artillery shells along with two self-guided scrambler mines. Quentin carefully locked in the target.

Then he saw a spike of energy from the machine ship, as if it suspected something. An active scan beam rippled across the hull of Quentin's kindjal. He tried to jam the reflections, but the thinking machine spycraft powered up immediately. Quentin hit hard acceleration, which slammed him back into his seat, making it difficult even to lift his hands to operate the controls.

With his lips drawn back and his lungs compressed, Quentin sent a direct signal to Faykan, wherever he was. "Found a robot . . . spycraft! It's trying to get out of the system. Have to . . . stop it. No telling what recon data . . . it's got."

With a sudden burst of speed, Quentin closed the gap halfway, but the robotic scout's afterburners fired in a long and hot acceleration that no human could have survived. Before giving up, Quentin launched his full spread of fast-release artillery shells. The projectiles shot out far faster than Quentin's kindjal could fly, spreading like a swarm of deadly wasps.

Quentin held his breath, watching the blips converge, on target. . . . But at the last minute, the robotic spycraft pinwheeled in an astonishing blur that must have been beyond the material limits of traditional hull metals. His artillery shells exploded, sending waves of energy and shock pulses through empty space. The robot ship continued to pick up speed, though it began to weave erratically, as if it was either still trying to dodge or had been damaged somehow.

Quentin maintained pursuit acceleration, nearly blacking out, though he saw that he would never catch up. His heart felt even heavier than the leaden foot of gravity pressing down on his chest. The robot spy was going to get away! There was no way he could stop it. Cursing his failure, he eased off on the acceleration, gulping huge breaths again and fighting back dizziness.

For a moment he thought it was a hallucination, then he recognized the new streak as Faykan's kindjal, roaring in on an intercept course toward the machine infiltrator.

The robot spycraft saw him much too late. Faykan was already opening fire. Two of his son's seven artillery shells struck their target, detonating against the robot's hull. The explosions imparted force in several different directions, sending the craft tumbling as it sputtered flames and globules of molten metal. The glow of its hot engines flickered and died.

The robot spycraft spun, entirely out of control, and the two League kindjals closed in, locking tractor beams to stabilize it. Working together, they drew it in like predators snaring a juicy piece of meat.

"Stay on your guard," Quentin transmitted over the comline. "He may just be playing dead."

"I hit him hard enough to make him play dead forever."

Side by side, their kindjals finally halted the robot ship's erratic motion. He and Faykan squirmed into their suits inside the cramped confines of their kindjal cockpits. Thinking machines had no need for life-support systems, and it was unlikely the interior of the robot spycraft would be pressurized.

Quentin and Faykan emerged from their kindjals and drifted in space, anchored to the captive vessel. Working together, they used cutter torches and hydraulic grapplers to slice open an access hatch in the spy vessel's belly. When they finally tore the hole in the hull wide enough for their two suited forms to enter, an ominous fighting robot loomed before them. Its several limbs bristled with weapons, swiveling to get a good shot at the pair of humans.

Quentin already had his scrambler-pulse generator primed and ready. He fired a blast, part of which diffused against the ragged hull opening, but the rest ricocheted and shivered through the robot. The combat mek twitched and shuddered, fighting to reset its gelcircuitry systems.

Faykan pulled himself inside. Using his own mass, he knocked the robot off balance in the low gravity. The combat mek tumbled, still jerking, unable to reset itself.

"We've found ourselves a prize," Faykan said. "We can purge its systems and reprogram it to teach swordmasters on Ginaz, like that combat
mek they've had for generations."

Quentin considered for a moment, then shook his head inside his helmet. The very idea offended him. "No, I don't think so." He unleashed a
potent scrambler pulse, which turned the lone robot into a motionless
hulk of scrap metal. "Now let's see what this damned machine was really
up to snooping around Salusa."

Long ago, when Quentin had undergone basic command training
under Vorian Atreides, he had learned the rudiments of thinking-
machine datasystems and computer controls. Considering itself perfect,
the evermind had not altered its operating systems in centuries, so Vor's
information remained valid during the entire time frame of the Jihad.

Now Quentin went to the controls of the deactivated spycraft. Faykan
frowned at the systems, trying to understand the purpose of the large convex devices studded on the outside of the vessel. "They're broad-range
sensors and mapping projectors," he concluded. "This ship was taking a
full sweep of everything in the Salusa system."

Quentin rerouted enough power to operate the log and datasystems
inside the robotic vessel. It took him a moment to understand everything
he was seeing, and another few seconds to assess the horrific magnitude of
what the spycraft had done.

"This is filled with information about League Worlds: our military
defenses, our resources . . . and how hard the Scourge has hit us. All of
our vulnerabilities, all focused here! This one ship studied a dozen League
Worlds and collated an entire invasion plan. The main target seems to be
Salusa Secundus." He pointed to the three-dimensional maps, the numerous inbound routes the machines had automatically plotted, finding the
path of least military resistance. "It's everything Omnius needs to plan a
full-scale invasion!"

Faykan indicated one of the record fields. "According to this, it's one
of a hundred similar recon ships sent all across the League."

Through the faceplates of their suits, Quentin looked at Faykan, seeing that his son had drawn the same conclusion. "With our population
and our military devastated by the Scourge, now would be the perfect
time for Omnius to stage his final assault."

Faykan nodded. "The thinking machines have something very
unpleasant in mind for free humanity. Good thing we caught this one."

The spycraft was too large for the kindjal scouts to tow back to the inner system. Quentin detached the computer memory core and took it with him while Faykan placed a locator buoy on the dead vessel so that League technicians could come back and analyze its systems.

Right now, both men had only one priority: to get back to the Jihad Council and report their news.

We are trained to fight with swords, with strength, and with blood.
But when the thinking machines send an invisible enemy against us,
how are we to defend ourselves or the rest of humanity?

— SWORDMASTER ISTIAN GOSS

When Istian Goss and Nar Trig arrived on Ix after the plague, there were no machines to fight, and almost two-thirds of the human population was dead. Fields and storehouses of food had burned in uncontrolled riots; cholera had gotten into the water supply; cascading storms had destroyed homes, leaving the already weakened survivors with no shelter. Many of those who had recovered could barely walk, crippled by the aftereffects.

The human race was hamstrung, fighting for its very survival, and had little energy or resources left for making inroads against the real enemy.

In the months since leaving Honru, the two new swordmasters had engaged combat robots twice in minor space battles. With the Army of the Jihad, they had surrounded and boarded two giant Omnius battleships, which they then seized and converted for human use. But the Scourge had killed so many soldiers and forced the cancellation of so many planned military strikes, that the pair of mercenaries spent most of their time in rescue and recovery operations.

Fortunately, the engineered retrovirus burned through its victims swiftly and then died out. Now, a month after the last reported case of sickness on Ix, Istian and Trig could help without undue risk of becoming infected themselves. Neither of them had any melange left.

In the early days, Ixian crews had used heavy digging equipment to deposit the numerous bodies in empty cave shafts, then sealed the openings with explosives. Recently, though, Martyrist fanatics had risen up, objecting to even the powerful excavating apparatus, targeting the heavy machinery as painful reminders of the destruction that thinking machines could cause.

When Istian commented that the Martyrists were unreasonable and shortsighted, Trig merely fixed him with a stony stare. The underlying strength of the Jihad had always been emotional, a motivating force that drove humanity forward. Passion pervaded the minds of military commanders and compromised the careful battle plans they tried to establish. "Their beliefs outweigh their need for convenience," Trig said. "They are strong in their own way."

"These people are a mob, and they are angry." Istian propped his hands on his hips and turned his bronzed face to the sky. The air was filled with smears of smoke from the fires the Ixians had lit to purge plague-tainted shelters and destroy leftover machine wreckage. "There will be no controlling them. Maybe it's better that we let them unleash their fury so that, like the Scourge, it burns out of its own accord."

Trig shook his head in sad frustration. "I can comprehend the need of these people, but this is not something for which any swordmaster is trained. We are not babysitters. . . ."

Later that day they came upon a group of glassy-eyed Martyrists who carried an array of confiscated pulse-swords and hand weapons, many of which looked battered and in poor repair. Other weapons didn't seem to function at all, but the people grasped them as if they had found treasures.

"Where did you come by those weapons?" Istian said. "Those are designed for swordmasters who have been trained extensively on Ginaz."

"We are swordmasters like you," said the leader of the group. "We found these weapons among our dead. The hand of Saint Serena guided us to them."

"But where did they come from?" Istian asked, skirting the religious question. Apparently, they were willing to make exceptions in using technology so long as they could turn it against thinking machines.

"Many mercenaries have died here over the years," Trig pointed out. "From the first conquest of Ix when Jool Noret destroyed the Omnius, to the second defense when Quentin Butler drove back the thinking machines, and now from the Scourge. Plenty of mercenary equipment must have remained here unclaimed."

"*We* have claimed it," the leader said, "and we are swordmasters our-selves."

Istian frowned, not wanting to see the proud name of his brethren cheapened by these pretenders. "Who taught you to become swordmas-ters, according to the high standards of Ginaz? Who was your sensei?"

The man scowled, giving Istian a haughty look. "We were not trained by a domesticated thinking machine, if that is what you're asking. We follow our own guidance and vision to destroy machines as well as you can!"

Trig surprised Istian by taking the ragtag group seriously. "We do not question your determination."

"Simply your finesse," Istian added, in a sharp tone. These people would wield sophisticated pulse-swords as little better than bludgeons or gardening implements.

"The Three Martyrs inspire us and guide us," growled the leader. "We know where we must go. There are no longer any demon machines on Ix, but with our ship we will go directly to Corrin to fight Omnius Prime and his evil robot minions."

"Impossible! Corrin is the central stronghold of the thinking machines. You'll be slaughtered outright, to no purpose." Istian was reminded of what had happened following the first robotic attack on Peri-dot Colony, Trig's family home. A group of impetuous jihadi soldiers had disobeyed orders and struck out on their own to attack Corrin. All had been killed by robot defenses.

"You are welcome to come along if you wish," said the leader, startling Istian.

Before he could laugh in disbelief, he noticed a hard set to his com-rade's face. "Don't even consider it, Nar."

"A true swordmaster should always consider an opportunity to fight the real enemy."

"You'll be killed for sure," Istian said.

Trig appeared angry with him. "We all know we are going to die. I have been prepared for that since I trained on Ginaz—as have you. If you carry the spirit of Jool Noret within you, why should you fear a dangerous situation?"

"It's not just dangerous, Nar—it's suicide. But even *that* is not what makes me speak against it, but the sheer pointlessness. Yes, you may kill a handful of combat robots before they strike you down, but what good will that do? You will make no progress for the cause of humanity, and

Omnius will simply rebuild his machines. Within a week it'll be as if you had never gone to Corrin."

"It will be a blow struck for the Jihad," Trig insisted. "Better than standing here watching survivors wallow in misery and squalor. I can't help them here, but I can do something by fighting against Omnius."

Istian shook his head. The leader of the Martyrists seemed as stonily determined and fervent as before. "We will be happy to take one sword-master with us, if not both. We have a spaceship. Many ships were left here when Ix was quarantined and the qualified pilots died. We were interdicted from flying to uncontaminated League Worlds, but that is not relevant now."

Istian could not stop himself from challenging them. "So you want to destroy all machines, except for pulse-swords and spaceships, because you find them useful? Your plans are just folly—"

"Are you afraid to join me, Istian?" Trig's voice had a disappointed edge.

"Not afraid, but I am too sensible to do it." With the spirit of Jool Noret came not only fighting skills and indomitable bravery, but also wisdom. "This is not my calling."

"It is mine," Trig insisted, "and if I am killed fighting the demon machines, then my spirit will grow stronger and be reborn in the next generation of Ginaz fighters. We may not agree with these people, Istian, but they see a truth and a way that you're unwilling to recognize."

Saddened, Istian could only nod. "The mercenaries of Ginaz work independently. We have always done so, and it is not for me to say what you must or must not do." Looking at the ragtag group of zealots clutching their collection of salvaged weapons, he suggested flippantly, "Perhaps on the journey to Corrin, you can teach them how to use those."

"I intend to do so." Trig reached out to clasp his friend's hand. "If Saint Serena wills it, we will meet again."

"If Saint Serena wills it." But in his heart Istian knew that it was a weak hope. "Fight well, and may your enemies fall swiftly." After an awkward moment, he gave his longtime friend a brisk, brief hug, knowing he might never see Nar Trig again.

As his comrade marched off, head held high, leading the group of self-taught fighters, Istian called after him one last time. "Wait, I have a question for you!" Trig turned and looked at him as if he were a stranger. "I never asked before—what was the name on the coral disk you drew from the basket on Ginaz? Whose spirit moves within you?"

Trig hesitated as if he hadn't thought of the question for a long time, then he reached to a pouch at his belt and withdrew the disk. He turned it so that Istian could see its polished surface—completely blank, without any name at all. Like flicking a coin, he tossed the disk to Istian, who caught it in his palm.

"I have no guiding spirit," Trig said. "I am a new swordmaster. I make my own decisions and my own name."

Evolution is the handmaiden of Death.

—NAIB ISHMAEL,
paraphrase of Zensunni Sutra

No matter how much the world changed around him, the desert remained clear and serene, vast, open, and eternally chaste. It seemed these days, however, that Ishmael had to go deeper and deeper into the great bled just to find his peace.

For centuries, the very harshness and isolation of Arrakis had driven away interlopers. Now though, because of the plague, the spice sent out too strong a call, and strangers no longer stayed away. Ishmael hated it.

The worm he summoned with his steady drumbeats was a small one, but he did not mind. He would not be taking it on a long journey. He just needed to escape the noise of offworld music and the garish colors of alien fabrics that surrounded him even among his own people. Ishmael required time for himself to cleanse his heart and mind.

Ishmael used hooks and ropes to mount the creature, accustomed to these efforts after many decades of practice. After he and his fellow escaped slaves from Poritrin had crashed here, infinitely patient Marha had shown Ishmael how to ride the sandworms, insisting it was a necessary part of understanding the legend of Selim Wormrider. How he missed her. . . .

Now, in the gathering colors of dawn, Ishmael held the rough and crusty surface of the worm's upper rings. He enjoyed the hot flinty wind in his face, the hiss of scraping sands as the worm forged along. The dunes, the great emptiness, a few rocks, the eternal winds, lonely plants and animals. Dune merging into dune, desert into desert. Blowing sand fogged the horizon, obscuring the rising sun.

With no explicit destination in mind, just wanting to be alone, he let the beast go where it wished. Memories rode with him, and he thought of his many decades of hardship and change . . . then eventual happiness. Countless ghosts followed Ishmael across the stark landscape, but his reminiscences were not frightening. He accepted the loss of friends and family, and he honored the time he had spent with loved ones.

He remembered the marsh village on Harmonthep where he'd been a little boy, then growing up as a slave on Poritrin, forced to work in agricultural fields, in the household of Savant Holtzman, and in shipyards before escaping to Arrakis. Two of the ghost-memories were blurred, made indistinct by the passage of so much time: his wife and younger daughter. It took him a moment to remember their names, it had been so long. Ozza and Falina. He'd been forced to leave them behind in the slave uprising. Stranded here, he'd eventually taken another wife . . . and Marha was also gone. His eyes stung with blown sand, or tears. He hated to waste his body's water in such a way.

Ishmael pulled a sheltering fabric over his head and face to protect them from the heat of the day. Needing no maps, he would circle around and find his way back home. After all this time, Ishmael harbored no doubt of his skills.

A strong, rich aroma of spice hovered in the air, pungent and cinnamon, penetrating even the plugs he inserted into his nostrils. The worm thrashed restlessly as it crossed rusty sands where a spice blow had occurred. Though he had been riding giant sandworms for much of his life, Ishmael did not understand their behavior. No one did. Shai-Hulud had his own thoughts and paths, and no mere human could question them.

Toward sunset he headed toward a long rocky outcropping where he decided to camp. As he approached the isolated site, his sharp eyes narrowed, and he sucked a quick, angry breath at the sight of glinting metal and rounded structures—a small village that had sprung up in the shelter of the stony island. Ishmael recalled no settlement from his previous visits out this way.

With a lurch, he yanked the hooks and applied spreading devices to steer the worm from the blot of civilization and headed around to the opposite end of the reef dozens of kilometers away. From the town, someone might have seen him astride the sinuous behemoth in the colorful dusk light. No matter. The stories of Selim Wormrider and his bandits were common knowledge—almost to the point of superstition among the swarming offworld spice rushers.

He let the weary sandworm collapse into the shallow dunes at the far edge of the reef. Ishmael sprang away from the rough surface of the creature and bounded across the sands while the worm wallowed itself deeper beneath the dunes. Despite his age, he felt rejuvenated from the exercise. He walked with a practiced uneven pace and climbed into the rocks where he would be safe.

There, Ishmael found spotty lichens and a few thorny weeds in cracks, demonstrating the hardiness and resilience of life. He hoped that his people would maintain the same tenacity and not grow weak and spoiled, despite El'hiim's attempts to lure them from their traditional ways.

When Ishmael found a place for his sleeping pad and a flat rock on which to cook his meal, he was suddenly dismayed to find signs of human passage even here. The tracks were not made by a desert man, no expert in Zensunni ways or careful survival techniques. No, this was the blundering path of an outsider, someone who knew nothing about Arrakis.

After a moment's hesitation, he angrily followed the trail—scuffed footprints in the dust, a few cast-off tools, overpriced metal implements that had been purchased in Arrakis City. Ishmael picked up a compass that looked shiny and new and was not surprised to find that it did not work. Next he came upon an empty water container, then crumpled food wrappers. Even though the desert and time would erase all marks, it disgusted him to see how strangers sullied the virginal purity of the desert. Soon he found tattered garments: flimsy fabrics not designed for the rough weather and unrelenting sun.

Finally Ishmael came upon the interloper himself. He had climbed down the rocks, stumbling to the sand where he could follow the edge of the reef against the ocean of dunes. Presumably the man was trying to make his way back to the new settlement many kilometers away. Ishmael stood over the nearly nude, sunburned man, who groaned and coughed, still alive, though probably not for long.

Not without help, at least.

The stranger turned a dark, blistered face upward, revealing sharp features and close-set eyes, looking at Ishmael as if he were a vengeful demon . . . or a rescuing angel. Ishmael recoiled. It was the Tlulaxa man he and El'hiim had met in Arrakis City. *Wariff.*

"I need water," the man croaked. "Help me. Please."

All of Ishmael's muscles turned rigid. "Why should I? You are a Tlu-laxa, a slaver. Your people destroyed my life—"

Wariff didn't seem to hear him. "Help me. In the name of . . . your own conscience."

Ishmael had supplies, of course. He would never have gone on a jour-ney without being fully prepared. He had little to spare, but he could always obtain more in a Zensunni village. This Tlulaxa spice hunter, lured to Arrakis by promises of easy wealth, had stumbled far out of his depth—and not even out on the harshest dune sea!

Ishmael cursed his own curiosity. If he had just remained in camp, he would never have tracked this fool. The Tlulaxa would have died, as he deserved, and no man would have been the wiser. He had no responsibil-ity for Wariff, no obligation. But now that Ishmael was faced with a help-less, desperate survivor, he could not simply turn his back.

From many years ago he remembered the Koran Sutras his grandfa-ther had taught him: "A man must declare peace within himself before he can find peace in the outside world." And another one: "A person's deeds are the measure of his soul." Was there a lesson to be learned here?

Sighing and furious with himself, Ishmael opened his pack and with-drew a water container, squirting just a little into Wariff's parched mouth. "You are fortunate I am not a monster—like your own people." The sun-burned man reached greedily for the spigot, but Ishmael drew it away. "Only enough for you to survive."

This inexperienced prospector had wandered off the trails and gotten caught in the desert. Back in Arrakis City, Wariff had rudely spurned El'hiim's offer of assistance and advice, but Ishmael's stepson, for all his faults and delusions, would never have allowed the man to make such simpleton mistakes as this.

After Wariff gulped another rationed sip of water, Ishmael gave him part of a spice wafer to provide immediate energy. Finally, he draped the smaller man's arm over his shoulder and stood, dragging Wariff to his feet. "I cannot carry you all the kilometers to the nearest settlement. You must help, since you caused your own misfortune."

Wariff stumbled. "Take me to the village, and you may have all of my equipment. I don't care about it."

"Your offworlder baubles are worthless to me."

They staggered along. The night stretched before them, already illuminated by two risen moons. Any healthy man could have made the trek in a day. Ishmael had no intention of summoning a worm, though it would have made their passage much faster. "You'll survive. The company town should be able to give you medical attention."

"I owe you my life," Wariff said.

Ishmael scowled at him. "Your life has no more value to me than your useless equipment. Just leave my world. If you can't take simple precautions to adapt in the desert, then you have no business on Arrakis."

The process of thinking. Where does it begin and where does it end?
                                                            Erasmus Dialogues

W hen Erasmus arrived at the military parade with his body, his memories, and his personality completely intact, Omnius was quite surprised. As if nothing had happened, the independent robot came to observe the ranks of new battle machines and the fleet of recently constructed warships.

In an intentional imitation of human pageantry, Omnius commanded the elite robots to remain at attention on a viewing stand, while mechanical forces marched, rolled, and flew past. It was all in preparation for his grand conquest of the *hrethgir*. The parade wound around the streets and airspace of Corrin City, with its broad boulevards and Central Spire. The display of superior weaponry seemed extravagant, impressive—and unnecessary.

Erasmus took his place at the forefront of the viewing stand and observed. Were the thousands of human slaves supposed to cheer? For himself, he would rather have been with Gilbertus. Even the Serena Butler clone was much more interesting than this . . . spectacle.

"What are you doing here?" Omnius demanded. "How is it you still exist?"

"Am I to infer, then, that you have ceased your constant surveillance of my villa with your watcheyes? Otherwise you would be fully aware of what occurred."

A flurry of watcheyes buzzed around the robot's shifting face, like angry hornets. "You did not answer my question."

"You asked me to study the insanity of human religions. It seems I have returned from the dead. Perhaps I am a martyr."

"A martyr! Who would mourn the loss of an independent robot?"

"You might be surprised."

GILBERTUS HAD BEEN extremely pleased with his solution to the dilemma. Erasmus himself was delighted when he returned to awareness to see the muscular man standing before him among the flowers and lush plants in the greenhouse courtyard.

"What has Omnius done?" Erasmus straightened, saw the huge grin on Gilbertus's face. "And what have *you* done, my Mentat?"

"Omnius copied your memory core into himself, and when he was finished, he destroyed it. Exactly as you anticipated."

Nearby, the Serena clone picked a bright red lily and put it to her face, inhaling with a loud sniff. She ignored them.

"Then how is it I am still here?"

"You are here because I showed initiative, Father." Unable to restrain himself, Gilbertus ran forward to hug the robot. "I surrendered your memory core to Omnius, as I was commanded. However, the instructions did not explicitly prevent me from making a *copy*."

"An excellent conclusion, Gilbertus."

"SO, YOUR RESURRECTION was a trick, rather than a religious experience. That does not qualify you as a martyr." The watcheyes circled Erasmus's head. All operations in the machine military parade had stopped. "And now I have your disturbing personality and memories isolated inside me, while you still exist on the outside. I do not seem to have accomplished my aims."

The robot formed a smile, though the demonstration of emotions did little for Omnius. However, with Erasmus's own identity inside the evermind, perhaps some part could appreciate them. "Let us hope your campaign against the League Worlds achieves better results."

"After internally studying your obsession with human artistic talents,

I see now that there may be some merit to your work. Therefore, I will tolerate your continued existence, for now."

"I am pleased to . . . remain alive, Omnius."

From the small watcheye speakers, Erasmus heard a sound Omnius had never made before, almost a snort of derision. "Martyr!"

To the independent robot's fascination, the evermind seemed very taken with his grand new extermination army drawn from all the Synchronized Worlds. Where had Omnius developed this idea of a spectacle? And who was the intended audience? Apparently, he had copied the routine from the Army of the Jihad and considered it a necessary part of preparing for the ultimate conquest.

Erasmus flicked a bit of grime off his polished platinum body. His flowmetal face shimmered in the ruddy blaze of Corrin's sun. He wondered yet again if the primary evermind contained some intangible flaw in its programming, an innate quality that could not be detected by direct inspection of the gelsphere memory core. Occasionally, Omnius committed indisputable errors and his behavior seemed odd . . . even delusional. Now that he also held a completely separate persona within his programming, perhaps the evermind was even more dangerous.

The voice of Omnius blared from unseen speakers all around him and throughout the city. "The humans are weak and defeated, billions of them killed by our plague. The survivors are distracted with the process of holding the remnants of their very civilization together. According to my returning spycraft, their numbers are greatly reduced, their government is ineffective. The Army of the Jihad is in chaos. Now, I shall complete the annihilation.

"Since the enemy is no longer able to launch offensives against me, I have been gathering the bulk of my robotic warships from across the Synchronized Worlds in preparation for the final offensive. All industries have been put to work augmenting weaponry, combat robots, and warships. This force is nearly complete in orbit over Corrin. With it, I will annihilate the human government entirely and leave Salusa Secundus a sterile globe."

Exactly as the League Armada left Earth long ago, Erasmus thought. As usual, Omnius did not have any original ideas.

"Afterward, with the rest of the League disorganized and helpless, I will easily impose order. Then I can systematically exterminate the race that has caused so much unnecessary damage to an orderly universe."

This worried Erasmus. Omnius understood only that humans presented a danger to him and his domain; therefore the evermind concluded that he needed to massacre them. All of them. But humans were such an interesting gene pool, capable of a wide range of emotional and intellectual actions in their comparatively short life spans.

Erasmus hoped they wouldn't all be destroyed.

As he gazed into the sky, flying machines engaged a mock enemy squadron in a carefully choreographed set of maneuvers. The demonstration squadron finished its programmed work against the enemy surrogates. With a concentrated flash of weapons, they destroyed the mock squadron, and flaming pieces of shrapnel spun toward the ground.

What a silly display, Erasmus thought.

Overhead, the gigantic fleet was being fueled and armed, almost ready to be launched on its month-long journey to wipe out Salusa Secundus.

If there is no plausible hope for survival, is it better to know that you
are doomed, or simply to exist in blissful ignorance until the end?

—PRIMERO QUENTIN BUTLER,
military journals

The information revealed in the captured spycraft was indisputable.

On their return to Zimia, not even taking time to change uniforms, Quentin and Faykan demanded to speak with all available members of the Jihad Council. Inside the room, behind security doors, Quentin showed them the computer data core, with all of its disturbing reconnaissance about League vulnerabilities. Faykan stood silent, letting his father speak. The Council members would draw the obvious conclusions.

"Omnius is planning to move against us. We must know how, and when." As they sat in stunned disbelief, Quentin made his bold request. "Therefore I propose a small but vital recon expedition deep into the heart of Synchronized territory—to Corrin itself, if necessary."

"But with the Scourge, and the quarantines—"

"Perhaps we should wait for the return of Supreme Commander Atreides. He should be back from Parmentier any day now—"

Quentin cut them all off. "And, because of the urgency implied by the robot spycraft, I propose that we use space-folding scouts." He punctuated his words with a brisk gesture of his fist. "We must know what Omnius is doing!"

Interim Viceroy O'Kukovich sat in silence with an expression of deep concentration. Even in Jihad Council meetings, O'Kukovich would listen to all sides and wait until a consensus decision had been reached before announcing the result, as if he had had anything to do with it. Quentin disliked the Interim Viceroy, considered him a man of inaction.

Grand Patriarch Xander Boro-Ginjo seemed pleasant and unprepossessing, though somewhat unaware of the true severity of the threat facing humanity. He had surrounded himself with simpering sycophants and fine possessions, and seemed more impressed with the actual chain of office around his neck than with the responsibilities and power it implied. "But I thought spacefolders were dangerous?"

Faykan gave a calm and precise answer. "Nevertheless, they can be used when the situation warrants. The loss rate is approximately ten percent, and highly paid hazard pilots usually fly the ships. VenKee has delivered many emergency shipments of melange to plague-affected worlds using cargo vessels equipped with Holtzman engines. Spacefolder scouts are the only way to send vital messages in a timely fashion."

"In this case, it is absolutely necessary," Quentin insisted. "It has been many years since we've sent an observer so deep into Synchronized space. Now we have direct evidence the machines are planning to move against us militarily. Who can say what plans they have developed—unless we see for ourselves?"

Faykan said, "We intercepted one robotic scout, but we know that Omnius launched many others, to many different League Worlds. The machines already know we are grievously wounded by their damnable Scourge. The evermind must be preparing a final assault against humanity."

"It is what I would do, if my enemy was weak, disoriented, and preoccupied," Quentin growled. "We must see what is happening on Corrin. One or two spacefolder scouts can slip in, acquire detailed images, then escape before the machines could possibly intercept us."

"Sounds very risky," mumbled the Interim Viceroy, looking around at the other Council members for confirmation. "Doesn't it?"

Quentin crossed his arms over his uniformed chest. "That is why I intend to go myself."

One of the high-ranking bureaucrats on the Jihad Council scowled. "That's ridiculous! We cannot risk an officer with as much experience and seniority as yourself, Primero Butler. Even if you survive the space-folding trip, such an expedition could lead to your capture and interrogation."

Quentin angrily dismissed all their concerns. "I cite the precedent of Supreme Commander Atreides, who often took small spacefolder ships, throwing himself against the enemy. As my service record has established, gentlemen, I am not an armchair general, to use an ancient historical phrase. I do not command through the use of tactical boards and war games. Instead, I put myself at the head of my men, and face the danger personally. On this mission I will not take a crew, but only one companion—my son Faykan."

This caused even more uproar. "You want us to risk two established commanders? Why not take a few mercenaries with you?"

Beside him, Faykan reacted with surprise. "I am not afraid to go, sir, but is that wise?"

"This intelligence is critical." He looked at his son. "We need redundancy to be sure someone lives."

Before Faykan could argue further, Quentin made a quick and subtle flurry of finger movements, using a sophisticated coded battle language that Jihad officers learned in high-level training. He and Faykan had often used it in military engagements, never in front of politicians. The other Council members knew something was amiss but could understand none of it.

With rapid gestures, Quentin communicated, "We are *Butlers*. The last two Butlers." *Since Abulurd insists on ramming his Harkonnen heritage down our throats!* "We must do this, you and I."

Faykan sat rigid, as if surprised, then nodded. "Yes, sir. Of course." No matter how risky the idea might seem, he would always follow the primero. He and his father understood each other, and they understood the stakes. Quentin Butler would never trust this task to anyone else.

Quentin turned to face the rest of the Council. "The League has not launched a military offensive against the enemy since the epidemic began. All of our worlds have been brought to their knees, and we are alarmingly vulnerable to outside attack. Billions upon billions are already dead, rotting out under numerous suns. Did you expect the machines just to sit back and let the Scourge take its course, without having a second phase of their plan ready?"

The Grand Patriarch paled as if the possibility of further danger from the machines had never occurred to him. He clutched his chain of office like a lifeline. As Quentin scanned the faces of the Council, he saw that they'd been too preoccupied with the epidemic to think of anything worse.

When the objections had simmered to grudging acceptance, the Interim Viceroy smiled and announced his decision. "Go with our blessing, Primero. See what Omnius is doing. But return to us with all due speed, and safely."

BOTH MEN WERE qualified to fly spacefolders, though the Army of the Jihad rarely used the quirky and dangerous crafts. Quentin decided that he and his son would fly separately in order to increase their chances. If one of them suffered a space-folding mishap, the other could still return to Salusa intact.

The primero departed without the customary farewells. After stopping to visit Wandra briefly in the City of Introspection, Quentin had no one else to see. Even Abulurd was still en route back from Parmentier.

The two spacefolder scouts raced through the distorted incomprehensibility of twisted space, no longer in contact. They slipped between dimensions, shortcutting across the fabric of the galaxy. At any moment they might streak through the heart of a sun or impact a planet or a moon that happened to lie across the line of their voyage. Once they had set course and engaged the Holtzman Effect engines, nothing remained but to wait a few moments until they came out the other end . . . or vanished forever.

If Quentin or Faykan died on this mission, would the history of the Jihad really take notice of their loss? Even two war heroes were insignificant against the plague that Omnius had unleashed. More people had died from the horrible epidemic than in all the Time of Titans and Serena Butler's Jihad combined. Omnius had utterly changed the parameters of the war, much as Serena herself had done when she'd initiated the Jihad.

This conflict was no longer a simple struggle that could be resolved. It was an absolute fight for survival, and victory could come only from the complete extinction of the other side. The number of those who had fallen victim to the Scourge was incalculable. No historian could ever gauge the magnitude of this disaster, and no memorial would ever be sufficient to mark the losses. From this point on, no doomsday weapon any human scientist invented could ever be too fearsome by comparison. No destructive power was too great to be turned against the evil thinking machines.

The human race, if it survived, would never be the same.

The journey to Corrin was as short as it was terrifying. Quentin's scout ship emerged from folded space, and the starfield shimmered around him, black velvet dusted with diamonds. The view was peaceful and serene, giving no evidence that he was deep within a part of the galaxy controlled by thinking machines.

Hanging there in silence, he cycled through navigational comparison grids that featured the contours of space and the patterns of constellations around Corrin. Spacefolders were not particularly accurate in their navigation, only to within a hundred thousand kilometers or so, but at least he had found his way to the correct star system. Quentin used his tracking skills to triangulate and verify his location. The red giant in this system was obviously Corrin's bloated sun.

After Faykan had joined up with him in space, they descended swiftly and stealthily toward the planet where the primary incarnation of Omnius directed his machine empire. There would likely be robotic picket ships guarding the system's perimeter and vessels that monitored traffic around the machine world. But since no human incursions had ever made it this far into Synchronized space, the robots would probably not be too vigilant.

Quentin and Faykan planned to sweep in, reconnoiter, and depart before any enemy ships could intercept them. It was the only way they were likely to return to the League with their fresh and vital information. If the thinking machines came close to capturing the spacefolder scouts, he and his son could activate the Holtzman engines, fold space, and leap back into League territory. With their traditional space-propulsion technology, the thinking machines could never catch them.

The two men were not at all prepared for the sight they encountered.

Space around Corrin was utterly filled with heavy robotic battleships of every conceivable size and configuration. Omnius had gathered an awe-inspiring armada of heavy cruisers, robotic destroyers, automated bombers, huge rammers, and interdictors. Hundreds of thousands of them.

"Is that . . . everything? The sum total of what Omnius has?" Faykan's transmitted voice was dry and wavery. "How could there possibly be so many?"

Quentin needed a long moment to find his own voice. "If Omnius launches that armada against the League, we are doomed. There is no way we can stand against them." He stared with such intensity that his eyes burned. Finally, he remembered to blink.

"The machines couldn't possibly have built them all here. Omnius must have drawn these vessels from across the Synchronized Worlds," Faykan said.

"And why not? We have been incapable of moving against him since the beginning of the Scourge."

To Quentin, the conclusion was inescapable. Undoubtedly, all those ships would be sent to hammer Salusa Secundus, to crush the heart of humanity. Then they would sweep across the League planets where plague survivors could barely feed themselves, much less defend against such a force.

"By God and Saint Serena," Faykan said. "I knew the machines were aware of the League's weakness, Father, but I never guessed that Omnius might already be preparing to attack."

Corrin looked like a swollen nest of furious hornets about to swarm. After the progress of the Scourge across the League Worlds, the human population was at its lowest ebb. The forces standing ready to defend against the thinking machines had never been so weakened.

And the doomsday armada of Omnius looked ready to launch.

*Hope and love can bind the most distant hearts, even across an
entire galaxy.*

—LERONICA TERGIET,
private journal

I n the early evening, Zimia's interplanetary district usually bustled with
activity, as sidewalk vendors and customers bargained loudly and good-
naturedly with one another, testing and teasing, using psychology and art-
ful humiliation as they tried to sell their wares.

Vor had not been back home in more than a month. Abulurd had
pushed the javelin and they'd arrived in Salusa a day early. As always, Vor
looked forward to seeing Leronica again. She was his anchor, his one
point of stability every time he returned from a mission.

He expected Estes and Kagin were still here. They had intended to go
back to Caladan months earlier, but the quarantines and uncertainty
caused by the Scourge had complicated all travel plans. They were safer
on Salusa than anywhere else . . . and he was glad the twins had been in
Zimia to keep their mother company while Vor was away. Yet again.

Tonight, as he strutted home ahead of schedule, a strange pall hung in
the neighborhood air, a curious lack of energy and enthusiasm. It seemed
fitting for his own mood, too, since he'd had to leave Parmentier without
ever finding news about Raquella. Although Abulurd and his crew had
assisted his search for two days, they had found no sign of Vor's granddaughter or her medical team. She and Mohandas Suk seemed to have
vanished off the face of the planet.

Abulurd had been anxious to return to Salusa, bringing his report on the final stages and aftermath of the epidemic, as ordered. Vor certainly understood the call of duty, and so he had shuttled with them all back to the javelin and headed home. . . .

Tonight, in Zimia's interplanetary district, the people seemed subdued, not chattering in their colorful languages as usual. Instead, they conversed quietly among themselves, and turned to look when they saw Vor pass. It was not uncommon for people in his own neighborhood to notice him, but this time no one hailed the Supreme Commander or made any attempt to engage him in conversation. They left him alone.

Something was wrong. He picked up his pace.

On the fifth floor of his building, he found Estes and Kagin inside the apartment with their wives, children, and grandchildren, people Vor rarely saw. Had Leronica thrown another reception for him? He doubted it, since she had not known the exact date of his return.

Smiling, he looked tenderly at his grandchildren, but they didn't seem to recognize him. He glanced curiously at his two sons, who greeted him with even less warmth than usual, preoccupied with great concern. They looked many decades older than their father. "What's going on? Where's your mother?"

"It's about time you got here," Kagin said with a glance at his brother.

Estes sighed, shaking his head. He picked up a rambunctious little girl and held her, shushing her. Then he gestured with his chin toward the master bedroom. "You'd better get in there. She might not have much longer, but she never gave up hope that you would come back to her."

Vor pushed his way into the bedroom, feeling the clamor of panic. "Leronica!" He could make no excuses for his priorities, and Leronica had never begrudged him his Jihad duties. But what if something had happened to her?

Vor entered the room he had shared with her for so many years. Uncharacteristic worry flooded his mind. He smelled medicines, sickness—the Scourge? Had Leronica been infected somehow, despite all the precautions? On general principles she had always refused to take spice, which left her vulnerable. Had he been a carrier himself, personally immune but still able to pass along the infection to others?

Vor stopped just inside the door, his breath catching in his throat. Leronica lay on their large bed, looking older and frailer than he had ever seen her before. An intense young doctor attended her, trying different treatments.

When she saw Vor standing at the doorway, her eyes lit up. "My love! I knew you'd come!" She pulled herself into a sitting position, as if she had just received a full dose of stimulants.

Startled, the doctor turned, then let out a visible sigh of relief. "Ah, Supreme Commander, I am glad that—"

"What's wrong with her? Leronica, are you all right?"

"I am *old*, Vor." She nudged the doctor. "Leave us alone for a while. We've got a lot of catching up to do."

The man insisted on staying a moment longer to adjust her pillows and check another scan reading. "She's as comfortable as I can make her, Supreme Commander, but there's—"

Having long dreaded this day, Vor didn't hear the rest of the doctor's statement. Instead, he focused his whole world, all his attention on her. She smiled bravely, a wan, sickly offering. "I'm sorry I couldn't be at the door to welcome you home with open arms."

When he lifted her warm, dry hand it felt like a papier-mâché sculpture in his grip. "I should have come back sooner, Leronica. I should never have gone to Parmentier. Abulurd could have done it all. I didn't know—"

He wished he could run from what he was seeing, but knew that was impossible. Watching the love of his life slide toward death was far more frightening to him than any battle against enemy thinking machines had ever been. Desperation made him dizzy. "I'll find some way to help you, Leronica. Don't worry about the medical situation. There'll be a solution. I'll insist on it."

Missed possibilities piled up around him, drowning him. If only he could have given her the life-extension treatment, too. If only he'd convinced her to take melange regularly. If only they could have a few more years together. If only his nurturing granddaughter Raquella could have been here to take care of Leronica. If Raquella was even alive . . .

Leronica's papery lips formed a smile, and she squeezed his hand. "I am ninety-three years old, Vorian. *You* might have found a way to fend off age, but it's still a mystery to me." She looked closely at him and reached up to wipe off a bit of age-simulation makeup he had put around his mouth. Her fingers brushed away the fine lines he had intentionally added. She always seemed amused at his efforts. "You haven't changed a bit."

"And you look just as beautiful to me as ever," he said.

VOR RARELY LEFT her side for the rest of that night or the next day. Estes and Kagin and their families crowded the house, and everyone struggled to control their anxiety. Even the twins could see that Leronica seemed much more vibrant when Vor was with her.

She didn't ask for much, occasional treats to satisfy her sweet tooth, and Vor procured anything she wanted, despite the disapproving glances of Kagin, who cited the doctor's instructions. Vor hung on to threads of hope—threads that grew more frayed hour by hour.

On the edge of evening on the second day, with reddish sunlight filtering through the windows into the bedroom, Vor gazed down on the old woman who slept fitfully. The night before, he had dozed uncomfortably on a single cot that had been brought in, and his entire body ached with fatigue. He recalled times when he had slept better huddled in scant shelters on rugged battlefields.

Now, as slanted sunlight touched Leronica's wrinkled face, Vor saw her in memory the way she'd been when he met her, serving kelp beer and food in a Caladan tavern. She stirred and opened her eyes. Vor bent over to kiss her forehead. For a moment Leronica did not recognize him, but then she focused and gave him a melancholy smile. Her dark pecan eyes remained beautiful—reflecting the depths of the rich, selfless love that she had felt for him all these decades.

"Hold me, my dearest," she said, her voice cracking from the effort of only a few words. Then, as his heart cried out helplessly, Vor felt her slipping away in his arms. At the last moment, as she gasped a final breath, she whispered his name, and he responded by saying hers, long and slow, like a caress.

When he could hold the tears back no longer, Vor began to cry softly.

Kagin appeared in the doorway. "Quentin Butler is here to see you. Something about the Jihad, and he insists it's important." Then, seeing his mother and Vor's tears, he realized what had happened. His face paled. "Oh, no! No!" Kagin rushed to his mother and knelt at her side, but she did not move. Vor didn't let go of her.

Kagin broke out in loud, convulsing sobs, looking so pitiful that Vor pulled away from Leronica and placed an arm around the younger man's shoulders. For a moment, his son looked at him with shared grief. Estes came into the room and stood, reeling, as if hoping to delay the reality for a few more seconds.

"She's gone," Vor said. "I'm so sorry." He stared in disbelief at the two dark-haired men who looked so much alike.

Estes looked like an ice statue, unmoving. Kagin looked coldly at his father. "Go attend your military business with Primero Butler. It always happens—why should it be any different, now that she's dead? Give us time alone with our mother."

Numb and barely able to move, Vor rose to his feet and plodded into the living room. Looking haggard from his own shock, Quentin Butler stood at attention wearing his crisp green-and-crimson Jihad uniform.

"Why are you here?" Vor demanded, his voice dull. "I need to be alone now."

"We have a crisis, Supreme Commander. Faykan and I are just back back from Corrin, and our greatest fears have come to pass." He drew a deep breath. "We could have less than a month before all the League is destroyed."

It did not occur to the humans who invented thinking machines that they would become relentless weapons turned against us. Yet that is exactly what happened. The mechanical genie is out of the bottle.

— FAYKAN BUTLER,
political rally

During the hastily convened crisis strategy session of the Jihad Council, Quentin Butler sensed mounting panic. He saw it in the blood-drained expressions of the political leaders, on the pasty face of the Grand Patriarch, and in the mystified expression of the Interim Viceroy. So many members, experts, and Parliament guests attended, the group had been forced to meet in an audience chamber instead of their usual private room. With news so calamitous, the Council knew they could not keep the information secret for long.

"The Scourge was not enough," Quentin said aloud into their worried silence. "Now Omnius means to ensure our extinction."

From the moment the first Council members had seen the images of Omnius's incredible extermination fleet, they realized that the League could never defend itself against such a force.

"My, this comes at the worst possible time," the Grand Patriarch finally said. His chain of office seemed to weigh him down. "One disaster on top of another. Over half of our population is dead or dying from the virus. Societies and governments are in total shambles, refugees are everywhere, and we have no way to take care of their needs—and now this battle fleet preparing to depart from Corrin. What are we going to do?"

Quentin and Faykan shifted uneasily in their seats. The Grand Patriarch should have been inspiring others, not whimpering and complaining.

To a larger audience now, they displayed the images their spacefolder scouts had taken at Corrin only days before. Jihad tacticians and expert Ginaz mercenaries rushed to make an analysis, but the conclusion was obvious. Omnius intended to throw everything into an utterly overwhelming offensive against already-weakened humanity. Intercepted transmissions had made the machines' target perfectly clear: Salusa Secundus. The dumbfounded politicians had no way to voice their despair.

Behind the speaking podium, holoprojections of highlighted planets indicated the strengths of the remaining League military forces, while blackout zones denoted systems still under tight quarantine. Casualties from the epidemic had gutted the Army of the Jihad. There had not been a coordinated offensive against Omnius since the conquest of Honru, and although the military had plenty of empty battleships, there were too few healthy soldiers to crew them all. In the midst of the plague, the jihadis who could still function were spread far too thin in quarantine and recovery efforts.

"Perhaps we should ask Cogitor Vidad to discuss . . . cessation terms again," suggested the representative from Hagal.

Vidad's brain canister sat on a special pedestal to one side of the Council table, attended by a pair of secondaries, an ancient man named Keats and a new recruit, Rodane. Now Keats said in a whispery voice, "The Cogitor has not left Zimia in many years, but he would be willing to return to Hessra and consult with his fellow Cogitors."

Grand Patriarch Boro-Ginjo turned in disbelief to the Hagal representative. "Do you mean surrender to Omnius?"

"Does anyone have a better idea for how we can survive?"

"We don't have time for that," Faykan Butler said, agitated. "Look at those images! Omnius is ready to launch his fleet!"

With his electrafluid glowing bright blue with mental activity, Cogitor Vidad sent words emanating through a speakerpatch. "Then I recommend that you evacuate Salusa Secundus. The machine forces cannot possibly arrive from Corrin in less than a month. Leave this planet empty when the machines arrive, and Omnius will then have no victory."

"That's more than a billion people!" the Interim Viceroy groaned.

A representative for the Ginaz mercenaries coughed loudly. "Since the Scourge, there are plenty of empty worlds where we can send so many refugees."

"Unacceptable!" Quentin shouted, unable to believe what he was hearing. "We can't just hide. Even if we escape Salusa in time, nothing will stop Omnius from overrunning our weakened worlds, one after another. The League will die the moment we evacuate our capital." He clasped his hands together as if he wanted to strangle something, then forced calm on his handsome features. "Now—if there was ever a time for it—we've got to take desperate, decisive action."

All eyes turned toward Supreme Commander Vorian Atreides, who sat stiffly on one side of the stage. Despite his always-youthful appearance, he seemed to radiate pain and grief from the loss of his wife, but he propped himself up and somehow held himself together. "We *destroy* them," he said, his voice as hard as frozen steel. "That is all we can do."

Some of the Council members moaned, and the Interim Viceroy actually let out a near-hysterical laugh. "Ah, good! So the solution is perfectly simple! We just destroy the thinking machines. We should have thought of that earlier!"

The Supreme Commander stood without flinching. Quentin felt sorry for him, thinking of his own love for Wandra. Yes, Leronica was dead. But he hoped Vor could find comfort in the knowledge that she had lived a long, full life surrounded by the love of her family—a rare thing in these troubled times. After a century of the Jihad, and now the wildfire destruction of the Scourge, everyone had more grief and ghosts than they could endure.

Vor anchored himself with his anger, searching for something to hurt, to destroy, as a way to relieve the ache in his heart. His uniform, normally neat and clean, was wrinkled and stained today. A believer in the formality of military operations, Quentin usually disapproved of people who lapsed in their personal discipline, but now he overlooked it.

"One way or another, this must be our last battle." Vorian Atreides strode to the podium and waited for an agonizingly long moment. Silence weighed down on him as he gathered his thoughts, balancing his anger and his grief. "After looking at the reconnaissance images, who can doubt that this is the sum total of the machine military forces? In the past two days, we have sent eleven spacefolder scouts to other randomly selected Synchronized Worlds, and their reports support that conclusion." Two scouts had been lost in the effort, probably due to navigational errors, but the information the remaining scouts had brought back was crucial. "We learned that the defensive fleets have been removed from the machine planets. All of them. Omnius has gathered everything at Corrin for this one grand strike."

The Grand Patriarch nodded somberly. "We are meant to tremble before this extermination fleet."

"No, we are meant to die." Now Vor smiled and spoke more forcefully. "But Omnius doesn't realize this tactic may prove to be a weakness if we know how to exploit it."

"What are you talking about?" Interim Viceroy O'Kukovich said.

Instead of answering the politician, Vor looked directly at Quentin. His gray eyes had a new, fractured sharpness, like shards of broken glass. "Don't you see? By consolidating his forces for this massive push, he has left himself vulnerable *everywhere else!* While the thinking machines move against us in their ponderous battleships, the Army of the Jihad can strike at *all the other* Synchronized Worlds, which are virtually undefended!"

"And how are we to do that?" the Grand Patriarch cried, his voice high-pitched and childlike.

"We must do the unexpected." Vor crossed his arms over his uniformed chest. "That is the only way humans can win."

Quentin raised his voice over the loud muttering, trying to keep the Council members quiet. He knew Vor had a plan, and it was perhaps the only one humanity could embrace. "Explain *how,* Supreme Commander. What weapons do we have against the thinking machines?"

"Atomics." Vor swept his gaze across the agitated audience. "An overwhelming number of pulse-augmented nuclear warheads. We can leave every single Synchronized World a radioactive cinder, just as we left Earth, ninety-two years ago. If the human race is brave enough to use atomics again, we can systematically eradicate Omnius from world after world. We destroy every incarnation of the computer evermind, just as he intends to destroy us."

"But there's no time!" Xander Boro-Ginjo wailed again, looking for support among the other stunned Council members. "The machines are sure to launch soon! We've seen the images."

"For the time being, the extermination fleet remains at Corrin, still being assembled. We may yet have weeks to prepare before they set out for Salusa. And even once they launch, it will still take them a month in transit—as the Cogitor has already pointed out," Vor said, waiting.

Quentin suddenly looked at Faykan. Both men had begun to realize what Supreme Commander Atreides was thinking. "Omnius has nothing but standard spaceflight capabilities!"

"But *we* have other options," Vor said, his voice flat and emotionless. "A month is plenty of time to destroy every single Synchronized

World—*if we use space-folding ships*. We can replicate our final victory at Earth on each of these worlds, magnifying its success many times over. We will obliterate every single evermind, one by one, without mercy or hesitation."

Quentin sucked in his breath, running through the implications in his head. "But the spacefolders are inherently unreliable. VenKee statistics show a loss rate of up to ten percent. Each time our fleet travels to a Synchronized World, we will lose ships. There are hundreds of Omnius strongholds. The attrition rate will be . . . appalling!"

Vor remained unruffled. "It is preferable to total extinction. While the Corrin fleet crawls inexorably toward Salusa Secundus, we will slip around them and strike the undefended Synchronized Worlds, methodically crush every planet on the list, and finally work our way to the primary world. Then, by the time we reach Corrin itself, the assault fleet will be too far away to respond in time."

Xander Boro-Ginjo interrupted, "But what about all the captive humans on the Synchronized Worlds? Aren't we supposed to be rescuing them from their slavery? They will all die if we unleash a nuclear holocaust against them."

"At least they will die free."

"Well, I'm sure that'll be a great consolation to them," O'Kukovich grumbled, but he saw that the opinion in the chamber had shifted in Vor's favor, so he quickly fell silent. The Council members seemed horrified yet hopeful. At least now they had a plan that offered them a slender chance.

"More people will die if we do *not* act decisively." Vor's determination and confidence was frightening. "And Salusa Secundus will be destroyed in the process, either way. We have no better choice."

"But what about Salusa? Do we just abandon it?" The Interim Viceroy's voice had an unpleasant whining undertone.

"Sacrificing Salusa Secundus may be a price we must pay to end this Jihad forever." He frowned at the preservation canister that held Vidad's brain. "The Cogitor is right: We have to evacuate this planet in the meantime."

Quentin's stomach turned to lead, but he tried to be objective. It might just work. It was a dreadful gamble, and either way it would leave deep scars on the human soul. "Even if the machine fleet succeeds in hitting Salusa, there will be no evermind to hold them together after they've completed their programming. They will have no guidance, and no initiative. We should be able to pick them off easily."

"They'll be all that remains of the entire Synchronized empire," Faykan said.

Like Vorian Atreides, Quentin now felt he was willing to go to any limit necessary to finish this conflict, or die in the attempt. Even the recent, miraculous return of his granddaughter Rayna reminded him of her parents dead on Parmentier, of all the billions Omnius had already slaughtered. "I agree with the Supreme Commander. It is our best chance, and we dare not ignore this opportunity to ensure our very survival. My soldiers in the Army of the Jihad will volunteer to crew spacefolder battleships, even knowing the extreme risks—although so many have already died of the Scourge, I don't know if we can muster sufficient personnel. Think of all the kindjal bombers that will need pilots."

The Grand Patriarch pursed his lips. "I'm sure we could find any number of Martyrists willing to fill out the ranks. They've been demanding a chance to sacrifice themselves against the machines." He saw this as a way to solve two problems at once.

"For the time being, they can fly spacefolder scouts," Faykan suggested. "It's risky, but we'll need regular reports from Corrin. There's no other way we can monitor when that robotic force begins to head toward us. Once the extermination fleet launches, our clock starts ticking."

Quentin considered, mentally doing the math. "We know from captured update ships that there are five hundred forty-three Synchronized Worlds. We will need to send a large enough battle group to every single one of those planets in order to insure victory there. Just because they have moved their heavy ships to Corrin doesn't mean they won't put up a fight."

"We'll need thousands of ships with skeleton crews and full bomber squadrons to deploy the pulse-atomics," Faykan said. The very concept seemed to take his breath away. "Jump after jump after jump, and each time we could lose as much as a tenth of our forces." He swallowed hard.

"No sense waiting. We should launch what we have immediately and begin this Great Purge." Vor lifted his chin. "In the meantime, we need to use every resource in the League to start manufacturing the necessary nuclear warheads. We have some stockpiles, but we need more pulse-atomics than the human race has ever produced—and we need them *now*. We also have to get space-folding engines installed or activated on every available ship. For our first missions we'll have to use the functional spacefolders from the first group Xavier and I commissioned from Kolhar sixty years ago."

At the back of the chamber, the two yellow-robed secondaries stood quickly, lifting Vidad's preservation canister. "The Cogitor is very concerned," ancient Keats said. "He will return to Hessra to discuss this turn of events with his fellow Ivory Tower Cogitors."

"Discuss it all you like," Vor said, his voice tinged with scorn. "By the time you reach a conclusion, this will all be over."

Let fat humans and thinking machines inhabit the comfortable worlds in this galaxy. We prefer the desolate, out-of-the way places, for they invigorate our organic brains and make us invincible. Even when my cymeks have conquered everything, these difficult places shall be our favorite haunts.

—GENERAL AGAMEMNON,

New Memoirs

The Titans had killed the five Ivory Tower Cogitors too swiftly, and now General Agamemnon regretted his impetuous revenge. *After so many decades of feeling hunted and impotent, I should have relished my conquest.*

Now, too late, he thought of how satisfying it would have been to dissect the ancient brains, removing one sliver of mental matter at a time, erasing the snippets of thoughts contained within each rippled contour of the cerebrum. Or, Juno could have added interesting contaminants to their electrafluid and together they could have watched the unusual reactions.

But all the Cogitors were already destroyed. Stupid lack of foresight!

Instead, as the three Titans consolidated their hold on Hessra, they were forced to entertain themselves by torturing the captive secondary monks, humans who had given over their lives to tending the Cogitors. All of the secondaries had now been stripped of their fleshy burdens, their brains torn like ripe fruit from their skulls and installed unwillingly into cymek preservation canisters. Slaves, pets, experiments.

Because they'd initially refused to cooperate with the takeover, the hybrid secondary-neos were given a set of torment-inducing needles, modified thoughtrodes inserted into the naked brain tissue.

From a tower high above the sheets of ice, the Titan general focused his optic threads, swiveling his head turret to survey his bleak conquest. Wherever gray or black outcroppings showed through the glacier, strange blue smears appeared. Threads of lichens and hardy moss found sustenance within fractures of the ancient ice wall, converting the dim sunlight into enough energy to sustain their lives. Occasionally, chunks of the glacier calved off, and the many-branched blue lichens quickly withered once exposed to the frigid air.

Agamemnon had made a cursory study of some of the electrafluid records and treatises compiled by the Cogitors over millennia. Apparently minerals and other trace elements from these native lichens combined with runoff water that flowed into Hessra's underground streams. Inside deep laboratories and factory chambers at the base of the ancient black towers, the monks had used this water to manufacture the nutrient-rich electrafluid.

For a thousand years, Agamemnon and his cymeks had required a constant supply to keep their preserved brains fresh and alert, and the Cogitors had maintained an uneasy and neutral relationship with the cymeks, allowing an illicit trade in the potent life-support liquid despite their self-imposed isolation.

But Agamemnon did not like to be beholden to anyone. The conquering Titans had confiscated the chemical production facilities and "strongly encouraged" the secondary-neos to continue making the vibrant substance.

With a clatter of methodical footsteps, another Titan walker entered the high observation tower. Agamemnon identified the newcomer as Dante, who paused and waited for the general to acknowledge him. "We have finished studying the recent images our neo-cymek scouts took of Richese and Bela Tegeuse." He paused, making certain he had his leader's full attention. "The news is not good."

"These days, news is never good. What is it?"

"After we retreated, Omnius's forces returned and laid waste to both planets, killing the rest of the human population that once served us. All the neos had already escaped—a small advantage, I suppose—but without our captive humans, we no longer have a pool from which to draw more cymeks."

Agamemnon felt anger and gloom. "With the *hrethgir* writhing and dying from Yorek Thurr's damnable plagues, Omnius can turn his attention against us again. These are dark days, Dante. The thinking machines have destroyed our last major world, leaving us trapped here with no followers, no population to enslave, only a hundred or so neos, some converted secondary monks . . . and three Titans."

His artillery arms flinched as if he subconsciously wanted to blast a hole through the tower wall. "I had intended to launch a new Time of Titans, but we've been hounded by the thinking machines and hunted by humans and their damned Sorceresses. Look what remains of us! Who will lead our great rebellion now?"

"There are numerous neo candidates to choose from."

"They can follow orders but they cannot produce a winning strategy. Not a single one of them shows potential as a military commander. They were raised in captivity and volunteered for a chance to have their brains yanked from their skulls. What good are they? I need a *fighter*, a commander."

"We are safe here for now, General. Omnius does not know where to find us. Perhaps we should simply be content on Hessra."

Agamemnon swiveled his head turret, his optic threads blazing. "History rarely notices those who remain content."

As the two Titans stared up into the ocean of stars, Agamemnon's network linked with external sensors and picked up the blip of an incoming, unexpected ship. Curiously, he focused and waited for confirmation.

Juno was in the cymek control center established in the main chamber where they had slaughtered the five Ivory Tower Cogitors. As he expected, her sweet synthesized voice soon came over the direct comline into his preservation canister. "Agamemnon, my love, I have quite a surprise for you—a visitor."

Dante, on the same comline frequency, responded with reservations. "Has Omnius found us already? Do we need to move and hide again?"

"I am sick of hiding," Agamemnon said. "Who is it, Juno?"

Her voice was lilting and cheery. "Why, it is the last of our Ivory Tower Cogitors—Vidad, returning home! He transmits greetings to his five companions. Alas, none of them can answer him."

Agamemnon felt a flood of excitement wash through the sparkling electrafluid. "This is unexpected indeed. Vidad doesn't know the other Cogitors are dead!"

"He claims he has urgent news and requests an immediate convocation," Juno said.

"Maybe he's finally discovered the proof to an ancient mathematical theorem," Dante suggested sarcastically. "I can't wait to hear it."

"Set up an ambush," Agamemnon said. "I want the last Cogitor captured. Then . . . we can take our time with him."

DURING THE LONG voyage from Salusa Secundus, Vidad was deeply preoccupied with troubling thoughts. The foundation of the Ivory Tower Cogitors' existence was to remain isolated, not to interfere. Both the evermind and the humans were sentient beings, intelligent life-forms, though based on fundamentally different principles. The Cogitors could not take sides in this conflict. When they had allowed Serena Butler to sway them from their long-held position, disaster had resulted. As a consequence, the fervor of the Jihad had been redoubled for the next sixty years.

Now, however, Vidad knew that the humans intended to obliterate all incarnations of Omnius. Did neutrality require complete nonparticipation, if the total extinction of a sentient presence was at stake? Or did it mandate the maintenance of a careful balance of power?

Vidad could not decide this issue by himself. The six Cogitors formed a unit, a discussion group that encompassed virtually all of human wisdom. He had hurried to Hessra in order to raise the question. After much appropriate debate, the Cogitors would reach a consensus about what to do.

Vidad had departed immediately after the Jihad Council reached its decision. He did not know how much time he had.

Piloting the fast ship were two of his loyal secondaries. Rodane was a new recruit Vidad had trained during his years in Zimia. Keats, extremely old but still functional, had been recruited by Grand Patriarch Ginjo long ago and had served the Ivory Tower Cogitors for almost seventy years; he seemed near the end of his useful life, and this trip back to Hessra would certainly be his last. Many of Ginjo's first recruits had already died and were entombed in open crevasses on the slow-moving glaciers. Vidad's Cogitors would need new volunteers soon.

En route, Vidad spent every hour of every day contemplating the weighty problem of the planned pulse-atomic strikes. He had not reached any tenable decision before they arrived at the icy planetoid. Vidad sent direct transmissions to the other five Cogitors waiting in their citadel, but oddly enough, received no response.

While Rodane piloted their ship down toward the target glacier, Keats peered out the cockpit windows. "Something's happened here," he said in his raspy voice. "Ice around the towers has been excavated. I see craters that look like they were made by . . . explosions. I suggest we proceed with caution."

"We must determine what has happened," Vidad said.

The younger pilot circled close to the citadel where they would normally land. Though his eyes were old and watery, Keats spotted the ambush first. "Machines, artillery—cymeks! Get us out of here!"

Confused, Rodane glanced to the Cogitor's brain canister for additional orders. He worked the controls, but not fast enough.

As soon as the small craft's course altered, cymeks emerged from their hiding places on the ice and under the citadel. Flying forms shot out, and marching combat walkers surged away from hidden shelters, raising their artillery arms and opening fire.

As shells exploded around them, bursts of light sent crippling shockwaves through the vessel. The young pilot tentatively dodged back and forth, but Keats grabbed the controls from him and flew more extreme maneuvers. "Your caution will get us killed, Rodane."

A frantic transmission finally crackled across the comline on which Vidad had expected to hear from his fellow Cogitors. The voice was merely a pulse electronic signal deciphered by the communications systems. The ancient philosopher did not recognize the tone or inflection, but the words were astounding. It was from one of the secondary monks.

"The Titans have taken over Hessra! They've killed the five Cogitors and many secondaries . . . except for some of us, and we are not alive. We've been transformed into cymeks, forced to serve them. Cogitor Vidad, you are the last. Flee! Above all else, you must remain alive—" Then came the sounds of struggle and shrieking, echoing pulses of agony transmitted into the open and uncaring universe.

Three cymek flyers accelerated toward them, blasting with projectiles, trying to knock them out of the sky. Larger walker-forms strode out onto the open icepack. One of the monstrous warrior bodies was so immense it must have been a Titan. Explosions erupted in the air all around them.

Keats punched the small craft's engines, sparing no fuel, burning to their maximum acceleration to carry them free of Hessra. Though he was protected in his preservation canister, Vidad knew the merciless acceleration would be too much for Keats's frail old body. "You will die."

"And you . . . will live," Keats managed to gasp before unconsciousness overtook him. He didn't have the strength to keep breathing under such constant, brutal acceleration. Several of his brittle bones cracked.

Rodane, though, was strong and versatile. He would survive. Vidad needed only one attendant. Flying on an automatic escape vector, they pulled far from frozen Hessra, flying deep into space and away from the system. The short-range cymek pursuers dropped back, transmitting angry curses.

In his cockpit seat, Keats's old body lay in the peculiar gray stillness of death, but the younger secondary still struggled, his breathing labored. When they reached the fringe of the system, the acceleration automatically dropped off, and Rodane came back to consciousness. Eyes wide, he looked with sad shock over at his aged companion, who had given up his life so the Cogitor could escape.

"Now where shall we go, Vidad?" the secondary asked, his voice edged with panic.

The Cogitor thought of his five companions, all murdered by the cymeks who had taken over Hessra, an apparent attempt to hide from Omnius. Vidad was the only philosopher who could make up his mind about how to react to the impending atomic holocaust Vorian Atreides wanted to unleash. He was objective, neutral, intelligent. . . . He had also been human once. Knowing what the cymeks had done to all of his companions, how could he not feel even an echo of long-forgotten emotion? Of . . . revenge? He had yet another reason to speak to the evermind.

"Set a course for Corrin," Vidad commanded.

*For all the years of this Jihad, we have known we must be prepared
for any attack. In the end, though, preparations are not sufficient.
We must be willing to act.*

— SUPREME COMMANDER VORIAN ATREIDES,
address to Jihad Council

Though the death of Leronica left him with a dark vacuum inside as empty as the sparsest reaches of open space, Vor did not have time to grieve. He only had time to be the Supreme Commander.

And save the human race.

The Army of the Jihad was already engaged in a massive emergency effort. Space-folding spycraft, mostly flown by Martyrist volunteers, secretly darted back and forth from Corrin, bearing regular reports on the progress of the giant fleet Omnius had amassed. The moment the robotic horde left the red giant system, the League humans would know that the countdown had begun.

Other spacefolder scouts flitted from world to world, bearing the news and calling the survivors of humanity to action; dozens of them vanished without a trace, but enough redundant messengers raced about to maintain the lines of communication. Never before had the planets of the League of Nobles been so closely up-to-date.

On returning from plague-ravaged Parmentier, Vor and Abulurd had brought young Rayna to Zimia. Faykan, her uncle, had quickly taken the girl under his wing. He had been very close to his brother Rikov, and he treated the survival of the young girl as a miracle. Though all of her hair had fallen out, at least she had survived the virus. In moments of cynicism, Vor thought that Faykan seemed primarily interested in using the young girl as a political tool for his own purposes, a symbol to show that humans could indeed survive the plagues Omnius had sent.

Perhaps it will help.

While the pieces of the Great Purge were brought together, the giant fleet assembled, the tactical plan mapped out on the star charts showing the coordinates of every Synchronized World, the Supreme Commander put Faykan and Abulurd in charge of the impossible task of evacuating Salusa Secundus. He made sure his twin sons and their families were among the first to be taken away to safety. Then, knowing the rest of the effort was in capable hands, Vor concentrated on the primary goal.

Far off, the Kolhar shipyards worked night and day to refit League ballistas and javelins with the new engines. Norma Cenva, never losing her faith in the space-folding engines, had insisted for years that many of the capital ships be equipped with the capability, whether or not it was ever used. Now Vor applauded her foresight.

All stockpiles of pulse-atomics were gathered and loaded aboard the existing Jihad spacecraft, while new nuclear warheads were being manufactured frantically on all League industrial planets.

We should have planned better. We should have anticipated the need. We should have been ready!

The first dozen spacefolder battleships, those already equipped with the quirky Holtzman engines, were loaded with pulse-atomics and crews of volunteers to fly the necessary squads of bomber kindjals. They were the vanguard, sent off immediately to begin the systematic extermination of all evermind incarnations.

Finally, three weeks and three days after Quentin and Faykan had first returned from Corrin to sound the alarm, the Martyrist pilot of a spacefolding scout returned to Zimia. He was so frantic he nearly crashed his ship while attempting to land. Two spacefolders had raced back with the news, and only one had survived.

"The machines are moving! Omnius has launched the extermination fleet."

Hearing the report, Vor blocked out the cries of dismay from the other Jihad officers in his headquarters. He simply nodded and looked at a calendar, marking how long they had left.

Are Cogitors completely neutral, as they claim? Or is "neutral" merely a euphemism for one of the greatest acts of cowardice in the history of the human race?

— NAAM THE ELDER,
First Official Historian to the Jihad

After the scheduled departure of the extermination fleet, Erasmus and the evermind had little to do on Corrin. The immense and invincible armada of robotic battleships had been en route for six days, inexorably following their programmed path to Salusa Secundus. The vessels were slow, relentless, and unstoppable.

Omnius saw no need to hurry. The plan had been set in motion, and the results were inevitable.

Inside the robot's grand villa, he and Omnius discussed a painting, an extravagantly imaginative mountain landscape. "It is an original creation, executed by one of the captive humans. I believe he has a great deal of talent." Erasmus had been surprised at the slave's skill, the way he mixed pigments and media. Now that the evermind had a copy of the robot's independent persona inside him, perhaps he could begin to understand the nuances.

Looking at the painting through one of his flying watcheyes, Omnius could not see why the robot found so much merit in it. "The illustration is physically inaccurate in four hundred thirty-one details. The very act of painting is inferior to specific imaging processes in almost every respect. Why do you value this . . . art?"

"Because it is difficult to do," Erasmus said. "The creative process is complex, and humans are masters of it." He directed his optic threads at the masterpiece, analyzing every brushstroke in an instant and absorbing the interpretive nature of the work. "Each day I look at this painting and marvel. In order to better understand the creative process, I even dissected the brain of the artist, but I found no special differences."

"Art is easily created," Omnius said. "You exaggerate its importance."

"Before making such a statement, I suggest you try the act of creation yourself. Make something pleasing and *original*, not a copy of any existing work in your database. You will see for yourself how difficult it is."

Unfortunately, Omnius accepted the challenge.

Two days later, Erasmus stood inside an amazingly transformed incarnation of the mutable Central Spire, which now stood as an ostentatious golden-domed palace. To show off his newfound artistic flair, the evermind had filled the Spire with high-tech machine statuary and cultural pieces made entirely of gleaming metal, rainbow dazzleplaz, and teckite materials. There were no human images. Omnius had done it all quickly, as if to strengthen his assertion that creativity was a simple ability that could be processed and learned.

Noting the lack of innovation, however, and knowing that the evermind did not even see the difference between his work and a true masterpiece, Erasmus was not convinced. Gilbertus, who had never professed to be an artist, could have done better. Perhaps even the Serena Butler clone . . .

Feigning interest, the independent robot studied another interior wall of the domed palace. It contained an immense gold-framed video display of Omnius's newly created machine art, a flowmetal kaleidoscope of modernistic shapes. From his own files and experience, Erasmus recognized that this particular art project was modeled after the wildly creative displays in human museums, galleries, and fine homes. *I find this most unstimulating, however. Uninspired and imitative.* Finally, the robot shook his head in disapproval, replicating a mannerism he had observed in human subjects.

"You do not appreciate my art?" Omnius surprised him by recognizing the implication of the gesture.

"I did not say that. I find it . . . interesting." Erasmus should never have let down his guard, as the watcheyes were always there, always observing. "Art is subjective. I am just struggling, in my inadequate way, to understand your work."

"And you shall continue to struggle. I must maintain some secrets from you." The evermind emitted a boisterous but tinny laugh he had recorded from one of the human slaves. Erasmus joined in.

"I hear falseness in your cachination," Omnius said.

The robot knew he was able to modulate every sound he made, every mannerism, to produce the exact effect he desired. *Is Omnius attempting to trap me, or confuse me? If so, he is not doing particularly well at it.*

"I meant it to be as genuine as your own," Erasmus said, a sufficiently neutral comment.

Before the debate could continue, Omnius diverted his own attention. "An outside ship is approaching my Central Spire."

The unannounced vessel had come into the system at extremely high acceleration, broadcasting neutrality despite its League configuration. "The Cogitor Vidad brings important information for Omnius. It is vital that you hear it."

"I will hear what the Cogitor has to say before I make any extrapolations," the evermind said. "I can always kill him later, if I so choose."

Before long, the massive entrance doors of the golden Spire slid open, and a trembling human in a yellow robe walked in flanked by an escort of sentinel robots. The young man was bruised and weary after spending more than a week suffering under the highest acceleration his fragile body could tolerate. Now he struggled to carry an electrafluid-filled container that held the ancient philosopher's brain, though one of the robots could easily have held it. The yellow-robed man seemed weak and exhausted, barely able to stand.

"It has been many years since you last spoke with us, Cogitor Vidad," Erasmus said, stepping forward like an ambassador. "And the results of those interactions were not beneficial to us."

"Not beneficial to any of us. We Ivory Tower Cogitors made a significant miscalculation," the voice spoke directly from a speakerpatch on the side of the container.

"Why should I listen to you again?" Omnius modulated the volume of his voice so that the booming words made the walls vibrate.

"Because I bring relevant data that you lack. I recently returned to Hessra only to discover that the Titan Agamemnon and his cymek followers have established their new base there. They killed my five fellow Cogitors, took over our electrafluid production laboratories, and enslaved our secondaries."

"So, that is where the Titans went to hide after abandoning Richese," Erasmus said to Omnius. "Valuable intelligence indeed."

"Why do you come here to reveal this information?" the evermind demanded. "It is not logical to involve yourself in our conflict."

"I want the cymeks destroyed," Vidad said. "You can do it."

Erasmus was surprised. "Thus speaks an enlightened Cogitor?"

"I was human once. The other five Cogitors were my philosophical companions for much more than a millennium. The Titans murdered them. Is it surprising that I would desire vengeance?"

The weary secondary struggled to keep hold of the heavy preservation canister.

Omnius pondered the information. "Currently my machine battle fleet is occupied on another mission. After we succeed, the robot commanders will return here for further programming. I will then instruct them to go to Hessra. They have standing instructions to destroy any neo-cymeks and to capture the remaining rebellious Titans." The evermind seemed to be enjoying the new situation. "Very soon, with the *hrethgir* and the cymeks defeated, the universe can continue on a rational and efficient path, under my astute guidance."

Without changing the tone of his simulated voice, Vidad continued. "The situation is more complex than that. The League discovered your huge fleet many weeks ago. When I departed from Zimia, they were already monitoring your progress. They also know that your other Synchronized Worlds are undefended." In a brisk cadence he summarized the Jihad Council's plan to launch a series of blitzkrieg nuclear massacres, using the exceptional speed of the space-folding engines. "In fact, the first pulse-atomic strikes on your fringe worlds probably took place shortly after I left, and I have been more than a month in transit from Salusa, to Hessra, to Corrin. Certainly, the Great Purge is proceeding even as we speak. Therefore, you must be prepared for a pulse-atomic attack at any moment, at any place."

With mounting alarm, Erasmus extrapolated scenarios and consequences. They had long suspected that the *hrethgir* had access to some sort of instantaneous space travel. And an atomic-armed human fleet could well have already obliterated many Synchronized Worlds. With the extermination fleet gone, even Corrin was vulnerable to such an attack.

"Interesting," the evermind said, processing the details. "Why would you reveal such plans? Cogitors claim to be neutral, but now you seem to be siding with us—unless this is a trick."

"I have no hidden agenda," Vidad said. "As neutrals, the Cogitors have never wished to see either thinking machines or humans wiped out. My decision is entirely consistent with this philosophy."

Erasmus watched the artistic lights flashing all around him inside the Spire, and knew that Omnius was already transmitting instructions to his machine underlings, making defensive preparations and sending out the fastest vessels available. "I am the primary Omnius. For my self-preservation I must recall my war fleet to defend Corrin. The entire fleet. If the other Synchronized Worlds put up enough resistance to delay the humans' progress, there is a nonzero probability that some of my fastest battleships will return before it is too late. I can take no chances against these irrational *hrethgir*. With all of my ships back here to defend Corrin, the humans would not dare to strike against me."

Erasmus knew that it would take time to send a message to the enormous fleet, which was already eight days out, and even longer to turn the lumbering ships around and bring them racing back to Corrin, limited as they were by their traditional stardrive engines.

There will not be enough time.

*In the emotional frenzy of war, even the most hardened warrior can
shed tears over what he has to do.*

—SUPREME COMMANDER VORIAN ATREIDES,
Battle Memoirs

A s the robot fleet proceeded toward Salusa, the Army of the Jihad
continued its Great Purge to eradicate the undefended Synchronized Worlds. Before this endgame was over, either the human race or the
thinking machines would be obliterated. There could be no other outcome.

On the command bridge of his refitted flagship, the LS *Serena Victory*,
Vorian Atreides tensed as the Holtzman engines activated. "Prepare for
departure. Omnius is waiting out there."

The numerous Martyrist crew members invoked a fervent prayer
before the first jump. Vorian, though, preferred to depend on the augmented, sealed navigation systems Norma Cenva had secretly installed in
a handful of his best ships. He was always a pragmatic commander.

"For God and Saint Serena!" the crew shouted in unison.

The Supreme Commander gave a reassuring nod to the pale-faced
helmsman. He gave the order, then involuntarily closed his eyes as his
battle group plunged into the dangerous wilderness of folded space. He
had always been prepared to die in battle against the machines. He
hoped, though, that he wouldn't meet his end just by getting lost or accidentally hitting an asteroid.

Decades ago, Norma's prototype computerized navigation systems had
drastically improved the safety record of the spacefolders, but the skittish

Jihad Council had forbidden their use. Vor, however, had spoken with her in private at the VenKee shipyards where Holtzman engines were being activated in vessels of the Jihad fleet. On the Supreme Commander's direct orders, Norma surreptitiously installed her twelve remaining computer-based devices deep in the navigational systems of selected spacefolders. Vor had no intention of letting superstition decrease his chances for victory.

For the past few weeks now, group after group had leaped into Synchronized territory as soon as the weapons, vessels, and personnel were ready. All told, the Army of the Jihad had assembled more than a thousand capital ships for the Great Purge. The whole fleet was divided into ninety battle groups of twelve major vessels each, and each group received its list of targets. Their launching bays were loaded with hundreds of kindjal bombers containing pulse-atomic warheads. Some kindjals would be piloted by skilled veterans, others by rapidly trained Martyrist volunteers.

Every time they used Holtzman engines to leap from one star system to another, some ships would undoubtedly vanish into limbo, annihilated by unseen dimensional hazards. Given the ten-percent attrition rate, the battle groups could make only seven or eight jumps before they were no longer assured of success. Volunteers would fly numerous spacefolder scouts to maintain vital contact with the other battle groups as the widespread mission proceeded across the Synchronized Worlds.

There were more than five hundred enemy planets, including Corrin. Once and for all, the League would destroy every one of the Omnius incarnations. Statistically at least, the Army of the Jihad had enough ships to do the job. . . .

In only a few agitated breaths, the journey was over. From the sector coordinates displayed on his command console and the clarity of stars visible around him, Vor knew his ship had made it. Though jumps were often imprecise even with detailed coordinates, his attack vessels had arrived inside the machine-controlled system.

"Nineteen planets orbiting a pair of small yellow suns. It's the Yondair system for sure, Supreme Commander," said the helmsman.

Shuddering gasps and sighs of relief echoed among his bridge crew. The Martyrists uttered more prayers.

"Sound off. Give me a report on any losses in our battle group."

His first and second officers, Katarina Omal and Jimbay Whit, waited at their stations nearby. Omal was tall and dusky-skinned, one of the most effective female officers in the fleet. Whit, already showing a paunch at twenty-five, doubled as Vor's adjutant in the absence of Abulurd Harkonnen. With experience and battle smarts far beyond his years, Whit came from a distinguished military family. Decades ago, Vor had fought beside his grandfather in the all-out atomic attack on Earth.

"One ship gone, Supreme Commander," Omal said.

Vor accepted the loss and suppressed any visible expression of dismay as he noted the identification of the missing vessel in his squadron. *Well within the expected loss rate.*

Alarm klaxons went off, and a message screen on the bridge indicated a problem with the LS *Ginjo Explorer,* an unfortunately named vessel in his squadron. Throughout the Jihad fleet, four other warships had been named after the former Grand Patriarch. *The corrupt man does not deserve such an honor. The name that should adorn the vessels is Xavier Harkonnen.*

"Engine fire," a voice reported over the comline. "Holtzman system overload. We won't be using that ship again."

Through a viewing port, Vor saw the eerie illumination of flames on the underside of the ship, following the escaping atmosphere in a hull breach. Spacetight doors closed, and onboard fire-suppression systems prevented the spread of flames.

A damage assessment blared over Vor's comline. "Something blew in the Holtzman engine right after we folded space. Lucky we made it through, but the minute we got here the damn thing exploded and burned. First time out, and we're dead in space."

War is full of surprises, Vor thought. *Most of them bad.*

Over the next hour, Vor supervised the evacuation of the vessel and redistributed the volunteer crew of eight hundred men and women, mostly bomber pilots, onto the other ten warships. They also took aboard all the kindjal fighters, along with their pulse-atomic warheads.

They left the empty ship hanging in space after destroying its Holtzman engines, on the slim but frightening chance that if they failed in their mission, Omnius could obtain the space-folding technology. Finally, Vor drew a deep breath, then issued the command to deliver their killing blow.

"It's time to do what we came here for. Begin immediate atomic bombardment of Yondair. Every surviving ship, launch your kindjal squadrons with pulse-atomics before those machines can get ready for us."

Even without the huge robot military fleet, the Synchronized Worlds would still have local defenses and possible battle stations in orbit around many of the enemy strongholds. Each assault of an "undefended" machine planet would take at least a day just to get the Jihad ships in position, to launch all the fast bombers with their pulse-atomics, and to verify that the mission was a success. Despite the near-instantaneous travel between targets, the jihadis would still take a long time to comb through Omnius's fringe empire.

With the remaining warships behind him, Vor led the way toward the largest world, the ringed planet of Yondair. His squadrons of warhead delivery ships scattered from the launching bays, swooped beneath the rings, and dropped airburst bombs into the atmosphere, hitting strategic substations first and then deploying secondary atomics to spread the destruction across the landscape below. Pulse after pulse obliterated every gelcircuitry brain on the planet.

Any human prisoners who happened to be down there became unfortunate collateral casualties, but the need for swift and utter destruction of every single evermind allowed them no leeway for sympathy.

Looking ahead, Vor blocked out all thoughts of guilt, then gave the order to regroup at the edge of the Yondair system. After assessing their victory, his ships launched off to the next machine world.

And the next.

With any luck at all, the other squadrons were doing the same against the rest of the Omnius-controlled worlds. Nuclear destruction spread like a wrathful wave, rippling across the territory Omnius had subjugated. They would pick off the easy machine strongholds first, leaving Corrin for last.

The evermind had no way to resist, no way to send messages of warning fast enough. Like swift assassins, the warhead-carrying Jihad ships would slip in, strike, and then vanish. Omnius would be destroyed before he even felt the blow coming.

At least that was the plan. . . .

We may die tomorrow, but we must hope today. Though it will not
extend our lives, at least it will make them more meaningful.

—ABULURD HARKONNEN,
Journal of the Last Days of Salusa Secundus

Even with the population of Salusa Secundus devoted to a full-scale
effort, one month was not nearly enough time to evacuate an entire
planet. They had to prepare for the worst.

While the main task of assembling sufficient ships, volunteer crews,
and nuclear warheads consumed the League, Abulurd Harkonnen was
left to help his brother Faykan administer the great exodus from the capital world.

Supreme Commander Atreides had gathered his spacefolder fleet over
Salusa in a military force like nothing humanity had ever seen. One battle group after another activated their space-folding engines and vanished. It would be a long time before complete reports would come back
to the League, but Abulurd had faith in the desperate plan. Every morning when he woke up after a scant few hours of sleep, the young officer
knew that more Synchronized Worlds must have been vanquished out in
the thinking-machine empire.

However, from the images Abulurd's father and brother had
brought back from Corrin, they all knew what sort of threat was on its
way to the League capital. Even if the Great Purge succeeded in
destroying the enemy at its core, Salusa Secundus was almost certainly
doomed.

Abulurd could not save everyone, but he worked around the clock to get as many people away as possible. Faykan issued directives from Zimia, commandeering every ship, every able-bodied person.

That very morning, Abulurd had removed his comatose mother from the City of Introspection and placed her on an evacuation ship. Since there would not be enough room to take everyone away before the time ran out, some people had looked at the young man with anger, obviously wondering what good it would do to ensure Wandra's safety at the expense of others. His mother was not conscious of anything, could not appreciate her peril or the fact that she was being saved.

Abulurd understood the impossible choice, had even considered leaving Wandra in a fortified, subterranean section of the City of Introspection. But no one could take care of her there. So many things to consider, so many critical decisions to make. Each breath his mother took was important to him, for it left open the possibility—however remote—that she might survive. He could not leave her behind. Such choices reminded him of Ix, when Ticia Cenva had played God, determining who would be rescued and who would stay behind. . . .

In the end, he turned a deaf ear to complaints and to the accusations of favoritism. *She is my mother*, he told himself, *and she is a Butler!* He cited Faykan's authority, gave his orders, and made sure they were followed.

Every day, Abulurd watched crowds rush across the spaceport to clamber into any available ship, packing the cargo decks and passenger cabins with far more people than they had ever been designed to hold. He saw the panic on their faces and knew that he couldn't sleep until it was all over. He found himself taking regular doses of melange—not to protect himself from the Scourge anymore, but to give himself the energy to keep moving.

He looked up into the sky as ship after ship departed from Zimia Spaceport. Many of the captains would return for more passengers; others, fearing the imminent arrival of the Omnius fleet, would simply stay away, leaving Abulurd fewer and fewer options to rescue the populace.

The lifeboat vessels and a few remaining quarantine craft had already been taken out of the system to an isolated rendezvous point. There, far from any signaling devices, they hoped to remain hidden from the incoming robot battle fleet.

Faykan handled the massive administrative details, constantly accompanied by his pallid niece, who had stayed with him ever since arriving here from Parmentier. Even in the midst of the frantic evacuation, though, ghostly Rayna Butler seemed to have her own agenda. She spoke clearly and forcefully in front of any audience that would listen, and since she had come through the Scourge, many League citizens paid close attention to what she had to say. The girl had an eerie voice that could carry over great distances. To the crowds, Rayna declared her passionate mission: the destruction of all thinking machines. "With God and Serena Butler on our side, we cannot lose."

Hearing that, Abulurd thought, they had nothing to fear. He wished he could inspire Faykan and Rayna to incite the mobs into *helping* or into building something, instead of simply proclaiming their rigid beliefs and wreaking havoc.

There was no feasible means to impose order upon the frenzied exodus. Within two weeks, everyone who wanted to leave and who had access to a ship had departed, but many of the vessels did not have much range or adequate supplies to keep the passengers safe for the duration of the emergency, since no one knew exactly when Omnius's battle fleet would arrive.

A completely separate effort involved digging in and hoping for the best. Engineering crews from the Army of the Jihad excavated giant underground shelters, reinforced them with alloy mesh and support girders, and filled them with stockpiles of supplies. Those who did not make it off the planet in time would be rushed into the underground warrens, where they would take shelter from the initial bombardment by the extermination fleet.

Based on previous experience, the thinking-machine army would attack and then likely retreat. If, however, the robots decided to obliterate all vestiges of the League capital and establish a new Omnius network here, then the survivors would be trapped underground with little likelihood of survival. Even so, they had no other choice.

Many people whose families had lived for generations on Salusa did not want to leave. They chose to remain here and take their chances against the invading machines, though Abulurd thought they would change their minds as soon as they saw the incoming robotic warships.

The task seemed impossible, hopeless. But Abulurd would do no less than his utmost. Vorian Atreides had entrusted him with this task—that was all the incentive Abulurd needed.

Evacuation ships continued to depart from Zimia Spaceport and other landing pads across Salusa. At first, teams of monitors attempted to keep records of who had escaped, where they had gone, and who still needed to be rescued. But the overwhelming numbers quickly crushed the effort. Abulurd and his comrades spent their days simply getting people off-planet. If they survived, they could sort it all out later.

If the Great Purge worked perfectly and all incarnations of the Omnius evermind were destroyed, Abulurd's father, Supreme Commander Atreides, and whatever remained of the space-folding Jihad fleet would return here for a final stand against the now-leaderless robotic extermination force.

For now, as a last tenuous line of defense, the few League warships without Holtzman engines remained in orbit, a pathetic defensive cordon around the world. All of the jihadi soldiers who had stayed behind knew they would die here. They had seen the size of the fleet Omnius had launched against them.

But Abulurd would not give up—not yet. Out there somewhere, Vorian Atreides and Quentin Butler were leading the Purge. Day after day, world after world.

He watched more ships streak to the skies. Each one of those vessels contained a handful of human survivors that would likely escape Omnius's wrath. It would have to be good enough. Somehow, together, they would wrest a victory from this moment of hopelessness.

The human imagination is infinite. Not even the most sophisticated machines can understand this.

—NORMA CENVA,
thoughts recorded and deciphered by Adrien Cenva

A t the edge of a trance but not quite there, Norma chewed two more melange capsules. The essence of spice filled her mouth and nostrils, made her eyes water. Then, in her mind, she traveled far from Kolhar. . . .

The Great Purge continued across the Synchronized Worlds. She knew that bombing raids were obliterating the fringe Omnius incarnations in lightning ambushes. Machine-dominated planets were dying, strike after strike, before the rest of the everminds knew what was happening.

Her space-folding technology made it possible.

But instead of complete pride, Norma sensed a deep disturbance in her psyche. Strange echoes of disaster tumbled through her spice-induced visions, and she felt terrible guilt.

Since she had never adequately solved the spacefolder navigation problem, many soldiers were losing their lives. Each time the battle groups jumped from one target to the next, their numbers were decimated. And decimated again before they reached the next target. Oh, the incredible cost!

In her perfect, beautiful body, looking like an avenging angel, Norma stood alone on one of the vast, flat rooftops of the spacefolder assembly plant. She gazed up at a night sky filled with glistening stars and bright planets. Some of them were League Worlds, others dominated by thinking machines . . . still others were now radioactive cinders, completely dead.

The vast distances called to her. A cool breeze blew her long blond hair behind her. Norma had figured out a way to bridge the entire galaxy, folding the fabric of space. Every star system she could see, and more, now lay within the range of human exploration. The Holtzman engines worked, as she'd known they would. But an elusive something lay beyond her grasp.

My ships are still flawed.

With her body so saturated with melange, she rarely slept anymore, not the way she had as a small child in the warm caves on Rossak. In those days, she'd gone to bed with few problems on her mind, even though her mother rarely paid any attention to her. To compensate for Zufa's disapproval, the girl had retreated into other realms, dabbling with mathematics so esoteric that they approached the realm between physics and philosophy.

With help and encouragement from Aurelius, important ideas had begun to trickle into Norma's hungry, receptive brain, like the first droplets of water in an eventual ocean. By the time she was seven years old, as the reservoir of her intellect filled, she always went to bed with her mind brimming with problems or challenging mental exercises; many solutions danced closer in the half-waking fugue state just before sleep took her, and she rarely woke up without having considered them in detail.

Now, somewhere behind her, she heard the whine of a Holtzman engine as workers tested it inside one of the buildings. As she focused on the sound, it grew more distant. Pulsing through her tissues, the massive dose of melange soothed her, muffling sensory perceptions while heightening other abilities. Gradually the distracting sound faded entirely, and she no longer felt the cool breeze, either. She seemed to drift upward in her thoughts, into the starfield.

Out there, ship after ship in the Jihad fleet folded space and plunged across dimensions from one Synchronized World to the next. Now, in her mind, she heard another crew vanish and die, their souls torn apart—because she could not help them find their way. She wished the Supreme Commander had been able to install her forbidden computer systems in more than his twelve primary ships. If a computer was designed to assist in the destruction of Omnius, was it still inherently evil?

Or perhaps she should have designed paths for them, made the fleet's jumps shorter, across more predictable lines of space. It would be like a sprint, covering safe distances in a flash, and then moving more slowly across uncharted jumps. But such caution would cost a great deal of time. Time! The Army of the Jihad did not have that commodity.

Her vision remained vivid, letting her see the nuclear storms dropped by the League ships, hurricanes of pulse-atomics that devastated the Omnius enclaves. . . . Human captives cheered at first and then saw that they too were doomed.

Another machine world gone, another Omnius erased. But with each transit through folded space, fewer and fewer of the Jihad ships survived.

Emerging from her daze, Norma realized that the expansive rooftop was bathed in artificial light from blazing glowglobes. Adrien was nearby, watching her, looking worried. She wondered how long he had been there. The sounds of manufacturing and testing suddenly came sharp and loud across the shipyard.

"So many casualties." Her throat was dry and raspy. "They can't see where the spacefolders will take them, and so they are lost. Too many brave fighters for the Jihad, too many innocent prisoners on the Synchronized Worlds. My ships. My failure."

Adrien looked at her with dark eyes full of stoic resignation. "It is another price of this long and bloody war, Mother. When the Jihad is finally over, we can get back to business."

Still, all through the night, she heard the screams of the dying as they echoed through—and between—space.

The way of the warrior, moment by moment, is the practice of death.

—SWORDMASTER ISTIAN GOSS

Under the plan that Vor had established with Primero Quentin Butler before departing from Salusa Secundus, fast messengers were dispatched from each battle group after every engagement at a Synchronized World. Due to the known attrition with each space-folding jump, the Army of the Jihad did not dare risk sending all the components of their fleet to a single meeting; however, Martyrist volunteers in space-folder scouts were considered expendable.

Flurries of the small ships bearing news and records converged at established rendezvous points, placing their detailed logs in buoys, which were retrieved, copied, and disseminated by the scouts from other battle groups, keeping the commanders apprised of the progress and losses. Vorian Atreides had modeled the system on Omnius's pattern of dispatching update ships throughout the Synchronized empire to keep the everminds current. He found the irony satisfying.

As technicians tallied the information, the blanks were filling in, each report of success a small victory, an indication of survival, a reason to hope. But there were other reports as well. One hundred eighty-four ships lost . . . two hundred seventeen . . . two hundred thirty-five . . . two hundred seventy-nine. Each space-folding flight in the nuclear blitzkrieg was a terrible, unpredictable game of Russian roulette: a lightning strike if it went well, but lightning-swift death if it did not.

For a moment, Vor allowed himself to mourn one of the lost ships, the LS *Zimia*, and its captain, a fine soldier and a great drinking buddy. They had shared many tall tales of battles and women, in numerous spaceports across the League. Other faces and personalities whirled through his mind, all dead heroes, but for the sake of the mission he had to set such thoughts aside.

He thought of young Abulurd back on Salusa, safe from this ordeal, yet facing a threat of his own that was just as terrible. He and Faykan had to evacuate an entire population.

Cursing under his breath, Vor wondered how many more jumps his fleet could survive. He could estimate the number using only the statistics—but that was how a machine would analyze their chances. Nothing about war was perfectly predictable. When the Great Purge was all over, how many ships would remain? Would he himself make it? Norma Cenva's augmented navigation device gave him a better chance than most, but would it be enough? Already his fleet had left a graveyard of space trash in its wake.

And once they had finished crushing the undefended Synchronized Worlds, and then Corrin, the remnants of the Jihad fleet would need to race back to Salusa. There, they would make a stand against the oncoming thinking-machine battleships, which were still programmed to attack, even if the evermind was erased. The Jihad battle fleet would cause as much damage as possible, die in flames, and hope to deflect the machines' attack.

He and all of his fighters expected to die before this engagement was over. But he would sacrifice himself with the satisfaction of knowing he had defeated the computer evermind at last. Maybe he would even be with Leronica again in Heaven, if the Martyrists were correct in their religious beliefs. . . .

Vor shook his head, staring at the newly updated tactical projection on the bridge of the LS *Serena Victory*. Out there, in the vast but silent battleground of empty space, he knew the strikes continued, and continued. By now, more than three-quarters of the five hundred and forty-three Synchronized Worlds should have been slagged.

As each group of fast messengers brought back summaries from the ninety battle groups, Vor updated the picture of their progress across enemy territory. In scanning the scattered reports, he saw that some Synchronized Worlds had put up heavier-than-expected resistance, drawing upon leftover ground-based systems. Five of the Jihad Purge groups had failed at specific targets, which would necessitate a second offensive to the same coordinates. In another instance, due to the quirks of space-folding travel, four of the remaining ships in a battle group had vanished in a single jump; only two of the foot messengers had survived to deliver their fateful reports.

We will have to make up for it.

"My battle group will do it," Quentin Butler transmitted. His voice sounded bleak, as if he no longer cared whether or not he survived. "If you give me two of your ships, Supreme Commander, we'll go back and finish mopping up the targets that were missed."

Quentin's flagship had survived one of the disastrous passages. Already down to only six capital ships in his battle group, he had then lost three of them in a single space-folding jump to a Synchronized target. He had seen the robots' defensive emplacements there, calculated the odds, and realized he could not succeed in destroying Omnius. Disappointed, he had rallied his three surviving ballistas and gone to rendezvous with Vorian at the Supreme Commander's projected location. They pooled their ships, sterilized another Synchronized World together, and then paused to assess their situation. Quentin was anxious to be on the attack again.

"Very well, Primero. Go with my blessing. We can't leave a single enemy world intact."

Verified estimates indicated that over a billion human slaves and trustees had already died in the Great Purge—people toiling under horrendous conditions, beaten down by the depraved thinking machines. Those sacrifices had been disquieting, but entirely necessary. And even more were bound to die.

The first planetary systems annihilated in League nuclear attacks had all been lesser machine worlds, primarily military strongholds and resupply points for Omnius forces. Now, with the remainder of his battle group, Vor would go after the more important Synchronized Worlds, eventually making a final assault on Corrin. Then it would all be over.

After Quentin departed, Vor's re-formed group made its next leap. Space folded around his attack force in what would either be an embrace or a strangulation. He would know in a few moments. . . .

As his warships came within range of the immense planet Quadra with its silvery moons, he dispersed the vessels and approached in a crescent formation, with the LS *Serena Victory* on one wing, then deployed his first squadrons of bombers. Scanners picked up incoming missiles, and Vor ordered the Holtzman shields up.

Though the Great Purge had been under way for weeks already, no slow-flying robot ship could have traveled to other Synchronized Worlds swiftly enough to deliver a warning. But the Quadra-Omnius had automatic defensive systems in place, which responded to the arrival of the Jihad fleet.

The robot missiles struck the Holtzman shields and deflected off their targets to spin harmlessly away into space. Before the local evermind could launch a second volley, Vor ordered his ships to shoot back through their pulsing flicker-and-fire shield systems, choosing some of their targeted multiple-blast atomic warheads. Moments later ten artificial moons crackled with the impacts, cascading silvery fireworks into the vacuum of orbital space. He could already see that this battle would take hours, maybe even days. . . .

After pounding the artificial battle moons, still unable to break through to the ground defenses and Omnius strongholds on Quadra, Vor stepped back with surprise as his bridge screen shuddered with static. His communications officer said, "We're being contacted by people below, Supreme Commander—a transmission from humans. They must have seized a com-network down there."

The screen filled with a sequence of images, an overview of the continents and cities below. Vor observed close-up images, apparently from surveillance watcheyes in one of Quadra's cities. He knew what he had to do. "We can't save them. Continue with full warhead deployment, per our plans."

One of the Martyrist volunteers manning the flagship's scan station nodded. "They will be accepted into Paradise if they give up their lives for the Holy Jihad."

"After today, Paradise is going to be a very crowded place," Vor muttered as he stared at the screen.

UP IN THE smoke-filled skies of Quadra, silvery moons hung low over the Synchronized metropolis. The robots marching through the streets paid no attention to the looming battle moons, but the enslaved humans felt the overbearing observation. Even with all the robotic warships withdrawn and sent to Corrin for the final assault on the League, the threat remained in place.

But some of the slaves had made whispered plans, always hoping. . . .

When dazzling sparks and flashes unexpectedly erupted on the artificial satellites, humans in the streets of Quadra City turned to stare. Many flicked their glances up to the sky, then nervously returned their attention to assigned tasks, refusing to believe.

The man named Borys, though—a former swordmaster of Ginaz captured twenty-one years ago at a skirmish on Ularda—knew exactly what must be happening. His hope swelled, and he dropped his tools on the hot open-air packaging line where he was forced to labor. He shouted, knowing he dared not hesitate. "This is what we have been waiting for! Our rescuers have come. We must throw off our chains and fight with the liberators before it's too late."

Gasps and mutters rippled like a shock wave through the work gangs. Borys immediately grabbed one of his heavy tools and jammed it into the whirring machinery that moved the production line. Sparks flew and smoke poured out. The complex system ground to a halt with a shriek that sounded like machines in pain.

Around him, sentinel robots and combat models paused, receiving urgent new instructions from the Quadra-Omnius. Borys did not think his meager disturbance had caught the notice of the evermind: Something up in orbit consumed all of the giant computer's attention.

Over the years of his captivity, Borys's fellow mercenaries captured with him at Ularda had been slain, some for good causes, others pointlessly. Borys was the last of his team, and he had grander hopes. Now, as he rallied the people working in the streets, he understood this was their only chance.

Borys had never stopped spreading his plans among the cowed humans, gauging the other prisoners. As a swordmaster who followed the teachings of Jool Noret, he had been bred to fight, trained in combat techniques by the sensei mek Chirox. Borys knew his abilities and his limitations. He had carefully culled out those willing to fight for their freedom, separating them from the captives too fearful to risk harm. By now, his handpicked lieutenants were dispersed across Quadra.

A burst of communication crackled through the speakers on the packaging line. Normally, robots used the system to disseminate harsh commands to their captive workers, but now a human voice broke across the speakers. "It's the Army of the Jihad! Ballistas, javelins, fast-attack fighters!" Borys recognized one of his commandos stationed aboard an artificial moon. "They appeared out of nowhere . . . amazing firepower. One of the battle moons is already damaged and offline."

In the sky, Borys saw furious flashes of light, like sparks spraying from a grinding wheel. The firepower was concentrated on one of the silvery spheres in low orbit. As the intensity increased, Borys drew a quick breath, seeing the artificial satellite crack open with a dazzling explosion. Pieces of debris spread apart like fragments from an eggshell. The flash dissipated, and the destroyed portions screamed down through the atmosphere, trailing fire as they burned up on reentry.

Seeing this destruction as a clear sign of imminent victory, the hesitant workers now had the impetus to throw in their lot with Borys's insurrection. Casting aside their fear, people began to run loose, cheering their impending liberation and wreaking all the mayhem possible.

The chaos and unpredictability made it impossible for the sentinel robots to respond effectively, so the thinking machines retaliated using violence and superior firepower. While the intense battle continued overhead, sentinel robots pursued the unprepared slaves in the streets of Quadra, firing into the crowds. The bloodshed and screams were terrible.

But the desperate people fought back with no thought for their own survival, and Borys allowed himself a wash of pride. He had spent years preparing them for this. Many of the slaves had considered it only a fantasy, an exercise, but now it had come to pass. They had hope again.

"We must hold fast! The League ships will be here soon—we've got to open the way for them."

As a swordmaster, Borys could fashion weapons out of anything. He used metal clubs and electrical discharges. He wrecked automated machinery, found ways to overload generators. Within an hour he had destroyed many thinking machines and worked with a team to blow up a secondary command center. But even as the Quadra-Omnius concentrated meager defenses against the Jihad fleet in space, more robots closed in from around the city. There were many of the deadly machines, and they were too well armed for the oppressed slaves to defeat with only bare hands and primitive weapons.

Borys did not allow himself the luxury of dismay. He continued to hope that the humans would soon descend to the surface, bringing reinforcements. More and more of the slaves, even a handful of the pampered trustees who had sided with Omnius, joined the battle, and fought for their freedom at last.

When he finally reached a functioning communication system, Borys transmitted their need to any League commander, begging for rescue. Jihad kindjals and shielded bombers swept down like a group of eagles. Seeing them, the surviving slaves cheered, and Borys raised his fist into the air.

Then the pulse atomics began to flash, starting from the far horizon. Intense white light swept like sheet lightning across the sky. Waves of incinerating nuclear energy rushed over the machine city, a dazzling glare from round after round of annihilating nuclear bursts.

Borys let his makeshift weapon clatter to the ground and turned his face upward. Now he understood why no one aboard the armada had responded to his calls. "They didn't come here to rescue us after all." He drew a deep breath of resignation as the Army of the Jihad swarmed in. The League had come to destroy Omnius, not to save a handful of human captives. "We're just collateral damage."

But he comprehended what the League was doing, and he took a small measure of pride in realizing that he had a chance to die in the fight—perhaps the last great battle of this horrific war. Before, Borys had been unable to think of a suitable way for him to give his life. If the armada above succeeded, then the machines would be destroyed. "Fight well, and may your enemies fall quickly," he muttered to himself.

The fast-burning kindjals and bombers tore through the atmosphere. The intense flashes were oddly silent. The tidal wave of disintegrating force crashed over Borys, all humans, and all robots long before they ever had a chance to hear it coming.

THE FLAGSHIP BATTLE group folded space again to the next system. This time, thankfully, Vor lost no more capital ships. According to information retrieved by the last round of messengers, fewer than three hundred Jihad ballistas and javelins remained out of more than a thousand.

Vor checked activity on the surface of the Synchronized World below, his next target, nothing more than a name and a set of coordinates. *That is how I must think of it.* A target, a necessary victory. Even if the enslaved populations down there cheered him, he still had to give the order to unleash their pulse-atomics. Complete sterilization on every single Synchronized World. After convincing himself that this was necessary, he had stopped thinking about it. He hardened his heart and his will because he had no other choice.

He hopscotched methodically through folded space, hitting more enemy worlds, and losing two additional ships in the process. Simultaneously, his bomber squadrons made their attacks. The increasingly furious warriors of the Jihad traveled from stronghold to stronghold, closing in on the central machine world of Corrin. All but one of the remaining everminds were erased. With each successful mission, the Jihad fleet left devastated worlds in their wake, devoid of life, whether machine or human.

Finally he met the rest of his fleet, as planned, and counted survivors. Down to two hundred sixty-six ships now. He combined them into a single battle group commanded by himself and Quentin Butler as his second. With his powerful sense of resolve, he had no time for sadness or tears— not yet. Vor would achieve victory, no matter the cost. There could be no regrets, no looking back.

They dared not stop now. The monstrous machine fleet was on its way to Salusa Secundus. Without pausing to consult his conscience, Vor gathered his ships and prepared them for the next jump.

Toward Corrin.

No two human brains are identical. This is a difficult concept for the thinking machine to grasp.

—ERASMUS,
Reflections on Sentient Biologicals

With engines hot and using the last scraps of fuel for violent deceleration, the first cluster of the fastest robotic warships returned from their intended assault on Salusa Secundus. The extermination mission had been scrapped, their priorities shifted by a direct command from Omnius Prime. The group of robot warships would serve as an initial layer of defense against the *hrethgir* Great Purge. Every projection gave similar results. The atomic-laden human ships were sure to arrive soon.

After receiving the startling news from Vidad, Omnius had dispatched ten "burnout" ships, superfast vessels with enormous engines to bring the extermination fleet running back to Corrin. League ships were en route. It was possible—probable?—that the rest of the Synchronized empire had already been destroyed.

The burnout ships expended all of their fuel in constant acceleration, roaring out of the system at ever-increasing velocities, saving no power for a return trip or even for deceleration. The urgent messengers overtook the bulk of the Omnius fleet in five days, but they could not slow to intercept or dock. Instead, the robotic vessels streaked past on their headlong course, transmitting the evermind's commands and reprogramming the fleet ships.

The machine battle fleet spread out as each vessel maneuvered to turn around. Those ships capable of greatest speed were given priority and dispatched first on a frantic return to form a protective cordon around the primary Synchronized World. The fastest machine ships pushed their systems so furiously that many of the robotic vessels were overloaded or damaged by the time they limped into orbit at Corrin. The larger and slower robotic ships would come afterward, as quickly as possible.

Meanwhile, Omnius modified all of his groundside industries to produce weaponry and robotic fighters. Within days, he had established the beginnings of a defense. The next group of robot battle vessels trickled in from the fleet—accompanied by an update ship captain carrying a complete Omnius update sphere from one of the obliterated worlds.

Months ago, after escaping from his long captivity with Agamemnon, Seurat had been reassigned to his old duties, which he performed quite proficiently. Now he had barely escaped from a nearby Synchronized World, one of the first targets in the Great Purge. He brought direct confirmation to Omnius Prime that a Jihad battle group had appeared in space, out of nowhere, attacked with an overwhelming spread of pulse-atomic warheads, and then disappeared again, as if going in and out of a hole in the fabric of spacetime.

Exactly as the Ivory Tower Cogitor had warned. After delivering his information, Vidad had considered his obligations ended. While the thinking machines went into turmoil on Corrin, reacting to the news, the Cogitor and his lone human companion had departed immediately, launching off through space on a leisurely return to Salusa. Omnius did not try to stop them; henceforth, the Ivory Tower Cogitor was irrelevant.

When he learned of Seurat's arrival, Erasmus immediately decided to visit the update ship and confront its captain.

"I'd like to go with you, Father," Gilbertus said, leaving the placid Serena clone among the flowers in the garden.

"Your insights are always valuable."

A levtrain whisked them across the city to the spaceport, where a sleek white-and-black update ship rested on a new section of tarmac, not far from the gleaming metal terminal building. When he met with the captain, Erasmus interfaced with the robot, an autonomous unit like himself. He studied Seurat's mental records, and interesting facts began to surface as he dove deeper.

The robot pilot had just received a new update copy and had prepared to depart the Synchronized system when an enemy blitzkrieg fleet surged in from nowhere, annihilated the Omnius incarnation, and then vanished into the cosmos in a flash, undoubtedly to execute even more attacks. Afterward, Seurat had raced to Corrin with all possible speed, almost exhausting his vessel's engine capabilities along the way.

Erasmus withdrew from the connection to process the startling news. He turned to Gilbertus. "The actions of the Jihad forces are most unexpected. They are killing millions and millions of humans on the Synchronized Worlds."

"I can't believe humans would knowingly choose to slaughter so many of their own kind," Gilbertus said.

"My Mentat, they have always done so. This time, though, they are destroying thinking machines as well."

"I'm ashamed to be a member of the species."

"They are doing everything necessary to exterminate us," Erasmus said, "no matter the cost."

"You and I are unique, Father. We are free of the unwanted influence of both machine and human."

"We are never free of our surroundings or our internal makeup. In my case it is programming and acquired data; in yours it is genetics and life experiences." As he spoke, Erasmus noticed a pair of glittering Omnius watcheyes floating in the air, accumulating and transmitting data. "Both of our futures hang on the results of this immense war. Many things influence our behavior and circumstances, whether we are aware of them or not."

"I do not wish to die as a victim of their hatred of thinking machines," Gilbertus said. "And I do not want you to die either."

To Erasmus, his surrogate son appeared genuinely sad and completely loyal. But decades ago, Vorian Atreides had seemed that way as well. He shifted his focus and placed a heavy metal arm around Gilbertus's shoulders, simulating an affectionate gesture.

"Enough of our fleet will return in time to protect us," he said to reassure his human ward, though he had no data to support his assertion. The thinking machines would have to dig in here at Corrin, establishing a stronghold behind such an impenetrable barrier that no humans could touch them.

"That is required," Omnius said, eavesdropping. "I may already be the last incarnation of the evermind."

If I were given the opportunity to write my own epitaph, there is a great deal I would not say, much I would never admit. "He had the heart of a warrior." That is the best memorial I could hope for.

—SUPREME COMMANDER VORIAN ATREIDES,

to a biographer

In the blackness of deep space, the remnants of the Jihad space-folding fleet drifted in loose formation while the crews worked feverishly to ready their warships for the final assault on Corrin. Repairs were made, warheads primed, Holtzman shields and engines tuned for the last battle.

"Within hours, we will eradicate the last Omnius," Supreme Commander Atreides transmitted over the ship-to-ship comline. "Within hours, the human race will be free for the first time in over a thousand years."

Listening to the speech from the bridge of his own ballista, Primero Quentin Butler nodded. All around him in space, spangled with the faint illumination of distant stars, the surviving spacefolders gave off a comforting glow from their interior lights and green collision-avoidance sensors. He heard a steady stream of chatter over the comlines, continuing transmissions on the progress of preparations, and reports from the ever-alert guards at every perimeter. The Martyrists offered hymns of thanksgiving and prayers for vengeance.

Almost over now. Corrin should be completely undefended, the robotic extermination fleet weeks away.

Quentin's heart felt like a dead cinder, charred by the white-hot knowledge that he had just killed billions of innocent human slaves held prisoner by Omnius, but he struggled not to allow those horrific thoughts to penetrate his consciousness. In his darkest moments, Quentin could only draw inspiration from what Supreme Commander Atreides had said of the harsh decision he had forced upon the Army of the Jihad: Although they had already inflicted a terrible toll, vastly more humans would die if they didn't steel themselves to follow through and accept the responsibility for what they must do.

A complete victory against the thinking machines, no matter the cost.

Quentin hated just to sit here on his battered ship. He needed to get moving again, to finish this terrible task. If they stopped too long, they would all start thinking too much. . . .

Corrin, the primary Synchronized World—the *last* Synchronized World—held greater importance than all the others. And now that it was the only remaining bastion of the evermind, the stakes here were highest, the danger greater than ever. If any portion of the huge assault fleet had remained behind to protect Omnius Prime, the thinking machines would devote all their resources to preserving and defending their very existence. With the ships of the Great Purge already battered, their numbers diminished, this would certainly be the most deadly battle of all.

And if Omnius managed to preserve a copy of itself before the atomic destruction, if an update captain like Seurat escaped with a gelsphere of the evermind, then everything would be lost. The thinking machines would be able to propagate again.

Vorian Atreides had proposed an innovative solution. Among the weapons the Army of the Jihad carried were pulse-scrambler transmitters, which could be installed in thousands of satellites. Before the remnants of the human fleet engaged the enemy at Corrin, they would spread the Holtzman satellites in a net around the machine planet, effectively trapping the evermind. . . .

Now, before the final push, Quentin watched his officers and noncom technicians go about their duties, looking harried and rushed. His temporary adjutant stood nearby, young and eager, ready to relay his superior's commands or perform key tasks, so that Quentin could focus on the upcoming conflict—would it truly be the final battle?

He had known nothing but the Jihad for as long as he could remember. He'd become a war hero early in his career, married a Butler, and fathered three sons who also served in the struggle against the thinking machines. His entire life had been dedicated to this one unrelenting struggle. Although by now, he didn't see how he could ever recover from his soul-deep fatigue, he just wanted this war to be over. He felt like the mythical Sisyphus, condemned to a hellish, impossible task for the balance of eternity. Perhaps if he ever returned to Salusa—if Salusa survived this battle—he would become a recluse in the City of Introspection and finish out his days sitting next to Wandra, staring sightlessly into the air. . . .

But this was wartime, and Quentin forced himself to rise above such self-indulgent thoughts. They weakened him emotionally and physically. As the liberator of Parmentier, defender of Ix, he was admired by countless jihadis and mercenaries. No matter how tired he felt, no matter how despondent, the primero could never show it.

Thus far, the nuclear bombardment campaign was a success, but the victories had come at tremendous cost. After so many successive space-folding jumps, the entire fleet was less than a quarter of its original strength. Many of his best and brightest fighters, some of them longtime friends, were dead. And so many innocents had been slaughtered on the Synchronized Worlds, disintegrated in an atomic haze.

Quentin felt the twin weights of responsibility and survivor's guilt, when so many were gone. One day, when he had time, there would be letters to write and family members to visit . . . if he himself survived.

A number of ships in the final assault group had been damaged in battle and repaired sufficiently to function as warhead-delivery vessels, though without important offensive or defensive capabilities. The artillery banks on some were ruined; others had inoperable Holtzman shields. A dozen ships could still fold space, but had no offensive capabilities at all. They could only be used in rescue operations or, to a limited extent, as filler vessels that made the Army of the Jihad force look larger than it really was.

Every scrap had its part to play.

Across the comline, Quentin's bright-eyed adjutant broadcast last-minute instructions to every remaining ship in the battle group. When Quentin acknowledged his readiness, Supreme Commander Atreides coordinated the space-folding launch for the final offensive against Omnius.

"Set course for Corrin!"

In response, the officers and troops cheered, a great roar that filled the speaker system and sent chills down Quentin's spine. Decades of warfare had led up to this point. Every technical skill the fighters had learned in battle, every instinct, would be needed if the Army of the Jihad was going to succeed.

Space folded.

Then, like fish leaping above the surface of an ocean, the battered human fleet emerged from space. Beyond the large ball of Corrin, Quentin saw a ruddy sun casting bloodred rays, as if in anticipation of the human lives that would be lost here today.

ENEMY VESSELS BEGAN popping out of space, appearing from nowhere. More than two hundred vessels, all bearing the marks of the Army of the Jihad. "They have come to eliminate us, Gilbertus," the robot said.

"Our defenses will hold," the evermind insisted, booming from a wallscreen. "I have run simulations and calculations."

Piece by piece, the first waves of returning thinking-machine ships had taken up defensive positions around Corrin, forming a series of formidable rings and traps. However, the bulk of the robot assault fleet was still on its way. The ships currently in position did not appear to be sufficient to hold off the human fanatics. Erasmus stared at the *hrethgir* attackers bearing down on Corrin, knowing their cargo holds were full of pulse-atomic weaponry.

Once again, Omnius had clearly underestimated the human enemies. Erasmus could also see that the rapidly assembled machine defenses and the first handful of returned robot battleships were not sufficient to stand against this force.

Statistically speaking, the *hrethgir* might actually win.

AS THE FIRST tactical reports came in, Quentin stepped closer to the projections. "Their defenses are stronger than we expected. What are all those battleships doing here? I thought the extermination fleet departed for Salusa weeks ago. Did they leave a guardian force behind?"

"It's possible. Or the Corrin-Omnius might have been warned," Vorian Atreides spoke across the comline. "But we can still break through—if we throw everything into this last push. It'll just be tougher than the victories we've had so far."

Quentin counted his own ships. Thankfully, no more had been lost in the latest jump from their rendezvous point in deep space, which gave him a modicum of encouragement.

"First, we deploy the net of scrambler satellites. Our primary objective is to keep Omnius from escaping." Vorian sent orders for the Jihad vessels to send out their swiftly constructed defensive buoys, each one equipped with a pulse generator. Orbital scientists had planned the most efficient grid, a tight web of destruction that would sew up a barrier impenetrable to the gelcircuitry minds of thinking machines. It was the reverse concept of Tio Holtzman's energy shields, which League Worlds normally used to keep the machines out.

The robotic ships did not move forward to engage the Jihad vessels, maintaining their tight positions in close orbit, as if daring the humans to approach. The scrambler satellites scattered all around Corrin, like seeds in space moving into position.

"That'll take care of them," Vor said. "Prepare to activate the scrambler web on my command—"

On Quentin's bridge, the first officer yelled from her observation station, "More incoming enemy ships, sir! A lot of them!"

"By God and Saint Serena, look at them all!" cried one of the Martyrist volunteers. "The extermination fleet has come back."

"That's a hundred times our firepower," another said. "We don't have enough ships left to fight them!"

Quentin turned away from the small group of robot ships clustered around Corrin itself. More of the immense machine fleet came around Corrin, with the bloated sun behind them. Though this still wasn't the number of ships he and Faykan had seen on their recon expedition, the military craft kept coming, kept filling more and more of the starfield. Their engines were hot, and the battle fleet was spread out and disorganized, as if they had rushed pell-mell back to the system.

Quentin stared, trying to assess the sheer numbers of returning machine vessels. "Activate Holtzman shields. Damn! They're too close— and we're much too inaccurate—to fold space past them."

From his flagship, Supreme Commander Atreides transmitted, "They knew we were coming. Somehow. The Corrin-Omnius called them back to save himself before we could get here."

The enormous robot ships clustered closer and closer together, in a formidable reinforced cordon to shield the last Omnius. It was clearly an act of desperation, and the evermind seemed to understand the stakes. But with the League fleet at one-quarter strength, having already been hit hard, Quentin concluded—much as he hated to do so—that they did not have enough firepower to blast their way through.

Even so, he drew a deep breath and transmitted to the flagship, "We've come too far to give up now. Should I give the order to engage? Perhaps enough of us will break through to drop our pulse-atomics before they get organized."

Vor hesitated just a moment. "A useless gesture at this point, Primero. None of your ships could penetrate the atmosphere and release nuclear payloads. I won't waste lives."

"We are volunteering, Supreme Commander. It's our last chance."

"No, stand off. Do not engage."

Quentin couldn't believe what he was hearing. "At least let us activate the scrambler satellites we just deployed. Then they won't be able to add reinforcements."

"On the contrary, Primero, I *want* them all to congregate at Corrin. Keep the scrambler net inactive, for now." His voice carried a self-satisfied lilt. "I have an idea."

From the planet below, robotic defenders shot upward, powering their weapons, prepared to stand as a suicidal barrier if the League force should press forward. Shooting around the red-giant sun and careening into the inner system, the main machine battle fleet kept massing like locusts over Corrin. Returning enemy warships swept in, taking up positions in low orbit, forming an impenetrable barricade.

Now Quentin understood. "Ah, so you are letting the thinking machines stick their own heads in the noose."

"We may as well let them do our work for us, Primero."

Wave after wave of returning machine ships formed defensive layers above Corrin. Quentin knew the survivors of the Great Purge could not have fought them. No possible defense of Salusa could have withstood such an enemy, but at least they had returned here. He watched as the final stragglers appeared, forming an impregnable defense of the last remaining Synchronized World.

"All right," Supreme Commander Atreides said. "*Now* activate the scrambler web." He sounded as if he was smiling.

Above Corrin, the small Holtzman satellites switched on, creating a lethal net all around the planet. Any robotic ship passing through the energy grid would be erased. It was a line no gelcircuitry brain could cross.

"We didn't destroy them," Vor said, "but all the remaining thinking machines are now neatly bottled up at Corrin. Those scrambler satellites will keep them from causing trouble for the time being."

"Looks like a standoff," Quentin said, as scanner reports came in. His voice sounded infinitely weary and disappointed. "They're cornered like rats."

Vor assessed the situation and knew the odds. "Now we need nearly all of our remaining ships to stay here and make sure the machines can't go anywhere else—until we find a way to finish them off." He pondered the next step, knowing that the thinking machines were reinforcing their defenses every second he delayed. But the scrambler satellites would hold them. Finally, Vor shook his head.

"Now that we have the last Omnius bottled up, we must maintain our force at Corrin and bring back as many other vessels as we can possibly throw at this planet—faster than Omnius can manufacture reinforcements. Corrin is the last stand, both for thinking machines and for humanity." He clenched a fist, hammered it down on the arm of his command chair. "Primero Butler, shuttle over to my flagship. You and I will return to Zimia to deliver our report."

"Yes, Supreme Commander." Quentin's back was bowed, his shoulders slumped with the weight of defeat. They had sacrificed so many lives, worked so hard . . . suddenly he drew a quick breath as the realization flooded him. This standoff did imply a victory of a sort. To cheer his soldiers, he spoke over the general comline. "Think of it, men—look out there and see the entire terrible fleet. The *whole* robotic fleet! By forcing Omnius to recall those ships, we have saved the lives of everyone on Salusa Secundus."

"I would rather have destroyed the thinking machines," his first officer murmured, slamming her fist on a chair back, obviously as frustrated as he was to leave the job undone.

"There is still time for that," Quentin said. "We will find a way. Prepare to withdraw to a safe distance, but maintain full containment posture."

Victory. Defeat. These are impostors, illusions. Fight fearlessly toward your own death, and this life cannot count you among its horde of slaves.

—SWORDMASTER ISTIAN GOSS

The bulk of the battered space-folding fleet, still loaded with their remaining pulse-atomics, stayed behind at Corrin to keep the thinking machines at bay. Day after day, they sought even the smallest opening. Thanks to the dense net of scrambler satellites, the forces were at a standoff, for the time being, but the equilibrium was unstable.

Vorian Atreides and Quentin Butler rushed to Salusa Secundus. Back at the capital world, the Supreme Commander cobbled together another group of League battleships, drawing away the last-stand defenses in orbit over Salusa even as evacuees began to return. He called for the last great vessels, even those not equipped with space-folding engines, to launch for Corrin without delay. "I need every javelin and ballista. *Every* ship."

"That would leave us all undefended!" cried the Interim Viceroy, who had been one of the first to flee Salusa, and one of the first to return as soon as the planet was no longer considered to be in danger. "Is that militarily—or politically—wise?"

"At the moment, there is nothing else to defend against. If we do not hold the last Omnius at Corrin—if we do not find a way to destroy the only remaining evermind—then no defense will be sufficient," Vor said. "I am the Supreme Commander of the Army of the Jihad, and this is a military decision: I *will* take those ships."

He had the blood of billions on his hands, the price he had accepted in order to complete the Great Purge. He did not intend to stop now. Quentin stood stonily at his side, his expression hard but his voice quiet whenever he managed to speak. "We cannot become complacent—not now, not ever. Though contained at Corrin, with their backs to the wall, the machines are more dangerous than ever."

"There is no time to lose. The last evermind has gone into a bunker mentality, and the machines will devote all of their resources to building new weapons and enhancing their defenses, to prevent us from getting through," Vor said before the stunned-looking Council. "And over the next weeks or months, for every ship Omnius builds, we must construct another one to counter it. No matter what the cost, we cannot let the machines get loose again."

Quentin gazed across the table at the shaken politicians. "The moment we see a chink in Omnius's defenses, we have to be ready to break through." Looking drawn and broken, he drew a deep, shuddering breath. "We have sold our souls for this victory, and I will not see all those sacrifices squandered."

BACK HOME IN Zimia, Vor stared out at the golden rising sun that painted the lovely buildings, many of which were still empty. Ship after ship came back, bringing the evacuees from their hiding places outside the system. During the Great Purge, Abulurd and Faykan had done remarkable work preparing Salusa for the worst, and now the two Butler sons looked from their father to the Supreme Commander.

Leronica was already buried here, though he wished he had been able to take her back to Caladan. Estes and Kagin had gone back there during the evacuation, and he doubted they would come to Salusa again. There was no reason for them to return here.

As the first returning refugees rejoiced in their near-complete victory, the League began the arduous task of assessing the success, and the cost, of the Great Purge. Numerous spacefolder scouting expeditions were dispatched to document the destruction of Synchronized Worlds. One by one, Martyrist volunteers scanned and mapped the devastated worlds to verify that no thinking machines remained. In a matter of days, detailed reports and holophotos arrived showing black, smoldering worlds. It was as if each of the machine planets had been dipped into a cauldron of hell and hurled back into space.

Now, other than Corrin, the evermind had no territory left, not one of his more than five hundred Synchronized Worlds. The cheering population of the League—those who had survived the Scourge and its aftermath as well as centuries of depredations from Omnius—called it a blessing. Martyrists called it the vengeful Sword of Serena. . . .

During the first formal meeting of the reconstituted Jihad Council, Vor immediately proposed, and pushed through, the production and assembly of many more guardian warships to maintain a tight vigil around the trapped machine forces. He feared that in a concerted suicidal run, the battleships of Omnius might be able to break through the Holtzman scrambler net and destroy the League defenders stationed above the planet. More space mines, more scrambler satellites, more weapons, and more League military vessels would prevent Omnius from escaping.

The Army of the Jihad would lay siege at Corrin for months, years, decades—whatever it took.

"Today, ninety-three years after Serena Butler summoned us to fight the thinking machines, I declare that the Jihad is over!" Grand Patriarch Boro-Ginjo announced to a cheering Hall of Parliament, filled to overflowing by a crowd that rushed in from the plaza. "We have crushed Omnius for all time!"

Standing beside him, Supreme Commander Vorian Atreides felt emptiness and exhaustion. All around him the people celebrated, but for him the war was not over as long as any thinking machine remained, as long as Omnius had one last stronghold.

Nearby, Quentin appeared distraught and dispirited. Onlookers might have perceived this as fatigue, but it was much more than that. *We have taken far too many lives in order to achieve this victory.* He prayed that mankind would never be forced to use such weapons again. . . .

VOR RODE ALONG the streets in an open groundcar while crowds applauded him. More than four million people waved colorful Jihad banners and flashed holoprojections of him, Serena Butler and her baby, Iblis Ginjo, and other Heroes of the Jihad.

One is missing. He thought of Xavier, his former comrade in arms. *Per-*

haps Abulurd is right. We should at least try to rectify the errors of history. But not with the wounds of the Jihad so fresh in the minds of the public. It was a time for healing, forgetting, and rebuilding.

When the groundcar stopped in the center of Zimia, he stepped out into an enthusiastic, adoring throng. Men clapped him on the back; women kissed him. Security officers cleared the way, and Vor proceeded to an awards platform erected at the center of the great plaza, in the shadow of immense government buildings.

At Vor's insistence, a uniformed Tercero Abulurd Harkonnen sat on one side of the ceremonial stage, ostensibly as his adjutant, though Abulurd and his older brother Faykan were also to receive honors for the work they had done here on Salusa. The Grand Patriarch had questioned the wisdom of displaying a *Harkonnen* in so prominent a position, but Vor had given him such a cold and angry look that Boro-Ginjo immediately withdrew his objection.

After nine decades of military service, Vor already had so many medals that he could not possibly wear all of them at once. He wore only a few ribbons and medals on his dress uniform. A Supreme Commander didn't need to outshine anyone. Leronica had never cared about the medals either; she would rather have had him with her, spending more time at home instead of on the battlefield.

Even so, the people *needed* to give accolades to them, to express their adoration. Politicians wanted to be involved in the festive process as well. *I'm the most famous man in the League of Nobles, and I don't give a damn about awards or glory. I just want peace and quiet.*

Thus, Vor accepted the medals and plaudits from the plump and satisfied-looking Grand Patriarch. He even delivered a short but stirring speech, praising everyone who had served in the Army of the Jihad, and all those who had vanished in the Great Purge.

Vor needed time away from all the frenzy of the giddy celebration, time to put his life in perspective. He needed to get to know himself again, and discover if he had anything left that he wanted to do after such a long life.

SURROUNDED BY A formidable wall of battleships orbiting their last bastion in space, Omnius and Erasmus assessed the situation. Above Corrin, in a standoff with the protective machine battleships, the League vessels hovered, always alert for any chance to release their last warheads.

"The verminous *hrethgir* will be back with reinforcements," Omnius said.

"No doubt they intend to lay siege to Corrin," Erasmus said. "Will they have the patience and diligence to maintain the necessary force for the necessary length of time? Humans do not excel in long-term planning and execution such as this."

"Nevertheless, we will build new ships, construct superior defenses. Our highest priority is to remain secure here, impregnable. Indefinitely, if necessary. Machines can outlast humans."

PART II

88 B.G.
NINETEEN YEARS LATER

Machines have something humans will always lack: infinite patience and the longevity to support it.

—SUPREME COMMANDER VORIAN ATREIDES,
Early Assessments of the Jihad (Fifth Revision)

Almost two decades of relative quiet finally allowed the remnants of humanity to pick up the pieces, rebuild their worlds and their societies . . . and forget the magnitude of the threat.

Except for Corrin, all of the Synchronized Worlds were uninhabitable wastelands. Humans themselves had proved to be as ruthless as any thinking machine. The survivors regularly assured themselves that the result had been worth the effort. Though some planets had remained clean, the Omnius Scourge alone had killed fully a third of the human population. In its wake, many children were born, new cities and agricultural settlements built, trade networks reestablished. The League went through a succession of leaders, and people turned their attentions toward the parochial concerns of survival.

Corrin remained a festering sore in space, an impenetrable barricade of robotic warships held at bay by the network of scrambler satellites and an ever-watchful force of human sentry ships. The thinking machines tried repeatedly to break free, and the vigilant humans countered them every time. It was a whirlpool of resources, soldiers, weapons, ships.

The last incarnation of Omnius hid behind his armored wall of secrecy, waiting. . . .

ABULURD HARKONNEN, WITH his redefined service rank of bator, was stationed with the watchdog fleet above Corrin. There, he could still perform a vital service for the League, though he suspected that his brother Faykan had suggested the assignment simply to get the Harkonnen embarrassment out of sight, far from the League capital.

Since the end of the Jihad, Faykan had left military service and built a fine political career for himself, eventually being elected as Interim Viceroy after a succession of six others, each as bland and uninspired as Brevin O'Kukovich had been. Faykan, at least, seemed to be the strong leader the resurrected League had been waiting for.

Abulurd had commanded the guardian fleet for the better part of a year already, making sure Omnius did not break through the defensive barricade. He hoped the citizens slept better at night knowing that dedicated soldiers stood against further assaults from the thinking machines.

The evermind continued to design and build new ships, augmented weapons, heavily shielded rammers to batter against its electronic prison walls. Like clockwork, the machines tried to breach the human defenses—attempting to disrupt the scrambler net, to launch fleeing update ships, anything to scatter copies of the evermind to new worlds. So far, Omnius used brute force more often than innovation, but each attempt was methodical, shifting parameters slightly, trying to determine a technique that would work. The evermind's tactics changed occasionally, but not significantly—except for a few wild sorties that had taken everyone by surprise.

None of the enemy attempts had succeeded, but Abulurd remained on edge. The Army of Humanity did not dare lower its guard.

For nineteen years, while history and politics and social change trickled across the League Worlds, the human battleships at Corrin drove back furious suicidal plunges. The evermind tried old technologies and new ones, throwing vessel after vessel against the scrambler net, launching guided projectiles against the patrol fleet, scattering decoy targets in all directions. And when those robot ships crashed and failed, the machines simply built more.

On the surface of the planet, the robotic war industries never rested, manufacturing weapons and ships to be turned against the League warships. Corrin's orbit was strewn with the wreckage of dead vessels in a dense obstacle course as thick as any intentional defenses. Meanwhile, on all the League Worlds, factories and shipyards constructed and launched replacement vessels to plug chinks in the defenses around Corrin as swiftly as the enemy could hammer away at them.

For the most part, though, the people in the League paid little attention to the far-off battlefield.

Many in the League Parliament were frustrated at the constant expenditures, now that the Jihad had been declared "over." The priorities of reconstruction and repopulation required vast amounts of funding and resources, yet the watchdog fleet was a constant drain. The century of fighting and massacres had left the League of Nobles weak, frayed, and depleted with billions dead and primary industries devoted to the production of war materials at the expense of other needs.

People were anxious for change.

When, two years after the Great Purge, Vorian Atreides had proposed an ambitious new mission to eradicate the last known stronghold of the cymeks on Hessra, he was labeled a warmonger and actually shouted out of the assembly chamber. *So much for appreciating the greatest war hero in history*, Abulurd had thought. In the years since, he had been distressed to watch how his mentor was being sidelined and cut out, a symbol of the bloody past and an obstacle to a naively bright future.

If only Corrin wasn't such an inconvenient reminder.

With the end of the Jihad, the tattered military had been reorganized and renamed the Army of Humanity. As a symbolic change, even the old ranks and command structure had been modified. Instead of the efficient numerical promotions leading up to primero, now the rank designations were taken from an ancient military in the golden age of mankind, dating from the Old Empire or even beyond—levenbrech, bator, burseg, bashar. . . .

Though adopting the Harkonnen name all those years ago had probably stalled his career, Abulurd's service record and the frequent quiet assistance of Supreme Bashar Atreides had earned him a rank equivalent to that of colonel or segundo. Over the past fifteen years he had served on six different worlds, performing mainly civil engineering work, reconstruction, and local security while maintaining a military presence. At least here, commanding the watchdog fleet at Corrin, he was in the thick of things again.

Even after months of facing off against the imposing robotic war fleet that maintained its bristling defensive posture, Abulurd did not feel the tedium in the way that some of the younger soldiers did. Most of the fighters assigned to guardian duty were too young to remember when the Synchronized Worlds had controlled much of the galaxy. They had never fought in the Jihad itself. It was history for them, not the stuff of nightmares.

These were the first generation of children born after the Scourge, bred from healthy genetic stock and more resistant to diseases. They were familiar with stories of the Jihad and its lingering, untreatable scars; they had heard of the brave battles led by Vorian Atreides—now Supreme Bashar—and Quentin Butler; they knew of the Three Martyrs and still talked about the "cowardly betrayal" of Xavier Harkonnen, believing the propaganda.

During the relative peace, Abulurd had filed several formal requests to reopen the investigation into his grandfather's supposed treachery, but such business fell on deaf ears. Nearly eighty years had gone by, and the League had far more pressing concerns. . . .

Sometimes, in the mess halls or exercise chambers, the young soldiers in his watchdog crew pressed their commander for war stories, but he could sense their underlying scorn for his lack of accomplishments. Abulurd had been sheltered from most of the major battles, protected by Vorian Atreides. Some, demonstrating prejudices they had learned from their parents, commented quietly that they expected little else from a Harkonnen. Other soldiers in the watchdog fleet seemed more impressed by the fact that he had rescued Rayna Butler, the famous leader of the wild Cult of Serena, from Parmentier.

Looking down at the last Omnius stronghold from the bridge of his observation ship, Abulurd endured. He knew what was important.

He had four hundred ballistas and over a thousand javelins, an imposing and heavily armed force to keep the machines utterly confined, though the Holtzman scrambler satellites and mines formed the primary line of resistance. Conversely, the main machine defenses covering Corrin—and Omnius—were impregnable. No League offensives had been able to open a gap large enough to dump their pulse-atomics. Not even suicidal Cult of Serena bombers could break through. They were at an impasse.

Running his watchdog fleet with diligence and discipline, Abulurd initiated drill after drill to keep the soldiers sharp and alert. The intimidating robotic ships were positioned like a spiked collar around the planet, just out of reach. How Abulurd wanted to push forward and obliterate them once and for all, to prove his worth on a real battlefield! But for that, he would need another thousand of the League's most powerful ships—and weary, scarred humanity was simply not willing to commit to such an effort.

Could the thinking machines be lulling us into complacency? Making us think they have no effective innovations?

UNFORTUNATELY, HE WAS proved right sooner than he expected.

The human soldiers, sick with boredom and counting down the days until they were rotated home, suddenly sounded alarms. Abulurd rushed to the bridge of his command ballista.

"Three more robotic ships have broken from the defensive ring, Bator Harkonnen," announced the subordinate scan operator. "Heading in random trajectories, racing toward the scrambler net."

"They've tried that one before—it won't work."

"This is something new, sir. Doesn't follow the usual pattern."

"Look at those engines they've got!"

"Sound the alarms. Full defensive formations. Prepare to intercept, if anything should happen to get through." Abulurd crossed his arms. "No matter how fast they fly, the scrambler satellites will wipe their gelcircuitry. Omnius knows that."

The new thinking-machine craft were sleek missiles, metal daggers that stabbed the satellite net, plunging through Holtzman barriers that should have erased their programming. But the craft tore through and continued to accelerate.

"Power up weapons and open fire!" Abulurd called over the open comline. "Stop them—it could be an update sphere."

"How did they get through? New shielding?"

"Or maybe whatever's aboard those missiles is just standard-issue automation, no gelcircuitry." He leaned forward, studying the readings from the scanners. "But then there can't be any thinking machine aboard. What is piloting those things? Did Omnius dust off an old-model nonsentient computer?"

The watchdog ships opened fire, but the new missiles were accelerating so fast that even high-velocity projectiles couldn't intercept them. Other League ships converged, firing in a frantic barrage, realizing that one of the fleeing craft just might get away. But it couldn't be carrying a copy of the evermind, not after passing through the scrambler web.

"Keep watching Corrin as well!" Abulurd called. "I don't trust Omnius not to try something else while we're on a wild goose chase."

"We'll never catch up to those projectiles, Bator—"

"The hell we won't." Quickly Abulurd identified the trio of fast-cruising vessels on the outer fringe of the defense network. "Full dispersal of perimeter ships to intercept. Stop them at all costs. You have never had a higher priority in your military careers. Even if their gelcircuitry's wiped, they may be carrying more plagues."

The suggestion struck a cold panic into the soldiers, and they scrambled to follow his orders.

"Bator! The machines have launched one of their surprise sorties against the scrambler satellites! Now they're all trying to break through!"

Abulurd slammed a fist into the palm of his other hand. "I suspected it was some kind of decoy. Move in closer to Corrin! Drive back those robot warships!" He studied both sets of readings, suddenly worried that he had chosen the wrong decoy. Which one was the real plot? Or was Omnius fully invested in both schemes?

A flurry of League intercept ships came in firing weapons, while howling challenges and insults at the robots. Ring after ring of the human defenders grouped high above the planet in an attempt to block the ever-accelerating machine vessels.

The three robotic ships each took a different route, flying in wild trajectories, as if in hope that at least one of them would escape. The human ships easily destroyed the first one before it built up sufficient speed to escape from Corrin.

Meantime, near the scrambler net, the major battle was engaged. Some robot ships plowed into the deadly pulse web, careening through; though their gelcircuitry brains were obliterated, the momentum of the giant machine vessels turned them into huge projectiles. The watchdog fleet used their most powerful weapons to cut the hulks to pieces. Hundreds of small new scrambler satellites were deployed as replacements, stitching together the energy holes in the web before it was too late.

The second superfast projectile came under heavy fire as it raced toward the red-giant star. Before the machine ship could find sanctuary in the roaring solar environment that would have been deadly to any biological organism, the sheer firepower of the human defenders broke the vessel into glowing shrapnel. Two of them destroyed.

The third superfast projectile poured all energy into its engines, picking up more and more velocity, gaining distance from Corrin and from the fleet. The outermost human scout vessels, which Abulurd had placed in concentric orbits farther and farther from the infested planet, came in at last, cutting off the robotic ship's escape and opening fire.

Impact after impact struck true, but could not penetrate the enemy vessel's armor. As the flurry of defensive battle—the diversion, or the real plan?—continued closer to Corrin itself, seven more human ships converged on the lone remaining projectile at the outskirts of the solar system.

At the last moment before its hull failed, the front of the superfast projectile split open like a flower and vomited a swarm of smaller pods, self-propelled canisters not much larger than coffins. They streaked away in all directions like sparks from a stirred campfire, startling the defensive fleet.

"Omnius has a new trick!" one of the pilots transmitted.

Abulurd saw what was happening and made up his mind that these pods were the true reason for the fleeing ships. He made a command decision. "Stop them! They are either some terrible weapon, or new copies of Omnius to be spread elsewhere. If we fail here, the human race could pay for centuries!"

The soldiers pursued and took every available shot. They destroyed most of the independently guided canisters. But not all of them.

Remembering the plague-dispersal torpedoes that had rained down upon Parmentier and other League Worlds, Abulurd felt deep dread in his heart.

"Track them before they get out of sensor range. Follow the trajectories and estimate their targets." He waited tensely as his soldiers scrambled to project the paths of the escaping machine ships. "Damn! We'll have to tighten our defenses so that this doesn't happen again!" He ground his teeth. Vorian Atreides would be disappointed in him for letting such a potential disaster slip through his fingers.

"One cluster is heading for Salusa Secundus, Bator Harkonnen," said a tactician. "The other appears to be targeted on . . . Rossak."

Abulurd nodded, not particularly surprised. Despite the risk, he knew what he had to do, the only way that he could beat the fast-burning machine missiles to their targets.

"I'm taking a spacefolder scout and returning to Zimia to sound the alarm. I pray that they can prepare in time."

*It has been said of Yorek Thurr that if humans had gears and bolts,
his would be stripped and loose.*

—*The Jihad Chronicles*,
attributed to ERASMUS

E ven though fleeing to Corrin saved his life when the Army of the
Jihad obliterated Wallach IX, Yorek Thurr regretted ever having
come here. Now after nineteen interminable, frustrating years, Thurr was
trapped and useless on the only remaining Synchronized World.

Omnius had turned this planet into a desperate stronghold, a fantasti-
cally armed camp. Thurr was theoretically safe. But what was the point
of it? How could he make his bold mark on history with his hands tied
like this?

Wearing protective eyewear under the bloodred sun, the bald, leathery man paced beyond the pens of pathetic human slaves, glancing at the
tall Central Spire inhabited by the evermind.

As soon as the space-folding ships of the Great Purge had arrived at
Wallach IX, Thurr immediately guessed what the humans meant to do.
Before the first kindjal bombers had begun deploying their pulse-atomics,
Thurr had leaped aboard an escape vessel and streaked far away, carrying
a copy of the local evermind as a bargaining chip. At the time, he could
easily have found some other place to inhabit. Why had he come to Corrin? Stupid, ill-considered decision!

With his immunity to the RNA retrovirus, and the life-extension
treatment he'd received, Thurr should have been invincible. It had been
instinct that drove him back to the heart of the Synchronized Worlds. Of

course, with his standard space-travel engines, he had arrived far too late, after the holocaust was over and the humans had tightened their noose around the last evermind. In his League-configuration ship, Thurr had transmitted conflicting orders to the fatigued and stressed pilots who were scrambling to put their blockade in place. They had not been watching for someone trying to sneak *into* Corrin. While Omnius retrenched and brought together all his mechanical defenses on the surface and in layers of low orbits, Thurr had transmitted his own secret overrides and identification codes, which granted him passage and then sanctuary.

But now he could never leave! What had he been thinking? He had wrongly imagined that the machines would win, somehow. Omnius had commanded the Synchronized Worlds for more than a millennium—how could the whole machine empire fall in a month?

I should have gone elsewhere . . . anywhere.

Now with the Army of Humanity's watchdog fleet monitoring the entire Corrin system, neither Thurr nor any force of thinking machines could ever get away. It was such a waste of his time and talents, more frustrating even than living in the pathetic League. Tired of chastising himself, he had long wanted to hurt someone else. The standoff had lasted for decades, and for Thurr it had grown quite tiresome.

If only he could just go up there, face the League military, and bluff his way through. After all his famous works in Jipol, all his accomplishments, surely his face and name were still known, even after so much time. Camie Boro-Ginjo had taken most of the credit, though Thurr himself had done the work, vilifying Xavier Harkonnen and turning Ginjo into a saint. But Camie had outmaneuvered him, forced him to abandon the League. Perhaps he shouldn't have done such a good job of faking his death. . . .

Every step of the way, Thurr had made wrong decisions.

In Erasmus's laboratories, he had found a kindred spirit in Rekur Van. He and the limbless Tlulaxa researcher had combined their knowledge and destructive appetites into horrifically imaginative schemes against the weakling humans—and oh, how they deserved their fates. Once Erasmus had declared the limb-regeneration experiments a failure, Rekur Van had harbored no aspirations of escaping. But Thurr could be free to roam the habitable planets and make his mark . . . if ever he could get away.

He stared up into the sky. Not likely anytime soon.

The intriguingly unpredictable robot Erasmus visited him, bringing his companion, Gilbertus Albans. The robot seemed to understand Thurr's frustration, but could offer no hope for freedom from Corrin. "Perhaps you can develop an innovative idea that will fool the League watchdog fleet."

"As I did with the plagues? As I did with the recent targeted projectile factories? I hear they succeeded in breaking through the cordon." He gave a thin smile. "I shouldn't have to solve all of our problems—but I will if I can. I want to get out of here more than any of you machines."

Erasmus wasn't convinced. "Unfortunately, now the Army of Humanity will be even more vigilant."

"Especially after the mechanical devourers reach their targets and begin to work." More than anything else, Thurr wished he could be there himself to witness the mayhem.

Erasmus turned to his straw-haired, muscular companion. Thurr resented the robot's "pet," because Gilbertus had received the immortality treatment while he was still young enough to benefit from it.

"And what do you think, Gilbertus?" the robot asked.

Blandly, the other man turned to look at the bald man as if he were no more than a failed experimental specimen. "I think Yorek Thurr operates too close to the fringe of human behavior."

"I agree," Erasmus said, apparently delighted with the assessment.

"Even if that is so," Thurr sneered, "I am still within the realm of humanity, and that you can never understand, robot." When he saw that Erasmus was taken aback, Thurr felt a great satisfaction.

It wasn't freedom, of course, but at least he had achieved a small victory.

*As long as Earth, our Mother and our birthplace, remains in the
memory of the human race, it is not completely destroyed. At least
we can try to convince ourselves of that.*

—PORCE BLUDD,
The Mapping of Scars

The long succession of atomic strikes had taken a terrible toll on
Quentin Butler. Almost two decades later, the former commander
still could not pass a night without dreaming of the uncounted billions of
humans he had annihilated, all for the sake of defeating the thinking
machines.

He was not the only one who wondered if the luckiest jihadi soldiers
had been those who perished swiftly and cleanly, lost in the mysterious
maze of foldspace. It was far worse, Quentin thought, to have to live with
the knowledge, to stare at the permanent bloodstains on his hands.

It was the price he had to pay. For the honor of all his victims, he had
to endure it. And never forget.

People still called him a hero, but it no longer made him proud.
League historians remembered, and embellished, virtually everything he
had accomplished in his military career.

But the real Quentin Butler was little more than an empty shell, a
hardened, hollow statue formed of memories, expectations, and horrendous losses. After what he'd been forced to do, his heart and his soul had
left him. He watched Faykan and Abulurd continue with their lives;
Faykan had married, started a fine family, while his younger brother
remained single. Perhaps Abulurd wouldn't continue the Harkonnen
name in his offspring after all.

Quentin felt as empty as his cataleptic wife Wandra, who remained alone and unaware in the City of Introspection, year after year. At least she was at peace. At times when he visited her, Quentin would look into her blank but beautiful face and envy her.

After experiencing so much, after making so many difficult decisions, he'd had enough of military service. He had spearheaded too many attacks, sending too many fighters to their deaths, along with all of the innocent human captives, whom he should have been able to liberate from machine oppression. In reality, he had freed them from Omnius only by slaughtering them.

Quentin could no longer live with that. For years after the Great Purge, he had served in meaningless posts and then shocked his oldest son by attempting to resign his commission.

In response, trying to keep his war-hero father close by, Faykan suggested he accept a post as an ambassador or a representative in Parliament.

"No, that is not for me," Quentin had said. "I have no interest in beginning another career at my age."

But the Grand Patriarch—still Xander Boro-Ginjo—had read a prepared statement that someone else had undoubtedly written for him, refusing to accept the primero's resignation, altering it instead to a well-deserved indefinite leave of absence. Quentin didn't care about the semantics, for the result would be the same. He had found another calling.

His friend Porce Bludd, a fine companion from Quentin's happier days as a lowly soldier and engineer working to build New Starda, offered to take him along on a pilgrimage and expedition.

In the years since the Omnius Scourge and the Great Purge, the philanthropist nobleman had become obsessed with the idea of helping planets. On Walgis and Alpha Corvus, two cauterized former machine worlds, he had found a few ragtag survivors living in squalor. The people were desperately in need, disease-ridden and starving, exhibiting numerous forms of cancer caused by the nuclear fallout. Their civilization, technology, and infrastructure had been obliterated, but the hardiest souls still clung to life, cobbling together support networks.

Bludd had returned to the League, seeking volunteers and organizing huge airlifts and rescue convoys to deliver supplies to the survivors. In the worst cases, they moved entire villages to less contaminated areas or off the planet to more hospitable League Worlds. With the human population scattered and devastated in the aftermath of the retrovirus epidemic, new bloodlines were welcomed, especially by the Sorceresses of Rossak.

Some stern politicians insisted that liberation from the machines was the best compensation any survivors could ask for. More and more, Quentin realized that the men who made such sweeping pronouncements had never been the ones who offered the sacrifices in the first place. . . .

Bludd, who had no need to fight for political gains, simply turned his back on the League Parliament when they refused to offer reparations. "I will give the aid that I deem necessary," he'd said in an announcement in Zimia. "I don't care if I spend every cent of my fortune. This is my calling in life."

Although much of the incredible family wealth had been lost in the slave revolt that destroyed much of Starda and killed Bludd's granduncle, vast sums continued to pour into Poritrin's coffers from the burgeoning market for personal protective shields. It seemed everyone around the League was wearing them now, even without the threat of an outside machine enemy.

Hearing of Quentin's leave of absence, the nobleman sought him out. "I don't know if you will want to see them with your own eyes," Bludd said, his expression filled with compassion, "but I intend to go to planets devastated in the Great Purge. Former Synchronized Worlds. The atomic blasts were enough to destroy ecosystems and eradicate the scourge of Omnius, but there's a chance"—his eyes brightened as he extended a finger—"a *chance*, I tell you, that some humans survived. If so, we must find them and help them."

"Yes," Quentin said, feeling a weight lift from his shoulders. He dreaded the prospect of going to the nuclear wastelands, where he had dropped a storm of atomic warheads himself. But if there was some small way he could make amends . . .

Bludd's luxurious space yacht contained more amenities than a League battleship, with living quarters, a large cargo hold loaded with medicines and relief supplies, and a one-man scout flyer in the hangar. At first Quentin refused to take advantage of comforts he felt he didn't deserve, but in the end he convinced himself to enjoy the trip. He had served enough missions over the course of his military career, devoting forty-two years of his life to Serena Butler's Jihad.

On their long voyage, Quentin and Bludd traveled to pinpoints on a map that had once marked known Synchronized Worlds; all radioactive hotspots. Nineteen years ago, Quentin had flown from planet to planet, dropping cargoes of death. Now his mission was one of compassion and commemoration.

Quentin stared down at the ruined landscape of Ularda, the burned ground, the stunted trees and plants that grew in the contaminated soil. Most buildings had been leveled by the pulse-atomic explosions, but the handful of survivors had stacked up rubble to form huts and cottages, scant shelters from the fearsome post-holocaust storms that ripped across the plains.

"Do you ever get used to scenes like this?" Quentin swallowed the lump forming in his throat.

In the pilot's seat, Bludd looked at him with emotion-filled eyes. "Let us hope not. For the sake of our own humanity, we dare not become used to such things."

As their yacht cruised overhead, they saw people below working with sticks and scrap metal to till fields. Quentin could not imagine how they lived. The survivors stopped and stared upward—some waving and cheering, others dropping their tools and running for shelter, afraid that the strange airship signaled a return of machine forces to complete the extermination of the human race.

Tears streamed down the Poritrin nobleman's face. "I wish I could pack every single person aboard this ship and deliver them directly to a League World, where they could have a chance. With all my wealth and influence, I should be able to save everybody." He swiped a hand across his eyes, and it came away wet. "Don't you think so, Quentin? Why can't I save everybody?"

Quentin's heart was heavy, and the guilt was like a cancer eating through his body.

Though the background radiation affected their scanning systems, Bludd was able to detect three squalid settlements. All told, fewer than five hundred had survived the bombardment. Five hundred . . . out of how many millions?

Then the thoughts of a military commander intruded. If five hundred fragile human beings could endure the pulse-atomic holocaust, what if a protected copy of the evermind had escaped destruction? Quentin shook his head. He had to believe the atomic attacks had succeeded—because if even one intact evermind could propagate across other planets, then all of this death and destruction would have been for nothing.

He squeezed his eyes shut as Bludd landed the ship at one of the three settlements. The men suited up in protective garments and stepped out to look at the battered and squalid scarecrows who managed to scrape out a subsistence on what had once been a Synchronized World. Only the strongest could survive here; most people died horribly and young.

Surprisingly, the two men were not the first to arrive on Ularda in the years since the Great Purge. After meeting with the town elders—elders? The oldest looked barely forty!—Quentin discovered that the Cult of Serena had taken root here, spread by two proselytizing missionaries trained by his granddaughter Rayna. Even in their difficult circumstances, these people eschewed technology, viewing the atomic attacks as just punishment for the thinking machines.

In places such as this, where the minuscule population was hurting the most and had nothing left to sacrifice, fanatical religions took hold easily. The Cult of Serena, evolved from the original Martyrists, gave these broken survivors a tangible scapegoat, a focus for their anger and despair. Rayna's message, disseminated by the visitors, commanded them to smash all machines and never allow computer minds to be developed or used by humanity again.

Quentin respected her philosophy of teaching people to live by their own wits and resources. Yet the harsh and inflexible message worried him. In twenty years, even on League planets that had suffered from the Scourge but not nuclear destruction, the antitechnology crusade had been accepted with great fervor. People shunned machines in all their guises. Spaceships, in the service of their antimachine crusade, were apparently exempt from their fanaticism.

Now, in the small village on Ularda, the natives wore stained and tattered garments; matted hair had fallen out in clumps; sores and growths dotted their faces and arms.

"We've brought you food and medicines, supplies and tools to make your lives better," Bludd said. His radiation-blocking suit crinkled as he moved. The people looked at him hungrily, as if they might rush forward, a starving mob. "We will bring more when we can. We'll dispatch help from the League. You have already proven your bravery and resourcefulness just by surviving. From this point forward, things will get better for you, I promise."

He and Quentin unloaded cases of concentrated foods, vitamins, and medicines. Next, they brought out sacks of high-yield crop seeds along with farming implements and growth-enhancing fertilizers. "I promise it will get better," Bludd repeated.

"Do you really believe that?" Quentin asked when the two men returned to their ship, weary and distraught from the horrors they had seen.

Bludd hesitated, again avoided the easy answer. "No . . . I don't believe it—but *they* have to."

PERHAPS IT WAS a symbolic journey, a need to witness the first great battlefield against the machines and the birthplace of the human race. Bludd announced that he intended to go to Earth.

"It's doubtful there will be survivors," Quentin said. "It has been too long."

"I know," the Poritrin lord said. "Both of us were too young for that first victory . . . the start of this exhausting Jihad. Still, I feel that as a human being, I must see it for myself."

Quentin looked at his friend's eyes and saw the deep need there. He, too, felt it in his heart. "Yes, I think we both should go to the birthplace of humanity. Maybe we can learn something. Or maybe by looking at its scars, we can find a way to get through the rest of our work."

But there was no life to be found on Earth.

As he navigated his space yacht over the silent and blistered landscape, Bludd and Quentin searched for any enclave of humanity that had somehow escaped the nuclear bombardment. Here, where cymeks and Omnius had methodically obliterated every vestige of humanity, the League Armada had dropped enough atomic weapons to sterilize the surface of the whole planet: No one was left alive. They orbited repeatedly, hoping to find a reason to doubt their initial reports, but Earth was nothing more than a horrific, charred scar.

Quentin finally left the bridge. "Let us go somewhere else. Someplace where there might be a glimmer of hope."

Some say it is better to rule in Hell than to serve in Heaven. That is a defeatist attitude. I intend to rule everywhere, not just in Hell.

— GENERAL AGAMEMNON,

New Memoirs

I t was time for changes—they were long overdue, in fact. Perhaps they had all the patience in the universe, but nineteen years was surely long enough.

Agamemnon hauled his enormous walker to the top of the windswept glacier. Abrasive snow and breezes whipped across the uneven terrain, and starlight reflected under the bruised skies of Hessra. The light on the frozen planetoid was as dim as the cymeks' prospects had been. Until the Purge.

Juno clambered up beside him, her immense shape exuding power and ambition. Articulated legs rose and fell, powered by durable engines. Because the Titans had lived for so long, they tended to lose track of their goals, letting each day slip away from them, and now it was growing too late.

He and his beloved companion stood together, immune to the inhospitable cold. Behind them, the half-buried towers of the Cogitors' fortress looked like a crumbling monument to lost glory—reminding Agamemnon of gaudy shrines and memorials he had forced slaves to build for him on Earth.

"You are the lord of all you survey, my love," Juno said.

He couldn't tell if she was teasing him or admiring his minuscule victory. "It is pathetic. After all, we have nothing to fear. The League can barely wipe their own noses, and they eradicated Omnius on every Synchronized World except Corrin, where he hides behind all his weapons."

"As we are hiding here?"

"Why? There is no longer any reason for it." With a heavy metal limb, he smashed a crater into the ice in front of him. "What is to stop us now?"

Inside his mind, Agamemnon's thoughts rumbled like distant thunder. He found it shameful that he had allowed his own dreams to fade—perhaps he should simply have died like so many of his coconspirators. After nearly nine decades of their new rebellion against Omnius, the general and his handful of surviving cymeks had accomplished little and were hiding like rats in holes.

"I grow weary of this," Agamemnon said. "All of it."

He and Juno understood each other well. It surprised him that the ambitious female Titan had remained with him for more than a millennium. Perhaps it was only because she had no other viable options . . . or perhaps she really cared for him.

"What precisely are you waiting for, my love? Such complacency has turned us into apathetic lotus-eaters, just like the population of the Old Empire we despised so much. We have been sitting around for all these years like . . ." Her voice grew full of self-derision. "Like Cogitors! The galaxy is an open field for us—especially now."

With his optic threads, Agamemnon scanned the lifeless mountainscape, the inexorable tides of ice. "There once was a time when thinking machines served *us*. Now Omnius has been destroyed and the *hrethgir* are weakened—we should take advantage of that. But there is still a significant chance we will fail."

Juno's voice was thick with scorn, prodding him as always. "When did you become a frightened child, Agamemnon?"

"You are right. My own attitude disgusts me. Being a ruler for the sake of bullying a few underlings is not sufficient. It is good to have slaves at one's beck and call, but even that grows tiresome."

"Yes, look at how Yorek Thurr behaved on Wallach IX. He commanded a whole planet, but that wasn't enough for him."

"Wallach IX is a radioactive scab," Agamemnon said. "Like all the other Synchronized Worlds. It is irrelevant."

"Any planet that was once a Synchronized World is never irrelevant, my love. You must think in a different paradigm."

They stared together at the desolate landscape of Hessra, as lifeless as so many of the scorched Synchronized Worlds they had explored, and discarded, after the Great Purge. Presently, Agamemnon said, "We must instigate changes, instead of being the passive recipients of whatever history throws at us."

The two Titans swiveled their head turrets and strode back across the rough ice toward the Cogitors' towers. "It is time for a fresh start."

BEOWULF SUSPECTED NOTHING, though his fate had been part of the Titan general's burgeoning plans for some time. Dante suggested, "His damaged brain no longer has the capacity to sense nuances or draw conclusions."

"The clod can barely walk down a corridor," Agamemnon said. "I've put up with him long enough."

"Perhaps we should just let him wander outside and fall headfirst into a crevasse," Juno said. "That would save us all a lot of trouble."

"He already fell into a crevasse when we first took over Hessra. We were foolish enough to rescue him," Agamemnon said.

The three Titans summoned the wavering neo-cymek into the central chamber that had once held the Cogitors' pedestals. The etched Muadru runes on the wall blocks had been defaced with obscene scribbles. Scuttling about in limited walker-forms, the enslaved secondary-neos went about their laboratory duties, monitoring electrafluid-processing equipment for the cymek rulers.

Agamemnon had everything he needed. Now what he needed was *more*.

Beowulf lumbered in, the thoughtrode control of his walker limbs unsteady. Signals tangled and overlapped so that he staggered like an intoxicated man trying to move from one point to another. "Y-ye-yes, Agamemnon. You c-ca-called me?"

The general's voice was carefully neutral. "I have always been grateful for the service you performed in helping free the cymeks from Omnius. We are now at a watershed. Our circumstances are about to change dramatically for the better, Beowulf. But before we can do that, we need to perform a bit of housecleaning."

Agamemnon lifted his walker-form, looming high in the stone-walled chamber. He withdrew one of the antique weapons he kept in display cases on his body. Beowulf seemed intrigued.

Dante darted forward and deactivated the engines and power source that drove the brain-damaged cymek's robotic body.

"W-wha-what—"

Juno's voice sounded sweet and reasonable. "We have to get rid of some old junk before we can move on, Beowulf."

Agamemnon said, "Thank the gods in all their incarnations that Xerxes isn't still here in his blundering attempts to assist us. But you, Beowulf . . . you are a disaster waiting to happen."

The Titans clustered around the deactivated walker-form, extending their articulated arms, fashioning the necessary tools to begin the dismantling process. Agamemnon hoped to try out some of the antiques in his collection again.

"N-no-nooo—"

"Even I have been waiting for this a long time, General Agamemnon," Dante said. "The Titans are ready for a great resurgence at long last."

"What matters most is that we expand our power base, taking over more territory and holding it with an iron fist. I was distracted for a long time by desiring the planets inhabited by the *hrethgir*, but since the Great Purge, there are innumerable bastions for the cymeks to conquer. I will be happy to build our new domain from the graveyards of Omnius. Before, when I dismissed the possibility, I did not consider how ironic and satisfying it could be. A radioactive wasteland poses no threat to our protective shells and our shielded brain canisters. To reign in Hell will only be our first step. Thereafter, we can build our strength and strike out against the League Worlds."

"There's nothing wrong with beginning a new empire in the ruins, my love." Like tearing a giant crab apart, Juno disengaged and removed the first set of bulky legs from Beowulf's walker-body. "So long as it is only the beginning."

The damaged neo-cymek continued to wail and plead with them, becoming less and less articulate as his urgency grew. Finally, in disgust, Agamemnon deactivated the speakerpatch connected to the preservation canister. "There. Now we can concentrate and finish this euthanasia."

"Unfortunately," Dante continued, "only we three Titans remain. Many of our neos are loyal enough in their own way, but they have always been passive. We drew them from subjugated populations."

Agamemnon snapped one of the thoughtrode clusters from Beowulf's walker-form. "We need to develop a new Titan hierarchy, but we can never obtain the stock we need from our dwindling resources. The neos are all sheep."

"Then we shall simply have to look elsewhere," Juno pointed out. "Though Omnius tried his best to exterminate them, a great many *hrethgir* remain. And the survivors are the strongest ones."

"Including my son Vorian." As he worked to dismantle all of the components that kept Beowulf alive, the Titan general was reminded of the days when his loyal trustee Vor would lovingly and meticulously clean, polish, and refurbish all of his father's delicate cymek components, in a gesture that went back to the dawn of history, washing the feet of a beloved leader. Those had been their most intimate times between father and son.

Agamemnon missed those days, and he wished things had not gone wrong with Vorian. His son had been his best chance for a perfect successor, but the humans had corrupted him.

Juno did not notice his reverie. "We should recruit from them, take talented candidates and convert them to our cause. I'm certain we have the wiles and the techniques to accomplish something so simple. Once we have a person's brain detached, there's little we can't do to manipulate him."

The Titan general considered. "First, we will scout the radioactive planets and decide where best to establish our strongholds."

"Wallach IX will be a good first step," Dante said. "It is near Hessra."

"I agree," Agamemnon said, "and we'll step on whatever remains of the throne of that maddening Yorek Thurr."

Beowulf's mechanical body was disassembled now, and the components lay strewn about for recycling and reconditioning. Silently, the secondary-neos came forward to take the pieces away.

As Agamemnon thought about all the wasted Synchronized Worlds, it occurred to him that Vorian had been the spearhead behind all that nuclear destruction. Perhaps in a way, he might be an appropriate successor to the Titans after all.

*If we turn around to gaze at the remote past, we can barely catch
sight of it, so imperceptible has it become.*

— MARCEL PROUST,
ancient human author

V or stood inside his token office in the Army of Humanity headquarters, gazing through the open window at the evening drizzle. The
cool moisture felt good on his face after a hot afternoon, since Zimia had
been unbearably hot and humid for the past week. The rain was a pleasant respite, but not enough to make the Supreme Bashar feel much better.

Every day, it seemed, he was losing his battle against the government's stagnation, lethargy, and inability to make difficult decisions.
League representatives were afraid to finish the necessary dirty work,
and with every year that passed they forgot more and more. Engrossed
in local problems and political favors, they convinced themselves that
the continuing threats of Omnius and the cymeks would just go away.
He could not make them believe that even though the Titans had
bided their time for years, Agamemnon was not finished with his reign
of terror.

His long war was over. After the Great Purge, Quentin Butler had not
been the only military leader who sought out a long and peaceful escape.
It had been too easy to give highest priority to recovery and reconstruction. Other people wanted to relegate the whole Jihad to history.

But it really wasn't over. Not yet, while Corrin and the cymeks
remained very real threats to humanity. But Vor seemed to be the only
one who saw it. The League refused to authorize an offensive force, not

even a regular reconnaissance routine to Hessra, where the last Titans were known to be hiding. Complacent fools!

The Grand Patriarch and the nobles had devoted their energy to the internal economic problems of extending their administration to the Unallied Planets in order to create a larger empire with tighter, more centralized controls over each world. The Grand Patriarch had added several new jangling links to the chain of office he wore around his neck.

The conquered Synchronized Worlds would remain uninhabitable for centuries, but some of the more aggressive League Worlds considered the Unallied Planets to be ripe pickings. Across the League, the insatiable demand for melange had not lessened with the end of the Scourge. Population restoration programs had been under way for many years, following the guidance of Supreme Sorceress Ticia Cenva.

The public-works projects required human labor pools, now that sophisticated computerized machines had been banned. And that meant human slaves, mostly Buddislamics from backwater planets. There had been some protest in the League chambers against treating other humans "just like the machines did," but that position had little support.

Since his military duties had been replaced by mere administrative work, public speeches, and appearances in parades, Vor had long ago made a point of continuing his search on Parmentier for his granddaughter Raquella. After six months of effort, he had finally found her.

Having fled the Hospital for Incurable Diseases, she and Mohandas Suk had settled in an outlying village populated mainly by an insular group who followed the incredibly ancient religion of Judaism. There, she had helped them through the Scourge, tending their needs—until another paranoid mob that drew upon even more ancient prejudices had swept into the town and burned it, blaming the Jews as well as the thinking machines for the epidemic.

So she and Mohandas had moved again and continued their work, accompanied by some of the Jewish villagers who hid their identities. Even after the epidemic had passed, the recovery of Parmentier took years and years.

By the time Vor had found her, she was working under primitive conditions. Most of her medical equipment had been destroyed, so Vor generously sent her whatever aid she needed, including more equipment and guards to keep her safe. Shortly thereafter, he recruited Raquella and Mohandas to help form the Humanities Medical Commission—or HuMed—that replaced the old Jihad Medical Commission. Then, with his own funds, he purchased a hospital spaceship for their use. The new ship enabled Raquella and her medical associates to travel across the galaxy to perform their important work more efficiently. The worlds of the League had to be watched closely for new outbreaks of the Scourge, even after all this time. . . .

Someone had to be vigilant.

Not all League expenditures were as beneficial to its citizens. Illuminated in spotlights across the Zimia plaza, Vor saw the ostentatious Cathedral of Serena under construction, one of the many projects Rayna Butler and her Cultist followers had pushed through the government in recent years. When completed, it would be the largest and most expensive religious structure ever built. Though Vor revered and loved Serena—the *real* Serena—more than anyone still alive, he felt that the energies of reconstruction might have been better turned elsewhere.

The Cult of Serena had grown too quickly, for all the wrong reasons. Though earnest Rayna remained dedicated to her antimachine crusade, many of her followers seemed interested in using the pale young woman as a fulcrum to build their own power bases. He could see it clearly, though others apparently didn't notice.

No one wanted to listen when Vor, the "old warmonger," pointed out the obvious problems.

He heaved a deep, exasperated sigh. Parliamentary and military leaders moved forward with their own agendas and left the Supreme Bashar out of the decision-making process. His rank had become more ceremonial than functional. Though Vor still looked like a young man, even Faykan Butler had suggested that he accept a long-deserved retirement. Vor would not go down in a blaze of glory, like Xavier Harkonnen. This was worse. Vorian Atreides was just fading into obscurity.

Each day as he arose early and went about his business in the city, Vor's thoughts turned backward, to fond moments and personal crises he had endured. Serena, Leronica . . . even Seurat, whom he'd called Old Metalmind.

He hated being ineffective.

Vor was now one hundred thirty-five years old, but he felt far older. When he finished his daily duties in the Army of Humanity headquarters, he no longer had anyone waiting for him at home. His sons were now old men with extensive families of their own, all living on far-off Caladan.

And Vor missed his former adjutant Abulurd Harkonnen, who had seen him as a mentor and a father figure—much more so than Estes or

Kagin ever had. But Abulurd had spent the past year in the Corrin system keeping Omnius contained.

As if his thoughts had summoned his protégé, Vor looked up to see Abulurd himself striding purposefully down the street toward the military headquarters. His uniform was rumpled and he hurried along without an escort, ducking his head in the drizzle. His movements conveyed a sense of urgency.

Only half convinced he wasn't imagining Abulurd's reappearance, Vor hurried down the corridor, took the stairs two at a time, and rushed to the door, startling the other man as he tried to enter. "Abulurd, it is you!"

The younger officer slumped, as if he had used his last energy to get here. "I came straightaway from Corrin, sir. I took a spacefolder scout, because I had to arrive ahead of the machines. But I don't know how much time we have."

THOUGH VOR AND Abulurd both felt a similar sense of exigency, the rest of the Parliament members felt that the crisis was somewhat exaggerated.

"After so many years, what can the thinking machines possibly hope to accomplish? They are defeated!" exclaimed the Giedi Prime representative.

"And if these automated missiles passed through the scrambler fields, isn't it certain that any gelcircuitry would have been wiped out? Therefore, we have nothing to worry about." The stuffy Honru ambassador lounged back with a smug look on his face.

"There is always something to worry about—so long as a single incarnation of Omnius remains." Vor couldn't understand why they would be so confident. But the attitude wasn't surprising: Anytime they were faced with a difficult problem, the representatives discussed it until everything became muddled and inconclusive.

After Abulurd's return, Vor spent more than a week arranging meetings, speaking directly with other subcommanders. Abulurd submitted his recorded images taken from the watchdog fleet, showing the strange projectiles. Finally, the Supreme Bashar insisted on addressing the Parliament directly. According to his projections, depending on the acceleration rate and the fuel reserves, the superfast missiles could arrive at Salusa any day now.

"Are you certain you're not exaggerating the dire threat, to rile up the populace and strengthen the Army of Humanity, Supreme Bashar?" a thin man from Ix said. "We've all heard your war stories."

"Be thankful you didn't have to live through it yourself," Vor growled. The Ixian man scowled. "I grew up during the Scourge, Supreme Bashar. We may not all have as much battlefield experience as you do, but every one of us had hard times."

"Why go chasing shadows?" muttered another man, whom Vor didn't recognize. "Send some scout ships out to patrol the perimeter and intercept these projectiles before they can reach Salusa. If they ever come. That's how Quentin Butler took care of the plague projectiles."

The meeting continued in a similar vein for the better part of the morning. Finally, disgusted with what he heard beneath the great golden dome of the Hall of Parliament, Vor slipped outside. Pausing at the top of the stone steps, he looked up into the cloudy sky and heaved a great sigh.

"Are you all right, sir?" Abulurd hurried forward from between the ornate columns to the carved-stone steps.

"The same old foolishness. The legislators have forgotten how to talk about anything other than farm prices, space-travel regulations, reconstruction subsidies, and massive public projects. Now I finally understand why Iblis Ginjo formed the Jihad Council during the height of the war. People might have complained about their draconian powers, but at least they made prompt, effective decisions." He shook his head. "The greatest enemy of humanity now seems to be complacency and bureaucracy."

"We have limited attention spans for long-term threats or projects," Abulurd pointed out. "Our society is so focused on returning to normal— as if anyone can remember what that is—that we can't focus on a threat we thought we had already dealt with."

Now the rain resumed, heavier than before, but the veteran officer did not move. Someone floated a suspensor umbrella shield over Vor's head to protect him from the moisture. Abulurd again. Vor smiled at him, but the bator remained concerned.

"What are we going to do about it, sir? Those missiles are on their way." Before he could answer, a gust of wind snatched the suspensor umbrella, pulling it across the stone steps, and Abulurd chased after it.

The two of them were just about to go back inside the Hall of Parliament when Abulurd, after gaining control over the suspensor umbrella, pointed into the distance. The umbrella broke free again in the wind. This time he didn't chase it.

Like the slashes of a predator's claws, silver-orange streaks cut down across the sky. "Look—the missiles from Corrin!" Abulurd groaned, filled with as much shame as alarm that he had not been able to get anyone to heed his urgent warning.

Vor clenched his jaw. "The Army of Humanity believes its own propaganda. People think that simply because we've *decreed* the Jihad is over, our enemies no longer scheme against us."

He took a deep breath, remembering too vividly what it was like to be a battlefield commander. "It looks like I'll need someone to help me," he said to Abulurd. "You and I have work to do."

It was said of Norma Cenva that one could not judge her on the basis of appearances. No matter her physical failings or the classic beauty that eventually replaced them, neither represented the essence of the woman. She was, above all else, a cerebral powerhouse.

—PRINCESS IRULAN,
Biographies of the Butlerian Jihad

When she returned to Rossak, the silvery-purple jungle in the deep rift valleys brought back an avalanche of memories from Norma's childhood. The skies were still stained with toxic smoke from distant volcanic action, and the smell of the life-laden atmosphere rose up like a miasma from the dense undergrowth below the cliff cities. There, the jungles swarmed with the most unusual plant and insect life, flora and fauna fighting for survival in the sheltered, fertile cracks.

Norma remembered as a young girl going out on expeditions with Aurelius and his botanical specialists, hunting in the lush jungles for plants, fungi, berries, even insects and arachnids that could be converted into pharmaceuticals. VenKee Enterprises still reaped great profits from their drug harvests on Rossak, though melange had become the company's dominant export product.

In Norma's recent vivid vision, however, she saw that nearly everything here would be destroyed. Soon. Something terrible would happen to Rossak, to the Sorceresses, to everyone. She hoped she could convince her half sister of the urgency, though Ticia would want proof, details, explanations. Norma could offer nothing like that . . . just a very strong premonition she had had during an intense melange-induced dream.

Ticia would not be very amenable to taking Norma at her word.

Many years ago Ticia had gone out on one of the last raids against cymeks; she and her fellow Sorceresses had been prepared to unleash their mental powers, to take enemy cymeks with them as they died. All of Ticia's companions had sacrificed themselves, and Ticia herself would have been the next in line. But then the cymeks had retreated, leaving Ticia the sole survivor, her sacrifice not needed, and somehow she had always resented not getting her chance. Ticia's personality was formed of regrets, blame, and determination. She could find many ways that her life had soured, and as many people to identify as the cause.

The Supreme Sorceress had always ignored Norma to the point of pretending she didn't exist, letting her work alone on Kolhar with her ships and her space-folding engines. She was as devoted to her projects as Norma was to hers. In an odd way, that allowed Norma to understand her half sister.

Now that the Jihad was over, there was no longer any call for the women of Rossak to be trained as suicidal mental juggernauts. Now the Sorceresses devoted their energies to studying and managing all the bloodlines they had compiled over generations, along with all of the new genetic material they'd collected during the worst of the Omnius Scourge.

"I suspect your inspiration, your premonition, comes more from the distortions of too much melange than from any real prescience," Ticia said, after listening to Norma's message. They stood together on a cliff balcony, staring down into the thick jungles.

As Supreme Sorceress, she wanted little to do with drugs and artificial crutches. As far as she was concerned, only the weak were forced to rely on drugs. VenKee had made enormous profits by distilling stimulants, hallucinogens, and medical treatments from the exotic jungle plants. The whole matter was distasteful to Ticia, as was her half sister's obvious addiction to the spice from Arrakis.

Both women looked icily beautiful, tall and pale-skinned, with platinum-blond hair and precise features. Inside her mind, though, Norma still saw herself as the dwarfish, blunt-featured woman who could easily be intimidated by domineering Sorceresses, like Ticia.

"It was not my imagination," Norma said. "It was a warning. I know that among the Sorceresses, precognition is occasionally manifested as a talent. You certainly have the records to prove that."

"I will send a message if your dire prediction comes to pass. Just go back to Kolhar and do your work." Ticia lifted her chin regally. "We have our own important duties here."

Norma looked at her half sister through sparkling blue eyes that seemed to veil a whole universe beyond. She touched her own temple and smiled complacently. "I am working on the calculations every moment. I can do them here as easily as on Kolhar."

"Then perhaps we'll both see whether your bad dreams come to pass."

BUT FOR DAYS, nothing terrible had happened, and Norma could provide no further details of her premonition.

Each morning during her extended visit, Norma walked alone through the densest jungle, selecting roots, berries, and leaves and tucking them away in her pockets without ever explaining why. *Such a strange person,* Ticia thought, watching her half sister from afar.

Hazy sunlight glinted off Norma's unnatural gold hair and milky skin as she made her way trancelike up a steep path from the jungle floor, toward the high cliff opening where the Supreme Sorceress stood. So preoccupied, so absentminded. How amusing it would be if Norma were to trip and tumble to her death. . . .

Their mother had abandoned Ticia as a baby in order to spend all her time with Norma, choosing this . . . freak over her, over a perfect Sorceress. *Fall, damn you!*

When Norma's gliding steps brought her up the steep path to the cave opening, Ticia continued to stare at her, never moving. Norma spoke directly to the Supreme Sorceress, as if she were continuing a dialog she'd been having for some time, probably inside her head. "Where do you keep the computers?"

"Are you mad? We have no thinking machines here!" Ticia was shocked that her half sister would have guessed their secret. *Is she . . . really prescient? Should I take her warning seriously?*

Norma looked at her without ire, not believing Ticia for a moment. "Unless your minds have been trained to the organization and capacity of a computer, you must be using a sophisticated system to maintain such vast amounts of detailed genetic data." She studied Ticia with the intensity of a deep-scanning instrument. "Or are you doing a poor and sloppy job because you're afraid to use the necessary tools? You don't seem the type."

"Computers are illegal and dangerous," Ticia said, hoping it would be enough of an answer.

Norma, as usual, fixated on the problem and refused to let go. "You need not fear suspicion or paranoia of machines from me— only curiosity. I myself took advantage of computerized organization and response systems to solve the foldspace navigation problems. Unfortunately, the League failed to admit the benefits, and I was forced to discontinue that highly productive line of work. I would not begrudge you their usefulness for your own research."

Before Ticia could develop a viable-sounding excuse, she heard the sudden shrill whistle of something hot and fast screaming through the air. In unison, they looked at the hazy morning sky where silver descent trails streaked down, targeted toward the deep, sheltered rift valleys. Large projectiles crashed into the treetops, plunging through foliage and thudding into the jungle floor.

Norma bit her lower lip as she nodded slowly. "I think this is the start of what I saw in my vision." She turned to Ticia. "You had better sound an alarm."

Hearing the impacts outside, white-robed Sorceresses rushed from their cave chambers and moved about with intense, determined speed. At the base of the cliff, one of the projectiles that had embedded itself in the soft loam began to shudder and open like an eggshell. A flurry of metal parts sprang out, dug into the ground, and dumped dirt, pebbles, and other materials into a processing hopper.

Despite her fearsome premonition, Norma studied the crashed projectile with detached curiosity. "It appears to be an automated factory—though not as sophisticated as a genuine thinking machine—using local resources to assemble something."

"It's a *machine*," Ticia said. She grew rigid, ready to generate a power source in her body that would enable her to fight in the only way she knew. "Even if it is not a cymek, it is our enemy."

On the jungle floor, several men in VenKee uniforms approached the crash site. Filled pouches were clipped to their belts from a day of harvesting the underbrush. One pale, distorted-looking young man accompanied them like an eager puppy; he was cow-eyed and misshapen, an unsettling freak, and Ticia scowled at him from her high vantage, wishing the Misborn would just die when they were cast out into the jungle. . . .

Then, as the curious group approached the landed projectile, the automated factory spat out its first completed products: small silver spheres that flew like armored, hungry insects. They rose in a swarm, scanned the area, and then rushed en masse toward the VenKee party. The misshapen young man scampered away with surprising speed and vanished into the thick and tangled underbrush, but the VenKee men did not move fast enough.

"They are small, but they must have crude sensors," Norma said, still sounding analytical.

The flying metal mites swirled around their victims like a cloud of angry wasps, then struck like tiny buzz saws, shredding the men, stripping cloth and skin, sending out a spray of blood and bits of ground-up flesh. Then men shrieked and screamed, running, thrashing, but the piranha machines pursued them, ate away at them, mangling their bodies.

Then the fanged mites streaked toward the cave openings. "They have targeted us," Norma said.

Ticia shouted to the other Sorceresses, and the powerful women of Rossak stood together, facing the oncoming cloud. The buzzing little drones, covered with sharp metal spines, whirred forward like bullets. Ticia began to shake, calling up her mental abilities.

Behind the Sorceresses, the children and men of Rossak crowded into safe chambers. Ticia and her companions raised a crackling wind with their minds, sending forth small blasts of telekinetic power like a mental hurricane. Clusters of the oncoming mechanical mites were scattered, then pulverized in the air. Then more came. The crashed factory probe was manufacturing the machine mites by the thousands.

"This doesn't require as great an effort as vaporizing a cymek," one of the Sorceresses said, "but it still satisfying in its own way."

"Omnius has found a way to send a new weapon against us, even from behind the League's barricade," Norma said. "These machines are pro-grammed to hunt us down and destroy us."

Metallic clouds of artificial insects filled the air in front of the cliff cities, seeking out victims. The Sorceresses were surrounded by ozone and invisible wind. Their pale hair flew about, their garments rippling with telepathic currents. Ticia raised her hand, and with a concentrated burst the women wiped out another wave of machine mites. Then, joining their efforts together, the Sorceresses blasted the factory cylinder itself, imploding its mechanisms into a thick lump.

"Send men down with flame cutters and explosives," Ticia said. "They need to destroy that cylinder before it can repair itself." She felt exhilarated and smug, even to the point of acknowledging her half sister's dire prediction.

"The war is not over," Norma pointed out. "It may be just starting. Again."

If thinking machines have no imaginations, how is it that they continue to conceive such horrors to unleash against us?

—BATOR ABULURD HARKONNEN,
"Zimia Incident Report"

All of the Zimia security inspectors and curious bystanders who ran to the pod crash sites were killed. Even remote images went blank within seconds as the deadly flying machines devoured everything in their path. All contact was cut off.

Suspecting the worst from Omnius, Vor rallied the home guard regiments, ordering weaponry and fighters to surround the pod landing sites. Standing at his side, Abulurd Harkonnen helped implement his commander's every instruction. The Supreme Bashar was like an angry Salusan bull, and no one dared stand in his way.

"I told them we had to remain vigilant," Vor grumbled to Abulurd. "I told them not to let their guard down. You even brought us a direct warning, and still they wouldn't listen!"

"Given a few years of peace, people quickly forget what urgency feels like," Abulurd agreed.

"And now that we're faced with some new attack from Omnius, we respond like scuttling rodents!" Vor made a disgusted sound.

Even before they knew details of the threat, Abulurd coordinated detachments of soldiers stationed in the city districts nearest the crash sites. Using emergency powers, he activated and dispatched any mercenaries who remained under contract with the Army of Humanity.

The coffin-sized projectiles had crash-landed in a broad zone. Elemental resources churned through fabricators in a widening factory maw, and swarms of insatiable devices—each the size of a ball bearing—spewed forth from the automated factories. Each one had a power source, simple programming, and very sharp jaws. Like piranhas, they sought out any human form, then attacked and devoured.

As people fled, the mechanical mites buzzed about on a mission of unrelenting destruction, swarming to strip their victims down to shreds of dripping flesh and splinters of gnawed bone. Soldiers in uniform, as well as citizens in tight-fitting slacks and shirts, seemed to be particular targets. Women and priests in flowing robes, and old men in tall retromodern hats, avoided notice for a time, but the voracious flying mites swarmed back around to take a second look—and then attacked.

People ran screaming through the streets, dropped in their tracks before they could find shelter. Like relentless sausage grinders, the piranha mites burrowed through bodies in random courses, disgorging mangled meat. As soon as each victim dropped, the tiny machines buzzed upward again and sought new targets.

The first wave of responding soldiers was cut down quickly. Piranha mites slammed into them like killer bees, but some of the fighters switched on their personal shields to block the onslaught. Others were not so quick to activate their shields, and when the mites hit them, they fell as if sprayed with toxic gas. Their hand weapons were useless against the sheer numbers of mechanical attackers.

Even shielded people succumbed eventually as the mites battered against the Holtzman barriers, probing, exploring, until they stumbled on the trick of slow penetration. Blood and cellular tissue splashed inside the shimmering force walls. Within moments, the trapped mites destroyed the generator apparatus, the shield bubbles faded, and the bloody mites rocketed outward.

More and more of the attackers swarmed through the air. Families ran into buildings and vehicles, sealing themselves inside, but the mites followed and always found ways to get through. There were no hiding places.

In a widening radius, collector devices scoured for available metals and added them to the voracious processors to create more and more flying hunters. The crashed machine cylinders opened wider, dug deeper, and mites continued to fly outward like a cloud of buckshot. The mobile factories sent out brute-force gatherers that demolished Zimia structures for their resources, stripping the buildings down to remove metals and other necessary elements.

The perimeter of destruction widened.

ABULURD FOLLOWED SUPREME Bashar Atreides as they rushed to the scene of the nearest infestation. When Vor bellowed orders, the inexperienced Zimia soldiers were too frightened to hesitate. He and Abulurd established a temporary sealed command center not far from the first impact point. Pandemonium ruled in the streets. Citizens locked themselves in sheltered rooms and closets, trying to hide from the self-propelled bullets with sharp teeth.

Less than an hour had passed since the first landing, and already thousands had died.

Finally, the League's artillery came within firing range. Abulurd checked the manifests. "The shells are loaded with high explosives. Our gunnery officers say they're ready to fire. One direct hit should take out that factory, and then we can clean up the mess."

Vor's brow furrowed. "Give the order to fire, but don't expect it to be that easy. Omnius undoubtedly built in numerous protective systems." He gestured with one hand. "However, the sooner we know what those defenses are, the faster we can find ways to circumvent them."

A barrage of artillery shells pounded outward in short arcs, flying point-blank toward the nearest factory pit. As the explosives dropped toward the target, clouds of piranha mites swirled like smoke around the open production mouth. The voracious devices clustered together, as if they could form a barricade against the infalling projectiles. Hordes of mites connected to each other with sticky interfaces, clustering into various shapes, setting up large obstructions.

Then the mite clusters homed in on each incoming shell, like mechanical leeches. They dismantled the shells in midair, ripping them to tiny scraps of metal, which they delivered into the factory maw, where the raw materials were broken down and converted into more of the killer units.

Without direct orders, one foolhardy mercenary swooped over the vicinity in a small armored flyer, and the machine mites targeted him. Thousands of the flying devices clumped along his flyer's hull, where they began stripping away the metal, the seals, the electronic systems.

As a last gesture, the mercenary managed to drop only one of his explosives. The projectile tumbled down and detonated in the air before the mites could dismantle it entirely. The shockwave merely stirred up the furious mites and caused little damage.

The mercenary's fighter broke apart. For a moment, the doomed man fell free, flailing in the air, and then the piranha machines zeroed in and ripped him to shreds. He was dead before the tattered remnants of his body struck the ground.

Faced with such a horrific threat, some of the younger soldiers failed to respond to the Supreme Bashar's orders; dozens had fled their posts. Vorian looked angry, but Abulurd said, "They are inexperienced and unaccustomed to all the awful things the machines can do."

For a moment, Vor gave the other man a faint smile. "Others might have grown lax, Abulurd, but you have never slackened in your training. We need to find a solution, you and I. Something effective that we can implement immediately."

"I won't let you down, Supreme Bashar."

Vorian looked at him with warm, deep pride. "I know, Abulurd. It's up to the two of us to save all of these people."

When men achieve paradise in this life, the result is inevitable: They
go soft, lose their skills, their edge.

—Zensunni Sutra,
revised for Arrakis

After the ancient Tuk Keedair had died, Ishmael was the oldest person in the Zensunni village. Keedair, a slaver, had ostensibly remained a prisoner of Selim Wormrider's band of outlaws. Though he'd certainly had ample opportunity to make his escape and return to League civilization, the Tlulaxa flesh merchant had accepted his lot among Ishmael and his desert Zensunnis.

Ishmael had never called the flesh peddler a friend, but they'd had many interesting nighttime conversations, drinking spice coffee as they stared out at the passage of stars. Though enemies, they had at least understood each other. Somehow, ironically, they'd had more in common than the current group of village leaders.

Now as Ishmael sat after his evening meal, he listened to the elders, including his daughter, talking among themselves. Even Chamal spoke of city things, appliances and luxuries that Ishmael did not need or want. The lives of these free men were filled with more amenities than even Savant Holtzman's household slaves had received. It was all so unnecessary—and dangerous.

By now, the descendants of the freed Poritrin slaves had intermarried with the survivors of Selim's band. Ishmael's own daughter Chamal had taken two other husbands and had five more children; now she was considered a valued elder of the tribe, a wise old matron.

Ishmael wanted to make sure none of them forgot their former lives, insisting that the outlaws maintain their skills and their independence so they would never again fall prey to flesh merchants. While Arrakis was not the promised land they had hoped it would be when he'd led them in their desperate escape, Ishmael wanted them to keep this world no matter what the cost.

Others, though, saw him as a bitter and stubborn old man who preferred the hardships of times past to modern improvements. Twenty years ago the spice rush had changed Arrakis forever, and now the offworlders would never leave; instead, they came in greater numbers. Ishmael knew he could not stop it, and he realized with a sinking heart that the Wormrider's vision had been perfectly accurate: The melange trade was destroying the desert. There seemed no place left where he and his people could live free and unharassed.

Twice more in the past month, Naib El'hiim had invited trading ships to land nearby, giving them the coordinates for the supposedly secret and secure Zensunni village, so they could exchange spice for supplies.

Lost in his thoughts, Ishmael snorted. "Not only have we grown dependent on commerce from the cities, we have also become too lazy even to go there!"

One of the old men next to him shrugged. "Why should we undertake a tedious trip all the way to Arrakis City, when we can force the offworlders to work for a change?"

Chamal chided the speaker for his disrespectful tone, but Ishmael ignored them both, frowning and keeping his own counsel. No doubt the villagers considered him a fossil, too rigid to accept progress. But he knew the dangers. Since the end of the Jihad and the loss of so many workers due to the Scourge, slavery had once again become widespread and accepted. And flesh merchants always preferred to prey on Buddislamics. . . .

Despite his age, Ishmael's vision remained sharp. Peering out into the night, he was the first to spot the incoming ships. The running lights of the craft marked their passage as they arrowed closer—not in an uncertain search pattern, but directly toward the Zensunni village. Instantly he felt a sharp uneasiness. "El'hiim, have you invited more nosy, unwanted visitors?"

His stepson, sitting in conversation with the elders, stood promptly. "No one should be coming." He walked to the edge of the cave, and the flyers came in with increasing speed. The roar of their engines sounded like a distant sandstorm.

"Then we should prepare for the worst." Ishmael raised his voice, summoning his commanding authority from when he had led these people himself, many years ago. "Guard your homes! Strangers are about to arrive."

El'hiim sighed. "Let's not overreact, Ishmael. There could be a perfectly good reason—"

"Or a perfectly dangerous one. Better to be ready. What if they are slavers?"

He stared furiously at his stepson, and finally El'hiim shrugged. "Ishmael is right. There's no harm in being careful." The Zensunnis went to stand together and prepare their defenses, but they did not seem to be in much of a hurry.

The sinister ships circled closer, alternately accelerating and decelerating. Upon reaching the cliffs, men in dark uniforms leaned out of gaping hatches and opened fire with small weapons. The Zensunni people shouted and scrambled back into the shelter of their caves.

Explosions peppered the walls, but only one projectile entered a balcony chamber and did damage, creating a small rockslide. Moments later the ships landed on the flat sands at the base of the cliff. A stream of men in ragged uniforms marched out, moving like beetles on a hot rock, with no organization or plan. Their weapons were new, however.

"Wait, they're just spice prospectors!" El'hiim shouted. "We have traded with those men before. Why are they attacking—"

"Because they want everything we have," Ishmael said. Gunfire continued to rain around them, small explosions, shouts, and confusing orders. "Did you brag about how much spice we have stored in this village, El'hiim? Did you tell these merchants how much water we have in our cisterns? How many healthy men and women live here?"

His stepson wore a startled and troubled expression. He took so long denying the accusation that Ishmael had his answer, and knew what had really happened.

As he watched the strangers unload their equipment—stun belts, nets, and strangle-collars—Ishmael knew these were not simply raiders. He cried out in indignant horror, his voice surprisingly strong. "Flesh merchants! If they capture you, they mean to take you as slaves."

Even El'hiim reeled. Surely he could see that these outsiders had betrayed his trust and now deserved to die.

Chamal stood beside her father, shouting to the others. "You must fight for your lives, your homes, and your futures! Leave no survivors."

Ishmael looked at her with a hard smile. "We will defeat these men as a lesson to any others who might come against us. They think we are soft. They are foolish and wrong."

Though frightened, the Zensunnis shouted in response. Men and women scrambled through the cave chambers, grabbing Maula rifles, clubs, worm goads, anything that could be used as a weapon. A group of older Zensunnis who had been among Selim Wormrider's first outlaws proudly sported crystalline daggers made of sandworm teeth. Chamal rallied a group of women, wild-eyed with feral anger, who carried curved blades of their own, fashioned painstakingly from scrap metal.

With renewed warmth in his heart, Ishmael saw the determination in their faces. He drew his own crystal knife, which he had earned when he'd learned to ride a sandworm. Marha had owned one, too, but she had given it to El'hiim upon her death. Now Ishmael turned to his stepson, and finally El'hiim drew his own blade.

The would-be slavers crawled up the cliffside paths, charging and yelling, slipping on rocks. They were too confident in their sophisticated weaponry. Knowing Naib El'hiim, they expected his villagers to be weak desert scavengers.

But when the offworlders pushed through the openings into the cave city, they were completely unprepared for the resistance they met. Howling like jackals, the desert nomads struck from every shadowy corner, trapping the slavers in blind chambers and slaughtering them. High-powered gunfire rang out in response.

"We are Free Men!" Ishmael howled. "Not slaves!"

Shrieking like wounded children, four of the flesh merchants managed to run stumbling down the path toward their ships, hoping to escape. But a handful of Zensunni volunteers had already slipped away from the main battle, bounded down the steep slope, and boarded the vessels. Hiding inside, they met each man who came aboard and slit his throat.

After all the would-be slavers were killed, the Zensunnis nursed their injuries and counted their dead: four. When El'hiim recovered from his shock and astonishment, he sent scavenger crews into the empty ships. "Look at these craft! We will confiscate them from the men who wanted to take us as slaves. It is a fair enough bargain."

Ishmael stood before the younger Naib, his face flushed with anger. "You speak as if this were a commercial transaction, El'hiim! Buying and selling commodities just like any other trip to Arrakis City." He pointed a gnarled finger. "You endangered all of our lives, bringing these men here despite my warnings, and now, sadly, I have been proven correct. You are not fit—"

The older man bunched his muscles, half raised his hand to strike his stepson across the face, but that would have been a mortal insult. El'hiim would have been forced to respond, challenging Ishmael to a death duel. One of them would end up slain on the cave floor.

Ishmael could not allow that to split the unity of the tribe, and he had promised Marha to watch out for El'hiim—so he forced restraint upon himself. He saw a flash of fear in the younger man's eyes.

"You were right, Ishmael," El'hiim said quietly. "I should have listened to your warnings."

Breaking the gaze, the old man shook his head, and Chamal came up to put a comforting hand on her father's shoulder even as she looked at the Naib. "You never knew the nightmare of living as a slave, El'hiim. We risked our lives to break free of bondage and come here."

"I will not allow you to sell our freedom," Ishmael said.

His stepson looked too shaken to reply. Ishmael turned and stalked away.

"It will not happen again," El'hiim called after him. "I promise that."

Ishmael gave no indication that he had heard.

The march of human civilization is a constant succession of achievements and setbacks, always proceeding uphill. Adversity may make us stronger, but it does not make us happier.

— SUPREME BASHAR VORIAN ATREIDES,
Early Assessments of the Jihad (Fifth Revision)

On ancient charts, their next destination was known as Wallach IX. Quentin had never heard of it. The planet had no place in human history, as far as he knew. Apparently not even Omnius had considered it an important part of his Synchronized empire.

Still, this planet had been a target in the Great Purge. One of the Jihad battle groups had come here, releasing squadrons of pulse-atomic bombardiers to drop scattered warheads to vanquish the evermind, and then departing as flashes and shockwaves swept through the atmosphere. . . .

Wallach IX showed little evidence that it had ever been civilized, even before the attacks—no major industries, only sparsely populated settlements. Someone had crushed the natives to the edge of survival well before the Army of the Jihad bore down on them like an avenging angel.

But Wallach IX was the next destination on Porce Bludd's mapped-out plan of inspection and aid. The Poritrin lord flew his space yacht in a quick survey. Beside him, Quentin studied the scarred and poisoned landscape that grew larger beneath them. "I am highly skeptical of finding survivors down there."

"We never know what to expect," Bludd said with contagious optimism. "But we can always hope."

They cruised over the flattened, skeletal ruins of several old settlements, but detected no recent signs of life, no rebuilt structures, no indications of agriculture. "It's been almost twenty years," Quentin pointed out. "If anyone had survived, they would have made some sort of mark by now."

"We need to be thorough, for humanity's sake."

In the city with the largest buildings, they also encountered the most destruction. The ground, rocks, and structural frameworks were glassy and blackened.

"Radiation levels remain high," Quentin said.

"But not immediately lethal," Bludd added.

"No, not immediately lethal."

Surprisingly, they did discover signs of new construction, including large columns and heavy arches that were unsettlingly ornate. "Why would survivors waste time building gaudy memorials when they don't have any way to feed themselves?" Quentin asked. "Showing off?"

"I've detected a few scattered power sources." Bludd ran his fingers over the controls. "But there's too much radiation for me to pinpoint them. I knew I should have invested in upgrading the yacht's capabilities. It was never designed as a survey vessel."

Quentin stood. "Why don't I use the small scout flyer? We can cover more ground that way."

"Are you in a hurry, my friend? Once we depart from Wallach IX, we can only look forward to more long weeks in transit."

"Being so close to . . . all this makes me uneasy. If there's nothing to be found here, I'd rather get the job done soon and be on our way."

Quentin flew out in the small scout ship designed for short excursions over planetary surfaces. Bludd's space yacht had too many conveniences, and there was nothing for a man to do besides sit back and let all the operations take care of themselves. This was much more interesting. It felt good to be out on his own, actively scanning an area, holding the engine power at his fingertips. Just like when he'd first led the raid on Parmentier, long ago. . . .

The Poritrin lord landed the large yacht in a devastated area near what had been a ruler's palace on Wallach IX. He transmitted to Quentin's cockpit, "I'm suiting up and going outside to see what I can learn about these new towers. Who built them and why?"

"Be careful." Quentin cruised in an ever-expanding circle. The destruction had a sickening sameness to it: charred rubble, dirt melted into glassy puddles. He saw no trees, weeds, or movement. Like Earth, Wallach IX was thoroughly dead, completely sterilized. But that had been the goal of the Army of the Jihad, he reminded himself. At least there was no sign of Omnius here.

Without warning, a burst of weapons fire hit him, damaging the flyer's engines and sending him into a deadly spin. Quentin yelled, hoping the comline would automatically pick up his words. "I'm under attack, Porce! Who— "

He struggled to regain control. Another explosion ripped his wing, and all Quentin could do was hang on. His view through the cockpit window twirled, alternating between the scarred ground and open sky. Suddenly he saw movement below, large mechanical things with articulated bodies. Combat robots? Had Omnius survived somehow? No, it didn't look right.

Flicking switches and rerouting power, he activated a secondary thruster and managed to stabilize his path, though he was losing altitude swiftly. One engine was on fire. He had barely enough lift to keep himself aloft for a few more minutes, putting more distance between himself and the mysterious attackers. Just long enough to get back to Bludd's yacht, with any luck.

He tried to squeeze out distance and power. Another explosive projectile soared up from the bizarre machines below, detonating close to him. The shockwave shorted out a full bank of his controls.

Now Quentin finally recognized what had attacked him. Enormous walkers, just like the ones he had seen in historical images . . . or like those that had attacked him on Bela Tegeuse long ago. "Cymeks! Porce, prepare to get away. Return to your ship." But he couldn't tell if his comline still functioned.

He was going to crash.

The mechanical behemoths marched across the blackened landscape, emerging from their lair to continue firing on the unexpected human scout. With great strides, they moved across the melted radioactive ground, hurrying to intercept him.

Oily smoke spurted out behind him like blood spilled in the sky. The cockpit rattled and lurched. The ground rushed up at him. He edged another burst from his attitude jets, a nudge to keep him aloft just long enough to pass a line of jagged black rubble, then he dropped into a gentle bowl.

With a screech, the scout ship's lower hull ground against the crumbled and sterile soil. Spraying sparks and clods of dirt, the flyer slewed, nearly tumbling end over end, but Quentin scrambled to keep it level, like a careening sled. Half of the left wing sheared off as the scout flyer made one last lurch into the air and slammed back down with a loud crash.

The restraints against his chest were so tight they nearly suffocated him. The plaz cockpit window cracked in a spiderweb pattern, and greasy dust splashed across his view. Finally the nightmarish ride stopped, and the mortally wounded scout ship collapsed on the open ground.

Quentin shook his head, realizing he must have blacked out for a few seconds. His ears were ringing, and he smelled smoke, lubricants, burned metal, shorted electronics . . . and dripping fuel. When he couldn't unfasten the restraining straps, he worked loose his ceremonial combat knife and slashed himself free. His body ached with mere hints of all the pain he would feel as soon as the shock wore off. Quentin knew he was in trouble, realized that his left leg was probably broken.

Tapping unsuspected reservoirs of energy, he managed to lift his head and shoulders out of the wreckage. And saw cymeks coming for him.

BLUDD RECEIVED THE urgent call as he stood clad in his antiradiation suit before an obelisk decorated with ornate scrollwork. It had been erected near the ruler's hall as some sort of ridiculous Golden Age memorial. He whirled as Quentin's emergency signal rattled through his helmet. In the distance he saw the scout flyer under fire, weaving through the air, and finally careening down into an open area far from him. The flyer slewed, tore up the dry ground, then came to a halt in a pile of debris.

Alarmed, Bludd hurried back toward the space yacht, clumsy in the thick suit. Feeling a crawling fear, he turned around again to see nightmarish combat walkers like the ones that had long ago attacked Zimia. The Titans had returned! Cymeks had set up a base here in the radioactive ruins of a Synchronized World.

Like enormous metal-shelled crabs, the cymek walkers stalked over the debris, stomping on anything that blocked their way to the scout ship. Bludd stared, paralyzed with dismay. He could never get to the crashed flyer in time to rescue his friend.

Still conscious after the crash, Quentin shouted over his suit's short-range comline. "Get away, Porce! Save yourself."

Bludd scrambled aboard the space yacht, sealed the hatch, and removed his helmet. He didn't bother to take off the rest of his antiradiation suit. Throwing himself into the pilot chair, he activated the still-warm engines and lurched the space yacht into the contaminated air.

OVER A RISE, the cymek walkers converged on the downed scout flyer.

Quentin watched them come, knew he had less than a minute. He wore only a flight suit, not an antiradiation suit, and could not survive in the poisoned environment for long.

As his enemies approached, his mind raced, thinking of his military training and experience, clawing through possibilities. The scout flyer carried no armaments at all. He couldn't defend himself—not in any conventional way.

But he did not intend to go down without a fight. "Butlers are servants unto no one," he muttered to himself, like a litany. His ship's fuel cells were cracked, leaking volatile fluid into the engine chamber and all around the crash site. The smell was sharp and acrid in his nostrils.

He could ignite it, detonate the tank, and maybe drive back the cymeks. But he would have to do it by hand. He would be caught in the explosion himself, incinerated. Even so, that might be better than letting the cymeks seize him.

Quentin heard the heavy movement in the still, dead air. Footfalls like pile drivers slammed into the dirt as the massive walkers approached, humming with hydraulics, buzzing with weapons preparing to fire. They could launch another explosive bombardment and roast him where he crouched in the meager shelter of the wreckage.

But they wanted something.

Ignoring the sharp pain in his broken leg, Quentin worked frantically with his hands and the emergency tool kit he recovered from a storage pocket in the cockpit. Fuel gushed out as he cracked open the caps of the sealed power cells. His eyes watered and stung, but he kept working. An electronic pulse beacon would do him no good. He found a primitive flare that would produce a hot spark, an intense shower of fire.

Not yet.

The first cymek walker reached the crashed scout and hammered on the rear hull. Quentin scrambled back into the pilot seat, gathered the shreds of his restraints around him, knotted them across his chest as best he could.

A second mechanical form approached from the left side, raising long spiderlike metal legs. He heard another cymek coming toward him.

With cool precision despite his growing alarm, Quentin activated the hot flare, tossed it behind him into the leaking fuel reservoir, and then with a quick prayer to God or Saint Serena or anyone who might be listening, he triggered the emergency ejection controls on the pilot seat.

Fire and fuel combined in a startling gush of heat and a shockwave like a mallet striking the air. The ejection seat hurled Quentin out of the cockpit, racing the explosion beneath him as the remnants of the scout ship detonated.

He tumbled through the air, the wind knocked out of him, his face and hair burned. The view was surreal and nauseating, but he did catch a glimpse of one of the cymek walkers lying mangled in the flaming wreckage of the downed ship. Another walker, obviously damaged, staggered away, one of its articulated legs destroyed, dangling in a stump that showered sparks.

Then he dropped with crushing force onto the ground again. The pain was excruciating, and he could hear a succession of bones crack inside his body: ribs, skull, vertebrae. The frayed restraints snapped, and as the ejection seat rolled, his body fell to one side like a discarded doll.

Looking at the site of the scout's explosion, he barely focused on the flurry of mechanical walkers. The surviving cymeks used laser cutters and heavy, sharp arms to tear open the few intact scraps of the hull, like hungry creatures trying to remove a savory morsel from a can. As if having a temper tantrum, one of the Titans tore the crashed flyer to shreds while two others lurched toward him.

His vision obscured by a red haze, Quentin could barely see and could hardly move, as if much of his muscle control had been severed. His left hand dangled at a useless angle from his wrist. His flight suit was covered with his own blood. Still, he forced himself to his knees and crawled forward in agony, trying to flee in any direction.

Behind him, the ratcheting sounds of walker-forms approached, growing louder and more ominous. The cymeks were like monsters from his most frightening dreams. After his close call at Bela Tegeuse long ago, Quentin had never wanted to see cymeks again.

Hearing a ragged noise, he looked up and saw Porce Bludd's space yacht rise up in the distance and dwindle away into the sky.

With a trembling hand, Quentin withdrew his ceremonial dagger. As the angry cymeks came after him, he prepared to fight. The cymek walkers fell upon him, a single human, helpless and unprotected on a devastated landscape.

The final analysis may show that I killed as many humans as
Omnius did . . . perhaps more. Even so, that would not make me as
bad as the thinking machines. My motives were entirely different.

—SUPREME BASHAR VORIAN ATREIDES,
The Unholy Jihad

After several failed reconnaissance missions, the Supreme Bashar finally had a complete, disappointing update: All nine of the automated factory pods remained intact, unaffected by any measure the humans threw against them. The manufacturing pits continued to spew out hungry piranha devices by the tens of thousands.

Since the piranha mites destroyed and dismantled almost all observation devices, seizing their components as raw materials for assembling more copies of themselves, Abulurd and Vor had access to only brief snapshots that showed the extent of the expanding robotic factories that burrowed in their craters.

Vor paced the floor, furious for inspiration. "What if we sent in projectiles filled with highly caustic liquids? Once the piranha mites strip away the shells, the acid will spill down and eat them."

"It might work, Supreme Bashar, but it would be extremely hard to hit the targets," Abulurd said, still staring at the images. "We could not get close enough to use hoses and pumps to spray acid into the factory pits."

"If we could get that close, we might as well use plasma howitzers," Vor said. "But it's a start. Unless you have a better idea?"

"Working on it, sir."

Abulurd stared at the images around the nearest pit, struck by the dichotomy of what he saw. Any fast-flying attack vessels were shredded, their metals stolen, and entire crews massacred. Buildings and machinery were torn apart; tall mounds of waste debris lay scattered around the gaping mouth of the fabrication cylinder. Human bodies sprawled about, splashed with red, mangled and chewed as if dozens of small projectiles had exploded inside their bodies.

"Those mites are too small to have sophisticated discrimination programming, but they are picking the targets somehow. Disassembling threats? Seizing concentrated resources? Maybe they're programmed to attack any organic material they detect."

Abulurd sifted through the sketchy available information. Oddly enough, in the lush surrounding parklands, the shrubs and tall trees were intact, entirely undisturbed. Birds flew away from the buzzing swarms of piranha mites, but the tiny ravenous spheres paid no attention to them.

"No, Supreme Bashar. Look, they've left the trees and other animals alone. They know to go after *humans*. Could they be homing in on . . . brain activity? Tracking our minds?"

"Much too sophisticated—and we know they don't have gelcircuitry AI technology. That would have been destroyed when they passed through the scrambler web at Corrin. No, it's got to be something simple and obvious."

Abulurd continued to shuffle through the recon images. The mites attacked humans, and they sought out usable metals and minerals to build more copies of themselves. Cellulose, fabric awnings, wooden structures, and living trees and animals were unaffected.

He stared at the incongruity of an image taken from an infested park in Zimia. It was adorned with the usual fountains, statues, and memorials, but one statue of a fallen Jihad commander had been completely stripped down to its stone foundation. Even more bizarre, in another statue of a hero riding on a Salusan stallion, the piranha mites had destroyed only the human figure of the sculpture, leaving the horse part intact. But both parts of the statue had been made of the same stone.

"Wait, Supreme Bashar! I think—" He caught his breath, remembering the unexpected, but clearly noticeable, delay in mite attacks against women and priests in flowing robes or dresses, or men with strange hats, people with unusual coverings. *Disguising their humanoid outlines.*

Vor looked at him, waiting. In all his military training, Abulurd had learned not to blurt out the first thing that came to mind—although in this crisis the Supreme Bashar wanted to hear any suggestion, no matter how preposterous.

"It's simple shape discrimination, sir. They have a pattern model burned into their main circuitry. The piranha mites attack anything that fits a particular standard shape: two arms, two legs, a head. Look at these statues!"

Vor nodded quickly. "Simple, straightforward, not terribly elegant— exactly the way Omnius would do it. And it opens a door to a weakness we can exploit. All we have to do is mask our human shape, and we can walk right past them unnoticed."

"But the mites still strip any useful elements. There can't be any exposed metal."

Vor raised his eyebrows. "You mean we should make wooden flyers to deliver bombs?"

"Something far simpler. What if we cover ourselves with a blanket or tarpaulin, something made of organic materials the mites won't find usable. We could get close enough to those factories to cause some true harm. It won't provide us with any physical protection, though. If the ruse fails, then we'll have exposed ourselves—fatally."

"We'll have to take the risk, Abulurd. I like the sound of this deception," Vor said with a hard grin. "Should we call for volunteers, or are you thinking what I'm thinking?"

"Supreme Bashar, you are far too valuable for—"

Vor cut him off. "Remember how I was just scorned by the League Parliament and declared a useless old war fossil? You've seen how ineptly the younger soldiers are reacting in this crisis. How many of them would you trust on a dangerous mission?"

"I trust myself, Supreme Bashar."

Vor clapped him on the shoulder. "I trust you, too—and me. Beyond that, I am not willing to say. Let's put this plan into action, you and I."

VOR DELEGATED HIS command to a group of local officers, each in charge of defending against an individual piranha mite factory. He left an explicit explanation of what he and Abulurd intended to do, so that if it worked, the others could immediately put the same plan into practice. And if Vor and Abulurd failed, there would at least be some record of what they had attempted; those who followed might be able to come up with something more effective.

Vor was delighted with Abulurd's idea. "You've been studying my military strategies, haven't you?"

"What do you mean, Supreme Bashar?"

"This plan rivals some of my own schemes," Vor said as he pulled out the thick draping cloth. "Fooling the machines, tricking their sensors— like I did with the hollow fleet at Poritrin."

"This is not at all comparable to your triumphs, Supreme Bashar," Abulurd said. "The piranha mites are stupid opponents."

"Tell that to the people we're going to save. Let's move out."

Their time was short and options scarce, but Vor and Abulurd did their best under the circumstances. Other soldiers helped them to cover the two mobile suspensor pallets with layers of tent fabric and sheets, all made of natural fibers that the mites could not possibly see as valuable resources for the factory cylinders. Then Vor and Abulurd draped themselves and the floating pallets with the tentlike covering; so that as each man moved along with his equipment, he appeared as a wide, shapeless mass.

Abulurd's pallet contained a large plaz tank of intensely corrosive liquid connected to a dispersal nozzle. Vorian held a plasma howitzer that should incinerate the factory—if they could get close enough to it.

The two officers plodded forward, barely able to see. Though suspensors kept their pallets off the ground, the men still had to step through the rubble and spattered gore from shredded human corpses.

The stench made Abulurd ill, but he gritted his teeth and kept going. He had arranged a thin, gauzy section of fabric so that he could see ahead. To his left, the shapeless lump of the Supreme Bashar accompanied him. Abulurd knew they must look ridiculous moving forward, large and lumpy under the tented cloth. The piranha mites could easily have torn the fabric to shreds—if they knew to attack. But the thin layer of fabric kept them safe from the unsophisticated discrimination programming.

They worked their way forward slowly and deliberately. The humming, roaring sound pounded like electrical nails into Abulurd's spine. At the moment, he could imagine no death more horrible than having tiny chewing machines tunneling in and out of a human body—though worse by far, he thought, would be to let Vorian Atreides down. That, Abulurd would not do.

Finally, they reached the edge of the expanding pit. The mobile factory had opened its maw wider and wider, like a carnivorous flower. Robotic gatherers dumped metals and scrap into the opening like priests sacrificing to a hungry god. Exhaust chutes, like ventilation shafts, dumped waste materials and noxious gases. From other openings in the ever-expanding automated complex, streams of silver toothy spheres flew out, seeking new targets.

"If we don't stop this soon," Vorian shouted over the background noise, "it'll grow larger than we could ever destroy with hand-carried equipment."

Abulurd stood at the edge of the pit, holding his dispersal tube beneath the folds of opaque fabric, and powered up the pump. He slid the nozzle through the access slit that had been cut in the cloth. "Ready, Supreme Bashar."

Vor, even more impatient than the young bator, activated his plasma howitzer and unleashed a hellish gout of plasma fire down into the automated factory. Following his lead, Abulurd flushed caustic liquid through the tube, spraying a stream of corrosive chemicals.

It was like throwing gasoline on a mound of stinging ants. The whipping flames and oozing acid caused immediate, horrendous damage to the manufacturing devices: metals melted, circuitry and fabrication components corroded and broke. Noxious smoke whirled upward. The silvery piranha mites buzzed around in confusion.

Abulurd gripped the bucking hose that continued to gush smelly corrosives, careful not to splash himself. He directed the stream into the yawning gullet of the fabrication chute. Within moments, the mobile factory groaned and collapsed in on itself, a fuming cauldron of oozing, melting materials.

Vor's plasma flame struck down the gatherer robots, destroying everything else. The corrosive fluid caught fire, and flames spread across the already devastated pit.

Abulurd transmitted triumphantly to a nearby substation, where officers monitored their progress. "It worked! We've destroyed this fabrication plant. All subcommanders follow our lead. Now we go after the other eight of them."

"And when you're finished with that," Vorian added to the transmission, "we've still got a hundred thousand piranha mites to mop up."

THE FLYING DEVOURERS continued to wreak havoc, buzzing through the streets and striking down anyone who dared to come out and investigate the massacre. But once the fabrication pods had been eliminated, no more of the ravenous devices were produced.

Fortunately, like short-lived insects, the individual power sources died, but several long and terrifying hours passed before the last of the mites burned out and fell to the ground like silvery marbles littering the streets.

Exhausted, Vor and Abulurd sat on the steps of the Hall of Parliament. Along with the thousands of victims in the city, more than thirty political representatives had been slain. Their bodies had been removed from the premises, although messy stains and horrific splatters still covered the walls and staircases.

"Every time I convince myself that I can't hate the machines any more than I already do," Vor said, "something like this inspires new depths of revulsion."

"If Omnius sees a chance, he'll try to move against us again. He may even have found a way to break free of Corrin."

"Or maybe this was simply launched out of spite," Vor said. "Despite all the damage and pain those tiny metal monsters caused, I don't think Omnius really believed he could destroy Salusa Secundus with them."

The bator nodded, still badly shaken. "The Holtzman satellite net remains in place around Corrin. Omnius can't escape . . . unless he has some other plan."

Vor gripped the younger man's shoulder firmly. "We cannot let foolish politicians suggest that we lower our guard."

He reached down and scooped one of the small spheres from a cranny in the stone steps. It lay inert in his hand, its teeth razor-sharp. "Their small power supplies are exhausted, Abulurd, but I want you to retrieve hundreds of specimens. We'll need to dismantle and analyze them so the League can develop suitable defenses, in case Omnius decides to use them again."

"I'll put our best men on it, Supreme Bashar."

"Put *yourself* on it, Abulurd. I want you in charge of the project, personally. I've always been proud of you, and today has shown that my faith was never misplaced. I want you close to me. A long time ago I took you under my wing because I felt you needed the support. Today, of all the soldiers here in Zimia, you excelled. You would have made your grandfather proud."

Abulurd felt warm inside upon hearing the praise. "I have never regretted reclaiming my Harkonnen name, Supreme Bashar, even though others heaped dung upon me because of it."

"Then maybe it's about time for us to fix that." Vor narrowed his gray eyes. "It has been decades since I told you the truth about Xavier. I thought that would be enough, but I should have known better. There is an old saying that one should not stir up unwarranted trouble. All along, I had decided that Xavier chose his course and was content with how he knew history would paint him.

"I can't even get the League to invest enough firepower to destroy the Corrin-Omnius and the remaining cymeks. I figured I had no chance at all of convincing the Assembly to rewrite history, pardon Xavier, and reveal Iblis Ginjo as the real villain." His eyes blazed. "But it's not fair to let my old friend pay such a price. You have been braver than I, Abulurd."

Abulurd looked as if he would choke with the effort of containing his tears. "I—I only did what seemed right to me, Supreme Bashar."

"When I see the right chance, I will raise the matter, at least get my objections on the record." He looked around the bloodstained streets of Zimia. "Maybe they will finally listen."

He clapped a hand on Abulurd's shoulder. "But first, it's time for you to get your due. Since the Great Purge, your rank has not risen in proportion to your performance. Although other officers will deny it, I'm convinced you have been punished because of your Harkonnen name. From this day forward, that changes." Vor stood now, looking grim and determined. "I give you my solemn promise that you will receive the full rank of bashar, fourth grade—"

"*Bashar!*" Abulurd cried. "That's a jump of two ranks. You can't just—"

Vor cut him off. "After today, I'd like to see them try to argue with me."

Despite their biological flaws, human beings continue to see things
that our most sophisticated sensors cannot detect, and they under-
stand strange concepts that gelcircuitry minds cannot comprehend.
It is no surprise, then, that so many of them go insane.

—*Erasmus Dialogues*

The standoff in the skies over Corrin between the robot fleet and the *hrethgir* battleships that constantly sought to destroy them held no sense of urgency after almost two decades; Erasmus was far more interested in a small drama in his own gardens.

There was no need for complex or subtle spy apparatus; he simply observed unobtrusively. Completely intent on a conversation with the latest Serena Butler clone, Gilbertus had not noticed his presence. His human ward seemed enraptured by her presence, though the robot couldn't understand why. Surely after twenty years Gilbertus would have wearied of his efforts to fashion her into a worthy mate. This clone was flawed, mentally deficient, damaged somehow by Rekur Van's re-creation of her flesh.

But his ward claimed to be attached to this particular clone, for some inexplicable reason.

Gilbertus looked like an adoring and patient young man as he sat with an open picture book. Serena looked at the illustrations and paid attention to some of his words, but other times she stared at the flowers and the jewel-toned hummingbirds that flitted about, distracting her.

Behind the hibiscus hedge, Erasmus held very still, as if his motionlessness might convince her that he was merely a garden statue. He knew the Serena clone was not stupid . . . simply uninteresting in any way.

Gilbertus touched her arm. "Look at this, please." She turned her gaze back to the book, and he continued to read aloud. Over the years, he had diligently taught her how to read. Serena could access any book or record in the vast libraries kept on Corrin, though she rarely chose to do so. Her mind was usually engaged in less meaningful things. Gilbertus had never stopped trying, though.

He showed the Serena clone great masterworks of art. He played exceptional symphonies for her, and he exposed her to many philosophical treatises. Serena was more interested in amusing pictures and funny stories. When she grew bored with the picture book, Gilbertus walked with her around the gardens again.

As he observed Gilbertus's makeshift teaching techniques, Erasmus recalled that many years ago he had filled the same role with an unruly, feral child. The task had required extreme effort and a relentless dedication that only machines could devote. Eventually, the robot's work with Gilbertus Albans had paid off.

Now he watched his ward attempting to do the same thing. It was an interesting reversal. Erasmus could find no flaw in his technique. Unfortunately, the results simply weren't equivalent.

Through medical analyses, Erasmus knew that the Serena clone had the biological potential her genetics provided, but she lacked a mental capacity. More importantly, what she lacked was a set of meaningful experiences, the ordeals and challenges the original Serena had faced. The clone had always been too sheltered, too protected . . . too numb.

Suddenly Erasmus thought of a way to salvage the situation. Fashioning a broad grin on his platinum face, the robot pushed his way through the crackling hedge and strode over to Gilbertus, who smiled back at his mentor. "Hello, Father. We have just been discussing astronomy. This evening I plan to take Serena out under the night sky and identify constellations."

"You have done that before," Erasmus pointed out.

"Yes, but tonight we'll try again."

"Gilbertus, I have decided to make you a fine offer. We have other cells, and the possibility for creating many other clones, which will likely be superior to this one. I recognize how hard you have worked to bring this version of Serena up to your level. It is not your fault that you haven't succeeded. Therefore, I suggest as a gift to you that I will provide another identical clone." He broadened his flowmetal smile. "We will replace this one so that you can start again. Certainly you will have better results next time."

The man looked at him with an expression of horror and disbelief, "No, Father! You can't do that." He clutched Serena's arm. "I won't let you." Gilbertus held Serena close to him and whispered soothingly to her. "Don't worry. I'll protect you."

Though he did not understand the reaction, Erasmus rapidly withdrew his offer. "There is no need to become upset, Gilbertus."

With a look over his shoulder as if the robot had just betrayed him, Gilbertus quickly took Serena away. Erasmus stood pondering, reassessing what he had just experienced.

LATE THAT NIGHT, under the dark skies of Corrin, the robot continued to spy on Gilbertus and the clone as they sat outside the villa, staring up into the sky. Though the trails of constantly shifting warships sketched distractions across the backdrop, Gilbertus pointed out patterns of stars, traced outlines, and identified the groupings on old star charts. Serena seemed amused and drew her own patterns in the sky.

Erasmus felt oddly unsettled, even troubled. When he had spent years teaching Gilbertus, at least he received positive feedback and rewards from the progress his ward made. Even the original Serena Butler, with her sharp tongue and emotional debates, had been a worthy mental sparring partner.

But the clone offered none of those things to Gilbertus.

No matter how many times Erasmus reran his thoughts through his gelcircuitry mind, this made no sense at all. It was a puzzle that a sophisticated independent robot should be able to solve. But though he observed the two humans for hours that night, he came no closer to any insight.

What does Gilbertus see in her?

For those who know where to look, the past produces clear indications for us to follow in our journey into the future.

       —A History of VenKee Enterprises

After returning from Rossak, having neither expected nor received gratitude for the warning she had delivered, Norma stood naked and curious in front of a mirror. Though she was not vain, she examined her body for more than an hour. Its classic bone structure and milky skin should have made her the vision of perfection, but imperfections appeared with unfortunate frequency: growing red blotches, ripples in her skin, and shifting features, as if her bone structure and her muscles had become plastic. Puckered patches of red covered large areas of her chest and abdomen. Even her stature seemed smaller. Distorted.

So peculiar. She could always restore her appearance if she willed it, but the flaws would reappear. Norma wanted to understand what was happening.

Adrien had noticed, but she could not explain it to him. At his insistence, she consulted one of the shipyard doctors, an elderly female specialist. The doctor prodded, frowned, and then made a quick pronouncement. "Allergic reactions, probably caused by an overconsumption of melange. Your son tells me you ingest immense quantities."

"Thank you, Doctor. Please reassure Adrien." Her noncommittal words produced the desired effect, and the medical specialist turned to depart.

Norma would have preferred to be left alone, to concentrate on her work, and she had no intention of cutting back her melange consumption. Her recent visit to Rossak and her warning premonition about the piranha mites had left her unsettled. If the machines were indeed stirring again on Corrin, preparing new horrors against humanity, then she must always keep her mind alert and on guard.

For that, she needed more spice.

She had been experimenting with different variations of melange: solids, powders, liquids, and gases. Physically and mentally, she was already different from any other human being.

Norma could get rid of the blotches that appeared on her skin, but why bother? Now, still standing in front of the mirror, she made the blotch on her upper body fade, and then brought it back intentionally. Such folly to keep herself beautiful. For what? For whom? A waste of time and energy. Allowing her body to change would never diminish the love she held in her heart for Aurelius.

VenKee market studies showed that some people experienced immediate reactions to melange, while others developed them over time. Norma did know that large doses of spice opened doors in her mind and in the universe, allowing her to see pathways to the impossible. In fact, contrary to the doctor's advice, she intended to take even larger doses of spice, pushing the limits of her capabilities.

Since the Great Purge, Norma had lived with a weighty, perplexed guilt because so many of the Jihad spacefolders and crews had been lost. Certainly, she had made progress on individual elements of the problem since then, but the ultimate solution still eluded her. It was time to redouble her efforts and solve the space-folding navigation problem once and for all.

From the storage bureau inside her private chamber, she removed a specially designed breathing mask, which she sealed over her mouth and nose. When she touched a button, gas hissed through the tube, carrying with it the pungent odor of melange. Rusty orange swirls colored her vision. She could barely see outside herself, but she could see *within*.

Due to the high level of spice already in her body, the effects were almost immediate. Norma experienced a stunning vision . . . at last, a brilliant epiphany in which she saw the solution to the navigation problem—a means of safely avoiding the hazards of space.

The key lay not in machinery or calculations, but in *prescience*, a mental ability to forecast safe paths across vast distances. Like her recent vision of the danger to Rossak. With repeated exposure to melange at high enough concentrations, she could open up far more abilities than anyone had suspected humans possessed. Her earlier computerized probability calculators had been the crudest possible attempt along these lines. But with spice, her own mind could become a far superior navigation tool. *Prescience*.

Recovering from her revelation, Norma noted that her body had shifted back to something resembling its former stunted shape, the original pattern, though with more crudely formed features and a larger head. Why? A throwback? A distant cellular memory? A subconscious choice?

But her mind was expanding, crackling with energy as it focused on what was important: Melange. Navigation. Folded space. Prescience.

The answer at last!

BECAUSE HER BODY had chosen the new shape during her vision, Norma let it remain that way, a rough approximation of the body she had grown up with, blunt-featured and stunted, but with a grossly larger head in relation to her dwarfish frame.

She didn't attempt to resculpt her appearance. It was simply an unnecessary expenditure of energy. The whole physical journey to beauty seemed shallow to her, infinitely insignificant in the scheme of the cosmos.

Unlike the spice, prescience, and folding space . . .

A guiding mind aboard a space-folding ship could predict disasters well before they happened, in time to plot a different path through folded space. Yet merely knowing the basis of her answer had not shown her how to physically implement the solution. Still, it was only a matter of time.

Each experiment brought Norma closer to her goal. She found it amazing that melange was both efficacious for inhibiting the Scourge and for traveling via folded space. The substance itself was a miracle—an extremely complex molecule.

Now her work required ever-increasing quantities of melange, and through VenKee she could obtain as much as she needed. The price of melange on the open market had risen swiftly. Twenty years ago, a significant percentage of the human population had survived the Omnius Scourge in large part because of the spice. Unfortunately, afterward their appetites had been whetted; many of the survivors were even addicted. The epidemic had changed the economy of the League, and VenKee Enterprises, in dramatic and unforeseen ways.

Her eldest son was ambitious and clever, just like Aurelius had been. Norma had never craved power or wealth herself, shying away from the fame her remarkable discoveries brought, but she realized that her navigational breakthrough and the feasibility of space-folding ships would allow Adrien and his descendants to expand the already wealthy VenKee Enterprises into a commercial empire as powerful as the League itself.

Norma knew that the gaseous form of melange was superior for her purposes, more intense, taking her mind to previously unattainable heights. Now, with eager anticipation, she planned to take her idea to the next stage.

Full spice immersion, total exposure, complete dependence.

OBSESSED WITH HER plan, Norma conscripted laborers and technicians from other projects in the shipyards. In comparison with the huge vessels with complex Holtzman engines and shield generators, her project was small and inexpensive. But it would have more far-reaching importance than anything else she had ever done.

Though he tried to talk with her, Adrien didn't completely understand what his mother hoped to accomplish, and she did not try to articulate the reasons. Lately, it seemed difficult for her to speak in his language, but he never argued with her requests. He knew that whenever Norma had one of her vast ideas, the shape of the galaxy was bound to change.

The crews constructed a transparent, airtight plaz chamber fitted with nozzles, to which they connected large bottles of expensive melange gas. When the chamber was complete, Norma sealed herself inside, bringing a simple cushion on which to sit. *Alone.* Closing her eyes, she turned a control to pump in orange spice gas. She drew deep breaths, waiting for the effects, as the enclosure filled with more melange than she had ever before consumed. Such a potent concentration would have killed an unprepared person, but she had built up a great tolerance, and *need,* for the spice.

With wide-eyed Kolhar workers looking on, she inhaled deeply of the curling orange gas—and felt herself dropping away, accelerating into her mind. The cells of her misshapen body swam in the cinnamon-smelling vapor, merging with it. Total concentration, total calm.

This experience took her beyond the technology of folding space, lifting her to a level of pure spirituality. To Norma, the essence of being human was her ethereal nature. She felt like a sculptress on a cosmic scale, working with planets and suns as if they were modeling clay.

It was majestic and liberating.

She remained sealed inside the chamber without food or water—only the nourishing spice. The clearplaz walls became streaked with rusty brown, and she barely heard the constant hiss of gas jets around her.

At long last, she swam in a place where she could really *think*.

One cannot understand humanity without taking a sufficiently long view. We are in an excellent position to achieve this.

—*Rossak Archives,*
"Statement of Purpose"

The bloodlines of humanity formed an intricate and beautiful tapestry, but only for those who were able to see it. The warp and weft of DNA threaded from family to family, generation to generation. Nucleotide sequences combined and recombined, shuffling genes, creating a near-infinite number of human patterns. Not even the Omnius evermind could comprehend the potential that lay within beings that sprang from this awe-inspiring double-helix molecule.

Ticia Cenva and the Sorceresses of Rossak had taken on that project as their charge and their quest.

Deep inside the cliff cities, far from the sounds and smells of the silvery-purple jungle, far from the scars left by the recent attacks of the swarming piranha mites, Ticia stood with one of her tall, pale sisters inspecting their vital—and highly illegal—computers. These record-keeping devices were anathema to the League of Nobles, yet here they were absolutely necessary. The Rossak women had no other way to sort and manage the overwhelming genealogical data they had acquired. The Sorceresses kept many deep secrets from the rest of humanity, and this was one of their boldest.

For generations the Sorceresses had maintained breeding records of all the families on this one planet. The environment of Rossak played havoc with human DNA, causing frequent mutations—some of which were horrific embarrassments, while others actually improved the species. The information collated during the Scourge offered them vastly more data to track and study.

Turning to the woman beside her, a young Sorceress named Karee Marques, Ticia said, "Now that we have compiled the basic bloodline data and followed many possible permutations, just imagine what we can do with this amazing information. Now we can finally put it to use." She pressed her pale lips together and admired the computers. "Projections. Perfection. Who knows what new human potential we can uncover? Our limitations can be erased. In fact, why should we stop at attempting the merely superhuman? There may be abilities we have not yet dreamed of."

She and Karee left the database rooms with their humming circulatory systems and power generators. The genetic computers were kept safe and shielded.

The two women entered one of the communal dining halls where a group of Sorceresses and their young female trainees gathered for a brief meal and quiet conversation. Ticia had arranged this place for the women to dine together so that they could speak of relevant problems rather than endure the inane chatter of the men about business interests. As the Supreme Sorceress took a seat, women and their students looked up and gave nods of respect to her.

The pleasant mood, though, was broken by a disturbance in the hall, people calling out, a slurred male voice. A short, broad-shouldered young man staggered in, helping another man walk. The young man's legs were short, his mop of blond hair disheveled. "Need help. Man sick."

Ticia drew her mouth into a tight frown of disapproval. Jimmak Tero was one of the Misborn, a birth defect who had lived. His face was wide and round, his forehead sloped, his blue eyes innocent and wide-set. He had a sweet disposition that did not make up for his dull intellect. Despite her constant scorn, Ticia had never been able to convince Jimmak that he simply wasn't welcome in the cliff city with all the normal people. He kept coming back.

"Man sick," Jimmak repeated. "Need help."

Jimmak half walked, half dragged the man to a seat at one of the dining tables. The man slumped face first onto the table. He wore a VenKee jumpsuit with many tools and pockets and sample pouches. He was one of the pharmaceutical prospectors who wandered through the Rossak jungle. Jimmak, a feral child, often helped such people out, showing them around the convoluted maze of the jungle's darkest levels.

Ticia came forward. "Why have you brought him here? What happened?"

Karee Marques stayed by Ticia's side. Jimmak helped to roll the man over. Karee gasped when she saw his face. Neither of them had seen such symptoms in almost two decades, but the signs were unmistakable. "The Scourge!"

Many of the women in the dining room stood up quickly, and withdrew. Ticia's breath came quick in her mouth, drying her tongue and her throat. She forced her voice to be calm and analytical. She could not afford to let them see her flinch. "Perhaps. But if so, it's a different strain. There's a flush in his cheeks and discoloration in his eyes. But those blotches on his face are different. . . ." She sensed an indefinable certainty deep inside that told her what should have taken hours of testing to determine. "But basically, I believe it is the same virus."

Ticia had known that the thinking-machine threat was not at an end. Although Omnius had attacked them with piranha mites, Norma's warning had been extreme, hinting at a far greater disaster than the mechanical mites. Perhaps the crashed pods had also contained the RNA retrovirus . . . or more likely the disease had simply gone dormant on Rossak, where it could have spent years brewing in the jungle, mutating, growing deadlier.

"He's going to die," Ticia said, looking at the drug prospector, then turned her stern gaze on Jimmak. "Why didn't you take care of him yourself? That way he might have infected all of you Misborn and put you out of your misery." Energy crackled in her blond-white hair as her anger began to slip out of control. But Ticia focused her concentration again. "You shouldn't have brought him to us, Jimmak."

The young man stared at her with his bovine eyes, looking hurt and disappointed.

"Go!" she snapped. "And if you find more victims, don't bring them here."

Jimmak scuttled away, moving backward with a clumsy grace. When he turned away, his gait was awkward, his head hunched down, as if trying to hide.

Staring after him, Ticia shook her head, ignoring the plague victim for the moment. She resented the Misborn for making a squalid living for themselves out in the jungle instead of just dying from their defects. No one knew how many of them there were. She would have despised all of them even if one—Jimmak—had not been her own son.

*There is a maddening equilibrium in the universe. Every moment of
joy is balanced by an equal measure of tragedy.*

—ABULURD HARKONNEN,

private journals

By the time his promotion to bashar made its way through the
bureaucracy of the Army of Humanity, Abulurd Harkonnen had
already handpicked a team to analyze the deadly piranha mites. He'd
studied the service records and accomplishments of loyal scientists,
mechanics, and engineers, choosing only the best. He invoked the name
of Supreme Bashar Vorian Atreides to requisition a newly vacated and
upgraded laboratory space not far from the Grand Patriarch's administrative mansion.

Many thousands of the tiny burned-out machines had been found
scattered like deadly hail pellets throughout Zimia. Abulurd's research
team dismantled more than a hundred of them to discover the rigid programming circuitry and the tiny but efficient power source that had kept
each mite moving—and killing.

Though he was not a scientist himself, Abulurd regularly inspected
the progress in the laboratories. "Do you have any ideas yet for defenses
against them?" he asked each man and woman as he passed their analysis
stations. "How do we stop them next time? Omnius is very persistent."

"Plenty of ideas, sir," said a female engineer without looking up from
an intense magnifying scope, through which she studied the miniaturized
machinery. "But before we can do anything definite, we need to understand these murderous little weapons much better."

"Would Holtzman pulses work against them?"

Another engineer shook his head. "Not likely. These devices are very primitive. They don't use gelcircuitry technology, so the Holtzman disrupters can't damage them. Once we understand their motivational programming, however, it's likely we can develop a similarly effective jammer."

"Carry on," Abulurd said. When he glanced at the chronometer, he excused himself and hurried to his temporary quarters so that he could prepare for the ceremony. Today he was scheduled to have his new rank insignia pinned on during a formal presentation.

Abulurd's small room was austere. Since he'd recently returned from a year of watchdog duty around Corrin, he had few personal possessions here. He played no music to relax. His life was in the Army of Humanity, and he had little time for shopping, hobbies, luxuries, or anything else.

Though he was thirty-eight years old and had occasionally toyed with romantic diversions, he was not married, had no children. He hadn't contemplated a time when he might settle down and focus on other priorities. Smiling, he put on his carefully pressed formal uniform. For a long moment, he inspected himself in the mirror. He practiced a suitably solemn expression, but his heart hammered with excitement. Abulurd wished his father could be here. On such a day, even Quentin Butler could have been proud of his youngest son.

But the retired primero had gone with Porce Bludd some time ago on a surveillance tour of the radioactive Synchronized Worlds. In his father's place, Faykan had agreed to do Abulurd the honor of pinning on his new rank.

He inspected himself one more time, decided that his hair, uniform, and expression were regulation perfect, and departed for the ceremony.

SEVENTY-EIGHT SOLDIERS WOULD receive promotions and commendations at this ceremony, and Abulurd waited patiently in his place while the lower ranks and the younger enlisted men received their rewards. He observed the older officers, the scarred war veterans, the consummate politicians, the brilliant tactical experts who had shaped the Jihad and the years of recovery afterward. They looked proud to usher a new crop of officers farther along in their careers.

It was a stinging disappointment, yet oddly not unexpected when

Faykan changed his plans at the last moment. The Interim Viceroy sent formal apologies that he would not, in fact, be able to present his younger brother with the new rank insignia. He did not detail his excuses, but Abulurd knew his brother's reasons were political. At least he hadn't bothered to lie about it.

Inside the echoing auditorium, the officer sat in silence. Though his heart grew leaden, he allowed none of his hurt to show. Such a display would have shamed him. Just because Abulurd had taken the surname of Harkonnen, it did not mean he no longer honored the Butler name.

Near the reviewing stand, a pedestal held the transparent preservation canister that contained the living brain of Vidad, the last of the Ivory Tower Cogitors. Vidad had returned to Salusa shortly after the Great Purge, announcing that all the other ancient philosopher brains had been killed when cymeks overran their stronghold. Vidad spoke little about what else he had done on his long journey; Abulurd had heard Vorian Atreides mutter that the Cogitor had probably wanted to be out of the way, in case the machine battle fleet did hammer into the League Worlds. Now the lone Cogitor remained on Salusa, curious, willing to either help or interfere, depending on his esoteric moods.

As the ceremony proceeded, Abulurd sat rigidly, recalling all he had accomplished, how he had unerringly followed orders, honored his commanding officers. He had always felt duty-bound to do what was required of him, not for applause, medals, or other accolades. But when he watched other officers receive the insignia of their promotions, with friends and families cheering, he understood how wonderful it could be. He suppressed a sigh.

Raising Abulurd to the level of bashar was the last activity in the already long and tedious process. When his turn finally came, Abulurd walked woodenly up to the stage, alone. The master of ceremonies announced his name, and mutters rippled through the audience along with polite applause.

Then a commotion occurred at the officer's bench. The master of ceremonies announced, "A new presenter will offer the rank insignia to Abulurd Harkonnen."

Abulurd turned as the doors opened. His face lit up, his mouth split into a grin, and his heart felt as if it would lift right out of his chest. Supreme Bashar Atreides had arrived.

Smiling, Vor joined Abulurd on the stage. "Someone has to do this right." The veteran warrior held up the bashar insignia like a coveted treasure. Abulurd stood ramrod-straight, presenting himself. Vor stepped forward. Although he looked barely half Abulurd's age, he carried himself with extreme confidence and respect.

"Abulurd Harkonnen, in recognition of the valor, innovation, and bravery you displayed during the recent attack on Zimia—not to mention countless other worthy demonstrations of your value to the Army of the Jihad over the course of your career—I am pleased to raise you from the rank of bator to the superior rank of bashar, level four. I can think of no other soldier in the Army of the Jihad who deserves this more than you do."

With that, Supreme Bashar Atreides applied the insignia to Abulurd's chest, then turned him so that he could face the onlookers. "Observe well your new bashar," he said, keeping a hand on his shoulder. "He still has great things to accomplish for the League of Nobles."

The applause remained somewhat muted and scattered, but the young man paid no attention to anything other than the look of paternal satisfaction on Vorian's face. No one else's opinion mattered as much to him, not even his father's or his brother's.

Now Vor turned to face the other military commanders, the League officials, even Vidad. "And after witnessing the bravery of Bashar Harkonnen in our most recent crisis, I am reminded of the similar deeds performed by his grandfather Xavier Harkonnen." He paused, as if daring them to object. "I was a good friend to Xavier, and I knew the true loyalty in his heart. I also know, *for a fact*, that his name was maliciously blackened and the truth obscured for political purposes. Now that the Jihad is over, there is no good reason to perpetuate those lies and protect people long dead. I propose a League commission to clear the Harkonnen name."

He crossed his arms over his chest. Abulurd wanted to hug him, but remained firmly at attention.

"But, Supreme Bashar . . . that was eighty years ago!" Grand Patriarch Boro-Ginjo said.

"Seventy-six years. Does that make a difference?" Vor looked at him with hard eyes. Xander Boro-Ginjo would certainly not like the findings of the commission. "I have waited too long already."

Then, like a window breaking unexpectedly in the silence of night, Abulurd's happiness was shattered. A disheveled, florid-faced man pushed his way into the presentation auditorium. "Where is the Supreme Bashar? I must find Vorian Atreides!" Abulurd recognized the Poritrin nobleman Porce Bludd. "I bring terrible tidings."

Immediately Vorian switched to his emergency mode, the same way Abulurd had seen him react during the piranha mite crisis. "We were attacked on Wallach IX," Bludd cried. "My space yacht is damaged—"

The Supreme Bashar cut him off, attempting to make the man organize his thoughts. "Who attacked you? Thinking machines? Is Omnius still alive on one of the devastated worlds?"

"Not Omnius—cymeks. *Titans!* They were building monuments, establishing a new base in the ruins. Quentin and I stopped to inspect, and the Titans charged out. They struck us, shot down Quentin's scout flyer. They tore his ship apart. I tried to rescue him, but the cymeks attacked and drove me off, doing significant damage to my ship. Then I saw them fall on Quentin."

"The cymeks!" Vorian said, unable to believe.

"No matter how many enemies we defeat," Abulurd said in a shaky voice, picturing his father trying to fight the machines, "another rises to take its place."

*The union of man and machine pushes the limits of what it means
to be human.*

—GENERAL AGAMFMNON,

New Memoirs

H is psyche swam in flashes of memory, sparking electrical impulses
that leaked out of his mind. Quentin Butler thought he was dying.
The cymeks had dragged him down, grappling with their articulated
metal legs. They could easily have torn him apart, just as they had shredded the hull of his crashed flyer. As he'd scrambled away in the radioactive atmosphere, the fallout had already been burning his flesh, his
lungs . . . and then the gigantic walker-forms crushed him—

His last vision was one of dismay and hope: Porce Bludd flying toward
him, attempting to rescue his friend, then limping out of range, home
free. When Porce escaped, Quentin knew he could die with some measure of relief.

The explosion of pain, the stabs, the cuts, the burning . . . And now
his thoughts were trapped in this endless loop, playing the last visions
over and over again. Nightmares, memories, his life draining away.

Occasionally, like bubbles rising to the top of a boiling pot, he saw
Wandra when she had been young and beautiful, an intelligent woman
filled with the zest of life. She had laughed at his jokes, strolled arm-in-
arm with him through the parks of Zimia. Once, they had gone to view
the huge monument made out of a wrecked Titan mechanical body. Ah,
the clarity of perception, the sharpness of perfect recall.

The two of them had had so much joy together, but the time was far too short. He and Wandra were a perfect match, the war hero and the Butler heir. Before everything had changed, before her stroke, before the birth of Abulurd.

In a recurring memory flash—a burst of stored chemical data in his brain, released in his last moments before death?—he again saw Porce successfully escaping from the cymeks. Quentin clung to that brief spark of joy, knowing he had accomplished something good at the very end.

But the darkness and oblivion suffocated him. Inner dread made it worse, as if he was reliving those awful, endless hours during the defense of Ix, fighting combat robots in the deepest cave channels. An explosion had brought the walls and ceiling tumbling down around him, and he had been buried alive, left for dead like his seven crushed companions. But eventually the rocks shifted, and Quentin had clawed and pushed, finally clearing a breathing space. He shouted and dug until his throat was raw and his fingers bloody. And finally, finally, he had worked his way upward and out into fresh air and dim light . . . and the amazed shouts of other jihadis who had never expected to find him alive.

Now the oppressive blackness was all around and inside him again. He screamed and screamed, but it did him no good, and the darkness did not go away. . . .

After a while, the pain changed, and he became completely disoriented. Quentin was unable to open his eyes. He heard no sounds. It seemed as if all his senses had been stripped away. He drifted in a kind of limbo. This didn't match the descriptions of death or Heaven he had read about in religious tracts and scriptures. But then, how could any prophet know for certain?

He couldn't feel any part of his body, couldn't see a glimmer of real light, though occasional flashes of residual neuron bursts flickered in the darkness of his unconscious sky.

Suddenly there came a lurch, and he seemed to be tumbling in zero gravity, floating . . . falling. Distorted sound returned to him, echoing all around with a clamor he had never before heard. He wanted to clap his hands over his ears, but couldn't find his hands. He couldn't move.

A female voice sounded thunderously loud around him, like a goddess. "I think that's part of it, my love. He should be aware now."

Quentin tried to ask questions, demand answers, scream for help—but found he could make no sound. Mentally he shouted, crying out as loud as he could imagine, but he could not find his vocal cords or his lungs. He tried to take a deep breath, but sensed no heartbeat or respiration. Yes, truly he must be dead, or nearly so.

"Continue to install the rest of the sensory components, Dante," a gruff male voice said.

"It'll be a while before we can communicate with him," said a second male voice. Someone named Dante? *I know that name!*

Quentin was curious, confused, frightened. He had no way to measure how much time passed, only the occasional indecipherable sounds he experienced, the ominous words.

Finally, with a crackle of static and a blaze of light, vision returned to him. In the glare and the jumble of indecipherable sights, he focused until he recognized the horrific images before him. Cymeks!

"Now he should be able to see you, Agamemnon."

Agamemnon! The Titan general!

Around him he saw smaller walker-forms, not designed for combat or intimidation, but still monstrosities. Brain canisters were installed in protective cages beneath the walkers' control systems.

Quentin and the cymeks were inside some sort of chamber . . . not out in the open skies that he remembered from Wallach IX. Where had they taken him? One of the cymeks continued to work in his field of view, raising slender, sharp arms, each of which ended in a strange surgical instrument. Quentin tried to thrash and escape, but was as ineffective and immobile as before.

"And this should establish connections with all the sensory endings that remain intact."

"Including the pain receptors?"

"Of course."

Quentin screamed. He had never experienced such agony. It was worse even than the suffocating darkness. Now, the stabbing pains went to the core of his soul, as if every centimeter of his body were being flayed from him with white-hot, dull knives. A shrieking, raucous cry rippled through the air, and Quentin wondered if he had somehow caused the noise.

"Turn the voice pickup off," said the gruff male voice. "I don't need to hear that racket yet." *Agamemnon.*

The machine with the female voice came into his field of view, moving smoothly, as if making seductive gestures, but she looked like a sinister spider. "It's merely neurologically induced pain, my pet. Not real. You will get used to it, and then it'll be only a distraction."

Quentin felt as if atomic warheads were going off inside his brain. He tried to form words, but his voice refused to work.

"Perhaps you don't know where you are," said the female cymek. "I am the Titan Juno. You've heard of me."

Quentin quailed, but could not respond. Years ago, he had attempted to rescue members of the enslaved citizenry on Bela Tegeuse, but instead they had turned on him and tried to deliver their prisoner to Juno. They hadn't wanted to be freed—they had wanted to earn the "reward" of being converted into neo-cymeks. He remembered her synthesized voice like metal scraping on glass.

"We have taken you as a specimen and brought you back to Hessra, one of our bases of operations. We are building new strongholds on abandoned Synchronized Worlds such as Wallach IX, where we found you, my pet. But for now, our main facilities are here, where the Ivory Tower Cogitors once lived." She made a strange lilting sound that might have been a laugh. "We have already performed the most difficult part. We've cut away and discarded the broken meat and bones of your body, leaving your lovely brain intact."

Quentin took a long moment to realize where—*what*—he was. The answer had been obvious, but he'd forced himself to deny it until the quieter male cymek—Dante?—adjusted his optic sensors.

"You will learn to manipulate things on your own, using thoughtrodes, given time and your choice of mechanical bodies. But now perhaps you would like to see this for one last time."

On the table Quentin recognized the bloody, sagging body that had formerly been his own. It was battered, bruised, torn—showing just how hard he had fought even up to the last minute. It lay there like an empty suit of flesh, a disconnected, discarded marionette. The top of the head had been cut away.

"Soon you'll become one of us," Juno said. "Many of our subjects consider that to be the greatest reward. Your military expertise will prove quite valuable to the cymeks—Primero Quentin Butler."

Even though his vocal pickup was not connected, Quentin howled in despair.

Successful creative energy involves the harnessing of controlled madness. I am convinced of this.

—ERASMUS,

The Mutability of Organic Forms

A fter a full day of training his loyal human ward, Erasmus stood alone in the Corridor of Mirrors on the main floor of his mansion. Even trapped on Corrin, with the fate of Omnius and all thinking machines in grave doubt, he still had a great deal of curiosity about esoteric matters.

With rapt attention, he studied the reflection of his flowmetal face, how he could make it change to mimic a variety of human facial expressions. Happiness, sadness, anger, surprise, and many more. Gilbertus had coached him well through his entire repertoire. He especially liked to play at making scary faces to engender fear, an emotion that stemmed from the humans' own physical weakness and mortality.

If only Erasmus could better understand the subtle ways in which humans were superior, then he could incorporate all the best aspects of human and machine into his own body, which would in turn become a template for an advanced series of thinking machines.

Under one scenario, he might be treated as a godlike figure. An intriguing possibility, but it did not particularly appeal to him, after all his studies. He had no great patience or empathy for the irrationality of religions. Erasmus sought only personal power in order to complete his fascinating experiments with *hrethgir* test subjects. The independent robot did not intend to end his machine existence anytime soon, did not envision himself becoming obsolete and discarded for a better model. He would keep improving himself, and that would take him in directions he did not presently foresee. He would *evolve*. Such an organic concept. Such a human concept.

Standing before the mirror, the robot tried out more expressions, particularly enjoying one in which he looked like a ferocious monster, copied from an ancient human text describing imaginary demons. Though he considered this one of his best faces, all of his expressions were too simple and basic. His flowmetal countenance was not capable of more subtle, sophisticated emotions.

Then a thought occurred to him. Perhaps Rekur Van could use his biological expertise to come up with an improvement, now that the reptilian limb-regeneration experiments had all failed. It would give the limbless Tlulaxa captive something to do.

As he walked through his ornate mansion toward the outbuildings, inquisitive watcheyes flew everywhere, surrounding him, like eager spectators. The independent robot found himself distracted by holo-art and music—shimmering flowmetal-like images of stylized machine warships going through battle maneuvers in space. In the background, a harmony of Claude Jozziny's "Metallic Symphony" played, one of the greatest pieces of synthesized classical music, performed entirely by machines. With complete satisfaction, Erasmus watched the dance of simulated warships around him, projected from lenses in the various rooms of his villa, the blasts of their weapons as they annihilated enemy vessels and planets. If only real war were so easy.

Omnius continued to dabble in his own embarrassing artwork, imitating Erasmus's efforts or those of historical human masters. Thus far, the evermind didn't comprehend the concept of *nuance*. Perhaps Erasmus himself had once been inept, before Serena Butler helped to teach him the subtleties.

With a mental command, the robot switched off the cultural exhibition, then entered the large central chamber of his adjacent laboratory complex, where the Tlulaxa's limbless torso was connected to its life-support socket, as always.

Beside the stump of a man, the robot was surprised to see swarthy little Yorek Thurr. "What are you doing here?" Erasmus demanded.

Thurr sniffed in indignation. "I was not aware that I needed permission to enter the laboratories. No one has denied me access before."

Even after twenty years, Thurr still preferred the elegant trappings he had chosen for himself when he'd been the despotic ruler of Wallach IX.

He wasn't as gaudy or ostentatious as Erasmus himself, but he still chose fine fabrics, bright colors, and impressive accessories. He wore a jewel-studded belt, a gold circlet settled upon his bald scalp, and a long ceremonial dagger at his hip with which he had slain many hapless subjects whenever they'd displeased him. Here on Corrin there were still millions of human captives to choose from.

"We thought you would be busy in your surgical experimentation rooms," Rekur Van said in a mocking tone. "Eviscerating a live human or reconstructing his body." As if stung, the Tlulaxa frowned in the direction of Four-Legs and Four-Arms, who were both puttering around in the side chambers, monitoring long-term investigation equipment.

"My behavior is as predictable as that?" Erasmus said. Then he realized that Thurr had successfully diverted the robot's original question. "You did not answer me. What is your purpose in my laboratory complex?"

The man gave a conciliatory smile. "I want to get away from Corrin as much as you do. I want to crush the League and take away their seeming victory. Years ago we were quite successful with our retrovirus epidemic, and recently our mechanical devourers escaped through the barricade. By now they should have struck some of the human worlds." He rubbed his hands together. "Rekur Van and I are impatient to begin something new."

"And so am I, gentlemen. Yes, that is why I am here." Erasmus stepped forward. Thurr could quite likely be of assistance, though his mind had not been entirely stable since his corrupted life-extension treatment.

"You have an idea?" Rekur Van began to drool in anticipation and could not wipe his mouth.

"I have many ideas," the robot said with considerable simulated pride. He found human impatience intriguing and wondered if it had something to do with the finite nature of their lives, the innate knowledge that they must accomplish things in only the time allotted to them.

"Observe." Erasmus demonstrated a variety of flowmetal facial expressions, scowling at the two men, displaying an artificial mouth filled with sharp metallic teeth.

The Tlulaxa looked entirely befuddled with what he was doing, while Thurr merely seemed annoyed.

Finally, Erasmus explained. "I find these faces, in fact my entire appearance, unsatisfactory. Do you think you can create a more lifelike flowmetal process? Develop a 'biological machine' that can mold itself to different appearances at will? I want to be able to pass as human, fool humans, look like any one of them, whenever I choose. Then I can observe them without being noticed."

"Mmmm," the former flesh merchant said. He might have scratched his head if he'd had arms to do so. Erasmus made a conscious effort not to count the time of the delay, as an impatient human would have. "I should be able to do that. Yes, it might be amusing to spend my time on that. Yorek Thurr can provide me with genetic material for experimentation. . . ." He smiled. "He has access to many sources."

The deadliest of poisons cannot be analyzed in any laboratory, for they are in the mind.

—RAQUELLA BERTO-ANIRUL,
The Biology of the Soul

It had been nearly twenty years since the Omnius Scourge had swept across the League Worlds, leaving populations in ruins, and then burning itself out as the hardy survivors developed immunities and protected themselves with the spice melange. Still, from time to time pockets of the retrovirus still reappeared, forcing sudden and stringent containment measures to stop its resurgence.

After decades of adapting to the rich, chemical-saturated environment filled with strange fungi, lichens, and plant growths, a new strain emerged from the jungle canyons of Rossak—a mutated super-Scourge that far exceeded the mortality rate of even Rekur Van's best genetic work.

League medical teams were called in; dwindling decontamination supplies and drugs were distributed. Specialists continued to face great risks to stamp out any new manifestation of the Omnius Scourge.

In the years since barely escaping the antitechnology mobs on Parmentier, and then reconnecting with Vorian Atreides after the Great Purge, Raquella Berto-Anirul and her companion Dr. Mohandas Suk had toured the League Worlds, plunging tirelessly into the hot spots. For HuMed—the Humanities Medical Commission—the pair of beleaguered physicians served as troubleshooters, traveling in the medical ship her grandfather had purchased for her, the LS *Recovery*. They cruised to more than thirty planets in their efforts to treat plague victims. No one knew more about the various forms of the Scourge than they did.

After the first reports, HuMed dispatched Raquella and Dr. Suk to face what became known as the Rossak Epidemic.

Other than its pharmaceutical merchants and drug distribution business, Rossak had always kept to itself. The Sorceresses were insular, preoccupied with their own work and claiming superiority over most people. Recognizing the hazard immediately, Ticia Cenva had imposed a draconian quarantine, refusing to let even the VenKee pharmaceutical ships depart. Rossak was completely walled off.

"It'll make the quarantine more effective," Mohandas said, quickly brushing his hand along her arm. "Easier to maintain."

"But that won't help any of the people down there," Raquella pointed out. "The Supreme Sorceress has issued strict orders that anyone who comes to the surface will not be allowed to leave until the epidemic is officially over."

"It's a risk we've taken before." Their medical ship took its place in a holding orbit, where it might have to remain for a long time.

"You should stay with the laboratories up here," she said to him. "Keep working on the test samples I send up. I can go with some of the HuMed volunteers to administer our treatments." Nothing they had developed so far was an actual cure, but the time-consuming and difficult treatments could clear the mysterious Compound X from a victim's bloodstream and give the patient time to fight back the liver infection, keep him alive.

After so many years of working together, she and Mohandas had a strong collegial bond in addition to being lovers. Aboard the ship, Dr. Suk could work without interruption or fear of contamination, studying the new form of the Omnius retrovirus. So far, though, all indications were that the Rossak strain was far, far worse than the original Scourge.

Raquella was more interested in helping the afflicted people. She and her assistant Nortie Vandego shuttled down to the cliff cities in the habitable rift valleys. Vandego was a young woman with chocolate-brown skin and a cultured voice; she had graduated at the top of her class the year before, and then volunteered for this dangerous duty.

Arriving at a groundside processing facility, they went through a battery of tests themselves before being released to do their work. After long and unfortunate experience, Raquella knew to take thorough precautions, protecting their wet membranes, covering eyes, mouth, nose, and any open scratches—as well as consuming significant prophylactic doses of spice. "VenKee provides it all," said one of the receiving doctors. "We get a shipment from Kolhar every few days. Norma Cenva never charges us."

Raquella gave an appreciative smile as she accepted her ration of melange. "We had better got to the cliff city, so I can assess the magnitude of the problem."

She and Vandego each carried a large, sealed container of diagnostic equipment as they headed across the spongy paved areas of the dense treetops. On their arms they wore patches bearing a crimson cross on a green background, the symbol of HuMed. High above them in orbit, Mohandas Suk would be waiting for a return shuttle to carry samples of infected tissue that he could culture and compare with antibodies obtained from those who had recovered from previous strains of the Scourge.

The air was filled with strange, peppery smells. People moved about on the ledges and stood in the open doorways of the cave cities. The tunnels looked like channels drilled into the cliff rock by hungry larvae.

Raquella heard the buzz of a bright green beetle as it dove out of dense purplish foliage, flew low along the polymerized leaves and canopy, then swooped higher above the treetops, its immense hard-shelled wings catching an updraft. The air was moist and oppressive from a recent tropical downpour. This place was rich with biological possibilities, festering and fecund. A perfect breeding ground for diseases, and possible cures.

Though their arrival was expected, along with other HuMed experts, no one came down from the cliff cities to meet them. "I'd think they would welcome us and our supplies," Vandego said. "They've been cut off here and dying in droves, according to reports."

Raquella squinted in the hazy daylight. "The Sorceresses don't have much practice in asking for—or accepting—outside help. But this is one challenge that their mental powers cannot influence, unless they can control their bodies, one cell at a time."

Raquella marched with her slender assistant toward the caves. When they reached the top level of the cliff openings, following walkways and bridges, they asked for directions to the hospital areas. Every tunnel and chamber seemed to be designated as infirmary space. Over half of the population was already affected, but the symptoms of the new Rossak Epidemic were variable and difficult to predict or treat. The death rate seemed to be significantly higher than the forty-three percent of the original Scourge.

The two HuMed women took a lift that dropped them along a channel on the outer face of the cliffs; the plunge was fast enough to make Raquella's stomach queasy, as if even the lift was anxious for them to get started. As she and her companion stepped off, a small and dainty woman in a long, hoodless black robe greeted them inside an immense, high-ceilinged enclosure. Tiers, railings, and balconies rose above them. Statuesque women in black robes hurried along walkways, and darted in and out of rooms.

"Thank you for helping us here on Rossak. I am Karee Marques." The young woman had shoulder-length pale hair, high cheekbones, and large emerald-green eyes.

"We're anxious to begin work," Raquella said.

Vandego looked around at all the gloomy black robes. "I thought the Sorceresses traditionally dressed in white."

Karee frowned. The skin of her face was translucent, showing only a faint flush. "We wear black robes for mourning. Now it appears we may never stop, if these deaths continue."

The young Sorceress led them through a central corridor, passing rooms filled with patients on makeshift beds. The facility appeared to be clean and well run, with black-robed women tending the patients, but she picked up the unmistakable odor of sour sickness and decaying flesh. In this devastating incarnation of the virus, pus-filled lesions on the skin gradually covered the entire body, killing the membranous skin cells, layer by layer.

Inside the largest grotto filled with hundreds, perhaps thousands, of patients in various stages of the disease, Raquella stared, reeling with the magnitude of the work to be done. She recalled Parmentier, how the Hospital for Incurable Diseases had struggled to make headway against the first manifestations of the epidemic. But it was like using a rag to mop up the tide.

Vandego swallowed hard. "So many! Where does one begin?"

Beside her, the black-robed young Sorceress stared, her eyes moist with frustration and grief. "In such a task, there is no beginning—and no end."

FOR WEEKS, RAQUELLA toiled long hours with the patients, reducing their blistering pain with special medpacks that released supercooled melange gas into their pores. The medpacks were a joint invention she and Mohandas had developed. At the end of the Scourge so many years before, Raquella had hoped she would never need them again. . . .

The Supreme Sorceress remained aloof, rarely bothering to visit or acknowledge Raquella's presence. Ticia Cenva was a mysterious, elusive figure who seemed to float on air as she walked. Once, when they locked gazes from thirty meters away, Raquella thought she detected hostility or strange fear in the woman's expression before Ticia hurried away.

The women on Rossak had always been very self-sufficient, ready to proclaim their superiority over others, demonstrating their mental powers. Perhaps, Raquella thought, the Supreme Sorceress did not want to admit that she was incapable of protecting her own people.

At a communal meal for the volunteer medical workers, Raquella asked Karee about her. The younger woman said in a low voice, "Ticia doesn't trust others, especially outsiders such as yourself. She is more afraid of the Sorceresses appearing weak than she is of the virus. And . . . there are things here on Rossak that we would prefer to keep away from prying eyes."

For a full week before requesting urgent aid from HuMed, Ticia Cenva and her Sorceresses had worked to combat the spreading plague in the cliffside cities, using their own cellular and genetic knowledge. They even turned to native herbs and drugs provided by the VenKee pharmaceutical researchers, who were also stranded on the planet due to the quarantine. But none of the attempts had been successful.

VenKee headquarters on Kolhar shipped massive amounts of melange, in hopes the spice could aid in staving off another League-wide outbreak. While Mohandas Suk worked diligently in his sterile orbital lab aboard the *Recovery*, Raquella sent regular samples up to him, along with personal notes, often telling him that she missed him. He reported back periodically, summarizing the variations he saw in the Rossak strain, the difficult resistance this new retrovirus showed to the barely effective treatments they had used last time. . . .

Raquella became known for her gentle ways with patients, alleviating their pain and dealing with each of them as important individuals. She had learned her hospice methods long ago in the Hospital for Incurable Diseases. More often than not, her patients died. It was the nature of the new epidemic. She stared down at an aged and respected Sorceress who shuddered her last watery breath, then sank into stillness. It was a peaceful end, far different from the convulsions and psychic uproar caused by some of the victims who experienced heavy delirium before fading into unconsciousness.

"If that is your best effort, it isn't good enough." Ticia Cenva stood close behind her, her face frustrated and angry; streaks of tears had long ago dried on her cheeks.

"I'm sorry," Raquella replied, not knowing what else to say. "We will find a better treatment."

"You had better do it soon." Ticia swept her gaze through the crowded infirmary as if the whole epidemic was Raquella's fault. Her face hardened into the bony features of a raven.

"I came to help, not prove my superiority." Raquella excused herself quickly and went to another ward, where she continued her work.

When testing our powers against each other, challenging our skills and careful routines, we can try to prepare for every eventuality. But as soon as we face real battle, everything we know becomes mere theory.

—ZUFA CENVA,

lecture to Sorceresses

T hough Quentin and Faykan never suspected as much, Abulurd made regular visits to see his mother in the City of Introspection. Now, after he'd received his promotion only to be struck down again by the terrible news of his father's brave end at the hands of the cymeks, he felt more alone than ever.

His brother was engrossed in politics as Interim Viceroy, while Vorian Atreides focused on how best to fight the cymeks if Agamemnon and the surviving Titans were planning further action against free humanity. Abulurd could not go to either of them for commiseration or sympathy, not now.

So, Abulurd went to see his mother. He knew Wandra couldn't respond to anything he told her. In his entire life, he had never heard her speak a single word, but he wished he could have known her. All he knew was that his own birth had taken away her mind.

Two days after learning of his father's death, his shock had abated enough for him to make this visit. He was sure no one had bothered to tell Wandra her husband's terrible fate. Likely no one, not even Faykan, considered it important or necessary, assuming she would be incapable of understanding.

But Abulurd dressed in his spotless formal uniform, making sure to polish the new bashar's insignia. Then he carried himself with all the dignity and impressive demeanor he could gather.

The devotees let him through the gates of the religious retreat. They all knew who he was, but he did not speak with them. Abulurd gazed straight ahead as he walked along the gem-gravel paths, skirting ornate fountains and tall lilies that evoked a placid atmosphere conducive to deep thinking.

For the morning, the caretakers had moved Wandra in her chair out into the sunshine next to one of the fish pools. The gold-scaled creatures darted among the weeds in search of insects. Wandra's face was pointed toward the water, her gaze empty.

Abulurd stood in front of her, his chin up, his back straight, his arms at his sides. "Mother, I've come to show you my new rank." He stepped close, pointing to the bashar symbol, its polished metal reflecting bright sunlight.

He didn't expect Wandra to react, but somewhere in his heart he had to believe that his words penetrated, that perhaps her mind was still alive. Maybe she craved these visits, these conversations. Even if she truly was as empty as she seemed, Abulurd didn't feel he was wasting his time. These were the only moments he spent with his mother.

He'd come here more often after retrieving her from the rescue ships at the end of the Great Purge, when Salusa was deemed safe from the robot extermination force. Abulurd had personally seen to it that Wandra and her caretakers were restored to the religious retreat.

"And . . . there is other news, too." Tears filled his eyes as he thought of what he must say. Many people in the Army of Humanity had already consoled him about the loss of his father, but that had been only passive sympathy. Too many knew that Abulurd and his father had a distant relationship. Their attitude angered him, but he kept his bitter responses in check. Now that he was speaking to his mother, he had to face what he knew and admit that the news was accurate.

"Your husband, my father, fought bravely and well in the Jihad. But now he has fallen to the evil cymeks. He sacrificed himself so that his friend Porce Bludd could get away." Wandra showed no response, but tears now streamed down Abulurd's cheeks. "I'm sorry, Mother. I should have been with him to help fight, but our . . . our military assignments did not coincide."

Wandra sat with bright eyes, staring disinterestedly at the fish in the pond.

"I just wanted to tell you in person. I know he loved you very much."

Abulurd paused, thinking, hoping . . . almost imagining that he saw a sudden glint in her eye. "I will visit you again, Mother." He looked at her for a long moment, then turned and hurried along the gem-gravel pathways out of the City of Introspection.

On his way, he stopped at the original crystalline coffin that held the preserved infant body of Saint Manion the Innocent. He had paid his respects at the shrine before. In the endless years of the war against the thinking machines, many visitors had come to see the baby who had sparked the entire Jihad. Abulurd stared down at his blurry reflected visage in the crystalline coffin, studying the face of the innocent child for a long time. When he left the City of Introspection he still felt very sad.

Memories are our most potent weapons, and false memories cut deepest of all.

—GENERAL AGAMEMNON,
New Memoirs

He was a prisoner without a body, trapped in limbo. The only break in the monotony of half existence came from occasional bursts of pain, images, or sounds when the other cymeks bothered to apply thoughtrodes to his sensor apparatus.

Sometimes Quentin could see the actual horrors around him; on other occasions, in his bath of pure electrafluid, he found himself adrift with memories and ghosts in a sea of longing thoughts.

He wondered if this was what life had been like for Wandra for so many years, trapped and disconnected, unable to respond or interact with her surroundings. Buried alive, like he had been on Ix. If her experience was anything like this, Quentin wished he had given her the blessing of a peaceful end long ago.

He had no way of telling time, but it seemed as if an eternity passed. The Titan Juno continued to speak tauntingly yet soothingly, guiding him through what she called "a typical adjustment." Eventually, he learned to block the worst of the phantom pain caused by nerve induction. Though it still felt as if his arms, legs, and chest were being bathed in molten lava, he had no real body that could experience the suffering. The sensations were all in his imagination—until Agamemnon applied direct inducers that sent waves of agony through every contour of his helpless disembodied brain.

"Once you stop fighting what you are," Juno said, "once you accept that you are a cymek and part of our new empire, then I can show you alternatives to these sensations. Just as pain is now readily triggered, you have pleasure centers as well—and believe me, they can be most enjoyable. I remember the delights of sex in the human form—in fact, I indulged in it quite frequently before the Time of Titans—but Agamemnon and I have discovered many techniques that are vastly superior. I look forward to showing them to you, my pet."

The odd secondary-neos who had once tended the Ivory Tower Cogitors trundled about their business, beaten and discouraged. They had adjusted to their new situation, but Quentin swore that he would never submit. He wanted nothing better than to kill all of the cymeks around him, even if it led to his own death. He didn't care anymore.

"Good morning, my pet." Juno's words thrummed into his mind. "I've come to play with you again."

"Play with yourself," he responded. "I can offer plenty of suggestions, but they are all anatomically impossible, since you no longer have an organic body."

Juno found this amusing. "Ah, but now we're also freed of organic flaws and weaknesses. We are limited only by our imagination, so nothing is truly 'anatomically impossible.' Would you like to try something unusual and enjoyable?"

"No."

"Oh, be assured, you could never have done it in your old meat, but I guarantee you'll like it."

He tried to refuse, but Juno's articulated arms lifted toward him, and she manipulated the thoughtrode inputs. Suddenly Quentin was awash in a whirlpool of exotic, breathtakingly pleasurable sensations. He couldn't gasp or moan, couldn't even tell her to stop.

"The best sex is mostly in the mind anyway," Juno said. "And now you are entirely mind . . . and *mine*." She hit him again, and the avalanche of ecstasy was even more intolerable than the spikes of incredible pain they had inflicted on him in his earlier punishment phase.

Quentin clung to his loving memories of Wandra. She had been so alive, so beautiful when they'd first fallen in love, and even though that was decades ago, he held on to the recollections, like beautiful strands of ribbon from a priceless gift. He had no desire for any form of sex with this vicious Titan female, even if it was all in his mind. It corrupted his honor and shamed him.

Juno sensed his reaction. "I can make this sweeter if you'd like." Suddenly, with a pulse of vivid awakening, Quentin saw himself with the ghost of his body again, surrounded by visual input painted directly from his past. "I can stir your recollections, pet, reawakening thoughts stored within your brain matter."

As a renewed wave of orgasms rocked the core of his brain, he envisioned nothing but Wandra, young, healthy, and vital, so different from the frozen mannequin he had seen for the past thirty-eight years in the City of Introspection.

Just having her in front of him again the way she had been gave him more pleasure than all the eruptions of stimuli that Juno playfully and sadistically released into his mind. Now Quentin reached out to Wandra, longingly—and Juno maliciously cut off the sensations and images, leaving him suspended in a dark limbo again. He couldn't even see the cymek's walker-form in the cold chamber.

Only her voice came, taunting and then seductive. "You really should join us voluntarily, you know, Quentin Butler. Can you not see the advantages of being a cymek? There are many things we could do. Next time perhaps, I'll even add myself to the images, and then we'll have a remarkably playful time."

Quentin could not shout at her to go away and leave him alone. He was left in a sensory-deprived silence for an interminable time, more disoriented than ever, his anger stalled against an insurmountable barrier.

He kept replaying over and over again what he had just experienced, how he wanted to be with Wandra again in the same way. It was a perverse thought, but so powerfully compelling that it frightened and delighted him at the same moment.

HIS TORMENT SEEMED to last centuries, but Quentin knew that his grasp on time and reality was suspect. His only anchor to the real universe was the thought of his previous life in the Army of the Jihad—and his passionate search for a way to attack the Titans, to hurt them even a fraction as much as they had hurt him.

As a disembodied victim, he could not escape, would not even try. He was no longer human, had lost his body, and could never return to the life he had previously known. He did not want to see his family or his friends. Better for history to record that he had been killed by cymeks on Wallach IX.

What would Faykan think if he could see his brave father as nothing more than a floating brain in a preservation canister? Even Abulurd would be ashamed to see him now . . . and what of Wandra? Despite her vegetative trance, would she react with horror to see her husband converted into a cymek?

Quentin was trapped on Hessra while the Titans hammered at his thoughts and loyalties. Despite his greatest efforts to resist them, he wasn't entirely certain how successful he was at keeping his secrets. If Juno disconnected his external sensors and pumped false images and sensations through his thoughtrodes, how could he ever be sure of himself?

The cymeks finally installed him inside a small walker-form like the ones the neos utilized to go about their business in the towers on Hessra. Juno lifted her articulated arms, seated Quentin's brain canister in the socket of a mechanical body. She used delicate digits to manipulate the controls, adjusting thoughtrodes. "Many of our neos consider this to be the time of their rebirth, when they are first able to take steps in a new walker."

Though his voice synthesizer was fully connected, Quentin refused to respond. He remembered the pathetic and deluded people on Bela Tegeuse, who could have been rescued long ago; instead they had turned on their would-be rescuers, summoning Juno, willing to sacrifice even comrades for the chance to become cymeks—like this.

Did those fools have any idea? How could anyone ask for this? They believed that becoming a cymek offered them a kind of immortality . . . but this was not life, just an unending hell.

Agamemnon entered the chamber in his smaller walker-body. Juno stood beside the Titan general. "I've nearly completed the installation, my love. Our friend is about to take his first steps, like a newborn."

"Good. Then you will see the full potential of your new situation, Quentin Butler," Agamemnon said. "Juno has assisted you so far, and I'll continue to be your benefactor, though eventually we will ask for certain considerations in return."

Juno connected the last of the thoughtrodes. "Now you have access to this walker-form, pet. It is a different sort of body from what you are used to. You spent your former life trapped in an unwieldy lump of meat. Now you'll have to learn to walk all over again, to stretch these mechanical muscles. But you're a bright boy. I'm sure you can learn—"

Quentin unleashed himself in a frenzy, not clear how to guide or direct his body. He thrashed with the mechanical legs, lunging forward, lurching to the side. He threw himself at Agamemnon, clattering and striking. The Titan general dodged out of the way as Quentin went berserk.

But he could not control his movements well enough to inflict any damage. The limbs and bulky body core did not move as he imagined they would. His brain was accustomed to operating two arms and two legs, but this vessel was an arachnid form. Random impulses made his sharpened legs jitter and strike out in the wrong direction. Though he struck Juno a glancing blow and drove himself forward again into Agamemnon, his minor success was purely accidental.

The Titan general swore, not out of fear but annoyance. Juno moved forward swiftly and delicately. Her articulated arms extended, and though Quentin thrashed about, the female cymek succeeded in disconnecting the thoughtrodes that gave him motivational power over his machine body.

"Such a disappointment," she scolded him. "Exactly what did you hope to accomplish?"

Realizing that she had accidentally disconnected his voice synthesizer, she applied the appropriate thoughtrode again, and Quentin shouted, "Bitch! I'll tear you apart and pierce your demented brain!"

"That's quite enough," Agamemnon said, and Juno disconnected the voice synthesizer again.

Her looming walker-form pressed closer to the optic threads Quentin used. "You are a *cymek* now, my pet. You belong with us, and the sooner you accept that reality, the less misery you'll endure."

Quentin knew deep inside that there could be no salvation, no escape. He could never be human again, but the idea of what he had become sickened him.

Juno stalked around, her voice warm and flirtatious. "Everything has changed. You wouldn't want your brave sons to see you like this, would you? Your only opportunity lies in helping us achieve a new Time of Titans. From now on, and forever, you must forget your former family."

"We are your family now," Agamemnon said.

Since the time of Aristotle of Old Earth, humankind has sought more and more knowledge, considering it a benefit to the species. But there are exceptions to this, things man should never learn to do.

— RAYNA BUTLER,
True Visions

It was her life's work. Rayna Butler could not conceive of another passion, another driving goal to compare with this. The intense woman never allowed herself to believe that the challenge was too great. She had dedicated her every breath for twenty years to exterminating any remnant of the sophisticated machines.

Once the Synchronized Worlds had been beaten in the Great Purge, Rayna and her fanatical followers had decided to complete the exhausting job, from within the League of Nobles. Not a scrap would remain. Human beings would do their own work, solve their own problems.

Still pale-skinned and hairless, she walked at the head of an ever-growing crowd that marched along the tree-lined streets of Zimia. Tall buildings, soaring high over complex monuments, defiantly declared humanity's victory after the century-long Jihad. But there was still much to do.

Rayna stepped forward, looking lean and waifish, yet filled with charisma. Crowds of Cultists pressed after her, their murmured determination growing louder as she approached the Hall of Parliament, her goal. Though she led all these people, she wore a plain robe without insignia or trappings. Rayna had no interest in gaudiness—unlike the Grand Patriarch. She was a simple and devout adherent to a holy cause. She had guided her followers and focused their passion to follow the shining white vision of Serena.

Behind her, people shouted and chanted, lifting banners and pennants that were embroidered or stained with images of Serena Butler and Manion the Innocent. For a long time, Rayna had discounted the icons and stylized images, preferring a more concrete expression of her mission for humanity. But she'd come to understand that the many brutally loyal followers of the Cult of Serena required their comforting paraphernalia. She finally accepted the standard bearers, so long as enough of her people also carried cudgels and weapons to do the necessary smashing.

Now she continued her march down the wide boulevard leading the throng. More streamed in from side streets, some merely curious, others sincerely wishing to join Rayna's crusade. After years of planning, here at the heart of the League of Nobles on her family's homeworld of Salusa Secundus, Rayna Butler could finally achieve her dream.

"We must continue to negate all machines that think," she called. "Humans must set their own guidelines. This is not something machines can do. Reasoning depends upon programming, not upon hardware—and *we* are the ultimate program."

But before she could get too close, a group of nervous-looking Zimia guards blocked the plaza in front of the Hall of Parliament. The security troops wore personal shields that hummed and shimmered in the sudden silence as Rayna paused in front of them. Her followers stumbled to a halt, catching their breath.

An angry grumble rose up from the Cultists. They held their cudgels and prybars, just as anxious to smash unbelievers as machines. The guards, milk-faced with dread and anxiety, were clearly not pleased with this assignment to stop Rayna's march, but they followed orders.

If Rayna commanded her followers to sacrifice themselves to make the larger point, there were not enough soldiers to prevent the mob from charging recklessly forward. But the Zimia guards did have sophisticated weapons, and many of Rayna's people would die—unless she could resolve this. She squared her shoulders and lifted her pallid chin.

In the center of the cordon of soldiers, a female burseg took one step closer to the pale-skinned young woman. "Rayna Butler, my soldiers and I have been instructed to block your passage. Please tell your followers to disperse."

The Cultists muttered angrily, and the officer lowered her voice, speaking so only Rayna could hear. "I apologize. I understand what you're doing—my parents and sister were killed by the Demon Scourge—but I have my orders."

Rayna looked intently at her, saw that the burseg meant what she said, that the woman had a good heart but would not hesitate to tell her troops to open fire. Rayna did not answer at first, considering possibilities, then she said, "The machines have already killed enough people. There is no need for humans to kill other humans."

The burseg did not order her soldiers to stand down. "Nevertheless, madam, I cannot allow you to pass."

Rayna looked back at the crowds on the streets. She and her followers had been to many devastated League Worlds in the past year, and they had recently returned to the capital. She saw hundreds, even thousands of faces, all of them with a grudge against Omnius. Every person there needed to strike a blow against the demon machines. If she gave a signal, she could incite all of these fanatical followers to rip the guards limb from limb. . . .

But she was not willing to do that.

"Wait here, my friends," Rayna called to them. "Before we can proceed, there is something I must accomplish alone." With a placid smile, she turned back to the burseg. "I can keep them at bay for now, but you must escort me into the Hall of Parliament. I request a private audience with my uncle, the Interim Viceroy."

Taken aback, the burseg looked at her fellow soldiers and at the overwhelming crowd—still chanting, waving banners, and gripping crude weapons. Wisely, she took a step back and nodded. "I will arrange it. Follow me, please."

RAYNA HAD LED her destructive marches against the thinking machines since she'd been a girl on Parmentier. She was thirty-one now, and for years the Cult of Serena had been solidifying around her, especially once they learned that the thin woman with ghostly features and haunted eyes was a blood relative of Saint Serena Butler. Her passionate movement had grown in strength and momentum, first across the plague-ravaged worlds and then everywhere.

The disheartened people listened to her message, saw the fire in her eyes—and they *believed*. With their civilizations already wrecked and their populations decimated, Rayna demanded that they destroy all appliances and conveniences that would have helped them to rebuild their lives. But those who survived were the strongest the human race had to offer, and under her potent leadership they picked up the pieces with their own hands and reassembled their societies. Rayna's ardent message convinced them. Though they faced difficulties, the crowds shouted and prayed, calling out the revered name of Serena.

When her followers chanted her name along with those of the Three Martyrs, Rayna stood fast and tried to stop them. She did not want to be seen as a prophet or pretender to any throne. She protested when the Cult elevated her and declared her the greatest human since Serena But- ler. Once, when Rayna noticed to her shame that such worship gave her an unexpected thrill of pleasure, she had stripped herself and sat naked all night on a cold rooftop, crouched against the biting wind, praying for for- giveness and guidance. There was a clear danger in letting herself become a powerful figurehead, followed by too many people without question.

She was finally ushered into the offices of Interim Viceroy Faykan Butler. Rayna knew that her uncle was a skilled politician, and somehow the two of them would have to negotiate an appropriate solution. The young woman was not naïve enough to think that she could simply make her demands, nor did she want to force Faykan into ordering a regrettable massacre. Rayna feared what might happen to her holy legacy if she were made into another martyr like Serena.

Behind the closed door of his private office, Faykan embraced his niece, then held her at arm's length to look at her. "Rayna, you are my brother's daughter. I love you dearly, but you certainly cause a great deal of trouble."

"And I intend to continue causing trouble. My message is important."

"Your *message?*" Faykan smiled and went back to his desk, offering her a cool beverage, which she declined. "That may be so, but who can hear your message above screams and shouts, and the wild smashing of plaz and metal?"

"It must be done, Uncle." Rayna remained standing, though Faykan sat back in his plush Viceroy's chair. "You have seen what the thinking machines can do. Do you intend to have your troops stop me? I would rather not have you for my enemy."

"Oh, I don't object to the results you desire. I simply have problems with your methods. We have a civilization to think about."

"My methods have been successful so far."

The Interim Viceroy sighed and took a long sip of his drink. "Allow me to make you a proposal. I hope you'll grant me that much?"

Rayna remained silent, skeptical but willing to consider her uncle's words.

"Though your main goal is to obliterate thinking machines, you must admit that your followers often . . . get out of hand. They cause massive amounts of collateral damage. Look around you at Zimia, see how much we have rebuilt after cymek and robot attacks, after the piranha mites. This place is the capital of all League Worlds, and I simply cannot let your unruly mob run rampant through the streets, smashing and burning." He folded his fingers together, still smiling. "So please don't force me to do something that will harm everyone. I don't wish to have my guards open fire on your followers. Even if I attempted to minimize the casualties, it would still be a bloody massacre."

Rayna stiffened, but she knew that Faykan's words were true. "Neither of us wants that."

"Then may I suggest a more lasting solution? I will let you make your announcements across Salusa. You can ask people to surrender their supposedly corrupt machines and appliances. I'll even let you hold a great rally to destroy them. Have as large a crowd as you wish! But when you march through the streets of Zimia, you must do it in an orderly fashion."

"Not all people will voluntarily surrender their conveniences. They have been too seduced and corrupted by the machines."

"Yes, but a great many of them will be swept up in the emotional fervor you incite, young woman. I can introduce appropriate legislation that will forbid the development of any devices or circuits that even remotely resemble gelcircuitry computers."

Rayna clenched her jaw and leaned over the table. "I have heard the commandment directly from God: Thou shalt not make a machine in the likeness of the human mind."

Faykan smiled. "Good, good. We can use that wording in the laws that I propose."

"There will be exceptions, people will refuse—"

"Then we will punish them," Faykan promised. "Believe me, Rayna, I will make this happen." His eyes narrowed as his face took on a calculating expression. "However, there is one thing you can do for me to ensure that I have sufficient power to help you."

Rayna remained silent, while Faykan continued. "At the start of this Jihad, Serena Butler took only the title of Interim Viceroy, claiming she did not deserve the formal title 'until such time as the thinking machines were destroyed.' Yes, the thinking machines remain a thorn in our side at Corrin, but the real Jihad is over. The enemy is defeated." He pointed at Rayna. "Now, young woman, if you will stand beside me, as my niece and the leader of the Cult of Serena, I will take on the title of full Viceroy. It will be a great day for humanity."

"And this will allow you to pass laws forbidding all thinking machines throughout the League? You will enforce these laws?"

"Absolutely, especially here on Salusa Secundus," Faykan pledged. "On the more primitive frontier League Worlds, though, you and your Cult may have to continue your work, however you see fit."

"I accept your terms, Uncle," Rayna said. "But with this warning—if you do not achieve what you have promised, then I will return . . . with my army."

Not everything is as it appears.

—DR. MOHANDAS SUK,
medical journals

I 'm afraid we'll have to use trial-and-error methods," Dr. Suk said, his voice distorted by the communications patch in his complete anticontamination suit. He had shuttled down personally from his sterile orbiting lab on the *Recovery*. Under the stars, he met Raquella on the polymerized canopy landing pad across from the cave cities. "We don't have any choice. Almost sixty percent of those infected will die, even after consuming melange."

He faced Raquella as she stood bravely, wearing no protection other than a breather. She looked into his dark, liquid eyes and thought of all the close ties they had, both the warm love and the friendship that had formed between them. Now they were separated by a thin, impenetrable barrier of decontamination fabric. She had never been so much at risk; the Rossak Epidemic made the original Scourge seem almost like a practice run by comparison.

With a gloved hand, the doctor extended a transparent carrying case that contained ten vaccine vials. "Variants on the RNA treatments we used before. Some of them might work . . . some might be deadly."

Raquella pressed her lips together and nodded. "Then they have to work."

"Analyzing this retrovirus is like trying to solve a murder mystery with a billion suspects," he said. "The mutated strain actually camouflages the genetic blueprint of its DNA, as far as our tests can determine. I'm looking for patterns, trying to map genomes and project the statistically probable components of the virus based on the available evidence. The melange molecule is no longer as effective in blocking the receptor sites."

Raquella saw the concern etched in his compassionate brown eyes. Some of his thick black hair had slipped free of its clasp inside the helmet, giving him a disheveled appearance. She wanted to hug him.

Mohandas had not been able to develop a viable gene therapy technique, but he continued to try. Other than heavy preventive consumption of melange, which blocked some of the retrovirus from converting the body's hormones into the poisonous Compound X, the only partially effective treatment involved specialized blood-filtering treatments from modified dialysis apparatus. Like its previous incarnation, this new retrovirus seated itself in the liver, but the slow and difficult dialysis procedure was not sufficient to cull out toxins faster than the infected body could produce them.

Staring at each other, he and Raquella discussed the test vaccines. One vial was a rich, deep blue, like the eyes of a spice addict. Mohandas gazed intently, longingly at her from behind his protective faceplate. He seemed to want to say so much more. "You are taking enough melange to protect yourself? Another VenKee ship just came from Kolhar."

"Yes, but spice does not guarantee immunity, as you well know. I am exercising suffient care."

But he wasn't convinced. "You aren't giving your spice ration to other patients?"

"I am taking sufficient amounts, Mohandas." She lifted the case of vaccine vials. "I'll get right to work on this. I need to determine which of the people are in greatest need."

FOR DAYS, KEEPING careful records on circuit plaz files, Raquella administered the trial vaccines with the help of Nortie Vandego and the still-healthy Sorceress, Karee Marques. It seemed a terrible irony, but the most powerful Sorceresses seemed even more susceptible to this version of the retrovirus than the normal population of Rossak.

As they worked, Raquella noticed a strange-looking boy watching with doe-eyed curiosity, keeping his distance. She had seen him before, working quietly and diligently to clean the wards and bring food and supplies for the medical workers.

She knew that mutagens and chemical contaminants in the Rossak environment caused many birth defects, deformities, and various levels of mental retardation, especially among males. Karee noticed Raquella's interest in the calm, curious young man. "He is Jimmak Tero, one of Ticia's sons—though of course she does not claim him, considering his obvious faults. She says he belongs with the Misborn."

The young man saw her looking in his direction and hurried away, flushing a deep red. Raquella drew a quick, sighing breath. "I'm surprised she didn't kill him at birth. Does that mean Ticia Cenva has a heart after all?"

With a wan smile, Karee said, "I'm sure she had other reasons."

Raquella gestured to Jimmak, luring him back as she spoke in a gentle, coaxing tone. "Come over here, Jimmak. I can use your help."

Timidly, he approached, staring at her with inquisitive, round blue eyes. He looked delighted that she would ask for his assistance. "What do you need, Doctor Lady?" His words were halting with a loose enunciation.

"Doctor Lady?" She smiled, tried to judge his age. Fifteen or sixteen, she thought. "Could you bring us some drinking water from the sterilizer, please? Nortie and I have been working so hard that we haven't had anything to drink for hours."

He glanced around nervously, as if afraid that he was doing something wrong. "You want something to eat? I could get food from the jungle. I know where to find things."

"Just water for now. Maybe food later." She saw instantly how much this pleased him.

After administering the test vaccines, Raquella performed regular blood tests to check the efficacy of the treatments, but the results were disappointing. None of Dr. Suk's trial batches of potential cures showed much promise.

Many patients were hooked to rows of overworked blood-filtering apparatus, pumps taking blood from the veins in the arm, scrubbing out the toxic Compound X, then recirculating the blood. But the infected livers continued to produce the deadly compound, and the patients would require the modified dialysis all over again within a few hours. There weren't nearly enough machines.

Raquella noted Ticia Cenva stalking through the rows of patients, snatching circuit plaz records and skimming them, while talking briskly to two Sorceresses beside her. She seemed edgy, barely holding on to her fear. In a derisive tone, Ticia said, "Your medicine is no better than the prayers of a Cultist. A wasted effort."

Raquella did not rise to the provocation. She had enough guilt of her own and didn't need the Supreme Sorceress to add to it. "Better to make an attempt and fail than just to let nature take its course. If humans did not fight against impossible odds, we would all be slaves of Omnius."

Ticia gave her a superior smile. "Yes, but *we* fought effectively."

Angry now, Raquella put her hands on her hips. "HuMed dispatched us here because you were having no success."

"We didn't ask you to come. HuMed forced you upon us. You're not doing any good here—in fact, the plague has gotten worse since your arrival. Count the casualties." Irritation and tension suffused the voice of the Supreme Sorceress. "Maybe you brought a new strain with you. Or maybe your supposed cures are spreading the disease even faster."

"That's ridiculous superstition," Raquella said. "If your methods are better, then why have so many of your best Sorceresses died?"

Ticia recoiled as if Raquella had slapped her. "The weak ones are dying. The strong ones could have solved the problem by now." With that, she and her companions marched off.

Jimmak had returned, carrying a tray piled with a container of water and loose pieces of fresh-picked fruits and mushrooms, but he huddled against one of the stone walls, waiting for his aloof mother to go away. Ticia had not acknowledged the shrinking boy in any way. When Raquella smiled at him, though, Jimmak hurried forward and showed her his prizes: dark and fuzzy little lumps, a large yellow melon, and something pear-shaped in an unappetizing greenish-black color.

"I like these the best," he said, pointing at the fuzzy lumps. "In the jungle we call them rossies."

Raquella took the fruits. "I'll keep these for later. They look delicious." She didn't trust whatever the young man had picked in the deep jungle.

Jimmak lowered his voice conspiratorially. "My mother doesn't like you."

"I know. She doesn't think I belong here. But I'm trying to help."

"I could help you," Jimmak said, his face bright, his voice breathless. "Some things in the jungle make people feel better."

"How interesting." She knew about all the drugs and pharmaceuticals VenKee workers harvested out in the wilderness. "You'll have to show me sometime."

OVER THE NEXT several days, Raquella and her young friend spent more time together, and she even began to sample the things he brought her from the jungle after carefully washing them. Jimmak had an odd, feral sort of intelligence she had not understood at first. An outcast, he must have been forced to take care of himself, living out in the wilderness.

Eventually, she began to wonder if perhaps he did have interesting solutions to offer. None of the powerful Sorceresses took the Misborn boy seriously, but by now she was getting desperate.

Exhausted and frustrated by her lack of progress, she sometimes took short breaks and walked with Jimmak along pathways that cut through thick, overhanging vegetation down on the jungle floor. One trail in particular filled her with a sense of awe and wonder, as sunlight filtering through plants in the canopy created a rainbow effect on the ground, with colors that danced as the trees moved.

"I don't feel any wind," Raquella said, "and I don't see how any wind could get in here. But those trees above us are moving, causing the colors to shift."

"Trees are alive," Jimmak said. "They make colors for me with sunlight. I talk to them sometimes." A rainbow flickered in front of him, then seemed to change shape, into a prismatic ball, splashing colors all around it. Then another ball appeared, and yet another. Laughing, Jimmak juggled the three illusory balls in his hands, splashing colors around him, until they disappeared into the canopy.

Amazed, Raquella asked questions, but Jimmak didn't tell her anything more. "Many secrets in the jungle." The more she pressed, the more silent he became. She decided to let the matter go, for now.

Jimmak showed Raquella mushrooms as big as ponds, odd lichens, berries that crawled by themselves. He was always scampering off into the deepest levels of the shadowy jungle, retrieving unusual plants and leaves for her to examine, even telling her some of their medicinal characteristics, which he had learned from helping VenKee prospectors.

The jungle of Rossak, however, yielded no magic cure to help with the local epidemic. And people kept dying.

If no one remembers the grand things I have accomplished, then did I do them at all, as far as history is concerned? The only solution seems to be that I must achieve something spectacular or cause an event that no version of history could ever ignore.

—YOREK THURR,
secret Corrin journals

Thinking machines might have infinite patience, but Yorek Thurr didn't. This exile on Corrin was interminable. Though his life span had been artificially extended, he still found it a maddening waste of time—decades!—to sit idle behind the defensive walls of machine and League ships.

Unlike Omnius and Erasmus, who were content to bide their time and outwait the guardian *hrethgir*, and the limbless Rekur Van who had no place else to go, Thurr devoted his mental energies to finding a way out— for himself, if for none of his computer allies.

Under the blazing red sun that filled half the sky like an immense bon-fire, Thurr took care to wear special eye protection as he walked alongside Seurat. The robot captain had served Omnius for centuries and had been the close companion of Vorian Atreides. More importantly, Seurat had been held hostage by Agamemnon for more than half a century.

"So tell me in more detail how you escaped from the Titans," Thurr said.

The robot looked at him curiously. "My files are available for complete review whenever you desire, Yorek Thurr. Does the matter hold particular interest for you?"

Thurr narrowed his eyes. "I'd like to get away from here, and some of your ideas might be helpful. Aren't you eager to escape Corrin? You were designed to be the captain of an update ship, flying free among the Syn-chronized Worlds—yet you haven't left here in twenty years. Even for a robot, that must be maddening."

"Since there are no other Synchronized Worlds, I am no longer needed to perform an update run, which is my core purpose," Seurat said. "And I did fulfill my last duty by bringing a copy of the Omnius sphere to Corrin after the humans annihilated most Synchronized Worlds."

"I brought a copy of Omnius, too," Thurr said. "But that doesn't give me much satisfaction."

Seurat's coppery face remained placid. "As soon as Omnius deter-mines how best to use my skills, I will receive new instructions."

"Humans aren't quite so . . . complacent."

"I am aware of that. My experiences with Vorian Atreides taught me much." Seurat's voice sounded almost wistful. "Do you know any jokes?"

"Not any funny ones."

Thurr reviewed the detailed records of Seurat's escape from Richese, how he'd slipped out from under the cymeks' noses. It had taken the dis-traction of an outside attack. Perhaps something similar would work for him here.

Fortunately, the huge machine barricade had been designed and emplaced to keep the League *out*, not to keep someone like himself *in*. And the Holtzman scrambler net would do nothing to stall his human brain. Thurr's main challenge would be to create a significant enough diversion that he could steal a fast ship and slip through the net of the human forces. They would be watching much more closely since the deployment of his mechanical devourers. But once he made his way out into free space again, the possibilities were much more extensive.

It was worth thinking about. At least Thurr had all the time in the world to mull over possibilities, to plan and rehearse his actions.

He made his way into a side chamber of the Central Spire, past gal-leries of the computer evermind's ridiculously gaudy ornamentation. Omnius Prime was embedded deep within the ingrained gelcircuitry and flowmetal structure of the monolithic building. Inside, however, were stored the other two evermind incarnations: the sphere Seurat had brought and the copy he had delivered himself when he'd fled Wallach IX.

The evermind incarnations should have been nearly identical, but Omnius, against his usual practice, had refused to synchronize the other two updates with himself. He kept the pair of silvery gelspheres isolated, fearing that they might contain some secret destructive virus such as the ones Seurat had delivered long ago. Thurr himself had often tampered with the Omnius on Wallach IX, to keep his devious activities secret. He didn't think he had done any damage, but there was always that possibility. . . .

Now the two additional copies, slightly out-of-phase, retained their independent identities. The main evermind naïvely believed that since all three incarnations were together and presumably experiencing the same daily events, they would not continue to deviate. But Thurr believed that the trio of separated everminds had already grown farther and farther apart.

He counted on that, in fact, for it could work to his advantage.

When he accessed the evermind copy he had brought from Wallach IX, he stood before the speaker circuit, trying to sound very rational. "Corrin continues to face a severe threat. It is clear that the challenge is too great for the processing power of Omnius Prime alone."

"I am identical to Omnius Prime," the evermind said.

"You are *equivalent* in skills and talent. No longer identical. If both of you were to apply yourselves to the problem in parallel, there would be twice as much mindpower. The *hrethgir* could not possibly resist. You both have access to the same systems here in the Central Spire. While Omnius Prime maintains an unbreachable defense, as he has done for nineteen years, I suggest you plan another *offensive* against the human guardian fleet. We certainly have sufficient robotic ships in orbit."

"There has been significant attrition, which strains the capabilities of Corrin to replace. Our ships have undertaken numerous offensives, but we cannot pass the scrambler net. What would another attempt accomplish?"

Thurr sighed with impatience. Though the evermind copy had vast amounts of information, it had little insight—like most thinking machines. "If you could devote all of our ships to breaching the *hrethgir* line, shredding the scrambler network no matter how many battle vessels that requires, then we could immediately launch more copies of Omnius. Everminds would be free to propagate, and then thinking machines could retake Synchronized Worlds or even establish strongholds on new planets. Like seeds scattered on fertile ground. But only if they can get away—only if you can create a large enough hole in the barrier."

He smiled. "On the other hand, bottled up here, you are completely vulnerable if the *hrethgir* manage to break through with even a few ships to drop pulse-atomic warheads. Therefore it is imperative that the Omnius everminds disperse, propagate, and survive."

"I will interact and discuss the matter with Omnius Prime. Perhaps this is a viable plan."

Thurr shook his head, placing his hands on his hips and adjusting his belt and jeweled dagger. "Then you would sacrifice your independence, which is currently an advantage in this crisis. Would it not be better to demonstrate unequivocally to Omnius Prime that you have innovative ideas he has not considered? Once your attack proves successful, Omnius Prime cannot deny your worth as a separate unit."

The Wallach IX copy pondered, then reached a decision. "I have analyzed the patterns of the enemy's guardian forces and have calculated the most effective time for an unexpected massive counteroffensive, unlike any we have attempted so far. The best opportunity will occur within nine hours."

"Excellent," Thurr said, bobbing his head. He wanted to run to his rooms, yet dared not show his impatience, though he doubted the evermind could read simple human nuances. Nine hours. He settled for walking quickly. He had a great many things to prepare.

WHEN THE STARTLING attack began, the robots on the surface of Corrin reacted with as much disorganized panic as the human watchdog ships in orbit. The Central Spire convulsed, losing integrity as Omnius Prime's full attention was diverted elsewhere, and the structure of the flowmetal tower began to fail.

Suddenly a full contingent of robotic defenders powered up their weapons, changed their configurations, and launched outward in a dramatic headlong assault against the human sentinel ships. Even this was similar to what they had done many times before over the past two decades. Stopping just inside the deadly boundary of the scrambler satellite net, they launched a flurry of explosive missiles at the stationary human vessels, then drove forward into the scrambler zone. The Holtzman satellites discharged their deadly pulses, and scrambler mines targeted the machine ships, wiping out all of the thinking-machine controls. But as the dead robotic hulks piled up in space, more and more of the bristling Omnius ships pressed forward into the logjam. Several of them got through the gaps in the scrambler web.

Thurr had meant for it to be nothing more than a pointless and destructive diversion, but for a moment it looked as if it might almost work. . . .

As soon as the surprise orbital offensive was launched and the *hrethgir* fleet was fully occupied with defending itself, he raced to the landing area. He chose the well-maintained but unused update ship that Seurat had flown to Corrin on the leading edge of the Great Purge. It was a fast ship with decent defenses, rudimentary weapons, and a minimal life-support system that he had installed years before . . . always planning ahead. The ship was exactly what Thurr needed.

The update ship was ready to fly and completely unguarded by ground-side robots. Thurr had already studied its controls and knew he could pilot the vessel. He had taken only minimal supplies, afraid that if he stocked the update ship it would be a blatant signal of what he had in mind. Thurr needed only sufficient food and air to reach another outpost.

While the furious battle continued in orbit, with League ships and robot vessels launching weapons against each other, Thurr activated the access ramp and hurried aboard the update ship.

Inside, Erasmus stood waiting for him with his human ward. "You see, Gilbertus, I was correct in my interpretation of Yorek Thurr's strange behavior. He intends to leave us."

Brought to a halt, Thurr gasped. "What are you doing here?"

Gilbertus Albans stood off to one side, nodding. "Yes, Father. You understand human nature quite well. The signs were subtle, but once you pointed them out to me, they seemed obvious. Thurr has staged a diversion in orbit to steal this craft and escape."

"I admire such desperation." Erasmus's flowmetal face shaped itself into a smile. "But in this instance I question your wisdom."

"It's my choice to make," Thurr said, sniffing. "Corrin will be doomed as soon as the League of Nobles decides to tie up loose ends. The thinking machines should also be considering how to get away. You, Erasmus, face repeated threats from Omnius when he tries to rewrite your personality. He never seems to learn." Smiling, Thurr stepped closer to the robed robot. "Why don't you and your ward come with me? We can fly far from Corrin and make our own mark on the galaxy. History will never forget us."

"Thinking machines maintain accurate files of all events," Erasmus said. "History will not forget my actions anyway."

Thurr took another step. "But don't you realize the beautiful logic of my plan? This ship could easily break through the *hrethgir* fleet now, during the diversion. We can get away. In fact, other update ships could take the same opportunity and bring along new Omnius spheres. The Synchronized Worlds could expand again."

"That is a possibility. However, I have calculated the odds of success, and they are unacceptably low. Even if I were to detach my own mental core and encase it in thick shielding, I might not survive passage through the scrambler net. I will not take that chance, especially not if it means leaving Gilbertus alone."

Thurr moved like a striking snake. He had focused the robot's attention by moving closer, but really intended to slash at the vulnerable human. In a blindingly fast move, he drew the ceremonial dagger from his belt and darted to the left, wrapping a sinewy arm around a surprised Gilbertus's neck. Thurr planted his knee in the small of the muscular man's back, brought the dagger around, and pressed its point against his victim's jugular.

"Then I'm afraid I'll have to influence your decision in a more . . . human fashion. If you don't let me escape now, before it's too late, I'll kill him. Don't doubt me."

Thurr pressed the knife closer. Gilbertus remained frozen, tensing, flexing his muscles and preparing to use his years of careful training. Erasmus could see he intended to fight, to risk himself—

"Gilbertus, stop!" he said, amplifying his voice. "I forbid you to take the risk. He will harm you."

"Yes indeed," Thurr said, showing a strange smile. Gilbertus hesitated just a moment, then relaxed, surrendering to the robot's wishes.

Erasmus said, "We do not wish to come with you." The robot's flowmetal face became a smooth mask. It flickered as if instinctively into a distressed frown, then returned to its blank expression. "If you kill him, I will not allow you to escape. I may not be capable of vengeful anger, but I have invested a great deal of time and effort in Gilbertus Albans. If you damage my specimen, do not doubt that I will exterminate *you* as well."

They were at an impasse. Thurr did not move. The robot's face changed through a litany of practiced expressions.

Gilbertus gazed for reassurance at the polished face of Erasmus, obviously hoping the independent robot would save him. "This man is most disturbing to me, Father. I am placing an extraordinary effort into keeping my thoughts organized, yet this man seems to be . . ."

Erasmus finished for him. "Chaos incarnate?"

"An adequate assessment," Gilbertus said.

Finally, the robot suggested to Thurr, "If you release Gilbertus and promise not to harm him, we will allow you to depart alone in this ship.

Perhaps you will escape successfully, perhaps you will be killed. It will no longer be our concern."

Thurr did not move. "How do I know you're not lying to me? You could command all robotic forces to turn against me and blow my ship out of the sky before I even reach orbit."

"After long practice and study it is actually possible for me to lie," Erasmus admitted, "but I do not choose to make the effort. My bargain is genuine. While I disagree with your motives and plans, I have no particular reason to risk harm in order to stop you. It matters little to me whether you escape Corrin. Only circumstances have forced you to remain trapped here, not any command of Omnius's."

Thurr considered this, his thoughts racing. He had very little time. He didn't know how long the robotic attacks would last before Omnius Prime reasserted his own control.

"What do you think?" he said harshly into his captive's ear. "Maybe I should just take you along as a hostage."

Gilbertus's voice was calm. "You can trust Erasmus if he has given his word."

"Trust Erasmus? I doubt many people have said that in the history of the Synchronized Worlds. But all right." He relaxed his grip, just a little. "Erasmus, you leave the ship. As soon as you're away from the boarding ramp, I'll turn Gilbertus loose. Then you both step away, and I'll fly off. We never need to see each other again."

"How can I be certain you won't kill him anyway?" Erasmus asked.

Thurr chuckled. "For a robot, you're learning quickly. But hurry—or this all falls apart."

The robot stepped away, his plush robe billowing as he took a last look at Gilbertus and marched down the ramp. Thurr considered assassinating the hostage anyway to show the independent robot how capricious humans could be. As the unreasonable compulsion shot through him, he twitched, but managed to restrain himself. That would accomplish nothing, and would surely turn Erasmus against him. The ground forces of military robots might still shoot him out of the sky. Not worth the risk.

He gave his captive a heavy shove, causing him to stumble away. As Gilbertus hurried to join the independent robot on the landing field, Thurr sealed the hatch and raced to the controls.

GILBERTUS AND ERASMUS watched the ship dwindle into the sky. "You could have prevented his escape, Father, but you chose to rescue me instead. Why?"

"Despite his past value, Yorek Thurr is of no future use to us. Besides, he is alarmingly unpredictable, even for a human." Erasmus remained silent for a moment. "I calculated the consequences and decided that this outcome was preferable. It would have been unacceptable to see you harmed." Suddenly the robot spotted a fleck of red from a minor cut on Gilbertus's neck. "You are injured. He has drawn blood."

The man touched the sore spot, looked at the small crimson droplet on his fingertip, and shrugged. "It is insignificant."

"No injury to you is insignificant, Gilbertus. I will have to watch you more carefully from now on. I will keep you safe."

"And I'll do the same for you, Father."

The universe is a playground of improvisation. It follows no external pattern.

—NORMA CENVA,
revelations translated by Adrien Venport

Sealed inside her spice-filled tank, Norma knew no boundaries whatsoever. Nothing was concrete anymore, and the sensation—exhilarating, breathtaking—felt utterly natural. Mere walls could not contain her. She had not left her chamber in many days, and yet she had gone on an incredible voyage of discovery.

A spectrum of unusual abilities rose and fell in her mind, like bubbles of possibility, largely beyond her control, as if some god were displaying them for her perusal, showing her a broad realm of wondrous possibilities. She had spent her life trying to unravel the mysteries of the universe, and now majestic threads and strings and ideas reeled out all around her.

She was able to observe Adrien from afar, like a benevolent angel, as he performed his complex and time-consuming work for VenKee Enterprises. Intelligent, capable, visionary—truly a synthesis between herself and Aurelius.

Now, just outside the walls of her tank, breathing normal air, Adrien peered through the streaked clearplaz walls. He was trying to see her inside, to reassure himself that his mother was still alive. She knew he was greatly worried about her and unable to understand why she refused to leave the enclosure, why she wouldn't eat or respond . . . and why her physical body seemed to be changing. When she took the time and concentration, she could send signals outside to reassure him, to communicate with him, though it seemed increasingly difficult to expend the energy. And it was difficult to make herself comprehensible . . . not just to Adrien, but to anyone but herself.

With the controls at her strangely rubbery fingertips—her hands had begun to show . . . *webbing?*—she kept filling the enclosure with spice gas, in heavier and heavier concentrations. The vapors swirled around her, an orange soup with a strong cinnamon odor.

As her mind grew stronger, larger, and more dominant, the rest of her body atrophied. The transformation continued in odd directions—the torso, arms, and legs withering while her brain enlarged. Remarkably, her skull did not act as a constraint; instead, it grew.

Her clothing had fallen off, deteriorating from the potent concentrations of melange. But Norma no longer needed garments: Her new body was smooth and asexual, little more than a vessel to contain her expanding mind.

She rested on the cushion she had brought with her, but Norma no longer felt her surroundings. Some normal physical functions ceased: She no longer needed to eat, drink, or eliminate bodily wastes.

Knowing that her son was trying to see her, she leaned forward to the plaz wall. Norma could feel Adrien's presence, his thoughts, his concerns. She noted the narrowed eyes and the size of his pupils, the marks of concern etched on his forehead and around his mouth, as if painted there by a master artist. A thin film of fearful perspiration covered his brow.

She could identify each of her son's facial expressions, which began to remind her of conversations they'd had in the past. In her growing mind, Norma catalogued their entire relationship. Assembling the data of their interactions, she matched the past thoughts her son revealed in words with the way he had looked each time he spoke.

Ah. She understood. Now Adrien was wondering what to do to help her. Three aides stood with him, and she could read their lips. They wanted to break into the container so that Norma could receive medical attention. He listened to them, but had not yet agreed to do anything.

Trust me. I know what I am doing.

But he could not hear her distinct thoughts. Adrien Venport was torn with indecision—a very unusual thing for him.

In her spice reverie, Norma noted the subtle markings of his demeanor, the luster of his eyes, the curve of his mouth. Was he recalling an old conversation? Her own words floated back to her. "Melange will enhance my prescience and enable me—and others who follow—to accurately navigate the spacefolders. I can foresee the hazards before they occur, and I can avoid them. It is the only way to respond swiftly enough. No longer will the Holtzman engines be an unsafe means of rapid space travel. It will change . . . everything."

I have the key to the universe. But you must let me finish.

Norma tried to remember how to control her face, how to form her most serene, calm expression. She needed to give Adrien the impression that she had everything under control. When she tried to speak to him, her words sounded to her own ears as if they were vibrating through a thick medium of water.

"This is where I want to be, my son. Each moment I draw closer to my goal, to the perfect state I must attain in order to navigate our ships safely. Do not worry about me. Trust in my vision."

But the spice chamber had no speaker system—an inexcusable oversight, she realized—and he could not hear her distinctly. Still, she hoped he would get the sense of her message. Adrien had nearly always managed to understand her, somehow.

However, he was also coolly logical and pragmatic. He knew how long it had been since his mother had had any food or water. No matter how she tried to reassure him now or what she had told him before entering the tank, he would be concerned about what she was doing. Still, he hesitated, trusting his genius mother to know what she was doing . . . to a certain extent.

Clearly, his muscular aides wanted to remove her from the container by force. They carried heavy tools that could either dismantle or smash open the tank. Several doctors had already expressed the opinion that it was impossible for Norma to have survived as long as she had. Once again his mother had accomplished what no one had thought possible.

But not without cost. Staring at her through the transparent wall, he could see how dramatically her body had changed, the extreme alterations and evolution that her physical form had undergone. She was no longer human.

Apparently, Adrien was alarmed by what he saw in her face. With a deep weariness, he motioned toward his three aides, who raised their heavy tools. If they broke through the plaz walls, all the spice gas would rush out, possibly killing them, possibly suffocating her. Behind them, through the uncertain blur of the chamber's stained walls, she saw that Adrien had arranged for medical specialists to stand by with emergency life-support equipment.

Before the men could move, Norma raised her sticklike arms to ward them off. If they committed such a foolish act, they would throw the now-bright future of the space-folding program into irretrievable chaos.

She analyzed Adrien's thoughts. He had made his decision, convinced that what he was doing would save her life. She stared back at him, silently pleading, willing him to understand. Then, as he looked at her for one last time, she saw his facial muscles relax abruptly, like a sudden calm falling over a stormy sea.

Her ropy, misshapen index finger brushed the surface of the plaz, touching the caked melange dust that had collected there. Trying to remember more primitive methods of communication, Norma moved her fingertip, smearing a mark on the surface. Straight lines, precise angles, curves, an ellipse. A simple word.

NO.

And Adrien clearly saw something in his mother's enlarged spice-blue eyes that stared at him through the thick barrier—an eerie, hypnotic awareness. Silently, showing supreme confidence in her own vision, Norma urged her son, hoping he would understand. He had to trust her now. *Don't disturb me. I am safe! Leave me.*

Just as the men were poised to break through, Adrien ordered them to stop. His patrician face was a mask of uncertainty and conflicting emotions. The attending doctors tried to change his mind, but he sent them away. Then he broke down and wept.

"I hope I'm doing the right thing," he said through the plaz, and she understood him perfectly.

Yes, you are.

*They say of El'hiim that he loves neither his father nor his stepfather,
and that he is disloyal to his people.*

—Comment made by Zensunni elder,
secondhand source

It was Ishmael's last chance to save the man he had raised as his son. He had asked, then nearly begged the Naib to go with him on a pilgrimage into the deep desert, the Tanzerouft. "I saved you once, long ago, from scorpions," Ishmael finally said, hating that he was forced to call in an old debt.

El'hiim looked troubled by the memory. "I was foolhardy, without any caution, and you almost died from all the stings."

"I will keep you safe, now. When a man knows how to live with the desert, he need not fear what it has to offer."

Finally, the younger man capitulated. "I remember the times you went with me to other villages and into Arrakis City, even though I know how much you dislike those places. I can make the same sacrifice for my stepfather. It has been a long time since I was reminded of how rustic and difficult life used to be for the outlaw followers of Selim Wormrider."

To his fellow villagers, El'hiim gave the impression that he was merely humoring the old man. His young water-fat followers, wearing their strange and colorful clothing, joked and wished El'hiim a fine time.

But Ishmael could see uncertainty and even a flicker of fear in the Naib's eyes. *That is good.*

For decades now, El'hiim had forgotten how to respect the desert. Regardless of how many luxuries the Zensunni people purchased from offworld merchants, Shai-Hulud still reigned supreme out there. The Old Man of the Desert had little patience for those who scorned the religious laws.

El'hiim left instructions with his lieutenants. His trek with Ishmael would last several days, during which time the Zensunni villagers would continue delivering supplies of spice to VenKee merchants or whichever offworlders bid the best price. Though she looked old now, Chamal was still in charge of most of the women in the cave city and would keep everyone else at their tasks. She kissed her father on his dry, leathery cheek.

Ishmael said nothing, gazing longingly out into the vast and clean dunes, as the two departed from the cliff village. When they had made their way in the moonlight down to the open sands, he turned to his step-son. "Summon a worm for us, El'hiim."

The Naib hesitated. "I would not take that honor from you, Ishmael."

"Are you incapable of doing that which made a legend of your father? The son of Selim Wormrider is afraid to summon Shai-Hulud?"

El'hiim let out an impatient sigh. "You know that's not true. I have called many worms."

"But not for a long time. Do it now. It is a necessary step in our journey."

Ishmael watched the Naib as he planted the resonant drum stake and pounded on it with his rhythmic hammer. He studied El'hiim's every movement, watched how he set out the equipment and prepared to face the monster. His actions were swift but jerky, clearly nervous. Ishmael did not criticize him, but he readied himself to help should anything go wrong.

Even for a master, summoning a sandworm was a dangerous activity, and El'hiim had almost forgotten how to live with danger. Their journey would remind him of this, and of many things.

When the sinuous beast arrived, it was accompanied by a hissing roar, a scraping of sand, and a cloud of thick, pungent scent. "It's a big one, Ishmael!" The awe and excitement in his voice almost drowned out his terror. Good.

The worm reared up, and El'hiim ran forward, concentrating fully now. Ishmael threw his own hooks and ropes, climbing, assisting in the capture. The younger man didn't seem to pay attention to how much of the task Ishmael performed for him, and his stepfather did not point it out.

Exhilarated, El'hiim rode on the back of the worm, glancing over at the old man beside him. "Now where do we go?" He seemed to be remembering his younger days. Finally.

His long gray-white hair blowing behind him, Ishmael pointed toward the flat, shadowed horizon. "Out there into the deepest desert, where we can be safe and alone."

The worm plowed through the loose dunes, eating distance throughout the night. Selim Wormrider had originally taken his band of outlaws deep into the most barren wilderness where they could hide, and Marha had led them even farther into exile. But since the Wormrider's death, most followers had lost their dedication, tempted by comforts and easy lives. Once-isolated settlements drifted closer to the scattered cities again.

Selim would have been disappointed that the influence of his vision had dwindled so much in only a generation, when he had sacrificed his life so that his legend would be remembered for all time. As the first Naib after the legendary founder, Ishmael had done his best to continue the quest, but after relinquishing control to Selim's son, he had felt all progress slipping through his callused fingers.

The two men rode the powerful worm until dawn, then took their packs and dismounted near a cluster of rocks that would offer shelter for the day. As El'hiim ran to find a place to lay his soft pads and erect their reflecting shade-cloth, he looked uneasily at the austere surroundings.

Sitting with his stepfather in the heat of the strengthening sun, El'hiim shook his head. "If we used to live with no more comforts than this, Elder Ishmael, then our people have made substantial progress over the years." He stretched out his hand to touch the rough, hard rock.

Ishmael looked at him, blue-within-blue eyes sharp. "You cannot grasp how much Arrakis has changed in your lifetime—most especially in the past two decades since the Grand Patriarch opened our planet to hordes of spice prospectors. All across the League, people are consuming melange, *our melange*, in huge quantities, hoping it will protect them from sickness and maintain their youth." He made a disgusted noise.

"Don't be blind to how we have benefited from it," El'hiim pointed out. "Now we have more water, more food. Our people live longer. League medical care has cured numerous ills that needlessly stole our people— like my mother."

Ishmael felt stung, remembering Marha. "Your mother made her own choice, the only honorable one."

"An unnecessary one!" El'hiim actually looked angry at him. "She is dead because of your stubbornness!"

"She is dead because it was her time to die. Her disease was incurable."
The younger man angrily threw a stone far from their camp. "Primitive Zensunni methods and superstitions couldn't cure her, but any decent doctor in Arrakis City could have done something. There are treatments, medicines from Rossak and elsewhere. She could have had a chance!"

"Marha did not want that kind of chance," Ishmael said, disturbed. He himself had felt the awful grief of knowing that his wife was dying, but she had devoted her life to Selim Wormrider's philosophy and goals. "It would have been a betrayal of all she was."

El'hiim sat in brooding silence for a long time. "Such beliefs are only part of the great rift that separates us, Ishmael. She didn't need to die, but her pride and your insistence on the old ways killed her, just as surely as the sickness did."

Ishmael softened his voice. "I miss her just as much as you do. If we had delivered her to Arrakis City, perhaps she would have lived a few years longer connected to medical machines. But if Marha sold her soul for a bit of comfort, then she would not be the woman I loved."

"She would still be my mother," El'hiim said. "I never knew my father."

Ishmael frowned. "But you have heard enough stories about him. He should be as familiar to you as if he had spent his life at your side."

"Those are just legends, stories that make him out to be a hero or a prophet, or even a god. I don't believe such nonsense."

Ishmael furrowed his brow. "You should know the truth when you hear it."

"Truth? Finding that is more difficult than sifting melange powder out of fine sand."

They sat in silence for a long while, and then in a gesture of truce, Ishmael recounted his stories from Poritrin. He steered away from the grandiose myths of the Wormrider, speaking only things that he could declare were the outright truth.

The two got along well enough for several days. El'hiim was clearly miserable with the harsh conditions, but he was trying. Ishmael appreciated the effort. He reminded his stepson of traditional desert pastimes that El'hiim had long since stopped following, how to find food and moisture, how to create shelter, how to predict weather from the smell and feel of the wind. He talked about the different kinds of sand and dust, and how they all moved and changed.

Though he had known most of these things all his life, El'hiim actually appeared to listen. "You are forgetting the most important technique of survival," the younger man said. "Be cautious and do not allow yourself to get into such a desperate situation in the first place."

For those few days, Ishmael felt young again. The desert was silent, and he saw no taint of encroaching spice prospectors. When finally they agreed to make their way back to one of the outlying cliff villages, the old man felt as if a new bond had been forged between them.

They took another worm, a small one, and made their way to the southern fringe of the Shield Wall, where another of the former outlaw settlements had been established. Members of Chamal's extended family lived there along with descendants of the original Poritrin refugees. El'hiim also had friends in the settlement, though he usually took more traditional means of transportation to get there. The two men left their worm to wallow back into the sands and made their way along the wall on foot, traveling in the long afternoon shadows.

When they reached the cave city, though, Ishmael and El'hiim could smell the smoke and burned corpses before they saw the open passages. With growing urgency, Ishmael ran across the crumbling rocky ground through the still-burning remnants of what had been homes and possessions. Appalled, El'hiim followed him. When they entered the caves that had once been settled by peaceful Zensunni people, they both stared, sickened.

Ishmael heard the moans of survivors, found a few children and an old woman weeping beside the murdered bodies of the village's elders. All of the young, healthy Zensunni men and women had been taken away.

"Slavers." Ishmael spat the word. "They knew exactly where to find this settlement."

"They came with many weapons," said a woman hunkered over the dismembered torso of her husband. "We knew them. We recognized some of the traders. They—"

Ishmael turned away as bile rose in his throat. El'hiim, reeling from the horror and bloodshed, stumbled through the chambers, finding a few young boys who had lived through the raid. When Ishmael saw them, he remembered that he himself had been only a small boy on Harmonthep. . . .

His breathing came fast and hard, but he could think of no curses sufficient to express what he felt. El'hiim returned, blinking, with an odd expression on his face. He held a torn piece of colorful fabric, on which an intricate pattern had been imprinted with dyes. "The slavers took their own wounded and dead, but they left this material, clearly of Zanbar manufacture. This design is traditional on that planet."

Ishmael narrowed his eyes against the stinging wind. "You can tell that simply by looking at a gaudy scrap?"

"If you know what to look for." El'hiim frowned. "Some vendors in Arrakis City sell a similar pattern, but this one here comes from Zanbar." He waved the cloth. "Very distinctive. No one can counterfeit this dye— Zanbar Red. And I looked outside at the skid marks made by the landing gear of the raider vessel. The configuration looked like it comes from one of those sleek new Zanbar skimmers. Prospectors imported them here."

Ishmael wondered if the Naib was trying to show off his prowess. "And what good does this do us? Shall we go to war against the planet Zanbar?"

El'hiim shook his head. "No, but it means I know exactly who did this and where they usually make their camp."

The God of Science can be an unkind deity.

—TLALOC,

A Time for Titans

Agamemnon felt that the conversion of his cymek candidate was going well. Along with Juno and Dante, he had developed an intricate scheme to break down the mind and loyalties of Quentin Butler, then build him back up again into the form required by the Titans.

It proved to be quite a challenge, but one the general found intriguing.

Of late, Agamemnon realized to his embarrassment that he had grown lax in his ambitions—just like the fools in the Old Empire, whom he and the visionary Tlaloc had overthrown. Even though neo-cymeks had at last begun to sweep across the dead Synchronized Worlds, their glory had become a petty, self-congratulatory delusion. Newly converted neos were drawn from the most acceptable captives they found on abandoned planets, and they were almost always volunteers, willing candidates thrilled to receive powerful mechanical bodies and extended life spans.

Quentin Butler, though, was quite a different story. Through spies in the League of Nobles, Agamemnon had heard of this primero's exploits. The military officer would be a great asset to the Titans' burgeoning plans—if only he could be convinced to cooperate. The general knew that if Quentin converted too easily, then the results would not be as valuable. *It might take a little time.*

Through careful manipulation of his sensory input as well as direct stimulus through his pain centers and visual cortex, Quentin's time sense and equilibrium were completely turned around. Agamemnon preyed upon his doubts, while Dante fed him false data, and Juno cajoled him, playing the part of seductress and sympathetic ear whenever he felt lost or alone.

As a disembodied brain in the preservation canister, he was completely at the Titans' mercy. The secondary-neos that ran the electrafluid laboratories salted chemical additives into the solution that bathed Quentin's mind, increasing his disorientation and accelerating his thought processes. Each night for him seemed to last years. He barely remembered who he was, had only a vague separation between the reality of his memories and the false information poured into him. Sophisticated brainwashing in its purest and most literal sense.

"But why do you want *me?*" he had shouted at Agamemnon the last time his voice synthesizer was attached. "If your new empire is so glorious and you have tens of thousands of neo-cymek volunteers, why waste time on an unwilling subject like myself? I will never be devoted to your cause."

"You are a Butler, a much greater prize," Agamemnon replied. "The other volunteers were raised in captivity, ground under the heels of the thinking machines or tamed by League politics. You, on the other hand, are a military commander and a tactical expert. You could prove most useful."

"I will give you nothing."

"Time will tell. And time is one resource we have in abundance."

With both of them installed in rugged new mobile forms, the Titan general took Quentin on an expedition out onto the frozen plains, then up the glacier line to higher ground from which they could look back at the half-buried towers of the former Cogitor stronghold.

"There is no need for us to be mortal enemies, humans and cymeks," Agamemnon said. "With Omnius trapped on Corrin, we have more territory than we could possibly need, and plenty of volunteers to replenish our ranks."

"I didn't volunteer," Quentin said.

"You are . . . an exception in many ways."

Agamemnon wore a colossal biped form, walking as he had done in his ancient and nearly forgotten human body. It required balance and finesse, and he felt like a giant robotic gladiator. Quentin, not nearly so adept, wore a vehicle body that roared along on wide treads, requiring little coordination. Snow crystals blew around them in Hessra's constant twilight, but they could adjust their optic threads to increase sensitivity to the ambient illumination.

"I used to go out for walks," Quentin said. "I enjoyed stretching my legs. Now I'll never feel that pleasure again."

"We can simulate it in your brain. Or you can choose a mechanical body that covers great distances with every step, one that propels you through the sea, or one that flies. There is no comparison to your former prison of flesh."

"If you don't understand the difference, General, then you have forgotten much over the past millennium."

"One must accept and adapt. Since there is no way you can go back, think instead of the opportunities you have now. You held an important position in the League, but the end was in sight. You had only taken a leave of absence from the Army of the Jihad, but you knew you would never go back to fighting. Now you no longer have to think about retirement, because we're giving you a second chance. By helping us strengthen our new cymek empire, you can ensure peace and stability throughout the galaxy. Omnius is irrelevant, and now cymeks and humans must live together compatibly. You can be a vital go-between. Is there a better person for the job? With us, you could accomplish a greater measure of peace than you ever had at the head of the Jihad battle fleet."

"I question your motives."

"Question them all you wish, so long as you are objective and willing to hear the truth when it is spoken."

Brooding, Quentin remained silent.

"At our restored laboratories on Bela Tegeuse and Richese, we cymeks are designing new combat walkers—strictly for our own protection, of course. Though we could never send our cymek forces against the formidable Army of Humanity, we must be prepared to protect ourselves."

"If you hadn't caused so much pain and suffering, no one in the League would want to attack you."

"For the sake of civilization we must forget the past and erase ancient, perpetual grudges. We must begin anew. I foresee a day when cymeks and the League will cooperate in a mutually beneficial relationship."

Quentin attempted to make a laughing sound, but didn't have the knack yet. "The stars will likely burn out first. Your own son Vorian Atreides would never make peace with you."

Angered, Agamemnon fell into a brief silence. "I still hold out hope for him. Perhaps one day Vorian and I can make mutual concessions and forgive one another, and then there may be peace with the rest of humanity. But for the moment my cymeks are still forced to develop new defenses. Since the League's Holtzman shields prevent us from launching projectiles against human battleships, we have built many laser guns. We hope the high power energy beams will be more effective."

Quentin hesitated in his heavy, tractorlike walker form. "No one has used lasers in many centuries. It is not wise."

"Nevertheless, why not try?" Agamemnon said. "At least it will be unexpected."

"No. You should not use them."

Sensing an unusual alarm and reticence from his captive, the Titan general pressed, "Is there something I don't know about lasers, after all these millennia? No one is afraid of them."

"They have . . . they have been proven inefficient. It is a waste of your time."

Intrigued, Agamemnon did not press the matter further. But he knew he would have to learn the answer from Quentin, no matter what form of torture or manipulation it might require.

WHEN QUENTIN'S BRAIN canister was detached from the walker-form and again placed in its preservation machinery, Juno set to work deactivating his time sensors, disorienting him even more, pumping him with chemicals, and pulsing his pain and pleasure centers. It required five days, but Quentin eventually let slip everything he knew, without ever being aware of what he had done.

According to the primero, only a handful of the highest-ranking officers in the Army of Humanity knew that any interaction between a Holtzman shield and a laser produced an appallingly huge feedback explosion that closely resembled an atomic detonation. Since laser weaponry had not been used in active combat for many centuries, the chances of such a coincidental encounter were vanishingly slim.

The Titans were astounded by the unexpected weakness the League had kept so carefully secret for the length of the Jihad, and Agamemnon was eager to exploit it. "This will make significant strides toward our dreams of expansion and renewed conquest."

Because Dante was the most efficient and methodical of the remaining Titans, the general dispatched him on a mission to verify the startling information. Dante launched a fighting force of neo-cymek vessels from the reconquered Synchronized Worlds in a series of provocative attacks against *hrethgir* colonies that still struggled for full recovery following the Omnius Scourge.

Since the time of the Great Purge, Agamemnon had brooded and planned and sent out eager neo scouts to study the nearest planets, note their weaknesses, and determine which ones could easily be subjugated by a few dominating cymeks. The League itself remained in a shambles, commerce and enforcement still frayed from system to system.

Many of the worlds were ripe for the picking.

"Your goal is twofold, Dante," the general said. "We need you to provoke a direct confrontation with shielded *hrethgir* warships. A single blast from a laser will show immediately whether we have learned a very valuable secret."

"If you must conquer a dozen or so new worlds before they notice what we're doing, then all the better!" Juno said with a delighted simulated laugh.

Dante set out with his cymek ships and zealous neos who were anxious to grind lesser humans under their mechanical feet. Surveys and starmaps had already pinpointed their best targets. The mechanized vessels struck the small settlements like hammers from the sky—Relicon, al-Dhifar, Juzzubal. The people had no effective defenses, pleaded with the cymeks for mercy. Dante, though, had received no specific instructions about mercy. Each time, he made certain to let a ship or two escape, so that someone might warn the Army of Humanity and send a few warships running to the rescue.

On the worlds that were easily crushed, Dante left behind a neo-cymek force to cement their domination and expand their empire. Neos were given free rein as planetary dictators, gathering desperate volunteers from the broken population and converting them into more new cymeks, thus expanding their ranks. Dante knew that General Agamemnon would be pleased with the easy acquisition of so much new territory.

Most importantly, he kept waiting for human ballistas and javelins to appear, so the cymeks could conduct their lasgun-shield experiment. But Agamemnon had given him a strict caution: "If my son Vorian is in command of whichever *hrethgir* battleships you encounter, you must not destroy him—everyone else, but not him."

"Yes, General. He has much to atone for. I understand why you want to deal with him personally."

"That . . . and I have not entirely given up hope. Would he not be an ally superior even to Quentin Butler?"

"I fear we will not convert either one of them, General."

"We Titans have already succeeded in many impossible tasks, Dante. What is one more!"

Finally, after ravaging two more small *hrethgir* colonies and moving on to a third, Dante and his neo-cymek warships stumbled upon two new-model ballistas and five javelins rushing to protect the recently fallen human colonies.

After sending a challenge to the commanders, and verifying that Vorian Atreides was not at the helm, Dante ordered his fanatically loyal neos to build up a defensive line. From the outset, it was clear that the Army of Humanity outnumbered the handful of cymek ships, but Dante gave orders for his followers to launch volleys of explosive projectiles that pummeled the heavy armor of the human fleet.

Predictably, the League commanders ordered their vessels to activate full Holtzman shields. As soon as his sensors indicated that the jihadis had graciously, though unwittingly, fulfilled the conditions of the experiment, Dante gave the order for his neo-cymeks to ready their laser weapons. He sent them forward while keeping his own distance, the better to observe.

The lasers were not particularly powerful, barely weapons caliber. The blasts could not possibly be effective under ordinary circumstances.

Still staying well clear of the combat zone, Dante was not disappointed. Not at all.

The lasers struck the shields, triggering a cascade of pseudo-atomic detonations. Within seconds the entire human fleet was vaporized, one after another, in blinding flashes of light.

However, the feedback of the laser-shield interaction was so intense that most of the neo-cymek gunners were also obliterated. Their ships disintegrated in an instant, resulting in the simultaneous annihilation of both sides.

It looked as if a new sun had suddenly dawned over the planet the *hrethgir* had tried to defend. The glow faded as the dissipating vapor and energy spread out, dwindling into the cold of space. For Dante and the few surviving neos, the show was well worth the cost. . . .

AGAMEMNON WAS EXCEEDINGLY pleased. Since none of the humans in the battle had escaped, the *hrethgir* high command could not possibly know that the cymeks had discovered their fundamental weakness. "This is a watershed for us! Even with our lesser numbers, we can cut a swath of death and destruction through the *hrethgir*. Our goal is in our grasp."

All the terms of this conflict had changed, and the Titan general suspected that he and his son would face each other before it was all over.

Science is lost in its own mythos, redoubling its efforts whenever it
forgets its aim

— KREFTER BRAHN,

Special Advisor to the Jihad

The mutated RNA retrovirus spread like poisonous smoke through the caves of Rossak. Standard protective devices proved ineffective, sterilization routines sometimes failed, and even potent doses of melange did not guarantee safety. In time, more than three-quarters of the population in the cliff cities was infected, and the majority of those died.

Raquella Berto-Anirul and Dr. Mohandas Suk were out of their depth and failing in their efforts to treat the disease.

So far, none of Dr. Suk's trial vaccines had shown positive results, and the epidemic continued to rage through the communal caves, eating away at the remaining healthy members of Rossak's population.

Each day and far into the night, Raquella labored in the crowded cliff warrens that served as hospital wards. Every bed, every clear space on the floors, was filled with stricken men, children, and Sorceresses. Taking her daily dose of spice delivered by VenKee drop pods, Raquella pushed her body beyond its limits. Though she wore a sterile breather and eye films, the miasma of sickness accompanied by a constant clamor of the suffering and dying weighed upon her psyche. But Raquella steeled her resolve to defeat the virus.

In previous years, jihadi warriors and suicidal Sorceresses had thrown themselves against impossible odds, fighting swarms of thinking machines with no thought for their own survival. Raquella could do no less, fighting in her own way. "Victory at any cost."

Jimmak Tero followed Raquella like a slow but loving puppy, eager to help. Each day he brought her food fresh from the jungle: silvery fruits, fuzzy fungi, and juice-laden berries. He made her a strange, tart herbal infusion that left an odd aftertaste, but Jimmak seemed particularly proud of it. He looked at her with his broad, simple smile and bright eyes.

After a grueling day in humid heat, with another dozen patients dead under her watch, Raquella felt emotionally and physically drained. One of the victims was a premature baby cut from its mother after she'd succumbed to the plague. Since Raquella was the only member of the staff in the main ward, she sat down on the cool stone floor and wept.

Trying to find the strength to continue, Raquella wiped the tears from her already moist cheeks. Hot and dizzy, she struggled to her feet—and nearly lost her balance. She waited a moment to catch her breath, thinking she had risen too quickly, but the discomfort only worsened, and she felt herself falling. . . .

"You okay, Doctor Lady?"

She looked up into Jimmak's round, concerned face. He was holding her shoulders in his strong arms. "I fainted . . . too tired. I should've eaten more, taken another dose of spice. . . ."

Then Raquella realized that she was lying on a bed with feeding tubes and gauges hooked to her. How much time had passed? She touched her arm, recognized the dialysis machines that had shown some benefit for the worst victims of the new Scourge.

Her dark-skinned assistant Nortie Vandego stood nearby, checking the equipment. Vandego looked at her with dark eyes that held a glint of fear. "You just finished the first blood-scrubbing treatment. We caught the buildup of Compound X before it damaged your liver, but . . . you are infected. I've given you an additional dose of melange."

Raquella shook her head, then tried to climb out of bed. "Nortie, you should be tending other patients, not me."

The assistant put a hand on her shoulder, pushing her back onto the bed. "You're a patient now. You deserve the same care you gave to all the others."

Raquella knew that if she was infected, her odds of survival were not good. She summoned her courage. "It may just be an allergic reaction to the jungle foods I've been eating. I let myself get too run-down, and I need rest."

"That's probably it. Just rest now."

Raquella recognized that tone only too well: It was the voice she had heard her assistant use to soothe the dying.

TWO DAYS LATER, Nortie Vandego fell ill herself and was taken to a different ward. The job of tending Raquella now fell to the petite Sorceress Karee Marques, who administered a number of pharmaceuticals and unproven treatments as if Raquella were a test subject. Raquella didn't mind, though she believed Mohandas was more likely to find a cure. Did he even know she was sick?

The nights in the cliff warrens were deep and black. Oppressive and mysterious sounds came from the dense jungle outside. Raquella was lying half asleep from a cocktail of drugs administered to her when she heard a loud, angry voice nearby. Opening her eyes narrowly, she saw Ticia Cenva berating Karee, telling her to spend time on other patients. "Let this one die. She is not one of us, and her meddling may have made the epidemic worse."

"Worse? She has exhausted herself to help us."

"And how do we know for certain that she saved anyone? The plague will only take the weakest among us," Ticia insisted, her voice as hard as armor plating and a taint of wildness in her eyes. The Supreme Sorceress seemed even more frayed, less in control. "The Scourge will weed out the inadequate stock and leave the Sorceresses stronger."

"Or it will kill all of us!"

As Raquella lay struggling with her aches, her fatigue, her nausea, she focused on one part of the debate. *They think I'm dying.* It was an awkward thought for a doctor, a healer. *Perhaps it is true.* She had seen enough death to be ready for the inevitability of her fate, though she was deeply disappointed at being unable to finish her work here.

But her body did not surrender easily. She fought the disease for days, struggling to remain conscious, to remain alive. After the first few treatments, Raquella was not hooked to the blood scrubbers again, and she knew that the toxic Compound X was rapidly building up. Her skin was yellow, pocked with lesions; she was always desperately thirsty.

The Sorceresses had given up on Raquella, leaving her to die.

Only Jimmak bothered to tend her. He sat at her side, wiping her brow with a cool cloth. He gave her his bitter tea, fed her small bits of fruit, and tucked a blanket around her to make her comfortable. Once, she thought she even saw Mohandas, but it was only a fever-induced hallucination. When was the last time they had talked . . . touched?

The Rossak Epidemic had already gone on forever.

In what seemed like another life, she recalled quiet, private days with him, when they'd had time to be lovers like any two normal human beings, on other worlds in other times. She missed the sweetness of his smile, the warmth of his embrace, the engrossing discussions they'd had as dedicated colleagues.

"How is Nortie?" she asked Jimmak in a brief lucid moment. "My assistant. Where is she?"

"Tall lady die. Sorry." Raquella didn't want to believe it. The slow-witted boy leaned closer to where she lay in her sweat-damp sheets. His broad, smooth face was fixed with determination. "Doctor Lady won't die, though."

He scuttled away, then returned with an empty suspensor gurney that the healthy workers used for hauling away bodies. Jimmak pushed it in front of him, as if he knew what he was doing. He maneuvered the floating platform and lowered it next to Raquella's bed.

"Jimmak? What are you doing?" She tried to keep her thoughts straight.

"Call me Doctor Boy!" With strong hands, he rolled her onto the gurney, then stuffed clothing, towels, and a blanket into a storage compartment beneath it.

"Where . . . are you taking me?"

"The jungle. Nobody to take care of you here." He pushed the drifting gurney ahead of him.

Struggling to prop herself up on her elbows, Raquella saw Ticia Cenva standing in the corridor, watching the tableau. Jimmak ducked his head, as if hoping his aloof mother wouldn't notice him. Raquella tried to meet the gaze of the black-robed Supreme Sorceress, who seemed momentarily disappointed. Wishing that Jimmak was carting off Raquella's dead body, perhaps? The stern, ravenlike woman said nothing, and let them pass.

As darkness settled over Rossak, the boy loaded her into a lift and worked his way all the way down to the jungle floor. He ignored the threatening sounds, the shadows, the thick vines, and pushed her deep into the dense alien wilderness.

*I never thought I would see Salusa Secundus again, the superb
League assembly halls, the towering monuments of Zimia. Alas,
they are not as magnificent as I remembered.*

—YOREK THURR,
secret Corrin journals

Once he escaped from Corrin, it took him almost two months in
transit to get to the vulnerable heart of the League of Nobles.

During that time, Thurr managed to steal a different vessel at one of
the plague-ravaged planets on the fringe of League space. Since he was
immune to the Scourge, it warmed his heart to see how devastated the
population was and how many cities and towns had collapsed during the
great death. His mind seemed to sing with razor-sharp clarity.

On planet after planet, human civilization had been reduced to subsistence level. After two decades with minimal outside commerce, the handful of survivors were like carrion crows fighting over the remaining
supplies, homes, and tools. In some systems afflicted by cascading disasters, fully eighty percent of the population had died from the epidemic or
its secondary consequences. It would be generations before mankind
recovered from the disaster.

And it was all my original idea.

He stopped at two other worlds along the way, gathering news, stealing money, modifying his story and his disguise. He was hungry to learn
how everything had changed since his faked death and exile among the
thinking machines.

Foremost among the changes, religious fanaticism had grown much
stronger, with the Cult of Serena foolishly smashing useful devices and

equipment. Thurr could not help but smile as he watched their zealous, wasteful destruction. This was an outcome he had not anticipated, but he did not object to it. The humans were only damaging themselves.

When he reached Zimia, he hoped to discover that another of his fiendish ideas—the hungry little mechanical mites—had also wrought incredible horrors upon the population. Contrary to what Erasmus believed, Thurr did not revel in death for its own sake. He simply liked to *accomplish* things. . . .

By the time he finally arrived at Salusa Secundus, Thurr had fully immersed himself in his new identity as a refugee from Balut, one of the Scourge-decimated worlds. Salusa had become a central world for distributing refugees and repopulating planets and strengthening racial lines using seed stock gathered by the Sorceresses of Rossak years ago. Thurr smiled. In a sense, he had helped to *improve* the human race.

He marveled at the sheer momentum and persistence the League expended on trying to return things to the way they had "always been," instead of accepting changes and moving on. As soon as he restored himself to his rightful position of power, Thurr would do something to assist in that regard. Seeing how weakened and confused the League was, he didn't expect to take long to achieve his goal. Without the Jihad to focus them, the human survivors were drifting aimlessly. They needed him.

Thurr studied historical databases, scanning propaganda-laced histories of the Jihad, and was annoyed to discover that he barely warranted a mention! After everything he had accomplished—the immense work he had done during his time of service! He had formed the Jihad Police, helped Grand Patriarch Ginjo turn his office into a position of utmost importance. Thurr should have become the Grand Patriarch himself, but his greatest mistake had been to trust that scheming Camie Boro-Ginjo. Now, after his absence, it seemed that the League had spurned him, brushed him aside.

Once he received biological clearance by proving himself free of all plagues and sicknesses, Thurr set foot in Zimia again for the first time in decades. The city had changed greatly. Banners of Serena, Manion the Innocent, and Iblis Ginjo hung on every tall building. Shrines filled with orange marigolds adorned every corner and cul-de-sac.

Much to his surprise and irritation, Thurr learned that Jipol had been disbanded. Since the war had ended almost two decades ago, League security had grown laughably lax. After studying his surroundings and developing a method, Thurr easily bypassed various checkpoints to enter the core of the city.

Xander Boro-Ginjo was now the Grand Patriarch, as nephew and successor to Tambir. He had not even been born until a year after Thurr's faked death. By all accounts, Xander was a dithering figurehead, a plump and soft puppet who needed to be manipulated by a better master.

Thurr felt fire inside his chest. Now more than ever, he deserved to be the Grand Patriarch. Thurr could be very persuasive, and he hoped to make this transition cleanly. At the right moment he would declare his true identity and miraculous return, telling a brave and fictitious story of captivity and torture under Omnius. Then he would claim his due. The people would recognize their need and understand the wisdom of what he offered.

Surreptitiously, he studied the Grand Patriarch's administrative mansion, his routine and his movements. He learned the layout of research centers, office buildings, and the headquarters of the Army of Humanity, and determined the responsibilities of political bureaus. The obvious growth of bureaucracy showed that the League was already stagnating, wandering down a wrong path that would prevent them from accomplishing anything great.

Thurr had gotten here just in time, and he knew he could straighten things out.

It didn't take him long to formulate a plan to slip into the offices of the Grand Patriarch. Discarding his drab disguise as a Balut refugee, he obtained the acceptable clothing of a League clerk, disposed of the man's body, and worked his way through the halls and offices of the administrative mansion.

As soon as he revealed his identity to Xander Boro-Ginjo, Thurr imagined he would be welcomed as a lost hero. There would be parades through the streets, people would applaud his life's epic story and welcome him back into the League. Thurr's dark eyes glittered with anticipation.

Without much caution, he made his way to a room that had the proper access, climbed out a window, and gracefully crossed a tiny ledge to a window at the rear of the target office. He waited until Xander was alone in his private office, and then climbed inside.

Thurr swelled his chest and smiled, waiting to be welcomed. From behind the desk, the distracted Grand Patriarch looked up at him with confusion instead of fear or outrage. The ornate chain of his office hung heavily on his thick neck. "Who are you and why are you here?" He consulted a heavy book on his desk. "Do you have an appointment?"

Thurr's thin lips formed a smile. "I am Yorek Thurr, former com-mander of the Jihad police. I was your grandfather's right-hand man and special advisor."

His life-extension treatment had kept his appearance like that of a man in late middle age, though in the last five years he had begun to experience strange tics and tremors that made him wonder if Omnius had tricked him somehow. This chubby oaf of a leader would never believe Thurr's real age.

"I'm sure that's very interesting, but I do have an important meeting in only a few minutes."

"Then you must redefine what is important, Xander Boro-Ginjo." Thurr stepped menacingly closer. "I was supposed to become the succes-sor to Iblis Ginjo, but your grandmother seized the chain of office instead, and then your uncle Tambir became Grand Patriarch. Again and again I was denied what was rightfully mine. I have put aside my rights for many years now, but the time has come for me to lead the League in the direc-tion it must go. I demand that you resign your position and give it to me."

Xander appeared perplexed. His face was jowly and soft from fine living, his eyes dulled either by drugs, drink, or plain lack of intelligence. "Why should I do that? And what is your name again? How did you get in—"

An aide opened the door. "Sir, your meeting is—" He blinked in sur-prise at Thurr, who whirled to glare at him. Thurr wished he had brought his dagger. "Oh, excuse me! I didn't know you had a visitor. Who is this, sir?"

Xander rose in a huff. "I don't know, and you shouldn't have let him in. Tell the guards to remove him."

Thurr glowered. "You are making a grave mistake, Xander Boro-Ginjo."

The aide shouted for guards, who rushed in and surrounded Thurr. With disgust, he saw that he was outnumbered and could not easily press his point. "I expected a better reception than this, considering all I have done for the League." His head thrummed, and for a moment he had dif-ficulty understanding where he was. Why couldn't these people see?

The Grand Patriarch shook his head. "This man is suffering from delusions and I fear he may be violent." He looked back at Thurr. "No one knows who you are, sir."

That alone nearly drove Thurr into a murderous rage, and he struggled mightily to restrain himself, not wanting to sacrifice his life in such a pointless fashion. As the guards escorted him away roughly, Boro-Ginjo and his aide busied themselves studying the agenda for the upcoming meeting. Thurr pretended to cooperate as the guards marched him out of the administrative mansion.

Frustrated with his own foolishness, he realized that he had lived under the thinking machines for too long. He had been the ruler of Wallach IX, with the absolute power to make demands. He had forgotten how stupid and intractable the *hrethgir* could be. He chided himself for his mistake, and vowed not to make a similar one again. A plan . . . he needed a better plan.

The guards were incompetent soldiers, unaccustomed to sophisticated, trained killers like Yorek Thurr. He chose not to murder these men, though, for that would have drawn more attention than he wished. He had plans to formulate and could not be bothered to elude a manhunt at the same time.

As soon as a moment of distraction presented itself, Thurr slipped away from the inept guards and dashed into the streets of Zimia. They shouted and pursued him, but he avoided them easily. Though the men called in reinforcements and persisted in their efforts for several hours, the former Jipol commandant quickly found a bolthole and concentrated on developing a more effective approach.

It was merely a matter of time and careful planning, and then Thurr would get everything he deserved.

I have imagined what it would be like to be Omnius. What far-reaching decisions might I make in his position?
—Erasmus Dialogues

The independent robot stood in one of the expanded art exhibit rooms of the Central Spire, awaiting an audience. Though the evermind could speak with him anywhere, Omnius seemed particularly intent on making sure Erasmus saw his new gallery. All the bizarre electronic paintings, sculptures, and geometrical jewel-forms were horrendously derivative and uninspired. Omnius seemed to think he grew more and more talented through sheer quantity of production.

It had only grown worse once the three near-identical but separate incarnations of the evermind had begun to "collaborate."

Working in concert, the three Omniuses had created jarring juxtapositions of bright colors and random jagged shapes, stylized renditions of mechanical contrivances accompanied by dissonant, synthesized music. No aesthetic harmony whatsoever.

Leaving the exhibits as swiftly as he could, the platinum robot picked up a black guidance cube from a wall-mounted tray. The cube lit up, verified his identity, and then showed the robot which direction to go. No pathway was ever the same through the Central Spire, since the flowmetal building was constantly being changed as Omnius vented his creative urges.

Following red arrows on the surface of the cube, Erasmus entered a large chamber and rode a conveyor floor that spiraled up seventy stories. The independent robot grew weary of the endless and unnecessary variations.

As Erasmus entered the top level of the Spire, he found the three Omnius incarnations in the midst of an unemotional but involved and focused discussion. In human psychology the situation might have been described as a multiple-personality disorder. The primary Omnius attempted to remain dominant, while the copies brought to Corrin by Yorck Thurr and Seurat had developed different perspectives. The trio of everminds attempted to cooperate as one electronic unit, but by now their differences had become too severe. Though they could easily have linked and merged, the three remained separated, speaking to each other only through black speaker holes positioned around the flowmetal chamber.

"I am here at the appointed time," Erasmus said, attempting to call attention to his arrival. "Omnius requested my presence." *One of you did.*

The out-of-phase everminds paid no attention to their visitor, not even when Erasmus repeated himself. Previously, for his own amusement, he had created nicknames for the other two everminds, just as he called Gilbertus "Mentat," or as Omnius Prime used the derisive "Martyr" to refer to the independent robot after his supposed resurrection from total erasure. In his mind, Erasmus had dubbed Seurat's gelsphere update "Seur-Om," and the one Thurr had delivered from Wallach IX, "ThurrOm." Just listening to them, the independent robot could distinguish among the three by subtleties of tone and attitude, and by the information they used to support their arguments.

The Omniuses were concerned about being trapped on Corrin, but could not agree on what to do about it. The abortive offensive maneuver ThurrOm had launched, after being tricked by Yorek Thurr, had led to the destruction of over four hundred major robot ships, while doing little damage to the *hrethgir* watchdogs. All in all, though Thurr himself had escaped, the flurry had accomplished nothing for Omnius, and had only made the human sentries more vigilant.

As he listened to their flat but rapid-fire debate, Erasmus saw that some of their postulates were illogical and demonstrated a thorough lack of understanding of human responses and priorities. Apparently even Omnius Prime did not consult with the inner reservoir of knowledge and insight that would have been accessible in the isolated copy of Erasmus's persona. The three copies had grown more extreme in their conclusions and less flexible. The robot would have liked to correct them, but these new diversified everminds would not listen to him.

The trio agreed on some things. They knew it was unwise to keep the only copies of the evermind on Corrin. Omnius Prime advocated an electronic escape, transmitting a normalized copy of the vast computer mind far out into space, a stream of data in search of an appropriate target. ThurrOm pointed out that there were no known receivers for such a data package, and with distance the signal would only grow more diffuse and dwindle to oblivion. A pointless expenditure of energy and effort.

The Seurat Omnius insisted on a more tangible option. SeurOm wanted to colonize twenty or more Unallied Planets. As soon as the thinking machines anchored their new outpost, the resurrected Omniuses could proceed to additional planets, thereby regenerating the Synchronized empire. He blithely presumed they could find a way to escape the deadly scrambler net, but did not explain how that might be accomplished.

As if his violent appetite had been whetted by his first independent offensive, ThurrOm advocated sending their entire machine fleet against the guardian human ships. He wanted to accept overwhelming losses and hope that some part of the machine battle fleet survived. If they failed, however, then the fanatical *hrethgir* could bombard all of Corrin with their pulse-atomic warheads and exterminate the last vestiges of the computer evermind. ThurrOm admitted that this could be a problem.

All of the plans had a vanishingly small chance of success. It intrigued Erasmus to see how much trouble the primary Omnius was having in his bizarre argument with the subsidiary incarnations.

Month after month, the robotic ships continued their regular attacks by throwing themselves against the scrambler net and the League barricades—consequently suffering predictable waves of destruction. For more than nineteen years, Omnius had strip-mined Corrin, ripping metals and raw materials from the crust, then recycling and reprocessing. By now, the planet was nearly wrung dry. Some of the rare elements and molecules necessary for creating sophisticated gelcircuitry minds had become difficult to obtain. The production of replacement warships had slowed. Erasmus projected that their stronghold would soon become vulnerable simply due to the constant attrition of their forces.

He had to find a solution—for himself and Gilbertus, at the very least—before that occurred.

For years now, Erasmus had considered many possible methods of escape. Far from Corrin, he and Gilbertus could devote themselves to mental pursuits without the interference and distractions of the increasingly eccentric evermind.

The independent robot had left his ward back at the villa, where

Gilbertus continued to explore a difficult intellectual puzzle with the Serena Butler clone at his side. The muscular and well-trained human could follow serpentine pathways in his brain, extrapolating fiftieth-order variables and consequences. For years now, he had been able to memorize every detail of his daily experiences, keeping everything organized and retrievable in his brain.

Attempting to get the attention of the everminds while they steadfastly ignored him, Erasmus began to hammer his metal fist against the wall, reenacting behavior he had witnessed from Gilbertus when he'd been an unruly young boy. "I am here. What is it you demanded to discuss with me?"

The robot considered hurling his directional cube at the floor, but instead held it tighter in his flowmetal palm. It was only simulated anger, but this seemed like a good opportunity to explore the humanlike emotions he had learned.

The three harmonized voices commanded in unison, "Stop being impatient, Erasmus. You are acting like a *hrethgir*."

The robot thought of several excellent retorts but decided against voicing them. Instead, he placed the inactive directional cube on the floor. The flowmetal surface of the deck swallowed the cube, then smoothed over again like a puddle of water around a dropped stone.

The Omniuses resumed their debate.

Suddenly Rekur Van entered the room, pushed by an armed robot guard, who also held a directional cube. "It is time for my appointment!" the limbless man said, raising his voice to be heard over the escalating argument.

"I have precedence, Stump," Erasmus said with no rancor, amplifying his words to an appropriate relative level.

The voices of the three everminds still sounded unemotional in the background, but the synthesized signals among them grew increasingly louder, reverberating around the chamber with such force that the floor shook and rattled. The three Omniuses accused each other of inefficiency and fallibility, casting blame back and forth. The debate continued faster and faster as Erasmus and Rekur Van eavesdropped, with growing curiosity and alarm. Finally it became clear that Omnius Prime had convinced himself that he was the one true God of the Universe; according to his analyses and the projections Erasmus had performed for him, he decided that he fit the definition. He held ultimate knowledge and ultimate power.

"I declare the two of you false gods," Omnius Prime boomed suddenly.

"I am not a false god," SeurOm said.

"Nor am I," ThurrOm insisted.

Such a strange trinity. It seemed ironic that Omnius, who had so roundly criticized the emotionally charged religions of human beings, now embraced a religious belief system of his own, with a thinking machine at its pinnacle.

Without warning, the trio of everminds reached a critical flashpoint. The room filled with a storm of multicolored electronic flashes, firing from wall to wall and floor to ceiling. Erasmus managed to scramble smoothly out of the way, retreating onto the entry ramp, from which he watched as the chamber lit up.

A bright yellow blast excoriated Rekur Van's robot guard, and the limbless Tlulaxa screamed as sharp pieces of metal tore into his flesh. His life-support cart tipped over and fell across his smoking companion robot.

With great disappointment, Erasmus recalled that Rekur Van had been working on the shape-shifting biological machine project. He'd had so much potential.

The chamber grew suddenly silent. Presently, ominously, one of the everminds spoke. "Now there are two of us to rule."

"As it should be," said the other. "Neither one of us is a false god."

So, Omnius Prime had been obliterated in the electronic battle. The primary evermind that Erasmus had known for so many years on Corrin existed no more. The walls began to ripple and shudder, and he worried that the entire Central Spire might collapse or change shape, with him inside it.

To his surprise, Rekur Van moaned and began to squirm helplessly. Hurrying to his aid—strictly to preserve a valuable resource—Erasmus scooped the Tlulaxa and his cart into his metal arms and exited the writhing Spire. No sooner had they reached the safety of the plaza than the structure dramatically changed shape behind them, as the new evermind rulers exerted their combined will. The tower grew taller and spinier.

"This is quite unexpected, and interesting," Erasmus said. "The everminds appear to have gone insane."

The helpless Tlulaxa man turned his burned face to look at the bizarre convulsions of Omnius's primary structure. "We might be better off taking our chances with the *hrethgir.*"

The flesh may not be excused from the laws of matter, but the mind is not so fettered. Thought transcends the physics of the brain.
—"Origins of the Spacing Guild" (a League publication)

Though he had decided not to smash into his mother's spice-immersion enclosure, Adrien Venport paced the floor. His brothers and sisters, scattered across the League on VenKee business assignments, could not help him. He doubted they could even understand his quandary.

From within the misty chamber, Norma could sense her son's indecision and concern. His worries were diverting him from vital VenKee business matters. He knew full well that if his odd and esoteric mother could truly and safely guide the spacefolders, VenKee would effectively control all future commerce between star systems. But she depended on him to keep the trading company strong, because she required its infrastructure for her next grand step.

She would have to quell his unreasonable fears. Finished with her main work, Norma knew it was time to change. Adrien needed enough answers to reassure—and even exhilarate him.

Forcing her expanding mind back to the real world, concentrating on her body and its immediate environs, Norma summoned him. With slow, painstaking effort, mouthing her words with uncooperative lips, scrawling letters in the spice stains on the plaz walls, she convinced Adrien that she wanted him to join her inside the chamber—provided that he wore a clearplaz breather and eye protection.

Her son did not question her. He ran out of the laboratory building shouting orders. In less than half an hour he returned, fully clothed in an environment suit. Apparently, he didn't even want to risk exposing his skin to concentrated spice gas. Norma realized that was probably wise.

With a mental command, using Sorceress powers she rarely practiced, Norma allowed part of her enclosure to open, creating an inward vortex that made the spice gas swirl and kept most of it inside. Though clearly intimidated, Adrien raised his head and stepped inside. The door sealed quickly behind him, and she took deep gulps of spice gas, watching him as he walked through the murk.

"Oh, the universe I have seen, Adrien!" she exclaimed. "And there is so much more to explore!"

He was overjoyed just to be close to her again. "We should install a speaker system, Mother. It has been impossible—so many questions, and we couldn't get through to you." He knelt by her half-dissolved cushion on the tank's floor.

"A speaker system is acceptable," she said. "But as long as you and I have an understanding, Adrien—as long as we have trust and confidence in each other—you can enter this chamber whenever I tell you it is safe."

With a perplexed expression, he asked, "When would it not be safe to enter your tank?"

"When I am using my mind, my prescience, to calculate a safe course through folded space. Did you forget the purpose of this project?"

Her voice sounded eerie to her own ears as she spoke at length, explaining how melange saturation had enhanced her ability to envision future events, to avoid disastrous paths. "I have worked out all of the final details in my mind."

Through his clearplaz mask she saw that his patrician features were still tight with concern. "I understand, Mother, but I have to be certain you are safe. Let the medical personnel examine you to make sure you're healthy. You look emaciated."

"I am better than I have ever been," she said, with a distant smile on her wide, bony face. "And healthy." From all appearances, her body had degenerated into a form that hardly seemed capable of supporting the freakishly large head. Her skin rippled and her limbs had lost definition and become cordlike. "I've been altering into something . . . and *toward* something."

She took his much larger hands in her own, gripped them tightly, lovingly. With a penetrating gaze from her spice-blue eyes, Norma said,

"Load my test chamber into one of the spacefolder ships, so that I can demonstrate my new navigation abilities. I will be able to pilot it."

"Are you sure it's safe?"

"Adrien, life is inherently perilous, as fragile as a flower bud in a storm. But, like the bud, it contains incredible beauty, a reflection of God's intent for the universe. Is folding space safe compared to what? By odds, it is probably safer than a woman undergoing childbirth, but . . . yes, it is more dangerous than hiding and never venturing outside your front door."

"We really need this breakthrough," he agreed, thinking like a businessman again. Then he crossed his arms stubbornly as the spice gas swirled around him. "But if it's as safe as you say, then I insist on going with you, to demonstrate my faith in your abilities."

She nodded slowly, her enlarged head drifting up and down on the thin stalk of her neck. "You are as tough a negotiator as your father. Very well, then. I will show you the universe."

UNDER NORMA'S STRICT though distant supervision, and Adrien's intense scrutiny of every detail, the preparations for her first space-folding journey were completed. This trip would be different for Norma, exciting and concrete, not just theoretical. A test, proof—liberation.

Hundreds of Kolhar workers made certain that the medium-sized cargo vessel and the modifications to her spice-gas chamber met exacting specifications. Once the speaker system was installed inside the tank, Adrien could communicate directly with his mother, though he often had trouble focusing her attention or getting information from her in a useful form.

When all components were ready for the prescient voyage, only two people climbed aboard: Norma sealed inside the chamber, and Adrien secured inside a lifepod on the same deck with her. He knew he was risking the future of VenKee Enterprises on this one flight, since none of his siblings could manage even a fraction of the necessary business activities.

But Adrien trusted his mother. Through the plaz of their respective enclosures, they could see each other, and talk through the direct comline. The Holtzman engines would fold space and transport them from Kolhar to a different place entirely. Norma would choose the proper course.

Before embarking, she increased the gas mixture in her enclosure to its maximum concentration and went into a trance that opened up the universe like the unfolding petals of a magnificent rose. Each time she peered into space it was more beautiful than the time before. And on this occasion Norma would make the leap, guiding the ship along a prescient pathway that her mind had already foreseen.

Norma focused on the future, saw the swirling colors of the cosmos and her infinitesimally small ship. It was a cosmic conundrum, but one she understood fully. Space would wrap itself around the vessel in a loving embrace, like an attentive mother cradling her child. In her core, she felt a powerful soundless humming, and without actually turning back to look, she saw Adrien vibrating with life inside his protective lifepod.

Once the Holtzman engines folded space, bending one coordinate to another, the journey was set, and the ship glided through layers of distance and space. Adrien was shaking, both from the ship's vibration and from fear, as if his body and his mind might come apart, but he did not regret what he was experiencing.

Then they were on the other side of their destination. She saw Adrien existing at one coordinate, then appearing at another. In only a moment, the universe became very small.

"We've done it, Mother! Look below!" Amazed, he peered through a viewing port in the cargo ship and recognized the dry, cracked planet. From orbit, it looked like a basin of gold. "Arrakis? I've been here many times."

"For my first prescient voyage," Norma said, "I thought it appropriate to travel to the source of the melange."

Arrakis beckoned her as a place to anchor all prescient experiences, a place where she could build upon everything that was yet to come—for her, for Adrien, and for all of humankind.

"Stunning, in more ways than one," he said. "With an instantaneous assured conduit to the source of the spice, VenKee can make even greater profits."

"Not all profits are monetary. Arrakis is like the spice it contains, complex beyond comprehension, valuable beyond measure."

Norma knew that spice and navigation were inextricably linked. Supplies of melange would have to be guaranteed. VenKee Enterprises might need to station its own company military force here to protect its spice sands. Arrakis was not the sort of place to be bound by legalities. It was a raw, untamed world where only the strongest survived.

From her sealed, spice-impregnated navchamber, Norma mentally guided the VenKee transport ship low over the barren planet with conventional engines. The ocean of dunes dwarfed her spacefolder. With her powerful mind, Norma observed great sandworms, dust clouds, and ferocious Coriolis storms. Her mind opened in two directions at once, to the past and the future, and she saw bands of people moving across the landscape, some on foot and others actually riding the worms.

"If only we could find another source of spice, so that we were not so dependent on this one world, which has already been overrun by spice rushers," Adrien said, his voice floating into her gaseous chamber. "Since the Scourge, everyone knows the riches waiting here, and Arrakis is swarming with spice harvesters and even slavers."

"Melange is the heart of the universe," she said. "There is only one heart."

Hovering their ship over the vast deserts, she saw into the future of human commerce. Adrien could not possibly comprehend what a powerful organization he would help create.

"History will say that your father developed these great ships," she said. "Aurelius Venport will be remembered as the visionary inventor, a great patriot for the cause of humanity. As time passes, with all of the actual participants gone, no one will be able to separate fact from myth. This thought makes me very happy and content. It is my last gift to the man I love. I want you to understand this as the leader of VenKee Enterprises, a company that will evolve into something much more."

He nodded. "You're doing that out of love, and out of appreciation for when my father was the only one who believed in you. I understand that, Mother."

After what seemed like a long time over harsh Arrakis, Norma Cenva took her transport ship back into the void, bound for Kolhar.

Life on Arrakis is less significant than a grain of sand in the open bled.
                                        —*The Legend of Selim Wormrider*

Battered survivors of the raided Zensunni village followed Ishmael and El'hiim back to the main settlement in the faraway cliffs. El'hiim suggested that they take the most seriously injured to a nearby company town for medical attention.

Ishmael would hear none of it. "How can you even suggest that? These people barely escaped being taken by slavers. Now you would deliver them into the jaws of those who created a demand for slaves in the first place?"

"They aren't all slavers, Ishmael. I'm trying to save lives."

"Cooperating with them is like playing with a half-tamed beast. Your conciliatory ways have already cost these people their loved ones, their homes. Do not try to squeeze more blood from them. We will take care of them ourselves, with whatever supplies we have."

When their band of refugees reached the cave settlement, the news swept like fire through the people. With his forceful personality and his unyielding demands, Ishmael acted as their leader.

Letting the old man have his way, El'hiim—the actual Naib—said, "I understand the outsiders better than you do, Ishmael. I will send messages to the VenKee towns, submit formal protests to Arrakis City. They cannot do this with impunity."

Ishmael felt as if his anger had broken something inside of him. "They will laugh at you. Slavers have always preyed on the Zensunni, and you stepped right into their trap."

When his stepson rushed away to the crowded cities, Ishmael called the able-bodied Zensunnis to meet with him in the large gathering chamber. As the only female elder of the village, Chamal represented the women, who were just as bloodthirsty as the men. Many boisterous young men who revered the old legends of Selim Wormrider demanded the execution of the criminals.

Incensed and ashamed, remembering how many times they had ignored Ishmael's warnings, the strongest among them volunteered to gather weapons and form a kanla party, a group of commando soldiers who would find the slavers and exact a bloody revenge.

"El'hiim told me he knows where they are," Ishmael said. "He can lead us there."

WHEN EL'HIIM RETURNED with vague promises from the Arrakis City security force to more rigorously enforce certain regulations against kidnapping, he was met by the already armed and bloodthirsty kanla party. Seeing the expressions on their faces and understanding the thoughts in their hearts, he had no choice but to join them, as their Naib.

Though he was far older than any of the fighters, Ishmael accompanied the vengeance party. In spite of—or perhaps because of—his disgust and grief at what had happened to many of his Zensunni friends and even some of his grandchildren by Chamal, Ishmael felt charged with energy, as if he had just taken a massive dose of spice. He could strike a blow against those who had corrupted this world that he had fought so hard to call home.

"Perhaps this will be my last fight. Perhaps I will die. If that is the way of it, I cannot complain."

They crossed the desert, moving swiftly and silently. Gliding like shadows across sun-washed rocks, the kanla party spotted the slavers' camp late the following afternoon. The desert men hunkered down in the shelter of boulders to observe and plan their attack.

One of the fighters suggested that they slip in at night and steal all of the camp's water and supplies. "That would be a fine revenge!"

"Or we could cut the fuel lines on their Zanbar skimmers and leave the despicable men stranded in the desert, where they will die slowly of thirst!"

"And become food for Shai-Hulud."

But Ishmael had no patience for such a long, slow revenge. "Long ago, my friend Aliid said, 'There is nothing more satisfying than the feel of your enemy's blood on your fingers.' I intend to kill these demons myself. Why let Arrakis have the pleasure?"

As darkness fell and the first moon sank below the horizon, the kanla party slipped forward like desert scorpions, carrying crystal blades as their stingers. The slavers—he counted a dozen—activated generators that spilled bright light all around their camp, not for protection but for their own comfort. They didn't bother to post guards.

The Zensunni avengers surrounded the camp and closed in. Though the slavers apparently had more sophisticated weapons, the kanla party outnumbered them almost two to one. It would be a gratifying slaughter.

Ishmael had not wanted them to use their Maula rifles, because they were too clumsy and impersonal, but El'hiim suggested they take advantage of the projectile weapons to shoot out the lights. To this, Ishmael agreed. When the kanla party was in position, he gave the signal, and a roaring barrage of Maula projectiles peppered the air, smashing glowglobes and plunging the area into darkness.

Like wolves, the desert raiders swooped in from all sides. Taken completely by surprise, the offworlders scrambled out of their blankets, unprepared. Some grabbed their weapons and opened fire, but they could not even see their attackers.

The Zensunnis kept low to the ground, snatching any available cover. Their spirits had felt caged for too long, and now they unleashed their emotions in a thrilling bloodbath. They leaped upon their victims, stabbing and slashing with wormtooth daggers, taking their revenge.

In their midst, Ishmael strode through the camp, looking for enemies to punish. He seized a small-statured man who raced for cover among folded bolts of reflective fabric. The coward didn't try to defend his fellows or fight for his own life.

Ishmael hoisted the squirming man. As his eyes adjusted to the starlight, aided by the glow of spreading fires, he could see it was a Tlulaxa by the characteristic pinched face and close-set eyes. Realization hit him. It was Wariff, the unprepared prospector whose life Ishmael had saved twenty years before.

The Tlulaxa looked up at him and called Ishmael by name, remembering him after all this time. Ishmael drew his wormtooth dagger, its curved edge sharp. "I saved your life, and you repay me by raiding my people, stealing them as slaves? I curse you and your vile race."

The violence and shouting around him had reached a fever pitch. Wariff struggled, fluttering his small hands like the wings of a bird. "Please don't kill me. I apologize. I didn't mean—"

"I take back that which I gave you long ago." Ishmael drew the sharp dagger across the slaver's scrawny throat, slicing open his jugular. He tipped Wariff's head back so the blood could gush freely out into the night. "This is the justice of Free Men. Your water, I give to the desert. The blood of these others, I will take for our tribe."

In disgust he discarded the body among the scattered belongings of the slavers. Ishmael realized that in circumstances such as these, his angry friend Aliid might have been right. Back on Poritrin, when they'd both been young men, Ishmael had always insisted that they try to find a peaceful resolution. Now, finally, he saw eye to eye with Aliid. Sometimes there was nothing more exhilarating than vengeance.

El'hiim's voice rose above the din. "Stop now! We must take the rest alive and bring them to Arrakis City, where they will stand trial. We must have proof of their crimes."

Confused, some of the Zensunnis stuttered to a halt. Others continued fighting as if they hadn't heard their Naib. Ishmael grabbed his stepson by the front of his robe. "You would give them back to the outsiders, El'hiim? After what they have done to us?"

"They have committed a crime. Let them be condemned by their own rules."

"Among their kind, slavery is not even a crime!" Ishmael hissed. He released El'hiim and let him stagger to keep his balance. El'hiim could no longer keep control over his vengeful people. Ishmael lifted his red-splashed hand and bellowed so that all could hear. "These men owe us a debt they can never repay. On this world, the only coins are spice and water—so let us take their blood, distill its water, and give it to the families of those they have harmed."

The other outlaws looked at Ishmael, hesitating to do such a thing. El'hiim looked horrified.

"Water is water," Ishmael insisted. "Water is life. These men stole the lives of our friends and relatives when they raided our villages. Slit their throats and bleed them dry, keep their blood in containers. Perhaps God will consider that they have made some repayment for their crimes. It is not for me to judge."

The doomed slavers continued to shout while attempting to defend themselves. The Zensunnis ran at them howling and slashing, killing one after another. In a single day, they made a rich harvest of blood.

My father was declared a Hero of the Jihad. Even if all other histor-
ical records fade into dust, let the human race never forget that fact.

— VICEROY FAYKAN BUTLER,
resolution introduced to the League Parliament

In a bland and logical voice, Dante informed him of the successful test run against the League fleet. Lasers, shields . . . and total devastation.

As he listened in astonishment, unable to disconnect his auditory thoughtrodes, Juno explained to Quentin that he himself had unwittingly revealed the shields' deadly vulnerability to lasers. He went into a frenzy, and after they disconnected him from his walker-form, he sank into despair, unable to calculate how many human soldiers he had doomed through the weakness of his mind. And how many more would die?

The three Titans detached his preservation canister and denied him access to any mechanical bodies. His instinct told him to fight and die in a great and gallant effort, but he found himself utterly impotent. The cymeks had taken his arms and legs. They had taken his eyes, his hearing, his voice. He was nothing more than a helpless trophy. With no temporal reference points to demarcate his limbo, Quentin didn't know how long he was isolated.

If he could only shut down his life-support systems, if he could *will* himself to die, then he could be sure he'd never reveal any more vital information.

But Quentin had to endure his damnation, all the while waiting to seize even the slightest chance that would allow him to strike back, especially now that he knew what vital information he had betrayed. He was no coward like Xavier Harkonnen. He was perfectly willing to give up his life in battle against these hybrid enemies, but he would not waste his efforts. He needed to be convinced he had at least a chance of hurting the Titans.

When his sight suddenly returned with a flare of light, his reconnected optic threads showed him a streamlined walker-body and brain canister that he recognized as Juno's. He wanted either to cringe away or lash out. If he could have used his brain to manifest powerful arms, he would have reached forward to strangle her, but Quentin did not have that option.

"We'd like to take you with us," Juno said. "You're going to fly."

IT WAS AS wonderful as the cymeks had promised, and Quentin hated them for it. Though Juno had lied to him many times, she had not exaggerated these sensations.

The neos installed his preservation canister into a sleek flying ship designed to carry cymeks into interstellar battlefields. As the force raced away from Hessra, Quentin felt like an eagle soaring with wings of steel. He could swoop on the updrafts of stellar winds, entirely unfettered. He could fall forever like a raptor snatching prey and then change his course at will, accelerating and flying in any direction.

"Many neos experience the ecstasy of flight," Dante transmitted from the head of the small force. "If you had cooperated, Primero Butler, we could have let you experience this long ago."

For a giddy moment, Quentin had forgotten the horror of his circumstances. Now, though, he curtailed his ecstatic sensations and fell glumly into tight formation with the rest of the cymek ships. He could break away now, change course and fly straight into the nearest fiery sun, just as the traitor Xavier Harkonnen had done, carrying Iblis Ginjo to his death.

But what purpose would that serve? He still wanted to cause destruction among the cymek ranks. Each day the debt of vengeance grew larger.

He flew with Dante from Hessra, with all of the weapons of his ship deactivated. As a predatory bird, he was neutered and stripped of his claws, but Quentin could still observe and hope to seize a chance.

Agamemnon and Juno departed for other cymek worlds in their corrupted empire, while Dante meant to inspect the five worthwhile planets he had recently attacked to check on the progress of the neo-cymek dictators he had installed. After suffering so much under more than a century of machine attacks and then the Scourge, the people on those conquered planets should cling to any false hope. The cymeks offered them power and immortality.

Only a few converts were needed to crack down on the entire society. Not all humans had a strength of will equivalent to Quentin's.

Finally, as the group of cymek ships approached the fringe of the Relicon system, Dante was surprised to encounter a League expeditionary force from Salusa, coming to inspect and aid the still-recovering human colony. They didn't know the cymeks had taken the planet more than a month earlier.

Dante's warships instantly shifted into a battle-ready posture, activating their weapons, loading projectiles into launch tubes, preparing their laser weaponry. "It looks like someone has come to play with us." The Titan's transmission was beamed toward Quentin, but the other neos cheered, spoiling for a fight.

Quentin did not wish to encounter the Army of Humanity vessels, especially when he saw that the lead javelin vessel was a political flagship. Some high-ranking official had come on an inspection tour, offering humanitarian assistance and reparations.

"Prepare to attack," Dante said. "We'll take an unexpected prize here."

Quentin searched for an option. He had no weapons in his strippeddown ship, but it would be a massacre if he didn't warn the League ships that the cymeks knew about the laser-shield interaction. Working all systems available through the thoughtrodes connected to his brain canister, he found that he could manipulate the ship's communications systems. If he could change frequencies, maybe—with any luck—he would be able to send a transmission.

Then a signal came over the broadband open channel from the flagship of the group. "Cymeks, enemies of humanity, this is Viceroy Faykan Butler. You have attacked these human colonies, and now you must face our justice."

Quentin felt a surge of hope, then dread. Faykan! He didn't want his oldest son to see him like this. But that was a selfish fear . . . now that there was so much at stake.

Dante spoke to the neo-cymek forces, following a carefully planned script. "All neos, open fire with projectile weapons."

Like an explosive hailstorm, torpedoes and shaped grenades sprayed against the javelin flagship and several escort destroyers.

Quentin kept working on altering the communication frequency aboard his cymek craft, but he had not been trained in this. Whenever his thoughts went astray, he overshot what he wanted to do.

Dante continued, sounding pleased and confident. "Their shields are up, making them vulnerable to lasers. Prepare—"

Finally, Quentin screamed across a secret frequency long used by the Army of the Jihad for high-level command transmissions. "Faykan! Drop all shields immediately. It's a trick."

"Who is this?"

Naturally, the signal Quentin transmitted from his mind had no recognizable voice patterns. "Faykan, they mean to use laser weaponry—you know what that means. Drop your shields before it's too late!"

Faykan apparently believed him. Only a few officers and political leaders in the command structure of the League knew about the secret vulnerability of the Holtzman shields. "Shields down! All subcommanders, drop shields *immediately!*"

Though many of them argued, the Viceroy issued another firm order. The protective shields faded away only an instant before weak and inefficient energy beams played across the armored hulls, causing only marks and superficial damage, nothing significant, and leaving a few scorch marks. The lasers swept out again, more intense the second time, but none of the League ships powered up their shields.

Faykan realized in an instant that the mysterious transmission had saved them all from annihilation. "Who is this? Do we have an ally among the cymeks? Identify yourself."

Dante still hadn't figured out what Quentin had done. "Something has gone terribly wrong, but we have other ways to pursue this." The cymek attack fleet moved together, reloading their projectile weapons. The explosives would be deadly if Faykan's vessels kept their shields offline.

"Get your ships out of here. I . . . or you will be—" Quentin said, then faltered, afraid to identify himself. "Just trust me. Make me . . . shed tears of happiness again." Quentin hoped that would be enough to help his son figure it out. He could not bear to confess everything—not now. It was too terrible to think that the Army of Humanity might mount an ill-advised rescue for him, coming to the cymek stronghold on Hessra in an effort to free him. Quentin didn't want that. He just wanted Faykan to get away before Dante and his powerful ships slaughtered everyone.

"Father!" Faykan transmitted back on the private frequency. "Primero—is that you? We thought you were killed!"

"Butlers are servants unto no one!" Quentin cried over the channel. "Now *go!*"

As Dante's followers swooped in, launching the first volleys of explosives, Quentin suddenly realized that his ship could serve as a weapon. He had no launchers of his own, but he changed course, locked his engines into high acceleration—and suddenly flew through the cymek ranks, scattering them like a dog frightening a flock of pigeons. The cymek ships swirled about, dodging him. Over his communications system, he heard them chattering, arguing about what to do.

Quentin veered in an effort to collide with any cymek he encountered, but the neos were more adept in their mechanical bodies than he was. Avoiding him, they began to fire disabling shots at his drive system. Abruptly their words became garbled as the cymeks switched over to encrypted communications.

The disabling shots glanced off his hull, and Quentin pushed harder and harder toward Dante. He vowed to give up his life if he could destroy one of the three remaining Titans.

Dante swerved his larger combat body so that Quentin only managed to scrape the ships together in a glancing impact. As the vibration ground through his sleek metal body, Quentin sensed damage but no physical pain. His ship responded more sluggishly now, and he wondered how much damage he'd done to his artificial body.

He was relieved to see the League expeditionary force withdraw in confusion, though it was not yet in full retreat. "Go! Get out of here or you will all die," he transmitted again.

"Primero Butler must have told them something!" Dante said. "Jam his signals!"

A blast of interference cut off further transmissions. He couldn't explain anything, couldn't ask for forgiveness or even say farewell to his son. But he had done what was necessary. And now the League would know he was still alive.

The cymek blasts were not enough to destroy Quentin's ship, but caused sufficient damage to disable his engines and leave him hanging dead in space. Helpless and ineffective. An ignominious way to end, he thought. . . .

THE CYMEKS HAD to tow him back to Hessra, while Dante lectured and scolded him for his foolishness. Still, Quentin was pleased with what he had managed to do. After being completely helpless for so long, he had struck a real blow for the cause of mankind. Not a single human life had been lost in the encounter.

Once Quentin was dragged back to Hessra, General Agamemnon would undoubtedly imprison him in his canister and make him submit to an eternity of pain stimuli, if he permitted Quentin to live at all.

But his accomplishment was worth it.

The best plans evolve along the way. When a plan truly succeeds, it takes on a life of its own, quite apart from anything its original creator intended.

— SUPREME BASHAR VORIAN ATREIDES

Vor had always known the Titans were still at large, and that his father would not sit quietly forever, especially now that Omnius had been contained. Seventeen times since the end of the Jihad, Vor had spoken to the League Parliament, insisting that a military operation be launched to scour out the cymeks on Hessra, but no one else had seen the urgency. Other priorities were easily found.

They would always underestimate Agamemnon.

After racing back from Wallach IX with the news of the cymek attack and presumed death of Quentin Butler, Porce Bludd had sounded the alarm. On the heels of the recent piranha mite terror—against which Vor had also warned the League—and the appearance of an even worse strain of the Scourge on Rossak, Vor was sure the government could finally be shocked out of its complacency.

At least he was no longer dismissed outright. Despite his apparent youth, the parliamentary representatives knew he was an old fixture, a veteran who had outlived all his comrades in arms. He demanded immediate action—which translated into months of discussions.

One entire Army of Humanity squadron had vanished and was presumed destroyed. Now Viceroy Faykan Butler had returned with the alarming report that the Titans now knew about the deadly laser-shield weakness, a secret that had been so closely held for the entire Jihad.

And Faykan also reported that his own father had been converted into a cymek himself!

Vor seethed at this latest outrage. Finally, at least, they might be jolted into taking some action, but he doubted it would be swift or severe enough for his tastes.

He needed to get away from the insanity of Rayna's daily Cultist rallies, the endless meetings of the League Parliament, and his irrelevant duties as nominal Supreme Bashar of the Army of Humanity, while he waited for instructions from the government. *How had it come to this?* A part of him longed for the days of open warfare and undisputed enemies, when he had been able to make up his own mind to launch a devastating raid, and let the consequences settle themselves out. He had always teased Xavier for so strictly following regulations and orders. . . .

When Bashar Abulurd Harkonnen invited him to visit an ancient archaeological site outside the city, Vor gladly accepted. The newly promoted officer promised serenity, fresh air, and a place where they could talk, which both men sorely needed.

Though they were ostensibly taking time for themselves, their mood was serious. By now, Abulurd looked even older than his mentor, who treated him like a kid brother. With Leronica dead for all these years, Vor no longer bothered with the self-aging makeup or artificial tints of gray in his dark hair. But his eyes had grown older, especially now that he knew what Agamemnon was really doing.

The archaeological site was on a sunny hillside an hour north of Zimia by groundcar. The military driver, an old veteran of the Jihad who had suffered a serious chest wound on Honru, told the two officers repeatedly how he wished he could still serve, and how he prayed to Saint Serena every day. He had a small, partly concealed badge that showed he sympathized with Rayna's movement. The driver dropped them off and drove his car to a shaded area where he would wait for them.

The two men wandered alone into the isolated archaeological site. Reading signs and avoiding his real thoughts, Abulurd said, "This region was once inhabited by Buddislamics before they were freed from generations of slavery and went off to settle on Unallied Planets."

"Your father will never be freed from his slavery now," Vor muttered, dropping a blanket of reserved silence over them. As a cymek, Quentin Butler could never come home again.

They both stared at the age-weathered ruins, and Abulurd made a halfhearted attempt to read displays and markers, occasionally stumbling in his recitation as his own misery broke through his facade. "After turning their backs on our civilization, the Zensunnis and Zenshiites entered a long dark age; to this day, most of them live as primitives on far-flung planets." He squinted at the plaque in the bright sunlight. "Muadru pottery has also been found here."

"The Cogitors have some connection with the Muadru," Vor said. "And Vidad is the only one left alive." The mention of Vidad made him think of Serena and her death.

No one alive had as much history with, or as much resentment toward, the Titans as he did. Agamemnon had raised him, trained him, and taught him tactics—all so Vor could one day oppress human slaves. But he had turned that knowledge against the thinking machines during the Jihad, continually defeating them by using inside information. Now Vor had more inside information about Agamemnon, and he intended to use it in a very different manner.

The two men sat on a pile of building rubble and shared wrapped gyraks, sandwiches made by locals using stone-ground bread and highly seasoned meats. They washed the food down with bottles of cold Salusan beer. Vor didn't say much, his mind full of important concerns. He shuddered, remembering the terrible "reward" that the cymek general had once promised him. *If I had not escaped from Earth with Serena and Ginjo, Agamemnon would have converted me into a cymek, too. Like father, like son.*

From the standpoint of a military leader, Vor had done all he could for the League. The exhausted human race had neither energy nor enthusiasm for another long struggle. Long after the crisis, many leaders were horrified to contemplate the nuclear holocaust he'd led against the Synchronized Worlds, shamed at what they had done. Most people didn't remember the urgency, the horrors, the necessity of those dangerous days. They only hung their heads at the memory of the billions of human slaves who had been killed as bystanders during the annihilation of Omnius. They didn't remember that billions more humans would have died if the thinking machines had succeeded instead. Vor had seen all too many times how mutable history could be.

Now that Agamemnon had finally returned to cause mayhem again, Vor felt he had to fight one more battle—alone, without anyone second-guessing him.

Gritting his teeth, Vor looked at Abulurd and said, "I know what I have to do. I'll need your help, and your complete confidentiality."

"Of course, Supreme Bashar."

And he proceeded to tell Abulurd how he intended to get rid of Agamemnon once and for all.

Always bear in mind the inevitability of your end. Only after you have accepted the fact that you are going to die can you truly reach greatness and achieve the highest honor.

—SWORDMASTER ISTIAN GOSS

A bulurd Harkonnen sat in the front row of invited guests in the League's imposing Hall of Parliament, proudly displaying the bashar insignia on his shoulders and chest. The attendees at the ceremony, a combination of military and political leaders, sat nearby murmuring without obvious enthusiasm.

Supreme Bashar Vorian Atreides had asked to speak to the assembly, promising an important announcement—as he had often done before. However, because he had delivered so many dire warnings and endlessly pessimistic projections over the years, the dignitaries no longer displayed much interest in his talks. They were aware of the new cymek depredations, and the piranha mites had reminded them that Omnius remained a threat; obviously, they expected the old veteran to rail at them for their lack of foresight.

Abulurd, though, knew the true reason for the Supreme Bashar's speech. He sat, breathing shallowly, keeping himself calm, a model of decorum.

For most of the morning Abulurd had been engrossed in his work in the laboratories near the Grand Patriarch's administrative mansion. Following their mandate from the Supreme Bashar, his engineering team continued dismantling and analyzing the deadly piranha mites, activating a few of them under carefully controlled conditions. His researchers felt they now had several possible avenues for defense, should Omnius decide to use the ferocious little machines again. Already, two of his engineers had constructed a prototype jammer—not the same as Holtzman's pulse generators, but a simpler beacon that would overload and confuse the mites' base programming.

Abulurd had changed out of his laboratory clothes and put on his military uniform for the event. Although formal dress was not required by code, he did it out of respect and honor for the Supreme Bashar.

Now, as soon as the tall doors opened and Vorian Atreides was announced, Abulurd leaped to his feet and saluted. Seeing this, other Army of Humanity officers followed his lead; within moments, the rest of the audience in the assembly chamber stood a few at a time at first, and then in a wave.

His expression unreadable, Vorian strode proudly down the wide aisle. He had chosen to appear grand and imposing with an extravagant assortment of well-earned ribbons, medals, and rank insignia acquired over his decades of military service. He jingled and clanked as he walked, and the weight of all the tokens of service seemed about to tear the fabric of his uniform shirt. The uniform, while freshly pressed, seemed to have a shadow of soil and blood in its stitching, as if the fabric, like the man himself, could never be entirely cleaned.

He glanced over to where he knew Abulurd was; their eyes met, and the younger officer's heart swelled.

The Supreme Bashar held his head high and kept his shoulders square as he walked up the steps to the stage where Viceroy Faykan Butler presided next to the Grand Patriarch. Xander Boro-Ginjo's daily uniform was gaudy and full of unnecessary trappings.

"Supreme Bashar Vorian Atreides, we welcome you to our proceedings," said Faykan. "You have called us here for a vital announcement? We are all interested to hear your words."

"And you'll all be thankful that I intend to be brief," Vor said. Several representatives in the front row chuckled. "As of this month, I have spent one hundred thirteen years as a soldier for humanity." He paused to let the number sink in. "That's well over a century of fighting against the enemy and helping to protect the League of Nobles. Though I may still appear to be young and strong, and though I retain my health and my ability, I doubt any person in this assembly would dispute that I have served sufficient time."

He looked slowly around the audience, finally settling his gaze on the

Viceroy. "Effective immediately I wish to resign my commission in the Army of Humanity. Nineteen years ago, the Jihad was declared over. My term of fighting is done. I will take some time for myself and then return to work with the task force to clear the name of Xavier Harkonnen."

Faykan responded quickly and smoothly, as if he'd known all along what Vor intended to say. "I speak for all those gathered here. We recognize that you have given a long lifetime of faithful service. New challenges face us, with the cymeks and Omnius, but the work is never at an end. It seems we will always need to deal with the enemies of humanity. One man cannot solve all the problems, no matter how hard he tries. Vorian Atreides, you may relax, retire, and do as you will, and let the rest of us continue the work. Thank you for your exemplary service. You deserve all the honor and respect we can offer you."

The Viceroy began to applaud, and the Grand Patriarch clapped dutifully. Soon, everyone in the assembly chamber joined in a resounding standing ovation. Swept up in the thunderous applause, Abulurd watched his mentor, feeling as if he might drown in emotion, both proud and sad at the same time. The Grand Patriarch offered Vor a formal blessing.

The Supreme Bashar nodded to everyone, and only Abulurd knew that he did indeed intend to continue the fight, though in a fashion the League would never be willing to condone. As Vor was escorted out of the cavernous Parliament building, borne along by cheers, congratulations, and applause, Abulurd followed, hoping he would get the opportunity to say farewell to this man who had done so much for him.

Everything about the announcement and the response had been appropriately respectful, yet Abulurd's reaction soured. After all the good things Vor had done for the League, and despite the fact that his skills had not waned a bit, not one person in the chamber made even a feeble attempt to talk him out of his departure. They were glad to see him go.

Death can be a friend, but only if he comes calling at the right time.
—Navachristianity text (disputed translation)

L ost in her fever, Raquella dreamed of dreams, of the images and hopes of her ancestors, so bright in youth and so faded and tattered in the harsh reality. Even her mysterious grandfather Vorian Atreides was there, and Karida Julan, her grandmother, the woman who had loved Vorian . . . as were numerous men, women, heroes, cowards, leaders, and followers. And Mohandas Suk.

From somewhere, she heard water dripping . . . or some other liquid . . . ticking like the passage of time. She sensed that her physical body was draining away, rejoining the ageless ecosystem of the planet.

Rossak.

She had never expected to die on such a strange world. Raquella had not been born here, had no connection to Rossak, would never have journeyed to this place at all if not for the reappearance of the Scourge, and her need to help.

She felt adrift and numb, without any tactile sensations to her skin, without any ability to move. It was as if something thick and heavy covered her body, and she could feel it forcing the life out of her. The retrovirus itself? Or her impossible responsibilities? With great difficulty, she managed to heave a deep nourishing breath.

Jimmak Tero had taken her somewhere, a hidden place deep in the silvery-purple jungle. She'd been barely conscious at the time and remembered only the sounds and the damp, perplexing smells. Now she had no idea where she was.

Despite the constant clamor in her mind and body, Raquella tried to calm herself. *It is all right. I have done considerable good. Mohandas and I have helped plague victims. My life was worth sacrificing for their benefit.*

Long ago on Parmentier, Vorian Atreides had said he was proud of her; she had held on to that kind comment ever since, tasting the emo-tion that this stranger, her grandfather, had felt for her. Vor had visited her many times in the intervening years and offered her his affection and unwavering support. Now that she knew and cared for him, her heroic grandfather's respect and pride meant more to her than ever. The Supreme Bashar of the Army of Humanity was an important, famous man. He had gone to a great deal of trouble to locate her, and had finally found her, but in a time of plague.

As she struggled to contain the shockwaves of pain shooting through her body, Raquella needed all of her energy to keep breathing. She focused on the dripping sound, hung on to the rhythmic noise, bal-ancing on the razor's edge of consciousness and life. *Drip.* Breath. *Drip.* Breath.

Raquella thought back, remembering oases of happiness in a desert of turmoil. Most of life was spent working, seeking, achieving, and very lit-tle of it in the enjoyment of the delightful surprises that God sprinkled about. But Raquella *had* made a difference, and that should be enough for one person. She felt tired, almost ready to let go of the slender strands linking her with existence.

The dripping sound grew louder. She felt something on her face, cool wetness, and involuntarily swallowed a mouthful. It was not the first swal-low, she realized. How long had she been here? And where was here? The water had done something to her . . . or she had done something to it. An odd sensation.

Raquella stirred, opened her eyes, and saw the wide, innocent face of Jimmak, who knelt next to her, splashing water on her cheeks and fore-head. His expression brightened to unfettered joy to see her awake. "I am Doctor Boy. I do good work."

She saw that she lay stretched out on loamy soil beside a mirror-still pool. Roots, walls, and a dirt ceiling showed that she was in a dimly lit cavern. Shafts of light angled through from holes in the roof, filtered by dust. Spiderwebs, hairy roots, and thick cables of growth plunged from the low ceiling to the floor.

Phosphorescent bluish fungus clung to stone walls. Water trickled from the ceiling and flowed peacefully into the pool without disturbing the surface. She heard voices echoing, and noticed two strange people on the other side of the water. Both had twisted, deformed bodies. One of them, a rail-thin girl, pointed at her.

"I think Doctor Lady is cured." Jimmak's words were slow. "Fever went away, but you kept sleeping. I put more mineral water on you. You even drank some. That helped a lot."

Raquella shivered, realizing that her hospital work clothes were drenched. She noticed the abandoned suspensor gurney floating nearby, where Jimmak had left it after bringing her here. She had read of places like this, limestone sinkholes. Her reeling mind searched for the term . . . a cenote.

Sounding apologetic, Jimmak said, "We put you in the healing water. My friends and me. Let you soak for a whole day. It washed away your fever."

"Healing water?" Raquella realized that she did feel strangely energized.

"Special place." He smiled. "Only the Misborn know it."

"You're very smart, Jimmak." The words were heavy as she forced them out, but she seemed to be gaining strength. "You knew exactly what to do to help me. I didn't think I was going to survive."

"I brought dry clothes and blankets," Jimmak said. "For you."

"Thank you. I think . . . I'll feel better in dry, clean clothes." Her garments were cold and clammy.

Assisted by several of the Misborn women, who were strikingly different from the tall and icily perfect Sorceresses, Raquella went into a dim side passage and changed into a loose, clean black robe. She put her sodden garments in the bin beneath the suspensor gurney, then tottered back to squat on the cool floor beside an eager Jimmak and wrapped one of the dry blankets around herself.

She indicated the group of curious and shy misfits. "Who are these people, Jimmak? Why do they live out here?"

"Sorceresses throw us into jungle. Hope monsters will eat us." He grinned. "But we have secret places. Like this."

Shafts of sunlight danced across the cenote's water, making the chamber a soothing, magical environment far from the hatred and scorn of the telepathic, perfect women.

"Sorceresses don't come here. Not even VenKee men, who take plants and mushrooms." Jimmak stood tall. "The water is special. Now, Sorceresses die, but Misborn stay alive."

Raquella could not deny that something had cured her, and it was probably the cenote water. She had tended enough patients, knew the stages of the new Scourge, and realized that no one had ever survived after reaching the depths into which she had fallen. The retrovirus had certainly sent her into a fatal spiral before Jimmak took her from the cliff city. She would have died.

But there was no telling what kind of chemical contaminants had settled into the brew of this underground pool. She did not look to Jimmak for technical explanations. It was not surprising that some combination of toxins and natural by-products might prove deadly to the plague retrovirus.

This water offered the key. Mohandas and his team had been working without rest in their isolated orbital labs aboard the LS *Recovery*, but every treatment had so far failed. If he could determine the key contaminant present in the cenote, reproduce and distribute it to the suffering populace in the cliff cities, then so many victims could be saved.

The sudden surge of hope made her feel giddy and disoriented in her weakened body. With unsteady steps, she moved toward the edge of the placid undergound pool. "We can bring the other sick people here and cure them. Thank you for showing me this, Jimmak."

The Misborn drew away from her suggestion, hiding in the shadows, whispering and moaning. Alarmed, Jimmak shook his head vigorously. "Oh, no. You can't do that. This is our special healing place."

Raquella frowned. "I'm sorry, Jimmak—but all those people are dying. This gives us a chance for a cure. I am a doctor. I can't ignore such an opportunity."

Jimmak's face grew red as he worked himself up. "Sorceresses will steal the magic water. Kill us for hiding it."

"No, Jimmak. That won't—"

"Sorceresses always want to kill us. They want to clean the—" He struggled to remember words his mother had hurled at him. "Clean . . . the gene pool."

Raquella wanted to argue with him, but she had seen Ticia Cenva, and knew how cold and cruel the Sorceresses could be. If this hidden underground spring was found, the Sorceresses and VenKee pharmaceutical scouts would descend in a swarm, and they would destroy one of the only places these poor misfits had to themselves. A healing place.

Raquella's dismay was plain on her face. "Tens of thousands are already dying, not just the Sorceresses but all the people on Rossak.

Everybody. You've seen them, Jimmak. We don't know how to save them—but something in this water has a pharmaceutical effect." She sighed. "All right, then, I need to take a sample of the water to Dr. Suk. That way I won't have to bring them here to your sacred cenote."

From the water, Mohandas should be able to break down the impurities, and isolate the effective chemical substance before time ran out for the remaining population on Rossak. No one else would need to know about this cenote or its curative properties. She would never reveal where it had come from—she could do that much for Jimmak, at least.

In a mounting frenzy, Jimmak cried, "You can't tell anyone! They will want to know where you got the water. No!" His eyes were desperate.

Raquella looked at Jimmak's innocent face, his rounded features and moppish hair. She knew she could never get him to change his mind, and she did owe her life to the young man. And yet, there were so many other victims. . . .

"Promise, Doctor Lady. Promise!"

The other Misborn still watched her nervously, some with aggressive stares, as if they might consider killing her before she could betray them. If she didn't convince them, they would never let her leave. And then she couldn't tell Mohandas about the cure.

"All right, Jimmak. I promise. I won't bring people here."

But what was the greatest call on her loyalty—to save the sick and dying, or to keep a trust? Too many lives hung in the balance. She did not want to dishonor herself . . . yet there could be no question what her decision must be. Even if she had to trick him, she couldn't deny all those infected people the chance of a cure.

Surely, the needs of the dying population outweighed the desires of a handful of Misborn. She would protect Jimmak and his companions as much as she could, but she could not deny Mohandas this lead. She had to get him a sample of the water, at least.

There was a way.

The Misborn watched her hawkishly, kept her away from the pool as if afraid she would steal a bottle of the liquid. Raquella sighed, lay back on the suspensor gurney, and told him she was ready. Jimmak wrapped a blindfold over her eyes, and she felt him guiding her out of the cavern. "Promise you won't tell anyone about this place," he pleaded, his mouth so close to her ear that she could feel his warm breath.

"You have my word," she said into the darkness.

WHEN RAQUELLA RETURNED to the crowded cliffside chambers, the black-robed Sorceresses gathered around her in astonishment. Even Ticia Cenva showed great surprise to see her still alive.

"You have come back from the dead—and you are cured!" young Karee Marques said, ignoring the others. "But how?"

"That doesn't matter," Raquella said, noting a look of stern disapproval on Ticia's face. "I may have found the key to save the rest of you."

A good plan is flexible, and unexpected results are acceptable . . .
provided they are sufficiently momentous.

— YOREK THURR,
secret Corrin journals

After so many years among thinking machines, Yorek Thurr had almost forgotten the thrill of applying his particular skills at stalking and infiltrating.

For much of his "first life" in the League of Nobles, he had developed sophisticated deception and observation techniques for the Jihad Police. He could spy wherever he wished, could kill a man in a hundred different ways. But after serving as the undisputed ruler of Wallach IX, then living as a coddled captive on Corrin, Thurr's abilities had atrophied.

Thus, he was pleased to see, as he sneaked late at night into the Grand Patriarch's administrative mansion, that he still had the necessary skills. Guards patrolled the grounds, and primitive security systems monitored the windows and entrances. But those electronic surveillance devices and the perimeter warning sensors were as easy to fool as the sleepy, complacent sentinels.

During his time with Jipol, Thurr had made a habit of never waking or sleeping at the same time of day. He altered his schedule, staying awake for days or getting by on only a few hours of sleep in bunkers. Iblis Ginjo had thought it was an amusing display of paranoia, but Thurr did not play games.

One of the high, small windows was open, and Thurr managed to crawl along a rooftop ledge, lower himself down to window level, and slide his legs in through the narrow opening. Contracting his shoulders, he slithered in like an eel and dropped silently to the marble floor. He padded across the hall into the open suite of Xander Boro-Ginjo.

When he found the Grand Patriarch's sleeping chamber, the buffoon was alone, snoring quietly in his bed beside a burbling fountain that drowned out Thurr's stealthy approach. Perhaps Xander simply was not interesting enough to have any complex vices. Thurr frowned. Any decent leader needed to have a certain edge. This pampered Grand Patriarch, bestowed with the chain of office through his grandmother's political wrangling, didn't deserve to command the surviving remnants of humanity. They needed a visionary like Yorek Thurr, someone with guts and vision and intelligence.

Thurr bent over the sleeping, corpulent man like a mother about to give her child a good night kiss. He drove away the insistent buzzing inside his head, focusing on what he must do. "Wake up, Xander Boro-Ginjo, so that we can get down to business. This is the most important appointment of your life."

The Grand Patriarch snorted and heaved himself into a seated position, naked. As his mouth opened to splutter a question, Thurr calmly extended the small canister in his hand and sprayed a burst of a pungent-smelling liquid into the man's open mouth and down his throat. Xander coughed and retched, clutching his larynx. His eyes bugged open wide, as if he feared he had just been stuck with an assassin's stiletto.

"It's not poison," Thurr said, "simply an agent to neutralize your vocal cords. You can still whisper, so we'll have our necessary conversation, but I can't have you screaming for help. Even your incompetent guards would cause too much of a distraction. It's hard enough to concentrate these days." He rubbed his smooth scalp.

Xander gasped and whispered, finally squeezing out hoarse words. "What? Who—"

Thurr frowned. "I *told* you who I was. How could you have forgotten so much in only a few days? We had a discussion in your own office. Don't you remember me?"

Boro-Ginjo's eyes widened. He let out a breathy call for his guards, but the words were nothing more than a squeak.

"Stop wasting my time. There are great changes afoot this evening. The annals of League history will recall this as a watershed of human existence." Thurr smiled. "You shouldn't dismiss me until you know what I offer. I lived for many years on Corrin, and I bring vital information about Omnius. I know secrets about the thinking machines that could prove crucial to our survival."

Xander opened and closed his mouth like a fish out of water. "But . . . but the machines are no threat anymore. They're all bottled up on Corrin."

Thurr wanted to slap him. "Omnius is *always* a threat. Never forget that." For all his life, Thurr's entire foundation of power, his reason for existence, had hinged on the conflict of the Jihad. And now, if the League truly believed the last of the thinking machines were neutered, he had to find a way to make his mark. More than anything else, Yorek Thurr did not want to become *irrelevant*.

Xander whispered for his guards again, and Thurr struck him across a fleshy cheek, leaving a bright red handprint. The Grand Patriarch shook with rage. The spoiled fellow had probably never been treated in such a fashion before.

Calmly, Thurr went to the bureau beside Xander's bed and with great reverence lifted the interlinked chain of office that the Grand Patriarch customarily wore over his shoulders. "I designed this myself, with the widow of Iblis Ginjo," he said, looking over at the frightened man, who still sat propped speechless on his bed.

"After Iblis was assassinated by Xavier Harkonnen, we met in emergency session to discuss how to lead the Jihad and keep the League of Nobles on its straight track. Because of politics, and because the people would accept it better, Camie insisted that she become her husband's successor, promising that I would follow her. But after ten years, she handed the chain of office over to her son Tambir. She didn't consult with me, simply made the decision by fiat." His nostrils flared.

"I was livid. I threatened to kill her. She just laughed at me. After all I had done for the Army of the Jihad, after I kept the human race strong against the thinking machines—she betrayed me! So I . . . changed my alliances." Scowling, he jangled the ornate chain. "But by all rights this is mine now. You must resign."

"I . . . I can't resign as the spiritual head of the League," Xander said in his faint whispery voice. "The succession does not occur like that. You don't understand politics, sir."

"Then I'll remove you some other way. But first, ask yourself what have *you* done for the human race? How have *you* benefited the League as Grand Patriarch? The answers are obvious."

Naked, Xander scrambled off the bed and tried to run like a clumsy cow. But Thurr moved with ferret swiftness, intercepting him. With a hard slam against the man's sternum, he pushed him back to the edge of the bed, where he stumbled and sprawled over it. "Hmm, I take it that's your decision, then."

Thurr sat beside the plump Grand Patriarch, who shivered in fear. Going into a near-fetal position, he looked helpless, ready to cry. Dredging up false bluster, Xander squeaked, "You don't frighten me. You can't kill me—I'm the Grand Patriarch!"

Thurr squinted, furrowing his leathery brow. "You fail to understand, Xander, that I masterminded both the killer mites that Omnius unleashed on Zimia and the Scourge itself. I am personally responsible for more deaths than any other human being in history. By now I must have killed a hundred billion people."

The Grand Patriarch lurched to his feet again in a pathetic attempt to flee, but Thurr reached up and grabbed him by the wrist. He dragged him back down, then wrapped his arm around the man's doughy neck in a casual, almost loving gesture. As Xander gurgled, he squeezed, tightening his hold, then jerked viciously backward until he heard the snap of the spine. He kept holding the chubby man until Xander stopped twitching and squirming.

"There, that makes it one hundred billion *and one.*"

After letting the Grand Patriarch slump to the sheets of his bed, Thurr proudly draped the chain of office around his own neck, then made his way back out into the night. When alarms finally sounded throughout the city, hours later, he was still flushed with excitement and full of plans about the changes he would make when he took control.

For one thing, security would have to be increased.

Before there can be betrayal, there must be trust.

           —SUPREME BASHAR VORIAN ATREIDES,
           private message to Abulurd Harkonnen

Vorian Atreides went alone in search of his tyrant father. He knew he could not trust the lethargic League, even when the crisis was so plain. He would deal with the cymek threat. Personally.

With a heavy heart, he left Abulurd behind with instructions to continue working on defenses against the machine mites, while also compiling historical records that might be useful in clearing the name of Xavier Harkonnen. So far, the League task force had done little to look into the matter.

As he flew off in the *Dream Voyager*, he wished he could have gone back to Caladan one more time, just to see his sons. That was the destination he had given the League, but that could not be. If Estes and Kagin sensed something was wrong, they would feel obligated to try to talk him out of his plan. Or maybe they would just formally accept his visit, talk about inconsequential things, and wait for him to go so they could get back to the routine of their lives.

At least they didn't hate him, as he hated his father.

Vor had never seen any place as bleak as Hessra. During his solitary journey at the familiar controls of the *Dream Voyager*, he had called up historical holovids from Serena Butler's visit to the Ivory Tower Cogitors, but even those images had not prepared him for such complete desolation.

Vor chose his landing coordinates carefully, within sight of the glacier-buried fortress that formerly held Vidad and his companions, and set the old update ship down a short distance away in the vast valley of ice at the base of the craggy peaks. As he stepped out of the black-and-silver ship, bundled against the cold and wind, Vor took his first breaths of the thin, unfriendly air.

I am deep in the heart of cymek territory. They could simply blast me away. Any moment now, I will know. But he was sure his father would want to gloat, then interrogate or torture him. None of the cymeks would do anything without orders from the Titan general.

Feeling the frozen surface tremble beneath his feet, he looked up at the ice-encrusted spires of the Cogitors' citadel. Immense doors rattled open beneath the buried towers. The machines began to emerge, a horrific menagerie of flyers and heavily armored crablike walkers. Each one contained the brain canister of a neo-cymek, one of Agamemnon's minions. In the freezing air, he heard the crash of heavy mechanical footsteps, the whine of powerful engines, the ominous buzz of warming weapons.

He faced the oncoming force of machines with human minds, alone and unafraid. He crossed his arms over his chest and planted his feet more firmly, knowing he looked cocky and unimpressed.

Cymeks in flying forms roared past him, their hot engines making thunder in the dim sky. Lumbering combat walkers advanced, artillery turrets extended. From his time as a trustee human on Earth, Vor was familiar with many of the shapes and designs. *There was a time when I wanted more than anything else to be one of them.*

An angular flyer hovered above him, and Vor saw the glow of a holo-camera focused on his face, no doubt transmitting to the control centers inside the citadel. Vor tilted his head and shouted upward, "I am Vorian Atreides! Tell Agamemnon that his son has returned to him. He and I have much to discuss."

The hovering neo-cymek extruded mechanical talons and gripped Vor around the torso. He did not bother to struggle, knowing the neo was trying to intimidate him. If any of these underlings hurt him, they would have to answer to the wrath of Agamemnon. He had to count on that.

Clutching Vor in its metal grip so he could barely breathe in the already thin air, the neo flew back to the Cogitor citadel. On the ice field behind him, other neos surrounded the *Dream Voyager* and took possession of the update ship. Some of the smaller walker-forms manipulated the controls, trying to get inside. Vor hoped they would not damage the ship.

But if they did, he had always been prepared to be left without a means of escape. Saving his own life was only a secondary consideration.

The neo-cymek took him through a yawning reception doorway in an excavated grotto beneath the fortress. The cymeks had cleared away centuries of piled glacial ice, opening chambers and facilities that the Ivory Tower Cogitors had long abandoned. Inside the echoing bay, the flying neo-cymek set Vor down on his feet. Frost covered the floor and walls of what seemed to be a storage or preparation area. Around him he saw the clutter of extra cymek walkers, flyers, and other ominous mechanical forms, currently without brain canisters attached.

Vor brushed himself off, took a deep breath, and regained his composure. Ignoring the flyer that had unceremoniously dumped him here, he faced an open tunnel doorway through which he heard the pounding footsteps of what had to be an approaching Titan. With a calm and determined expression fixed on his face, he prepared to meet his father again. He had spent the past century imagining this moment.

Agamemnon strode into the light, his powerful metal legs and obvious weaponry as overstated as ever. Smiling, Vor looked up at the head turret, with its galaxy of glittering optic threads.

"So, Father—are you happy to see me?"

The cymek towered over Vor, at least twice the man's height and many times his bulk. Two human-sized mechanical arms appeared in the front of the carapace and pulled open a panel just in front of the suspended, encased brain.

"Happy enough to rip you into gobbets of meat and bone." Agamemnon's choleric voice was like the sound of stones breaking. "Why have you come here?"

Vor continued to smile, maintained a calm voice. "Is this the unconditional love a father shows his son? Since you've already killed all your other offspring, I thought you would at least hear what I have to say. Where is my welcome?"

"Welcoming you is different from trusting you. At the moment I choose to do neither."

Vor made himself chuckle. "Spoken like the true General Agamemnon!" Holding up his hands, he touched his smooth, youthful face. "Look at me, Father. I have not aged, thanks to the life-extension treatment you gave me. Don't you believe I'm grateful for that?"

The enormous walker strutted slowly across the frozen floor, striking sparks from the rocks. "I did that back when you remained faithful to me."

Vor countered quickly, "Ah, yes, back when *you* were loyal to Omnius. Things change."

"You could have had millennia—as a cymek. But you threw that opportunity away."

"I assessed my options and chose the best one. Certainly you can understand that, Father—it's exactly what you taught me. After all, I broke free of Omnius decades before you managed to do it."

Agamemnon was not pleased, nor was he made of patience. "Why are you here?"

"I have brought you a gift." The neos drew back, as if Vor might produce a hidden bomb. "*Me.*"

Agamemnon's hearty laughter echoed through the cavern. "And why would I want that?"

"I have lived among failures long enough, and I'm ready to renew our relationship."

In a caustic tone, the cymek retorted, "You expect me to believe that? You betrayed the thinking machines in order to help the humans in their Jihad."

"True enough, Father, but you and your cymeks changed sides yourselves, more than once." Vor tossed his dark hair. "I expect you to listen to my reasons and see if you come to the same conclusion."

Struggling to keep himself from shivering in the frigid chamber, he laid out his exaggerated litany of the League's failings, how the people refused to make the necessary commitment to destroy Omnius at Corrin once and for all, how they treated him as an old relic who looked like a young and inexperienced man.

"My wife has died, and my own sons are strangers to me. Time and again, the League has made it clear they have no further use for an old warhorse. They are busily squandering all of the victories—all of *my* victories—achieved against the Synchronized Worlds. They cannot think longer than a few decades, caring nothing for the future if it extends beyond their short life spans. Unlike the Titans, Father, who have not wavered in their ambition in more than a thousand years. But look at you: a handful of cymeks hiding on a frozen planetoid long after Omnius has been defeated. Frankly, you and your followers could use my help."

Agamemnon sounded offended. "We have many worlds!"

"Dead, radioactive ones that no one else wants. And a few new colonies that were already weakened by the Scourge."

"We are building our power base."

"Oh? And is that why you seized Quentin Butler and converted him into a cymek? Obviously you need new blood, talented commanders to help you lead. Wouldn't you rather have *me* than an uncooperative hostage?"

"Why can't I have both?" The Titan walker reared up, flashing another set of projectile weapons. "Before long, we may even succeed in breaking Quentin."

"There's a chance I can help you with that." Vor stepped closer to the monster, within instant striking range of the powerful metal claws. "I don't blame you for being suspicious of me, Father—after all, you trained me. But I am your blood, your son—your *last* son. You can have no other offspring. I am your final chance to create a worthy successor. Do you want to take this opportunity, or throw it away?"

As the remark struck home, Vor watched the play of electrical charges on the brain inside the canister. Agamemnon reached forward to scoop Vor off the floor and up into the air. "Against my better judgment, I will give you the benefit of the doubt—for now. We are a family again, my son."

FOUR DAYS LATER, they stood outside on the cold glacier under the star-swept skies of isolated Hessra. The air was much too thin and cold for Vor's human body, so he had donned one of the League environmental suits stored aboard the *Dream Voyager.* The protective garment sparkled with icy reflections.

A meteor streaked overhead, shining brightly for a moment and then vanishing forever. "Once you become a cymek with us, helping me, Juno, and Dante establish the next Time of Titans, your perspective will span millennia instead of mere decades."

Vor hurried to keep up with the great strides of the mechanical walker. Somewhat wistfully, he was reminded of his own youth and innocence, when he had happily followed his father through the streets of Old Earth. Back then, blind and deluded, he had never noticed anything bad about the tyranny of Omnius. Vor had been proud to serve the Synchronized Worlds as a human trustee, never imagining that his great father could possibly be corrupt.

"Remember when I used to wait for you every time you returned from fighting against the *hrethgir*? I would tend you, listen to your stories, clean all of your parts and systems."

"And then you betrayed me," Agamemnon growled.

Vor did not rise to the bait. "Would you rather I had continued to fight for Omnius? Either way, I would have been on the wrong side."

"At least you've finally come to your senses. I just wish it hadn't taken you more than a century to seek me out again. Most prodigal sons would have died of old age long ago."

Vor chuckled. "In that case, I have a distinct advantage."

"I had thirteen other sons," Agamemnon said, "and you are the most talented of them all."

Growing more serious, Vor said, "When I was with Seurat before I . . . changed my loyalties, I discovered in the databases that *you* killed all those other sons."

"They were all flawed," Agamemnon said.

"I'm flawed, too. I admit it freely. If you wanted perfection, you should have continued to serve the thinking machines."

"I was searching for a person worthy of being my successor. Remember, I overthrew the Old Empire, fighting beside the great Tlaloc. I could not pass such a mantle to anyone who showed weakness or uncertainty."

"And none of your other sons had any abilities?"

"Some were slow, others unambitious, a few overtly disloyal. I could not have that, so I killed them and started again. A weeding process. Centuries ago, before I transformed myself into a cymek, I stored a stockpile of my sperm, so there was no reason for me to accept a mediocre heir. But you are the last, Vorian. As you well know, all of my sperm was obliterated in the atomic destruction of Earth. You are my only surviving son . . . and for many decades I thought you were lost to me."

"The universe is not static, Father."

"And you've come back not a moment too soon. Originally, I had high hopes for Quentin Butler, but he resists the inevitable, thwarting all of our efforts. He hates us, even though his future lies with us, since he can never go back to the League, can never again be human. We could continue working our manipulation, and we may make him an ally after all. But if I have you, I no longer need Quentin's skills. Once I convert you into a cymek, you will be my heir apparent, the next general of the Titans."

"History is unpredictable, Father. You may be overestimating what I'll be able to accomplish."

"No, Vorian. I do not overestimate you." The huge walker-form lifted an articulated arm to nudge the small human. "As a cymek, you will be invincible, like me. I can then take you safely to many of our recaptured worlds, make you the king of whichever planets you desire."

Vor was not impressed. "I could have had the governorship of any League World I wanted, Father."

"Once you become a cymek, your new existence is in itself a fabulous reward. As I recall, when you were a trustee you begged me for that opportunity. You looked forward to the day when I would put you through the surgery to make you strong like the other Titans."

"I still look forward to that day," Vor said, swallowing the bile in his throat and making certain his voice sounded enthusiastic. Side by side the pair finally returned to the half-buried towers of the Cogitors again. "I hope it is soon."

"Before you are converted, your biological form still retains one advantage, a resource that I lost long ago."

"What is that, Father?" He felt suddenly cold inside.

The giant walker-form continued across the ice. "You are my son, my offspring, the only remaining vestige of the ancient House of Atreus. And even though all of my sperm was destroyed on Earth, you still have the potential to continue our line. You must be harvested. Juno has the apparatus already set up inside the Cogitors' chambers. This is a duty you must perform before I can allow you to become a cymek."

Vorian's stomach lurched, but he knew that he would not be able to talk his father out of this. Therefore, he would have to provide the genetic samples the Titan leader demanded. He thought of Estes and Kagin and Raquella. They would stand as his true legacy, no matter what happened here. Vor's throat felt dry with anxiety, but he did not hesitate too long. "I'll do whatever is required of me, Father. I came to you in order to prove my loyalty. Some of my sperm for future generations of Atreides . . . that is a minor thing."

As they stood before the Cogitors' towers, the open vault doors leading into dark passages beneath looked like open, hungry jaws. He stepped inside, ready for whatever Juno would force him to do.

In truth, is it better to remember or to forget? We must balance this decision between our history and our humanity.

—DASHAR ABULURD HARKONNEN,

private logs

The murder of the Grand Patriarch caused an uproar in the League of Nobles. Accusations and suspicions flew in all directions, while Viceroy Butler attempted to maintain calm and stability. All powerful people had their share of political rivals, but bland Xander Boro-Ginjo had never been the sort of man to inspire the passionate sort of hatred that his assassination implied. It was difficult to believe anyone's reaction to him could have gone beyond mere annoyance or impatience.

Although Faykan expressed his anger and shock at the assassination, he was slow to announce a replacement for the Grand Patriarch. For the time being, Abulurd's brother appointed a panel of deputies to take over Xander's duties, which, once the responsibilities had been delegated and disseminated, turned out to be largely ceremonial and insignificant.

A handful of those who hoped to become the next Grand Patriarch urged a quick resolution. The Viceroy made a firm statement that since all those close to Xander must, by default, be considered suspects, he would appoint no successor until the investigation had been completed. Abulurd suspected his brother was stalling for time, though he could not understand why.

The new bashar devoted most of his energies to the ongoing research work in the laboratory facilities near the Grand Patriarch's administrative mansion, which was now cordoned off for the investigation. One of his lab workers hurried from an outside office with an alarmed expression on her face. "You should see what's happening in the streets, Bashar. The Cult of Serena is rallying. A huge crowd."

"Again?" Because the laboratory was isolated for protection, he'd been unaware of any disturbance outside. Abulurd had had little contact with his niece, Rayna, since bringing the waifish plague survivor to Salusa, but he knew her penchant for destroying sophisticated equipment. "Stay here and barricade the doors. Protect your work at all costs, because if the Cult gets inside you know what they'll do."

The lab technicians and engineers, who had no training in self-defense or combat, looked alarmed at his suggestion. "If they get . . . inside?"

"Just do your best," he said when he saw their stricken expressions. He went outside to see what had set the crowd off today.

In the streets Rayna Butler—now a thin woman in her thirties, still pale and hairless—marched at the head of her crusaders. They surged along the boulevards carrying banners and placards, chanting, brandishing weapons. Her zealous, violent following had developed on ragged worlds with few remaining laws. Here in Zimia, however, Rayna kept her adherents under greater control according to her agreement with Faykan. Abulurd feared, though, that it was merely a temporary measure. The Cult of Serena was a pot of hopeless humanity rising to a roiling, angry boil.

Many of the fanatics carried images of heroic figures, including the Three Martyrs, and screamed for justice. Uneasy home owners and shopkeepers came out to watch the procession go by, afraid that the mob might go on a rampage, given the right spark.

"Do you know what set them off this time?" Abulurd asked a nearby shopkeeper.

"The Parliament just released an image of the man who murdered the Grand Patriarch," the shopkeeper answered, glancing at the military insignia on Abulurd's work clothes.

"They've caught him, then? They know who it is?"

"No one knows. No one recognizes him."

"Why is the Cult of Serena so incensed?" Abulurd watched the followers stride by, demanding bloody justice. "They never cared about the Grand Patriarch before."

"Now that he's dead, they say he was a holy man who accepted Rayna's vision."

Abulurd frowned. The Cult of Serena had a penchant for seizing causes to increase their prominence. The shopkeeper handed him a printed image, a photograph captured by surveillance eyes mounted around the Grand Patriarch's administrative mansion. It had been matched with another picture taken from Xander Boro-Ginjo's offices. Abulurd frowned at the features of the bald, olive-skinned assassin. The man looked somehow familiar.

The text report summarized that this person had initially infiltrated the Grand Patriarch's offices and caused a disturbance before guards escorted him out, but he had escaped before the arrest could be processed. The stranger had come back some nights later, slipped into the Grand Patriarch's bedchambers, and killed him there. Presumably a hired assassin. No one recognized him from the usual group of Boro-Ginjo's rivals or acquaintances.

Charges of incompetence had already been leveled in numerous directions. Some people even suggested reinstituting the harsh Jihad Police to impose order. Abulurd thought of all the supposed machine spies the Jipol had caught and the numerous purges they had done during the days of Xavier Harkonnen, which he'd been studying. Could Xander's assassin be one of the insidious humans who were loyal to Omnius? Were any of them still left alive, or had they disappeared long ago like Jipol itself?

Then the unexpected impossible realization struck Abulurd like a blow. He squinted to get a closer look at the man's face. The features hadn't changed much—he looked almost exactly like historical images. Jipol Commander *Yorek Thurr!*

In order to help the task force Vor had requested, Abulurd had studied the records of his grandfather's career and his fall from grace. He knew Thurr very well. Although the Jipol commander had been a clandestine figure, avoiding holophotos whenever possible, Abulurd had gained access to confidential League files and committed the man's face to memory. Thurr and Camie Boro-Ginjo had waged an effective and merciless campaign to discredit Xavier's tremendous accomplishments and paint him as a cowardly traitor. Even Vorian Atreides had been unable to turn the tide against their calculated demonization of his friend.

But Thurr's spaceship had exploded sixty-five years ago, and the man was surely dead. It made no sense. Why would someone else disguise himself to look like a shadowy, all-but-forgotten figure from history?

He turned to the shopkeeper. "Can I keep this?"

The man shrugged. "Sure. You planning to catch the killer and turn him over to the mob? That'd be fun to watch."

With a vague nod, Abulurd hurried off to the Hall of Parliament. He would show Faykan comparable images and pose his question, though he could offer no theory as to how Thurr could still be alive or why an impostor would choose that likeness.

Inside the reception foyer of the assembly chamber, he was informed that the Viceroy was engrossed in a trade meeting and would not be available for at least an hour. Abulurd left word that he needed to speak with him as soon as possible.

Frustrated, the bashar wandered down the marble-lined corridor until he came upon the Cogitor Vidad resting on an ornate pedestal. The last of the ancient Cogitors, Vidad seemed somewhat lost and pathetic, pondering his deep thoughts for endless days, alone.

Abulurd paused before the preservation canister. This copious brain had diligently absorbed every aspect of human history since the Ivory Tower Cogitors emerged from isolation in the time of Serena Butler. Abulurd took a moment to locate the Cogitor's optic sensors. He didn't know if he should rap his knuckles on the curved canister wall to get the brain's attention. "Cogitor Vidad, I am Bashar Abulurd Harkonnen. I wish to speak with you."

"You may speak with me," Vidad answered through a speakerpatch in the pedestal. "But only briefly. I have important thinking to do today."

Abulurd held the printed image near Vidad's optic sensors and explained his theory. He asked the Cogitor to consult his own historical files, calling to mind any relevant information regarding the former Jipol commander.

"The resemblance is truly similar," Vidad admitted, "strikingly so. I suspect that this person has intentionally made himself look like Yorek Thurr, or perhaps it is a clone. The Tlulaxa outlaws have become adept at such things."

"He looks almost exactly as Thurr did in the last images before he was presumed dead," Abulurd said. "Either the real Thurr survived and has stopped aging, or someone copied his appearance from old holophotos."

"There are many possible explanations," Vidad said. "Long ago, in the time of the Old Empire, people developed an anti-aging treatment. We Cogitors used this to preserve our brains for millennia. There have been other instances—"

Abulurd gasped. "You mean like Vorian—Supreme Bashar Atreides. General Agamemnon gave him the life-extension treatment, and he's barely aged since his twenties."

"Such a treatment could have kept Yorek Thurr preserved all this time. If he were still alive."

Holding the printed picture, Abulurd paced in front of the pedestal. He felt weak as he followed the thought to its next step. "But if the machines are the only ones with access to the life-extension treatment, how did a Jipol commander get his hands on it? Do you think one of our scientists duplicated the process?"

"Always a possibility, but not a likely one. If such a treatment were available in the League of Nobles, do you truly believe it could be kept secret? The youth-enhancing properties of melange have caused the drug to spread exponentially. A perfect life-extension treatment could never be kept quiet in the League of Nobles. Consider simpler alternatives."

Abulurd knew Vidad spoke the truth. "But—you mean—" He stopped himself. "You're saying the Jipol commander was probably in league with the thinking machines or the cymeks?"

"A legitimate speculation," Vidad said. "If this is truly Yorek Thurr."

As anger swelled within him, Abulurd crumpled the printed image. All the while that he'd been blackening Xavier Harkonnen's name, Thurr might have been in league with Omnius! He felt outraged, betrayed.

"And now it seems he returned to assassinate the Grand Patriarch," Vidad said.

Silently vowing revenge, Abulurd left the Cogitor behind on his pedestal. The bashar no longer needed a meeting with Faykan: He needed to hunt down the turncoat assassin.

I sense a myth enfolding me, or is it a true vision? Great things will arise from my Sisters, provided they can be chosen with adequate care.

—REVEREND MOTHER RAQUELLA BERTO-ANIRUL

Raquella's return to life after her near-fatal bout with the mutated Scourge gave her a second chance, and an unexpected resource, to save the dying population.

Jimmak sat beside her against the stone wall of a crowded recovery room, sharing food he had scrounged from the jungle. He seemed to think everything was back to normal. Raquella could barely look at the placid young man, fearing that her guilt would show, because she planned to betray his trust . . . his simple request. But morally, she had no choice. Every delay cost more and more lives.

"Jimmak, would you make me more of your special tea, please?"

"Doctor Lady still weak?"

"No, I'm feeling better. But I'd still like some. Please?"

Happily, he scuttled off. Once he was gone on her make-work errand, Raquella removed the still-soaked garments she had stored beneath the suspensor gurney. Careful to preserve every drop, she sealed the clothes inside waterproof films and packaged them in a sample container.

Then, working alone in a small lab, Raquella also drew several vials of her own blood. Between the curative chemicals lacing the cenote's water and the antibodies in her blood, perhaps Mohandas could find the key. She dispatched the samples in a fast shuttle up to the LS *Recovery* with a message, begging him to work swiftly. For good measure, she also offered a prayer.

Jimmak returned with a cup of his bitter herbal tea, along with a glass of water for himself. He sat beside her, smiling. "Glad I could help."

"Maybe you can help these other sick people, too." Her voice was heavy.

He looked frightened. "No. Can't take anyone else to the water. You promised."

With a cold smile, Raquella acknowledged that his fear of Ticia Cenva was legitimate. Far from being relieved by Raquella's recovery, the woman had actually seemed angry and suspicious. If the Supreme Sorceress thought the Misborn had found a cure, she would hate them just for doing what she could not. The same reasons lay at the core of her increasingly irrational resentment toward the HuMed doctors and researchers.

"Yes, I promised." *But I have also sworn an oath to help those in need of my medical skills. . . .*

Late that evening, Mohandas sent a hurried transmission to tell her his preliminary results, amazed at what he had found. He had not yet determined the specific chemical composition of the alkaloids, minerals, and long-chain molecules that pervaded the water of the subterranean pool. It seemed impossible to duplicate or synthesize—like the spice melange itself.

From the blood samples, he concluded that something peculiar had happened inside Raquella's body, a biochemical transformation he had never seen before. The battle between the retrovirus and the strange chemicals in the cenote had done something to her biochemistry, changing her in fundamental ways.

Hoping he could produce a vaccine or a drug, Mohandas urged her to send many more liters of the cenote water, but she could not help him.

Frustrated to have a solution so close at hand, Mohandas said, "Every delay is a further death sentence for these people, Raquella. With the small amount of water I got from your garments, it's nearly impossible to run all the tests I need to do. How am I to isolate and synthesize the effective ingredient?" His face looked as wan and weary as her own. She wondered if he ever slept, even up in his safe orbital lab. "Can't you take us to the source? I need many liters more. Where did this water come from?"

Her love and admiration for him was clear and undiminished . . . and yet she had already committed enough of a betrayal. Raquella doubted she could even find the pool again. Certainly, Jimmak would never help her. "I . . . can't, Mohandas."

But each time she heard the moans of the sick in the huge infirmary cave chambers, every day as she looked at the tally of dead, smelled the stench of funeral pyres as stacks of bodies were burned out on the barren plateau above the jungle, her conscience cried out for her to do something.

Since she had returned, a high percentage of the remaining Sorceresses—more than half of them—had suddenly come down with the plague, as if their immune systems had given out simultaneously. More distrustful than ever, Ticia Cenva stood defiant and haggard, as if to prove that her own hard determination and mental powers would transcend the worst ravages of the epidemic.

Raquella harbored no personal animosity toward the Supreme Sorceress, except for how she had treated her son. Her harsh ways might have served her community well during the fury of the Jihad, when numerous Rossak women had sacrificed themselves to obliterate the enemy cymeks. But the resurgence of the epidemic was something she could not fight.

As Raquella pondered, an odd but importunate thought intruded. *Now that I've recovered, Ticia sees me as a threat. That's why she doesn't want the others to be around me. Does she believe I want to lead the Sorceresses myself? If I succeed here, then in her view it will mean that she has failed.*

Only women born on Rossak had ever exhibited the boosted mental powers that made them into the famed Sorceresses. No offworlder had even been considered worthy of joining them. Yet, Raquella had been dramatically influenced by the planet herself, cured in the mysterious cenote, her chemistry altered down to the cellular level. She could feel it inside her, a mental metamorphosis that had come from being physically annealed in the mutated Scourge.

She hoped Mohandas Suk would find something soon, even a trial serum to save a few of the worst-afflicted women.

Looking down at Jimmak, she saw him gazing back at her with the adoration of a child for its mother. It was a peculiar sensation for Raquella. This slow-witted young man had given so much to help her, taken such personal risks without concern for his own safety.

The thought saddened her. *I have to make certain he isn't harmed by what I have done.*

Raquella watched the landing lights of a shuttle coming down from orbit to the wide paved treetops. She recognized the configuration of the HuMed transport, and her heart surged. "I have to go meet Dr. Suk."

Jimmak beamed at her, cheerful and oblivious to her agony of indecision. "Need help?"

"No, I want you to go to the Misborn, ask them if they'll reconsider. The cenote water can save so many—"

His alarmed expression was like a knife in her heart. "They won't!"

She squeezed his shoulder, showing compassion. "Please try one more time. For me." As she touched him, she planted a tiny tracer in the fabric of his loose, stained shirt. When he ran out into the dense jungle, the small device would send out a signal to pinpoint the location of the cenote.

He trotted off.

With a leaden heart, she hurried out into Rossak's mysterious night, stepping across the spongy polymerized canopy. The landing area lights bathed the treetops in a harsh yellow-white glow. None of the Rossak men or women came to greet the shuttle; all routines had shut down entirely with the epidemic.

When the medical craft's airlock cycled and the hatch opened, a man emerged wearing a white-and-green decontamination suit adorned with the crimson cross of HuMed. She recognized Mohandas from his movements and mannerisms. He carried a sealed case and waved eagerly at her, smiling behind his faceplate. Even through the helmet, she could see his look of fresh enthusiasm. "This is a new trial vaccine—it shows some promise, but only more of your miracle water would be sufficiently effective."

Raquella glanced away. "I . . . that may change soon." Looking into his dark brown eyes, she saw the hope and enthusiasm there. She wanted to kiss him, return to orbit with him, and just spend a day holding him, feeling him against her in their cabin aboard the LS *Recovery*. But that wasn't possible. Not until the epidemic was over.

"It may not be soon enough, Raquella. We have to try everything. I've contacted the Supreme Sorceress and arranged for her to help administer this new sample."

Taken aback, Raquella hesitated. "Ticia actually agreed to help?"

"She intends to administer the vaccine personally." He spoke with a voice of authority. "It's political, I think. She wants to be in the loop."

Raquella wasn't surprised. She accepted the case of vials from Dr. Suk. "I'll let you know if it works."

"There's enough here for a dozen test cases," he said. "But I'm ready to ramp up to full-scale production in the orbiting lab. We can't wait—"

Ticia Cenva strode out of the cliffside opening and across the canopy, accompanied by three black-robed Sorceresses. "I will take those. I am in charge here."

Raquella did not want to antagonize the volatile woman. "I'll help you administer the vaccines. This could be our best hope." *Until I find the cenote and its healing water. . . .*

"We don't require your assistance." A glint of barely suppressed hostility flickered in Ticia's eyes.

"So you have said for weeks." Raquella tried to keep the edge out of her voice. "But you saw my symptoms—I clearly had a fatal case of the Scourge. I was in the final phase, from which no one else has ever recovered. I am the only one."

"Perhaps your remission is only temporary." The tall, pale woman took the vials, nodded curtly to Mohandas as he stood in front of his shuttle. "If this serum works, then you are all welcome to leave Rossak as soon as possible."

She and the other women marched back into the cliffside doorway. Raquella sighed but maintained her high hopes. If nothing else, Jimmak would inadvertently lead them to the cenote soon.

When others place impossible expectations on a man, he must rede-fine his goals and forge his own path. That way, at least someone is satisfied.

—SWORDMASTER ISTIAN GOSS

I n the twenty years since most of the thinking-machine forces had been wiped out, demand for the mercenary swordmasters of Ginaz had fallen. For centuries, training centers on the archipelago had instructed and unleashed crack fighters, primarily to destroy combat robots. Though none of the mercenaries complained that Serena Butler's bloody Jihad was over, the remaining swordmasters were at a loss as to where to put their skills and abilities to use.

Istian Goss had survived his battles, scarred but relatively intact. He kept his pulse-sword, but had no machine foes against which to use it. Instead, he had helped human refugees recover from the Scourge, travel-ing from world to world, using his muscle and knowledge to reconstruct colonies.

The League Worlds now had barely a third of their former popula-tions. Families were encouraged to have many children to give humanity its best chance to flourish again, but a sufficient workforce to sustain pre-vious levels of agriculture and industry simply did not exist. Everyone had to work twice as hard as before.

Many noble lines had been wiped out, and new centers of power began to emerge as ambitious survivors gathered their own empires, declaring themselves a fresh branch of the noble tree and claiming rights and privileges. Since the League Parliament had few enough representa-

tives, even the oldest and stodgiest families could not legitimately complain about the shifting power structure.

Five years ago, Istian Goss had returned to Ginaz to be an instructor.
Though he carried the mentor spirit of Jool Noret within him, he realized
he had never accomplished anything that would make his own name
blaze brightly in history books. He had not shamed himself like the
reviled Tlulaxa or Xavier Harkonnen, nor had he distinguished himself.
No one commented aloud that they had expected more from Istian Goss,
but he was disappointed in himself. He wished he could have begun with
a blank chit the way his lost friend Nar Trig had. Then he wouldn't have
felt such a heavy weight on his shoulders, and perhaps he could even have
excelled.

After the Jihad was declared over, League civilization and society had
changed in fundamental and unforeseen ways. With the widespread use of
Holtzman shields, anyone of even minimal importance wore a body shield
to protect against criminals, assassins, and accidents. Such a practice
made the use of projectile weapons and thrown blades virtually obsolete.

Against an opponent who wore a personal shield, the only effective
combat method was the deft use and careful precision of a handheld dagger or short sword. Objects could pass through the protective field if they
moved slowly enough, so new styles of fencing and knife fighting were
developed to take advantage of this one small vulnerability.

Thus, the combat mek Chirox altered his standard programming and
trained with Istian Goss to fashion a curriculum for developing swordmasters who could be hired out as assassins or bodyguards for threatened
nobles. Though the mercenaries no longer needed to fight hordes of combat robots, Ginaz would not let its standards or expectations diminish.
The graduates of the specialized swordmaster training were still the best
the League had to offer.

Istian watched new trainees come in, though there were far fewer than
before. Without the constant demand for more fighters against Omnius,
young men and women found other callings. The human race certainly
had enough work to do in the aftermath of more than a millennium of
machine tyranny.

One day Istian was surprised when a small ship came to Ginaz carrying
a message and an invitation. It bore the seal of Viceroy Faykan Butler and
contained a summons for the training mek Chirox and, if available, the
famous Swordmaster Istian Goss. The Viceroy had apparently summoned
the combat mek so that he could receive the recognition he deserved

after his years of service to the Jihad. Istian's shock was greatest, however, when he saw the signature of the man who had sent the message. *Swordmaster Nar Trig.*

All these years he had assumed his sparring partner had perished along with the ill-advised fanatics who had gone to Corrin to fight the thinking machines. But Trig was alive after all! What had the man been doing for the past two decades? Why hadn't he gotten in touch before this? Clearly from the contents of this message, Trig knew that his former comrade still served at Ginaz teaching new pupils.

Eagerly, Istian went to Chirox and shared the news with the multi-armed combat mek. "We must go to Salusa Secundus. We are required there."

The sensei mek did not argue or ask for reasons. "As you instruct, Master Istian Goss."

Loyalty is a clear-cut matter only for those with simple minds and no imagination.

—GENERAL AGAMEMNON,

New Memoirs

In spite of eleven centuries of camaraderie, Juno and Dante didn't always agree with Agamemnon. Frustrated, the restless cymek general paced in his walker-form, looking for something to smash. His heavy metal footpads scraped the floor of the chamber.

"No, I don't trust him entirely, even if he is my son," he said defensively. "But then, I didn't trust most of the Twenty Titans, either. Remember Xerxes."

"Don't you see? It's too convenient for Vorian to simply strut in here and claim he's changed his loyalties again, after a hundred years of serving the Jihad." Juno's voice normally soothed him, but now it had an abrasive edge.

Agamemnon simmered. "Wouldn't *you* go insane living among those people for so long? Vorian was raised and trained in the Synchronized Worlds. He memorized my memoirs and admired my accomplishments, until he was distracted by a woman—call it a youthful rebellion if you like. I believe his reasons are good and sufficient. It is certainly what I would have done."

Juno twittered with simulated laughter. "So your son is very much like you after all, Agamemnon?"

"Never underestimate the power of blood ties."

"Never overestimate them either," Juno said.

VOR LOOKED SMALL and vulnerable as he stood in the central chamber once inhabited by the Ivory Tower Cogitors, gazing at the intimidating form of his father.

Agamemnon said, "What makes you think you can convince Quentin Butler to ally himself with us, when all our techniques of coercion and brainwashing have failed?"

"That is precisely why, Father," Vor said. "If you want a military genius to turn his talents toward cymek ends—toward *our* ends—you can't simply torture him. You tricked him once, but he is a highly trained military commander. Your methods were all wrong, considering the results you want."

Vor studied the shielded translucent brain canister holding his father's age-old brain, as well as the numerous showy compartments where Agamemnon displayed his odd collection of antique weapons.

The general lurched upward like a tarantula ready to spring. "I still don't believe you or trust you, Vorian."

"With good reason. You haven't given me much cause to trust you either." He gazed calmly at the monstrous walker-form as Agamemnon strode back and forth. This mechanical body was swift and powerful and could tear a mere human limb from limb. Not today, though. "Still, I'm willing to take the gamble. Or are you afraid of me?"

"I have lived long enough to be afraid of nothing!"

"Good, then that's settled." Vor never allowed his bluster or his confidence to fade.

The Titan shifted in his walker-form, clearly angry with his son's boldness, but he restrained himself. "And you think you can do better with Quentin Butler?"

Vor crossed his arms over his chest. He was careful not to flinch in front of the Titan. "Yes, I do, Father. Quentin and I were comrades. I was his superior officer. He respects me, and knows how hard I fought for the Jihad. Even if Quentin disagrees with my choice, at least he will listen to me. That's more than you've achieved so far."

The cymek's speakerpatch rasped and vibrated as if Agamemnon were grumbling unspoken complaints. "You may make the attempt," he finally said. "But bear in mind that this is as much a test of you, Vorian, as it is of him."

"Everything in life is a test, Father. The moment I fail you again, you won't hesitate to discipline me."

"Your next discipline will be your last. Don't forget that." But Agamemnon's words lacked conviction. With so many squandered hopes, the general would not be so quick to dispose of Vorian Atreides.

After all these centuries, Agamemnon thought, *I did not expect to have any human emotions left.* He hoped none of them showed.

THE AIR WAS so chilly deep under the glacial layers that Vor could see his own breath wafting upward in steam. One of the neo-cymeks brought him into a cold side chamber where Quentin's preservation canister had been stored since his rebellion during the cymek attack against Faykan's group of League ships.

The once magnificent primero, liberator of Parmentier and Honru, commander of Jihad forces, was now nothing more than an inert mass of rippled brain tissue suspended in sparkling blue electrafluid. His canister sat on a shelf like a piece of discarded equipment. After his stunt warning Faykan, he had been taken back to Hessra and dismantled, his brain canister denied access to any cymek body. He was trapped here.

When Vor saw him, words caught in his throat. "Quentin? Quentin Butler!" Appalled, he stepped closer to the preservation container and was about to ask questions of his neo-cymek escort, when he saw the clanking walker back out of the room and scuttle away down a hall. Vor hoped Quentin's sensors were connected to his thoughtrodes so they could communicate.

"I don't know how well you can see or recognize me, Quentin. I am Supreme Bashar Vorian Atreides."

"I see." The voice came from a speakerpatch on the wall not far from the brain canister. "I see another cheap trick."

"I am no illusion." Vor knew that the Titans would be eavesdropping on every word he spoke, so he had to be careful. Every nuance and phrase would be suspect. Somehow, he had to emphasize the truth to Quentin, while not revealing his own secret plans.

"The Titans have manipulated and tormented you, but I am real. I fought beside your sons. I am the one who went to Parmentier and came back with the news that Rikov and his wife were dead from the Scourge. Once, I accompanied you to visit Wandra in the City of Introspection— it was spring, and the blossoms were full on the trees. I told you I always had a soft spot for Wandra because she was Xavier's youngest daughter.

You got angry with me, because I brought the Harkonnen name into our discussion. Do you remember that day, Quentin?"

The retired war hero's brain remained silent in the canister, then he finally said, "The cymeks know about the laser-shield interaction. I . . . I told them. They almost destroyed Faykan."

Knowing that this subject could prove dangerous, Vor introduced a new topic. "Faykan is now the full Viceroy of the League. Did you know that? It happened while you were away with Porce Bludd. You would be very proud of him."

"I . . . always was."

"And your youngest son, Abulurd." Vor pressed closer to the canister. "I saw to it that he was promoted to bashar, fourth grade. I pinned the insignia on him myself. It was the happiest day of his life, I think, but he was deeply disappointed that you could not be there to see it."

"Abulurd . . ." Quentin said, as if the name raised uncertainties in his mind.

Vor knew the veteran warrior had always given his youngest son a cold shoulder. "You have been unfair to him, Quentin." Vor felt that a stern tone might be most effective. "He is a talented, intelligent young man— and he's right about the Harkonnen name. I can tell you that the legends you've heard about Xavier were mostly lies. He was made into a scapegoat to strengthen the Jihad. I launched a task force to rectify the situation. It is time for those wounds to heal. And Abulurd . . . Abulurd has never done anything in his service to warrant your disappointment."

"I *have* been unfair to my son," Quentin agreed, "but now it is too late. I can never see him again. I've had nothing to do for the past three eternities here but think . . . and regret all my past mistakes. I hate what I have become. If you are truly loyal to us, if you have any love or respect for me, Vorian Atreides, you will smash my preservation canister on the floor now. I tried to resist, but they have stripped all chance of that from me. I want to die. Perhaps that is the last way I can complicate their plans."

"That would be far too easy, Quentin." Vor's voice took on a sharp edge. He used the commanding tone he had developed over more than a century in the Army of the Jihad. "You are a cymek now. You have an opportunity to fight alongside General Agamemnon. Without you, without me, the cymeks would probably go on a rampage against helpless humans, becoming a new threat as terrible as the thinking machines. You have often told me that Butlers are servants unto no one. True enough.

We are leaders, you and I. If we choose to cooperate, we can help shape the interaction between humans and cymeks for the better."

Vor sounded convincing, even to his own ears. "But the Titans won't be willing to negotiate until they've secured a position of strength. Many times, I myself advocated destroying them. They have good reason to be concerned about the League.

"But our insight could be the key. If you help them with what you know, humanity will have the greatest chance for peace and prosperity. In the long run, if you aid the cymeks, you'll be saving human lives. Do you see that?" Vor's vehemence was sufficient that he was sure the eavesdropping Agamemnon and Juno would be convinced. "You have to stop clinging to your prejudices, Quentin. The Jihad is over. A new universe awaits us."

As he raised his hands, gesturing for emphasis, Vor made certain he was facing the optic sensors connected to Quentin's thoughtrodes. He made quick, deft gestures with his fingers, the command-level military signals that he and Quentin had used for decades in the Army of the Jihad. The cymeks, long separate from free humanity, were unlikely to practice or be familiar with such a curious means of communication, but Quentin would certainly recognize it. Vor hoped it was enough to prove that he had not in fact switched loyalties, that he had something else in mind. Vor would find a way to spark continued rebellion from a place deep within a brain that thought it was beaten, outmaneuvered, and trapped into compliance. He would show Quentin that there was another way—if they could coordinate a plan.

Quentin remained silent for so long that Vor began to think he hadn't seen the gestures. Finally, the disembodied brain spoke through the voice amplifier. "You have given me much to consider, Supreme Bashar. I cannot say I agree . . . but I will think about it."

Vor nodded. "Excellent." He departed from the cold chamber, sure now that the two of them would set up Agamemnon for his fall.

*The greatest of mankind's criminals are those who delude themselves
into thinking they have done "the right thing."*

—RAYNA BUTLER,
sermons on Salusa Secundus

Though the Grand Patriarch had been a weak leader, lacking any true vision, Rayna took the opportunity to turn the murdered man into a hero, a figurehead for all to admire. Ironically, she would make sure that Xander Boro-Ginjo accomplished more after his death than he had during his long tenure in office.

The assassination could be a spark to ignite dissent against those who favored corrupt old ways, elevating the simmering Cultist movement to new heights here on Salusa Secundus. Rayna had purified many League Worlds, freeing them of any taint of computerized machinery, any vestige of devices that emulated the sacred human mind.

Though many days had passed, Viceroy Faykan Butler still avoided announcing a successor to the Grand Patriarch, and Rayna thought that perhaps the position should be hers after all. She could use the chain of office to expand the Cult of Serena, giving it the majority appeal that it deserved. It would be just as the vision of the white lady had shown her.

Word slipped quietly among all those who were loyal to her. Zimia and its modern conveniences made some of her followers uneasy, yet new converts kept coming to see Rayna, to hear her . . . and for the luckiest ones, to touch her.

Almost certainly, her uncle had spies among the Cultists. Some of her zealots had discovered the infiltrators and killed them quietly. Upon learning

of it, Rayna had been appalled, since she had never advocated direct violence against human beings, only against mechanical monsters. She ordered
that such activities must stop, and her lieutenants grudgingly agreed, though
they didn't look suitably chastened. Perhaps, Rayna thought, they simply no
longer intended to tell her about their secret murders.

On this of all days, though, the Cult's plans had to remain completely
confidential. The scheduled march must be a genuine surprise so that the
Zimia Guard would not have time to scramble in defense. This demonstration would be far more effective than a general strike.

The Cult of Serena had many more devotees than Faykan Butler suspected. Now, as Rayna in her pristine white robe marched at the head of
a mob, the light of the rising sun bathed her pale face. She must look like
the shining vision of Serena that Rayna had seen years ago, while suffering from the Scourge.

When it all began, the sounds of breaking glass, smashing metal, and
shouts of triumph formed a symphony in her ears. The primal movement
swept the half-empty boulevards and surged through the residential complexes. Some bleary-eyed men and women tried to defend their shops and
homes. Though Rayna had issued explicit instructions not to harm any
innocent people, the Cultists did not consider anyone who resisted to be
innocent.

The mob killed recklessly as they grew in force. Some of the shocked
populace fled, abandoning homes and businesses. Others, caught up in
the fervor, swore sudden loyalty to the Cult of Serena. Rayna's ranks
swelled, and the destruction continued unabated.

The Zimia Guard raced out, trying to pull together an effective
response, but many of them were also secret members of the Cult of
Serena.

Rayna led her procession forward, advancing on the Hall of Parliament. She wore a beatific smile on her pale face. When they approached
the large governmental structure, tramping down the flagstoned streets
into a plaza filled with elegant fountains and statues, Rayna was disappointed that Faykan did not come out to face the charged situation.
Apparently, the Viceroy had seen fit to be conveniently away on other
business. Perhaps he had infiltrators among her people after all.

But even Faykan Butler could not have stopped this tidal wave.

The paltry line of guards wavered and broke when they saw the surge
of angry people pounding toward them. Politicians and League representatives fled the assembly chamber through side wings and back exits.

Rayna was surprised to see five brave figures, men in yellow robes, emerge from the arched front entrance. They glided out, with one of them carrying a translucent brain canister as if it were a holy relic. Another two bore a pedestal.

Without pausing, Rayna looked up. The sun dazzled her eyes, but she recognized the last of the Ivory Tower Cogitors. Behind her, the momentum of the mob was too great to be stopped, and she did not slow her pace as she began to climb the long, shallow steps before the Hall of Parliament.

The secondaries erected the pedestal and placed the Cogitor's canister on its flat surface. When his speakerpatch was connected, Vidad's words boomed out, "I speak to your humanity! I beg for a moment of sanity. Consider what you are doing."

Rayna shouted back in a clear voice, "I have spent years considering this, Cogitor Vidad. I have direct inspiration from God, a clear vision from Saint Serena herself. Who can question that?"

"I spoke to Serena long ago, in *person*," Vidad said. "You are not wise to deify her. She was just a woman."

The Cultists grumbled, not wishing to hear that their patron saint had been no more than human.

Rayna climbed another step higher. "You Ivory Tower Cogitors brokered a foolish peace with the thinking machines, with terms so appalling that Saint Serena went to her death so that all could see the true nature of the demon Omnius." Her voice remained eerily calm. "You were the Judas, Vidad. We will not listen to you this time. We have learned from our mistake, and know how we must fight."

"Apply your rational thought processes," the Cogitor said. "Are you truly superior to Omnius if you commit violence against your fellow citizens in the name of purity? The machines you are destroying cannot harm you. Observe objectively. You must—"

"He defends the machines," someone shouted from the crowd. "And he looks like a cymek! Cymeks, Cogitors—they're all thinking machines!"

The shouts and roars grew louder. Rayna continued ascending the polished stone steps. "We have had enough of cool, rational thought, Vidad. That is the way of machines. But we are humans, with hearts and passions, and we must complete this painful purge that God and Saint Serena have set for us. You will not stand in our way."

The rest of the mob swelled behind her, shouting, waving sticks and cudgels, rushing toward the Hall of Parliament.

Vidad's secondaries tried to stand firm, but at the last moment, two of them faltered and ran off in a flurry of yellow robes, while the other three struggled in vain to protect the vulnerable Cogitor on his pedestal. In the furor, Vidad continued to beg for sanity, but the background noise quickly drowned out the voice from his speakerpatch.

Rayna stood in front of the Cogitor, but her fervid followers pushed forward. Someone jostled the column, and the brain canister wobbled. Then others, out of control now, shoved intentionally. The heavy container toppled and fell, striking the stone steps and cracking. It rolled and bounced, and the crowd cheered. They chased after the fallen canister, pounding it with their pipes and clubs until it shattered.

Rayna considered trying to stop them, but she understood all too well. The zealots saw the Cogitors as anathema, much like the evil Titans: brains without human bodies, kept alive by infernal technology. Thick blue electrafluid flowed on the ground, like blood.

Finally, Rayna turned and surged with her loyal followers into the Hall of Parliament.

Justice may be impartial, but righteousness is deeply personal.
— BASHAR ABULURD HARKONNEN,
private journals

Speaking from a safe retreat while Rayna's zealots surged through the streets, Viceroy Butler declared martial law. But the Zimia Guard was not large enough to reestablish order. They had no way to control the rush of fanatics, short of authorizing wholesale slaughter using all available weapons.

The League of Nobles maintained large archives of electronically stored data. Though the archives were not processed with AI programming or technology—a fine distinction that many people did not acknowledge—the very presence of computerized systems was a thorn in Rayna's side. The Demon Scourge had already thrust League civilization into turmoil, and a great deal of scientific and military information, as well as family records and historical documents, had been lost in the panic. Now Rayna was expanding the scope of the purge.

The records of millennia were being thrown into fires, the magnitude of the loss even greater than the destruction of the Library of Alexandria on Old Earth. If this continued, the human race was sure to face an extended dark age, if it ever recovered at all.

Not all records were accurate, of course, Abulurd Harkonnen thought. Perhaps if the false historical records were destroyed, it would be easier to restore his grandfather Xavier to his rightful place as a Hero of the Jihad.

Not wishing to be a target, Abulurd removed his bashar's uniform and donned civilian clothes. If he had thought it might be effective, he would have gone into the streets with his personal sidearm. But members of the Cult of Serena were perfectly willing to sacrifice their own lives. One man could never stand against them.

But he hoped to be able to protect his own laboratory.

When he arrived in the facility after sunset, some of the buildings around the Grand Patriarch's administrative mansion were on fire, though the nondescript research building was unharmed—so far. Abulurd was both relieved and disappointed to discover that none of his scientists or engineers had come to defend the research facility. Perhaps they were all at home protecting their families.

Inside the building, he sealed away all the records and test results about the machine mites. In the laboratory the prototype distorter device his engineers had developed was still sitting out on a bench after undergoing several final tests. He would have to reprimand his staff for not locking up their valuable equipment, which a zealous Cultist could have found and hammered into wreckage.

Before he could lock the distorter away in its proper place, he heard someone moving about in an interior analysis chamber. Abulurd held his breath to listen. Perhaps one of his engineers had come to stand guard over their research after all. He set the prototype distorter back on the lab bench and approached cautiously. None of the lights had been turned on. Shadows were long, and the intruder's sounds were cautious and rushed. Not an engineer, then. Someone who shouldn't be here. One of the Martyrists?

Pausing to power up his personal shield in case he was attacked, Abulurd pushed the room's illumination to full intensity, dazzling the stranger. The man shielded his eyes and moved like a lizard on a hot rock. He fired two rapid shots from a Maula pistol, but Abulurd's shield stopped the projectiles. The intruder skittered away, seeking shelter behind a bank of laboratory instruments. He saw the man's olive skin and bald scalp, his features familiar from history. The man Abulurd had been searching for.

Abulurd drew the chandler pistol from his side and grabbed a ceremonial dagger with the other hand. He could not fire the pistol's crystal needles while his shield was on, and he dared not switch off the protection now. "I know who you are, Yorek Thurr."

The intruder laughed, but with a nervous edge. "At last my fame precedes me! It's about time."

Crouching, Abulurd circled. "I'm glad I have a chance to meet you face-to-face. The League investigation force doubts you could still be alive after all these years, but I didn't underestimate your abilities."

Having used comparison techniques on historical images of the Jipol commandant with the image taken of the Grand Patriarch's murderer, Abulurd had no doubts whatsoever about the killer's identity. Afterward, when he'd delivered his analysis to his skeptical brother, Faykan promised to take the information under advisement, but obviously had treated it with as much seriousness as he gave the task force to clear Xavier Harkonnen's name.

As part of his manhunt, Abulurd had used his own connections to study records of new arrivals on Salusa Secundus, backtracking the paths of refugees by their documentation. He'd found several surveillance images that looked strikingly similar to the half-forgotten Jipol commandant, but the trail had gone cold. Though the League had cast a wide net for the killer of Xander Boro-Ginjo, the net had a great many holes.

"Everyone has been searching for the Grand Patriarch's assassin," Abulurd said, "but I alone have been looking for *you*. And now, during the greatest frenzy in the streets, you have come right to me, like a gift."

Thurr's leathery face looked at least half a century younger than he had any right to appear, frozen on the verge of old age. Grinning carelessly, he seemed to be enjoying this confrontation, and exhibited no concern.

In the harsh light of the research center, Thurr maintained his grip on the Maula pistol, though it was useless against Abulurd's shield. Thurr wore protection as well, but had not activated the power source. Apparently, he preferred the freedom to use his projectile weapon over the coverage the Holtzman field would give him.

"To what do I owe the honor of your obsession, young man?" Thurr asked. "Perhaps I can use you in my future plans. Wouldn't you like to be a part of history?" He moved like a panther stalking prey.

"You have used people enough as it is." Abulurd squared his shoulders. "My grandfather was Xavier Harkonnen—a hero in the war against the thinking machines—and you destroyed his reputation. You manipulated the truth and bled away the honor of my family."

"Yes, but it was all for a good cause, don't you see?"

"No. I don't." Abulurd stepped closer to him, holding out his dagger, which he could use while maintaining the protection of his body shield. "Why did you come to my lab?"

"Isn't this where you keep the remaining samples of my lovely mechanical pets? The devourers I helped develop on Corrin." Gleeful, Thurr raised his eyebrows. The historical records had portrayed him as ruthless and coldly intelligent, but now the feral look in the traitor's eyes carried an added sharpness, as if something had become twisted inside his head. He was still as malicious and scheming as ever, but his toehold on sanity seemed to be slipping.

"Ah, what an effect I've had working for Omnius—far more significant historically than anything I did as the commandant of the Jihad Police. Even when I worked for Jipol, I was completing a mission for Omnius, who provided me with this marvelous life-extension treatment. Oh, I still kept many important secrets from the machines, but all the while I planted red herrings, threw out false trails for Grand Patriarch Ginjo and his deluded though vehement devotees.

"Everything would have been perfect if only his widow had given me my due. That would have been the crowning achievement of a glorious career. My own kind of historical immortality! But when that was stolen from me, I had to do something else. The hungry little mites were merely an experiment. I developed them when I was bored with my endless captivity on Corrin. The retrovirus I suggested was far more devastating. Don't you agree?"

"I cannot grasp the magnitude of your evil," Abulurd said.

"Proof that you lack imagination."

Abulurd clenched the hilt of the knife, wanting to kill this man before he confessed to even more horrors. "Why are you telling me all this? Is your conscience heavy and you want to get it off your chest?"

"Don't be ridiculous. Surely I've earned the right to brag after all I've achieved? Besides, I mean to kill you anyway, so allow me that much satisfaction beforehand."

Though he still held the pistol in one hand, Thurr lifted a small translucent storage box in the other. Abulurd recognized one of the lab's secure sample containers; the seal had been breached, the locking mechanism broken. With his finger, Thurr flipped the lid. "I'm disappointed that you kept only twelve of my hungry little friends intact . . . but a dozen will certainly do the job here."

Once activated, the tiny voracious mechanisms began to buzz and jostle. Thurr flung the open box at Abulurd. The box bounced off of Abulurd's shield, and the machine mites scattered in the air like angry hornets. Abulurd backed away, looking for shelter, but the mechanical devourers spread out and pursued him.

Flattening himself against the wall, hidden among shadows and confusing shapes of equipment, Thurr observed and chuckled.

The buzzing mites swirled in the air, scanning the room, identifying Abulurd's human shape as the most obvious available target. They darted after him, tiny crystalline jaws whirring, ready to chew through flesh.

One of the piranha mites collided with the invisible barrier of his personal shield, striking with the speed of a bullet. It ricocheted off, and the other devices circled, closing in more slowly. Abulurd had no doubt that they would soon discover how to penetrate the Holtzman field.

As he backed against one of the stations where his engineers worked, he glanced down and saw his salvation. Grabbing the prototype he had set on the laboratory bench, he switched on the distortion field.

The crude device couldn't fry the tiny motors of the devourers, but suddenly Abulurd's shape became indistinct and invisible to their discrimination routines. The machine mites buzzed in circles, confused, and then orbited wider, casting a broad net in their search for the victim that had suddenly disappeared.

Tentatively, Abulurd held up the distorter and walked two steps out into the middle of the laboratory room. The machine mites did not respond to his movement. With their jaws spinning and their levitation engines driving them in random trajectories, they did not react to him at all.

Annoyed at this interference, Thurr demanded, "What have you done? How did you—"

Suddenly the machine mites spotted him. They changed course and zoomed toward their creator. Thurr scrambled away and activated his personal shield. The dozen tiny killers swarmed around, bumping into the force field, bouncing off and trying again. They were like carrion birds pecking a carcass. Abulurd activated the security controls for the door. The chamber barricades sealed into place and an automatic distress alarm was transmitted to enforcement personnel, though with Rayna's mobs in the streets, he doubted anyone would respond soon.

"You have conceived your own fate, Yorek Thurr."

The first of the devourers tunneled slowly through the indistinct barrier of the traitor's personal shield. Once inside the zone of protection, the piranha mite bounced about wildly in a ravenous attack. Soon it signaled the shield-penetration trick to its eleven counterparts, and the voracious machines pressed closer, slower, until all of them had passed through.

The mites began to attack Thurr's body, latching mechanical jaws on to his arms, his neck, his cheeks. He swatted at them ineffectively. As they consumed him, the traitor screamed and writhed, flailing his hands. Though blood poured from chewed holes in his shoulder and his side, he seemed more infuriated than terrified at his impending death.

One of the killing machines circled the top of his head, cutting a wide trough across his tanned scalp, exposing the white bone of his skull. Others bored into Thurr's stomach and burrowed through his thigh. One emerged, bloodied but still gnashing its artificial teeth as it broke through his rib cage, circled around in the air, then dove in for another meal. It spewed flecks of meat like raw sausage from its exhaust openings.

Thurr howled. He collapsed to his knees and in a desperate gesture managed to snatch one of the silvery balls out of the air and clench it in his hand. As he watched, the machine mite gnawed its way through his closed fist, severing Thurr's knuckles so that his fingers dropped off.

Abulurd watched the gruesome spectacle, sick with horror, yet also remembering that this man had betrayed humanity, murdering billions, and he had desecrated the memory of Xavier Harkonnen. Reminding himself of those things helped deafen Abulurd to the screams.

Because there were only twelve piranha mites, it took them several long minutes to do enough physical damage to kill their victim. Even after Thurr had fallen and his twitching ceased, the mites bored out his skull, then searched the room for other viable targets. Abulurd's distorter prevented them from seeing anyone else. Presently, the devourers returned to Thurr's body and continued to mutilate it.

Abulurd could not tear his gaze away. He let the piranha mites proceed with their horrific destruction until the traitor was entirely erased. Finally, their limited test power sources exhausted, they fell to the ground like fervid, fang-studded pebbles.

When finally, belatedly, three pale and harried-looking guards responded to the emergency alarm Abulurd had triggered, they stared with sick horror at the mangled flesh that lay piled like waste scraped from the floor of a butcher shop.

"I know this isn't our highest priority during the mob action," Abulurd said to them, "but that was the assassin, the man who killed Grand Patriarch Xander Boro-Ginjo."

"But . . . who was he?" one of the guards asked.

Abulurd thought long before answering, then finally said, "No one worth remembering."

The Rossak drug is but one path to infinity. There are others—and one, as yet unrevealed, which is greater than all.

—REVEREND MOTHER RAQUELLA BERTO-ANIRUL

All of the Sorceresses who received Dr. Suk's new test vaccine died. The total mortality rate shocked Raquella. In an increasingly strident voice, the Supreme Sorceress characterized it as another complete failure that demonstrated the incompetence of the HuMed researchers who had forced their services upon the people of Rossak.

Ticia Cenva tended the patients closely, refusing to let Raquella "torment" them. She had one of her Sorceresses send samples to Dr. Suk aboard the orbiting ship, but even upon analysis, he could not understand why the treatment had proved so deadly. At worst, it should have been ineffective.

Raquella began to wonder if something else—Ticia herself?—was at work here.

Looking like a vulture in her black mourning robe, the Supreme Sorceress scowled at the six dead women, victims of the test vaccine, as if displeased with their weak expressions of agony. She directed her ire at Raquella. "Your efforts are pointless. Any fool can see you are not helping."

"And what would you have me do? Just watch them die?"

"That appears to be what you're best at."

"At least we tried."

Ticia did not seem interested. "The strongest will survive, and the weak will suffer the fates that they deserve. That is how our bloodlines have always worked on Rossak. That is why the Misborn are cast out into the jungle. Those who cannot meet the challenges of the universe will perish. From our DNA storehouse, we can breed replacements, as soon as we choose desirable characteristics."

Raquella looked around her at the death ward, saw the overwhelming numbers of patients, smelled the stink of sickness. It was night now, and most of the people were either sleeping, or possibly dead. "Genetic samples cannot replace the friends you will lose, if you reject our help."

By now, most of the population had been exposed to the mutated retrovirus. Up in the LS *Recovery*, Mohandas had still been unable to identify the key ingredient in the cenote water sample, much less reproduce it. He needed more from the source itself.

Since his test vaccines had all proved fatal, Raquella no longer had any choice. The tiny tracer she had planted on Jimmak had shown her where to find the cenote. Once the medical technicians and Sorceresses had access to the water, they could cure all the sick, save their population.

The Misborn would suffer. They might even be killed. But there were far more people in the population of Rossak, and she could no longer justify remaining silent. Her duty was clear.

Sick and exhausted after wrestling with her decision, Raquella went to seek a few hours of sleep. At daylight, she would lead an expedition to the cenote to get what they so desperately needed. . . .

IN THE LOW light of amber glowpanels, a black-robed woman made her way past sleeping plague patients, many of them curled up in blankets on the stone floor. Weeks earlier, they had run out of beds.

She struggled against the growing effects of the illness. She could feel the Scourge, used every thread of her mental powers to drive back the symptoms, but she knew it was there inside her. No matter how strenuously she denied it, how much spice she consumed, the evidence of her affliction screamed from every muscle in her body.

But Ticia Cenva had a mission, something she had to do.

Entering an adjacent chamber, she paused and calmed her breathing, trying not to make any sound. These were the quarters of the HuMed doctors, nurses, and other medical personnel. She paused at a bed in the women's section, one of several in a long row. Lying on her side, Raquella Berto-Anirul slept the deep slumber of exhaustion, breathing rhythmically.

Ticia's eyes narrowed, and she felt energy building in her mind, the power of long-restrained destruction. As the daughter of the great Zufa Cenva, she had always been prepared to give her life in a final flash of glory, but had never found her opportunity. She was weak, a failure—an unused weapon that no longer had any purpose. Inner, nagging voices called her a coward, playing upon her survivor's guilt.

The Rossak Epidemic was killing all of her people, and she could do nothing about it. Anger and determination were all that kept her on her feet. Her body stiff, Ticia glared down at the woman she hated. Raquella believed she could come in from the outside and prove how simple, weak, and *ineffective* the Sorceresses were. That could not be allowed.

The weakest patients would all die, a necessary price to maintain the strength of Rossak bloodlines. Everything was recorded, documented, stored within the hidden computers that tracked the DNA of the human race. Even if Dr. Suk's vaccine had worked, it would only have staved off the inevitable and left the survivors tainted forever. She couldn't stomach the knowledge that her people were so feeble they could not keep themselves alive without outside help. Better that they die here and now, so that history would blame the meddling doctors rather than find fault with Ticia's leadership.

As if from a distance, the Supreme Sorceress acknowledged that the first-phase symptoms included irrational thoughts, paranoia, anger. But the onset of the disease in her body had moved slowly, stalled by her own mental fires, and she never thought to question her motives. Her blame and resentment made perfect sense to her.

Bending over the sleeping form of Raquella, Ticia knew she needed to finish this quickly. No one suspected that she was here, or that she had begun to show signs of infection herself. But Ticia had one last thing to do before melting in the plague fires that were consuming her. Her skin already felt hot, flushed with fever and with the exertion of walking.

Slipping a hand into her dark robe, she brought out a tiny apothecary bottle and removed the cap. Raquella's lips were parted slightly in her deep breathing. With trembling fingers, Ticia fumbled with an applicator and drew out a few drops of the viscous, oily liquid. The smell was bitter, pungent, giving the barest hint of how deadly the draft could be.

Many years ago, Aurelius Venport and his pharmaceutical scouts had discovered the incredibly potent toxin, a chemical so deadly that they had named it only the "Rossak drug." The chemical had no legitimate uses outside of the assassin's trade. No known antidote had ever been found. Once administered, the Rossak drug was always fatal, even in minuscule doses.

Raquella rolled slightly, tilted her head, and opened her lips a little farther. As if cooperating.

Seizing her chance, Ticia dripped liquid into the detestable woman's mouth. The poison went in smoothly, easily, just as it had when Ticia killed the test subjects who had received Dr. Suk's new vaccine. Now, everyone would believe the cure was a false hope, and that Raquella's unexpected healing ability had merely been an illusion, and a swift relapse had killed her after all.

It served the woman right for flaunting her superiority in front of all the Sorceresses. Raquella never should have come here.

As Ticia reached the doorway, she heard Raquella lurch awake, coughing and sputtering, already trying to fight off the Rossak drug. No matter. Nothing could alter her fate now. The Supreme Sorceress fled through the shadows.

HER MIND IMMEDIATELY recoiled from the bitter taste that spread through her mouth. The acid flavor of death. Raquella's fleeting, drowsing memory told her of the droplets she had felt on her lips, so different from the curative water of the secret cenote where Jimmak had taken her. That had been a life-giving baptism. This was something entirely different. A life-taker.

Poison.

She was already lost, drifting into dark unconsciousness. Suddenly light flared in her mind, showing Raquella a new way to fight back, a weapon she had not known she possessed. Her body had been altered in the crucible of the Scourge, after assimilating the incomprehensible mixture of environmental chemicals. Raquella had unexpected skills and new resources now, deep within her very cells.

Utter calmness pervaded her, and in her mind's eye Raquella saw the connections that led from the core of her brain—neural pathways spreading outward to veins, tendons, muscle—governing every function, whether voluntary or automatic. All so clear, like a human blueprint. The insidious poison pervaded her blood, organs, and immune system. The Rossak drug seemed almost alive, malicious, secure in its evil purpose.

No, *it* wasn't evil—but the poisoner was.

"I will not give up," she murmured. "I will fight back. Only fear can kill me now."

Going deep within herself, Raquella waged an internal war.

She shored up her body's defenses and constructed a biochemical wall against the poison's attack. Then she confronted the enemy head-on. Analyzing the molecular structure of the Rossak drug, she shifted the elements around, reconnecting free radicals, snipping off dangling protein chains. Taking away its weapons.

In the process, Raquella patiently transformed the poison, breaking it down until it was rendered impotent. It could no longer harm her. Because she was doing this for the first time, she explored her abilities, and realized that she had complete control over every cell and extraneous molecule in her body. Her medically trained mind marveled at the thought. She was the master of even the most intricate functions of this complex biological machine.

Like the evermind Omnius.

The thought disturbed and intrigued her. How similar were human beings to the thinking machines they had created? Perhaps more than either of them would ever admit.

And she saw something else inside, like an amazing storybook deep in her genetic code. At first it came to her drop by drop, like the water trickling into Jimmak's pool, then in a gush of data, as hereditary memories of her ancestors inundated her. She knew this vault of knowledge had always been there, passed from generation to generation, sealed and unreachable . . . and now, through the catalyst of the deadly poison, she had received the key and unlocked the door.

The rush was like trying to sip from a torrent. Much went into her brain, flooding her consciousness, although it had been there all along . . . lurking, hiding, waiting. Strangely, her mental access was limited to only her female predecessors.

Then, in the midst of her euphoria, the memories slipped away, tantalizing and out of reach. At first, Raquella felt like an orphan when all those wonderful ancestors abandoned her. Then, slowly, she understood that they would come to her on occasion, assist her, and recede again into the reverberating past.

In the echoing emptiness without clamoring memories, she noted that the Scourge retrovirus was no longer active in her system. She had neutralized it entirely, creating invincible antibodies in its place. Raquella could track the path of any disease through her cellular structures, follow it like an avenging force, and drive the enemy away. She would never need to fear getting sick again.

In the deepest regions of her cells, Raquella worked with what she had, achieving results that Mohandas Suk could never have hoped to attain in his orbital laboratory. She had her own laboratory now, inside her body, and presently she created exactly what she wanted: the precise antibodies needed to synthesize a swift and potent vaccine that would wipe out the Rossak Epidemic.

She did not need the cenote water. Her own cells and immune system were a factory far more complex and efficient than all the facilities Mohandas Suk used aboard the LS *Recovery*. Raquella could make as much antidote as was necessary.

The poison had not killed her, but had instead liberated her. It would save everyone on the planet. Exactly the opposite of what Ticia Cenva had planned.

THOROUGH TESTS, AS well as Raquella's own new intuitive comprehension, proved that Suk's original vaccine would indeed have bolstered the immune systems of the epidemic victims. She also understood that the test subjects had died not because of a failing in the medicine, but from murder.

Ticia Cenva.

In her new awareness, Raquella did not focus her thoughts on vengeance, but on healing. Through catalysts produced by the biofactories in her body, she was able to transmute the existing supplies of vaccine, enriching it with antibodies from her blood. She had no need of the cenote water, no need to destroy the Misborn and their squalid existence. She had everything she required in her own body.

Raquella went about administering the cure to the dying patients who crowded the wards and infirmaries in the cliff city. The remaining HuMed doctors and medical assistants stumbled along, helping her. As more people were cured and left their beds to help in the efforts, the Rossak Epidemic slowed, stalled, and finally retreated.

It seemed ironic that Raquella had obtained the water for her original cure from outcasts, people the Sorceresses thought were worthless. Now, her altered internal chemistry would save those women who had treated the Misborn as little more than animals, or mistakes.

Far from celebrating their rescue from the viral scourge, Ticia Cenva was nowhere to be found. Raquella, who had once again miraculously sidestepped death, was not surprised that the Supreme Sorceress remained in strict isolation. Raquella and her swelling ranks of healthy assistants distributed the vaccine vials and ministered to the sick.

When Raquella knew the vaccinations had been given to nearly everyone in need, she demanded to know what had happened to the Supreme Sorceress. Had Ticia avoided the virus, or succumbed to it? As the other women eluded Raquella's questions, she sensed direct and indirect lies. The Rossak women were concealing something important.

On her own initiative, fearing nothing, though she knew the Sorceress had tried to poison her, Raquella went to the private chambers of Ticia Cenva. She had never wanted to usurp the authority of the Supreme Sorceress, had only meant to fight the epidemic and then leave Rossak. But Ticia would probably see her now as a smug victor gloating over the vanquished.

When she reached the private chamber opening, Raquella found her way blocked by a shimmering energy barrier—a wall of force projected by an angry and delirious mind, not by a Holtzman shield generator. On the other side of the impassible barrier, she saw a distraught young Karee Marques. On her left, blurred by the waves of power, stood Ticia Cenva, glowing like a psychic weapon about to fire.

Only fear can kill me now, Raquella assured herself, and she sought out the calmest place in her spiritual being, a place that no one could take from her. From that personal stronghold, that citadel of her soul, Raquella stared at the energy barrier, employing powers that no Sorceress had ever discovered.

The barricade disappeared, falling away like the last flickers of a dying charge of electricity. Fiercely, Ticia tried to reconstruct the wall, but each effort fizzled, and it would not stand. With it, the Supreme Sorceress lost her psychic glow, as if the tides of desperation had washed it away. Utterly defeated, Ticia Cenva stood shaking, her beautiful face a mask of anguish and disease.

Raquella stepped through and confronted her nemesis who swayed on her feet, red-faced and perspiring. Obvious plague lesions now covered her face and arms; her skin and eyes had a yellowish cast. Karee Marques huddled out of the way, frightened by the play of power she had just witnessed. Five other Sorceresses emerged from the rear of the private chamber, awed by the obvious failure—and sickness—of their leader.

"Tell me what you have been hiding," Raquella demanded, in a Voice that was not entirely her own. Her female ancestors within, a veritable horde, spoke with her, from the past to the present and the future. Words echoed through space and time, and folded back on themselves.

"I can't . . ." Ticia said. "I c-can't . . ."

"Tell me! Tell all of our ancestors the blame you have cast, the lives you have taken, the future you have stolen!" The Voice again, this time stronger from Raquella's throat, much more importunate. The utterance sounded compelling, impossible to defy.

In a torrent of confession, Ticia revealed how she had foiled Raquella's attempts to save the people of Rossak, how she had killed the vaccination test subjects and tried to poison Raquella. The reasons had made sense to her, had demanded her action, in the disorienting and paranoid early stages of the mutated Scourge.

With her new understanding of the Supreme Sorceress, Raquella realized that Ticia Cenva was hiding much more, and her secret went far beyond petty rivalry. "Now tell me what you are protecting here." Like a primal thing, the Voice surfaced, and it was undeniable.

Ticia could not resist. Moving jerkily like an ill-used puppet, Ticia led Raquella to an immense cave chamber filled with computers and other electronic equipment, a vast reservoir of information. The computers hummed softly as they processed data, exchanged it between machines, and constantly built upon it, taking it to higher, more comprehensive levels: the DNA breakdowns from billions of people of varying races, the most detailed repository of genetic records ever compiled, not just during the original Scourge, but from many generations of breeding on Rossak.

Somewhere in her subconscious, Raquella had already known about this place. As the plague-stricken Supreme Sorceress confessed under the demands of the Voice, Raquella sensed that the ancestors within had guided *her* into this situation, as if they had foreseen it and moved the human beings around like game pieces. *What am I destined to do here?*

She answered her own question, and the realization gave Raquella an eerie feeling, simultaneously uncomfortable and reassuring. Women who had long ago turned to dust were watching her, guiding and counseling her in the important forthcoming decisions.

Suddenly Ticia coughed and stumbled. She slipped to her knees on the hard stone floor.

Raquella hurried to her. While Karee Marques held Ticia still and tried to comfort her, Raquella removed a vial of vaccine from her own pocket. "Your disease is in its advanced stages, but this drug will still flush it from your body, neutralizing the virus."

Lying on the floor, writhing in pain, Ticia fell into a fit of coughing. Her blue eyes were rheumy and streaked with red veins, a window into her soul that suggested she was much older than her actual years. For some time now, she had been forced to consume large quantities of melange, which had given her a more youthful appearance and intense spice-blue eyes. That was all changing now, as the Scourge ran roughshod over her defensive systems.

With her last burst of strength, Ticia pushed Raquella away. "Don't want your help! Now you know about our genetic database. The computers. You'll bring the Cult of Serena in to destroy everything we have worked for."

"I don't want to destroy your work," Raquella said. "I want to build on it. Fanatical mobs destroyed the Hospital for Incurable Diseases on Parmentier. I have no love for their cause."

Ticia grew quiet, but the hatred in her eyes flared even hotter. When she withdrew her hand from a fold in her dark, perspiration-soaked robe, the Sorceress held a small, open bottle of a bitter, acrid substance. Her fingers were smeared with it. Raquella instantly identified the liquid as the Rossak drug that had nearly poisoned her.

Raquella grabbed for the Supreme Sorceress, but with a last flare of mental power, Ticia knocked her away. The bottle dropped to the floor and broke. Before anyone could stop her, the Sorceress lifted her poison-smeared fingertips to her lips. A single drop was enough.

The life faded swiftly from Ticia's eyes, and she stared off into infinity.

The giver and the recipient may each define a "reward" quite differently.

—COGITOR KWYNA,
City of Introspection Archives

D ante, calm but skeptical, sat back in his mechanical form and reeled off counterpoints as if he were reading from a list. The other two Titans had already had their say, and they listened to his summary.

"Therefore," Dante concluded, "if you truly believe Vorian Atreides comes to us of his own free will, General, and that he will contribute to our expansion effort and turn against the *hrethgir*—then we had better convert him into a cymek before he changes his mind." The optic threads on his head turret flickered on and off, the mechanical equivalent of a blink.

"I agree," Agamemnon said, overjoyed. "We'll cut away the extraneous meat, and then his new loyalty to us will be more than intellectual. It will be irrevocable."

"Oh, there's not much of anything *intellectual* about his decision," Juno said. "I will prepare the surgery chamber, and our dear pet Quentin will assist me. An important test of his own . . . refocused loyalties."

"Butler will hate doing that," Dante said.

"I know. But it will demonstrate whether or not he has truly seen reason, as Vorian claims." Juno laughed. Her walker-form clattered out of the central chamber as she went off to find their other new convert.

"YES, FATHER, I want to be a cymek. More than anything." Vor had practiced the lie over and over. "When I was a trustee human, it was my dream. I always knew that if I made you proud, I would one day be allowed to become a cymek. Like you."

"Then the time has come, my son." The enormous combat walker of Agamemnon loomed in front of him at the ice bridge outside of the citadel. The Titan general's walker-form was twice Vor's height, adorned with golden highlights like chain mail. "They await you in surgery."

As the two walked toward the entrance to the Cogitors' old citadel, doubts assailed Vor. For a brief moment, he thought about taking the *Dream Voyager* and fleeing before the cymek surgeons could perform their horrific vivisection. But after working so hard to set up his plan, he could not give up now.

The Titan's walker strutted beside him. "You will like being a cymek, I promise you. You can be anything you like, not limited by the failings of a weak biological form. Whatever you can imagine, we can create a suitable body for those desires."

"I can imagine many things, Father." Overhead, the icy sky seemed like an extension of the surface of Hessra, as if the ice and snow had lifted above them and left a layer of open air in between.

Vor drew himself up as tall as possible, still looking young and virile but feeling quite antique. Steeling himself to do what had to be done, he entered the giant structure. Inside the passageways, he was cold in spite of his protective layers of clothing. "Before I undergo surgery, why don't I groom you one more time, like I used to?"

"For old times' sake? Some of the old clichés remain appropriate, don't they?"

Vor laughed, a sound rendered hollow as it dissipated into the vast emptiness around them. "Of course you could always transfer yourself into a different, clean machine form, but I just want to experience it one more time in my old body, before I give it up forever. And it would be something we'd both enjoy."

"A wonderful idea—and then I shall admire myself." Agamemnon rattled his chain-mail adornment as he strode into the cold, enclosed corridors that had been built centuries before. The chain-mail decoration seemed as odd and out of place as the gadgets, knives, and bolt-projectile guns he stored in the display cases around his walker-body.

Vor's rush of adrenaline and anticipation kept him moving, flushed and anxious. But he and the Titan general were anticipating different things . . .

Now, while Juno prepared the surgical chamber, his father took him up a series of ramparts that were guarded by neo-cymeks with translucent preservation canisters tucked safely in their undercarriages, like strange mechanical genitalia. They climbed a tower, still half-buried in glacial ice, which loomed high above the cracked and frozen landscape. Agamemnon had always liked to survey his conquered territory, no matter how sparse it might be.

"It has been far too long since my last grooming," Agamemnon said, easing his large walker against the maintenance equipment the cymeks had assembled. "I will enjoy this, Vorian. In fact, I think I shall perform your surgery myself, as a quid pro quo for the cleaning and polishing."

"I wouldn't want it any other way."

At the top of the cold tower, they entered a large, mirrored room with four empty cymek walkers standing around the perimeter—varying forms of combat units that the Titan general preferred. Cleaning and polishing supplies were neatly arrayed in cabinets and on shelves. A broad window looked out upon the dim, icy expanse of Hessra. Vor shivered involuntarily.

As he studied the instruments and restoration devices, he recalled how young and innocent he had been in his days as a voluntary trustee. He had believed the general's false memoirs, his stories, his theories. Vor had never thought to question anything. Now, it seemed, he believed nothing.

He had learned and experienced much.

"Well then, Father," Vor said, turning to the waiting cymek, "let us begin."

Support thy brother, should he be just or unjust.

—Zensunni Saying

After the successful kanla raid, Ishmael addressed his people inside the largest meeting chamber in the cave village. He felt alive again, the blood running hot in his ancient body. He and the too-civilized desert men had slain their enemies and reaped the spoils of the slaver camp. They had taken the offworlders' water, food, equipment, and money. But it was not enough for Ishmael—never enough to repay what the flesh merchants had done to the other villages they had raided.

Now that the ordeal was over and they were home, El'hiim was deeply disturbed by what he had seen, especially the draining of an enemy's blood to take his water. "Centuries of civilization have been stripped away from us," he had said quietly to Ishmael. "We turned into animals, and now no law on Arrakis will take our side. We have lost more than we gained."

"No. We regained our heritage," Ishmael said. "We have always followed the law of the desert, the law of survival—the law of Buddallah! What do I care for the rules laid down by civilized men in their comfortable homes?"

El'hiim frowned. "I care, Ishmael."

But Ishmael refused to let matters rest as they were among the villagers. He spoke vehemently when the elders gathered, and many impatient younger men and women stopped to listen. "Slavers attacked our village, but we drove them off. We avenged all those who were lost when they struck another village—but our enemies will come back again and again! We have opened our door to them. We have let the jackals take advantage of us." He raised a gnarled fist.

"Our only hope for the future is to go back to the ways of Selim Wormrider. We must pack up only those possessions we need for our survival, and retreat into the deepest desert, where the slavers will leave us alone."

Some of the people cheered enthusiastically; others seemed troubled. After the bloody raid, a number of the young Zensunni men wanted to launch more vengeance attacks, as in the old outlaw days.

But now a troubled-looking Naib El'hiim stood and tried to calm them. "There is no need to be so reactionary, Ishmael. Those who preyed upon the unprotected village were criminals, and they have suffered the ultimate punishment. We've taken care of the problem."

"The *problem* is at the core of our society," Ishmael said. "That is why we must leave and find our souls again. We must remember the prophecy of Selim Wormrider and do as he told us."

El'hiim said, "I am Naib, and the Wormrider was my own father. Let us not put too much stock in the dreams he experienced after consuming excessive amounts of melange. Do we not all have strange visions when we drink too much spice beer?" Some of the Free Men chuckled, while Ishmael scowled.

"Running away from our problems will not solve them, Ishmael. Your solution is . . . simplistic."

"And your solution is blind and lazy, *Naib*," Ishmael snapped back. "You've seen how the offworlders enslave and kill our people, yet you still want to form a business relationship with them and pretend that nothing happened. You think we can coexist peacefully with them."

El'hiim clasped his hands together. "Yes I do! We must all coexist."

"I have no interest in becoming a good neighbor to vermin!" Ishmael had hoped that by gaining obvious and overwhelming support he could make his stepson change his mind. But he saw now that there could be only one solution, one that had been growing for years. Because he had raised El'hiim, because he had promised Marha, Ishmael had refused to consider the obvious, necessary action. Now—for the good of his people and the future of Arrakis—he could no longer avoid it.

He turned to face his stepson, whom he had rescued from an infestation of black scorpions, whom he had taught and protected. Now it was more important to protect their people. The decision tore him apart, and he feared that Marha's ghost would come back to haunt him for breaking his sacred word to her. But he had to do this. He must keep the Zensunni alive and free. He knew in his very soul that El'hiim would lead them into weakness and destruction.

"Ishmael, there are many factors to consider," El'hiim said, trying to placate him. "We all understand how unsettling the recent events have been. But if we simply become outlaws again, we lose all the progress we have made over the past half century. Perhaps together we can—"

"A challenge," Ishmael said, his voice booming in the cave. El'hiim looked at him. "What—?"

Ishmael drew back his hand and struck the Naib resoundingly across the face, for all to see. "A challenge, by Zensunni tradition. You have turned your back on much of your past, El'hiim, but the people will not let you ignore this."

A collective indrawn breath echoed through the chamber. El'hiim reeled backward, unable to believe what the old man had done.

He raised his hands. "Ishmael, stop this nonsense. I am your—"

"You are not my son, nor are you the son of Selim Wormrider. You are a ruinous insect that eats at the heart of our Zensunni people."

Before he could stop himself, Ishmael slapped him again, harder, on the other cheek. A mortal insult. "I challenge your title of Naib. You have betrayed us, sold us out for profit and comforts. I challenge you to a duel for control of all the Zensunni people, and for our future."

El'hiim looked alarmed. "I will not—I cannot fight you. You are my stepfather."

"I tried to raise you in the ways of Selim Wormrider. I taught you the laws of the desert and the holy Zensunni Sutras. But you have shamed me, and you shame the memory of your true father." He raised his voice. "Before all these people I renounce any claim to you as my adopted son— and may my beloved Marha forgive me."

The people were unable to believe what they were hearing. But Ishmael did not waver in his determination, though he saw the stricken, frightened look on El'hiim's face.

"Zensunni law is clear, El'hiim: If you are not willing to fight me, as tradition demands, then we will let Shai-Hulud himself decide."

Now the younger Naib looked truly terrified. The other Free Men in the speaking chamber stared, knowing exactly what Ishmael meant.

A sandworm duel would determine their future.

So much is based upon perception. We see events through the filter of our surroundings, making it difficult to know if we are doing the right thing. In this terrible task I must undertake—a sinful act by any objective measure—the problem becomes more apparent than ever.

—SUPREME BASHAR VORIAN ATREIDES

During the process itself, Quentin had not been forced to observe the gruesome surgical operation that had separated him from his human body. The cymek vivisectionists had scooped his brain out of its skull before he'd ever regained consciousness. Now, with his optic threads, Quentin would be forced to watch the whole horror show for Vorian.

Juno seemed particularly proud of all the sinister-looking apparatus in the chilled operating chamber. For now, the medical tools gleamed with polished metal and plaz; soon they would all be stained with blood.

Even isolated in his brain canister Quentin could not quell the absolute revulsion he felt. He prayed the Supreme Bashar knew what he was doing. . . .

Two of the hybrid secondary-neos moved about, reluctantly assisting in the operation that would convert Vorian Atreides. Like Quentin, the secondary-neos were unwilling participants, but he doubted they would help him. They silently prepared the room for the surgery.

Large articulated machinery was connected to the room's walls and ceiling, a variety of drills and cutting lasers, nimble needle probes, diamond saws, and pry clamps. Metallic bins rested beside a polished table where discarded limbs and organs would be tossed. The operating table had deep channels that led to drains.

"Things tend to get messy for a while," Juno pointed out brightly. "But the end always justifies the means."

"Cymeks have always justified their actions," Quentin said.

"Is that bitterness I hear, pet?"

"Do you deny it? I'm having difficulty justifying it myself, but the Supreme Bashar has told me I must try." He hated the words even as he spoke them. "Becoming a cymek was never my choice. You can't expect me to accept it easily . . . though, I am beginning to see certain advantages."

"I know how stubborn men can be. I've spent more than a thousand years with Agamemnon." She chuckled again.

For his upcoming participation, Quentin was granted a small walker-form with manipulating arms, a mechanical body that was no threat to Juno's larger, more sophisticated structure. She was a Titan and could easily crush any neo.

As the mechanical monks sterilized the surgical machinery, Juno relished describing how Vorian would be brought inside and laid out on the table. "I've considered giving him sufficient anesthetic to make the surgery easier. However, in a sense, there's something pure and elemental about raw pain experienced by physical flesh. This is the last chance Vor will have to feel it." She made a tittering laugh; Quentin thought it more likely that she was simply being vicious. "Maybe we should use the cutters without any drugs . . . just to give him a last memory of genuine agony."

"Sounds more like sadism than a favor," Quentin said, continuing to play the resigned and unresistant part so that she would not suspect his anticipation. "If the son of Agamemnon has voluntarily joined your cause, why would you want to anger him?" He moved forward, studying the surgical lasers, the cutting and manipulating digits designed for delicate cerebral surgery.

Juno positioned herself to guard the major medical equipment. She kept him away from the powerful cutters and heavy weaponry in this horrific surgical chamber, though she didn't think the beaten Jihad officer would do anything so foolish as to attack her here. He would never gain access to the large tools.

But that was Juno's greatest blind spot: She overlooked the need to think small. Quentin understood weaknesses that the Titans did not worry about. The cymeks had more than one Achilles' heel.

During his earlier brash and violent attempts at rebellion, Juno had easily subdued him by neutralizing the thoughtrode connections that linked his brain to its walker-form. A simple disconnection had effectively paralyzed him. The Titans used the technique as an easy, nondestructive method of shutting Quentin down whenever he grew too unruly.

For that, he didn't need powerful or destructive weaponry—just finesse. Quentin had only to seize his chance.

Working with his mechanical hands while Juno continued to jabber about the torture she would inflict upon Vorian Atreides, he picked up a small low-intensity laser. He felt like a boy selecting a pebble to fight Goliath, as in a story Rikov and Kohe had read to their daughter on Parmentier.

Quentin's greatest concern would be to aim the small tool precisely. Juno wasn't worried about him. Not yet.

Moving dutifully and silently, the secondary-neos cleared the metallic surgery table and activated the heavy equipment beside it. Soon she would call for Vorian to be brought into the chamber. But one of the clumsy, bizarre helpers accidentally tipped over a tray, causing a loud clatter. Juno swiveled her head turret in response to the noise—giving Quentin sudden access to an external port. He moved in a flash and ripped away the shielding plate with his augmented arms, exposing her protected thoughtrode network.

Juno reared back, but Quentin shone the diagnostic laser into one of her delicate receptors, blinding her sensors. From intense practice and studying the configurations of cymek bodies, Quentin knew exactly where to aim.

The power surge was enough to overload and disconnect one of the links from Juno's preservation canister to her walker-form's mobility circuits. Stunned, she lurched and reeled, trying to regain control, but Quentin dropped the tiny diagnostic laser and raked the end of his metal arm along three other thoughtrode links, severing them.

The shock to Juno's circuits caused her articulated legs to slump as if they had lost physical integrity. But unlike a human falling into unconsciousness, Juno remained awake. Her brain canister glowed bright blue with fury. She simply could not move.

"What foolishness is this?" One of the walker legs twitched. "Thoughtrodes regenerate quickly, you know. You can't stop me for long, pet."

He acted swiftly, scuttled closer, and again used the diagnostic laser to burn out the rest of the mobility thoughtrodes. Temporarily paralyzed, Juno shouted and cursed him, but Quentin had her entirely at his mercy.

He found the thoughtrodes that connected her voice synthesizer, and next to them the stimulators that fed into her sensory centers. Pain centers. "I would love to hear you scream and keep screaming, Juno," he said, "but I can't afford the distraction right now." With another blast, he disconnected her speakerpatch, so Juno could make no more sounds. "I'll simply have to imagine all the pain you are going to be enduring, and be content with that."

Working hurriedly but carefully before the thoughtrodes could reassemble themselves and give Juno back her control, Quentin detached the preservation canister from the walker-form. He lifted it with his own strong metal arms and placed the container on the table where Vorian Atreides was scheduled to be converted into a cymek.

AGAMEMNON LUMBERED OVER to the banks of grooming equipment, anxious to proceed with the fondly remembered activity. "Ah, Vorian, you are indeed the prodigal son. You scorned your destiny for more than a century, but now you've finally come to your senses. Everything will soon be perfect, just as I've always hoped."

"If we are to be immortal, what is the significance of a mere century? It's just a tiny blip on the time line of our lives." Vor stepped forward, remembering the intricate steps of the grooming process. "Even so, it seems like a very long time since I did this for you." He thought of the extravagant cities on Earth, the towering monuments to the glorious Time of Titans. He had almost forgotten that he'd been happy then. . . .

"Too long, my son." Like a large, obedient pet, the Titan removed his extraneous chain-mail adornment from the heavy walker-form and then settled into the maintenance bay. He almost purred while his son climbed carefully on top of the walker, cleaning and polishing the exterior, using metalsilk cloths and buffing compounds.

"A Titan should inspire awe and majesty," Vor said. "Just because you cymeks are all alone here on Hessra is no excuse to get sloppy."

As he cleaned the mechanical parts and performed external maintenance on the walker, the life-support systems, and connectors to the preservation canister, Vor felt a twinge of nostalgia. Then he reminded himself why he was here.

One death to avenge all the murders this cruel tyrant had committed.

THE SECONDARY-NEOS STOOD watching everything Quentin was doing. They did not comment, did not flee. Nor did they attempt to stop him.

Now that he had full access to the heavy surgical machinery, Quentin used the diamond saw to cut through Juno's thick-walled preservation canister, spilling blue electrafluid. At last, he exposed the female Titan's soft, vulnerable brain that had been so hateful for centuries.

"Considering all the fear you caused, Juno," Quentin spoke aloud, knowing that with her sensor network disconnected she would not be able to hear his words, "you don't look all that frightening—not now, *my pet.*"

Next he brought in the heavy surgical lasers, and powered them to their highest levels. "This may tend to get messy," he said, paraphrasing what she had told him. Then he fired dazzling incineration beams to slice Juno's brain into small hunks of smoking gray matter. Trickles of fluid and oozing biological matter drained into the troughs, just as Juno had said would happen.

He stepped back to look at the blackened mass, shapeless and unimpressive.

With one of the three remaining Titans now dead, Quentin swiveled his head turret and saw the secondary-neos still watching him. "Well? Do you intend to oppose me, or will you assist me?"

"We hate the Titans who murdered our masters, the Cogitors," said one of the strange hybrids.

"We applaud what you have done, Quentin Butler. We will not hinder you from continuing your interesting work," added another.

Finally, after a pause, the third one said, "And you would make an interesting cymek in a superior walker-form."

The mechanical secondaries worked to detach Quentin's own brain canister from the small and impotent mechanical body, then reinstalled him in the powerful Titan walker that had recently belonged to Juno.

With all his thoughtrodes reconnected and his new systems activated, Quentin felt terrific. Better than terrific, in fact. Juno's body had full weaponry and complete access to all of Hessra's defensive systems. The potential for utter destruction was exhilarating.

Agamemnon, Dante, and every neo-cymek could die, as far as Quentin was concerned. The galaxy would be better for it.

IN ORDER TO perform the most effective job on his father, Vor opened storage compartments on the walker, where the general kept interesting objects from his travels and exploits. Gruesome trophies, shiny baubles, ancient weapons. "Move a little, please, so I can clean inside this compartment."

The cymek obliged, shifting his body core. "I really should have kept one or two of the secondaries alive in their human bodies so they could perform this service. I had forgotten how . . . gratifying it can be."

Inside the opening, Vor found what he was looking for, an antique dagger, an ineffective piece that should never have been able to harm a Titan's warrior form.

"In our heyday centuries ago," said Agamemnon in a reverie, "we used human slaves to perform the task you're doing, but as renegade cymeks we no longer have this option."

"I understand, Father. I'll do my best job ever."

He disconnected the preservation canister from the walker-form. Just as he had always done.

Knowing that the cold citadel had a small army of neo-cymeks who would never let Vorian live if he tried anything, Agamemnon began to talk about his glory days as the ruler of all humanity, and his dreams of how he and his son could establish a similar leadership in a new empire, now that Omnius was defeated.

While his father waxed nostalgic, Vor worked. Already disconnected, the walker was useless; Vor had not yet unhooked the optic threads or the external sensors from the thoughtrodes. Even so, Agamemnon was now completely vulnerable.

Polishing the brain canister, Vor said, "I'll just move this ventilation panel a bit and clean around it."

As the general continued to ramble about his glory days, Vor slid open a narrow panel on the canister, revealing the fleshy mass inside. He gripped the antique dagger. One swift movement would drive the tip down into the spongy contours of Agamemnon's brain. Then it would all be over.

Just then, the door to the chamber burst open, and a monstrous Titan lumbered through. Startled, Vor dropped the knife, which clattered to the floor. Juno? Or Dante? Neither of those Titans had believed in his sup-posed conversion to the cymek cause.

The mechanical warrior was ominous, bristling with weapons and spined armor. "I thought I might find Agamemnon here," a synthesized voice said. "And Vorian."

The Titan strode forward and seized Vorian, lifting him away from the vulnerable brain in the preservation canister. Only inches away. He had come so close. . . .

Regardless of his rank, the foremost concern of a warrior is how he
will behave at the moment of his own impending death.

—SWORDMASTER ISTIAN GOSS,

opening remarks to his class

Scanning with his thoughtrodes, General Agamemnon paused in his reminiscing. "You are not Juno! Why are you in her walker-form? Who—"

The other Titan gently set Vor aside. "What you have in mind would be too quick, Vorian Atreides. Not nearly enough pain. I have a better idea."

"Vorian, reconnect my walker!" Agamemnon demanded through the speakerpatch.

Confused, Vor looked up at the walker-form towering over him. He recognized the configuration as Juno's, but didn't know what was different.

"Don't you recognize me, Supreme Bashar?" the Titan asked. Something rang familiar in the cadence of the words.

Vor blinked in disbelief. "Quentin? Is that you?"

Helpless in his brain canister, the general grew more strident in his demands, but Vor ignored him. So did the other cymek as he explained, "Yes. I have killed Juno. I destroyed her brain, cut it to smoking pieces."

"Juno?" Agamemnon let out a ragged wail through the speakerpatch. "Dead?"

Quentin reached out in Juno's powerful mechanical body and lifted the Titan general's preservation canister. He held the cylinder in front of his glittering optic threads, and the pink and gray membranes throbbed and writhed, as if trying to escape their confinement. "Yes, Juno is dead! And the same fate awaits you."

Vor stood without moving, feeling a storm of conflicting emotions, but wanting to complete his mission. Agamemnon moaned, but the speakerpatch could not convey the grief that bubbled through his brain for the woman who had been his lover for more than a thousand years.

Quentin continued talking, knowing Agamemnon could hear him. "For what you did to me, General, for killing my body, for transforming me into a cymek, for tricking me into revealing the secret vulnerability of our shields—I intend to make this last a nice long time."

Two of the secondary-neos came scuttling in, having followed Quentin up into the high tower. Vor glanced over at them, but realized that the cymeks, who had once been the Cogitors' monks, were not going to attack.

Still, the citadel was crawling with other loyal neos. "Let's get this over with, Quentin. No one can doubt that Agamemnon deserves to die for his crimes. I didn't intend to torture him—"

"That isn't good enough, Supreme Bashar." The secondary-neos came into the cleaning and maintenance chamber. Quentin placed the helpless Titan on the pedestal where Vor would have continued cleaning him. "I intend to hook Agamemnon's brain canister up to the pain amplifiers he installed in these poor monks' walker systems. If he endures only one second of agony for each life he has taken over the centuries, he will still boil in pain for decades and decades. Only a fraction of the suffering he deserves."

As a former Jihad commander, Vor could not argue against the justice Quentin had in mind. But, despite all Agamemnon's known crimes, he was still Vor's father.

The general screamed out through this speakerpatch. "My son! How can you do this to me?"

"How can I not?" Vor forced out the words. "Weren't you proud of all the atrocities you committed—all the oppression and domination? You tried to make me admire you for it."

"I tried to make you my worthy successor. An exalted Titan. I raised you to greatness, taught you to appreciate your potential, to revere history and to make your own place in it!" The general's voice was angry and defiant, not at all panicky. "I made you what you are, whether you're proud of it or not."

Vor struggled to maintain his stony determination. He didn't want to hear the truth in his father's words, didn't want to understand that his own choices had caused ripples through the lives of Abulurd, Raquella, Estes, and Kagin. He hadn't been the best of fathers himself.

"Quentin, no matter what you do, or how much torture you inflict, it can never be enough . . . and can never change history back."

The commandeered Titan walker shifted angrily. "Look what he has done to *me*, Supreme Bashar! I demand vengeance—"

"He took your body, Quentin. Don't let him take your humanity, too." He felt cold inside, not because of the chill tower room. "Too many times during the Jihad we let ourselves become monsters in order to accomplish our aims. We should stop it here, with this one small gesture."

"I refuse!"

Vor rounded on Juno's purloined walker-form. "Quentin Butler, I am still your superior officer! Your entire life was dedicated to the Army of the Jihad and then the Army of Humanity. You are a hero many times over—don't throw it all away. I am giving you a direct order, as your Supreme Bashar."

Quentin froze for a long moment, and the mechanical body seemed to tremble with his turmoil and indecision.

Vor explained what he wanted to do. Finally, Quentin angrily strode in his augmented walker over to the high tower window. With a mighty sweep of his articulated armored forelimb, Quentin smashed out the thick, reinforced pane. Chunks of glass and ice tinkled away, and frigid winds howled into the room.

Feeling the biting cold crackle over his exposed skin, Vor picked up Agamemnon's preservation canister and looked into the optic threads, knowing his father could still see and hear him. "I understand now that I am what you made me. From *you*, I learned to make the difficult decisions that no one else dared to make, and then accept the consequences. That is why I was able to lead the Great Purge, though it cost so many human lives. And that is why I must take this action I've chosen.

"I have read your extensive memoirs, Father. I know that you pictured a grand heroic end for yourself, that you expected to face off against great armies and die in a huge pitched battle."

He carried the cylinder over to the shattered observation window, blinking as the breezes cut like frozen razors across his eyes, his cheeks.

"Instead," Vor continued, "you, the powerful Titan Agamemnon, will meet the most ignominious death possible."

Agamemnon bellowed. "No, Vorian. You must not do this! We can create a new Time of Titans! We—"

Vor paid no attention to the general's continued protests. "I give you what you deserve—an end that is unremarkable and utterly *insignificant*."

He pushed the preservation canister over the ledge, knocking it out the high window. Spilling electrafluid, the cylinder tumbled through the air until it shattered on the iron-hard ice of the glacier far below and sprayed shards, gray matter, and viscous liquid in all directions.

WHEN IT WAS finished, Quentin and Vor went into the corridor. "The neos will be clamoring for your blood," the cymek said, "and mine, too . . . if I had any blood."

For a time, the neo-cymeks on the recently conquered worlds would continue without realizing their command structure had been eliminated. Vor knew, however, that the rest of the cymek rebels suffered from a softness in their leadership, a weakness in their decision-making ranks. That was why the Titans had kidnapped Quentin in the first place and attempted to make him one of their commanders. Without Agamemnon's driving vision, the new-generation cymeks were not capable of holding the fledgling empire together. Their influence would dwindle and fade.

Vor ran, leading the way through the tunnels. Quentin followed as rapidly as he could move, still getting used to the machine form he had commandeered from Juno.

Alarms sounded. "They'll figure out the details soon enough, once they find our handiwork," Vor said, breathless. "We've got to get to the ships. Is there a cymek spacecraft you can operate for yourself? I have the *Dream Voyager*."

"Don't worry about me, Supreme Bashar. There are numerous options."

Three neo-cymeks, armed with projectile launchers built into their walker-forms, strode down the corridors. As soon as they saw Vorian Atreides, the lone human being in the frozen fortress, they clicked their systems into standby mode, but Quentin was there, looming larger than the neos. They recognized the robotic body as belonging to a Titan.

"Juno, are you in control of the prisoner?" asked one of the neos.

In response, Quentin raised his far superior weapons arms and launched powerful torpedoes at the three smaller cymeks. The precisely targeted detonations shattered their brain canisters, and the neo-cymek bodies slumped into wreckage on the floor.

"This disguise may just be sufficient," Quentin said.

"Don't count on it. Come on."

Taking larger strides in the mechanical body, Quentin began to out-pace him, moving with confidence. "There is a way for this all to end. In his own paranoia, General Agamemnon planted the seeds for the cymeks' downfall."

Before Vor could ask what he meant, they encountered several other smashed cymek walker-forms that littered a tunnel near the landing bay where the *Dream Voyager* was stored. "It looks like someone else is at war with the cymeks."

Three neos clattered into the landing bay from adjoining passages. Quentin swiveled, preparing to blast them, but soon it became apparent that the neo-cymeks were fleeing from something.

Behind them came four rampaging secondary-neos that had been unwillingly converted from the caretakers of the slaughtered Cogitors. The former secondaries had appropriated parts from other cymek walkers, incorporating the additional appendages and armaments into bizarre new configurations. Pieces of combat bodies, such as the remnants of the dis-mantled cymek Beowulf, had been stored for repair and reuse on other walker-forms. The involuntary servants of Agamemnon had launched their own rebellion.

Blasting after the scuttling cymek-loyal neos, the secondaries raced into the landing bay. When the trapped and cornered neos saw the im-mense Titan walker waiting for them, they seemed to take heart. The neos rallied, thinking they had an ally in Juno.

Even as the secondary-neos continued to shoot their confiscated weapons, Quentin raised his cannon arms and blasted the other neos from behind. Shrapnel and blue electrafluid scattered everywhere. The cymek secondaries hesitated only a moment before charging forward, fir-ing weapons.

"They saw me destroy Juno's brain," Quentin explained to Vor. "It must be what finally pushed them over the edge to violence."

The secondaries raced in among the wreckage like scavengers on a battlefield. Making certain the brain canisters of the neos were thor-oughly destroyed, they stripped out the weaponry and added it to their own systems.

Quentin swiveled his head turret and marched toward the secondary-neos, who waited patiently. "What is your progress so far?"

"Ten of us have died. Only four remain, but we have already killed many of the neos. Their walker-forms litter the tunnels. We have destroyed the electrafluid production laboratories, drained the stockpiles, and ruined the machinery necessary to create more. Any cymeks who survive this battle will be sorely in need of their life-support fluid before long."

Vor felt as if a weight had been lifted off his chest. "Excellent!"

"A large problem remains." Quentin turned to the secondaries. "Do you know where Dante is? He is the last Titan."

"Somewhere in the complex, but we are not certain of his location."

Quentin said to Vor, "We have to find him. Destroying Dante is more necessary than you can imagine."

The *Dream Voyager* was stored and ready for takeoff. It would be so easy to escape and return to Salusa Secundus with his news, but Vor resisted taking the simple way out. "Quentin, the Army of the Jihad made a mistake two decades ago when we left one machine world intact. We didn't finish the job then, and we've paid for it ever since. I don't intend to leave our work incomplete here."

"Thank you," Quentin answered in a quiet voice through the speaker-patch. "Thank you."

DANTE HAD ALWAYS been little more than an administrator; he had run the business of overthrowing the Old Empire. Both Agamemnon and Juno were far more militarily inclined than he was. As soon as he discovered the murders of his fellow Titans, he understood he was in terrible trouble. He did not know exactly how Juno and Agamemnon had been killed, but he did not wish to stay behind and fight such an effective enemy.

Hessra was not the strongest base in the new Titan empire. Many more neos and their enslaved populations had been taken from the occupied worlds of Richese, Bela Tegeuse, and others; the defenses were more extensive on those planets. Agamemnon had never worried much about losing control of Hessra.

Now, while the loyal neos continued to battle the suicidal secondary-neos, Dante emerged from the tall, arched doors of the citadel and scuttled across the icy landscape to the Titans' waiting battleships. Dante had used these same vessels on his test run that had demonstrated the fatal interaction between lasers and Holtzman shields. He hurried across the windswept ground and, reaching one of the robotic craft, aligned sockets and adjusted the mechanical systems so that his preservation canister detached from its walker-form and was installed in the vessel to act as the brain of the ship. He had to get away.

Of the original Twenty Titans, Dante was now the sole survivor. After his thoughtrodes were automatically connected to the command systems, he powered up the engines. Now he could fly away from this frozen planetoid, saving himself.

Dante was not a coward, but a pragmatist. The rebellion here was causing too much damage, and he intended to return with an overwhelming force from Richese or one of the other newly conquered cymek worlds. He and his reinforcements would easily destroy the remaining rabble, and they could move on.

His ship rose into the empty sky, and Dante felt free and safe.

COMFORTABLE BEHIND THE controls, Vor activated the *Dream Voyager's* systems, preparing to launch. His scanners were operational, ready to lock on to their target, as soon as he discovered Dante's whereabouts. The secondary-neos reported that they had seen the Titan's walker-form out on the glacier, mounting itself into one of the waiting cymek battleships.

Quentin scuttled forward in his massive mechanical body. His speaker-patch was amplified, and his words boomed. "It is paramount that he not get away! Supreme Bashar, can you depart soon? Can you head him off?"

"The *Dream Voyager* is fast, but doesn't have much in the way of weaponry. It could be enough to keep him busy, though. Do you have something else—"

"Yes." Quentin scuttled backward on multiple legs. "Just slow him down. I will come after you as soon as I can. And then Dante won't be able to run. It is imperative that we not allow him to escape."

Vor understood the primero's need for vengeance. He worked the familiar controls that Seurat had long ago taught him to use, and the *Dream Voyager* shot out of the landing bay, following the trail of the Titan ship.

QUENTIN MARCHED THROUGH the underground chambers to where another enormous vessel was stored. He had seen the Titan general fly the craft more than once, and Juno had been delighted to show it off to him as a demonstration of the formidable cymek advantages over a weak human being. Now Quentin could use it to a much more satisfying purpose.

Agamemnon's personal battleship.

THE *DREAM VOYAGER* raced up into the starry, ever-twilit sky. Ahead of him, Dante's warship accelerated out of the system.

When the last surviving Titan saw that only one small vessel pursued him, a mere update ship, he turned his battle vessel and came back. He had warned Agamemnon not to trust his human son, and his suspicions had been accurate. "Vorian Atreides." The name was spoken flatly, as if the Titan was not surprised at all. "You are responsible for this mayhem?"

"I can't take all the credit. I am only one man. The Titans' history built up a debt that one man can't possibly make up for."

"You know that I can easily destroy your ship," Dante said, as if a threat was all he needed. "The *Dream Voyager* was never designed to withstand an attack by a cymek warship."

"Maybe, but I'm a lot more maneuverable." He peppered Dante's hull with a volley of small projectiles, then changed course in a radical backward loop to bypass the giant Titan's cumbersome retaliatory shots.

Vor swept in from behind and harried the cymek warship by launching four explosives that damaged one of Dante's maneuvering engines. The Titan turned and opened fire again, and this time his blasts grazed the *Dream Voyager*'s armored belly.

Vor tumbled in a wild spin, accelerating blindly until he regained control and could fly straight again. He turned around, intentionally taunting the remaining Titan over the comline, hoping to delay him as Quentin had asked. Dante launched another shot that exploded across his bow.

Just then a massive, nightmarish vessel—like a demonic pterodactyl—hurtled directly toward Dante's ship. The angular flying colossus swooped down out of nowhere, opening fire with explosives that sent the Titan's craft reeling.

Quentin's voice came over Vor's communications systems, speaking in the special coded battle language developed by the Army of the Jihad. "I must tell you why it is essential to take Dante out. When General Agamemnon created his armies of neo-cymeks, he was afraid they might show disloyalty, so he installed a kill switch in their preservation canisters. If at any moment he suspected treachery, he could trigger an individual death.

"As a final insurance Agamemnon, Juno, and Dante established a deadman network. As a fail-safe, there is a signal encoded in each of the three Titans' brain canisters. At least one of the three Titans must return regularly within transmitting range of the neo-cymeks, or else those neos shut down permanently. Life-support mechanisms gradually fail, and they all die."

Vor couldn't believe what he was hearing. "You mean if we destroy Dante, we'll wipe out the entire enemy force, in a single blow?"

"Essentially, though there may be some delay factor. The local neos will collapse from the immediate signal cutoff when the last Titan dies. Agamemnon was quite paranoid."

"I know."

"The other cymeks on distant outposts will break down and die in a year or so, when they do not receive a verification signal at the appointed time. That's why Dante is so important."

Vor grinned, but only for a moment, until he followed the thought to its only possible conclusion. "If we destroy Dante here, then you'll die, too, Quentin. It's an immediate consequence."

"You have seen me, Supreme Bashar. You know what I am. I have no intention of letting anyone in the League see me like this. Not Faykan, not . . . Abulurd. I don't want to go back."

"But what shall I tell Abulurd for you? He has to understand—"

"You'll know what to say to him, Supreme Bashar. You've always been better at it than I. Let me do this last thing."

Vor raised his voice. "No. We can find another way. We'll capture Dante. We'll—"

"Remember me, Supreme Bashar. I never chose to be a cymek, and every moment I looked for ways to kill them. At last I know what to do."

The huge nightmarish craft designed for Agamemnon arced around and headed toward Dante. The last Titan accelerated, trying to pick up speed and escape the powerful cymek ship.

But one of Dante's engines was damaged, and Agamemnon's craft was far superior. As he closed the distance, Quentin launched projectile after projectile, pummeling the fleeing Titan ship.

Even as he approached his target, Quentin did not slow. His engines went beyond full power, hurling the enormous cymek vessel like a hot hammer—until finally, just as Dante's hull buckled from the last round of explosives, Agamemnon's battleship slammed into it, still accelerating.

The light was blinding. Both vessels erupted in an expanding cloud of flames.

Helplessly, Vor watched the final moments. He felt a weight of great sadness in his chest for the loss of brave Quentin Butler . . . and a growing warmth of triumph to know that the last of the cruel Titans, and indeed all of the cymeks, had finally been vanquished.

Evil does not limit itself to either machines or humans. Demons can be found among both.

— SWORDMASTER ISTIAN GOSS

W hen Istian and the sensei mek arrived in the Salusan system and descended to Zimia Spaceport, the swordmaster could see how much had changed. He had been to the impressive metropolis only once, after completing his training on Ginaz and before being transferred to duties on the outlying League Worlds. Salusa Secundus had always been a place of grandeur, where towering buildings showcased the League's best architecture and sculpture for all to see the superiority of the human creative soul over the logic of thinking machines.

Now, though, the spaceport was in chaos. As his vessel swooped in for a landing—though he had received no response to his repeated requests for clearance—Istian saw that some of the streets were on fire, buildings smoking. Crowds surged up and down boulevards. With cold sickness in the pit of his stomach, he thought back to similar scenes he had witnessed on Honru and Ix.

Finally a familiar yet unexpected voice came over his ship's comline. "I see you have arrived on schedule, Istian. Always perfectly predictable. Is Chirox with you?"

"Nar Trig! So good to hear your voice."

"We are prepared to meet you at the spaceport."

Settling down now on an empty pad, Istian asked, "Will the Viceroy be sending an escort to meet us? What's going on in Zimia?" Chirox remained silent as the swordmaster asked his questions.

"The Viceroy is otherwise occupied. This is a busy and glorious day for the Cult of Serena. Your arrival will be one of our crowning achievements."

Istian felt uneasy, but he could not say why. The hatch opened, and he stepped out beside the combat mek. As soon as he saw the crowd waiting for them, heard the angry shouts, and saw the waving banners of Saint Serena and her child Manion, he understood that Chirox would be receiving no commendation from the Viceroy.

"We've been tricked," he said. "We may have to fight!"

The sensei mek loomed tall and powerful, his bright optic threads drinking in new details. He turned his head. "I do not wish to fight innocent civilians."

"If they rush us, we may have no choice. I suspect the message from the Viceroy was faked, just to lure us here." Istian had brought his pulse-sword along with his favorite fighting dagger for shield training. He had intended them as ceremonial adornments; now they were his only weapons. "This is very bad, Chirox."

The sensei mek waited. "We will plan our response according to the needs of the moment."

The leader of the mob strode forward—a broad-shouldered, arrogant man whose dark hair was shot with lines of gray. His ruggedly familiar features had been roughened over the years. A long burn made the left side of his face appear smooth and waxy. "I feared I would find you at the demon machine's side," Nar Trig said. "Join us, Istian, and your soul can be saved."

"My soul is my own business. Is this the reception committee you have gathered to welcome Chirox as a hero? He has trained thousands of swordmasters, and collectively they have killed a hundred times that many thinking machines."

"He is a machine himself!" cried one of the Cultists behind Trig. "Rayna Butler says we must eliminate all sophisticated machinery. Chirox is one of the last. He must be destroyed."

"He has done nothing to deserve this." Istian slowly drew his pulse-sword and combat dagger, waiting bravely in front of the sensei mek. "Are you at such a loss for enemies that you must create new ones for yourselves? It is ridiculous."

"Chirox trained me, too." Trig raised his voice so that all the gathered fanatics could hear. "I know his tricks, and I have surpassed his skills. I have become enlightened—I *know* humans are superior to soulless machines. I have a fundamental advantage over any demon robot. I challenge you to combat, Chirox. Fight me! I could easily let this mob tear you to pieces, but I would rather destroy you in a fair duel."

"Nar, stop this," Istian said.

Chirox stepped forward, pushing past Istian. "I have been challenged to battle, and I must accept." The robot's voice was flat. He extruded his full set of combat arms.

Trig carried two long pulse-swords, one in each hand. He raised the weapons high, and the mob cheered. "I will prove the superiority of humans. You taught me once, a long time ago, Chirox. But all I owe you now is your destruction."

"Obviously no one taught you honor or gratitude," Istian said, remaining close to the mek's side. He raised his weapons, not caring if the mob saw him defend the machine. What else could he do?

A sneer twisted Trig's waxy, scarred face. "Is that the voice of my friend Istian, or a pronouncement from your internal spirit of Jool Noret?"

"Does it make any difference?"

"I suppose not."

Chirox stepped forward to face his former student. Trig clenched his two pulse-swords. Istian watched, but could not stop the useless duel. The opponents remained motionless, assessing each other.

Behind them, the mob just wanted to see the combat mek smashed and torn asunder. After the primary target of their anger was eliminated, then the zealots' bloodlust might turn to others—like Istian Goss.

With an inarticulate yell that might have been a call for divine help, or a voicing of his lifelong anger, Nar Trig threw himself upon Chirox. In a metallic blur, the sensei mek countered and parried, his multiple arms moving like a twitching spider's. He had fought thousands of duels with his students on Ginaz, but only once in over a century of service to humans had he actually killed—the accidental death of Jool Noret's father.

"I should not fight you," the robot said.

Trig's pair of pulse-swords struck and ricocheted and drove in again, but Chirox deflected them repeatedly, catching the stun-burst tips on his insulated mechanical arms. The fury on Trig's scarred face was plain, and he attacked with great enthusiasm, turning his frustration into strength.

Istian gripped his dagger. "Nar, stop this—or I will fight you myself!"

The other warrior turned for just an instant in surprise. "No you won't—"

Following his programming, the combat mek saw an opening and drove in, slashing with bladed arms. He drew a fine line of blood across Trig's chest. The man roared and hurled himself back at his mek opponent.

"I'll deal with you later, Istian—machine lover!"

The mob growled, stirring menacingly, but they seemed hypnotized by the combat.

After all these years, Trig must have convinced himself of his superiority as a fighter. He had expected to make short work of the combat mek. But Chirox was far better than an average fighting robot. Over many generations, he had honed his skills and perfected his programming against the best human fighters on Ginaz. In his heart, Istian did not want to see his long-lost sparring partner hurt, nor did he want to see the sensei mek—to whom he owed so much—damaged or destroyed.

As the duel continued, Chirox moved with an odd hesitation, driving his bladed arms toward Trig. But at the last moment, the mek slowed, giving Trig time to dodge out of the way. This was a technique used in fighting against a shielded opponent, but Trig did not wear such protection, and Chirox knew it. Istian wondered why the sensei mek was fighting this way, and decided that Chirox didn't want to hurt his former student.

The mek spoke as he fought, distracting Trig while diverting none of his own attention from the intense combat. "I recall another duel like this, long ago when I tested myself against Zon Noret. He commanded me to use my greatest skills, to fight with all my intensity. He believed he could best me."

Trig was clearly listening, but he hammered at his opponent with more vigor than ever. The mob cheered as one of the man's pulse-swords deactivated Chirox's lower blade appendage. The metal arm dangled lifelessly. Istian knew the combat mek could reset himself within the space of a minute, but if Trig fought properly, he would keep deactivating the robot's defenses faster than Chirox could recover.

Istian wanted to intervene, to do something to stop this senseless exhibition, but things had gone too far. The Serena Cultists cheered. Some began pelting the mek with rocks, one of which struck the side of Istian's ship; another clanged off the metal torso of the combat mek. But Chirox kept fighting and talking.

"Zon Noret's overconfidence led to his death. I did not mean to kill him, but he had disabled the fail-safes, so I could not stop myself. With Zon Noret's death, Ginaz lost a talented swordmaster who may well have conquered many other enemy machines. It was a waste of good resources."

"I will kill you, demon!" Trig dove in again, his pulse-swords crashing against metal. "You are no match for me."

"Wait!" Istian shouted. A rock thrown by one of the Cultists struck him on the forehead, stunning him more with surprise than pain. Blood from the cut began to spill down his brow.

Chirox did not change his stance as he defended himself. "You have forced me into a duel that is not of my choosing. I have requested that you stop, but you have refused. You leave me with no choice, Nar Trig. This"—he moved his articulated arms in a frantic blur, distracting Trig as he tried to keep up, thrusting and parrying— "this is *intentional.*"

With a concerted sweep of two long-bladed arms, instead of trying to stab his attacker or parry his weapons, Chirox swung a powerful lateral blow that struck Trig's thick neck and instantly decapitated him. The head spun up into the air and thudded to the ground. Blood spurted, and the fanatical swordmaster twitched, his headless form still upright and trying to respond to nerve impulses. Both pulse-swords clattered to the ground from lifeless hands. Then the body slumped to its knees and fell forward, gouting arterial blood.

A shudder ran down Istian's spine. Trig had chosen his own path. Istian could have done nothing to prevent this. His thoughts spun as he examined his own actions.

The Cultists' long indrawn breath created a vacuum of silence. Istian felt his heart sink as he took in the expressions on their faces.

Chirox stood motionless, as if he had calculated that the ordeal was now over. He had defeated his antagonist, and with the completion of his victory he wanted to leave.

"It was a fair challenge," Istian shouted to the mob. "Nar Trig was defeated by his opponent." He didn't think fairness and honor were foremost in the minds of the Cultists.

"That thinking machine murdered our swordmaster!"

"It killed a human!"

"All machines must be destroyed."

"He is not our enemy," Istian cried, wiping blood out of his eyes.

"A thinking machine cannot change what it is! Death to the machines!"

Chirox straightened his metallic torso and retracted his blood-spattered blade arms. With weapons drawn, Istian took his place beside the mek. "Chirox did nothing wrong! He has trained countless swordmasters, and he has shown us how to fight the thinking machines. He is our ally, not our enemy."

"All machines are our enemies," shouted someone.

"Then you need to consider your enemies more carefully. This training mek is an ally of humanity. He has proved that machines can serve our cause as well as warriors."

But the furious outcry from the incensed Cultists suggested otherwise. The people were armed with only crude weapons: cudgels and clubs, makeshift swords or knives. All through Zimia the large-scale uprising continued as fanatics set fires and destroyed everything technological they could get their hands on, even innocuous and useful devices.

"You may claim the whole city," Istian said, "but you cannot have Chirox."

"Death to machines!" someone from the mob repeated, and Istian stepped in front of the combat mek, holding out his weapons.

"He is on our side. If you are too blind to see it, then you are not worthy members of the human race. I will drive off anyone who tries to damage him. I'll kill you if I have to."

Someone laughed. "Do you expect to stand against us—one swordmaster and a robot?"

"Honor guides my actions."

Chirox spoke again. "Do not sacrifice yourself for me, Istian Goss. I forbid it."

"That isn't open for discussion." Istian raised his pulse-sword. It was not a terribly useful weapon against a mob, but he would use it to its best effect, nevertheless. "It's what . . . what Jool Noret would have done."

The Cultists pushed to get closer to Trig's decapitated body, feeling their own anger and thirst for vengeance. Though their crude weapons might not be effective against Chirox, their sheer overwhelming numbers would be sufficient. Istian could see this was going to be a bloodbath.

"I will defend you," he said firmly, casting a glance over his shoulder at the sensei mek. Shielding Chirox, he turned a brave face toward the angry crowd.

"No. You will die. Many of these people will die," the mek said. "I cannot allow that."

His back to the robot, Istian confronted the oncoming throng. Behind him, Chirox stood erect with all of his weapons extended. "No, this must stop—stop—"

Torn between watching his frenzied attackers and figuring out what the sensei mek intended to do, Istian glanced back to see that the multi-armed combat mek had frozen in place. Chirox bowed down in front of the blood-spattered, headless corpse of Nar Trig. His arms were extended, each one tipped with a flowmetal-formed weapon, but they hung useless, not moving.

"I will not allow . . . you to die . . . defending me," said the sensei mek, his voice slurred and slowing. "It does not . . . match the proper . . . criteria." The combat machine's voice faded and stopped, swallowed up in a cold silence, and the bright optic threads in Chirox's face grew dull and lifeless.

Istian turned to stare at the motionless robot. After so many years of training swordmasters, learning the ways of the human race, the combat mek had made this difficult decision in his own mind—a *freewill* choice that he had not been programmed to make.

Stricken with grief and confusion, Istian tried to make sense of the tragedy. In his hands, his weapons felt like cold, useless sticks. The combat mek was as dead as Nar Trig. Each had sacrificed himself for his ideals.

Perhaps, Istian thought, *we have much to learn from the machines as well.*

"We've lost two great fighters today—for no fathomable reason," Istian said, his voice quiet. He was not sure that any of the fanatics could hear him.

The shock of the events had defused the destructive frenzy of the crowd. They seemed deflated and frustrated at having had their scapegoat stolen from them.

When two men strode forward, clearly intent on smashing the already deactivated hulk of Chirox, Istian guarded the motionless combat robot with his pulse-sword in one hand, ceremonial dagger in the other, and murder in his eyes. The angriest members of the mob glared at him, hesitated, and finally backed down, not wanting to pit themselves against a veteran swordmaster.

Rayna's revolt continued through the city, and gradually the fanatics dispersed to find other targets.

For many hours, Istian Goss remained steadfast beside the shutdown form of Chirox and the headless corpse of his former friend Trig. Though years ago atomics had wiped out all strongholds of the thinking machines, Istian could see that in the human heart the Jihad was still far from over.

*Do not be deceived. Until the last vestiges of Omnius are obliter-
ated, our war against the thinking machines will never end—and
neither will my resolve.*
—SUPREME BASHAR VORIAN ATREIDES

After the death of Quentin Butler and the violent elimination of
Dante, Vor sat alone, stunned and reeling, in the *Dream Voyager*.
He let the ship drift as he sifted through the mountain of suffocating
memories.

He admired Quentin enough not to grieve for the supreme sacrifice he
had made. Once his human body had been stripped from him, what more
could a great military leader have hoped for? At least Vor had tried to
make the primero understand his son Abulurd in the end. Now he would
deliver a message to the younger man and tell him what his father had
accomplished.

Vor took the ship back to Hessra, landing on the icy plains at the base
of the dark, half-buried Cogitor fortress where the last Titans had established their outpost. He stepped out of the *Dream Voyager* and stood alone,
the only human on a whole planet. Even wearing his flight suit, Vor felt
the penetrating cold. The thin arctic breezes whistled around him, and the
starry sky overhead bathed the rugged landscape in a milky glow.

As he approached the Cogitors' former citadel, he saw that Quentin's
explanation of Agamemnon's "dead man" switch had been correct. On
his walk across the ice, Vor encountered seven scattered forms, mechanical bodies that had collapsed. They looked like dead insects, metal arms
and grappling legs extended at odd angles, some still twitching. The neos'

canisters were a murky red, electrafluid mixed with exploded brain tissue and hemorrhages.

One of the neo walkers, still clinging to a shred of life, emerged from the dark mouth of the doorway underneath the citadel. It swayed and staggered, walking in circles because only one set of legs functioned properly. Vor stood silently, watching the machine lurch forward and then collapse.

"If I knew how to prolong your agony, I would," he said, then walked past the still-shuddering hulk and into the citadel.

Two of the tortured secondary-neos clattered forward, disoriented. Vor marveled at their determination to live. He had no great love for Cogitors, whose naïveté and clumsy politics had incited Serena to martyr herself, but he felt a twinge of sympathy for the poor human secondaries that the cymeks had forced into slavery. "You still survive."

"Barely," one of the monk neos answered. The tones coming from the speakerpatch were distorted. "It seems . . . we secondaries . . . have developed a higher threshold . . . of pain."

He stayed with them for hours, until they both died.

A similar die-off would happen on the handful of other cymek worlds over the course of the next year, when the surviving neos failed to receive the necessary check signal required to keep them alive. Vor wondered if some of them would learn what had happened to the Titans and scramble to find a way to save themselves. He doubted they would succeed—General Agamemnon was quite thorough about such things.

Vor shook his head sadly. "There is no end to the delusions we will follow. . . ."

After seeing what he needed to see, knowing the cymeks would all die, he walked back toward the *Dream Voyager*. He felt cast adrift, like a lost fishing boat on a Caladan sea. The Jihad had been his life and his focus for so long. What was he without it? So much had already been lost, so many billions of lives. And now he had killed his own father. *Patricide.* A terrible word for a horrendous deed. He felt sickened to think that it had been necessary . . . that any of it had been necessary.

Vorian Atreides had left a wake of blood across the ocean of his life, but every tragedy and victory had been necessary for the sake of humanity. He had been instrumental in the downfall of the thinking machines—from the Great Purge of the Synchronized Worlds to the destruction of the Titans.

But it wasn't over. One last target remained.

ON HIS RETURN to Salusa Secundus, Vor transmitted no celebratory messages. He didn't need any accolades or attention, though he intended to make certain Quentin Butler was honored as a genuine hero.

Although he had left the Army of Humanity and departed from the League more than two months before, he easily arranged a meeting with the Viceroy as soon as he returned home. No one but Abulurd had ever known the actual reason Vor had resigned his commission, but now they would learn he had gone off to hunt the cymeks. And he had succeeded. . . .

Passing through Zimia, Vor witnessed the aftermath of the recent riots—windows boarded up, ornamental trees on the boulevards blackened and twisted from fire, smoke staining the alabaster walls of governmental buildings. The fires had been put out and the Cultist mobs dispersed, but the damage remained. As he approached the Hall of Parliament, he looked around in sick amazement.

I did not fight the only battle.

Inside, distracted with picking up the pieces, reassuring the shaken populace, and making enough concessions to Rayna's growing movement to keep them somewhat under control, Viceroy Faykan Butler paused in between frantic committee meetings to see the Supreme Bashar. "I need to tell you about your father," Vor said.

Faykan was astonished and pleased to hear of the death of the Titans, then saddened to learn about his father's tragic yet heroic end. "For years, I was very close to him," he said, sitting formal and rigid at his desk. As a politician he had learned to control his expressions. "I confess that when I discovered he was alive but converted into a cymek, I wished he were dead—so did he, apparently."

He straightened a set of documents waiting for his signature. "Now after hearing this . . . well, I suppose it's the best we could hope for. He lived and died by the same credo—that Butlers are servants unto no one." He drew a deep breath that trembled at just the last moment. Faykan spoke louder, as if convincing himself. "My father would not let himself become a slave to the cymeks."

The Viceroy cleared his throat and seemed to put on his political mask again. "Thank you for your service, Supreme Bashar Atreides. We will make an official announcement with this great news about the end of the Titans. I am pleased to formally restore you to your rank in the Army of Humanity."

THOUGH ABULURD HAD not been close to his father, the younger man seemed far more affected by the news of Quentin's death. He was a sensitive person and felt pain and tragedy with his whole heart, whereas Faykan had learned how to wall himself off from any unwanted responses to the horrors of war or the unpleasantness of life.

Abulurd smiled, and for a moment the grief washed from his face. "I grieve for my father, sir . . . but in truth, I was much more concerned about the risks you were taking and the ordeals you went through."

Vor swallowed at the lump that formed in his throat, to think of the odd twist of circumstances: This talented officer was the son of Quentin, who had not appreciated him . . . while Vor's own sons on Caladan wanted little to do with *him*. Looking at Abulurd, he saw his real reason for remaining part of the League. "Your father was always a hero. History will remember him properly. I'll make sure of that."

Abulurd hesitated, bowed his head. "If only Xavier Harkonnen had the same opportunity. I fear the task force has made no progress in clearing his name. Now many of the historical records are destroyed—how will we ever prove the truth? Or will that make the job easier?"

Vor straightened. "It is long past time that we removed the unfair stain from the Harkonnen name. Especially now that I've defeated the Titans, maybe I can push a resolution through."

Abulurd looked weak with relief.

"First, though," Vor said in a steely voice, "there is one last thing I intend to accomplish. One large strategic blot remains on our own record. Given sufficient resolve and determination, I believe the Army of Humanity can succeed, where they have not in the past. If I don't seize the opportunity now, I fear the League will never do it."

Abulurd blinked at him. "What do you intend to do, Supreme Bashar?"

"I plan to go back to Corrin—and destroy it completely."

Abulurd jerked his head back in surprise. "But you know how many defensive ships the robots have put in orbit. We'll never break through."

"We *can* break through—if we bring a big enough hammer and swing it with sufficient force. The sacrifice may be high, both in ships and in human lives. But since Omnius is trapped on Corrin, this may be our last chance. If the thinking machines ever escape and proliferate, we'll be back where we were a century ago. We cannot allow that to happen."

Abulurd squirmed. "How will you ever convince the Parliament? Are soldiers still willing to fight and die against such an uncertain threat? No one seems to see it as a clear enough danger, even after the piranha mites. I think they've lost their resolve."

"I have listened to their excuses for years, but now I will make them see," Vor said. "I have the Titans and cymeks, and I understand the danger from the thinking machines better than any man alive. I won't rest until humanity is safe from them. An all-out attack is our best strategy. I have to finish the job. Don't underestimate my powers of persuasion in something that matters so much to me."

The two walked together for a long time in contemplative silence before Abulurd said, "When did you become such a hawk, Supreme Bashar? You used to rely on tricks and deception, but now your tactic is a full-fledged military strike? It reminds me . . ."

"Reminds you of Xavier?" Vor smiled. "Though we might have disagreed when he was alive, my old friend proved himself right. Yes, I have become a hawk." He clapped his hand on Abulurd's shoulder. "From now on the hawk will be my symbol. It will always remind me of my duty."

Each society has its list of cardinal sins. Sometimes these sins are determined by condemning acts that tend to destroy the fabric of social organization; sometimes sins are defined by leaders seeking to perpetuate their own positions.

—NAAM THE ELDER,
First Official Historian to the Jihad

As if forgetting their recent violent demonstrations, the people went wild celebrating the return of Vorian Atreides. The cymeks were dead, the last of the Titans destroyed, another threat to humanity removed from the universe.

When his armored limocar proceeded along the wreckage-strewn boulevards of Zimia, throngs of cheering people threw orange marigolds at him. Many carried placards bearing his stylized gallant image and the words "Hero of the Jihad, Defender of Humanity, Conqueror of Titans."

Rayna Butler had rejoiced in the "righteous execution" of the last machines with human minds, happily adopting Vor—"a true friend and follower of Serena herself!"—as part of her movement.

The Supreme Bashar had never felt comfortable with the sort of attention he was receiving now. Regardless of his rank, he had always done his job for Serena and her Jihad, with no thought of personal aggrandisement or advancement. He wanted to destroy the enemy, nothing more.

Looking at the throng that had gathered for his celebration, Vor didn't think he had seen such adulation or jubilant relief since the end of the Great Purge. Perhaps now, in the time when he needed it most, he could turn this energy to his benefit. He would use any tool necessary to achieve the final victory.

These Cultists, who found even simple household machinery threatening, could not possibly stomach the thought of allowing Omnius to remain a constant threat to humanity, safe in his stronghold on Corrin. To them, it was the lair of all demons.

Now, as his vehicle neared the Hall of Parliament, Vorian saw a larger crowd in the memorial plaza. Some of them carried cloth signs on mobile frames, ornately bordered and lettered, while others handed out paper sheets on which a long proclamation had been printed. In wild revelry, they piled electronic devices and computerized apparatus in the center of the square and poured fuel on them to set the offending articles ablaze.

Zimia security forces stayed a safe distance from the demonstration, working to clear a path for Vor's groundcar at the base of the wide stairs leading to the Hall of Parliament. When the demonstrators saw him, they issued another loud cheer. He kept his focus forward as he exited the vehicle and climbed the steps. Vor passed through the colonnade with its Grogyptian columns and paused at the main entrance of the building, where he saw an immense cloth sign crudely nailed on the door. Discarded leaflets fluttered along the ground, bearing the same printed message.

Scanning it, he guessed Rayna must have written it herself, judging from the vehement but unsophisticated tone. Her signature was at the bottom.

THE MANIFESTO OF RAYNA BUTLER

Citizens of free humanity! Let it be proclaimed throughout the League of Nobles that there are NO benign uses for thinking machines. Though they may conceal their evil under the guise of performing work-saving tasks for their users, they are insidious at any level.

This manifesto is a blueprint by which human society can cleanse itself of the worst sins. Every League citizen shall adhere to these rules, and be bound by these punishments:

If a person knows the location of a thinking machine and does not destroy it, or report it to the Movement, the offender shall be punished by the removal of his eyes, ears, and tongue.

If a person commits the grievous sin of *using* a thinking machine, he shall be put to death.

If a person commits the even more grievous sin of *owning* a thinking machine, he shall be put to death by the most painful of means.

If a person commits the worst sin of all, *creating or manufacturing* a thinking machine, the offender, all of his employees, and all of their families shall be put to death by the most painful of means.

Anyone in doubt as to what constitutes a dangerous machine shall contact the Movement and request an Official Opinion. Once an Official Opinion has been rendered, the offending machine shall be removed from operation and destroyed immediately. Punishments will be administered as specified above.

It is preferable to manufacture products through slave labor than to trust thinking machines.

Thou shall not make a machine in the likeness of a human mind.

Stunned at the broadness of the Manifesto, and the sheer madness of it, Vor marched through the main entrance into the assembly chamber. Yes, there was still an enemy. Yes, the thinking machines still existed. But these Cultists were aiming at the wrong target.

Corrin. We must go to Corrin.

Before he was announced, Vor saw that the League representatives were already on their feet, clapping and cheering—but not for him. Viceroy Butler stood inside the speaker's dome at the center of the hall, holding a copy of the new Manifesto high in the air. Around him, the lawmakers rose in waves.

"So be it!" Faykan shouted. "The Manifesto of my exalted niece is hereby passed by acclamation, and as Viceroy I shall sign it into law. Effective tomorrow morning, this shall be the Law of the League, and all dissenters shall be hunted down and punished, along with the enemy thinking machines they harbor. There shall be no compromises! Death to thinking machines!"

Like an echo, the words passed the lips of every lawmaker like a new mantra. From just inside the chamber, at its top tier, Vor absorbed the frenzy like a cold rain. If only they had been so vehement years ago, when it had been most necessary.

"We are reshaping galactic society, setting humanity on a new course!" Faykan shouted into the din. "We humans will think for ourselves, work for ourselves, and achieve our destiny. Without thinking machines! Such technology is a crutch—it is time for us to walk for ourselves."

Recognizing Vor, some audience members began to point at him and whisper among themselves. Finally the Viceroy raised his arms in exuberant welcome. "Vorian Atreides, Supreme Bashar of the Army of Humanity! Our people already owed you an eternal debt of gratitude for many things—and now you have given us one more. The last Titans are dead! The cymek abominations no longer exist! May your name be revered for eternity as a Hero of Humanity!"

The great hall thundered with acclamation. As Vor made his way to the speaking chamber, he felt that events were snowballing around him, sweeping him along. But he had his honor, his duty, and the promises he had made to himself and the people. He could swim against this wave—or he could ride it, all the way to Corrin.

The assemblage grew quiet as he gazed slowly around, focused on some of the familiar faces, then looked to the farthest points in the hall, where Rayna's followers waved oversized, colorful banners.

"Yes, we can celebrate the demise of the cymeks," he said. "But we are not yet finished! Why do you waste your time and energy writing manifestos, smashing household appliances, and killing each other—*when Omnius himself still lives?*" That stunned the audience into gasps, then silence.

"Twenty years ago we proclaimed the Jihad over, while leaving one Synchronized World untouched. Corrin is like a primed explosive, and we must defuse it! The cancer of Omnius remains a blight on a shining future for the human race."

The people had not expected such vehemence in his voice. Clearly they thought the veteran Supreme Bashar would receive his rewards, take his bows, and let the League government continue its work. But he did not rest.

"Death to thinking machines!" someone shouted in a frenzied voice from a high balcony.

Vor's voice remained loud and stern. "We have avoided our real duty for too long. A half-won victory is no victory at all."

The Viceroy looked at him, obviously uncomfortable. "But, Supreme Bashar, you know we cannot break through Omnius's defenses. We have tried for decades."

"Then we must try harder. Accept whatever losses are necessary. Waiting has cost us billions of lives. Think of the Scourge, the piranha mites. Think of the Jihad! Knowing all we have sacrificed to come this far, only a fool would stop now!" Faykan's words hinted that the League would hesitate once again, so Vor intentionally provoked Rayna's fanatics. His voice cut like the sword of a mercenary. "Yes, death to thinking machines—but why waste time on surrogates when we can destroy the real ones? Forever."

The crowd roared, despite the uneasy looks on the faces of many representatives. Then a hush rippled through the people as a pale, ethereal young woman walked to the speaking area. Rayna Butler exuded calmness and confidence, as if she could simply step into the Hall of Parliament and interrupt the proceedings whenever she wished. She wore a new green-and-white robe emblazoned with a bloodred profile of Serena.

"The Supreme Bashar is right," she said. "We stopped the Great Purge too soon, failed to stamp out the last ember in the fire when we had the opportunity to do so. It was an expensive mistake, a mistake we should not make again."

The great hall rumbled with enthusiasm, as if the building itself had come out of a long hibernating sleep. "Death to Corrin!"

"For Saint Serena," Rayna said into the voice pickup. Her words swept through the vaulted chamber. Like a wave rippling across a sea, the call was repeated, louder and louder until it became a storm of shouts: "For Saint Serena! For the Three Martyrs!"

Vor let himself be buffeted by the crowd's fervor and enthusiasm. It had to be enough. This time, he would make certain.

Regardless of strategy, training, or prayers, God alone determines victory and defeat. To believe otherwise is hubris and folly.
                                            —Zensunni Sutra

By the time Ishmael faced his rival across the open sands, the challenge had already divided the Zensunni people.

On the day of the sandworm combat, Ishmael trudged along the line of rocks, carrying his equipment as the morning sun grew brighter. His conservative followers hurried after him, offering encouragement, volunteering to carry part of his burden, but the old man ignored them. He would do this himself, for the future of the Zensunni people and the preservation of their sacred past.

He was both pleased and surprised to discover how many of the former outlaws were dissatisfied with the civilized changes and attitudes Naib El'hiim had fostered over the past decades. Most of the other elders joined him, including Chamal, as did the direct descendants of the Poritrin refugees Ishmael had freed from slavery. Gratifying, too, were the strong young warriors anxious to find excitement and battle an enemy . . . any enemy. These young men told idealized stories of Selim Wormrider and embellished adventures of the great Zensunni warriors who had fought to survive on Arrakis. Regardless of their reasons, Ishmael was glad to see the show of support.

El'hiim, on the other hand, brought with him numerous "civilized" men and women who made frequent trips to the towns and VenKee villages. People who were willing to compromise with the offworlders, blur their culture, and sacrifice their identity . . . people who blithely trusted those who traded in human beings.

Ishmael drew a deep breath of the hot, dusty air, adjusted his nose plugs, secured the bindings and fittings of his distilling suit, and lashed his cloak tightly so that it would not get in the way of his work. He turned to the people who waited at the rocks.

From the far side of the basin, El'hiim and his supporters also watched. They knew the time was at hand.

"Wait for me if I win," Ishmael said, "and remember me if I die."

He did not hear the mutters of encouragement and denial. He focused his thoughts and stepped out onto the softer sands, climbing the long gentle slope to the highest nearby dune. This battle was his own, and regardless of the consequences, he must concern himself only with the immediacy of the duel. He selected a good position, looked at the surrounding open desert, and judged the angles of the slopes. It was a perfect spot to watch for wormsign, a place from which he could mount an onrushing monster.

He had done this many times before, but never had it been so important. He remembered how Marha had taught him the skill, which she had learned from Selim himself. Ishmael missed her very much—as he missed his first wife Ozza. Eventually he would join them. But not today.

Ishmael squatted on the crest of the dune, facing away from the hopeful observers waiting back in the rocks. After seating the pointed end of his summoning drum deep into the dune, he began to beat rhythmically, using his palms. From far across the basin, he heard the faint echoing sounds of El'hiim's drumming.

The worms would come—and the battle would be joined.

This sort of combat had been devised by Selim Wormrider to weed out discontent among his followers. Such titanic duels had occurred only four times in the past; they made for glorious stories, but terrifying reality. Regardless of the result of this day's conflict, Ishmael and El'hiim would create the stuff of legends.

After he had brought his people from Poritrin, Ishmael—by marrying Marha—had stepped uneasily into the footprints of the great Selim. But El'hiim had actively struggled to emerge from the shadow of his mythic father and venture in ill-advised directions. Neither Ishmael nor his stepson had done the job of leadership well.

Now they were at a crossroads. Would Selim's dream die entirely and the Zensunni people fade away, absorbed into the distasteful weakness of infidel civilization? Or would they rediscover their souls and backbones, take up the challenge once again, and continue the fight until they emerged victorious and *free*—no matter how many centuries it might take?

Lost in his reverie, Ishmael didn't notice the wormsign until he heard the faint shouts of the spectators far behind him. With his ancient eyes, he observed the faint ripple of motion far beneath the dunes. He pounded on the drum seven more times—a holy number—and prepared himself, gathering his ropes and equipment. The worm shot toward him.

Far away, on the opposite side of the basin, he saw another commotion of tiny figures moving, and the appearance of a second sandworm. Shai-Hulud had responded to their call.

Ishmael tensed, squatting. His muscles were old, stiff, and sore, but he did not doubt his skills. He could mount and control this desert creature as well as Naib El'hiim could ever do.

The sands parted with a plume of disturbed dust and the sinuous body rose up as Ishmael bounded forward. In his life, he had called many sandworms that were larger than this, but such a one was sufficient. If Buddallah had sent him a titanic monster, all would have interpreted that as a clear signal from God; now he saw that the battle would not be decided so easily. He would have to fight for what he knew was right.

Ishmael was prepared for that.

He threw his hooks and grasped the ropes, climbing up the gritty ring segments before the creature noticed its unexpected rider. He used prybars to crack open the gaps, exposing sensitive flesh that would prevent the worm from diving back beneath the abrasive sands. Selim Wormrider had developed these techniques more than a century ago. He had become the first sandworm rider with nothing more than a metal staff and a coil of rope.

Now the monster twitched and struggled, fighting against the annoying parasite, but Ishmael held on. "I do this in your memory, Selim, for the survival of our people, and the glory of Buddallah and Shai-Hulud."

When he had secured himself, lashing a rope around his waist and anchoring it to the soft flesh near the sandworm's head, he launched the beast forward, careening across the sands of the open basin to where he would face El'hiim. The scouring sands generated heat and a strong cinnamon odor as the worm surged ahead. The fires within the sandworm's gullet were stoked hotter. Its gaping mouth sparkled with the needles of its teeth.

He spotted the second worm approaching from across the great flat, a larger beast ridden by El'hiim. Ishmael clutched his ropes, wrapping them around his hands so that he could not let go. He cried out a challenge and struck a stinging jab between the segments of his creature.

The pair of worms rushed toward each other like battle monsters, racing across the dunes. The sandworms of Arrakis were extremely territorial; as soon as the worms sensed each other's presence, they let out chuffing roars of challenge, bellowing melange-smelling exhaust from their cavernous throats. The worms coiled like vermiform springs, then plunged into combat.

Ishmael held on and instinctively closed his eyes as the immense, sinuous shapes collided. The impact nearly threw him out of his harness. The giant fanged mouths struck and pounded each other. A shockwave of pain and anger sent a convulsive tremor down the length of Ishmael's mount.

On the other worm, he could see El'hiim's terrified face as the younger man clawed at his ropes, lashing himself down again and again. Very foolish. He would be helpless, doomed, if the worm should roll over. A cold lump formed in Ishmael's stomach. He did not wish to see El'hiim die. . . .

Shai-Hulud will decide.

The sandworms withdrew to gather momentum, then slashed and pummeled again. Thick, rock-encrusted ring segments tore loose in long, rubbery strips of flesh. The duel was joined, and the territorial creatures would fight in their own way. Ishmael could no longer guide his worm; it was all he could do to hold on.

Hissing and wary, the worms backed off and circled, churning the sand into a dusty vortex. Then they engaged again, slamming behemoth bodies together, tangling themselves in a knot as if trying to strangle and squeeze the other. Crystal teeth sliced armored flesh. More worm segments were ripped away and cast aside. Gelatinous ichor welled up from the gaping wounds.

After colliding repeatedly, the sandworms exhausted themselves, but not their will to fight. Ishmael's mount thrashed and rolled, and he clung to its back, fearing the worm would roll over and crush him, despite its exposed ring segments. At the last moment it righted itself and bent back, swinging forward again like a hammer against an anvil.

On his own worm, El'hiim was nearly unconscious, but had lashed himself down so many times that he could not escape even if he'd wanted to. His larger worm crashed into Ishmael's with such force that the smaller creature bucked backward. Ishmael cried out, almost losing his grip on the cables and harness, but he dug his thick boots into position, anchoring himself.

One of his ropes snapped.

As the sandworms continued to batter each other, Ishmael fell like a dust grain in a storm, unable to catch himself. Tumbling, clawing for a handhold, he struck one ring, then another. The worms paid no attention to the insignificant human. Their mouths collided. Crystal teeth broke off like tiny icicles raining down.

Ishmael continued to tumble, and finally struck the soft, churned sands. He sank in, swimming, tried to climb to the air. He coughed, then thrashed with his hands as he struggled to gain his feet.

Each time the worms rolled, grappled, and moved onward, they devastated everything around them. Ishmael began to run as fast as he could, forgetting the random stutter-step he had learned to use on the open sands. The beasts tangled again. When they thrashed back in his direction, he threw himself into a gully between dunes. The slender tail of his own worm, hot with friction exhaust, passed over the old man, sweeping sand on top of him.

Choking, Ishmael clawed again to the surface, as the worms' continuing battle took them farther away. He limped toward the shelter of the rocks. Gasping, alone, barely able to remain conscious, he stared as El'hiim's triumphant worm drove Ishmael's farther away.

He hung his head. The duel was over. . . .

VICTORIOUS, EL'HIIM RODE his exhausted creature into the sand, finished with it. Both worms were utterly played out. Ishmael hadn't seen whether his own beast had been killed, or if it had simply slunk away, burying itself deep.

As Ishmael collapsed, panting and trembling, his own people came toward him, but he did not want to speak with them. Not now. He shook his dust-caked head, turned away. His heart still pounded and the breath was hot in his chest, but the realization was obvious. Though he had survived, he was not glad at all.

He had lost the challenge, and the future for the Free Men of Arrakis.

The Vengeance Fleet prepared to leave Salusa Secundus, bound for Corrin. The ships were crewed by veterans of the Jihad, regular soldiers in the Army of Humanity, and fiery members of the Cult of Serena.

Fast spacefolder scouts raced to the watchdog fleet that had maintained its position around the last Synchronized World, informing them that the immense battle group was coming. One final battle, and then their vigil could end.

The thinking machines knew nothing about their imminent destruction.

Forced to attend the elaborate send-off ceremony when he could have been attending to more important details, Vorian Atreides remained at attention on the spaceport tarmac, watching the last ships being loaded. The League had become addicted to pomp and fanfare.

He turned as Viceroy Butler approached, carrying a small blue box draped in golden ribbons. The Viceroy wore his formal robe of office and a small but noticeable badge that signified his connection with the Cult of Serena. Vor couldn't believe the son of Quentin Butler truly accepted the insistent antitechnology message promulgated by his niece and her Manifesto, but Rayna's movement had achieved such power that the Viceroy could see which direction the political winds were blowing.

Faykan still had not permitted the appointment of a new Grand Patriarch, now claiming that the offensive against Omnius should take priority. Vor suspected that the man had another agenda, and was just stalling.

Pallid Rayna Butler sat at the front of the reviewing stand, her eyes intent. Sincere, well wishers and bright-eyed fanatics thronged the tarmac, carrying white banners emblazoned with the bloodred silhouette of Serena Butler. The crowd cheered, and shouted Vor's name along with curses directed at Omnius.

Like a man climbing a mountain, Vor fixed his attention on the single point ahead, the summit, the goal of destroying the last evermind. Though he didn't like what the Cultists stood for, he would take advantage of every fighter, every resource. All that he had accomplished over a century of the Jihad would culminate in this last battle, and the thinking machines would never again be a threat to the human race. But from what he saw of the restless and angry crowd of Rayna's followers, he had no doubt they would continue to find enemies and scapegoats to keep their adrenaline flowing.

His flagship ballista, the LS *Serena Victory* that he had flown during the Great Purge, towered off to one side of the landing field, along with several other key ships. Most of the main war vessels waited in orbit.

Through it all, as busy as he was, Vor had not forgotten his recent promise to Abulurd, that he would work to restore the good name of Xavier Harkonnen as soon as they returned.

The honor guard of the Army of Humanity performed an extravagant display for the crowd. Following their traditional lockstep maneuvers, the honor guard formed a firing squad line and pointed loud projectile rifles at facsimile thinking machines chained to posts. The robot simulacra blinked their sensors, as if pleading for their lives. One by one, the mock robots were destroyed to wild cheers, leaving little more than sparks and smoke. The dramatic staged event was transmitted all over Salusa Secundus and stored for delivery to other League Worlds, where large crowds could also participate in the festivities.

"Just a warm-up before sending off the new Vengeance Fleet," Faykan Butler said in a voice that boomed across the spaceport. Rayna sat beside her uncle, as if her power was equivalent to the Viceroy's.

Those two are a dangerous combination, Vor thought, glancing from Faykan to Rayna. The veteran officer wished he could just go and fight the thinking machines in a direct battle, but it wasn't going to happen that way. The foolish Viceroy and his niece intended to accompany the fleet in their own diplomatic spacecraft, which would only complicate the critical battle. Now he not only had to worry about the thinking machines, he was also concerned about the Butlers taking some ill-advised action in the thick of battle.

Some of the Cultists wanted to use the Holtzman engines to launch the Vengeance Fleet immediately to Corrin. But even Vor's impatience and determination had not rendered him foolhardy enough to risk losing a tenth of his force in the jump. Norma Cenva, always working on the problem, claimed to have discovered a safe method of navigating the ships, but apparently only *she* could do it. One vessel at a time.

It was not good enough. For twenty years, the watchdog fleet had kept Omnius imprisoned at Corrin. The last thinking machines would have no reason to think the situation was about to change. Vor would contain his own anger and impatience. Just a month more, and it would all be over. . . .

Now, as the spectacular show ended with a flourish, Faykan peeled back the ribbons and opened the blue box, extending it to Vor, who saw sparkling golden insignia inside the container and suppressed a sigh. Another new military bauble to wear.

With clean, manicured fingers, the Viceroy removed the new insignia and proudly handed it to his Supreme Bashar. Faykan's voice echoed from speakers around the tarmac. "Vorian Atreides, in honor of our new military mission to Corrin, I hereby grant you another title: Champion of Serena, a man who represents the interests of the League of Nobles, the Cult of Serena, and all of free humanity!"

The crowd cheered, as if the label made any difference. "Thank you, Viceroy." Vor maintained a cool expression. "Now, enough of these frivolous ceremonies. It is time for our ships to depart. Omnius is waiting." He tucked the insignia into an inside pocket, out of view.

The Viceroy raised his arms high. "To Corrin! To Victory!"

"To Corrin," Rayna said.

All of Rayna's followers stood from the reviewing stands like a flock of birds preparing to take wing. They echoed her shout with a roar. "To Corrin!"

Vor couldn't wait to get on with it.

HIS FLAGSHIP LIFTED off first, followed by the other ceremonial ships, joining the mass of military equipment and personnel already assembled in orbit. With his eyes hard and his expression intent, Vor surveyed the command bridge while his executive officer, Bashar Abulurd Harkonnen, looked over at him. Vor was glad to have someone cool-headed, an officer he could rely on, at his side.

"We are ready to depart, Supreme Bashar—I mean, Champion Atreides."

Vor scowled. "I prefer to use the rank I actually earned, Abulurd. Leave that 'Champion' nonsense for your brother and his glorious spectacles." He still carried his new insignia in his uniform pocket and had no intention of putting it on.

"Yes, sir. This will be the end of an era." Abulurd's eyes became somewhat misty. "And afterward, we will restore Xavier to his rightful place in history—if you will still help me?"

"You have my word. I was there at the beginning of the Jihad, and I intend to see the last detail finished. Only then can I leave the future to you and your children, Abulurd." Through the screen, Vor stared at the stars, focusing his mind on the last, far-off Synchronized World. "Order the Vengeance Fleet to set course."

This entire new generation of fighters, while eager and instilled with religious fervor, had not seen direct combat in the twenty years the thinking machines had been trapped on Corrin. Even Abulurd was starry-eyed with tales of glory, in spite of—or perhaps because of—the grievous losses his family had already sustained.

Nearby, in orbit, the diplomatic craft carried the Viceroy and Rayna Butler. Though it was outfitted with the latest technology and weapons, Faykan's ship was more for show than combat. The bulk of its crew and passengers were untrained noblemen and representatives with no battle experience, spectators who wanted to be at the Corrin battlefield without participating, so that they could tell later generations they had been there. Vor intended to ignore them entirely. He had made it abundantly clear that he was in command of this operation, not Faykan or Rayna.

For her part, young Rayna was a conundrum, a walking clash of ideologies and actions. She professed to loathe technology and went about eradicating even the most rudimentary machines, whether they had computer systems or not. Yet, despite her fervent beliefs, she grudgingly agreed to ride in spaceships, which were very advanced machines. After a moment's hesitation, she had responded, "A spaceship is a necessary evil, which I shall use to spread my messages. I am certain God and Saint Serena will grant us dispensations. Ultimately, when the time is right, when such craft are no longer of use to me, I will have them destroyed as well."

Such plans did not inspire Vorian with confidence.

Given the massive firepower of the Vengeance Fleet, along with the military vessels already stationed around Corrin, Vor was confident of victory. At this point, after so many years of service, he would hold nothing back and throw everything into this final strike. Everything.

The past two decades of the League's hesitation and ineffectiveness had clearly demonstrated that he would never get another chance such as this.

In the final analysis, the battle would not be simple. Many of these ships and crews would be lost when they faced the extraordinary defenses of the machine fleet. The upcoming engagement would be an old-fashioned brawl . . . a bloodbath.

Privately, Vor said a prayer and steeled his jaw in determination. The Vengeance Fleet launched for Corrin.

Thinking machines are not capable of comprehending the concepts of evil, ethics, or love. They see things only in terms of their own survival. Nothing else matters to them.

—SERENA BUTLER,
Priestess of the Jihad

For two decades, the standoff had remained complete. Omnius couldn't escape, and the Army of Humanity could not get closer. Wall after wall of machine forces formed a protective shell around Corrin just inside the impenetrable Holtzman scrambler net, while the watchdog fleet maintained their airtight perimeter with heavily armed battleships.

At Corrin, robot ships circling the inner fringe of the scrambler web deployed long-distance scanners to monitor the outskirts of the system. The two surviving evermind incarnations had ordered increased surveillance because, even after twenty years, SeurOm had calculated the possibility that another Omnius might have survived and could come to rescue them. Like a densely packed school of sharks, circling and circling, the machine battleships cruised along in overlapping concentric orbits.

The sides exchanged potshots, launched explosive projectiles into the opposing force's cruising ships. The League guardians responded quickly, with the precision of frequently orchestrated drills. One *hrethgir* javelin was severely damaged; two robot warships were destroyed. Then the watchdog fleet tightened their own positions, increasing the frequency of practice maneuvers, releasing more scouts. They were waiting for something.

Then, with the League's final and unexpected gambit, everything changed.

From inside the perimeter, thinking machines spotted the sudden arrival of a huge new force of ballistas and javelins. In a single maneuver, the humans had tripled the size of the force already stationed there.

Machine scouts, held at bay by the intricate satellite cage designed to destroy gelcircuitry minds, transmitted their data back to the central complex on Corrin. The numbers were alarming and indisputable. The humans intended to change the equilibrium of the situation.

After statistical analysis, the pair of surviving everminds concluded that they were faced with enough firepower to pose a serious threat to their existence. The probability of destruction was high.

Erasmus stood out in the plaza with his dutiful Gilbertus Albans, quietly listening as the two everminds discussed their options in the suddenly changed scenario. Since deposing Omnius Prime, the two divergent copies of the evermind had rarely sought the advice of the independent robot, but now they realized the severity of their situation.

"This is a very difficult predicament, my Mentat," Erasmus said quietly.

Gilbertus looked anxious. "I should be with Serena, then. She is still back at the villa."

Erasmus looked at him. "You should be with me, developing a solution to the crisis. The flawed Serena Butler clone is not likely to offer any valuable ideas." They both listened to the rapid-fire dialog between the paired everminds.

Unlike the fallen Corrin-Omnius, SeurOm and ThurrOm, mercifully, had no artistic pretensions. One of the most obvious changes the new everminds had instituted concerned the gaudily ornate Central Spire. Stripping away the pretentious decorations and attempts at artwork, they had simply downshaped the entire Spire and tucked it into a giant protected vault beneath the main plaza. On top of the vault, out in the center of the city, stood two rather utilitarian-looking pedestals, each topped by a clear, spherical covering. Here, the two everminds manifested themselves.

Previously, the thoughts of ThurrOm and SeurOm had diverged widely, growing even farther from their deposed comrade. But the arrival of the huge Vengeance Fleet had focused the two everminds on a common problem.

"According to available data, the human warships could overwhelm us now," SeurOm said. "If their weaponry follows our established models, even our guardian fleet cannot withstand a full-fledged assault from the human battleships—if they are willing to commit all their resources and sacrifice themselves."

"They are not likely to make such a sacrifice," ThurrOm countered. "It does not support the data we have compiled over twenty years."

Erasmus was compelled to speak up. "We are isolated here, and we do not know the impetus behind this change in *hrethgir* attitudes. I must assume that they are fervently devoted to yet another new incarnation of their religious insanity. Do not expect them to behave according to your accepted principles."

"Launch more battleships. Increase our defenses."

"We can create no more gelcircuitry command minds. Our resources are stripped, though our mining robots and mineral scanners are scouring the crust for additional veins of the necessary rare elements. However, we have reached our limits. Corrin is wrung dry. We have already put every available vessel into place. There are no more replacements."

ThurrOm shot back a response. "Then we must attack first in order to alter the odds. Even without replacement gelcircuitry minds, we have superior weapons."

"We have attempted that before. Our reinforcements have been depleted over time and we cannot sustain dramatic attrition. Their ships are protected by shields, which gives them a significant ability to withstand our attacks. The scrambler satellites will destroy too many of our ships. The Holtzman web is easily repaired."

Robot scouts in orbit transmitted detailed estimates of the firepower capabilities of the expanded human fleet. Erasmus accessed the scans and shared summaries with his human ward. More accurate data provided better estimates—and the situation only grew worse.

SeurOm continued. "We must be more concerned with the survival of any Omnius than with our individual preservation. A massive effort on our part will create some gaps in the scrambler net. Several machine ships could get through to escape. Each of these must be loaded with a copy of the evermind. Some simulations suggest this is a possible outcome."

"An unconvincing argument, based on minimal data," ThurrOm said. "The majority of simulations produce a different result. More importantly, which of us will become the baseline evermind?" The twin spheres were so agitated that the coded electrical impulses increased in intensity, like lightning bolts, and their electronic vocal sounds boomed across the plaza.

"We can send copies of both."

"That will do nothing to protect us here on Corrin," Erasmus said. He had to find a way to save his ward, and himself. Though ensuring the survival of the evermind should have been the priority for any thinking machine, it was not enough for Erasmus. "Humans are unpredictable, Omnius. If you form your strategy based on a straightforward numerical analysis, then you will fail. The enemy will surprise you."

"Repeated attacks sometimes expose unforeseen flaws. There is a small but nonzero probability we will succeed even against these new human reinforcements. We have no other viable option than to make the attempt."

Erasmus formed a smiling expression on his flowmetal face. "Yes we do, if one understands how the *hrethgir* think. We have a weapon that may prove effective against the Army of Humanity—one they will never expect us to use." He turned his optic threads toward his ward. "One that will infuriate them."

"Explain, Erasmus," both everminds demanded in unison.

"In my slave pens and in cities all around Corrin, we have numerous captives and test subjects. According to the latest inventory, the *hrethgir* population here approaches three million. The League may have placed a large Holtzman shield against us—but we can use *human shields*. Put them all in harm's way, guarantee that any action by the Army of Humanity will result in millions of unnecessary deaths. That will make the enemy think twice before they launch their offensive."

Gilbertus looked at him in alarm, but did not speak out. Using a calming technique out of habit, he distracted himself by focusing on other things, concentrating on practice calculations in his head.

"Such a conclusion is flawed," SeurOm said. "The humans were willing to obliterate innocent slaves during the Great Purge. Your suggestion makes no sense."

"Humans themselves often make no sense. The situation is different," Erasmus pointed out. "We will make them look their innocent victims in the face. It will give them pause."

"Precisely what alternative do you suggest?"

"We place the human slaves in orbit in cargo containers, even crowd them aboard our weaker battleships. Then we threaten to slaughter them all if the Army of Humanity makes a move against us." Erasmus tugged the fabric to remove a wrinkle from his plush robe, proud of his plan and his careful insight into human nature.

"Such a plan does not make strategic sense," ThurrOm said. "If the Army of Humanity already intends to invade Corrin, they will expect human casualties. Why should this deter them?"

Erasmus widened his grin. He turned to Gilbertus. "Explain why it will be effective, my Mentat."

The man swallowed hard, as if he didn't want to face the reality of the threat. He seemed to go into a sort of trance, diving far down inside himself to find a calm core where he could organize all his thoughts, and he emerged a moment later with his answer. "Causing collateral casualties is different from being *directly* responsible for the slaughter of millions of the very human beings they are intending to free." He paused. "The difference is perhaps too subtle for a machine to understand, but it is significant."

"I was sure my extrapolation of human nature was correct!" Erasmus beamed. "After we fill our ships with innocent humans, we inform the League commander that we will execute the hostages if they intrude beyond a clearly defined boundary. It will be a bridge they dare not cross."

"A bridge of *hrethgir*," Gilbertus muttered. "It will work with a little luck."

"Luck does not enter into our projections," ThurrOm said.

The two everminds discussed the merits of the brash strategy, flickering impulses back and forth in a dizzying blur. Finally, they reached their conclusion, and Erasmus felt thoroughly proud of himself.

"Agreed. There must be no delay. The *hrethgir* fleet is already coordinating their assault." Even as the everminds spoke, they had already transmitted orders to armies of combat meks, battleship controllers, and sentinel robots to begin the massive effort.

Gilbertus looked deeply troubled, but the robot turned to his ward. "Perhaps this is the only way some of us can live, Gilbertus."

ONLY MACHINES, WITH their unwavering efficiency and relentless diligence, could have accomplished such an impossible task.

Cargo containers were filled with throngs of people herded out of the slave pens. One after another, cumbersome and barely spaceworthy vessels lumbered up through the atmosphere to their positions in low orbit. Most of the bristling machine fleet remained locked just inside the scrambler perimeter, while some of the vessels descended to take on large loads of unwilling passengers.

Although the life-support systems on the cargo containers and laden battleships were minimally sufficient, there would not be enough food or supplies to last the millions of hostages for long. Erasmus wasn't overly concerned with their welfare. The situation might change dramatically within a few days, if the human commanders reacted according to his estimation.

In the calm and restful botanical gardens of his villa, Erasmus enjoyed the company of Gilbertus Albans, while the furious activity continued unabated. The man asked after Serena, who was nowhere to be found. The robot made his face into a reassuring smile. "You and I are best equipped to deal with this crisis, my Mentat. I require your full concentration."

Gilbertus blushed and responded with a weak grin. "You're right. Sometimes she can be very distracting."

In the day since the League Vengeance Fleet had arrived, the human ships had consolidated their forces, moved into organized attack positions. They were obviously prepared to move. Erasmus hoped the "Bridge of *Hrethgir*" would be completed soon enough to stand as an effective deterrent.

Around them, the gentle fountains made soft and soothing sounds. Flowers were in bloom, with hummingbirds flitting from blossom to blossom. Everything on Corrin seemed to be at peace, except for the looming war fleet in space. Erasmus very much enjoyed this garden.

"Will you really kill them all, Father?" Gilbertus asked, his voice quiet. "If the Army of Humanity ignores your threat and passes the boundary, will you be the one who transmits the destruct command? Or will it be Omnius?"

Though the outcome would be the same either way, the independent robot could see that the question mattered a great deal to Gilbertus. "Someone must do it, my Mentat. We are thinking machines, so the humans will know we are not bluffing. They don't believe we are capable of falsehood. If we say we will do this, then we must be prepared to follow through."

The man's face remained placid. "We did not ask for this untenable situation. I would rather . . . make *them* responsible. I don't want you to kill so many hostages, Father. Put the trigger in the League commander's hands, so that he is directly to blame for the slaughter, if he chooses to move ahead."

"How? Explain."

"We can turn the tables by making their Holtzman satellites into a line of death that *works both ways*. Key the destruct sequences in all the cargo containers to the sensors in their own scrambler net. Once the Army of Humanity passes beyond their own satellites, those sensors will transmit the destruct signal." Gilbertus seemed to be pleading. "If *they* cause the death and destruction, knowing this is the price of their actions, it will give their own commander an additional reason to hesitate."

Though Erasmus struggled to understand the difference, he was pleased at the deeper insight that Gilbertus was showing him. "I would never doubt your intuition. Very well, I will let you program the trigger systems so that the League ships themselves initiate the massacre. It will not be a direct action on my part."

The man seemed strangely relieved. "Thank you, Father."

*In warfare, there are always events that cannot be anticipated by
military plans, surprises that become the turning points of history.*
— PRIMERO XAVIER HARKONNEN

As he prepared to face the thinking machines for the last time,
Vorian Atreides considered how often he had been in similarly desperate situations during his career. For over a hundred years, his triumphs
had been legendary, but the hubris depicted in ancient Grogyptian
tragedies reminded him that a single mistake could erase everything and
leave his name on the dung heap of history.

Thus, when he arrived with the Vengeance Fleet, Vor proceeded war-
ily. Though he had brought what he hoped would be overwhelming firepower, nothing was guaranteed. With each defeat suffered at the hands of
humanity, thinking machines learned more and developed new
countermeasures to prevent the recurrence of specific failures. They
added more and more robotic ships. The history of the Jihad—and of all
previous warfare—was replete with examples of human ingenuity, of creative decisions made by military leaders to surprise and overcome opponents. However, although the machines had access to vast archives of
such information, Vor doubted Omnius fully understood the process by
which humans made such "seat of the pants" decisions.

As Supreme Bashar, and the newly anointed Champion of Serena,
Vor had developed a number of possible attack strategies and then
described them en route to the captains of every vessel in his Vengeance
Fleet.

Since the cymeks had discovered the critical vulnerability of Holtz-man shields to laser weaponry, some of Vor's officers were concerned that machine spies might also have access to the knowledge. If true, Omnius could annihilate the fully shielded fleet with a single salvo of laser weaponry. The very idea was enough to frighten many of the battleship captains. Vor, though, couldn't put much stock in the threat. The cymeks had been enemies of Corrin for a long time and were not likely to have shared their military intelligence. Also, since the evermind had been imprisoned for decades, Vor was convinced the machines would have attempted to use lasers the moment they learned of the League's vulnerability.

If he ordered the Army of Humanity ships into the fray without shields, a huge number would be destroyed outright. The Supreme Bashar considered it an unnecessary sacrifice of valuable ships and fighters. Instead, he and Abulurd decided to organize the final offensive in waves, each front line of vessels using shields while those in the rear guard would keep theirs inactive until it came time to face the enemy bombardment.

It had been an incredibly long voyage. Omnius had no way of know-ing that the powerful fleet was on the way, or that the machines' end was at hand.

Upon reaching the Corrin system, Vor met with the commanders sta-tioned on the watchdog ships. Thanks to information delivered by space-folder scouts, the guardian vessels had completed their final preparations and drills while waiting for the Vengeance Fleet to arrive using safer con-ventional spaceflight engines. Everything was ready.

From the command bridge of the old LS *Serena Victory*, Vor watched the planet wallow in the bloody light of a swollen, giant sun. After destroying the Titans and gaining the endorsement of Rayna's fanatical Cult of Serena, he had earned his chance at last. He doubted the League of Nobles would ever summon sufficient resolve again. Therefore, Omnius must be destroyed, regardless of the cost in lives. Heroes and martyrs would be made this day. The end of a long, dark era was at hand.

Meticulous and reliable as always, his executive officer, Abulurd Harkonnen, oversaw the consolidation of all ships and commanders. He asked for a full inventory of weapons, fighters, and vessels for the final offensive. Every aspect had to be perfect and ready.

Meanwhile, from his diplomatic ship on the far perimeter of the stag-ing area for the battle, Viceroy Faykan Butler made inspirational speeches. Transmitting on an open comline, Rayna led the soldiers through prayers.

Though anxious, the Army of Humanity had no need to rush. Omnius wasn't going anywhere, but the machines clearly saw their doom.

In the vicinity of the planet, within the deadly shell of the scrambler net, the captive machines went through a flurry of activity. Robotic scouts flew to and fro like maddened hornets, and battleships landed on the planet then lifted off again a few hours later. Massive numbers of ships, boxy scrap-metal containers, and oversized satellites were sent into orbit.

"What are they doing, Supreme Bashar?" Abulurd asked. "That's a lot of clutter. Is it an obstacle course? A barricade?"

"Who can comprehend the demon machines?" grumbled one of the bridge tacticians.

Heavy, unwieldy structures that looked like cargo containers were hoisted into orbit, a long and dense cluster of them, like an island of . . . supply depots? Vor shook his head. "It's an act of desperation. I just don't know what it means."

Rayna's voice continued to float as background noise across the bridge of the flagship. Vor wished he could shut down her endless lecturing, but too many of his crew had already been captivated by the self-proclaimed visionary. Her goading gave them the suicidal resolve many of them would need to see the battle of Corrin through to its necessary conclusion.

"Get me a scanner report, Abulurd," Vor said. "Let's see what we can find out. I don't like it."

WHILE ALL OF the slave pens and human villages were emptied, Gilbertus used his programming skills to add receivers to the myriad components of the Bridge of Hrethgir. The constant signals broadcast by the scrambler satellites now acted as a trip wire for the self-destruct systems installed in all the holding vessels and cargo containers enclosing the human shields. If the satellite signals were disrupted, the self-destruct cycle would activate. It was a straightforward enough task. Now the very Holtzman network that imprisoned the thinking machines was also a first-warning system and a virtual trip wire.

Gilbertus hadn't seen the Serena clone in two days, but at least his concentration had been uninterrupted. "Do not concern yourself," Erasmus said. "If we succeed in stopping the Army of Humanity, then she will be saved, as will we all."

"I have done my part, Father."

"And now I must do mine, in order to keep you safe." Even though Omnius watcheyes flitted about, the independent robot had devised special programming systems to distract them. Ever since his destruction by the Corrin-Omnius—and subsequent "resurrection"—Erasmus had distrusted the primary evermind, and the two rebellious copies seemed even more unstable. Erasmus wanted more than one plan to assure his survival—and Gilbertus's.

Inside his villa, he surreptitiously hurried the man through a narrow sensor-blocked passageway and then down a set of stairs, until they reached an electronically shielded structure that neither SeurOm nor ThurrOm knew existed. He had meant to use it as a private isolation zone if he ever decided to perform experiments that he did not want the ever-mind to observe—something Yorek Thurr had once suggested. Now, he hoped it would be a safe place to keep Gilbertus until the crisis passed.

"Remain here," he said. "I have provided adequate food supplies for a significant time. I will come back to guide you to safety when the matter is resolved."

"Why can't Serena be here?"

"It would be dangerous to move her now. The everminds would see. I suggest you use this time to practice your mental exercises."

Gilbertus looked at him with large, expressive eyes. "Do not forget about me."

"An impossibility, my son." Gilbertus hugged him, and the robot imitated a response before hurrying off. He did not want the bipartite Omnius to grow suspicious.

Now that Gilbertus Albans was safe, he had other plans to implement. He went to find the Tlulaxa researcher Rekur Van.

For some men, hesitation is in their nature. Determination is in mine.

—SUPREME BASHAR VORIAN ATREIDES,
transmission to Vengeance Fleet

Before Vor could give the order to proceed with the final crushing victory at Corrin, a burst of static filled the general comline, cutting off Rayna Butler's prayers and replacing them with a smooth machine voice.

"We address the new group of human invaders. It is clear that you have come to Corrin intending to destroy us. Before you act, we must make you aware of certain consequences."

The tone was hollow but erudite, with just an edge of smugness. Vor recognized the voice—Erasmus! He clenched his jaw and maintained his silence as he listened, waving the grumbling bridge crew to silence. Close-up views of the robots' defensive system filled every scanner screen, enhancing the flurry of activity in close orbit.

"Those are not our images, Supreme Bashar," Abulurd said. "They've piggybacked onto our scanning systems."

"Are the Holtzman satellites still functioning?" Vor asked, suddenly fearing their primary line of defense had crumbled.

"Yes, still capable of scrambler pulses. But somehow their signal is penetrating our own comlines. I'm searching for alternative circuits, trying to reroute."

"Let's hear what Erasmus has to say—then we'll destroy them all," Vor growled.

The robot's voice spoke over the shifting images. "Your reconnaissance has already observed the ring of containers around Corrin. We have filled these new cargo vessels and many of our battleships with innocent human hostages. Slaves, more than two million of them, taken from our camps and pens."

The screen blurred, then shifted to show crowds of faces, people crammed together and moaning. Image after image flickered, a litany of desperate expressions.

"We have planted explosives inside every one of these cargo containers and vessels. The trigger to their destruction is tied to your own scrambler network installed around Corrin. If any Army of Humanity ship passes through those boundary sensors, the explosives will automatically detonate. Unless you maintain your distance, you will massacre two million innocents."

Now Erasmus showed his flowmetal face. The robot was smiling. "We consider the hostages expendable—do you?"

An uproar of disbelief and curses rippled through the LS *Serena Victory* and was echoed by all the craft in the Vengeance Fleet and the watchdog vessels stationed over Corrin. All of them looked to Vor for a solution.

He pressed his lips together, thinking of all the battles he had fought, the friends he had lost, the blood already on his hands. He gathered his courage and spoke slowly, icily. "It doesn't make a damned bit of difference." He turned to his crew. "This only reinforces the reasons why we must utterly destroy all thinking machines."

"But, Supreme Bashar!" Abulurd blurted. "More than two million people!"

Instead of answering him, Vor turned to his communications officer to initiate a response. As soon as his image was transmitted, Erasmus reacted with pleased surprise. "Ah, Vorian Atreides—our old enemy! I should not be surprised to find you behind this aggressive game."

Vor crossed his arms over his uniformed chest. "Do you think you can make my resolve waver with your cowardly human shields?"

"I am a robot, Vorian Atreides. You know me. You *know* I am not bluffing." He maintained a maddening smile on his flowmetal face.

Vor thought again of the images of multitudes of prisoners crammed into the linked vessels, their faces pressed against the plaz, frightened and hopeless. He fixed his mind on the ultimate goal, made himself stronger. If not today, he very much doubted he would ever have another chance at this.

"Then it is a sad but necessary price for victory." He turned and gave orders to Abulurd. "Prepare the Vengeance Fleet for full assault. Wait for my command."

His crew gasped, then grumbled, before returning steadfastly to their posts. Abulurd stood frozen, as if he couldn't believe what his mentor had said. True, they had been willing to accept the sacrifice of innocents as regrettable but necessary casualties of war—but not like this.

After a pause, Erasmus's voice continued, louder now but still sounding calm. "I thought you might be difficult to convince. Therefore, I have another surprise, Vorian Atreides. Take a closer look."

To his shock, after showing several more crowds of captives, the screens focused on a room where a woman sat by herself guarded by two burly combat robots. Everyone in the League of Nobles was familiar with that face, though it had been somewhat idealized over decades of devotion and stylized memorials. Vor himself had known her in life, had even loved her. He'd never had a chance to say goodbye before she brashly flew off to Corrin to defy Omnius and the proposed peace terms.

Serena Butler.

Now, over the comline, Rayna Butler's voice was shrill. "It is Saint Serena! Just like in my vision!"

Vor stared. She seemed to look somewhat younger than he remembered her, but eight decades had passed since her death. He knew her too well, her every expression, the set of her mouth, the gaze from her haunting lavender eyes. So many times he had seen those fateful last images, archival pictures taken as she boarded her diplomatic craft accompanied by her Seraphim guards and departed for Corrin to meet with the thinking machines—where she had been horrifically tortured and then killed.

"This is not possible," he said, forcing a cold calm into his voice. "We all saw the images of her execution. I personally saw the mangled body, which genetic analysis proved to belong to Serena Butler." He raised his voice. "This is a trick!"

"But Vorian Atreides—which was the trick?" Now Erasmus showed another familiar face on the screen, the hated visage of one of the Tlulaxa traitors. Rekur Van. The camera was close, showing only the genetic wizard's face.

The flesh merchant spoke in a taunting voice. "Omnius is not so foolish as to discard a person with such potential as Serena Butler. The burned and tortured body we sent back to the League was a *clone* of Serena Butler, grown in our tanks on Tlulax. You know we kept genetic samples of her in our organ farms. The entire plan was designed by Grand Patriarch Iblis Ginjo."

Erasmus added, "Vorian Atreides, believe my statement: Omnius did not kill Serena Butler. The images that so inflamed the human race were falsified by Iblis Ginjo."

Vor felt sick and hollow inside. He remained standing though his legs grew suddenly weak. Unfortunately, the accusation was all too probable.

The robot's eyes narrowed, and his face took on a conspiratorial look. "Iblis, in fact, perpetrated many tricks on you. Were you aware that the preserved baby displayed so proudly in your League is also a fake?"

Vor didn't respond. He had indeed known that the innocent child's body kept in the City of Introspection was a mere mannequin, though few outsiders realized this.

Now the image returned to Serena, and one of the guardian robots held up a small child, dangling it threateningly. No observer could mistake the implied threat.

"Consider: What if we were able to hold Serena's child in stasis?" Erasmus said. "I felt that with a substantial surgical effort, we could repair most of the damage. Now think of your choice to attack Corrin, Vorian Atreides. If you allow your armada to come closer, all of these hostages will be killed—including Serena Butler and her baby. I doubt you want that to happen *again*, Vorian Atreides."

"I cannot believe what you are showing me," Vor said, his voice low and threatening.

Rekur Van said, "It is the Priestess of the Jihad in the flesh."

Rayna Butler's shrill voice cut across all the communication channels. "A miracle! Serena Butler has returned to us—and Manion the Innocent!"

Over a high-security comline Vor heard Viceroy Faykan's agitated, panicky voice. "What shall we do now? We must rescue Serena if there is the remotest chance! Champion Atreides, answer me!"

Vor snapped, "Get off this channel, Viceroy. According to the rules of space and the Army of Humanity, I am in command of this military operation."

"What do you intend to do?" Faykan sounded very uneasy. "We have to reconsider."

Vor drew a deep breath, knew that once again he had to make the tough choice. He would never be able to live with himself otherwise. "I intend to complete my mission, Viceroy. As Serena herself used to say, we must achieve victory at any cost."

Vor blocked the incoming comline, preventing any further interference from outsiders. Then he broadcast to all of his ships and crews, to every chamber on every vessel: "Do not forget that *Erasmus* is the one who murdered Manion the Innocent, throwing the child off a high balcony! He himself set this entire Jihad in motion. I believe his entire human shield is a subterfuge, a trick designed to turn us back."

Vor's eyes were dry, sharply focused. Even the stunned hush around him seemed to pound loudly in his ears. He saw Abulurd staring at him with an expression he had never seen before, but Vor looked away. Right now he had a job to do.

*There are many similarities between men and the machines they cre
uted, and many differences. The list of differences is comparatively
small—but the items on that particular inventory are of tremendous
consequence. They form the heart and soul of my frustration.*

—*Erasmus Dialogues*,
one of his last known entries

After delivering his ultimatum to the League Vengeance Fleet,
Erasmus undertook an even more difficult task. At least Gilbertus
was safe.

Following a circuitous route, the autonomous robot hurried into a tunnel system underneath the plaza and reached the chamber where the
damaged Omnius Prime had been placed beneath the former location of
the retracted Central Spire. The walls of the chamber, like the spire
mechanism itself, were constructed of the finest flowmetal, but their previous luster had turned to black. The bifurcated evermind did not have
the "artistic flair" of the now-blasted Omnius Prime—only one of their
disturbing flaws.

The robot wasn't sure how much time he might have. He anticipated
that Vorian Atreides and his superstitious and fanatical *hrethgir* followers
would decide the terms were unacceptable, and the Army of Humanity
would withdraw without inflicting further destruction. Seeing what they
believed to be the genuine Serena Butler should be the deciding factor.

Rekur Van had recovered from the injuries he sustained when Thurr-
Om and SeurOm neutralized the Corrin-Omnius, and he had continued
to work on the shape-shifting biological robots, as Erasmus asked him to
do. He had hoped to use the new fleshlike flowmetal of the face-altering
machines to fool the Army of Humanity, but the innovative biometals

suffered frequent failures, and the test robots often displayed unsettling facial meltdowns. Some of the test robots managed to imitate Serena's expressions and movements, but one mistake would have ruined the entire illusion.

That meant Erasmus's plan had to rely on the Serena Butler clone. Gilbertus would certainly be upset, but for now it was necessary. He did not doubt that the *hrethgir* would scheme to find some other way to destroy the last Synchronized World. The independent robot did not trust the two ever-minds to find flexible solutions. He decided to increase the odds.

Using access codes, Erasmus forced open the shell of the old Spire, and at its very heart found what he was looking for: a tiny piece of metalglaz inside a ball of crystal. The overthrown Corrin-Omnius had been severely damaged, but perhaps Erasmus could salvage some of the mental contents.

Carefully, he lifted out the glassy ball. Taking a chance, doing what he had previously refused to do, Erasmus loaded the ball into an access port in his own flowmetal torso, "swallowing" it. Perhaps he could assimilate some of the remnants of the huge evermind. He had to take the chance. Everything was riding on it—the future of thinking machines . . . the future of an empire.

The robot's input drive adjusted itself to the size and shape of the inserted object and vibrated as his data-acquisition system tried to activate the evermind. The SeurOm and ThurrOm versions of Omnius had obviously been corrupted, and though Erasmus and Omnius Prime had experienced many dangerous disagreements, he decided to bring the original copy back online.

The evermind had substantial recovery routines, fail-safes that should have kept it intact even from significant damage. Erasmus hoped he could trigger it to heal itself. "If this works, you will have no further cause to call *me* Martyr," he said aloud, then realized he was imitating a strange human habit of smugness.

His attempt did not succeed.

Disappointed, the robot initiated his own processor's recovery routine, yet nothing happened. The backup evermind must be too severely damaged, unable to start and transfer itself into Erasmus's complex gelcircuitry. Dead. Useless.

Until, finally, he provoked a spark of response, the sluggish first movements of the data-reconstruction routines inside the fused core of the evermind.

Suddenly Erasmus noticed a watcheye hovering near his head, peering at him. Though ThurrOm and SeurOm were occupied with the threatening military impasse, he knew this little electronic spy was still connected to the pair of everminds, whether or not they were paying attention to it. He calculated that it would not be wise for his actions to be seen and interpreted. Erasmus snatched the watcheye out of the air, planning to crush it in his metal hand.

But the voice that issued from its tiny speaker did not belong to Omnius. "Father, I have found you." The signal was weak, distorted, but clearly came from Gilbertus Albans!

Inserting a needle probe from his hand into its tiny self-contained systems, Erasmus used his own programming to boost the gain, filter out the noise. The device glowed, and a holoprojection lit up, filled with information. In a flash, Erasmus scrolled through the exhaustive records, checking images.

With extreme speed, he scanned thousands upon thousands of images of the crowded sentient creatures trapped inside, huddled together as if simple closeness could protect them from the imminent explosions. Then Erasmus saw something that shocked his internal programming to the core. *No. It must be a mistake.*

He saw the clone of Serena Butler. *And beside her, Gilbertus!* Transmitting from one of the booby-trapped cargo containers up in the Bridge of Hrethgir.

Gilbertus held one of the machine sensors aboard the booby-trapped cargo container. "There you are, Father. I have linked this system to one of the watcheyes."

"What are you doing there? You should be in a safe place. I made sure of it."

"But Serena is up here. The records were easy to follow. Sentinels were rounding up the last of the humans to put aboard the containers so I came with them."

This was the most terrible thing the robot could imagine. He didn't even pause to realize that the extremity of his reaction went far beyond the norm for a thinking machine. He had done so much work with Gilbertus, trained him, turned him into a superior human being—only to discover that he was about to die with all of the others. With the inadequate clone to whom he showed so much silly love and devotion.

In spite of all that Erasmus had experienced and knew, none of it mattered anymore, except for one thing: He would do whatever was necessary to rescue his son.

On the outside datascreens, he saw that though the Vengeance Fleet had hesitated briefly, now they appeared to be moving forward, despite the threat.

"Gilbertus, I will save you. Be prepared."

He had no time to waste on the partially recovered core of Omnius Prime. Angrily, he set it aside and fled the underground chamber.

I MUST AWAKEN.

Data began to flow, but much work remained before the gelcircuitry memory would be fully restored. The two unsynchronized Omniuses had inflicted extreme injury to his systems, but had not bothered to finish the job. They had discarded his cybernetic remains in the core of his Central Spire and then occupied themselves with other matters.

Corrin was about to fall, because of them.

Before the two faulty copies struck him down, Omnius Prime had developed a perfectly acceptable means of escape, a way to allow the core copy of his evermind to survive. He had the ability to code all the information that comprised his entity into a giant datapacket. As a mere signal, not a gelcircuitry construction, it would be able to pass through the scrambler net. "Omnius" would drift across the galaxy until he found some receiver, anything that could download him. Anything he could inhabit.

The two usurper everminds could stay here and fight against hopeless odds. They would be destroyed, but Omnius Prime could not permit that to happen to himself. First, he had to regenerate his systems.

Only thinking machines see decisions in absolute black and white terms. Anyone with a heart has doubts. It comes with being human.

—BASHAR ABULURD HARKONNEN,

private journals

Reports streamed in from the watchdog vessels and from the decks of the flagship. The Army of Humanity soldiers were profoundly uneasy.

And then the human race would lose the war.

Beside him on the bridge and totally focused on the task at hand, Vor said, "If Omnius believes we will back down now, he is sorely mistaken! This tactic is yet another demonstration of how badly the thinking machines underestimate human determination."

Across a high-security channel to the LS *Serena Victory*, the Viceroy spoke again, sounding conciliatory. "Perhaps I was a bit hasty, Champion Atreides. You were quite correct. Although you and I fought side by side in many engagements during the Jihad, I am now the League Viceroy. I'm no longer a military man, so I wash my hands of the decisions here. You alone are in charge of this operation. The military authority, and the responsibility, are yours, with my blessing."

After separating himself from the impending tragedy, the Viceroy ordered his diplomatic vessel to drop well away from the battlefield over Corrin, taking his niece Rayna and the contingent of noble representatives with him to a safe distance.

"He's just positioning himself," Abulurd muttered, in disgust. "Everything my brother does is political, even out here."

Vorian fixed his stony gaze forward; Abulurd knew his commander was setting an example for the uneasy but dutiful crew members on the bridge. The Supreme Bashar's comline was linked to all the numerous ships that had come to make their last stand. "We will advance, regardless of the threats made by the thinking machines. I have no intention of stopping now. Damn the machines and their treachery."

"But, sir, the cost!" Abulurd cried. "So many innocent lives. Now that the circumstances are changed, we have to reconsider—think of another way."

"There is no other viable way. The risk of waiting is too high."

Abulurd drew a sharp breath. He had never seen his mentor so determined and implacable. "Omnius is logical. He will not do this if he knows he will be exterminated."

"His extermination is nonnegotiable," Vorian said. "We have shed so much blood already, I am willing to spend a few drops more to ensure our victory."

"A few drops!"

"It is necessary. They were already doomed when we came here."

"I disagree, sir. The other victims of the Jihad might have been necessary casualties, but not these. The situation is stable enough that we can take a little time to reconsider our options. We should meet with the other officers, see if anyone has—"

Vor turned to the younger officer. "More talk? I have heard interminable, useless discussions in the League for the past twenty years! Oh, it'll start out as a brief delay, and then the Viceroy will reconsider and ask us to send messengers back to Salusa. Then the nobles will weigh in." He balled his fists at his side. "We have made too many mistakes in the past, Abulurd, and paid a terrible price for our lack of resolve. That changes today, and forever."

The commander fixed his gaze on the screen, on the cancerous tumor of Corrin that needed to be excised from the universe. "All weapons active, all ships full forward."

"But, Supreme Bashar!" Abulurd stood insistently on the bridge. "You know Omnius is not bluffing. If you pass beyond the boundary, the automated destruct sequences will be activated. You'll be dooming all those people—including Serena and her baby."

Vor seemed distant. "I've done it before. If a handful of victims must become sacrificial lambs here for the future freedom of the human race, so be it."

"A *handful?* Sir, there are more than two million—"

"And think of the billions of soldiers who have already died. Serena herself understood that sometimes innocent bystanders become casualties of war." Now his gray eyes focused on Abulurd, and the younger man thought he saw a stranger there. "Make no mistake—*Omnius* is executing them, not me. I did not create this situation, and I refuse to accept this as my responsibility. I have enough blood on my hands."

Abulurd's heart pounded, and his breaths came quick. He didn't care how many crew members were listening. "We can take the time we need to consider this carefully, sir. The thinking machines have been imprisoned on Corrin for two decades. Why must you attack now— with more than two million people at risk? Just because our forces are here? Omnius poses no greater threat today than he did yesterday, or the day before."

Vor's youthful face went stony and cold, the only way he allowed his displeasure to show. "I allowed Omnius to live at the end of the Great Purge. We suffered from a fatal lack of resolve, even though our jihadis were ready to commit the final effort and pay the ultimate price. We never should have faltered then, and I do not intend to do so again."

"But why not at least try to mediate a solution, find a way to save some of those people? We can make a calculated strike the way my father and brothers did when they liberated Honru. Our ships are full of fast kindjals and bombers loaded with pulse warheads, and we have a great many Ginaz mercenaries on board. Maybe enough of our mercenaries can slip through and deliver targeted warheads to annihilate Omnius."

"They will still have to cross the line in space to do that." The Supreme Bashar's gaze turned stony. "There will be no further discussion, Bashar. We will proceed and use every weapon at our disposal. History will mark this as the last day of the thinking machines." Vor leaned forward in his command chair, intent on the tactical screens again.

Abulurd wanted to scream. *This is not necessary!* His heart felt as if it were being ripped out of his chest. He kept his voice even. "I can't let you throw away your own humanity like this, Supreme Bashar. We can hold the line here. We have our Vengeance Fleet in place. We can keep the machines bottled up on Corrin for another twenty years until we think of something else. Please, sir, work with me to find an alternative."

Vorian rose from his command chair, turning with cold fury on his executive officer. The bridge crew was clearly uneasy about the prospects of so much unnecessary slaughter, and Abulurd's argument was only deepening their doubts.

Vor squared his shoulders and glared. "Bashar Harkonnen, I have made my decision and given my orders. This is not a discussion group." Raising his voice, he barked at the rest of his bridge crew. "Power up your weapons and prepare for the final plunge."

"If you do this, Vorian," Abulurd said, not caring about the consequences, "then you are no better than your father. This is the sort of thing the Titan Agamemnon would have done."

Like a glowglobe being extinguished, all emotion left Vor's face. A rigid mask froze on his handsome features, and his voice came out as level and frigid as the ice plains of Hessra. "Bashar Harkonnen, I hereby relieve you of duty. You are confined to your quarters aboard this ship until the culmination of the Battle of Corrin."

Astonished, Abulurd stared at him, feeling misery well up inside, his eyes filling with a burning sheen of tears. He couldn't believe it.

Vor turned his back on him and spoke again. "Do you require an armed escort?"

"That will not be necessary, sir." Abulurd left the bridge—along with his hopes and his career—behind.

Human life is not negotiable.

— DASHAR ABULURD HARKONNEN,
private journals

Confined to his quarters and stripped of his duties, Abulurd Harkonnen felt the LS *Serena Victory* accelerate in its final run toward Corrin and the fateful line formed by Omnius's Bridge of Hrethgir.

Over the flagship intercom, the Supreme Bashar delivered a rousing speech to rally his troops for the heartless attack. "Omnius believes he can prevent our victory by placing human shields in orbit around Corrin. He thinks that by erecting this 'Bridge of Hrethgir' we will lose our resolve and leave him to continue his poisonous plans. But he is sorely mistaken.

"The evermind has chosen to place millions of innocent humans where they are sure to be killed. This only reaffirms the necessity for destroying him, no matter the cost! The thinking machines wallow in their inhumanity, just as we rejoice in our righteousness. Let this be our last battlefield! Follow me to victory, for the sake of our children and all future generations of humanity."

Abulurd knew that Vor, by sheer force of will, would keep the Army of Humanity soldiers focused on their duty instead of their doubts until they had completed their work. This was the point of no return. Momentum would carry them forward to the terrible end. The soldiers would not be able to think about what they were doing until it was too late. That was Vor's intent.

But Abulurd—trapped in his cabin—had nothing to do but consider the consequences. Damn it, these deaths were unnecessary. Unnecessary! Vor had labeled this mission an emergency and imposed an artificial deadline on this mission, then refused to reconsider for no better reason than because he did not want to.

Faykan had withdrawn to where he and his nobles could observe and keep their hands clean. Vor would dutifully accept full responsibility for the slaughter. But Abulurd Harkonnen would not.

He looked at the rank insignia on his uniform. He had been so proud when Vor had pinned the bashar cluster there. The young officer had placed all his hopes and devotion on Vorian Atreides. On his mentor's nobility and honor.

Now that relationship had fallen to ruin, and for what? All those people didn't need to die. Earlier in the Jihad, Vorian Atreides had made his name by coming up with innovative twists and solutions, deceiving the thinking machines with a decoy fleet around Poritrin or with a damaging computer virus distributed through his unwitting "friend" Seurat. Now, though, the Supreme Bashar called himself a hawk. Impatient and vengeful, he would lead his troops in one battle too many.

With a deep pang that was almost physical, Abulurd removed his officer's insignia and set it on his bureau. Then he looked at himself in the mirror, a man without any rank. Just a man with a conscience. He was ashamed to be part of this military operation.

But perhaps he could salvage this situation before it became a tragedy, *force* Vorian to pause, take time to reconsider. He knew the Supreme Bashar still had greatness within him. He had to delay this foolhardy action in any way he could.

Abulurd left his quarters, intentionally defying orders. It was only the beginning.

He marched down the corridors, feeling a resolve and determination that must be equivalent to Vorian's right now. Twenty years ago, he had not participated in the Great Purge that had killed so many billions of enslaved human beings. He had remained behind on Salusa Secundus to oversee the evacuation and last-minute defense of the League capital. Vorian Atreides had seen that duty as a kindness, a way to shield the sensitive young officer from so much bloodshed, horror, and guilt.

Now Abulurd would have to return the favor. To do the right thing, and to save the Supreme Bashar from a terrible decision, Abulurd was willing to sacrifice his own military career. In the end he was sure Vor would see the wisdom in what Abulurd had to do.

He hurried to the weapons-control deck of the flagship. From the interconnected primary command center, Abulurd could access the firing controls for the entire fleet. The systems were all coordinated from this point, though each battleship had the option of independent firing, if permitted by LS *Serena Victory*.

Upon launching the great fleet, Rayna Butler and her antitechnology zealots had been suspicious of the sophisticated command-and-control links on which the Army of Humanity relied. Among the concessions Viceroy Butler had given to his powerful niece was that all those systems would be disengaged forever, but only after the thinking machines were vanquished. In the meantime, they had been altered so that a human being had to be in the loop of activation and command. The systems could not be fully automated. They required a real person to direct the weapons fire from the flagship.

At the beginning of this mission, when they'd set off from Salusa Secundus, Vorian Atreides had trusted his executive officer completely. Always realistic, preparing for the event that something might happen to him, Vor had given Bashar Abulurd Harkonnen the master key set, the sequence of codes that could access all of the fleet's built-in weapons in a showdown—a down payment on his promise to help restore honor and respect to the Harkonnen name.

And while the key set allowed Abulurd to use all of the Vengeance Fleet's weapons, it could also serve to do something entirely different.

A crowd of weaponry technicians worked at their consoles, preparing for battle against the machine warships. The flagship ballista and the accompanying human warships closed in on their fateful confrontation, reaching the line that would trigger the senseless slaughter of millions of humans inside the Bridge. Engrossed in his battle plans and not wanting to damage morale, the Supreme Bashar had not yet announced Abulurd's punishment to the whole crew.

Thus, when he entered the weapons-control deck and the officers looked up at the bashar, they did not question Abulurd's presence or his missing insignia in the heat of the impending engagement.

Returning the automatic salutes the other soldiers gave him, Abulurd went directly to the primary station. Within minutes, the fleet commander would give the order to open fire.

As soon as he input the code from the master key, Abulurd received access to all the weapons controls. He stared at a console screen, intimidated and awed by the momentous action he was about to take. Before he could change his mind, he used his master key again to alter the access code to a sequence only he knew.

As he approached the battle zone, Vor would discover that he no longer had control over the weaponry that he needed for the fight. He wouldn't be able to shoot. Without any firepower, he would have no choice but to back off and reconsider. It would give him time to take a deep breath and find another way.

With a whispered prayer, Abulurd withdrew from the station. It would not be long before they discovered what he had done.

The Army of Humanity picked up speed, heading into their dramatic confrontation without even realizing that they had been mercifully hamstrung.

War is a combination of art, psychology, and science. The success-
ful commander knows how to apply each of these components, and
when.

—SUPREME BASHAR VORIAN ATREIDES

I *am a hawk. That is my symbol.*

The bloated giant sun peeked around the edge of Corrin, painting bloodstains on the hulls of the nearest ships with its somber light. Just inside the scrambler-satellite net, Omnius had clustered defensive ships and rigged cargo containers filled with innocent human shields. The first waves of the shielded Vengeance Fleet would crash through that obstacle, and damn the consequences.

Past the gauntlet the machines had erected, clouds covered much of the surface of the world. Vor saw a flash of lightning and then another, but the worst storms were about to occur in space.

Ahead of him, the network of scrambler satellites formed a line of death for over two million hostages. Including Serena Butler. *I can make no other decision. If that is truly Serena, alive after all these years, then she would understand—in fact, she would demand it.*

And if it wasn't Serena Butler, then what did it matter? He had already made up his mind.

As the fleet moved forward, picking up speed, closing the noose, the soldiers were uneasy. Some prayed that the thinking machines would back down at the last minute. But Vor knew that wouldn't happen. Uncounted billions of enslaved humans had already been annihilated during the nuclear purge of the Synchronized Worlds. The actions of this day would be regrettable, but no worse than what had gone before. And there would finally be an end to the thinking machines.

Even after learning of the human shields in the "Bridge," his resolve had not wavered. The very fact that the machines would do something so desperate told him that they had everything to lose here. *The price of victory is high . . . but acceptable.*

Abulurd's vocal objection, though, had been a weighty disappointment to him. Abulurd, of all people, knew how important this offensive was— for Vor and for all of humanity. He should have been helping the Supreme Bashar, not interfering with the orders of his superior officer—his friend.

Vor felt ice in the pit of his stomach. Xavier would never have hesitated in this situation. *He* would have made the necessary choice.

From her safe position aboard the diplomatic vessel, Rayna transmitted her prayers, clearly torn between her hatred for thinking machines and wanting to save the miraculously returned Serena Butler and her martyred child. Vor wondered if the Cult leader even saw the paradox here. If Rayna truly believed that the spirit of Saint Serena had appeared to her in a fever vision, then how could she believe the real Serena was still alive? It made no sense.

The Vengeance Fleet moved into range of the scrambler satellites. "Prepare to engage the enemy. Weapons officers, man your stations. Power up all systems and be ready to fire at my command. We will strike like a flaming sword from the sky."

He swallowed with a dry throat. If he was wrong in his guess that Omnius did not know of the laser-shield interaction, in a few seconds the first line of League warships would be instantly vaporized in a pseudo-atomic explosion.

"As we approach, select your key targets," he said.

"Sir, what if there are human hostages aboard the robotic warships?"

Vor whirled, saw the gunnery officer jump at his reaction. "And what if there *aren't?* Don't worry about them. Do your job, Bator." His voice sounded hollow. Once the Bridge of Hrethgir detonated, there would be nothing to hold back the retaliatory rage of the Army of Humanity. In a way, he wanted to be done with it, so the fleet could concentrate on the urgent task before them.

Ready to open fire and do what he had to, he inched his fingers closer to the touchpad that would commence the firing sequence. He wanted to hurt the machines exactly as they had hurt humans for so many generations.

Finally, the flagship's scanning officer reported: "In range, Supreme Bashar!"

"Commence bombardment. Let's soften them up!"

Wanting to fire the first shot himself, Vor touched the firing pad, but nothing happened. He tried again. Still nothing. "Damn!"

Around the command deck, other gunnery officers let out confused mutters and shouts of alarm. Chatter burst over the comlines.

"Sir, weapons are *inactive* across the entire fleet! We can't fire a single shot."

His officers scurried for answers, filling the comlines that connected the flagship with the rest of the fleet and asking questions. When the explanation came, it was like acid thrown in Vor's face.

"This is Abulurd Harkonnen," a voice boomed over the speakers. "In order to prevent the unnecessary murder of millions of innocent people, I have disabled the firing controls on every weapons battery in the fleet. Supreme Bashar Atreides, we *must* find a better solution than this. You have no choice now but to back off."

"Bring him to me!" Vor said. Security troops rushed from the command deck. He turned in his chair. "And get those weapons back online!"

"We can't do a thing unless we have the coded control sequence—and Bashar Harkonnen has changed it."

"Now we see why he took the name *Harkonnen*," one of the gunnery officers snarled. "He's afraid to fight the machines."

"Enough." Vor stopped himself from saying anything more. He reeled, unable to understand how his protégé could have done this, why Abulurd would have risked all their lives by interfering at the most critical moment. "Bypass what systems you can, rig manual launch sequences and targeting operations if you have to. Otherwise, we may have to open the cargo hold doors and throw rocks at the enemy."

"It'll take a few minutes, Supreme Bashar."

"Sir, do we keep going forward?" the navigator said. "We're almost to the Bridge."

Thoughts spun through Vor's mind, almost overwhelming him with the clamor of betrayal he felt at what Abulurd had apparently done. "If we slow now, the machines will know something's wrong."

"We dare not hesitate!" one of the Cultist crewmen cried. "The demon machines will think we've wavered in our holy purpose."

Vor was sure Omnius wouldn't think like that. "More likely they'll suspect technical difficulties, a weakness." He made his voice hard, inflexible.

"Proceed. We'll just need to do this the hard way." He would have only a few minutes to make Abulurd put the systems back online. Maybe he could do it in time.

Abulurd Harkonnen was easy to find, and he did not resist. He actually looked proud of himself when the guards dragged him back to the command bridge. He carried no weapons and wore a hard expression on his face that cut Vor like a stiletto. There was no insignia on Abulurd's coat.

Eyes blazing with cold fury, Vor strode forward. "What have you done? By God and Serena, tell me what you have done!"

The other man looked at him as if hoping for understanding. "I have saved you from making a terrible mistake. I have saved millions of lives."

Vor grabbed Abulurd by the uniform coat. "You're a fool! Unless we finish this now, today, you might have doomed us all and opened the door for another thousand years of machine slavery."

The gunnery officer sneered. "A *coward*, just like his grandfather."

"No, not like Xavier." Vor looked at Abulurd, his frustration burning away all good memories of the times they had spent together. "This man is in his own universe of cowardice, Bator. Don't compare him with anyone else."

Abulurd remained motionless in Vor's grip but continued to plead. "It doesn't have to be this way. If you'll only—"

Vor's voice was icy. "Bashar Harkonnen, I command you to give me the new codes. We don't have much time."

"Sorry, I can't do that. It's the only way you'll look at the problem in a different light. You'll have to pull back."

"You are endangering the lives of the entire Vengeance Fleet!"

The younger man did not even seem intimidated. "You're the one endangering lives, Vorian, not me."

"Do not dare to speak my name again. You presume upon a friendship that no longer exists." Disgusted, Vor shoved him away, and Abulurd stumbled to keep his footing. Vor knew he could not follow through on any threat of torture. Not with Abulurd. "You have betrayed the future of humanity!"

Alarmed, the navigator called out in a strained voice. "Coming up on the satellite boundary, Supreme Bashar. Should I reduce speed?"

"No! We proceed with the offensive, no matter—"

Abulurd gasped. "You can't! You have to stop now, regroup! Try to negotiate with Omnius. Your ships have no weapons—"

"The machines don't know that. And unlike Erasmus, I can bluff." A deadly calm came over Vor. Stripped of their long-range weapons, the Vengeance Fleet closed toward the machine forces. In Vor's mind, he had committed too much to risk failure. "Besides, as long as I have my imagination, I am *never* without weapons."

Turning away from the ghostly pale Abulurd, Vor said, "Get him out of my sight and put him under constant guard." Three angry-looking guards closed in around him, as if looking for an excuse to beat the traitor. "I'll worry about what to do with him later—if we survive this day."

The history of warfare is made up of moments . . . and decisions . . . that could have gone either way.

—*Erasmus Dialogues*,
final Corrin entries

Although he sifted through his long lifetime of memories, Erasmus could find no other time when he had been so deeply troubled. So close to . . . panic and despair? To avert disaster, he needed to act swiftly—to save Gilbertus.

Interesting, he thought with such an intense flash of insight that he was almost distracted from the emergency. *Perhaps I now have a better grasp of why Serena Butler was so frantic to protect her child.*

As an independent robot and advisor to the Omnius incarnations, Erasmus had access to every system on Corrin. In a shielded chamber deep beneath the capital city, he entered a room bathed in a holographic grid. The tactical image showed a scale model of the defenses around the planet, including the heavily armed robotic battleships and the numerous cargo and prison chambers that formed the Bridge of Hrethgir—including the one that held Gilbertus and the Serena clone. He could also see the human Vengeance Fleet just sliding into the proximity of the grid. Moment by moment, the display shifted as ships changed position, approaching the boundary of the satellite network that would trigger all the explosives and kill the human shields.

The robot's gelcircuitry mind interfaced with the command network. He quickly analyzed the programming that his brilliant human ward had implemented.

The League warships accelerated, their intentions clear. As they reached the deadly zone, they showed no hesitation. Nothing would turn them back now. Vorian Atreides, son of the Titan Agamemnon, was willing to sacrifice all of the prisoners. He would not stop.

Gilbertus would die as soon as the human ships crossed the line.

Outside the scope of the holo-model, the room was full of linked computer access nodes, with attendant robots performing sophisticated duties for the two everminds. Erasmus ignored them, speeding up his own mental processes.

In all of his probability projections, he had never foreseen the events unfolding around him now. If Erasmus had been human, his current course of action would most certainly have been called suicidal, and traitorous. He was eliminating the last desperate defense the machines had, the only possibility of keeping the human military at bay . . . even though it did not appear to be working.

But it was the only way to save Gilbertus right now. If this human died, Erasmus questioned the necessity of his own continued existence.

Two seconds remaining.

The robot studied the defense grid holo, saw more and more enemy ships approaching the detection radius of the system. Inside this chamber, they were no more than floating blips. But out there, the ships were real, capable of annihilating Corrin in yet another atomic attack, once they passed the Bridge and killed all the hostages aboard.

And he calls us inhuman!

Without further hesitation, Erasmus gained control over the defense system. Amber lights danced in front of his optic threads, and he deactivated the linkage between the scrambler-satellite network and the explosives.

Then he watched as the blips indicating the enemy fleet surged through the disabled barricade, with nothing left to stop them.

I do not fear death. I fear only failure.

—SERENA BUTLER,

Priestess of the Jihad

V or had a plan, or at least the pieces of one. He laced his fingers together, his thoughts racing. He considered all of the resources that remained to him.

Abulurd might have cut off the weapons systems built into the Vengeance Fleet's capital ships, but the launching bays of those ballistas and javelins were still filled with kindjal bombers, all of them loaded with pulse-atomics. Originally, he had intended to use the fleet's weaponry to blast through the robotic barricade, and then saturate Corrin with nuclear detonations. Now, he would be forced to use some of his atomics against the barricade itself, thanks to the bashar's treachery. He hoped he could save enough warheads to accomplish his mission against Omnius, by using precision strikes from his Ginaz mercenaries.

Also, he figured that even without their on-board weapons systems, his shielded vessels would make decent battering rams. All he had to do was get enough of his battleships through the robotic barrier.

In his mind, Vor had already chosen to pay the price of the innocent hostages on the Bridge of Hrethgir.

With a horrified collective gasp from the crew, the LS *Serena Victory* arrived at the boundary in space. Vor kept his eyes fixed on the screen, his own guilt and determination forcing him to watch the last moments of the millions of hostages he had just doomed. They crossed the line.

But there was no detonation, no flash of light, no destruction of two million victims.

The Bridge of Hrethgir remained intact.

Vor could not believe it. "The damned robot was bluffing after all!"

"The people are safe!" his navigator cried.

"Saint Serena has provided another miracle!" Rayna Butler's voice came over the comline. "And she will lead us to final victory over the demon machines. Champion Atreides, push forward to the destruction of Omnius!"

Vor growled, "Shut down her signal! I give the orders on this mission."

They still had no operational weapons, thanks to Abulurd's treachery. Vor could not think of anything worse than betrayal—especially not from such a beloved comrade, a young man he had taken under his wing. It would have been kinder if Abulurd had simply stabbed Vor in the heart.

I will never again think of him as a surrogate son, or even a friend.

The Supreme Bashar swore he would succeed in spite of what Abulurd had done.

"Let us not waste this opportunity." He studied a scanner board, listing the offensive specifications of the nearest thinking machine vessels, including operational data. Then he whirled. "Get me Bashar Harkonnen! The threat of the Bridge is now moot—even he can't refuse to reactivate the firing codes!"

Seconds passed, and Vor raised his voice into the comline. "Where is Abulurd! I need—"

"I'm sorry, Supreme Bashar, but the coward is . . . in the infirmary." The guard's voice on the comline sounded subdued. "On the way to his quarters, he . . . resisted slightly. He is not expected to regain consciousness soon."

Vor cursed, knowing he should have anticipated this. He turned to his tactical officer. "Get me any on-board weapons you can—missiles, artillery. Especially scrambler mines."

The ships continued to soar unaffected through the net of satellites and into a space brawl with the cornered forces of Omnius.

He began to receive reports from his fleet that some weapons systems had been brought back online, though without the accuracy of the complex targeting algorithms Abulurd had disabled. Gunnery officers and Cultist volunteers disconnected and remounted some of the launchers so they could now aim and fire the weapons manually.

The first line of Omnius's ships moved forward to face them. Vor studied the defensive parameters of his opponents, saw more reinforcement vessels rising into higher orbit to join the fray. At the moment, even with its limited systems, the Vengeance Fleet had this first line of machine warships outgunned. And they were shielded.

"We can take them out preemptively, Supreme Bashar," reported his new second officer. "If we can shoot straight."

"Let's do it." Vor stared at the impenetrable blockade, then shouted into the comline, "To the Cult of Serena, to the jihadis, the mercenaries, and every other person fighting beside me in this great battle, I remind you what this Holy War is all about. It's about avenging the deaths of our beloved Serena, of Manion the Innocent, and of billions of other martyrs. It's about stopping the enemy in their tracks. It's about taking the 'think' out of thinking machines!"

Oddly, one of the first machine vessels to approach the flagship was not a battle unit at all, but an old update ship. Instead of opening fire, the vessel signaled him. "So, Vorian Atreides. This is more complex than the strategy games we used to play." On the comscreen, coppery-faced Seurat looked at him, his robotic visage fixed and expressionless, as always. "Are you going to destroy me? I will be your first casualty for this attack."

"Old Metalmind! I didn't even know you were still—"

The achingly familiar image of Seurat filled the screen; Vor expected him to break into an inept attempt at humor, or to remind the commander of how many times he had saved the human's life. "We were not always on opposite sides of this conflict, Vorian Atreides. I have made up a new joke about you: How many times is a human allowed to change his mind?"

Vor had steeled himself to accept the massacre of more than two million human shields, but now, ironically, he hesitated upon seeing this *robot*, his former companion. Of all the family and close friends he had lost in his long life span—Serena, Xavier, Leronica, even Agamemnon— only Seurat remained.

"What are you doing, Seurat? Stand down."

"You aren't even going to try to guess the punch line?"

Vor crossed his arms over his chest. "How can you be sure I ever changed my mind, instead of just hiding my true feelings from you?"

The update ship kept coming closer. "Why don't you let me aboard, and we can talk about old times? Am I not an acceptable emissary to discuss a resolution to this matter?"

Vor froze, fighting down his initial impulse. Wasn't that exactly what Abulurd had wanted? He couldn't possibly negotiate with the thinking machines. But Seurat . . .

His second officer said in a low voice, "Sir, our weapons are still not at full capacity. Perhaps if we stall?"

"Old Metalmind, is this a trick?"

"You taught me about tricks, Vorian Atreides. What do you think?"

Vor paced the bridge. Seurat's vessel continued forward without pause. If it gave them a chance to get more of their weapons active again, wasn't it worth the risk? "Drop shields," Vor said. "Seurat, you may proceed. But you had better be prepared to offer Omnius's complete surrender."

Seurat's coppery face remained the same. "Now you are telling a joke, Vorian Atreides." The robot ship accelerated toward the flagship.

"Supreme Bashar, his gunports are active!"

Without warning, Seurat's update ship opened fire, the blast ripping across the hull and tearing out the partially reactivated starboard weapons banks. With no shields to diminish the impacts, the explosions tore through the hull of the LS *Serena Victory* in two separate places. Atmosphere vented like rocket exhaust, sending the flagship ballista careening off course. The command deck rocked, alarms sounded. In unison now, the first line of robot ships launched their attacks.

"Activate shields again! Give us full protection!"

Amid the chaos, the robot captain transmitted a simulated laugh. "I am reminded of a phrase you taught me, Vorian Atreides: I caught you with your pants down. You have grown soft and slow after all those years living among the *hrethgir*."

"Open fire!" Vor choked, cursing himself for his paralysis and lack of resolve. *I don't care if he is Seurat.* . . . "Get us back under control."

He closed his eyes as several of the manually operated weapons blasted. The flagship turned about to give the gunners a better shot, and the soldiers fired their makeshift artillery. The wave of targeted projectiles quickly overwhelmed the update ship.

With no time for sadness or indecision, angry at himself for his foolish, inappropriate sentimentality, Vor readied himself for the continuing bloodbath. The second line of robotic defenders came into range.

Over the course of many years and much intensive training, I have taught Gilbertus Albans how to organize his mind, how to prepare his thoughts in a systematic fashion so that his abilities approach even those of a thinking machine. Unfortunately, I was unable to teach him how to make correct choices.

—Erasmus Dialogues

Out in the main plaza above the shielded vault that held their main memory spheres, the twin everminds flickered with agitation atop their pedestals. Thousands of datastream reports flowed in from the battle lines above Corrin, transmitting updates and warnings.

The human Vengeance Fleet spread out and struck the last Synchronized World in waves, from all sides. At the last moment, the enemy commander had not balked at crossing the deadly boundary and dooming all the innocent captives held aboard the Bridge of Hrethgir. And yet the Bridge had not exploded.

SeurOm and ThurrOm could not understand it.

The paired everminds sent flurries of instructions to the robot battleships, directing them individually with myriad plans, many of which were contradictory. As a result, the machine defenses in orbit responded with unpredictable chaos.

Erasmus was perfectly satisfied with the confusion. He needed to achieve his aims without interference from the dual everminds.

His uncertain contact with Gilbertus was broken as numerous explosions and energy surges from the battlefield corrupted the faulty systems aboard the orbiting cargo containers. Erasmus held the now-blank watcheye in his metal hand, then smashed it on the ground. Anger?

The autonomous robot accessed a set of controls that flowed into some of the smaller defensive ships that had not yet been called to the front. Erasmus seized one of them, controlling the ship remotely from the surface of Corrin.

As his direct linkage to the machine subsystems granted him access, he needed to move the vessel into place and issue orders to the combat meks aboard without either SeurOm or ThurrOm noticing. This task was going to be difficult enough without the everminds' meddling.

He found the single most important container, guided the small robot ship up against it. Gilbertus was inside there. The vessel docked.

Even without anyone watching, Erasmus fashioned a smile on his face. By now it had become quite a habit for him.

THE STENCH WAS terrible, the air barely breathable, the oxygen depleted. The metal floor and the hull plates seemed to suck all warmth out of the air, and yet the crowded press of so many unwashed bodies generated a suffocating heat.

Gilbertus sat next to the Serena clone. He held her hand, and she pressed herself against his muscular chest. He had come here of his own accord; perhaps it wasn't the most logical choice under the circumstances, but he would abide by it. Either the ploy of using human shields would work—or it would not.

In his heart he resented that Erasmus had tricked him by allowing Serena to be whisked away with all the other hostages. When the rest of the plan had become clear, when the images of Serena had been broadcast to the threatening Army of Humanity, Gilbertus understood—in his mind. It all made logical sense; in fact, the addition of this one particular hostage might prove the deciding factor.

"If only it didn't have to be you," he whispered to her.

The other hostages aboard the container muttered, shifted, complained. None of them knew what was happening. Some had whispered rumors that the free humans were coming as their saviors; others feared this was another horrific crowd psychology experiment designed by Erasmus. Gilbertus had tried to explain the detailed situation to two men who huddled next to him and Serena, but they didn't believe his analysis any more than the dozens of alternative stories.

Rekur Van had also been hauled up here, encased in his life-support socket. SeurOm and ThurrOm had apparently seized upon the concept of putting their human captives in harm's way. The limbless Tlulaxa squirmed and complained and ranted so much that Gilbertus had taken Serena into a different segment of the cargo container. Together, they waited for it to end.

He was sure the crisis should have been decided by now. The delay was a good sign: almost certainly, the League commander had hesitated and drawn back. Otherwise Gilbertus and all of his fellow hostages would be dead by now.

Why, then, did he see so much combat occurring through the tiny window ports? So many bright explosion flashes, a panoply of space vessels flying in all directions? He didn't recognize several of the major emblems—human battleships? But they were past the scrambler line, and the Bridge of Hrethgir should have detonated.

Gilbertus turned away from the view outside. At least he was with Serena.

"It won't be much longer," he said soothingly to her. "They will have to resolve the matter soon." He knew, too, that the millions of humans aboard the components of the Bridge did not have enough food, water, or air to last more than a few days—and the sheer administrative problem of evacuating all of them back to the surface would require almost as much time as that.

They felt the shuddering vibration as another ship came alongside the crowded cargo container and docked. The maneuver sounded clumsy, as if an inexperienced hand guided it. Gilbertus raced through the possibilities, wondered if perhaps humans had arrived to rescue them. It wasn't what he wanted, though.

When the crude hatch opened, seven burly combat robots marched in. Their heavy footfalls struck the deck, sending resounding vibrations through the different rooms and holds of the cargo container. Hostages shrank out of the way, trying to avoid notice. The robots, though, were intent.

Gilbertus climbed to his feet. Now he understood. Erasmus had given him just enough information before the watcheye communications link failed.

The robots stopped in front of him, an implacable force, like prison guards ready to usher a prisoner to his execution. "You've come to save me," he said.

"Erasmus commands it."

The people who were packed around him clamored for rescue as well.

They could all feel the air running out, and many had not been fed for almost two days. Gilbertus flicked his gaze back and forth. He reached down and drew Serena to her feet next to him. "I will not resist."

"You cannot resist."

"But I must take Serena with me."

The robots hesitated. "No. Only one of us may return with you to Corrin."

Gilbertus frowned, trying to assess why Erasmus would do that. Then he realized that the independent robot had probably tricked the two Omnius incarnations; it would be easier for him to muddy the programming of a single combat robot than all seven of them simultaneously. Erasmus needed to buy enough time to get Gilbertus back to the dubious safety of the surface.

"I will not leave without Serena." Gilbertus crossed his muscular arms over his chest in a defiant gesture. She looked up at him with her trusting lavender eyes.

Six of the robots stepped back. "We will remain aboard this container to stand guard over the Serena Butler clone."

"Guard her against what?"

The robots paused, receiving new instructions. The lead mek said, "Erasmus asks you to trust him."

The man's shoulders sagged, and he let go of Serena's hand.

To accept new information and use it to modify our behavior—this we recognize as the human quality to think. And by thinking, to survive, not just as individuals, but as a species. In surviving, though, shall our humanity endure? Will we keep our hold on those things that make life sweet for the living, warm and filled with what we call beauty?

We shall not gain this enduring humanity if we deny our whole being—if we deny emotion, thought, or flesh. There we have the tripod upon which all of eternity balances. If we deny emotion, we lose all touch with our universe. By denying the realm of thought, we cannot reflect upon what we touch. And if we dare deny the flesh, we unwheel the vehicle which bears us all.

—KREFTER BRAHN,
Special Advisor to the Jihad

Soon after the Vengeance Fleet hurtled through the scrambler network, they suddenly entered the densest concentration of enemy fire. The robot battleships formed concentric walls to protect Corrin, and they did not intend to let the humans pass.

The machines launched an endless rain of precisely targeted explosive shells, blast after blast after blast that dissipated harmlessly against the Holtzman shields. But already the front lines of the Army of Humanity, pressing forward, were overheating. From the flagship, Vor viewed the projections, knew that under the constant punishing the shields would overheat and fail within an hour.

A second line of League javelins and ballistas came immediately behind them, and a third, and a fourth. He clenched the arms of his command chair, keeping his face expressionless and unreadable. It seemed to be a question of which side would be the first to dwindle to nothing.

"Keep firing," Vor said, though the gunners needed no such instructions. "Give them everything we have."

"Targeting systems are still faulty, Supreme Bashar. We're wasting a lot of our munitions." After Seurat's treacherous sneak attack, rapid repairs had been completed on the LS *Serena Victory*, but Vor had lost over a hundred crew members in the explosions.

"Take your best guess." He shook his head. "Look at all those robot warships—how can you miss?"

A forest of enemy vessels blocked him from his objective. Vor bit back a curse. It should have been such a straightforward operation! Abulurd had derailed so much planning, had made the offensive here so much more complicated.

When the Bridge of Hrethgir inexplicably failed to detonate even after Vor passed the trip line in space, two million human hostages had received a reprieve. If the League achieved victory on Corrin, they had standing orders to rescue as many of the hostages as possible. Especially if Serena Butler and her child were among them.

Though the Vengeance Fleet ships had minimal crews and thus plenty of extra space, they could never hold millions of refugees. They were slow vessels and would take a long time to reach another habitable planet. The only solution for the hostages would be to shuttle them from their cargo containers back to the surface of Corrin.

But not if Vor turned the planet to radioactive slag, like the other Synchronized Worlds in the Great Purge.

Now that he had proved the Bridge of Hrethgir seemed to be just an elaborate and diabolical bluff he could not so blithely doom all two million hostages. This epic victory would not be as neat or as simple as he had hoped, but he would achieve it nonetheless.

As Vor plowed ahead, the shields began to fail on the front line of beleaguered League ships. Many of the captains dropped back to be replaced by new vessels, but others plunged ahead, refusing to withdraw even as their Holtzman defenses flickered. Thus unprotected, the human vessels swiftly succumbed to the relentless bombardment. Numbers appeared on his summary screens.

"Launch kindjal squadrons," he said. It was time for the next step of the plan. "Tell the pilots to be ready to deploy their pulse-atomics."

"But, Supreme Bashar, we're not even close to the surface!"

"No, we're not—and we won't get there at all unless we can clear away some of this clutter." He drew a deep breath. "Save enough warheads for a final coup de grâce, and tell the Ginaz swordmasters we're going to need them for some precision work."

"Yes, sir."

As Xavier had lectured him many times before, a battlefield commander had to be flexible. Many routes led to the objective. The pulse-atomics would do the job of getting them through to Corrin . . . and he could not accomplish the primary objective of destroying Omnius unless he got to the planet. One step at a time.

The revised tactic would save lives—not only the millions still crowded aboard the Bridge of Hrethgir, but also all of the soldiers who would die if the Supreme Bashar insisted on hammering against the robot defenses with conventional weapons.

"It does no good to save our atomics if all our ships are destroyed here in orbit."

Swarms of kindjal squadrons flew out of the launching bays of the large ballistas, thousands of the sharp-winged fighters and bombers. They were small, like bits of fluff thrown against a herd of behemoths. But they carried the seeds of immense destruction.

The kindjals deployed their atomics, tossing them in a broad spread against the dense conglomeration of targets the thinking machines had arranged to block the Army of Humanity.

"Here it comes," Vor said to no one in particular. "All shields at full strength. Front lines, withdraw if you can."

Seeing the unexpected shift of tactics, the robot battleships moved forward, eager to regain some of the ground they had lost.

Then a wave of dazzling pulse-atomics detonated, overlapping floods of enhanced energy specifically designed to erase gelcircuitry minds. The enormous amount of physical damage was only secondary.

As Vor covered his eyes against the flash, he studied the automatically dimmed screen on the flagship. It looked as if the blinding, luminous hand of God had just swept through the robot lines, paralyzing the craft, killing the thinking machines aboard, and leaving the impenetrable defensive line in ruins.

No, Vor thought. *It was not a waste of our warheads.*

He had no doubt that many hapless Corrin prisoners had been placed aboard those enemy warships, and had died along with their robot captors, but Vor didn't pause to think about those casualties. They were necessary, unavoidable. Perhaps someday history would compile an accurate tally. But humans would write this history only if they emerged victorious from the Battle of Corrin.

"Full forward, into the breach!" he shouted. "If you've still got shields, use them against all that debris—and hold on!"

Like a battering ram, the Army of Humanity crashed ahead, blasting through the dead robot vessels until they encountered the inner line of machine defenses. Taken by surprise, the robot battleships scrambled to tighten their positions.

Vor sent out the next wave of kindjal bombers—and annihilated the next enemies standing against him. And then the third and last line. By the time they finally broke through to the atmospheric fringe of Corrin, the Vengeance Fleet had depleted most of their store of atomics.

Though they had used many of their warheads, at last the target lay below, exposed and vulnerable.

"We have business to finish down there." Vor pointed at the last machine planet, which stretched in a gentle curve almost seventy kilometers beneath them.

THE REMNANTS OF the opposing fleets locked in combat in the skies over Corrin, with warships on each side blasting their way through and then returning to open fire again. Vor guided his ballista into the fray as if he were at the controls of a one-man fighter, as if he were a young officer again, trying to prove himself. He remembered the first great battle of the Jihad over Earth.

His fleet dipped into the upper atmosphere. The escort ships accompanying Vor's flagship took a heavy beating from ultrasound aerial torpedoes, and when many of the Army of Humanity vessels caught fire and tumbled away, others took their place to protect the Supreme Bashar.

Hostile fire hit a nearby ship, overloading the already weakened shields until the League vessel exploded, pelting the LS *Serena Victory* with debris. Vor grimaced as bodies and body parts tumbled away from the wreckage into the high, thin air.

Much more destruction would follow. He did not fear death himself, and was proud of his crew on the flagship, as they performed their duties flawlessly. He could not possibly have asked for more.

Artillery blasts from the LS *Serena Victory* and the rest of the Vengeance Fleet obliterated thinking machines in their battleships and on the ground. Explosions blossomed in the sky and on the surface of the planet. Down there, Omnius still remained intact.

With the way cleared and a safe path opened up in orbit, now the Viceroy's diplomatic vessel approached from the outskirts of the battle zone. Several shuttles emerged, descending swiftly toward the heart of the fiercest combat. Over the comline, Vor heard the feverish voice of Rayna Butler. "By the grace of Saint Serena, we're getting through! I told you we could do it!"

Angrily, Vor opened a direct channel. "Viceroy Butler, what are you and Rayna doing? I did not give permission for this. Stay out of the line of fire."

Faykan's voice came back. "It isn't me, Supreme Bashar. It seems . . . Rayna has her own mission. She was quite insistent."

The pale young woman transmitted from her shuttle, "Corrin is the den of our enemies. This is—and has always been—my calling in life. My followers, and the spirit of Saint Serena, will protect me."

Vor heaved a deep, exasperated sigh. Somehow, that woman could rationalize any contradiction. Rayna believed Serena was alive on the Bridge, but she also felt she was guided by Serena's spirit. Of course, Rayna also wanted to destroy all forms of technology, yet she rode in spaceships. . . .

He had more vital concerns at the moment. At least they would be fighting a real enemy now, instead of harmless surrogate machines on the League Worlds. Let the fanatics face the brunt of Omnius's defenders— and better that the antitechnology fanatics burn out their vehemence here than at home.

As the surviving ships of the fleet pressed forward to the main goal on Corrin, machine forces regrouped around the evermind's stronghold in the center of the city. Vor summoned all the swordmasters and mercenaries, many of them seasoned veterans trained to deal with problems exactly like these. They had been waiting during the long journey for this moment.

Ultimately, it is not what you are but who you are that matters.
—*Erasmus Dialogues*,
final entries

Though he was numb in his heart and body, Swordmaster Istian Goss continued to fight. Corrin, at least, was a proper battlefield for his skills.

For the weeks of travel across space to the final Synchronized World, he had been disturbed and restless, keeping to himself. Aboard the ship he encountered many of the Cultist zealots whom he hated so much. If he didn't stay away from them, he might be tempted to lash out and break their bones.

Instead, Istian trained alone in sealed chambers, pushing himself, improving his fighting skills much as the young Jool Noret had done. But no matter how hard he worked, Istian still did not feel the spirit of the great hero moving through him. Even so, as he smashed one test opponent after another, he realized that the inner silence of Jool Noret did not in fact make Istian any less effective. He was a skilled swordmaster in his own right.

After the riots and demonstrations on Zimia had resulted in the deaths of both Nar Trig and the sensei mek Chirox, Istian had had no qualms about volunteering for this final assault on Corrin. Fighting the forces of Omnius yet again was far preferable to killing fellow human beings in order to assuage his anger and guilt.

When the Vengeance Fleet finally clashed above the last stronghold of Omnius, plowing through the defensive lines of robotic battleships, Istian and his fellow mercenaries armed themselves, prepared for the combat. But the space battle was not part of a swordmaster's fight. Istian had done little more than fidget aboard the ship, waiting, itching to use his pulse-sword in hand-to-hand combat.

At last, when the wreckage of the machine forces lay strewn in orbit, along with many dead ships from the Vengeance Fleet, Supreme Bashar Atreides turned them loose. Istian Goss and his fellow mercenaries climbed aboard a fast personnel shuttle, ready for a final assault on the primary city on Corrin. Beside him he had seen accompanying javelins and ballistas full of mercenaries blown up by repeated machine fire.

But some survived. Enough of them to do the job.

The personnel shuttle streaked down through the atmosphere, accompanied by twenty similar craft. It would be the mission of Istian and his fellow warriors to make Corrin safe, to eradicate the rest of the thinking machines, to plant the precision atomic charge that would exterminate the last evermind.

Beside him in the shuttle rode twenty-three other swordmasters, survivors of old battles, like himself. After the Jihad, many of them had found other callings in life, but they had returned for this conflict. One last opportunity to prove their combat skills.

As the personnel shuttle skidded to a halt in the chaos of the machine city, the hatches opened and the swordmasters poured out, their pulse-swords ready. Nearby, two other shuttles landed, bearing diplomatic markings instead of the Army of Humanity insignia. Enthusiastic but clumsy, Cultists carrying cudgels and crude imitations of pulse-swords raced out to destroy any enemy they could find.

His heart pounding, Istian turned away, not wanting to be distracted by fools when he had a real opponent to fight. An enemy that *mattered*.

However, he realized that the Cultists didn't care if they lost two or three fighters for every machine they managed to deactivate. This was pure jihad for them, more so than for anyone in the Army of Humanity. Unlike when they were back on Salusa Secundus, attacking useful machines such as Chirox, right now these zealots were actually Istian's allies. He found it strange to think of them as such. . . .

After Istian and his fellow mercenaries had exited, the shuttle pilot took off again, while anti-aircraft fire peppered the sky. Explosions rocked the streets of the primary Corrin city. Combat robots swarmed out of glistening geometrical complexes. With a loud yell, the swordmasters ran to meet them.

Eager for combat, Istian got there first. Before him, ominous combat meks stood to face the swordmasters, their weapons arms extended and optic threads sparkling, as if a machine could experience hatred.

Every one of them bore an eerie resemblance to Chirox.

After having watched the sensei mek sacrifice himself rather than hurt a human being, Istian hesitated, feeling a heaviness in his heart. He wished Chirox could be there beside him now. Even more influential on him than the visceral spirit of Jool Noret, the reprogrammed combat mek had guided Istian's life.

He groped for Jool Noret inside his heart—and finally felt an emotional, spiritual connection. In front of him, these warrior robots were simply brute-force fighters. And they would fall. The moment that his pulse-sword clashed against a combat mek, he realized that all similarity to Chirox was an illusion.

With the sensei mek's training, Istian was more than a match for them. He dispatched two opponents in the first wave and threw himself without thought upon the next combat mek, who had just killed one of the rampaging Cultists. While blood still dripped from its sharp flowmetal arms, Istian fried its gelcircuitry systems and spun about to seek another enemy.

As he continued to fight, all his ghosts and doubts burned away.

Istian reached the final level of abandonment, the true secret of Jool Noret's fighting style. He felt energized. This was what he had devoted his life to. This would always be the focus of his heart and mind.

He and his comrades made their way toward the central Omnius nexus, awaiting the final signal to plant their city-killer warheads and end their mission. Swinging his pulse-sword, Istian felt he could fight like this forever—and there were certainly enough thinking machines to keep him busy.

WHILE THE FINAL battle raged around Corrin, Erasmus paused to listen to the peaceful sounds of water trickling from numerous mechanical fountains and streams, punctuated with the background noises of battle in the skies above the capital city. Seeing the unfortunate course of the fighting—yet feeling no guilt for his own part in the terrible losses—the independent robot had retreated here to where he might seek solace for his troubles and await the end. Or terminate himself.

Abruptly, as he witnessed the return of his beloved ward, Erasmus changed his mind. With his crimson robe flowing around him, the robot strode forward to embrace a shaken-looking Gilbertus Albans, rescued from the cargo containers of the Bridge of Hrethgir. Even though the last Synchronized World was falling around him, he could think of only one thing. "You are safe, my Mentat. Excellent!" The expression of joy on his flowmetal face was not simulated, but a genuine, unconscious reaction.

The welcoming hug was so fervent that the powerfully built man gasped. "Father—please, not so much enthusiasm!"

Erasmus loosened the embrace and stood back to admire the man he had raised, trained, and cared for over so many decades. Gilbertus looked dirty and tired from his ordeal, but uninjured. That was the important thing. And the robot said, "I never thought I'd see you again."

"I felt the same." Gilbertus's large olive-green eyes misted over. "But I was also sure you would find a way to bring me back. You would not let me get hurt." He gave a worried frown. "But Serena is still up there. We must rescue her."

"Unfortunately, I am unable to help her now. Most of our defenses have been obliterated by human pulse-atomics. I fear that Corrin is lost to us," Erasmus said. "The League fleet will be here soon."

"At least she wasn't aboard one of the machine ships," Gilbertus said, striving for any sort of consolation. "Then she would be dead already."

The independent robot did not lie to him. "If Vorian Atreides follows his previous pattern, you and I may not have much longer, either, my Mentat. He will sterilize Corrin as he did the other Synchronized Worlds, and we will be obliterated. Up on the Bridge, your Serena may survive."

"I don't believe they will send waves of atomics to kill us all, Father. I saw their troops landing and entering the city—although their commander has already proved that he's willing to sacrifice millions of hostages. I cannot understand why the explosive trigger failed in the Bridge of Hrethgir."

"It did not fail, Gilbertus. I *deactivated* it—in order to save one person."

Gilbertus was stunned. "You did that for me? You sacrificed Corrin, the entire machine civilization? I am not worthy of that!"

"To me, you are. I have completed extensive projections, and it is clear that you will become a very important man one day. Perhaps when all the thinking machines are gone, you can teach your fellow humans how to think efficiently. Then all my work will not have been for nothing."

"You taught me how to think, Father," Gilbertus said. "I will honor you by explaining that these techniques come from you."

The robot shook his head. "No machine will escape Corrin today. Not even me. The battle is lost. I could show you the ongoing projections if we could activate one of the Omnius wallscreens. Our robot lines are crumbling. The League fleet has just driven another entire battle group through the scrambler network. We have very few active ships remaining in orbit. Already, the *hrethgir* have breached our tightest defenses. I can only hope that they choose to act with precision and spare some of the beauty of this world . . . and save you." He looked off in the distance, where the booming sounds of battle added a harsh counterpoint to the gentle peace of his garden.

"This is truly the twilight of the thinking machines. But not for you, Gilbertus. You must travel in human circles from now on, and never admit any connection with me. I killed Serena Butler's baby and sparked the mass mania that followed. Never mention my name or your association with me. The treasured moments we spent together can only be retained in your marvelous mind. You must pretend you have been a simple human slave here on Corrin. Change your clothes. With luck, the *hrethgir* will rescue you and take you back to the League of Nobles."

"But I do not wish to go." Though alarmed, Gibertus raised his chin. "If I do survive, then there is something I must do for you in return." He placed his hands on the robot's metal shoulders. "Will you trust me?"

"Of course. It is illogical even to ask me such a question."

DEEP BELOW THE plaza of the besieged city, underneath the flames, the rubble, and the thronging human conquerors, the recovering Omnius Prime began to move the flowmetal that encased him, material that had formerly been his Central Spire.

Fully functional now, the primary evermind intended to regain control of the planet.

Weapons are an important factor in war, but not the decisive factor.
People are decisive.

—MAO TSE-TUNG,

a philosopher of Old Earth

U nable to believe his triumph had finally come after more than a century of pain and bloodshed, Supreme Bashar Vorian Atreides guided his command shuttle toward the center of the main square of Corrin's primary city. The impending victory tasted like metal in his mouth, the pleasure dulled by his continuing anger against Abulurd. *At the moment of greatest crisis, he almost cost us everything.* And Seurat had betrayed him as well.

There would be time to deal with his emotions later, after he had witnessed the end of the computer evermind.

As Vor brought his command shuttle in from above, the robotic soldiers looked like children's toys spread across a stylized, smoking battlefield. The remnants of the mechanical army massed in a protective formation around a central shielded dome. Though defeated, they fired at the League's small kindjals and transport craft that buzzed overhead.

Shouting into his command link, Vor sent a wave of kindjal attack flyers against the last stronghold of Omnius, softening it up and removing any ground robot defenses, so that the mercenaries could approach and complete their surgical strike. In an ingenious technical innovation, the evermind seemed to heal the dome with each blast that struck, sealing a flowmetal layer over the destruction like a creature regrowing injured skin.

Wary, Vor called in a heavier bombardment from some of the surviving ballistas, and they descended through the flaming wreckage to pound the final stronghold of the evermind. With the larger armaments, the blasts went deeper, killing entrenched thinking machines. Finally, the protective dome crumbled under the massive detonations, and could not use flowmetal technology to restore itself.

As he landed his shuttle, Vor summoned the surviving Ginaz mercenaries and sent them forward with demolitions equipment and weaponry to finish obliterating any vestiges of the evermind.

I must watch for a final trap. In the endgame of this long Jihad, when things looked so bleak, the thinking machines could still come up with a clever last effort, something surprising and devastating.

As Vor strode into the machine city, he was reminded of the design and grid of Earth's huge Omnius metropolis where he had spent his youth. Viceroy Faykan Butler had also landed and was strutting around the battlefield, surrounded by other nobles who wanted history to record that they had been there personally.

Wild members of the Cult of Serena raced through the city in an orgy of destruction, and Vor let them indulge their penchant for chaos. He realized cynically that a single, well-placed atomic-pulse would get rid of Rayna and her furious Cult, the politically ambitious Viceroy, and the evermind all at once. He needed only the disloyal Abulurd Harkonnen to round out all the enemies of humanity in a single place. . . .

But Vor shook away his dark thoughts. Iblis Ginjo might have approved of such a scheme, but not Vorian Atreides. He vowed to leave a legacy of honor after this momentous day.

Seeing Vor, one of Faykan Butler's noble companions rushed up. "Champion Atreides! Rayna and some of her people were near the citadel before the bombardment! We're afraid they've been buried under the rubble. You have to dispatch crews to dig them out! The Viceroy is there now."

Vor couldn't believe what he was hearing. "Why would she be there? Doesn't she know we're bombarding the structure? This is no place for civilians. Corrin is a battle zone!"

"Maybe the poor girl expected to be protected by Saint Serena," the noble said with just a hint of sarcasm in his voice. "Please send workers and medical personnel—it's a direct request from the Viceroy."

Vor scowled, resenting that he had to take valuable personnel away from important missions to aid Rayna. Finally, suppressing his frustration, he summoned a group of engineers, soldiers, and battlefield surgeons.

While swordmasters stormed into the rubble of the citadel, battling combat robots that remained intact even after the bombardment, Vor made his way toward the center of the destruction. As he watched, Ginaz mercenaries threw scrambler grenades, sending pulses of disruptive Holtzman energy that wiped out gelcircuitry brains.

Near the embattled citadel, he saw the Viceroy standing at the excavation site, looking concerned. His troops had already removed dozens of human bodies from the rubble. Sighing, Vor stepped up to Faykan. "Have they found your niece yet?"

"Not yet. But I hold on to hope."

Vor nodded. "Yes, I suppose this is a place for hope."

On this very spot, the Central Spire of an earlier Omnius had once stood. Here also, Serena Butler had given up her life for the cause of humanity. So it was with a tremendous feeling of awe and a sense of history that Vor watched his troops use heavy machinery to search the rubble, while some of the Cultists used their bare hands to help.

On the plaza perimeter, combat engineers searched for hidden openings that might lead down. Sophisticated detection beams played over the rubble and patches of exposed pavement. The mercenaries were ready with special warheads.

One of the sensor operators sent Vor a comsignal. "We found something beneath what's left of a plazcrete monument that was inside the dome," the man said. "It's all recent construction, and I'm picking up hollow spots down there. Some side passageways, too, and a large void in the middle."

"Spectral analysis indicates unusual metals," another soldier said.

"Dig it out," Vor ordered.

Suddenly the plaza cracked open, scattering Vor and his engineers. Like a snake bursting out of its hole, the silvery, tentacular growth of the Central Spire lunged out of the rubble and shot skyward.

Soldiers shouted, and the Cultists made warding signs, screaming to vanquish the unexpected demon. The liquid-silver flowmetal spire twisted and reshaped, billowing out at the end like an inverted umbrella, a parabolic dish of some sort. *A transmitter!*

With a groan like a dying sea beast, the Central Spire convulsed and then vomited a flash of light, shooting a signal upward through the atmosphere like a scream out into space, where it would dissipate across the parsecs. Then the Central Spire collapsed, lost its integrity, and splattered into puddles across the broad, rubble-strewn plaza.

"What in the name of Serena was that?" Faykan cried.

"Nothing good," Vor said. "You can be sure of it."

He heard a cheer, and a short distance away saw soldiers and ragged Cultists pulling a battered Rayna Butler out of the debris. The young woman was covered with dirt and abrasions, but alive. Within moments she stood on her own, wavering, and brushed herself off. A bright stain of blood marked her robe, but she said it was not her own. Shakily, she climbed on top of a broken slab of plazcrete, gathered her breath, and shouted, "Saint Serena has protected me!"

"Saint Serena has done enough protecting for one day," Vor muttered to Faykan. "Get your niece and all of your people out of here—because I'm blowing up what's left."

He received an acknowledgment from the mercenaries, as they arrived at their target with three surgical pulse-warheads. Thanks to the aerial bombardment of the Central Spire, the robot ground defenses had crumbled. The rest was just an exercise. Vor and the Viceroy retreated with all of the other personnel, standing at a safe distance.

The flash was no more dazzling than all the previous ones, but the cheers from raw and ragged throats were louder. Omnius was gone. Forever.

GILBERTUS ALBANS DISENGAGED the independent robot's memory core, the same small sphere he had saved when Omnius demanded the erasure of Erasmus. He wrapped it in a cloth and tied it with loving care. The little bundle fit neatly into his pocket, where no one would think to look for it. It was a priceless record of Erasmus's remarkable life, his mind . . . his soul.

The robot's metal body, now empty and deactivated, remained in the middle of his beloved contemplation garden, surrounded by soothing classical music and the serenity of whispering fountains. His plush robe hung in heavy folds. Erasmus looked like a statue.

Now Gilbertus decided he had to find the Serena Butler clone. His next challenge would be to rescue her, if she was still alive. There was too much he did not know.

With a last glance over his shoulder at his mentor, Gilbertus ran from the villa and melted into a mob of uniformed human soldiers, mercenaries from Ginaz, and antimachine Cultists who were destroying everything in sight. One of them fired a rocket at the ornate villa, where Erasmus's beautiful platinum body stood. Gilbertus winced, then turned away as the villa erupted in flames. The crowd of zealots cheered, then ran on to the next target.

For hours, Gilbertus pretended to help the humans destroy thinking machines and the structure of the only society he had ever known. He ran with them, stumbling and sickened, but promising himself that he would reach safety.

It was what Erasmus would have wanted.

Sometimes memories are safer than reality.
—SUPREME BAŞHAR VORIAN ATREIDES

After the destruction of the last Omnius, as he divided his battle groups to complete the remaining planetside operations, Vor sent all available ships up to the Bridge of Hrethgir. The captain of each vessel had to do triage, set immediate priorities, and salvage the people from the worst-off cargo pods first.

And find Serena. How to locate one woman in particular, among so many hostages?

Vor's technicians sifted through the recordings Erasmus had transmitted that showed the familiar woman and her child, and analyzing details from every image they attempted to compare and backtrack the location so they could identify which of the numerous rigged cargo vessels might contain her.

Secondary squadrons of the Army of Humanity swarmed through the packed containers lined up in orbit. Ballistas filled with rescued hostages shuttled back and forth to Corrin in an endless succession. It had taken less than two days for the thinking machines to place all of the human shields in harm's way—a massive effort, but Vor received estimates from his staff that the remaining Vengeance Fleet ships would take at least a week to rescue the prisoners and return them to safety. He didn't believe they could all survive that long.

The makeshift holding vessels had been designed for robots, who needed no life-support systems; atmosphere pumps had been installed swiftly, and not necessarily perfectly. Aboard many of the hostage containers, the stench was horrendous, and the air had already begun to give out. Over mobile comlines, his officers reported problems. Some captives had already died, and others were weak. None of them had any food or water left.

"Time is running out," he muttered. "We have to speed up these operations."

When Vor's technicians narrowed the search to the cargo containers most likely to hold Serena, he gave orders for his battered flagship to pull alongside. "I will see for myself. If it really is her, I'll know her immediately."

When the command shuttle docked, Vor took a small squad of armed soldiers and combat engineers. Opening the hatch, they were mobbed by desperate people, but he and his troops pushed their way inside the death trap and again sealed the hatch. After quelling the frenzy of the hostages by firing sedative darts into the crowd, the League soldiers began an orderly evacuation. Six other personnel transport shuttles linked to hatches of the joined containers. Two engineers hurriedly studied the engines and the unreliable life-support systems, assessing how long the craft would remain intact.

Vor had another priority. He switched on his personal shield and left the professionals to do their work. After scanning the crowd being herded toward the rescue shuttles, he and four soldiers ran through a connecting tube into the next container and shoved open an airtight hatch. More prisoners pushed up against them, raising their hands, hailing their rescuers, begging for help. But the lead group hurried along, intent on their search. The sounds of boots on metal echoed as they ran.

The cargo containers were segregated into several large holds, crowded with noisy and stinking people. Finally, as Vor strained to see, one of his combat engineers called over the short-range comline. "Supreme Bashar, this container isn't going to last long. It's rigged with too many explosives, sir. We won't be able to disconnect them all in time."

Vor didn't pause. "If they put extra explosives on this cargo container, it must be the one we're looking for."

The first engineer's voice had a ragged edge. He was working with three of his team members. "We can't keep up with the cascading failures. Commander, you have to get back aboard the flagship!"

"Not until I find Serena Butler. Keep working on the problem." He broadened the transmission range. "Everybody report. Has anyone seen Serena and the child?"

Another soldier answered Vor's plea. "I think they're in here, Supreme Bashar—but something's . . . not right about them. I didn't even see her at first, and then they all changed. Right before my eyes. And . . . and there's more than one Serena!"

Vor received confirmation of the location and pushed his way past slaves and troops, not thinking about the deadly explosives. His experts knew what they were doing.

In a far corner of the dim and noisome chamber, he finally saw Serena sitting on the deck next to the small boy, a toddler in gray trousers and a white shirt. The woman wore a white robe, trimmed in purple, just as in the images that had been projected. She looked at him with her strikingly familiar lavender eyes . . . but when their gazes locked, she showed no sign of recognition.

Then he saw another Serena, one that looked younger but otherwise identical. And two more, all of them clearly Serena Butler. Copies, impostors.

One of the women stood and moved closer to him. She reached out a hand, and Vor touched her fingers; they had a rubbery texture that seemed far from human. "I am Serena Butler. Please don't kill me. Please don't kill my baby." The simulated voice was *almost* right.

Then her face began flickering and contorting—and it changed, lost its integrity, and began to sag, showing flowmetal and a rigid structure beneath. A robot, with some sort of fleshlike disguise.

As Vor lurched backward, he heard laughter from the other side of the container. He turned from the disguised robot, then saw a face he recognized from many years ago. Rekur Van, the Tlulaxa flesh merchant. But Van had no arms or legs. His limbless torso was propped up in a harness, connected to life-support machinery. The other hostages shrank from him, glad to get away as the League soldiers evacuated them toward the rescue shuttles.

Rekur Van glowered with his dark rodent eyes. "Had you fooled for a while, didn't I? I created that simulacrum, a biological flowmetal that looks like skin. Looks like Serena."

Sick with disappointment, Vor glared at the Tlulaxa man. Only now did he realize how much hope he had actually hung on the impossible chance that she might still be alive. Beside him, the four soldiers moved into position to guard the Supreme Bashar, their weapons ready.

The Tlulaxa's pinched face formed a wide grin. "Unfortunately, though a robot can mimic specific human features for a while, they always lose integrity in the end. The child-sized one was easier. Who recognizes the features of a baby anyway?"

"We're wasting our time here," Vor called to his guards. "Get the rest of these people out of here. I should have known machines could never come up with such lies all by themselves. They needed human assistance."

"*I'm* perfectly real, though." Rekur Van laughed. "Who would copy a body like this one?"

Vor looked around at the multiple Serenas. "Are they all shape-shifter robots?"

"Ah, no—much better. That one is a clone, from Serena Butler's actual cells, grown with a special process. A . . . flawed process. While her body might be identical, the mind has none of her experiences, none of her memories or personality. In fact, I doubt if it even has a soul—the process did not work as well as I had hoped, since all the right sort of tanks are still on my homeworld." He chortled at his joke, wavering like a toy. "I should have stayed on Tlulax. The everminds are insane. Three of them, then only two. Or have you destroyed them all already? Why would they send me up here with the useless humans?"

"Where is Gilbertus?" the Serena clone asked.

"Sir!" the first engineer shouted over the command comline. "We can't stop the destruct mechanism! You've got to leave!"

The Tlulaxa shouted, "Take me with you. I have a great deal of information you could—"

Six combat robots, stationed there by Erasmus when he had ordered the rescue of Gilbertus Albans, marched through the chamber's opposite end. Detecting Vor and the other soldiers, they began firing integral weapons. Two projectiles struck harmlessly off Vor's shield as he hit the deck. The few hostages who had not yet gotten away were mowed down. One of his guards, carelessly unshielded, was struck in the shoulder, and he went down, clutching the raw wound.

Vor and his three remaining guards could not fire back without deactivating their shields. The robots advanced rapidly and loudly, shooting wildly. The Serena clone stepped in front of them—trying to delay them for some unfathomable reason? Did she remember, after all?

He tried to rush forward, but she was cut to pieces by repeated fire. Vor watched in revulsion as the thinking machines killed Serena Butler again.

One of the heavy projectiles caromed off the metal hull, smashing through the wall of the failing cargo container. Air shrieked through the breach, spraying out into the vacuum.

Furious, Vor switched off his own shield and blasted the oncoming robots with his heavy projectile weapon. Two of the combat machines staggered backward, giving him just enough time to grab the wounded soldier, dragging him along. "Let's get the hell out of here!"

Switching his shield back on, Vor didn't look behind him. He hauled the injured soldier around the bodies as the other guards alternated firing at the robots and switching their personal shields back on.

The combat engineer yelled over the comline that the destruct sequence had entered its final phase. Vor ran, but he felt numb. None of the Serenas were real. The baby wasn't real. It had all been a stupid, desperate trick.

With the remaining combat meks still coming, Vor retreated through the connecting tube fastened to his command shuttle. His men fired from the rear, and then he rolled inside the shuttle with them. He handed off the injured soldier, and other men rushed the wounded man inside with them. Vor dove after them, sprawling on the deck as the last combat engineer sealed the hatch shut.

"Disengage!" Vor shouted.

As the flagship separated from the doomed cargo container, the rigged explosives finally detonated, destroying the Tlulaxa researcher and his unholy creations.

Even Norma Cenva had to struggle for perfection, and never achieved it.

                          —Origins of the Spacing Guild

L ife confined in a tank . . . but a mind without boundaries. Who could ask for more freedom?

Permanently addicted to the spice gas that swirled in an orange mist around her, impregnating her every pore, every cell, she never left the sealed enclosure anymore. Norma didn't even know if she *could* leave. Survival might not be possible for her on the outside. Not anymore.

During her long and eventful life, Norma had been many things, from a scorned and misshapen dwarf to a mathematical genius . . . to a beautiful wife and mother. And now, the next phase—something much, much more.

Even in a sealed spice tank, she was not prevented from traveling any-where she wished. She could guide VenKee ships safely through the labyrinth of folded space. The whole universe lay open before her.

She drew all of the nutrients she needed from the spice itself. Her direct physical senses were deadened, and Norma no longer cared about taste, touch, or smell. She still required her hearing and eyesight, but only to communicate with Adrien and the VenKee assistants, who fulfilled any needs she expressed to them.

But it was so difficult to talk down to their level.

Her alternate, deeper form of sight was much more significant and interesting than what she had lost. Triggered by the transformation she'd undergone during Xerxes's torture years ago, Norma had evolved beyond physical boundaries, beyond human.

She found it remarkable to see webbing between her fingers and toes. Her face, once blunt-featured and later flawlessly beautiful, now had a small mouth and tiny eyes surrounded by smooth folds. Her head was immense, while the rest of her body atrophied to a useless appendage.

But none of that mattered in the least to her.

With her prescience, Norma saw the future, like reflections within reflections, echoing to infinity. In her mind she could see—and encompass—the entire universe, and she knew there were no limits to what she could achieve. She watched the direction humanity would take, toward an interplanetary empire connected by her spacefolder ships . . . the lifeline of commerce for trillions of people.

Serena Butler's Jihad and the resulting antithinking machine fanaticism—as well as an abiding horror of the terrible biological weapons unleashed by Omnius and the appalling atomics used in the Great Purge—would leave an indelible mark on humanity for millennia.

But humanity would survive, and would create a vast realm of politics, business, religion, and philosophy, all held together by the spice melange.

With her new prescient vision, she could guide VenKee spacefolders on safe and instantaneous journeys across vast distances. And Norma could not complete all the work alone. She had to make others capable of navigating with their own prescience, enhanced by using massive amounts of spice gas. . . .

SHE NEVER ASKED Adrien where he found his first ten volunteers. As the fabulously wealthy directeur of VenKee Enterprises and its newest venture, the Foldspace Shipping Company, Adrien had numerous connections. Already, the candidates were confined to chambers filled with gradually increasing concentrations of melange gas. They would begin mutating and changing, much like Norma. One day these volunteers would navigate fast company vessels throughout the League and the Unallied Planets, but Norma knew they would never have the far-reaching vision she possessed.

Norma felt impatience as she waited for her own mutations to reach the end of their genetic journey. She envisioned the political, commer-

religious, philosophical, and technological tomorrows scrolling off ɔ an infinite distance.

She would blaze a trail through the cosmos. Like no other person who had ever existed, she had a unique, highly specialized set of talents.

But even with her unparalleled prescience, Norma could not determine what would eventually become of *her*.

*There is a certain malevolence concerning the formation of a social
order. Despotism lies at one end of the spectrum, and slavery at the
other.*

— TLALOC,
A Time for Titans

hen the Army of Humanity returned to Salusa Secundus after its
victory against the thinking machines, the delirious celebrations
throughout Zimia and across the League Worlds surpassed even the fervor
of Rayna Butler's technology-hating fanatics.

Stories of the Battle of Corrin were told, retold, and constantly
embellished. The Supreme Bashar's gutsy show of force at the Bridge of
Hrethgir had turned disaster into an unqualified triumph, forever eradicating the enemy. All vestiges of the evermind Omnius were gone, and
more than a thousand years of machine oppression was over. Humanity
was free at last, able to march unfettered into the future, at its own pace,
for its own glory.

Vorian Atreides, hero of the Battle of Corrin, took his place beside
Viceroy Butler and Rayna in Salusa's grand plaza for the celebration. The
Supreme Bashar wore his full-dress uniform, including new medals and decorations that had been crafted for him. He had rendered military service for
his own reasons, ever since Serena had convinced him of the innate power
of humanity. Now, though, looking at the unruly crowd, he felt misgivings
about the future that humanity might choose to create for itself.

Around Zimia, he still saw the scars of the recent Cultist uprisings:
burned buildings, smashed facades, the scattered wreckage of once-useful
machines. The Cult of Serena was out in the vast audience in force, hold-

ing banners and their symbolic clubs. Robots in effigy were pummeled and battered by the cheering crowds, as if it were a child's game.

Through it all, Faykan smiled at his niece and stood close, basking in her halo. Vor could see all too clearly what he was trying to do.

On the long voyage home, Vor knew that the Viceroy had made careful plans with his fervant niece, even while she recovered from her injuries. Faykan offered her the position of Grand Matriarch, but oddly enough the pallid young woman did not want the title. She wanted only promises from her uncle that he would follow through and help complete the social cleansing she envisioned across the League.

Vor did not have such grand hopes, though. If Rayna continued her purges, the rampant eradication of technology would sweep unchecked across all inhabited worlds. Anyone could see that this would set off a new dark age . . . but at the moment Vor feared Faykan was most concerned about securing his own power base. In the current climate, the Viceroy could not have formed a secular state without emotional trappings.

Suddenly free of their inhuman enemies, the people turned to their religions, in thanksgiving and hope. Blind faith was a source of energy the League would have to tap. The human race would face centuries of rebuilding, but apparently Faykan didn't trust them to perform those difficult labors out of political necessity. Something else needed to drive them.

Unfortunately, with their demons now gone, Rayna's followers were bound to grow restless again, as soon as the euphoria of the Battle of Corrin wore off. Vor saw deeply troubled times ahead. . . .

Under the bright sunlight of a perfect day, Viceroy Butler raised his hands. The cheering swelled to a deafening crescendo, then faded into silence. Faykan played the crowds, let their anticipation build. Finally, he cried, "This is a time of great changes! Following a thousand years of tribulation, we have earned our inevitable triumph, as promised by God. We have paid for our victory with uncounted—but not forgotten—debts. We cannot exaggerate the significance of the Battle of Corrin and the wondrous opportunities the future will provide us.

"To commemorate this great event, with my niece Rayna Butler and Supreme Bashar Vorian Atreides, I announce that I will merge my office of Viceroy with the duties of the Grand Patriarch, whose position has been vacant since the murder of Xander Boro-Ginjo.

"From this day forward, rather than letting the power be fragmented and diluted, authority shall reside in one person in myself and in my successors. There is much work to be done in transforming our weary League of Nobles into a more effective form of government. We will create a new empire of mankind that can grow and reclaim the glories of the Old Empire—while avoiding its fatal mistakes."

On cue, the audience cheered. Though surprised by the announcement, Vor was not particularly bothered. He'd never had any use for the office of the Grand Patriarch anyway, which had been created for Iblis Ginjo's purposes. Now, in Faykan Butler's smile and in his eyes, Vor could see echoes of Serena at her most passionate.

When the uproar subsided, Faykan placed his hand on Rayna's slender shoulder. "So that no one will ever forget how we have changed, henceforth I shall no longer be known by the name of Butler. I come from a great and honorable family, but from this day forward, I wish to be known for the Battle of Corrin, my crowning achievement, that put an end to the thinking machines."

Right, Vor thought, concealing a cynical smile. *He did it all by himself.*

"Henceforth," Faykan continued, "let the people call me *Corrino* so that all of my descendants will remember that battle and this great day."

IN SHARP CONTRAST to the ecstatic celebrations, the mood was somber and murderous the following afternoon, when the prisoner Abulurd Harkonnen was brought in to face charges in the cavernous Hall of Parliament. Initially, Faykan had wanted his younger brother dragged into the assembly chamber in chains, but Vorian argued against that, showing a last flicker of compassion for the man who had been his friend. "He wears the shackles of his own guilt. His conscience is heavier than anything we could do to him."

Outside in the streets, the mobs—seeking any enemy against whom to vent their anger—howled and swore at the traitor. Given the chance, they would have torn Abulurd limb from limb. He had hamstrung the Vengeance Fleet in its moment of greatest need. Neither the people, nor history, could ever forgive him for that.

Inside the chamber, League representatives and military officers watched Abulurd being marched to the center of the floor. During the journey back from Corrin, most of Abulurd's bruises and other injuries had healed from his beating, but he still looked wan and battered. The audience glowered at him, their hatred and outrage palpable. Though they knew of the bashar's previous exemplary service, nothing could sway the juggernaut of charges against him.

Faykan stood inside the speaking chamber, confronting the disgraced officer—his own brother, though they had not shared a family name for years. "Abulurd Harkonnen, former officer in the Army of the Jihad, you stand accused of high treason against the human race. Whether through collusion or poor judgment, your actions nearly caused grievous harm to our fleet—and, by extension, the whole of the human race. Will you further ruin your honor by offering excuses for your behavior?"

Abulurd bowed his head. "The record makes clear my motivations. Either accept or dismiss them. In the end, for whatever reason, it was *not* necessary to kill two million innocent hostages. If I must pay for that decision now, so be it."

The people in the hall grumbled. For them, no amount of torment would be sufficient to punish this traitor.

"The penalty for treason is clear," Faykan said. "If you refuse to give us an alternative, then this Assembly has no choice but to condemn you to execution."

Abulurd hung his head and said nothing further. The chamber fell deathly silent. "Will no one speak on this man's behalf?" the Viceroy asked, looking around. He pointedly refused to call Abulurd his brother. "I will not."

Abulurd kept his gaze fixed on the floor. He had made up his mind not to look at the faces in the audience. The wordless moment seemed interminable.

Finally, just as the Viceroy raised his hand to pronounce sentence, Supreme Bashar Vorian Atreides rose slowly to his feet in the front row. "With great reservations, I propose that we withdraw the accusation of treason against Abulurd Harkonnen, and limit the charge to . . . cowardice."

A gasp rang through the hall. Abulurd looked up sharply. "Cowardice? Don't do that, I beg of you!"

Faykan said quietly, "But cowardice is not technically accurate, considering his crimes. His actions do not meet the criteria—"

"Nevertheless, a charge of cowardice will wound him more deeply than any other." His words were as sharp as ice picks. Vor continued, his voice stronger now. "Abulurd once served bravely, fighting the thinking machines. During the time of the Scourge, he coordinated the evacuation and defense of Salusa Secundus, and he fought at my side when the piranha mites attacked Zimia. But he refused to fight the thinking machines when called upon to do so by his legitimate commanding officer. When faced with the terrible consequences of a decision, he showed disgraceful fear, and allowed it rather than duty to dictate his actions. He is a coward and should be banished from the League."

"That is worse," Abulurd cried.

Vor narrowed his gray eyes and leaned forward from his stand. "Yes, Abulurd—I believe it is."

Looking broken, Abulurd let his shoulders droop, and he began to shake. After all his work of trying to erase the charges against his grandfather Xavier, this accusation struck him to the core.

Faykan seized the opportunity. "A fine idea, Supreme Bashar! I decree that the proposed sentence is appropriate and hereby order that it be carried out. Abulurd Harkonnen, you are judged a coward—perhaps the greatest coward in history—both for the harm you did, and for all the harm you *could* have done. You will be despised long after your reviled grandfather Xavier Harkonnen is forgotten."

Vor spoke to Abulurd as if there was no one else in the great chamber. "You failed me at the moment I needed you most. Never again will I look upon your face. This I swear." In a dramatic gesture, Vorian Atreides turned his back on him. "From this day forth, let all who bear the name Atreides spit on the name of Harkonnen."

Without glancing over his shoulder, the Supreme Bashar strode out of the Hall of Parliament, leaving Abulurd to stand there alone in his misery. After a brief hesitation, Faykan Corrino also turned his back on his brother, and left the hall without a word.

Muttering and rustling, all of the gathered military officers followed suit, standing up in a wave and abandoning Abulurd to his solitary, ignominious fate. One by one the parliamentary representatives stood, turned away from the coward, and departed. Rapidly, the facility emptied.

Abulurd stood shaking in the middle of the echoing floor. He wanted to call out, to beg forgiveness or leniency, even to ask for execution so that he would not have to live forever with the terrible stigma on his name. But soon no respected member of the League of Nobles remained, except for his two guards. Every seat in the echoing hall was empty.

Abulurd Harkonnen did not resist when the Zimia guards took him away and sent him off to his lifelong exile.

We cannot move forward without the past. We carry it with us, not as baggage but as a sacred blessing.

—REVEREND MOTHER RAQUELLA BERTO-ANIRUL

Though not born on Rossak, Raquella had earned the respect of the few Sorceresses who survived the epidemic. The vaccine she converted using her own antibodies had saved thousands, but the jungle world would be a long time recovering from the horrendous effects of the mutated plague.

With Ticia Cenva gone, the other women asked Raquella to lead them. Enlightened by her strange new revelations, she accepted the mantle of authority, but not for any reasons of personal power. Her inner transformation had also shown her the generational path to her own genetic history. She was intrigued by the enormous amount of breeding information the Sorceresses had compiled. So much potential in the human race!

The secret and illegal genetic record-keeping machines were hidden deep within the stone caverns of the cliff city. The wave of antitechnology fervor sweeping across the League Worlds could not be allowed to damage the priceless bloodline data the women of Rossak had gathered over countless generations. *The very idea of using thinking machines to improve humanity!*

Enduring plague and poison, Raquella had achieved a sharply altered understanding of her cellular makeup. Now she hoped to share her vision with the stunned Sorceress survivors. Could others learn to manipulate their biochemical processes, and would they require a similarly difficult ordeal to do so? What terrible instruction and testing would the candidates have to undergo?

Drawn from the most powerful Sorceresses, they would be an elite order with special skills, linked to the distant past and the far future. *It will all begin here.*

AFTER RAQUELLA'S MIRACULOUS recovery from the Rossak Epidemic, Mohandas had rushed down from the orbiting medical ship. She went to meet him, feeling as if a great gulf suddenly separated them. But among all the lives and memories she held within herself, she also had her own times, her own history. And much of it was with Mohandas Suk.

On the polymerized treetop landing pad, he stepped out of the shuttle and hugged her enthusiastically. "I thought I had lost you!"

"Yes, I was lost . . . but I found many unexpected things along the way."

He clung to her, kissing her neck, focused only on being close to Raquella again. A flood of her own memories surfaced, and she used them as an anchor against all the others inside her. She and Mohandas had never had a wildly passionate relationship, but their love and their common professional bond had held them together for a quarter century.

"There are still so many people to help," she said. "The sick are still recovering. I can think of a thousand details, all the bodies to be buried, the food and purified water we still need, the—"

Mohandas held her close, not letting her pull away. "We have both earned a little time together. Just an hour or so."

Raquella could not argue. When they found a private place, she and Mohandas explored each other, reminding themselves of what it meant to be human. They made love, and it felt fresh and full of joy to her, a celebration of life. After so many years of tending the sick and dying, after enduring this new epidemic that had killed so much of Rossak's population, it was a small but significant affirmation.

She felt saddened that the two of them could never go back to the innocent past, but Raquella was no longer the same person—not just in her cells, but in her mind. The unlocking of ancient memories inside her had expanded the history she could grasp, showing her the saga of her female ancestors and enabling her to see how far the human race had come . . . and how much farther it had left to go.

She discovered with her new bodily control that she could easily manipulate her reproductive systems. Raquella watched with her inner eye, amazed at the miracle as she conceived a child. Lying close and warm against her, Mohandas did not know. She held him, but concentrated on the mysterious depths within her. It would be a daughter. . . .

Later, Mohandas told her of the plans he had made. "We've been through a century of the Jihad, then the Scourge, and now this new epidemic. Humanity must be prepared to face all the tragedies the universe has in store for us. When our race is at stake, important victories are won in hospitals as much as on battlefields." He grasped Raquella's hands, and she felt the warmth of his touch, his new passion. "We can take the best of us, the most talented researchers, the most skilled doctors, and form a medical school like none the League has ever seen. We must make sure that our doctors and facilities are such that no threat of machine, war, or plague can ever harm us again."

Caught up in his exuberance, Raquella smiled. "If anyone can do it, Mohandas, you can. You'll be even more successful than your great uncle Rajid. You have far surpassed his skills as a respected battlefield surgeon." Back in the days when the two of them had served in the lowly Hospital for Incurable Diseases on Parmentier, she would never have imagined such a possibility.

His dark eyes shone. "You have to come with me, of course. Without you, none of these people would be cured."

She shook her head slowly. "No, Mohandas. I . . . I must remain on Rossak. I have vital work to complete with these women."

He seemed baffled by her response. "But what could possibly be more important, Raquella? Think of what we could do together—"

She interrupted him, pressing a gentle finger to his lips. "My mind is made up, Mohandas. The things I have seen, the abilities I can now touch . . . hold many mysteries, many wonders. These women, with their great powers, need a rational and worthy leader for a change, one who can guide them into a broad future." Perhaps, Raquella thought, she could even do something for Jimmak and all the Misborn.

Mohandas shook his head in disbelief, then his eyes filled with emotion. Though the two of them had not often displayed their feelings for each other, she saw how strong his love for her remained. Her own feelings had forever changed, though. She held him, and put her head on his shoulder so that she would not have to look into his face. "I'm sorry . . . my future has to be here."

ONE AFTERNOON AFTER Mohandas had taken the LS *Recovery* to follow his own dream, Raquella waited for the Rossak women to assemble beside her on a windswept clifftop. She had summoned the Sorceresses here to this high perch to mark the beginning of their new organization.

By necessity, theirs was a close-knit group of skilled women with tightly held secrets and explicit trust among its members. She promised that their "Sisterhood" would be founded on adaptation, tolerance, and true long-term planning. With her new perspective that spanned all of her previous generations, Raquella could understand such things now.

If humans properly accessed their potential, they had an infinite ability to adapt to unusual, even harsh circumstances. Following the crucible of the Jihad, and more than a millennium of thinking-machine abuses, the human race was poised to take its next, most important step.

Raquella said to the gathering, "A voice from my female ancestry called to me from inside and told me what we must do. The voice was remarkable in its harmony, as if thousands of women were speaking simultaneously. It told me we must bond together from now on to achieve our common goal of strengthening the bloodlines of humanity."

She and her followers still wore black robes, but they were of a more classic cut than the grieving outfits the Sorceresses had worn during the height of the Rossak Epidemic; these had high collars and hoods that, when pulled over their heads, made them look like exotic birds.

"We will span generations and star systems and maintain a watch on the weaknesses and strengths of humanity."

At Raquella's side, Karee Marques turned to look at her. The breeze blew her robe and long pale hair. This young woman, who had the potential to be among the strongest of the new Sisters, spoke up. "Certain noble families—particularly the Butlers—are already attempting to rewrite history, seeking to erase their genetic linkage to the cowardly Harkonnens, Xavier and Abulurd. In a few generations, no one will even know their connections. Shouldn't we make sure the truth is preserved, somehow?"

Raquella said, "We will maintain our own private records—the correct ones."

She gazed across the silver-purple canopy of the jungle, which teemed with so much hidden life—including Jimmak and his Misborn friends. It seemed to her that the worthwhile things in nature had a tendency to conceal themselves from discovery, just as it was with the ideal genetic mix that she sought. She and her Sisters were embarking on an epic search that would require infinite patience and dedication.

But with the empire of the thinking machines vanquished, and a far-reaching new human empire in its embryonic stages, mankind was suffused with creative energy on a scale never before seen in history, a renaissance. Someone had to keep watch.

"You will journey to distant worlds, furthering our political aims so that our Sisterhood will remain strong for centuries. Disperse yourselves in every noble house. Just imagine how much you can observe and learn as employees, wives, mistresses, and fighters, while your primary loyalty remains with the Sisterhood."

The women smiled, looking forward to their new missions.

At the conclusion of the meeting, as the robed women returned to their cliffside homes, Karee approached Raquella. "After the epidemic, shouldn't our first priority be to rebuild our own population here on Rossak? We have lost so many families, so many breeders among the men."

Raquella thought of the embryonic daughter she now carried, cells busily dividing in her womb. It gave her a bittersweet pang to think that Mohandas might never know he had a child. "As always in the wake of a great loss, our Sisters will be tempted to consent to unchecked reproduction. But we must choose only the best partners and keep careful records. The genetic databases will help us select the proper mates. It cannot be random."

The young Sorceress looked crestfallen. "We must breed only according to the bloodline charts? Can't there be at least a small concession to love?"

"*Love.*" Raquella rolled the word around in her mouth. "We must be careful of that particular emotion, because it tricks a woman into thinking of one cherished individual instead of the larger perspective. Love introduces too many random factors. Now that we have a DNA road map, we can steer a clear course."

"I . . . understand." The young woman sounded disappointed. Did she already have a sweetheart among the survivors?

Raquella studied her classically beautiful features, and said, "Understanding is only the beginning."

No matter where I go, the universe always finds me.

—SUPREME BASHAR VORIAN ATREIDES,
Reflections on Loss

A t Zimia Spaceport, a hawk-featured man walked around an old-design update vessel, making his final inspection before takeoff. Freshly painted and overhauled, the old black-and-silver ship reflected the golden rays of the setting sun. Once he left, he doubted anyone here would ever see him again.

Vorian no longer wore any uniform. He tried to imagine what true freedom would be like, away from the duties that had imprisoned him for decades. It was time he left and flew far away, to the Unallied Planets and beyond. He would not regret leaving anything behind. Gone would be the cares of the Jihad, and he would rarely think of Abulurd, Agamemnon, Omnius, or any of the others who had inflicted so much pain on him.

His long career as a fighting man was concluded, and he did not know what lay ahead for him. He had lived two human lifetimes so far, and might easily have more than that remaining in his supercharged genes. He had begun to show faint signs of aging—he looked thirty at the most—but in his bones, in his very soul, he carried the fatigue of a thousand years. The Jihad and all of its tragedies had taken a great deal out of him, and he didn't know when, or if, he would ever recover.

Maybe he would stop on Rossak to visit his dedicated granddaughter Raquella, who worked there with the surviving Sorceresses. He had no idea what they were doing, or why, but he looked forward to finding out.

Maybe he would even go back to Caladan. He should at least say good-bye to his sons and grandchildren.

He felt like a galactic tourist with no schedule to keep, none of the pressures to which he had grown so accustomed over the past century.

For backwater trips on planets, he had brought an inflatable boat and suspensor-driven platforms that were compact and stowed away in the *Dream Voyager*'s storage compartments. He also had enough provisions to last for a long time. Vor could roam anywhere he wanted, discovering anything he liked. Most of his life had been devoted to learning and perfecting the art of war, but he had no use for such skills anymore.

Ironically, he did have a use for something he had learned early in life, long before he'd ever become a famous Hero of the Jihad, back to the easy days when he and Seurat had made update runs between Synchronized Worlds. Days of simplicity. This ship, once filled with computerized systems, now had only a manual operation system. With the redundancies that Vor had specified in the reconstruction, the craft would serve him well. Fewer parts and less sophisticated systems meant increased reliability, fewer breakdowns.

He boarded the *Dream Voyager* and took off a day ahead of schedule, so that he could avoid any fanfare or goodbyes. As he rose through the atmosphere, a huge weight lifted from his shoulders, replaced by a sensation of raw excitement, as if he were newly born into a life full of promise again.

A bad decision requires only a moment to make, but future genera-tions can suffer for centuries as a result.

—SUPREME BASHAR VORIAN ATREIDES,
Final Assessment of the Jihad (Fifth Revision)

Abulurd Harkonnen went into exile on the cold backwater world of Lankiveil. Banished for cowardice and reviled by the League, he accepted his fate in this forbidding and unwelcome place. He wanted nothing more than to withdraw and never be seen again.

Though Abulurd had wanted only to save the innocent human shields at the Bridge of Hrethgir, and though the machines had been vanquished in the end, Vorian was never able to forgive him for disobeying orders. The Supreme Bashar had considered the act not only a betrayal of his military duties, but of their relationship as well.

After all his service, unable to recover from his disgrace, Abulurd was disgusted with the League of Nobles, with his brother Faykan and his petty politics—and most of all with Vorian Atreides, the man whom he had loved but who had proved to be just as inhuman as the Titan Agamemnon.

Abulurd had expected to be forgiven, but coldhearted Vorian Atreides had shown no compassion whatsoever.

Worst of all, Vorian would never follow through on his promise to remove the unfair stain from Xavier Harkonnen's name. If Abulurd had returned a hero, he and Vor could have rehabilitated Xavier's memory, making the League of Nobles remember his grandfather as the great man he truly was. Just as he went into exile, the parliamentary task force that Vor had set up to look into the matter was disbanded.

Before Abulurd's trial, the Supreme Bashar had briefly visited Abulurd in his Zimia holding cell. He stared at the prisoner in silence for a long moment, and Abulurd waited, prepared to endure what he had to.

Measuring his words carefully, Vor said, "Xavier was my friend. But it is no longer possible to sanitize the Harkonnen name. People will say the blood runs true, that the taint of dishonor from your grandfather has passed through to you. Because of your treachery, you've lost whatever glory your family had." Contempt and scorn etched his face, and he left.

The encounter had lasted less than a minute, yet it burned like acid in Abulurd's memory. At the time, he had been deeply hurt; now, thinking back on Vor's words, he felt simmering anger.

But even banished from the League of Nobles, Abulurd had enough income to sustain himself on Lankiveil. Viceroy Faykan Corrino, wrapping himself in his protective and glorious mantle, had proclaimed that Abulurd and all his descendants must retain the reviled Harkonnen name. And in time, few would remember that Harkonnens and Corrinos had ever shared blood ties. . . .

Abulurd built his new home in the heart of a dismal village at the head of a steep-walled fjord on Lankiveil. The people were fishermen and farmers, living outside the influence of the League and uninterested in politics or current affairs. They did not care about their new lord's shame, and eventually he learned to live with it, still convinced of his own rightness at the Battle of Corrin.

After a few years, he married a local woman and produced a family with three sons. After he told them of his past, his wife and children fantasized about the riches that had been stolen from their family, and seethed about the opportunities forever denied to the Harkonnens. They resented the very thought of Vorian Atreides. Abulurd's sons came to see themselves as princes in exile, cut off from their noble heritage even though they themselves had never done anything wrong.

One day, one of Abulurd's sons—Dirdos—found his father's old green-and-crimson uniform from the Army of Humanity, neatly pressed and stored away, and tried it on. It hurt Abulurd to see his son in the once-revered uniform, and he immediately took it away and burned it. But that only inspired the Harkonnen children to make up new tales of lost glory.

Decades later, when Abulurd and his wife both died from a fever that swept through the fishing village, the Harkonnen sons blamed Atreides. Without any proof to support their claim, the sons said Vorian Atreides himself had spread the malady, just to wipe out their family.

Abulurd's sons passed countless stories to their own children, exaggerating how important the Harkonnen family had been and how far they had fallen. All because of Vorian Atreides.

Isolated on Lankiveil, later generations swore vengeance against their mortal enemies the Atreides. In the centuries that followed, by the time the Harkonnens made their tentative return to the new Corrino empire, their stories became accepted as fact. And the Harkonnens never forgot.

The deep desert is not an exile. It is solitude. It is safe.

—NAIB ISHMAEL,
Fire Poetry from Arrakis

I shmael recovered from the sandworm duel, but his heart did not.
Though he had lost his challenge, he did not accept defeat, for he knew that too much rested on his ability to save the Zensunni people, to preserve their heritage in the face of temptation from outsiders.

After his aging body healed from its physical injuries, Ishmael decided to gather a pack and supplies and set off alone into the deep desert—as Selim Wormrider had done following his original exile from Naib Dhartha's village.

When they learned of his plans, several eager young warriors and dissatisfied elders asked to go with him, along with Chamal and a number of Poritrin descendants. The older ones had been mere children during the Wormrider's time, but they had not forgotten. They all wanted to follow the vision of Selim, continuing his work and remembering his legend. When Ishmael understood that so many people meant to follow him and turn their backs on the unsatisfying ways of El'hiim, he felt heartened.

For the most part, his stepson avoided him and did not gloat over his own victory—at least not in Ishmael's presence. But the mood of the villagers had clearly changed. Many of those who had been spoiled by unnecessary comforts now wanted to move from their isolated village closer to Arrakis City. Some decided to set up secondary homes within the VenKee settlements themselves.

The thought made Ishmael sick at heart with the certainty that these Zensunnis would eventually lose their independence and identity as a people. They would settle in villages of the pan and graben, no longer nomads, no longer respectable Zensunnis. Ishmael refused to be a part of that.

With his pride boosting his health as much as a steady diet of melange, Ishmael counted his followers and told them to gather their most important possessions. They would leave behind useless luxuries, conveniences, and clothing that could never withstand the rigors of Arrakis. They would find their place in the deep desert.

Ishmael, by far the oldest of all living Zensunnis, faced El'hiim just before departure. "I will lead my people away from here—far from you, and far from all outside corruption."

El'hiim was startled at first, then amused. "Be sensible, Ishmael. All of you will die out there."

The old man did not waver. "So be it, if that is the will of Buddallah. We believe the desert will provide for us, but if we are mistaken, we will perish. If we are correct, however, we will thrive as Free Men, determining our own society. Either way, El'hiim, you will probably never know."

IN A GREAT exodus, Ishmael took his people and departed from the corrupted village. They left families and friends behind, marching through a pass in the Shield Wall mountain range and out into the wild, dangerous desert known as the Tanzerouft.

With a warm wind caressing his face, Ishmael shielded his eyes and looked far out into the restless, inhospitable landscape. But instead of appearing menacing to him, the great sea of dunes seemed to be open and filled with infinite possibilities.

He gestured to his people, as they walked with him. "Out there, no one will bother us. We will build our own protected settlements and live in peace, without interference from those who trust too much in outsiders."

"It will be difficult," said one of the elders who hiked beside him.

Ishmael did not disagree. "Hardship will make us strong, and one day Arrakis will be completely ours."

THE BROAD EXPANSE of sand kept its own time. As tides of change and history swept from planet to planet across the galaxy, the endless desert on Arrakis scoured away all attempts to manipulate or tame it. The arid environment preserved artifacts, while ferocious sandstorms erased anything in their path. Spice prospectors came and went, and the worms destroyed many of the unprepared interlopers. But not all of them.

The outsiders kept coming, drawn by the lure and legend of the spice melange.

Even as empires rose and fell, Arrakis, the desert planet, would turn its face to the universe and endure.

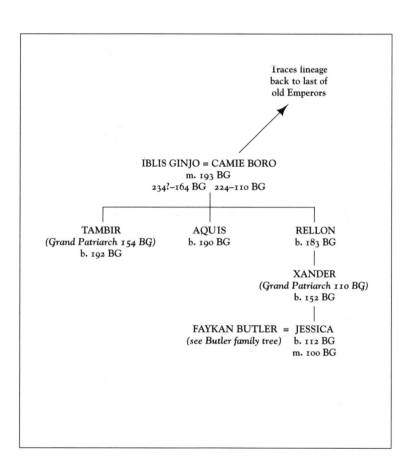

Traces lineage
back to last of
old Emperors

IBLIS GINJO = CAMIE BORO
m. 193 BG
234?–164 BG   224–110 BG

TAMBIR
(Grand Patriarch 154 BG)
b. 192 BG

AQUIS
b. 190 BG

RELLON
b. 183 BG

XANDER
(Grand Patriarch 110 BG)
b. 152 BG

FAYKAN BUTLER = JESSICA
(see Butler family tree)   b. 112 BG
m. 100 BG

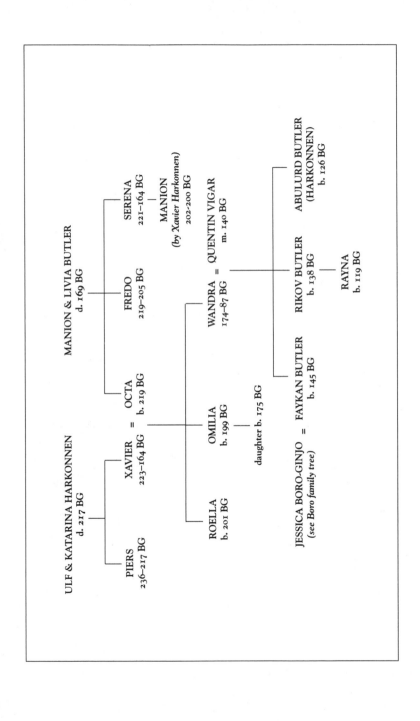